ISBN 978-1-780-20112-2

www.readersdigest.co.uk

Published in the United Kingdom by Vivat Direct Limited (t/a Reader's Digest),
157 Edgware Road, London W2 2HR

# of love & life

Three novels selected and condensed
by Reader's Digest

Reader's
Digest

The Reader's Digest Association Inc., London

# CONTENTS

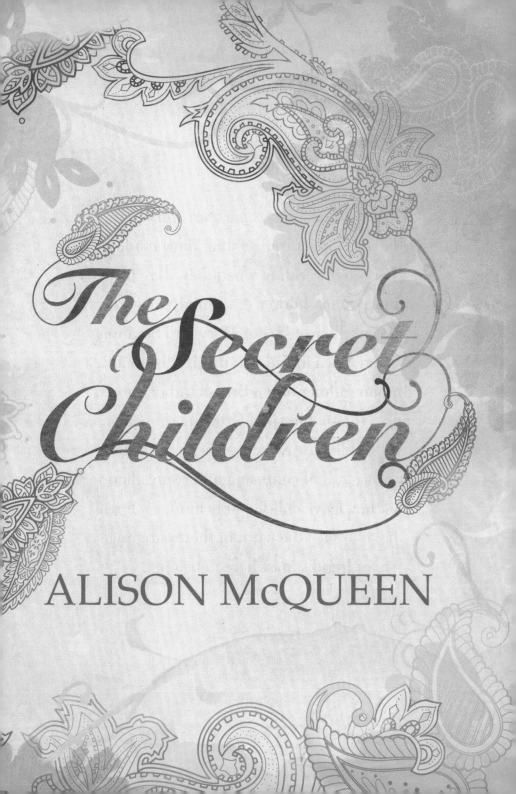

# The Secret Children

## ALISON McQUEEN

*'Not for as long as we both shall live.'*
This was the promise that Mary made to
her sister Serafina when they were little
more than children—a promise never to
reveal their past. For Mary and Serafina
were born in India in the 1920s, to an
Indian mother and a British father, more a
curse than a blessing. Growing up beloved,
yet hidden away from society, the sisters'
lives are full of confusion and contradiction.
As they leave childhood behind, each will
have to face the truth of their parentage
and find somewhere to belong . . .

# PROLOGUE

## Oxfordshire 2006

THE COLD, PERSISTENT DRIZZLE of the early English summer seemed fitting for such a tiny cloud of mourners. Silently they stood; Caitlin, sombre black coat drawn high around pale cheeks to shield swollen eyes, helped her ageing relative along the uneven path that wound its way between the gravestones set uniformly along this green hillside so far from home.

'I'm sorry about the phone call, Aunty. I should never have asked.' Caitlin's reluctant whisper hung heavy on the damp air.

'It's all right. You have nothing to apologise for. You can ask me anything you want to, although I am not sure whether I shall have the answers.'

Caitlin was silent for a moment, then could no longer help herself. 'She never told us *anything*. Never spoke of her life. It was as though she never existed before Daddy came along.' Her head dropped. 'I had so many questions, so many things I wanted to know. Ever since Daddy died, all she did was cry all the time and blame everyone around her. There was no comforting her, no matter how I tried. Then she got ill. And now it's too late.'

The old woman halted and looked Caitlin directly in the eye. 'You have to understand how difficult it was for her.'

Although her sight was failing her, there was not a single moment of almost four score years that Mary did not remember with perfect clarity; even those parts she might have wished to forget. Carefully she regarded Caitlin, almost middle-aged now, bereft in her loss. It was a child's right to know their heritage. Yet there was nothing to be done.

'You mustn't be cross with her.' Mary forced a smile. 'Try to think of your mother kindly. For her, it was the only way.'

'I don't understand.' Caitlin shook her head.

'We can only do the best we can,' her aunt said softly.

Caitlin sensed that she had said enough. With a resigned squeeze of her hand, they continued slowly along the wet path, finally coming to halt beside the few floral offerings laid out beneath a small plaque carrying the name SERAFINA CARLISLE.

Caitlin bent down to read aloud one of the tribute cards, a bland sentence from some distant friend of her father whose name she had not heard for many years, but the words caught in her throat and were lost to the biting wind. She cried small tears that fell freely like pearls, accepting frail comfort from her only aunt. With tiny brown hands flecked with the hallmarks of old age, Mary took a handkerchief from her handbag, and remembered a promise she had made a long time ago.

*Not for as long as we both shall live.*

## Part One

*Assam 1925*

## CHAPTER 1

THE COLOURS THAT FALL across the landscape of the remote northeastern corner of India are hewn from a different light. The eternal blue of the verdant hills sweeps up to meet mountains afloat on a sea of clouds, skimming the edges of the deep valley clefts, thick with wild green jungle.

The early mists linger across the highest peaks, where, for a while, it is impossible to tell where the land ends and the sky begins. The sun is slow to rise and cast its unhurried warmth upon the ground, sweeping away the fragile dew, revealing the colourful saris that pick their way along the high terraces, filling the baskets slung behind their heads with the leaves once prized for their healing properties, now cultivated for the silver-lined caddies of the white man.

As far as the eye can see, emerald tea gardens cling to the hillsides, mile upon mile of undulating curves, hugging the steep slopes like moss on an aged stone, paths zigzagging through the low-slung shrubs. Had it not been for the indigenous *Camellia sinensis assamica* discovered growing in its hills a century before, the British might have left this unforgiving, ungovernable place of ancient dynasties and tribal feuds where rulers come and go alone. There is no place like it on God's earth.

Some took these distant lands to their hearts and made them their own, their families becoming inextricably entwined with the jewel in their king's crown. This is the way it had been for James Macdonald, son of the most eminent surgeon in India's Doon Valley, born of these lands, thousands of miles from the Scottish shores that had spawned his father.

A tall, thickset man with jet-black hair slicked into daily submission with brilliantine, James Macdonald was among the first generation of Britishers delivered on India's burning soil. Every shred of his fabric had invisibly absorbed the intricacies of the British stronghold coiled round India's throat. Raised as a son of the Empire, his tongue moved easily between the language of the kings and the song of the natives. His skin, where exposed, had been baked by the sun into a permanent olive hue, lending his heavy brow a guarded impression of intensity. There was never any question that he would stay, and never any sense that he belonged either here or anywhere else. It was just his prescribed destiny.

The remote solitude of the plantation pleased James well enough, his predisposition towards introversion perfectly matched to the harmonious ebb and flow of the passing seasons. It had been a relief to loosen the ties to his family's influence and to shift eastwards, away from the dull, predictable introductions to the well-bred young women who came to the dances at the clubhouses, dispatched to the colonies like brood mares to provide wifely stock for those men who had not the time nor inclination to return to England in search of a suitable match.

That James's family had wished him to take a wife before he broke away from the fold could not have been made more plain, but his heart had not been in it. He had had no need of a wife, his vitality in no rush to see itself extinguished by an early marriage to a wide-eyed English girl who would serve only to remind him of the rigidities of his upbringing before producing a litter of children. Still two years from his thirtieth birthday, he concluded he had plenty of time to consider his future. Yet the gradual insistence of his stirring loneliness drew sighs when he least expected it; his thoughts all the while nudging him inexorably towards the deep cravings that plagued his every hour.

That a man must have a woman is as basic as his need for water or air, and there were no laws in this lonely province to rub against nature's grain. Here was a place where a man could satisfy his every desire without question or consequence. Of those precious commodities that the white man came to steal away, among the tea, the oil, the rich seams of coal and the rubies that lay hidden deep within the dry red earth, were other prizes, far away from the prying eyes of convention, of which few spoke. It would be an honour for any woman to be so chosen, to be permitted to serve her purpose unto one man and one man only. She must be grateful, for she had been born female, to live a hapless, passive life, and would never amount to anything until she became a man's possession.

The arrangement had been made at his own request, when the long nights began to stretch too far ahead, that a girl be found to satisfy his restlessness, that she be clean and pure, fair of face, and untroublesome of nature. He was not the first to have done so, and, most certainly, he would not be the last.

'Perhaps Sahib should take an orphan girl,' advised the old, bone-dry widow who lived on the outskirts of the ramshackle village nearby, spinning marriages for anyone who could afford her services. Her age and position excused her from the usual proprieties that prevented open talk from a woman on such matters. She eyed the man sitting in front of her, crosslegged on the floor, the small stone slab between them providing a low table on which their cups were set. She realised exactly who her intriguing new customer was, and smiled a shrewd smile.

'For an orphan girl will be most honoured by your master's attentions and is bound to show her gratitude, and there can be no complications from her family if she has none. Yes.' She nodded in firm agreement with herself. 'I think this would be a good match indeed. Just leave it to me.'

Shiva was not to be fooled and sat calmly, his slender face set with the same expressionless pose he had seen his master adopt when dealing with an adversary. For the past three years, Shiva had attended to James's every need, from his morning tea to the turning-down of his bed at night. The Sahib had arrived from the new plantations in the northwest, bringing no wife with him. It was only natural that he should wish for companionship, and Shiva was determined to serve his master well.

He had not liked the matchmaker from the first moment he stepped over the threshold into her grubby home. She was ugly, both of face and of manner, and her decrepit house carried a foul smell. His voice, steady and melodious, betrayed nothing of his sentiments.

'And see my master fobbed off with a filthy street urchin you picked up from the gutter? Would a wise man buy a cow without knowing the stock from which it had come, only to watch it die of disease and then wonder why?' Shiva set his pale hazel eyes upon her. 'I had heard that you were a reliable matchmaker. Now I see that you are just a sly old crone looking to take advantage of a man you must consider a fool.'

'Of course not.' She bowed to him. 'I merely raise the suggestion so that your master may consider all the options. This is not an easy matter. It will take great skill to find the right girl. Then, of course, there will be the delicate issue of dealing with the family. They will expect to be properly compensated, and not everyone is in such a hurry to rid themselves of their daughters, you know.' She took a noisy gulp from her tea. 'If your master can afford to be so choosy, then of course he will have to pay a little more. Even the poorest family may think twice before sending their daughter into the clutches of a white planter.'

'I doubt that very much,' said Shiva curtly.

'Then you do not know?' The old woman's eyes sparkled. 'They are frightened to death of them! I will have to use all my powers of persuasion to tempt the girl away from the simple life that she knows.'

Shiva refused to rise to her mischief, knowing that it was all merely a matter of money. 'The Sahib is a good man,' he told her, although he knew very well that this would be of no concern to her at all. 'The girl will be well looked after and she will have nothing to fear from him. You will find a suitable choice. But not from the hill tribe. That will only cause trouble.' The old woman nodded in small agreement. 'She must have a fine nose, not a great hook like a fish eagle, and her eyes must not be too slanted.' Shiva imagined that he knew the Sahib well enough to gauge his preferences in matters of beauty. 'And my master will have to see and approve her before the transaction is completed.'

'What? You ask too much!' The old widow yanked the short woollen shawl round her shoulders in irritation. 'Am I expected to search miles of jungle for this wretch, bargain with her family, feed her, clean her and bring her all the way back for nothing? And what am I to do with her if your master says no?'

'Of course, you will have expenses.' Shiva placed a cloth pouch on the table. She took it, peered inside, raised her eyebrows momentarily and settled with a small gesture of her hand. 'But choose carefully, old woman. You are dealing with a man who will not accept anything less than perfection.' Shiva left the tea untouched. 'And one final condition. You are not to go gossiping with the village hags and no one is to see her.'

The old woman smiled slightly, hiding her few teeth behind a wrinkled hand. 'I think we understand one another very well,' she said.

Shiva bade the hag goodbye and felt grateful for the fresh air outside.

The old widow rose from her seat, her movements surprisingly nimble, and watched Shiva through the crack in the wooden door, waiting until he had disappeared along the rough track. She congratulated herself for striking such a good bargain. Men were fools and made easy prey in matters of love. She tucked the pouch into her *choli* and settled herself on the floor to rest through the heat of the afternoon. There was no need for her to rush. She already knew where the girl was to be found.

**A** handful of languid blue days passed before the old woman chose to make the journey to the homestead of her cousin—a rough shack set precariously on a ridge between the paddy fields his family tended some miles to the east. She rented a pair of donkeys, and one youth to tend them, from the donkey-keeper in the village, and set out shortly after sunrise to arrive in good time before the light seeped from the day.

She was greeted with suspicious courtesy by her poor cousin, until she handed him two shining coins, a large bag containing dried red lentils, and a small parcel filled with fresh spices.

'You need not worry yourself that I have come to ask for your charity,' the old woman said, accepting a small bowl of rice with a thin spoonful of yesterday's dhal from her cousin's wife. 'I am here to pay my respects to you and to see your thriving sons. I have never seen two finer young men! How proud you must be, knowing that they will bring you such happiness and good fortune. You must tell me when they are ready to take wives and I will choose for you the finest girls in all Assam. But before then'—she came to her point, turning her eyes to her cousin—'I want you to take me back to the family you presented to me last time I visited.'

Four winters had passed since the old woman had come to her cousin's district in search of a wife for the son of a woman in the village. The old woman had accepted the commission easily and had made her way to her cousin's house, knowing that for a few annas he would be only too happy to pay visits to the scattered homesteads and bring her detailed information about the occupants. When her cousin returned home one afternoon and reported to her news of one family, saying that they would be certain to offer any of their daughters, she had thought that her job was as good as done. After walking for almost two miles the following morning, the old woman had discovered that the family's daughters were far too young to be of any use in her customer's household and had berated her cousin. Yet there was a slight girl among them who had burned an indelible image onto the old woman's memory. She had never seen such beauty.

With the purpose of her visit declared, the old woman demanded that they make the journey before her cousin's wife had lit their supper fire.

'But we have not yet eaten!' complained her cousin. 'We cannot go uninvited and take a poor family's food!'

'Nonsense,' said the old woman. 'In a few hours they will have more than enough money to fill their larder and one less mouth to feed.'

The old woman insisted that her cousin lead the way as she rode on one of the two donkeys to save her aching limbs, and display her wealth and authority. The second donkey followed behind on a tether, flanked by the youth, who hung his head and grumbled about his hunger.

Upon seeing their approach, the mother of the family recognised the far-off silhouette of the old marriage-maker. She leaped up from her supper fire and began to shout at her husband, for there was no other house nearby and the travellers could not have been on their way anywhere else.

The youth was given a piece of *roti* to stave off his hunger and told to tend the donkeys and wait. Just as she had predicted, the old woman was welcomed with every courtesy and begged by the mother to share the family's meagre supper.

'I have come to pay a great compliment to one of your daughters.' The old woman smiled. The mother glanced towards her husband, who immediately shouted towards the open doorway of their hut. Juvenile voices escaped from the hidden room before a girl appeared, moving towards them, freshly washed hair hanging in damp strands that clung to her bare arms.

The old woman pressed her palms together and bowed her respects to the girl. 'She is a fine young woman, but it is not this one that I have come to honour. Where is your second daughter?'

The girl rushed back inside, flushed with shame, and the father leaped up from his place and went after her. He reappeared in a moment, pushing his second daughter out into the light, where she squinted through the sudden glare of the low sun slicing through the trees before settling her black eyes on the strangers, refusing to smile.

The old woman saw that her memory of the girl had not been mistaken. Negotiations were opened with the merest nod of her head, and a deliberate glimpse of the pouch she adjusted at her waist.

'Who would want to take a bride with no dowry?' demanded the mother, suddenly suspicious. 'What is the name of the man our daughter will marry?'

'Ah,' said the old woman. 'That I cannot tell you, for his family wish to keep the arrangement secret until the last moment and I have been asked to remain silent on that matter. The family is very well-to-do. They have been in search of a suitable wife for some time, but the son has insisted that he wishes to marry a simple girl from your district, much to the delight of his mother.' The old woman smiled. 'Let your daughter come with me now, and you will soon receive the glad news of her marriage.'

Despite the girl's sullen manner, the father agreed to part with her without any further detail and did so quickly and cheaply, happy to be free at last of at least one of his dishonourable burdens.

The girl came without protest, her mother having scratched around to bundle together two threadbare saris, one blue, one yellow, and a small, old hair comb made from sandalwood.

The old woman allowed the girl to ride on the second donkey, and remarked that she had been smiled upon by the gods that day.

'I will pierce your nose when we return to my village,' she said. 'Then we shall see about adding some decoration to that pretty face of yours.'

The girl remained stony-faced.

'Why do you look so miserable, you ungrateful wretch? You are soon to enter the household of a very rich man. A white man.'

The donkey took fright beneath the sudden jolting grip of the girl, braying and throwing her from her seat.

'Catch it!' the old woman shouted at the boy. The animal reared away as he grasped hold of its loose tether, the boy digging his heels into the earth, gritting his teeth as the rope burned his hands. The girl pulled herself to her feet, her eyes searching for an escape.

'Do not run,' the old woman said, her voice all at once both gentle and commanding. 'You have been chosen to live a charmed life of great riches and comfort that you cannot possibly imagine, being of such low birth. Your parents would weep with happiness if they knew what blessings await you.' She eyed the girl's threadbare sari, the slender beginnings of womanhood beneath it. 'Anyone can see that you are ready to accept a man. Indeed, to possess him if you knew how, looking the way you do. So, what would you rather? To return to your parents' hovel and wait until they pass you into the hands of a rough peasant who will work you like a dog and breed you till you look like your poor worn-out mother? Or are you clever enough to accept this great gift of fate with a smile?'

Although shaken, the girl knew this to be the truth of it, reluctantly accepting the youth's helping hand to resume her mount.

'You have made a wise choice,' said the old woman as they continued on their way. 'All that you have known before will cease to exist. Your childhood is over now. Do you understand?' The girl nodded obediently. 'You must learn how to master the art of love and enrapture the man you have been chosen to serve.'

'When will we be married?' Her small voice, artlessly sweet, pleased the old woman, being as fair as her face.

'You will be taken to him when I deem you ready. The ceremony will already have been conducted. White people do not marry in the same way as we do. The bride does not need to be present.'

The girl frowned her confusion. 'I will not have a wedding?'

'Such ignorance!' The old woman laughed. 'Everybody knows that the Britishers have their own strange ways. You will soon get used to them.'

'There is a visitor to see you, Sahib.' Shiva bowed respectfully, interrupting James's evening routine, sitting out in the cool, relaxing with his sundowner, reading the week-old newspaper. Shiva spoke without glancing up from the teak floor, not wishing to catch his master's eye. 'An old woman from the village has a relative she wishes to introduce you to, Sahib. She is in need of somewhere to settle and the old woman wondered if you could take her in.'

After the briefest moment of confusion, James suddenly realised what

Shiva meant, but knew it would have been discourteous for his servant to voice it in any other way. His pulse quickened. He tried to recall the exact detail of the brief instructions he had issued to Shiva while bolstered by three glasses of whisky. He had subsequently put the conversation out of his mind.

'I see,' he said, the pit in his stomach beginning to cast a pall of doubt. 'And where is she?'

'They have been sent to wait at the summerhouse on the viewing point, Sahib.'

James rose from his seat, found that he was still clutching his newspaper and dropped it on his empty chair. 'I will go and greet them myself.' Shiva kept his eyes downcast, sparing his master the sight of the embarrassment flushing his face. 'Is everything ready, should she wish to stay?'

'Yes, Sahib.'

'Good.' James paused, his heavy brow suddenly clouded. 'You had better come and meet us at the viewing point with a bullock cart. It is too far to walk at this time of day and I expect she will be tired.'

'Yes, Sahib.'

The summerhouse, a small, open-fronted wooden affair, painted corn-flower blue, lay a short walk from the house, taking in the best of the views to the east. The old woman saw a shape approach—a tall, dark-haired man with broad shoulders and a purposeful stride, gathering pace as he moved towards them. She lifted her stick and prodded the girl sharply to stand up straight and mind herself, telling her that she would be sent back to the fields and her parents made to give back the money if he didn't like what he saw, warning her of the beatings she would receive.

The old woman watched James, eyes shielded behind the thin fabric of her black veil. She would be able to tell in a moment whether or not her merchandise was acceptable. There was no uncertainty about the girl's chastity: the old woman had checked that for herself. Yet although she was undoubtedly beautiful, the old woman feared that she might prove too highly spirited to make a suitable concubine. There was something about the way she held her head and stared without fear. The old woman put it down to her isolated upbringing and ignorant parenting. The girl would just have to learn to take her place and forget her insolent pride.

James slowed as he reached them, hardly glancing at the old hag as he began to fully take in the shock of the girl who stood before him. He had not expected her to be so young, juvenile in her awkwardness, yet with the unmistakable promise of the woman within, the soft outline of her breasts pressing through the thin fabric of her cotton *choli*. Her unsmiling eyes, black as the midnight sky, seemed to gaze right through him.

His breath caught in his throat. She was beyond compare, from the silken ribbon of black hair that flew from her head in the unexpected evening breeze, to the rising arches of her naked, dusty feet.

Finally, he found his voice to ask her name.

'*Aapka kya naam hai?*'

She was suddenly timid, unsure of herself, and looked to the old woman for instructions. All she received was a sharp nod. She turned back to James, all shyness.

'*Chinthimani,*' she said in her sweet voice, scented with the innocence of youth. '*Mera naam Chinthimani hai.*' Then, like a thousand suns breaking through a cloud, her red-painted rosebud lips parted and she smiled.

James handed a pouch of money to the old hag without another glance.

On a generous plot sitting just past the western estate road at the edge of the plantation, beyond the reach of the diminutive tea trees and the hands that attended them, stood a collection of simple whitewashed buildings, set about a dusty courtyard nestling within high, whispering trees. Beyond the trees lay the homestead's lands: paddy fields stretching all the way down to the river, where water buffaloes wandered unhindered, white paddy birds riding gracefully on their backs.

Shurika was happy to be here, having roamed for many weeks through the previous season's monsoon with her younger brother after their father had died from fever and left them without a roof over their heads. His remains had been taken to the village funeral pyre to be cleansed by the eternal flames. Broken and defeated by the loss of her husband, Shurika's mother had stood bereft as he burned and had then thrown herself upon the licking flames of her beloved husband's engulfed body, her terrible screams tearing the sky in two until, finally, the fire had silenced her.

In the ramshackle house that Shurika and her brother had returned to, there was not even a piece of stale bread for them to eat. Shurika had searched in vain, but had found nothing other than a handful of worn clothes and a string of empty promises left to the many people from whom her father had borrowed. There was little charity to be had from their neighbours, either. In her sixteenth year, Shurika should have been married off long ago, but Shurika's father had done little to remedy the absence of a match for his daughter. She was a good worker in a home of idle hands, and there was always something to be done.

The man who came for the goat before the ashes of her parents had cooled and blown to the wind told Shurika that he would take her and her brother in, out of the goodness of his heart. At his request, she had followed him inside to show him the exact spot where her father had ailed and died. He had then smothered her mouth with his hand and told her to keep still while he did what he had come to do.

Afterwards, Shurika had washed her weeping, bloodied body, searching for the courage to do as her mother had done. She prayed to the gods all night that they might give her the strength to put an end to her life, but they had forsaken her, whispering that she must now take care of her mother's precious son. At first light, she had woken her brother, and told him that they must leave that place and make a new life for themselves.

Shunned in the remote villages, they had wandered for many miles, the brother unwilling to work, Shurika reduced to begging for bread and gleaning what food she could from the land. She had come across the estate quite by accident, just when she thought her weary legs would not be able to take one more step. It was she who had insisted they go up to the house and ask for work, but her brother had shrunk from her suggestion, having never lifted a finger in his idle life, so Shurika had left him by the gates and gone by herself. She had found the cookhouse easily, the aroma of frying spices having beckoned her for hundreds of yards.

The cook was a jovial man with a sympathetic heart. He had given her a bowl of rice and vegetables and told her to sit in the shade and wait.

Shurika had sat for hours, watching the sun arc steadily across the afternoon sky, wondering how long her brother would wait before coming in search of her, or whether he would simply take off on his own and abandon her to her fate.

Towards the end of the afternoon, the cook had emerged from his kitchen and told Shurika to go and fetch her brother. She ran the whole distance and found him sleeping in the long grass. When the pair of them returned, they were taken on a bullock cart to a small enclave of buildings on the edge of the plantation. The gates were hanging loosely, and the courtyard around which the buildings sat lay unkempt and overgrown.

Shiva eyed the sullen youth as he jumped down from the cart and chose to address the young woman instead. 'There is plenty of work here and a home for you if you want it,' he told her. 'The Sahib wants this place to be cleaned up and made ready for habitation again. If you do a good job, you may stay and continue to work for the new mistress who will come to live here. You will have to clear the plot over there and make a new vegetable garden, repair the buildings and put up fences for the animals. There are paddy fields beyond those trees that have gone to rack and ruin. Have you worked paddies before?'

'No, sir.'

'It doesn't matter,' Shiva said. 'I can send someone to show you. It's easy enough. The irrigation gates are already there somewhere. Just overgrown like the rest of the place.'

Shurika had dropped to her knees and wept with gratitude, promising that she and her brother would work their every waking hour.

Since that first day, Shurika had offered *puja* to the gods, morning and night, for safely guiding her and her brother there. Before beginning the work that had been asked of them, she built a small shrine at the edge of the trees and laid gifts of food and flowers at sunrise and sunset.

Shiva visited every week to check on their progress, but never on the same day. Whenever he arrived, he would find Shurika hard at work and the brother either sleeping in the shade of the silver oaks or nowhere to be found. Shurika made excuses for him, saying that he was sick that day, or that he had gone to fetch reeds from the river bank to make a new roof. Shiva made a point of visiting two days in a row and, upon finding Shurika gone and the brother sleeping, he gently kicked him awake.

'Where is your sister?' he asked as the youth scrambled to his feet.

'She has gone to find dung to dry for the fire. Why do you want her?'

'I don't,' Shiva replied. 'I have come to tell you to pack your things and be gone by sundown. You do not want the work, so you will have to go. Your sister is a good worker, so she can stay, but your idleness has not gone unnoticed, and the Sahib does not care to be taken for a fool.'

When Shurika returned with the dung, she was surprised to find her brother busily pulling the overgrowth from the sides of the buildings. Naked down to his *lungi*, he had already cleared one wall completely.

**S**hurika crouched in the vegetable garden, tending the plants that had begun to show themselves two weeks ago. She picked the weeds from around each precious shoot and hummed to herself, making up a song in her head about harvesting the toil of her labours.

The distant sound of voices and distinctive clatter of rough wooden wheels creaking against the hard ground travelled to her sharp ears. Shurika was not expecting a delivery today. She stood up, shielding her eyes from the low sun, and peered into the near distance. Shiva, driving a bullock cart laden with furniture, called encouragement to the struggling beast as it staggered over the pitted track. Riding up on the front of the cart with him was a girl. Shurika's eyes widened, the weeds dropping from her hands. The cart pulled up by the wrought-iron gates, now hanging securely on their hinges and painted with thick black paint. Shurika ran and pulled them open, bowing her greeting to Shiva.

'This is your new mistress,' Shiva said, and stood down to help Chinthimani from the cart. 'You are to take good care of her and help her to settle in.' Shurika kept her eyes down. As her new mistress stepped to the ground, she could not help but notice her feet. They were small and fine, and above them, resting round the ankles, were silver chains hung with tiny bells. When her mistress took a step, the bells tinkled.

'*Namaste*,' said Shurika, palms pressed together, head bowed respectfully.

'*Namaste*,' replied Chinthimani.

At the sound of the soft, youthful voice, Shurika looked up to see her mistress's face. From beneath the shade of the pale yellow sari draped across her head, peered out the darkest eyes beneath perfectly arched brows. Chinthimani let her veil drop, revealing a fine nose hung with an ornate golden ring and a full blood-red mouth with rosebud lips. There was not one blemish on her heart-shaped face. Not a single fault to corrupt the perfection of her beauty. Shurika dropped her eyes to the ground again, wondering what age her mistress might be. She was perhaps a little younger or a little older than herself, but certainly no more or no less.

'You will be maid and servant to your new mistress,' said Shiva. 'This is her household now so serve her well. And know that the Sahib will be visiting, so you must keep the place clean and tidy.'

As Shurika nodded her understanding, she heard running footsteps behind her. Her brother slowed to a halt and began to stare.

'You!' snapped Shiva. 'What are you looking at? You do not stare at your mistress, is that understood?' The brother mumbled his apology and looked away. 'Now, get all this unloaded and see to it that your mistress is made comfortable.' Shiva waited until the brother, bent double beneath a large bundle of linen, had gone into the house, then addressed the two women. 'You must prepare for the Sahib,' he said. 'He will be here soon.'

It was an hour before sundown the next day before the heavy sound of cantering hoofs slowed at the gates.

'*Koi hai!*' shouted James. 'Is anybody there?' He threw himself out of the saddle, boots grinding grit against dust as he pushed open the gate and handed his horse to the sullen-looking boy who appeared from nowhere. 'Where is your mistress?'

Shurika's brother pointed towards the unpainted door at the far end of the courtyard. James crossed the short distance in confident strides, pulling the kerchief from his neck. He stood at the door for a moment, then knocked gently before entering.

Chinthimani sat on the single chair, facing a small table with a dressing mirror into which she gazed, transfixed by her own reflection in the magical glass. Shurika stood behind her, drying her mistress's hair with a small cotton cloth, untangling the knots with patient fingers. Both turned at the sudden intrusion and stared at James. His broad frame filled the doorway, his height requiring that he dip his head slightly to step inside, where he paused and looked down upon the two of them. Shurika felt herself begin to tremble, the wet cloth falling limp in her hands. It was the Sahib, that much she knew, for she had heard from the gatekeeper and from the boys who made deliveries that he was a powerful man with a dark, fearless expression.

Shurika knew why he was here. She clutched the damp cloth to her chest, her eyes rushing to her mistress's reflection in the looking glass, but, to her amazement, she saw not a trace of apprehension on the perfect face. Chinthimani stared back at him boldly, her mouth curved into a smile. She lifted her head and allowed her sari to slip from her shoulder.

Shurika soon learned what was expected of her. She stayed close by while Chinthimani spent her days resting and eating, then walked with her through the paddy fields down to the river to keep guard while she bathed, wading waist-deep into the water, her sari clinging to her curves, leaning her head back until her hair floated out on the surface like a wide black lotus leaf. As Chinthimani washed, she sang, her sweet, tuneful voice carrying across the water. She held her nostrils closed and submerged her head, sometimes for a minute or more. When her face finally broke through the surface, searching for a gasp of air, she would be smiling to herself, resplendent in her happiness and good fortune.

'You are afraid of the Sahib,' Chinthimani gently chided Shurika.

'No, mistress.' Shurika smiled at her mistress's gentle chide, having quickly forgotten the fear that had engulfed her upon first sight of him.

'Well, you should be,' she said proudly. 'He is the most important person in the region. A nobleman. And I was the one chosen to be his wife. Me! Of all people!' She paused. 'But it is a pity that they do not do things as we do. I should like to have had a grand wedding and to make my home in my husband's house, instead of having to keep to my own quarters.'

Shurika remained quiet.

'The old woman told me I would get used to it, but she was wrong about one thing.' Chinthimani smiled. 'There is no hardship to be found in this charmed existence. I am not even expected to have children in case it should spoil my body. Imagine that! I wonder what my mother would say if she could see me now, being waited upon by servants of my own. My sisters would die of jealousy.'

'Yes, mistress.'

'None of them shall ever have a proper bed like mine. It is like sleeping on a cloud. I could never go back to the old ways. It wouldn't suit me now that I have become a rich man's wife.'

'Does he call you wife, mistress?' Shurika did not seek Chinthimani's eyes in the mirror. She had heard in the village the word used to describe her mistress's position, and it was not wife.

'He does not use words like that,' Chinthimani said. 'He calls me by my name. Sometimes he even calls me "little woman". He doesn't like to talk much. It makes him tired.'

Each day, after bathing in the river, Chinthimani called for Shurika to comb her hair, and urged her to rub harder with handfuls of oil, perfumed with jasmine and the soft scent of cloves, massaging until her skin tingled and glowed, before helping her into a clean sari. Then together they would sit and wait peacefully, indulging in a little small talk of the day's events, but never for very long. The Sahib would hurry to Chinthimani when his day was done, striding into her cocooned world and leaving his own far behind. Shurika saw plainly that there was nothing more intoxicating to her mistress than the scent of her impassioned lover.

Shurika would leave them in peace, settling herself on the reed mat she had placed on the ground near the doorway of her own quarters, allowing herself to rest, her mind wandering freely as the day's fatigue left her body, sometimes pondering the work that needed to be done the next day, sometimes drifting to the man and woman who lay together a few yards away. She mourned that she would never have a husband of her own, her body ruined, its honour stolen by a stranger who had cared nothing for a worthless orphan, leaving her to drown in the endless abyss of her shame.

Hours later, when the Sahib was long gone, Shurika would rise from her mat and attend to her mistress once more. Chinthimani washed again, this time from the bowl of water Shurika brought from the well, squatting over it to remove the seed while Shurika turned away. The old woman had shown Chinthimani how to preserve herself, having bathed her roughly and demonstrated with her own hand what must be done.

Yet despite the ritual washing, Shurika knew that there would be no stopping what the gods intended, and no changing the laws of human nature. Chinthimani followed the old woman's instructions to the letter, and everything was fine for four whole seasons, then she missed her moon cycle, and another, and then a third.

'What is this?' The Sahib reached his hand down, passing it across the swelling of her belly. Chinthimani pulled away from him, quickly reaching for a sari to cover herself.

'It is nothing,' she said, the chill in the night air suddenly around her.

'Do not think me ignorant, woman.' He spoke softly, a taut strangeness in his voice. 'Did you think you would be able to conceal this from me?'

Chinthimani fell at his feet. 'Oh, Sahib!' she cried. 'I did everything I could to stop it! Forgive me for my stupidity! I would kill it if I knew how!'

James lifted her from the floor, taking the fabric from her to see for himself what could no longer be hidden. His heart came into his mouth. 'I think it is too late for that,' he said, pressing the soft mound of her abdomen, the skin on his face tightening with stark realisation. A child, of his making, having silently taken form while he took his pleasure. He cursed himself under his breath. He should have been more careful.

'You should rest,' he said grimly. 'And there will be no more talk of you doing yourself any harm. We wouldn't want you to go and kill yourself by accident, would we?' The heavy brow settled into a resigned frown. That she was now carrying his child was a complication he had not bargained for, but to have her death on his conscience would be intolerable. 'You will be well taken care of.' Lifting the sari fully from her hands, he opened its folds and wrapped it round her protectively, covering her nakedness. 'It is high time you had your own cook anyway, so I can be sure that you are eating properly.' His arms remained round her. 'And you are to send word to me if there is anything else you need.'

Chinthimani cried her relief, and promised to bear him a strong, healthy son.

# CHAPTER 2

CHINTHIMANI'S FIRST-BORN had not come easily. She had fought against the pain and torn at the bedclothes laid down for her comfort, refusing to give passage to the child that had clung to her womb for too long, fearful that the blight on her flesh would herald the death of her husband's cooled affections, feeling her body's destruction as the baby demanded to be released. When the agony had become too much for her to bear, she had cried out and reached for Shurika's hands, crushing her fingers until she, too, wept with pain. Then, finally, in the still of the night, the cry of a new life carried up into a stargazer's sky.

Word had been sent to the Sahib that his child had arrived, the message laced with undertones of the troubled birth in the hope that it would bring him to her, but James had not come. Instead, he had sent Shiva with the bullock cart laden with rich provisions, and a name for the child. A name that meant 'burning fire'.

Now, once again, Shurika prepared as she had done before to welcome

Chinthimani's second child into the world. Chinthimani had said nothing of this baby's coming, but Shurika had known the moment she saw her mistress's face that morning. She was unsettled and snapped ungratefully that her tea was too bitter and the bread too hard. Shurika recognised the signs at once—the tightness in her mouth as she pushed the tea away, the uncomfortable stretch of her hips as she rose from her bed. This was just the way it had been two years ago when the first baby came, although they had been younger then, Shurika unsure of what to do, Chinthimani more frightened than angry.

Shurika watched over her mistress like a hawk as she laboured quietly all day, pacing her quarters, barely speaking at all, except to emit a low moan and to bend to the wall when her breath came sharply. But this time would not be as difficult as the first. Shurika could tell that this baby was smaller and would cause her mistress less distress. The cook made sweets to tempt her appetite, but she hardly touched a thing.

When darkness drew in, the time came close and the baby let it be known that it was ready to be born. Chinthimani sank to the floor, leaned against Shurika and asked her to sing her a song. Shurika rocked her from side to side, humming softly, while her mistress lay quietly for an hour or more, breathing deeply, slipping in and out of a restless slumber. Then the pain came over her again, this time in great waves, tossing her hopelessly from sea to sea before she succumbed to the final moments. She roared, and with all her remaining strength expelled her second child from the depths of her body into Shurika's waiting arms. Shurika set her gaze upon the mother's joy, blinked the tears from her eyes and blessed the child with a softly voiced prayer song.

'Do I have a son?' Chinthimani's voice rose from her exhausted body.

'No, mistress. It is another girl. A sister for a sister.'

Chinthimani turned her head away in shame. 'I am cursed,' she said. 'My mother has set the evil eye upon me so that I may suffer the same humiliation as she did.'

'You must not say such things,' Shurika said. 'It is our own sorrow to wish for a male child, but this is not the way of the Sahib, mistress.'

Shurika bathed the infant and wrapped her in clean linen before giving her into the mother's arms, watching the tiny hand reach up to clasp the tip of Chinthimani's little finger, yearning to know the feeling for herself.

'She is perfect,' Shurika whispered. 'The Sahib will be pleased.'

The dim golden light thrown from the lamp cast a glow across the open doorway upon a small child, black eyes burning into the darkened chamber. Shurika had thought her asleep and hesitated at her presence, then smiled tenderly, rising to bring her into the room, leading her by her hand, encouraging her to peer within the bundle cradled to her mother's breast.

Serafina looked on silently at the squalling newborn with the squinting face and rooting mouth. It was of no interest to her, this thing that came in the night and caused the terrible, piercing noises that struck fear into her insides. She stared down at it and refused to smile.

'Come,' Shurika said, leaning in close to the child's ear. 'Kiss your sister, then we must take you back to your bed and let your mother rest.'

Serafina did as she was bid and kissed the baby, holding her breath to close out the sickly strange smells that cloyed at her throat. Before she could stand and flee the room, her mother reached a hand to caress the waves of her soft black hair.

'For you,' she smiled. 'So you may never be alone.'

The morning's work was over, and James had been sent for by one of the boys, who had run all the way from the house without pausing for breath. There was a visitor, the white man with the pale hair on his face, and he was in no mood to be kept waiting. The boy urged the Sahib to hurry, fearful of the punishment the man had threatened to mete out if he did not run like the wind and come straight back. James told the stricken youth not to concern himself unduly, and sent him off to the cookhouse instead with a message of no importance. That the news should have spread so quickly came as no surprise. There was always somebody in the village willing to impart a man's business for the price of a handful of grain.

James paused a while, removed the kerchief from his throat and doused it in water from his canteen, wiping his face cool. Felix could wait. Let him take a drink or two before testing their friendship again.

'You know I don't like to interfere, James.'

James watched Felix pacing the wide verandah, worrying at his extinguished pipe, his linen suit partially sweat-damp from the heat he still found intolerable after five long years.

'There's not a tea planter in the land with your competence. You have a way with these people, no question about that. If only every one of the company's managers was more like you, we'd have a lot less trouble. This place is quite the model of modernity. Excellent yields. Top-quality leaves.'

James studied Felix's awkward manner, calculating when the reprimand would come, a perverse sense of amusement touching him, just briefly, as he waited for the inevitable.

Shiva appeared from the house, set the silver tray down and served his master and his guest without so much as a murmur before retreating inside, the insect screen flapping lightly against the open door.

'I'm guessing you didn't come all this way to congratulate me on my management skills,' James said with a wry smile. 'Or the quality of my tea.'

Felix picked up his drink stiffly and made some pretence of looking out across the plantation. 'I hear you've got yourself another problem.' He failed in his attempt to veil the disapproval in his voice. James turned away in irritation. 'For God's sake, man, say something! I hardly recognise you these days! It's this bloody place, if you ask me. Stuck out in the middle of nowhere.' He fixed his eyes on James. 'You know very well that my high regard for you makes these matters all the more complicated. You want to be careful, James. Family like yours.' Felix pursed his lips.

'I'm flattered that you should think me so honourable.' James caught Felix's eye. 'But, alas, it would seem that I have disappointed you.'

It was a trite remark, James knew. To mix the heritage of his bloodline in this undisciplined manner would bring untold shame on his father's unblemished name. After two generations, the Macdonald title commanded the very highest respect in Dehradun. In James's early years, there had always been much high-minded talk of morals and the effects of one culture upon another. His parents had agreed wholeheartedly with the ancient wisdom of the caste system and opined, pointedly, that people should stick to their own kind.

Felix composed himself and lowered his tone. 'People will talk, you know. And it won't be doing your career any good, let me tell you. It's just as well that it's fallen to me to have a word with you about it before it went higher up the chain. There are others who would be a lot less tactful.'

'I stopped worrying about such tittle-tattle long ago.' James, his demeanour cool, did not move from his seat. 'And what should they care anyway? As you yourself said, I'm running the most profitable estate in the region. How I choose to conduct my private life is my own business.'

'Private? I wouldn't be so sure about that. These trees whisper, you know.'

'Then let the truth be known and be damned.'

'James.' Felix gave out a huge sigh. 'It could ruin you. You have to put an end to it. Get your affairs in order and sweep this whole unfortunate business under the rug before it can do you any more damage.'

'And what do you suggest I should have done? Drowned them in the nearest well?' James threw back his whisky. 'And we have the audacity to call *them* savages. You might not like it, Felix, but what's done is done. Now go back and tell them whatever you want, and let me get on with my job.'

Felix shook his head. 'I suppose it will do no good to rake over the same old coals again. I've made my point, and that will just have to do.'

'Yes, I'm afraid it will.'

Felix took a large swig of whisky and stared into his glass. 'Why don't you get yourself married and put all this nonsense behind you, eh? They like that kind of thing at the London office. I suspect it's the only obstacle holding you back from greater things.' He paused. 'I know it might sound like a daft suggestion given your current circumstances, but a wife makes a man complete.' James half raised an eyebrow, causing Felix to clear his throat uncomfortably and acknowledge his own unmarried position. 'Or so I'm told . . .' He cleared his throat again. It was a habit of his. 'Don't worry. All these things can be taken care of. It's not as though there aren't a thousand of these little bastards—'

Suddenly James reached out and rang the small silver bell, silencing Felix. Shiva appeared immediately, stepping silently from the shadows.

'Yes, Sahib?'

James nodded towards Felix's empty glass.

'What? Oh, yes. Splendid idea.' Felix thrust it at Shiva. 'And put some bloody whisky in it this time, eh?'

Shiva's eyes remained downcast. 'Yes, Sahib.'

Felix resolved to lighten the heavy mood. 'Look, there's a little group of us going off to Simla at the weekend. Thought we might see what's going on at the theatre up there. Why don't you come along?' He forced a smile, but James appeared not to be listening. 'Make a bit of a party of it, hmm? Get you out of this bloody jungle for a while and see if we can't find you a decent girl who can speak a bit of English for a change.'

James sat unhearing, consumed by a sudden urge to ride out to the homestead and check on the well-being of the new infant. His first glimpse of the bundle in Shurika's arms had brought his heart to a standstill. She was tiny, smaller than he imagined any life could be, the clasp of her hand barely covering the tip of his little finger. The sight of her vulnerability had left him unexpectedly moved, and he had bestowed upon her the most blessed of names, as if to capture her innocence.

Prompted by Felix's persistent throat-clearing, James finally seemed aware that he was being asked a direct question, of which he had no recollection. 'I'm sorry, Felix, I'm afraid I . . .'

'What do you say, old boy?'

There was nothing to say, of course, so the world stayed as it was, and the years rolled by.

## CHAPTER 3

ONE OF THE HOUSEBOYS picked his way cautiously a few yards ahead of the party, beating at the ground with a stick and poking at the parched, long grass. A baby cobra is born every ounce as poisonous as its mother, and much, much harder to see. To step on one would bring the day's outing to an abrupt halt. Better that everyone took the time to tread carefully.

Shurika had nothing to burden her today, the Sahib's bearers from the big house having taken charge of the fetching and carrying, and she took pleasure in swinging her arms freely as she followed the troop down to the river, keeping a watchful eye on her two young charges pulling at their father, demanding his attentions.

'Is it not a perfect day for a picnic?' Chinthimani appeared by Shurika's side, smiling proudly and nodding towards her master and children.

'Yes, mistress,' Shurika replied. 'It is a perfect day.'

The warm air circled in a gentle breeze, the sounds of Mary and Serafina's delighted squeals spreading toothy smiles across sun-drenched faces. The Sahib's servants trailed like a line of soldier ants, carrying furniture, baskets, tiffin boxes, richly patterned rugs, and games to play with the children after lunch.

'Do you ever wish for a husband?' Chinthimani asked.

'No, mistress.' Shurika turned her face away, hiding its sudden colour.

'No? But surely you must have wished for it sometimes?'

'My place is here with you, mistress, and with your children.'

Shurika followed Chinthimani's gaze towards James, now quite far ahead, his younger daughter perched on his shoulders, the elder carried in the same manner by Shiva. 'Did you leave everything prepared in my quarters?' Chinthimani asked.

'Yes, mistress.'

'I am certain that my husband will want to stay with me tonight.'

'Yes, mistress.'

Shurika knew better than to give voice to her own misgivings. It was wiser to smile and nod and play along with her mistress's pretence—it seemed to calm her beneath the brittle veneer that had settled upon her once perfect face as the Sahib's visits became shorter, more sporadic, gradually petering out altogether save these occasional, stolen days when he would arrive bringing half his household with him, obliterating all traces of the intimacy they had once shared. Whenever he came, Shurika would obediently prepare her mistress's quarters, collecting blooms from the trees to float upon dishes of crystal-clear water, twisting tapers of cotton for the tiny red clay oil lamps, burning sweet-smelling herbs while Chinthimani made the *burra-peg* as Shiva had once shown her.

But the Sahib did not stay. He had not done so in three years.

And Chinthimani no longer poured the drink away.

'He has been spending too much time working and travelling. I have told him that he must not neglect his family. I think he knows that we have been missing him. Perhaps that is why he has gone to so much trouble today.'

'Yes, mistress.'

Shurika was pained at the sight of Chinthimani's brief happiness. The smile that once lit up her face had become rarer. As the babies came, so the Sahib had stayed away. As the babies grew older, so her mistress had grown restless. Shurika had seen the change in many women from the village once their life purpose was fulfilled. Once a girl had crossed that divide into motherhood, no man would ever look at her again with the same eyes.

Reaching the riverside, the servants began to unpack their loads, laying down the rugs and setting out the table and chairs. Mary refused to get down from her father's shoulders and clung to his head with her tiny hands, staring down as the cook threw a big white cloth over the table and set out dish after dish, each one covered with a tin plate and tied with a welt of dry grass.

The river ran low at this time of year, the water flowing in gentle currents that swirled in the shallows and lulled calmly where the pools became deep in the shade of the trees. Shurika sat at the water's edge and slipped her feet into the stream. She would not be missed, for the children were fully occupied and the servants far too busy setting up the sun canopies and searching for the missing cricket stumps to notice her gone.

Chinthimani moved to oversee the servants, but they, perfectly practised in their roles, took little notice of her. Her eyes travelled to James, but his were always elsewhere, following his children, delighting in their joy. When she did manage to meet his gaze, he would look straight through her, or offer her only the smallest of smiles before turning away. It emptied her, slicing through her skin and sapping the shreds of hope she so desperately clung to, forcing in their place instead an insidious, bitter sense of envy for her daughters' higher position in his affections.

The cook's loud singsong voice was quickly followed by the crash of his picnic dinner gong: a pair of tin plates banged together with vigour. Mary, still too small to clamber onto the chair herself, reached her hands up. The cook lifted her with ease, swung her around his head for a moment, then landed her softly in the seat piled high with cushions.

'Hungry?' James spoke in her native tongue. She nodded. 'Good. Now let's see what we have here.' He lifted the first lid. 'Ah! Roast chicken.' He handed a piece to each of his children before passing the dish to Chinthimani. Mary had the chicken in her mouth before anyone could stop her. James laughed good-humouredly. 'You're supposed to wait until everyone has been served before starting, young lady.' She stared at him, mouth full, unable to understand this last sentence, spoken in strange words. Instead, she concentrated on the plate in front of her being loaded with spoonful after spoonful: potato salad with mint and onions, rice with fried brinjals, and spiced fritters covered with sweet chutney.

'Eat slowly,' Chinthimani scolded. 'You look like you're going to choke.'

'She's hungry,' said James. He winked at his daughters. 'Would you like me to take you for a dip in the river after lunch?' They nodded eagerly. 'Then eat carefully. We wouldn't want the pair of you to sink, would we?'

The servants sat on the ground to eat their simple lunch of rice and vegetables in the shade of the trees. One of the houseboys had brought with him a drum, and began to form a steady rhythm with his fingers before lifting his voice to sing a popular song. The servants clapped along happily and joined in with the choruses, breaking into laughter when the boy made a mistake and had to start again. Chinthimani sang for a little while in her sweet voice, hoping to catch James's attention.

'You know'—he settled a small reprimanding glance upon her—'we British consider it rude to sing at the table.'

Chinthimani silenced herself immediately, mortified by her mistake.

**A**ll the way home, the drummer kept up his steady, hypnotic beat. The party, pleasantly tired from the day, were glad of the song to encourage their weary legs over the rough terrain, the children's small, sleeping bodies slumped against strong shoulders.

'I will see them straight to their beds,' Shurika said, taking her leave of her mistress before she could answer.

James supervised the loading of the furniture back onto the bullock cart, which they had left at the homestead that morning.

Chinthimani watched him from afar, impatient for his company. 'Let the servants do that.' She approached him gently. 'Come inside and rest with me a while. I can make you a *burra-peg*, just the way Shiva does. I have a bottle of your favourite whisky. I sent for it from the house.'

'You know that I cannot,' James replied. 'It is already getting late.'

'You never used to mind that it was late.' Chinthimani opened her arms to him. 'Stay with me for a little while.'

**S**hurika waited outside, resting on the mat near to her mistress's door, but she must have fallen fast asleep, for when she woke the pitch black of the night sky had lifted, bringing with it the first lilac hues of morning. Perhaps the Sahib had stayed, for she had not heard him leave and had not been called to attend to her mistress afterwards. She crept inside the children's room and found them as she had left them, curled into their charpoys. She lay down on the floor between them. As she began to drift off, she heard small sounds from her mistress's quarters—the low, soft moan of her grief. Quietly Shurika slipped out to go to her, then stopped, pausing her hand on the door. There was nothing that she could do for her, and if the children woke to find that she was not beside them, they would become upset and cry for her. Shurika returned to the children, slid back onto the floor and closed her eyes.

With the tireless passage of one year upon another, life in the courtyard remained constant, cradled as it was within its own tiny world. The house, the mill for milling corn, the open-sided wooden barn that housed the big machine for winnowing rice, the cookhouse, the cowshed, the chicken run. There was space for other animals too—the goats, two fat pigs and the humped Brahmin cows that ambled wherever they cared to wander. Chinthimani's children grew stronger with each passing day, their paler skins and strange names marking them out from the village children they were permitted neither to befriend nor to play with.

Serafina was a proud and handsome child of seven summers. 'We want to go and see Papa.'

Shurika was used to Serafina's demanding ways and stood her ground in front of the petulant face. At the mention of their father's name, Mary began to jump up and down. 'Papa! Papa!' She reached up as Shurika scooped her up to a slender, cottoned hip.

'He's away on a hunting trip,' Shurika smiled, rearranging Mary's slight weight and dangling legs. 'You will see him soon enough. Be patient.'

Serafina's eyes burned. 'It's not fair. Mother said that he would come to see us. She said she went up to the big house herself and she promised us that he was coming.'

'If that is what your mother said, then you can be sure that it is true.'

Mary bounced in Shurika's arms. 'Papa soon! Papa soon!'

'Why does he have to go hunting? Why can't we go, too?'

Shurika was careful not to laugh at the girl's indignation. Serafina's waters ran deep and dark. She was not a child to be toyed with.

'You can't go hunting! The tigers will eat you up like a little rabbit!'

'No, they wouldn't. I would kill them with Papa's gun.' Serafina lifted an invisible rifle in her arms, took aim and shouted, '*Bang!*'

'You have the heart of a lion.' Shurika smoothed her hand against Serafina's neck, felt it stiffen and raised her eyes to follow the girl's gaze. Their mother had appeared from her quarters, her white sari fluttering under the afternoon sky. She walked towards them, her slow progress told by the sound of the silver bells that jingled around her fine ankles.

'*Maa! Maa!*' Mary clapped and smiled. Her mother reached them, kissed her younger daughter and stretched out a hand to place on Serafina's shoulder.

'The courage of your father.' Chinthimani smiled thinly. 'But the beauty of your mother.'

'Did you see him?' The urgency in Serafina's voice rang round the courtyard. 'Did you ask him if he was coming to visit? When will he—'

'Quiet, child.' Shurika raised a hand. 'Let your mother speak.'

'Soon. He will be here soon. So you must be sure that you are looking your very best. You want him to be proud, don't you? Go and get ready.'

Their squeals of excitement sent the chickens scattering. Mary struggled from Shurika's arms and the two girls ran off into the house.

Shurika waited until their voices were far away before asking their mother herself. 'Did you see him?'

Chinthimani shook her head quietly and looked down at the ground.

Shurika's hands flew to her cheeks in despair. 'Oh, mistress, do you not remember how upset they were last time? And the time before that?' Tears sprang to her eyes. 'It is cruel of you to torment them like this. You cannot let the children think that he is coming when he is not!'

Chinthimani's anger flashed a stinging slap across Shurika's face. 'Who are you to tell me what I can and cannot let my children think? You are just the *ayah* and you will do as you are told.' Her agitated hands wrung anxious folds through the unseated shoulder of her sari. 'He will be here. He always comes eventually. Now go and help the children wash and dress.'

**S**hurika finished brushing the girls' hair, her long, steady strokes pressing against their shining curls, then tied the satin sashes round their white cotton dresses. They were a perfect copy of the creased picture torn from the British periodical that had found its way to them, brought down from the big house by one of the boys at Chinthimani's instruction. The *darzee* had at first frowned at the illustration, before nodding his understanding, showing Shurika his finest cottons and agreeing his price. Serafina fussed that her sash wasn't tied right, undid it and began again, refusing any assistance. Mary giggled and found it all rather funny.

'Hold still,' Shurika scolded her, struggling to steady the child's constant fidgeting. Mary tried her best to stand still while Shurika settled the pink bow, her eyes wandering through to the next room. She could see her mistress standing listlessly by the door, taking in the coolness of the late breeze, looking out into the fading courtyard, drinking from the whisky glass she had once kept only for the Sahib.

'Let me clean that for you, mistress.' Shurika attempted to take the glass from Chinthimani's hand, but she snatched it away and glared at her.

'Huh!' she said. 'Do you think I don't know what you're up to?' The rosebud lips fell into a sneer. 'If you want some, why don't you just ask?'

'Please, mistress. You do not want the Sahib to find you like this.'

'Oh, that!' Chinthimani laughed bitterly. 'He won't come. He has far more important things to do than his whore and his bastard children.' She reached to the table and uncorked the bottle that stood there, pouring more. 'You should have thrown them into the river when they were born. Why did you let them live? What am I to do with two daughters that nobody wants? It is the disgrace of my family. No sons. What good is a woman without a husband or a son? I am cursed.'

'Please, mistress. Do not upset yourself. Let me bring you something to eat. You should rest.'

'Rest? What for? I have no reason to rest.' Her words were muffled, each one colliding with the next. 'I am nothing, a nobody, and my miserable children are merely an accident of one man's waste. A punishment sent by the gods because I served as a white man's harlot.' She drank from the glass again, her face grimacing against the burning sensation.

Shurika began to cry. 'Stop. I beg of you, please stop.'

'Fetch a knife from the cookhouse.' Chinthimani smiled at her, a cold smile with no mercy. 'Then cut my throat, and those of my unwanted children. When you are done, you can cut your own throat, too, if you want to, if you have the courage. Maybe you will rebirth as a white man and I will come back as the snake that bites you. Now go away.'

Shurika went back to the children and found Mary where she had left her, swinging her legs on the chair and trying to make a bow with the ends of her sash.

'Here,' said Shurika. 'I will show you how to do it, but you must be patient.' Her eyes flicked round the room. 'Where has your sister gone?'

Mary pointed to the darkest corner of the room, where Serafina hid, crouched beneath the table under the window, hugging her arms round herself. The expression on her face halted Shurika's breath.

'Serafina?' She left Mary's side and crept slowly towards the shape in the shadows. 'What is the matter?' Serafina shook her head violently and refused to answer. 'Have you been listening to things that you should not listen to?' Serafina turned her head away, her breathing heavy. 'Answer me!'

Shurika reached for Serafina's arm, but Serafina ducked away and hid herself deeper under the table. 'I heard what you said!' she shouted.

Shurika got down on her knees and craned her head to find Serafina's face. 'Your mother is upset. She doesn't know what she is saying.'

Serafina glared back at her. 'I heard everything.'

**D**arkness had fallen hours ago. Mary lay sleeping on the bed in her crumpled white dress, the pink satin sash crushed and tangled round her tiny middle. Shurika left her in peace. The dress was of no importance. She helped Serafina out of her clothes. The girl was crying. Bitter, angry tears that stung her eyes and spilled endlessly down her reddened cheeks. Shurika comforted her as best she could, stroking her hair and humming gently to quieten her shaking frame.

'Hush,' she said. 'Hush now. Do not upset yourself. Go to sleep and you will wake up to a new day when all will be well. And if your dreams are not sweet, wake me in the night and I will sing to you.'

Shurika remained beside her, humming a soft lullaby until Serafina's breathing fell slow and regular, before taking her place on the floor between the girls. In the semi-darkness, she settled herself, her half-dreams wandering to the time when the Sahib would come every day, throwing the household into an excitable burst of chaos each evening as they prepared for his arrival. Now there was nothing. Just the endless darkness, and the empty sighs of her pining mistress.

Chinthimani sat in sickly silence, her white sari heavily tarnished by the loose dirt beneath her, staring out listlessly towards the moonlit courtyard where all was still. Tomorrow she would take the children up to the white man's club, where they would be permitted treats, and Mary would fill her pockets freely and forget her disappointment. Her head began to spin. She leaned it against the cool stone of the wall beside her, closed her eyes and felt the breeze caress the damp of her fevered brow. It was like a deep sickness, this reeling feeling inside. It did not comfort her as it should. The glass slipped from her hand and rolled into the dirt. She must wait here awhile rather than try to stand. Shurika would come and help her soon, when the children were finally asleep.

The plantation house sat in an enviable position, occupying a spot midway between the lower gardens and the high terraces, taking in the very best of the heavenly views and displaying its glorious wealth for all to see, its green-tiled roof generously shading the open verandah surrounding the bungalow in grand surveillance. One would have thought that such opulence had no earthly place in such a simple land, yet the temptation of the Empire to display its superiority remained strong. The heat left the day the moment the sun dipped behind the highest hill to the west, taking the light with it. Night fell quickly here.

Shiva cleared away the remnants of his master's sundowners from the low table on the verandah, listening intently to the jazz floating through the open windows from the big brass-horned gramophone that graced the mahogany dresser in the drawing room. The rug had been rolled aside and Felix was clumsily leading the new girl who had arrived three weeks ago. Her aunt, Mrs Gardner, had chosen to stay on in India despite being widowed three years ago, and was pleased to have her niece's company.

'A supper invitation to the Macdonald house is always a welcome distraction,' Mrs Gardner whispered behind her hand to Mrs Edwards. 'And I don't mind telling you,' she confided, 'I've had my eye on James for quite some time.' She nudged Mrs Edwards's arm and nodded towards the dancing couple. 'Lucy is adamant that she expects to meet her future husband while she's in India, and I know that's exactly why her parents sent her out here. I'm hoping that she might catch James's attention.'

'I shall watch with interest.' Mrs Edwards's tone became playful. 'He doesn't strike me as the sort of man who'd be bothered with the usual inconveniences of courtship. It's all work, work, work with these types.'

'But of course he is! A man of his background is bound to be on the lookout for a wife. It's all a matter of timing, dear. I realise that Lucy's rather flighty.' She eyed her niece dancing boisterously with Felix. 'But she's terribly pretty and is bound to grow out of her nonsensical manner in another year or so. I think they would make a perfect match.'

Mrs Edwards nodded politely, but she had already seen that despite Mrs Gardner's effusive introduction of her niece, James had offered Lucy little more than a polite handshake.

'And how is your timid little houseguest getting along?' Mrs Gardner indicated with her glass the young woman sitting on her own in the corner of the room, looking rather uncomfortable.

'Who, Dorothy? Still quite overwhelmed, I'm afraid. I thought she might have made a few more friends by now.' Mrs Edwards sighed her disappointment. 'You know these bookish types. Her mother is quite at a loss to know what to do with her. She point-blank refused to settle in England. Said she'd rather take her chances with malaria than succumb to the humiliation of trying to make her mark in a profession where she's clearly not welcome. Geoffrey and I thought she'd be begging to be sent back to her family by now, but, credit to her I suppose, she appears quite determined to stick it out.'

James stood by the open window looking away towards the hills, their hazy blue outline becoming fainter against the dusk, forgetting his duties as a gracious host, allowing his mind to wander. The conversation among his guests was tiresome anyway. He raised his face slightly to the breeze, the cool of the evening refreshing his clean-shaven skin. The rains would be here soon. He could feel it in the air.

Dorothy watched him quietly from the corner where she sat, her eyes darting this way and that, flicking back to him whenever she thought his gaze elsewhere. A slight, fair-faced young woman of sufficient years to know her own mind, she had yet to meet a man who could hold her interest for more than a few minutes, and had resigned herself to the prospect of a long, happy spinsterhood.

She had been asked up to the big house only once before and had found herself strangely drawn to the quietly brooding man who spoke so politely yet seemed so very distant. Not one to put herself forward, Dorothy had to steel herself before rising from her seat to approach him. She crossed the room in silent steps hidden beneath the music, then, reaching his side, became immediately conscious of his preference for solitude. Her tongue tied in a moment and she found herself saying lamely, 'Penny for your thoughts?'

James, rudely roused from his deep trance, adjusted his manner immediately and smiled, noticing her discomfiture. Perhaps it was the way she held her drink with both hands, or found it hard to look him in the eye.

'I'm afraid I was miles away. Really. Quite unforgivable.' Dorothy smiled and hoped that the flush she felt rising to her cheeks was not noticeable. James spared her. 'It's Dorothy, isn't it?'

'Yes.' She reddened further.

'Thank goodness for that.' James exaggerated his relief and decided to enjoy the offer of her company, if only for a little while. She seemed charming enough, if a little plain. He lowered his voice. 'I'm usually hopeless when it comes to remembering names.'

'I expect you must meet lots of new people all the time.'

'No.' James sipped his drink and eyed her carefully. 'Not really. I find that the trick is to avoid meeting new people as one might avoid the plague.' He seemed quite serious. 'Then I don't have to worry about remembering who anyone is, and nor do I have to sit at a dinner table with a group of strangers and pretend to be interested in their small talk.'

'Oh!' Dorothy wasn't sure whether or not he was teasing her and wished that she had remained in her seat.

James smiled at her mischievously. 'Why so shocked? You don't strike me as the sort of young woman who's interested in small talk, or are you just like all the others who come out here to hunt among the unsuspecting for a husband?'

'No! I . . .' Dorothy floundered.

'It's all right.' James raised a hand in apology. 'You must excuse me. Felix says that I've been stuck in the jungle for far too long, and he's probably right. You'll find me nothing but a terrible bore, I'm afraid. I'd ask you to dance were it not that I have two left feet.'

'Nonsense!' Dorothy, suddenly seized by courage, took James's drink and put it down on the table with her own before leading him boldly into the middle of the room. 'There's nothing to it, is there, Felix?'

Burning cigarette hanging loosely from his lips, Felix spoke through the side of his mouth while dropping Lucy into an unexpected dip. 'Absolutely, old girl. Any chap can dance if he has half the brains he was born with.' He winked at James, who smiled back at him and took a firm hold of the surprised Dorothy. James could dance perfectly well, and set them both into a light foxtrot, much to the combined shock of his guests. Suddenly the room filled with laughter.

Felix eyed his old friend. 'Quite a beast you took down there yesterday, James.' James refused to acknowledge the compliment and concentrated instead on Dorothy's flushed, smiling face. With his attempt to engage with James rudely cast aside, Felix demanded the attention of Lucy instead. 'One clean shot. Took it down in an instant! You don't see that very often, let me tell you. It'll make a fine rug.'

'I've never been on a hunt.' Lucy sighed. 'Take me with you next time? I promise I won't get in the way. My aunt says that if a girl is to get along in these parts, she must learn to live like a queen and hunt like a man.'

Felix raised a mocking eyebrow. 'Have you any idea what it's like to ride out on the elephants at first light and be stuck out in the heat all day?'

'Not yet.'

'Then I suggest you keep it that way. There are some things that simply aren't meant for the fairer sex. The last thing we need is to be held up by fainting women just when the bag starts picking up, eh, James?'

'Quite,' replied James, without taking his eyes from Dorothy's. 'It wouldn't do to spoil a sweet nature like yours with a gruesome passion for bloodlust.' Colour rushed to her face again.

The music came to an abrupt halt and Shiva quickly changed the record, holding it gingerly by the edges and returning it to its paper sheath before placing the next one carefully on the turntable, winding the gramophone and setting the needle back down with a crackle.

'Shall we catch our breath for a few minutes?' James steered Dorothy towards the carved wooden seat beneath the window, the light from the flickering storm lanterns outside passing through the lattice to pattern the floor in a fretwork of gold. The breeze played with Dorothy's hair, prickling at the skin on her bare arms. Trying desperately to think of something conversational to say, she was thankful when suddenly the room filled with music again.

'Oh! I love this!' squealed Lucy. 'There's a new dance! It's all the rage in London. You absolutely must let me show you!' She pulled at Felix's arm while he tried to bat her away. 'Oh, come on, Felix!' she persisted, much to the annoyance of her aunt, who had noticed clearly enough that her niece might have missed her chance to dine beside James that evening.

Felix ignored her and looked around instead for Shiva, who was standing, as always, near to the door waiting to be of service to anyone's whim. As the only one of James's household to speak and understand English well, it was generally left to Shiva to relay instructions to the house servants, even though James spoke three dialects with unshakable fluency. Felix snapped his fingers at him. 'Bring out some more soda water, will you?'

'Yes, Sahib.'

Felix grunted and dropped himself into an armchair. 'And when's bloody dinner? I'm starving.'

An hour later, Felix was once again content, his claret glass full and his plate heavy with roast beef with no thought given to the politics of slaying a cow. He leaned drunkenly towards Lucy, seated to his right.

'Give me a good old waltz any day.'

'To jazz?' Lucy widened her eyes in warning. 'You'd never get away with it at the club. You might as well let me teach you or you'll look a complete fool when the next big dance comes around!'

Geoffrey Edwards laughed at her enthusiasm and patted his wife's hand. 'We really must do something about the servants, darling,' he addressed her. 'James handles his household so much better—'

'That's because he's a batchelor, dear. They really don't like taking orders from a woman, you know.' Mrs Edwards looked up. 'That's why I'm firm. It's the only language these people understand.'

Dorothy whispered conversation to James seated beside her, occupying the head of the table.

'I always knew what I wanted to be,' she said quietly. 'My mother was completely against it. Said it was no life for a woman of my upbringing.' She played with her beef, her appetite having deserted her. 'My father understood how I felt. He got round my mother by telling her I'd be better off getting it out of my system. Those early years in medical school were the happiest days of my life.' She cleared the memory with a sip of wine. 'And the toughest. My goodness. I'm sure I was made to work twice as hard as the men. And I was always the one expected to make the tea!'

'So what brings you to this far-flung corner of the earth?' James said.

'Ah.' She shrugged. 'Once I'd qualified, I found myself running the gauntlet of the old school tie so decided my services would be put to far better use elsewhere. Mother was horrified, but that's nothing new.'

James smiled. 'How are you finding the jewel in His Majesty's crown?'

Dorothy tipped her head in a so-so fashion. 'It takes a bit of getting used to. This heat!' She fanned herself mockingly with her napkin, although the evening air was cool enough. 'I haven't decided whether I want to stay yet. I'm just waiting to see how things work out. There's so much to take in. And you? I gather you've been here all your life.'

James twisted the stem of his glass and pursed his lips. 'Yes,' he said, pondering her question more deeply than she could possibly imagine. 'I suppose you could say that India is my lifelong love affair.' The words hung there for a while, out in the open, so easy to say. A small shiver passed over him. 'Or perhaps it was being shipped off to a freezing English boarding school with a trunk filled with thick grey socks that sealed my fate.' He offered her an explanatory laugh, pushing his demons aside. 'I think they must have been knitted from elephant hair.'

'I've heard a great deal about your father.' Dorothy became sheepish for a moment and blushed again. 'I've read a lot of his papers, too. Between you and me, I think I had a bit of a crush on him, especially during my training. I do feel rather ridiculous about that now. Does he still practise?'

'Yes, very much so. I hear he's been involved in pioneering some new procedure or other. I'm afraid I don't remember the details. There's a letter about it here somewhere—you would have a far better understanding of what it entails than I do.' He frowned at his forgetfulness. 'He stayed up in Dehradun. I have to confess that it's been some years since I've visited.'

'So you didn't want to follow in his footsteps?'

'Good heavens, no. With hands like these?' James held up a pair of handsomely manicured hands with strong, delicate fingers that would have done a surgeon's job perfectly well.

Dorothy laughed and, before she realised what she had done, daringly took one of them in her own.

James smiled back at her and wondered.

## CHAPTER 4

'WE SHOULDN'T BE HERE.' Shurika's voice trembled with warning. She watched nervously as the girls ran excitedly ahead, sensing that her mistress's proud defiance was terribly out of place. 'The Sahib has said—'

'Said what? That we are to remain within the confines of that prison while he ignores us year after year?'

'We want for nothing, mistress.'

'What I want is for my husband to treat me with the honour I deserve.'

'Mistress.' Shurika bowed her head. 'He is not your husband. You must not speak of him as such. We must be careful. There is nothing here for us except trouble.'

'Of course he is.' Chinthimani's voice hardened. 'Whether he likes it or not. I refuse to be silenced, to pace around and wait for his permission to take a glass of water from my own well.'

'The children should be at home, mistress.'

'Why? Because anyone can see whose children they are? Because their skin is too pale and their hair does not lie straight? Good. Let him be shamed into the truth of his family.'

'But, mistress,' Shurika implored her.

'Don't tell me what to do! Who do you think you are? It is me who tells *you* what to do. Do you hear me?'

They passed the ancient peepul tree where a holy man sat in the shade of its heart-shaped leaves, crosslegged in unblinking contemplation, hair matted, body daubed in the white ash of the village funeral pyres. Chinthimani dropped two annas into his begging bowl.

'Let the children have their treats, then we must take them home.' Shurika pulled her sari over her head, mindful of her mistress's lack of judgment, and quickened her pace.

'Be quiet,' Chinthimani hissed at her, smiling a greeting to the surly watchmen on the gate, ignoring her companion's nerves. 'We will do no such thing. My children have every right to be here, and then we will go and visit my friend Athira up in the village.' Shurika gasped her involuntary disapproval, then quietened herself before she could be punished. 'We will pay our respects and congratulate her on her daughter's forthcoming wedding. They have made her a very good match with the son of a cloth merchant. I hear that he has the face of a pig, but a girl with such a modest dowry should be grateful to be taken at all.'

Shurika shook her head gravely. 'I don't know where you hear of these things, mistress.'

'I hear everything,' answered Chinthimani with a wry smile. 'And much more besides. There is always somebody calling at my gate looking for a bowl of lentils in exchange for the village gossip.'

The two girls appeared from the back of the clubhouse, Mary's cheeks flushed and pockets bulging with biscuits. Serafina trailed behind her, picking at a piece of cake. She had barely uttered two words all morning. Shurika had tried to stay close to her from the moment they left home, but Serafina had walked away each time, rejecting Shurika's hand, yet constantly checking her surroundings as though deeply self-conscious, harried by her own thoughts. Shurika could not prevent her aching heart from returning to the words that had spilled from her mistress's slurring mouth the previous night. Yet this morning, Chinthimani had shown no recollection of the way she had sneered and spat her children's names.

'I think Serafina is unwell,' Shurika said quietly. 'Let us go back now and I will see that she takes some herbal tea and does not get any worse.'

'Unwell? There is nothing wrong with her. She is just temperamental today. She gets that from her father. Let her sulk all she wants to. It makes no difference to me. She'll soon become bored with it.'

'But, mistress, she has not been herself all morning. Please, let me take the children home now. You can go to the village if you want to. I can send for someone to go with you, or ask the cook to watch over the children and I will walk back with you myself.'

Shurika regarded Serafina anxiously. The child was seemingly miles away, lost in a daydream that creased deep worry lines into her face. A lone crow swooped down, landing by her feet to take the cake crumbs falling from her hands, shrieking its sudden melancholy caw and sending Serafina rushing into Shurika's swiftly opened arms.

'Still afraid of the crows?' Her mother smiled. Serafina did not answer, humiliated by her spontaneous display of weakness. She buried her face into Shurika's body, enraged by her mother's mocking smile.

The gatehouse was suddenly before them. Serafina did not want to leave, to go home, to the place where she was not wanted. She held back, pulling lightly on Shurika's arm.

'Shall we be staying for some tea?' she asked.

'No,' replied her mother. 'You have your biscuits?'

'Yes.'

'Then come along.'

Serafina dropped Shurika's arm and hung back, dawdling several paces behind, drawing tracks in the dust with her feet, glad to be left behind. She could slip into the trees and disappear in just a few moments. Nobody would miss her, and by the time they realised she was gone, she would be far away if she ran fast enough. She could find her way to her father's house from here. He would be pleased to see her and would pick her up and tell her how much he had missed her and apologise that he had not come to visit for so long. But in her heart she was uncertain, or she would have run all the way there last night, when everyone else had fallen asleep. She would have told him everything that she had heard, and he would have laughed at her and told her that she must have imagined it. Serafina stared at the thicket of trees and her courage deserted her.

The two guards on the gate smiled and waved her mother on, then whispered to each other and laughed as only men do. The taller of the two noticed Serafina watching them from lowered eyes.

'What are you looking at?' he called quietly to Serafina, his voice menacing. 'Are you a prostitute too, like your sluttish mother? Come over here. We will show you what we do with such low life forms.'

'Serafina! Where did you get to?' Shurika suddenly appeared. 'I turned round and you were gone!' The gatekeepers quietened, smiling and eyeing them both with disdain. Serafina clutched at Shurika's hand, holding tightly as she was led away. 'It's all right,' Shurika whispered. 'Do not look at them.' As they passed through the gate, she heard the same word that she had heard her mother use the night before, muttered clearly enough for them both to hear. Shurika ignored them, gripped Serafina's hand and walked quickly on.

'Come,' she said when they were far enough from the threat of the men. 'Your mother wants to walk into the village to see what is happening there.'

'Really? But you said that we were not allowed.' Serafina brightened a little. The village? That forbidden place filled with vibrant colours and foreign sounds and the delicious aromas of food? The two of them took the old road that led through the trees on the far left to the village beyond, bravely dismissing the eyes that watched them.

**M**ary was afraid of the threshing machine. She knew from the cook that her father had built it for her mother the season she was born six years ago, so that she might profit from the paddies. There was none other like it for miles around, so come harvest time, a steady stream of people would arrive bearing their crops, hoping to take advantage of the ingenious labour-saving device. Mary liked to hide behind the corn sacks when the villagers brought their rice for husking, and watched the cook's helper reach up and start the machine with the big handle. It made a ferocious noise, its deep first groan shuddering across the ground, travelling up her little legs and releasing a thousand butterflies in her stomach. It made her feel sleepy if she looked at it for long enough, its sound deepening into a swishing mechanical song, leaving her eyelids heavy.

She was not supposed to be there, but Mary was always to be found in the places that she should not be.

It was Wednesday. Provisions day. Cook had left for market soon after first light that morning. Mary's only occupation that day was to wonder what sweets the cook would bring back for her. He always brought them something. She had hinted yesterday that she had been suffering a hankering for *laddus*, deliciously sweet balls of coconut, saying that they tasted different from the market. Her mouth watered at the thought of them, freshly fried and piled into pyramids by the smiling street trader.

The hours stretched out, the sun gaining height and beating down upon her. Mary didn't mind waiting. She had a chicken settled in her lap. She thought it might be about to lay an egg, but she wasn't sure, so she hummed to it softly and kept it close by just in case.

'Come into the shade, little one,' Shurika said, one hand reaching for Mary, the other curved above her head to steady the bundle of clean linens she carried. Mary shook her head and concentrated on the chicken.

'Want Sera,' she mumbled.

'She will come and play with you soon.' Shurika put the bundle down and sat beside Mary. 'Maybe tomorrow, or the day after.'

'Want Sera to get up,' Mary said, her mouth pursed into a pout.

'Be patient, little one. She is not yet ready to play with you. You must remember that she is older, that she has to grow up first, and it is not always easy.' Shurika stood up, and bent down to take up the laundry bundle again. 'Let us go and see if she would like to hear a story, shall we?'

**S**erafina lay in her bed, eyes closed against her mother's cajoling voice. She wished more than anything to feel herself sliding back into the dreams where she felt safe from harm, to sleep until her spirit left her body and lifted her into the cool mountain streams that flowed down in clear, rushing torrents into the valleys and far away. Her mother's pitiful pleading filled her with fury, her murmured words of persuasion ringing hollow in the terrible new world in which she found herself. Serafina silenced her breath and kept rigid beneath the covers, the constant shape of her body set into stone. It was because of their mother that their father no longer came. Because of her shrill manner, her angry glances, her refusal to please him. Serafina felt her mother's hand on her hair. Her skin shuddered. She wished that she would go away.

'What is the matter with her?' Chinthimani demanded from Shurika the moment she came into the room. Shurika startled, surprised to see her mistress there. 'She has no fever. She should get up and enjoy the sunshine before the rains come.'

'I will look after her, mistress.'

'The doctor said there is nothing wrong with her.' Chinthimani's eyebrows twitched in irritation. 'Why does she pretend to be asleep like this?'

'Please, mistress. The child will be better in a few days. We must not force the sickness to let go of her. It will be gone in its own time.'

Mary slipped out of Shurika's arms and crept quietly to Serafina's bed. She leaned down close to her sister's face and watched intently as Serafina's eyes flickered against the wisp of her breath.

'Sera sick,' Mary said, placing a childish hand of concern on the bed. 'Poor Sera.'

'I will see to them.' Shurika examined Chinthimani's manner closely, aware of the barb of aggression placed in her voice by the whisky she smelled in the room. 'It is a beautiful day, mistress. Will you not go outside and admire the flowers growing in the garden? I will cut some and bring them to your room if you tell me which ones you like best.'

'Hmph.' Chinthimani dismissed her, then reconsidered. 'Perhaps I will.'

The gentle tinkling of the bells on her ankles grew fainter and disappeared as she crossed the courtyard.

Shurika crouched to the floor beside Serafina's bed and whispered to her. 'I will save the most beautiful flower in the garden for you,' she sang quietly into her ear. 'Although the gods never made a flower more beautiful than you, nor a bird that could sing more sweetly, nor a jewel that could shine more brightly.'

A small smile began at the corners of Serafina's mouth, lifting her cheeks into soft, pale mounds. Shurika pulled lightly at the velvet lobe of Serafina's ear, lifting her voice a little so the tune carried to fill the room. 'And the flowers will sigh, and the birds will fall silent, and all the jewels in the world shall be yours!' Serafina opened her eyes. 'Ah!' Shurika said. 'There you are!' Serafina pushed her covers down and stretched her arms round Shurika's neck. 'The flowers and the birds have been wondering when you will come outside to see them. We are all bored without you.'

'Sera awake!' clapped Mary. 'Sera play!'

'No.' Shurika smiled at her. 'Sera will not play today, but she will sit up and let me brush her hair, and then I will tell you both a very special story about the golden fishes who swim in the enchanted river. I have not told it to you before.' She hushed her voice to a whisper, drawing them both in. 'It is full of a rare magic that few people can understand.'

The sudden sound of the heavy gates squealing on their hinges snapped Mary out of her daydream. She gave a yelp of delight and ran from the room.

'Careful!' Shurika shouted after her, before returning her full attention to Serafina, still so quiet, leaning into her lap. 'There, now,' she said. 'Isn't it better to open your eyes and smile?' She felt Serafina's head nod slightly. 'It sounds like Cook is back, and I know that he will have brought you something special from the market. He was most unhappy that you wouldn't eat his cake yesterday.'

Serafina pulled herself up, slowly bringing her legs round to sit on the edge of her bed. There was hardly anything of her. 'Is he cross with me?'

'No! Of course not.'

'Is Mother cross with me?'

'No!' Shurika hugged her tightly. 'Why would you think that?'

'She doesn't want us. She lies and pretends. You all do.'

Shurika sat on the floor and took up Serafina's hands.

'Serafina, look at me.' Serafina's eyes wandered this way and that, uncomfortable with the sudden intensity of Shurika's expression. 'Listen to me closely.' She squeezed Serafina's hands hard. 'You must forget what you heard, child. You must put it out of your mind. You are not like other children, you and your sister. You must prepare yourselves to be strong for each other, and make ready to live your life when it comes to you, which it will.'

Serafina felt the urgency in Shurika's tight grip. It frightened her, deep down inside where no one could see it, but she knew from Shurika's voice that she must listen, for here lay trust; and, in that moment, she believed with all her heart that there was no one who loved her more.

Shurika settled her eyes deeply on Serafina's own, and with a voice filled with knowing said to her, 'You must not be afraid. The gods look after their own, Serafina. They will look after you as surely as they have looked after me.'

The rains came less than three weeks later, the skies darkening with the unimaginable weight of the clouds that gathered in great heavy blankets above. Serafina felt them moving near before the first drop of water fell. She yearned for the rains to break, watching the animals moving anxiously outside as they tensed against the building pressure. The cook peered out from the cookhouse, surveying the heavens with a wary eye. And so it came. The first thick, fat droplets hitting the dust, spattering one, two, three on the thirsty ground. Then, as though the skies had burst open, a mighty deluge cast down colossal sheets of water, setting the courtyard awash in a shallow lake, rich with the scent of the freshly bathed earth. Serafina stepped out into the rain. The might of the monsoon swallowed her up, drenching her in a moment, pouring in rivers down her outstretched arms, washing her troubles away.

Come September, the clouds parted and released infinite skies of iris blue. The sweetness of the rains left its peppery taste on the landscape, groaning with lush new growth, the rivers running high and filled with plump fishes that almost threw themselves into the fishermen's nets. After three months of rain, the air was fresh and new, the people smiling and happy, their lands habitable once more.

Felix liked nothing better than to make a show of things, and went to great lengths to parade his sophistications and pursue his passion for frivolities. It was folly to keep a motor car in an area almost devoid of the fuel on which to run it, or indeed the parts should anything break—an all too common occurrence given the non-existent state of the roads—yet he had insisted on bringing the Riley to drive them all to the clubhouse. He held the door wide open, helping Dorothy into the back seat before settling himself behind the wheel again.

'Don't just stand there!' he shouted at James. 'We haven't got all day!'

James hung back, absently pulling at his chin and looking out across the tea gardens. 'Just give me a minute, would you?'

'Come on!' Felix huffed his impatience, starting the motor and revving thick fumes into the air. 'Whatever it is, surely it can wait until later?'

James hesitated a moment before approaching the car window. 'It's no good,' he said. 'We've been having a few problems on the high terraces. One of the bull elephants ran amok last week, killing his mahout and injuring three of the coolies. We had to shoot it, and now the rest of the working herd is unsettled. If I don't go and check, I'll only worry about it. Why don't you two get going and I'll follow on a little later?'

Unable to mask her disappointment, Dorothy leaned her hand on the open window and frowned at him. 'Oh, really, James. Can't you send one of the boys to deal with it?'

A ridiculous urge to laugh assailed him. *Send one of the boys to deal with it.* Send one of the boys to deal with the consequences of his foolishness? To deal with the growing rumblings from a discontented mother and her two conspicuous children? He looked at Dorothy, her quietly pretty face, her disappointed smile. If only she knew, he thought. What would she think of him then? *Send one of the boys to deal with it.* No. Today he would not send one of the boys to deal with it. Today he would deal with it himself.

'Don't worry.' James smiled briefly. 'It really shouldn't take long.'

'Dorothy,' Felix barked. 'Talk some sense into this man of yours, will you? He certainly won't listen to a word I say.' James had already turned away, calling instructions to Shiva in his servant's tongue.

'I gave up on that long ago,' she said.

'Oh well.' Felix leaned his hand on the back of his seat and sympathised with her. 'It looks as though you're going to be stuck with me again, I'm afraid. Want to come up here and join me?'

Dorothy smiled dejectedly and slipped into the front seat beside him. 'I've spent enough time in his company these last few months to know when I'm fighting a losing battle. He's best left alone when he's like this.'

Felix concealed his concern, patting her hand, shouting merrily from the window, 'You're ruddy impossible, man! It would serve you bloody well right if I stole Dorothy from under your nose and made her fall in love with me instead.' He winked at Dorothy. 'I'd give him his marching orders if I were you. You're far too good for him.'

Felix pressed his foot to the accelerator and the car lurched away uncomfortably, kicking up a savage storm of red dust.

James watched the car turn and head towards the south gate, Dorothy's expression tugging at his conscience. He stood there long after the car had disappeared, pressing his chin into his palm, pursing his lips.

Shiva waited, out of sight behind the insect screen, watching his master's indecision, the sun beating down on his bare head. He should not stand out in it for too long. The minutes passed before Shiva finally showed himself, carrying James's hat.

'Can I bring you something, Sahib?'

James forced his attentions to Shiva. 'Hmm? No. No, thank you, Shiva.' He frowned at the ground, then suddenly changed his mind. 'Yes. Bring Titan. Quick as you can. And ask one of the boys to fetch my boots.'

'Yes, Sahib.'

The children played barefoot in the courtyard, running in between the cottons drying on the line and reaching for each other's hair, their untidy dresses smeared with the grubby marks of childhood freedom. Serafina ran to chase the waddling geese, sending them hissing angrily with outstretched wings while the cook shouted at her to leave them alone. Mary seemed unaware of the straw stuck to her clothes and bothered the chickens, picking each of them up in turn, looking for eggs. The white sun shone high in a cloudless sky, casting no shadow from the tall trees.

An earthy rhythm rolled in on the warm air, gathering pace like small thunder against the ground. The sound grew steadily until a powerful horse, flanks frothing, slowed and cantered heavy hoofs into the courtyard. The children looked up and ran towards the open gates, shrieking with excitement.

'Papa! Papa!'

'Whoa! Careful there!' James brought his mount to a halt, jumped down and lifted Mary with ease, swinging her round and kissing her smiling cheeks. She laughed and flung her arms round his neck, snuffling into his shoulder. Serafina broke pace and suddenly stopped short, her smile fading as the nightmarish feelings of anxiety that had held her to her bed for six days rose in her again. She hung back, eyes downcast, waiting her turn, her mouth fixed in serious repose. James noticed the rapid change in her demeanour and gently returned Mary to the ground. He looked down at Serafina and mimicked her doleful face.

'Oh,' he said solemnly. 'I see that I have come at a bad time.' He raised his hand to his chin and rubbed it thoughtfully. 'Perhaps you are so busy being serious that you do not have a kiss for your papa?'

Serafina could not help but break into a beaming smile. She rushed at him and threw her arms round his waist, holding on so tightly that he was for a moment left breathless. He pulled her arms away, lifted her with a kiss and put her into the saddle. In that fleeting moment, Serafina felt a hundred feet tall. Taller than her father. Taller than the silver oaks.

'You're not afraid of anything, are you, my little lionheart? Hold on tightly there.' James patted the front of the saddle, picked Mary up again and led the shining animal towards the stand by the cowshed.

Shurika came running from the house, almost tripping on the sari tucked so carelessly into the front of her waist.

'Sahib!' she cried. 'Oh, Sahib!' and rushed across the courtyard.

'Shurika.' James girded himself, the smile he readied for her overshadowed by the burden of his motive.

He put Mary down, threw the lead rein over the crossbar between the wooden struts and reached up for Serafina. She slid from the saddle into his arms and he returned her to the ground.

Shurika wished that he could have sent word of his arrival. Of all the days to have allowed the children to wear worn clothes and to let their hair fly loose! Chinthimani had refused to get up that morning, so Shurika had left her to sleep and had allowed the children to play in the vegetable patch. Her hands rose to her face in shame.

'Oh, Sahib! Can you not see for yourself? Are they not growing into the most beautiful daughters any Sahib could wish for?'

James forced a laugh and regarded his children with mock judgment, these creatures who had never asked to be born, who carried his resemblance and called him Papa, tugging at his heart with their guileless ways.

'Mmm.' He squinted down at the pair of them. 'Let's see now.' He looked at Mary. 'This one is a little skinny around the legs.' He leaned down and tweaked her knee. She laughed wildly, spinning in circles. James turned to face her elder sister. 'And this one is too serious. What do you think we should do with her?' Serafina blushed and smiled, glad of his sudden attention, but her smile disappeared as quickly as it came.

'Why have you not come for so long, Papa?' She peered up into his face, searching for the truth. 'You used to come and stay here with us and take us on picnics together. Now we never see you. Are you angry with us? Have I done something wrong? We once put on special dresses and waited for you until it got dark. I didn't eat any supper in case it spoiled my clothes.' She lowered her eyes to the ground, hiding their sadness.

James's expression became pained. He looked at Shurika, but she was unable to offer him anything other than a sympathetic shrug. He paused while he tried to think of an answer, then, instead of speaking, he wrapped his arms round Serafina's shoulders, bringing her close to him.

'Serafina, Serafina,' he whispered. 'Such a sensible head on such tender shoulders.' He pulled away and took her hands before speaking to her in the grown-up manner that she demanded. 'And where is your mother?' Serafina pointed towards the door leading to their mother's quarters. 'Let me go and speak to her for a little while. Then I'll come back and take you both for a long ride on Titan. We'll see if we can find you a tiger or two hiding in the trees, shall we?' He nodded at Shurika. She bowed her head respectfully and pressed her palms together.

Watching James walk to the house and disappear inside, Shurika and the girls fell silent. It was as though none of them dared to breathe. A few moments passed, then came a sudden shout from Chinthimani, the violent crash of objects being broken, a momentary raised voice from James. Then deathly quiet. Shurika took the girls' hands and led them away.

'Come,' she said. 'Let your mother and father talk. We'll go and ask Cook if he has a nice apple and a bucket of water for Titan. He must be hot.'

Chinthimani sat weeping in a chair, fragments of broken clay scattered on the floor around her. James paced the length of the room, up and down, up and down, exasperated, sighing, and firmly resigned to his decision.

'You're letting them run wild! What have I told you?' He stared down at her. Chinthimani cried and murmured prayers, rocking in her seat. 'Mary in with the chickens? Serafina chasing geese in her bare feet like a savage? What did you think was going to happen? This cannot go on any longer.'

'I don't understand!' she wailed. 'What is it that you wish me to do? Just tell me and I will do it! Have I not existed just for you? Have I not pleased you? Yet you cast me aside like yesterday's sour milk. You don't want me, that is clear. Why do you not just kill me and release me from this evil life?'

'None of this was supposed to happen.' James spoke as if to himself, hiding behind the English words that passed unheard.

Chinthimani got up as if to leave, then threw herself at his feet in a wave of contrition, grasping hopelessly at his boots, crying and begging.

'There is nothing more I can do,' James said stiffly, taking a folded piece of paper from his inside pocket and holding it towards her in a futile bid to make her understand. 'I have received a letter. You were seen in the village again with the children. What have I told you? Why did you not leave them here if you wanted to go and see that woman? Did you think you could get away with it again and again? There are eyes everywhere.'

How he wished that it were not so. That he could find another way. Any way except this. 'We spoke of this a long time ago. Do you remember?' He shook his head in fury. 'It was such a simple instruction. So long as they were kept hidden, there would be no one who could object and I would be able to protect you. But would you listen? No. And now look where your defiance has led them.' She refused to answer. Refused to look up at him. Just cried and held on to the floor.

He sighed and lowered himself to his haunches beside her, softening his voice. 'The time has come. You always knew.' He thought for a moment, and corrected himself. '*We* always knew.'

'What will become of us?' she wailed. 'Where shall we go?'

James reached down for her hands and brought her to her feet. He could not bear to see the ruin on her face, so he put his arms round her and closed his eyes to the sea of human wreckage that drifted in his wake.

## CHAPTER 5

'GET RID OF THE LOT OF THEM,' Felix concluded sternly, with a flick of his cigar. 'Unless you want to see your entire life blighted and your name dragged through the mud. God knows, nobody could count the number of men who have humiliated themselves by going public. They're nothing but a laughing stock. It's this sun, you know. Goes straight to the head and sends some men quite mad.' James laughed to himself softly. 'What? It's not bloody funny, James. No, best that you get it over and done with. Send them off and get on with your life. It's the only answer.'

'That's easier said than done,' James replied evenly. 'Like it or not, these are my children.'

'Only if you choose to acknowledge them.'

'Acknowledge? Is that what we're calling it?'

'Call it what you like. You know what I'm saying.'

'I'll be damned if I'm going to turn my back on them. God knows their lives will be hard enough as it is. What chance will they have unless I take the matter in hand myself?' An involuntary sigh escaped his weary lips.

'Well, I don't see what's so bloody difficult about it.' Felix puffed on his cigar. 'Money, James, that's all it takes. Just give her a hefty whack and tell her to be on her way. What she chooses to do after that is her own affair. They'll soon forget all about you. Let them go back to their own people and live a normal life.' He took a swig from his glass. 'Whatever that is.'

'A normal life? With two half-caste children? They wouldn't last five minutes, and I have no intention of spending the rest of my life wondering what became of them. That would be more punishment than even I deserve. It's out of the question.'

'All I know is that you can't keep stringing Dorothy along like this. You're starting to make the girl look like a fool. Anyone can see that she's potty about you.'

'And you'd be the expert on that subject, I suppose?'

'She's a wonderful woman, James. You'd be mad not to marry her. And if you won't, I will.' James smiled into his brandy. 'I'm serious!' Felix said. 'I can't think of anything more splendid than being married to a lady doctor.' He warmed to his own suggestion. 'God knows, most men would give their right arm to have a wife and physician all rolled into one. Old Mrs Edwards keeps telling me what a marvel she is. And, let's face it, the only reason Dorothy has stayed with them for so long is because she's hanging around waiting for you to make up your mind. Do you know, she's been offered a place at the Royal Free?'

'Has she?' The hairs on James's neck stood up. 'She hasn't mentioned anything to me.'

'I'm not bloody surprised. It seems that there's no talking to you about anything these days. If you weren't so wrapped up in yourself, you might even have bothered to ask her. No doubt she'll turn them down on the off-chance that you might make an honest woman of her. A woman can't have a career and a husband, and right now poor Dorothy has neither.'

'I should never have taken up with her in the first place, sweet girl like that. God knows, it was the furthest thing from my mind.' James shook his head in confusion, burdened again by the weight of this all-consuming worry. 'Oh, what a bloody mess.'

'You're damn right.' Felix stared at the glowing end of his cigar.

'I've tried to broach the subject once or twice, but where the hell to start?'

'What? Don't be an idiot! Keep your mouth firmly shut. What could you possibly gain? If you're hoping to absolve yourself of the guilt you so obviously feel, you're very much mistaken. This will be nothing but a whole heap of trouble, James, just you mark my words.'

An awkward pause fell between them for a while, souring the friendship that had grown through a thousand evenings like this.

'There are places, you know,' Felix said quietly. 'Good places, where you could be sure of their safety, if you are so determined to salve your conscience.' He stepped carefully, mindful of James's ill-hidden distress. 'If there is anything I can do to help, anything at all, James, you have only to say the word. But please, for the love of God, you have to spare Dorothy this humiliation. It'll be the end of it for both of you.'

'You're a good friend.' James smiled, a tired smile that had known too many lies. 'But that would be unconscionable. I shall have to tell her.'

'What? Have you not listened to a word I've said? I'd bet you a pound to a penny that she'd be on the first boat home.'

'There's no other way, Felix. She deserves to know, then she can make up her mind for herself.' James swirled the brandy in his glass. 'I should have taken my chances with a wife long ago. God only knows what was going through my head.'

'You're making a very big mistake, James.'

'Time will tell.' James drained his glass.

'Well, if that's the way you want it, so be it.' Felix rose unsteadily from his seat and slapped James heftily on the back. 'But whatever you do, for heaven's sake hurry up and do it soon, James.'

James eyed the dust on his shoes and cursed himself for agreeing to the trip, before returning his gaze to the passing scenery. Dorothy had gone to such trouble to surprise him, revealing with uncontainable delight at the eleventh hour that they were not going to Simla at all, but were instead heading many miles west to Mussoorie, perched in blessed splendour on a natural ridge in the Garhwal Himalayas overlooking the Doon Valley and the city of Dehradun. His father's city. She had seemed so pleased with herself that he had not the heart to tell her that he had kept his distance for good reason.

So sure was she that he would be thrilled at the prospect of seeing the family he had not visited for so many years that Dorothy had taken the brave step of writing ahead in the hope that they would be able to meet up and enjoy a grand reunion among the quiet charms of Mussoorie's spectacular setting. James sat quietly in the carriage and remembered it well. The clear and sunny days when the snow-peaked Himalayas seemed close enough to touch with outstretched hand, the sacred Ganga visible from one end of the saddle ridge, the Jamuna from the other.

Over the years, the distance between James and his family had widened into a gaping chasm filled with far too many unanswered questions and uncomfortable hints about his future plans for a family. *If only they had known*, he thought to himself as the train heaved its great length along, *what a conversation that would have been*. His thoughts returned to his last visit, soon before the birth of his second child. Edith, his elder sister, had taken him aside and casually mentioned that there were some men, of course, who did not care for the company of women. Her raised eyebrow had added a clear subtext, to which he had mockingly pretended to choke on his *burra-peg* and assured her that she need not worry herself on that count.

He now knew that he should have confided in Edith right then and told her of the mess he had made. Perhaps then he might have been spared this terrible journey and the torture of writing the impossibly brief letter that sat in his breast pocket, waiting to be handed to a messenger the moment they arrived. Edith would know what to do, even if he did not.

Dorothy looked across at James staring out of the window. She reached out and touched his hand. 'Penny for your thoughts?' She smiled at him.

James covered her hand with his own. 'So many memories,' he said. 'It will be good to see the place again. Why don't you close your eyes for a while? We still have hours to go.'

Dorothy settled a small cushion beside her head and allowed herself to drift with the lapping motion of the gently lilting train.

The journey was every ounce as arduous as James had anticipated, the final twenty miles from the railway station to the hotel an interminable jolting ride. Yet the magnificent views that extended without interruption as they reached the hill resort swiftly erased all memory of the discomfort.

The cool of the evening air reached Dorothy's skin as she stepped out onto the hotel terrace, and she wondered whether to return for her shawl before dismissing the thought, not wanting to conceal her new sage-green silk gown too quickly. English voices chattered amiably over drinks above the dramatic panoramic view, the Doon Valley glittering lantern jewels far below. Dorothy found herself unable to prevent her pulse from racing just a little, and began fussing unnecessarily with a lace handkerchief in her jet-beaded evening bag.

'Well! Don't you look a picture!'

Dorothy jolted, startled by James's voice. She had wanted him to catch her just so, standing on the terrace perhaps, looking out towards the twinkling lights, the moonlight settling a glow across her small features.

'Oh!' She blushed and accepted the kiss he offered her cheek. 'You caught me by surprise! I was just admiring the view. Isn't it magnificent?'

'Mmm,' he agreed. 'There's none other like it. If you have a fancy to get up early one morning, it changes every few minutes as the light comes up. We could ask to take early morning tea out here.'

'That would be lovely.'

'Is that a new dress you're wearing?'

'What? Oh, this!' Dorothy was suddenly terribly self-conscious. She had never known him to notice her appearance before.

'It's quite lovely. You should wear that colour often. It suits you well.'

'Thank you.'

James ordered a pair of gimlets from the boy and settled his full attention on Dorothy, touching her hand, admiring her modestly styled hair. Her heart thrilled.

'There is someone I'd very much like you to meet,' he said.

'Oh?' Dorothy's veins pounded.

'If you think you're ready to run the gauntlet of my family?'

'Of course! Oh, my goodness, I had no idea!' Dorothy's face flushed with excitement. 'I thought we wouldn't be seeing them for a couple of days. I've heard so much about your father that I'll probably babble on like an idiot. You must promise to nudge me if I start gushing.'

'Ah,' James said with some embarrassment. 'I'm afraid it's just my sister for now. I didn't think it would be a good idea to overwhelm you with the whole clan at once. Edith's quite a girl. One of those no-nonsense types who won't be forced to settle no matter what anyone says, much to everyone's chagrin. I expect you will have quite a lot in common.'

'Oh.' Dorothy's disappointment shamed her.

'It's all right,' James said reassuringly. 'It was quite proper for you to write ahead, and I have no intention of interfering with your plans. I sent a message to Edith as soon as we arrived because she'd never have forgiven me if I hadn't. She'll be travelling to London in a couple of months, so heaven only knows when we shall next see each other.' James tutted softly and shook his head, suddenly aware of the passing years. 'We were always close as children. She used to complain constantly about having been born female. Said that she would much rather have been a man so that she could live the high life without being remarked upon. I think she's had enough of this place and is looking forward to getting away.'

Dorothy, still lost in the romance of the moment, gazed out at the view and sighed. 'I don't think I could ever tire of it.'

'Fed up with being under the constant scrutiny of the family, I expect. She knows all about you, and I think the two of you will get along very well indeed.' Dorothy blushed with pleasure. 'I asked her to come along and join us for drinks this evening.' He glanced restlessly at his watch. 'I would imagine she will be here any time. You don't mind, do you?'

'No! No, of course not.'

'Are you sure?' James frowned. 'You must be tired from the journey. How thoughtless of me. I should have discussed it with you first.'

Dorothy smiled at him. 'Don't be silly! I'm simply dying to meet her.'

'Here.' James passed Dorothy her gimlet with a sly wink. 'Better see this off and we'll order another one at the double.'

They sat together, sipping their drinks and taking in the vast ink-blue horizon, peppered with pin-sharp stars. James reached for Dorothy's hand, squeezed it affectionately, then placed his glass on the table and moved his chair closer to hers. She almost dared not look at him, feeling so happy at that moment that she might cry like an overwrought child. She was so certain that she could make him happy, if he would let her.

James's face took on a new solemnity, the squeeze of his hand urging her to lean closer to him. 'My dearest Dorothy,' he said softly. Dorothy raised her eyes to his and forgot to exhale. 'You must realise that this has all been leading somewhere? All this wonderful time we have been spending together?'

'I suppose.' She tried to laugh a little.

'I have asked myself a hundred times over what on earth you must see in me. I realise I'm not the easiest of people to be around. I can be a bit, well . . .' He thought. 'Distant, I suppose.'

'Yes.' She smiled, touched by his admission. 'Sometimes it's as though your head is way up in the clouds somewhere. I don't mind. Really, I don't.' However distant he might be, she knew she could bear the loneliness, the silences, as long as they were together. She could never hope to love another man the way she loved him. Had she not felt it for herself, she would never have believed such devotion could have existed. 'It's true I often wonder where your mind wanders off to. It looks like a peaceful place. Perhaps you could take me there with you one of these days.'

'Well.' James straightened himself a little, picked up both her hands and kissed them. 'That, my darling, is what I want to talk to you about.'

As the words fell from his lips, Dorothy's whole world and every shred of hope that she had ever held for herself came crashing down around her.

'No,' was all she could say, whispering it over and over. The walls began to close in around her, the magnificent view stretching beneath them blurred by the tears that ran helplessly down her face as she felt the dagger twist inside. 'I won't believe it. You wouldn't.'

'Dorothy. I . . . I'm so sorry.'

She began to feel sick, then faint, finding herself unable to stand, as though swept away by an avalanche. 'It's not true.' She shook her head at him in disbelief, eyes wide with shock. 'Tell me it's not true.'

Amid the words, other noises escaped from her mouth—unrecognisable, pitiful yelps. The once laughing guests seated at the tables around them quietened, craning their necks to peer at the distraught woman, then accusingly towards James. At that very instant, Edith appeared. James stood the moment he saw her, left the table and rushed to her.

'James!' She threw her arms wide open to greet him, then, taking in the scene, her smile disappeared, her face flushed with concern. 'James? You haven't gone and . . .'

'Yes. Yes, I'm afraid I . . .'

'What, here? *Now?*'

'Yes, I . . .'

'Oh, for God's sake, James!' Edith glared at him. 'Why can't you men stop to *think*?' She shook her head and stared towards Dorothy, her head in her hands. 'I suggest you just stay out of the way and leave us alone.' She pushed him away. 'I think you've done enough damage for one evening.'

'Dorothy?' Edith bent over her, sliding a supportive arm round her shoulders and picking up the small jet-beaded evening bag from the table with her free hand. 'Come on now. See if you can stand up.' Her usually sharp voice was soft. 'I'm Edith, but I think you probably already knew that. I've sent James away. You won't have to see him.' She helped Dorothy to her feet, pressing a clean handkerchief into her trembling fingers, and steered her past the curious onlookers, through the hotel lobby and upstairs to the small suite of rooms James had taken for her.

Behind the closed door, Dorothy stood and stared at her puffy reflection in the mirror. Her make-up had run terribly, smearing her cheeks, dropping tear-sized stains all down the front of her new dress. Still weeping, she began to dab at them, then rubbed at them violently with a towel.

'Leave the dress.' Edith urged her towards a chair, but Dorothy refused. Her temper fraying, she tore at the dress, ripping it from her shoulders, buttons flying. She wrenched the dress from her body, splitting its green silk like paper, flinging it to the floor.

'How could he!' she wailed.

Edith quickly went to the door and shouted for a houseboy, before barking her order at him.

'Please, Dorothy. Try to calm yourself. You've had a terrible shock.'

'Shock? Is that what you call it? And I suppose you've known about this all along?' Edith sighed and sat heavily on the edge of the armchair. Dorothy's rage spilled over. 'I want to leave this instant. I shall not stay another moment in this godforsaken place. I must insist that a car be found for me at once.' She began lurching around the room, pulling at the case she had unpacked just that afternoon, indiscriminately throwing her belongings into it.

There came a small knock on the door. Edith answered it to take the tray she had ordered. She mixed the hot milk and brandy herself, adding a spoonful of honey and holding the warmth of the cup against Dorothy's hands. She was shivering in her petticoat, seemingly unaware of her undressed state. 'It's far too late for you to leave tonight,' Edith told her. 'And besides, you're in no fit state to travel.' She sat Dorothy on the bed and slipped a shawl round her bare shoulders. 'Drink it.' She pushed the cup towards Dorothy's lips. 'It will help you to sleep.'

'I don't want to sleep,' Dorothy said. 'I feel like I've been asleep for months. How could I not have known?'

'As far as I'm aware, nobody knows. Today was the first I'd heard of it, and, I must say, I can scarcely believe it myself.'

'How could I have been so blind?' Everything began to drop into place. His brooding silences. The unexplained absences.

'Don't,' Edith said. 'Don't blame yourself. I expect James has been worried sick about telling you. The longer these things are left, the harder they become.'

'Well, I hope he's satisfied. I shall never see him or speak to him again.' Dorothy began to cry once more.

'Sshh,' Edith said. 'You need time to think. You must stay here for a few days and gather yourself.'

'No. I want to go home.'

'All right. But don't force yourself into any decisions now. If you feel the same way in the morning, send word to me and I will come back and escort you myself to anywhere you wish to go.' Edith placed a silk eiderdown across Dorothy's exposed legs. 'I really am truly sorry, Dorothy.' She sighed heavily. 'Men can be such idiots. I'm certain that James would rather have stuck a knife in his own heart than hurt you like this.'

Dorothy buried her face in her hands and succumbed to the waves of grief that overwhelmed her.

'**W**ell,' Edith said to James, finding him alone in the bar and nursing a large whisky. 'I don't think I've ever seen a woman so upset in my whole life. Get me one of those, would you?' James nodded to the boy. 'You have no idea of the pain and misery you've inflicted on that poor girl this evening, James. I hope you're proud of yourself.'

'That's unfair, Edith.'

'Unfair? Hmph. You bloody men are all the same. That letter of yours would have been better addressed to your conscience.' Edith took up her whisky glass and swallowed half the contents. 'I burned it, you know. Before anyone else found it. Thought it was some kind of bad joke at first. My own brother, taking up like that with some . . .' She glanced around, lowering her voice to a whisper. 'What the devil were you thinking of?'

'I was lonely,' James admitted lamely. 'I wanted companionship.'

'Companionship, indeed.' Edith raised her eyes to the ceiling fan moving in slow, stealthy circles above their heads. 'You can save your euphemisms for the jury, James. Everyone knows what you wanted, and it wasn't fine conversation over a cup of tea, was it?' James bowed his head to his lap. 'Oh well. No point in crying over spilt milk.' Edith pursed her lips. 'Tell me about the children.'

'Two girls. The eldest, Serafina, is eight. The little one is six. Her name's Mary.'

'Serafina and Mary,' Edith repeated to herself quietly, as if to embed them in her memory. 'What about the mother?'

'I don't know. She's . . .' James struggled to find the words. 'I never thought about what this would do to her. I thought it would be a neat arrangement that would run its course with no one any the worse off.'

'Idiot.'

'They've been well looked after. And I am quite resolved to see that they should be provided for.'

'I can't even begin to imagine what our parents would say if they knew about this. As far as they're concerned, their darling, precious son has finally found himself a nice young woman to settle down with. Not that they're likely to so much as clap eyes on Dorothy after your little performance this evening.'

'Dorothy,' James said ruefully. 'Dearest Dorothy. What have I done?'

'Can you imagine how she must have felt?'

'No.' James hung his head in submission.

'No, I thought not. You should be thoroughly ashamed of yourself.'

They sat without speaking, James's indefensible position silencing him into quiet contemplation, unable to tear his thoughts from Dorothy.

'Is she all right?'

'No, of course she isn't! She wanted to leave immediately, but naturally that's out of the question at this hour. I promised to come back and escort her home tomorrow if she still wants to go, although I did try to persuade her to stay here for a little while, just long enough to gather herself.'

'Thank you, Edith.'

'Don't thank me. If I were you, I'd just keep my fingers crossed and hope that she comes round.' She watched the distress distorting her brother's face and smiled at him sympathetically. 'Oh, James. It really is wonderful to see you again. How long has it been?'

'Seven years.'

'Really? My, my. It's no wonder I've become so crotchety. I must have got older than I'm admitting to. I wish you luck with Dorothy. If only we could have met under more enjoyable circumstances, I expect things would have gone quite differently this evening. Write to me when you know what's happening.' She leaned over and kissed him on the cheek.

**D**orothy remained in her rooms for two days. The more she thought about it, the more she cried. Then she began to wonder, the seeds of doubt sown, whether the arrangement had remained in place while their own subtle courtship was gradually blossoming. She finally emerged from the solitude of her anguish and sat down to breakfast with James on the third morning.

'Thank you,' James said.

'What for?' Dorothy was unable to look him in the eye.

'For agreeing to have breakfast with me this morning. I've been worried about you.'

'I'm fine,' she said emptily. Her tears began to rise again, but she fought them back, determined that her crying was over. When she finally felt that she could trust her voice to serve her without cracking, she asked him outright. 'There is one thing I want to know, James.'

'Yes,' he said, relieved to engage with her at all. 'Of course.'

'And it is the only question I wish to ask of you on the matter.'

'Anything.' For a moment, James wanted to reach for her hands. As if sensing it, she moved hers from the table and placed them in her lap.

'The woman . . .' She hesitated, not sure of what she should call her. 'Were you still with her while we were . . .'

'No!' James was aghast. 'There has been nothing between us for years. Heaven only knows the number of times I have wished to be able to turn back the clock. The children arrived before I could . . .'

Dorothy lifted her hand.

'I don't want to know,' she said. 'All I was asking was whether or not you were still carrying on with her.'

'No.' James reached under the table and took her hand firmly, brooking no argument about it. 'I have not so much as looked at another woman,' he said. 'And nor will I. Not for as long as I live to take another breath.'

**S**hiva stepped down from the bullock cart, loaded high with the hard leather packing trunks that had been brought down from the big house by three of the servants, now filled with the clothes that had been sent for specially all the way from Hall & Anderson in Calcutta. All around, the seething spectrum of humanity teemed through the railway station, a bustling hub leading to the whole world.

James was content for Shiva to supervise the children's luggage being transferred to the platform and laid down by the red-shirted coolies. Sleep had eluded him last night. Instead, he had lain awake, hour upon hour, listening to the night sounds and worrying himself in and out of fitful meditations. That morning, as he had washed and dressed in the light brown suit he favoured for travelling, he had been unable to coax his thoughts away from his daughters for more than a few moments. He had told them himself several days earlier, the news disguised as a sweet surprise for two very lucky girls who would soon have more friends to play with than they could imagine. He spoke of another world, full of wonderful new things to discover. He spoke of the future as though it were a place that must be travelled to. Mary, too young to comprehend, had squealed and giggled in her usual way, but Serafina had fallen silent and run away before anyone could stop her. She was missing for the whole afternoon. James had immediately sent for Shiva and told him to organise a search party, telling him to take the four houseboys, the cook and his helper. Chinthimani threw clay pots, smashing them on the ground outside her quarters, and cursed herself and everyone around her before taking to her bed.

Much later, it was Shiva who discovered Serafina hiding beneath the idle threshing machine, curled up into a ball, exhausted from hours of useless tears. He had reached in and coaxed her out, then slowly, carefully, he had picked the stray pieces of twig and leaf from her dress and hair, tidying her and brushing her down before carrying her back to her mother's house.

James stared towards the parallel tracks and checked the time on his chain watch, tapping the glass for no good reason and forgetting what the dial said the moment he returned it to his pocket. The girls stood self-consciously, dressed awkwardly in their new cotton frocks and wearing the uncomfortable straw hats that felt much too stiff. Mary pulled at the strap beneath her chin, trying to set it in a less uncomfortable position, but it snagged against her ears each time she looked down to the heavy brown shoes on her feet. She had cried when they were first put on, and had kept pulling them off until Cook bribed her with a piece of cake.

Chinthimani stood silently, her sari barely moving in the insufficient breeze, its white cotton pulled high above her head to veil her face from the onlooking world and the idle groups of men who stared at her uninhibited. Inside, she was all emptiness, every grain of hope sucked from her. She was unable to feel the breath in her body, the blood in her veins. Just a cold space that felt like death.

Serafina loitered at the platform edge, waiting for the train that she knew would change everything. How she wished it would never come. That she could close her eyes and shut out the sounds around her, then wake and find herself lying in the darkness in the simple room she shared with her sister in their mother's house, Shurika asleep on the floor between them, quick to come to her side when the bad dreams began. She clenched her fists and screwed up her face, willing the tears not to come. She wished that Shurika were here. That she could run and hide in the folds of her sari as she had done so many times when she was small.

But Shurika was not here today. She had not eaten properly for two whole weeks, even though Cook had gone to the market specially and brought back jaggery and semolina and all the things that she loved. He had made more sweets in the last month than they had seen in the past year or more, but Shurika was not to be tempted, her grief refusing to be swallowed, and instead offered them to the gods with flowers and prayers, day and night, pleading with her head bowed as her already slight body faded before their very eyes. That morning, she had embraced the girls after dressing them and brushing their hair, her eyes red and swollen, her lips dry from fasting. Mary begged her to sing, but she had said that she could not.

The strange family stood together now, waiting and watching, until the huff-puff of the approaching train with its rising clouds of steam and smoke curled into view.

'Train!' shouted Mary, pointing and jumping around. '*Maa*, look! Train! Train!' Serafina envied her the luxury of her infantile ignorance and yearned for the courage to throw herself in front of its wheels.

The arrival of the train brought with it a rush of frenetic activity. People suddenly appeared from all quarters, whistles blowing and bells ringing. Hawkers offered food up to the windows as passengers crammed on and spilled off amid huge clouds of steam.

James saw that the trunks were loaded into the luggage car, spoke a while to Shiva, then guided his daughters and their mother towards the first-class compartment designated for ladies only. He lifted the girls in, one at a time. Serafina was perfectly capable of managing the big steps without any assistance, but stood and waited patiently to be carried up, wanting to feel the strength of her father's arms.

'What about you, Papa?' she asked.

'I'll be right here in the next carriage.'

'But why can't you travel with us? Why make us go in a carriage on our own?'

'It is the proper way,' he chastised her gently. 'Now you look after your mother and I will come and visit you each time we pull into a station. It will be a great adventure and a good opportunity for you to learn that there is a whole world out there. I want you to tell me everything that you see.' He busied himself, unable to meet their uncertain faces. Chinthimani reached her hand towards him. He looked at her briefly, admonished her with a shake of his head, then moved away to join the next carriage.

## Part Two

### *Haflong 1940*

### CHAPTER 6

THE GARDENS OF ST AGNES ran all the way round the perched, isolated buildings then fell sharply away, stretching down into the wide valley cleft below, leaving the whitewashed convent peacefully stranded above deep ravines of thick, mist-bound forest. Within these walls lay a place of sanctuary, far from the prying eyes of the outside world, dedicated to the glory of God.

Mary lay in her bed, willing the thermometer under her tongue to boil the mercury to a temperature of a hundred and one as Sister Margaret, resplendent in the long grey habit that flew about her, arranged her ample behind on the edge of Mary's bed, a large comfortable affair with three plump pillows instead of the single, thinner allocation on her usual bunk in the chilly dormitory. Of all the girls in the convent, it was Mary to whom Sister Margaret had grown most attached, Mary who had followed her around like a lost lamb when she and her sister first arrived six years ago, neither of them able to speak a word of English.

'Back in the infirmary again, Mary Macdonald?' Sister Margaret narrowed her eyes. Mary nodded solemnly, trying her best to appear very ill indeed. 'Sister Rosemary tells me that you were feeling sick during the night. Any better this morning?' Mary shook her head. 'I see.' Sister Margaret glanced deliberately at the crucifix bearing down upon them from the wall. 'And this wouldn't have anything to do with the maths lessons today now, would it, child?'

Mary gave her a look of all innocence, hoping to suggest that she had no recollection of the day's curriculum at all. The thermometer protruding from her mouth prevented her from speaking her answer, and she was glad of the excuse to remain honestly silent.

'Well, now,' Sister Margaret adjusted the rosary dangling into her lap, 'we can't all be as clever as that Albert Einstein fellow, I'll grant you, but every girl needs to know her times tables by the time she's twelve years old, otherwise the world might stop turning, and that would never do, would it?' Her pale lavender eyes twinkled kindly, the twitch at the corner of her mouth hinting at a hidden smile.

'There's nothing wrong with that one.' Sister Rosemary marched past Mary's bed, heading towards the door. 'At least, nothing that a good dose of castor oil won't cure. I'll be back in a minute, then we'll see how ill she is.'

Sister Margaret took the thermometer from Mary's mouth and held it up to the light.

'Mmm,' she said. 'And what do you think this might tell me?' Mary's bottom lip began to quiver. Sister Margaret sighed a small sigh and squeezed her hand. 'Sister Rosemary will have your guts for garters, child. She was a nurse in the Great War, you know, where thousands of men died for want of a clean hospital bed and a bit of care. She says there's nothing worse than a shammer who lies around pretending to be sick when they're not, and I have to say that I'm inclined to agree with her.'

Mary began to snivel, her eyes widening at the sight of Sister Rosemary heading towards her, armed with the dreaded bottle and spoon.

Sister Margaret stood suddenly, shaking down the mercury in the thermometer, clucking to herself thoughtfully.

'Would you just look at that, now?' She waved the thermometer briefly at Sister Rosemary. 'Almost a hundred and one!' She tucked Mary in firmly, pinning her down with the sheets and pressing her hand against her forehead. 'Red as a beetroot a moment ago, she was. I wouldn't go near her if I were you, Sister. The last thing we all need is for you to go down with a fever again, especially if we're on the verge of another outbreak of the chickenpox.'

'Really?' Sister Rosemary frowned. 'She seemed perfectly fine to me an hour ago.'

'I expect she just needs to sweat it out.' Sister Margaret threw an extra blanket across the bed, her broad back to Sister Rosemary, and winked at Mary. 'I wouldn't bother with the castor oil, Sister. She'll only bring it back up again and make a terrible mess. And as for you,' she spoke to Mary sternly, 'I'll come and check on you a little later, if I have the time. You had better keep yourself quiet now and not be any bother to Sister Rosemary. She's very busy, you know.'

'I won't,' said Mary, a little too quickly.

'Let's just get those pillows plumped up for you, then I'll be off. I can't sit around here all day playing nursemaid to you now, can I?'

Sister Margaret rumpled the pillows around Mary's head, shoving her hand beneath the pile momentarily, then mumbled half a prayer, crossed herself and swept out of the infirmary.

Mary closed her eyes and snuggled deep into the crisp, warm covers, feeling comforted by the reassuring smell of disinfectant. When she was sure that Sister Rosemary had left the room, she surreptitiously reached her hand up to feel beneath her pillows for the lump left there by Sister Margaret. Sliding out the rolled-up handkerchief, she put it under her nose and sniffed at the sweet, sugary scent, then quietly opened the tiny bundle to reveal two jelly babies hidden within.

The next evening, lying in her own flat bunk in the gloomy dormitory, Mary wished that all the beds could be as soft as the ones in the infirmary. She spread her arms out by her sides, feeling the relative narrowness of the thin mattress on which she lay, and wiggled her toes against the rough sheet, comparing its texture with the crisp, stiff cottons on Sister Rosemary's tiny ward.

'Have you heard the news?' Roley whispered, lifting her head a little to peer across from her pillow.

'No!' Mary quickly leaned up on her elbow, eager to hear the gossip.

Amelia sat up from the next bed. 'The Williamson girls are to be sent to Kalimpong.'

The whole dormitory rustled as half a dozen heads appeared beneath the hazy clouds of mosquito nets.

There had been many a night when they had all lain awake quaking at the stories, imagining the orphanage at Kalimpong, a great gruesome building where cruelty reigned and the terrified cries of forsaken children rose from the cold walls unheard.

'It's true.' Roley raised her voice just a little, sharing her news with everyone. 'I heard Sister Rosemary talking to Sister Ann in the chapel. They've been dropped by their father. He stopped paying the bills three months ago and now they don't even know where he is.' An icy chill blew through the dorm. 'That's why we haven't seen them for the past week. It wasn't malaria at all, and they're definitely not in the infirmary. Isn't that right, Mary?' Mary nodded, sending a small murmur of affirmation from bed to bed. 'It was decided that they shouldn't be allowed to mix with us any more. Not now that they're proper orphans.'

'Perhaps he's ill and can't get a message to them,' Mary whispered in disbelief. 'Perhaps he's *dead*.'

'Or he's been kidnapped!' A new English girl spoke from the darkness. 'It does happen, you know.'

'I heard Sister Rosemary saying that she never trusted the man and that he should be mighty ashamed of himself,' Roley declared. 'She called him a coward and said that she hopes his conscience eats him alive.'

'They can't be thrown out just like that!' said the new girl. 'For a start, it's un-Christian. What's the point of teaching one thing then doing the exact opposite?'

Everyone fell quiet. Mary pushed the corner of the sheet into her mouth and chewed on it, her heart thumping. Terrible fates were rumoured to befall those unfortunate souls who were abandoned and denied. She fought to expel the nightmarish pictures creeping into her head.

'Don't be so naive,' Roley said. 'What do you think would happen if everybody's father suddenly stopped paying? You know how it works around here. If you're dropped, you're out. Simple as that. After all, that's what the orphanage is for, isn't it?'

'But we didn't even get to say goodbye.'

'And what would be the point of that?' Serafina's slow, deliberate voice drifted from the far corner, its modulation steady and unwavering. Everyone quietened to listen to her, surprised as they were that she should have lifted her head from her book long enough to take an interest. 'Best to pack their bags and ship them out before they get wind of what's going on and run away. There's no helping them now.'

'That's the most awful thing I've ever heard. My parents would never—'

'Your parents?' Serafina cut off the new girl with a small laugh. 'You need never concern yourself about being dropped, I expect.' She returned to her book, holding it up to the moonlight, deliberately turning the page.

'Serafina, stop it,' hissed Jane. 'We're not allowed to discuss—'

'I didn't say a word,' Serafina said. 'I just don't see what she's got to get so upset about.'

'Not allowed to talk about what?' asked the girl.

'Our parents,' whispered Amelia.

'But that's ridiculous.'

'It might be to you,' Serafina said. 'Your parents are British.'

'It's the rules,' said Roley. 'Mother Superior says it's wrong to ask people personal questions and that we should respect each other's privacy about our families.'

'In other words,' Serafina said, 'we're not supposed to talk about girls like the Williamsons.'

'I don't believe it,' whispered the new girl. 'I don't believe that anyone could be so cruel and heartless.' She shook her small head incredulously. 'The only reason I'm here is because my father's taken a posting to Burma to work for one of the big oil companies and my mother refused to go with him. I said that we should go and take a governess, but Mother insisted that I'd be much better off in a proper school.' She looked around, unconvinced.

'Then you have nothing to worry about,' Serafina said lightly, swallowing the sour sickness that burned in her throat.

At the far end of the garden, where the grass had been left to grow high just before the small apple orchard began, a handful of girls huddled together under the shade of an old mango tree. Roley came puffing towards them, breathless with excitement.

'Flossie's father has sent a piano!' she blurted. 'I heard Mother Superior telling the house servants to make room for it at the end of the refectory.'

Serafina looked at her disparagingly. 'A piano? Whatever for?'

'Everyone knows Flossie's father's some kind of genius,' Amelia said. 'It must have driven him mad to have a deaf mute for a daughter.'

'Beethoven was deaf,' said Rose. 'Maybe he's hoping for a miracle.'

'He might as well have sent her a tree trunk for all the fun she'll get out of it.'

Serafina took a book from her pinafore pocket, opened it at the page where she had placed the small cross fashioned from a sliver of palm leaf, still pale green, and began to read. Not much happened here. One day segued into another with nothing remarkable to distinguish it from the next, and she had learned to while away the long hours by immersing herself in the foreign worlds of the novels she devoured. She could not leave her mind to wander, nor trust her dreams at night. So she read, or studied, or concentrated hard during the services she had memorised over the years, word for word. Anything to keep her thoughts from straying where she knew they must not, for there she would find nothing but sorrow.

Then, suddenly, there it was, softly, way off in the distance, carried in on the stillness of the air. *Umm . . . aah. Umm . . . aah.* The rhythmic chant of the porters.

Amelia scrambled to her feet. 'Quickly! Somebody give me a lift!'

All eyes fell on Roley, who grudgingly obliged by getting down on her hands and knees. 'Why is it always me?' she grumbled.

'Because you're the biggest. Now hurry up!'

Roley allowed the slight Amelia to stand on her back and pull herself up to peek over the high wall. Pressing the tips of her toes painfully into Roley's back, Amelia managed to steal a glance down into the valley below to a great black shape being heaved and hauled in the middle distance. The sun bounced shining rays from its polished surfaces, its legs bound in pale hessian sacking tied with ropes.

'It's huge,' Amelia whispered loudly, her eyes fixed on the path where the porters moved like a line of black ants, precise in their trajectory, some with enormous tied bundles, others with packing cases balanced effortlessly on their heads. 'There must be a hundred of them dragging it along, and a whole lot of other stuff, too.'

'Let me see.' Rose began to clamber onto Roley's back.

'No! Get off!'

'Oh, do be quiet, Roley. And for heaven's sake hold still, will you.' Rose pulled herself up and peered over the wall. 'At last!' she bellowed. 'They've brought parcels from home! I can see them!'

'Food parcels!' Rose gasped with delight and sank dramatically to the grass. 'Thank heavens! I'm so hungry I could just die!'

**A**nyone fortunate enough to have their name called after lunch gathered in the corridor inside the pantry house, watching as the mother superior unlocked the big, heavy doors with the old iron key that she kept tucked somewhere under her habit on a long chain with many others. Sister Rosemary took the parcels out one at a time under the mother superior's direction, reading the name on the tag aloud before handing it down.

'Maria Rowland.' Roley leaped forward and took hers off into a corner.

'Amelia Wilson-Hill.' Amelia stepped up and claimed hers with a smile.

'Serafina and Mary—' Serafina was there immediately. Mary stood back and let her sister take charge. Serafina set the package on the floor between them, tore at the brown wrapping paper and opened the box. Inside were big round cakes bound in greaseproof paper tied with string, Kraft cheese, brown paper bags filled with shining boiled sweets and twists of deep russet barley sugar, Lyle's golden syrup in dark green cans, two pots of jam, a tin of Staffordshire butter and all manner of other good things to eat. Serafina ignored the food and searched deeper, sifting through the layers of crumpled newspaper, looking for something else.

Sister Rosemary hurried the proceedings along. 'Take out what you want, girls. Hurry up about it. We don't have all day. You'll get them back after lunch tomorrow and then you can choose something else. And if anyone has something they'd like to keep out for breakfast tomorrow morning, let me have it now and I'll label it and give it to Cook for safe keeping in the pantry.'

**T**hat evening, Serafina lay on her shallow bed in a white cotton night-dress, a small woollen shawl pulled round her shoulders, the flame of the candle flickering on the table beside her, quietly reading aloud the letter sent from home. Mary knelt on the floor, hanging on her every word.

*A big cat has been going into the villages and taking pigs, and when it can't find a pig, a tasty little dog will do just as nicely. The villagers have been going out at night with torches, banging pots and pans to scare it away.*

*Shurika made you the bookmarks and hopes that you are studying hard. The Staffordshire butter is a gift from your Aunty Dorothy. She has just returned from England and says that the sea passage was rather awful. Enjoy the parcel, my darling girls. The holidays will be here soon and I will come to collect you. Cook has promised to make gulab jamuns for you and says he will prepare an extra special picnic on the first Sunday you are home.*

*It won't be long now. All my love, Papa*

Both girls fell silent, their father's words resonating around the dimly lit dormitory with its austere beds and small windows. The thought of having to wait even another day before travelling home for the annual holiday was just too much to bear, but bear it they must, as they had done each year from the moment of their arrival. Serafina turned over and stared at the wall, hiding her face and tucking the letter inside her shawl, close to her heart. Her body became still, except for the small shudder that passed over her shoulders. Flooded with homesickness, Mary looked down at the big piece of cake in her hands and picked at it half-heartedly, its crumbly sweetness now sitting uncomfortably in her mouth, dry and unwanted.

Nobody ever pretended to be ill on a Sunday, yet Serafina had barely spoken a word since rising, rejecting the rare offer of butter and jam at breakfast, hardly touching her lunch, saying that she was not hungry, before taking herself off to the gardens, book in hand, and hiding herself away. She hoped she had done enough to avoid the tedious Sunday walk that she knew would be setting off at any moment.

Two white-veiled novices walked by on their way from chapel, and Father Lazarus stood in the shade of the tall agarwood, watching the monkeys throwing themselves from tree to tree, babies carried in sinuous arms. Big, gruff and German, with a long white beard reaching almost down to his midriff, Father Lazarus recognised the figure sitting quietly in the far corner, and wandered in that direction.

'Good afternoon, Serafina.' He smiled down at her. Caught unawares, Serafina quickly slapped her book shut and pulled herself to her feet.

'Good afternoon, Father Lazarus.'

'Mother Superior tells me that you've been very quiet lately.' He concentrated on his pipe, the surface of the tobacco glowing orange with each draw, then leaned back on his heels and let out a great aromatic cloud from his mouth. He took the pipe from his bearded lips and peered into the bowl. 'Now, I know that quiet can be a good thing, but I also know that it can be a bad thing. Is there anything that I can help you with, Serafina?'

Serafina felt her throat tighten. She shook her head sharply and looked away. Father Lazarus did not press her. Instead he held his place and continued to enjoy his pipe, looking up now and again into the branches of the trees to admire the chattering birds. 'I want to show you something. I have a feeling that it may be the answer to your troubles.'

'I have to go on the Sunday walk, Father.'

'Ah,' he replied kindly. 'I think you can be spared for one afternoon. Unless you would prefer to go marching around the hills with Sister Margaret? I am sure if you ran you could catch up.' At last Serafina smiled. It was no great secret that she found the Sunday walk tedious.

Before she could reply, Father Lazarus had headed off, calling over his shoulder, 'Come on. If we're lucky, we might have a whole hour to ourselves before our noisy womenfolk get back from their walk.'

The refectory was eerily quiet, the tables bare, the windows locked closed. Father Lazarus went to the far end of the room, pulled the cover from the piano and raised the enormous lid, propping it on the long stick as though opening a huge sarcophagus. He set himself down on the stool, lifted the fall, and then, from those big, gnarled hands, there flowed a few notes, hesitantly at first, as his fingers awakened and remembered.

Serafina stood spellbound, watching his hands as they began to glide with effortless grace through the tangle of a thousand notes, the likes of which she had never heard. The claustrophobic walls of the cold refectory seemed to break open under the intensity of the sound.

She had never heard anything so uplifting. She felt the music flow through her, deepening with every breath she took, lifting her away from the unbearable burden of her sorrow, and stared in amazement as the priest unleashed these few moments of unrestrained passion, daring to tell the whole world of his place here on earth as a man who could be moved. Then, almost as quickly as he had begun, he closed his eyes and stopped, placing his hands in his lap, dropping his head for a moment. Serafina held her breath, barely able to conceive of what she had just witnessed, willing him to forget her presence in the room and continue. He turned his head to her slowly and lifted his finger to his lips with a smile.

'Father Lazarus!' She shook her head in disbelief.

'Shh. I could not resist it.' He laughed a little. 'Come and sit,' he said, removing himself from the stool and indicating her to take his place.

'But I can't play.' Serafina stared at the seat nervously.

'Not yet.' He smiled at her. 'Not yet.'

During the final month of school, trunks would be fetched down from the storage spaces in the attics and outhouses, and the packing would begin amid much speculative whispering and excitement, signalling the imminent arrival of the three-month holiday when the girls would leave for their homes, spread far and wide across the state and beyond.

Mary knew the time was coming near when the bright green parrots arrived, flocking to Haflong as they did each year for a little while, circling in the sky like an emerald cloud, taking roost in the trees of the lower hills where they could be heard screeching for a full hour before nightfall. Chinthimani knew the time was coming near when the rice hung heavy in the ear, leaning towards the earth, ready to harvest. Unable to settle herself, she would order the cook to bring in far more supplies than they would ever use, her agitation becoming constant, the bells on her ankles sounding their silvery notes long into the night as she paced the dark courtyard and felt the pull of her daughters' spirits.

The convent gates were opened to welcome the gradual influx of parents and chaperones, the pupils gathering to the east-facing windows of the school house waiting for their escorts, pressed to the panes from where they could see the open road to freedom. Soon the gates would be crowded with the porters who had made their way from the railway halt, talking among themselves cheerfully, assured as they were of a busy day with generous payment. Piles of packing trunks lay stacked precariously beside the high perimeter wall, their tags bursting into a flutter of tiny flags with each passing breeze.

Sister Margaret burst in, holding her list aloft. 'Serafina and Mary! Your father is here!' She raised her arm in a wide beckon. Mary stared at her friends, then turned and ran as fast as her legs would carry her without stopping to say goodbye.

On sighting his children, James lifted the hat from his head and held it high, waving it towards them, their shouts of joy drowning out his call of hello. He opened his arms as they crashed against him, hugging him tightly, loosening his footing.

'Goodness me!' he laughed, dropping his hat on to Mary's head. 'How much have you grown?'

'My clothes are all too small for me!' Mary pulled the hat lower, covering her eyes.

'Then we shall have to buy you some new ones!'

Serafina did not move, still pressed against his jacket, her face buried into his chest. James tightened his arm round her while he continued to jest with Mary, feeling the small convulsions of Serafina's tears.

'Did Mother come with you?' Mary looked past her father towards the gates.

'She is at the station waiting for you,' James said. 'So we had better hurry along. Your trunks have already been taken down. Shall we go?'

'Yes!' she shouted.

'Then lead the way, young lady!'

Mary danced ahead a few paces, holding his hat proudly on her head, turning constantly to check for his presence. James leaned down and took a handkerchief from his pocket. 'Here,' he whispered to Serafina. 'Dry your tears. There's nothing to cry about. I'm here now.'

Serafina took the handkerchief, laced with his scent, and put it to her face. *Nothing to cry about.* What would he know of her tears? What would he know of her agony? Of the blood she had begun to shed three months ago as she came into womanhood? What would he know of the whispers that passed from bed to bed at night? She dried her eyes and offered the handkerchief back to him with an empty smile.

Chinthimani listened to the porters' squabbling while slowly pacing the ladies' waiting room, sari held over her head, obscuring her face, peering out from the small window in the thin fabric at the commotion outside. She soon tired and sat, curling like a chrysalis as she leaned into the bench and allowed herself to slacken.

Among the softening colours of the watery figures on the platform, the dark shadow of a man appeared. He bent down for a moment, then thrust his arms forwards, releasing two smaller figures towards her.

'*Maa!*' Mary saw her in an instant and broke into a run. '*Maa! Maa!*'

Chinthimani's hands flew to her face. She stood and became immediately unsteady on her feet, leaning to the arm of the bench for support, then, unable to stop herself, sank back into the seat, opening her arms, the howl from her throat overwhelming her.

'Maa!' Mary felt herself swept into the soft cotton of her mother's sweet perfume, its wide white veil lifting up like a cloud and enveloping her completely, vanishing the world around them.

'Mary!' wept Chinthimani. 'Mary, *main tumse bohat pyar karti hou! Tum jawan aur balshaali ho!*'

'I love you, too!' Mary mumbled into her body, the rich scent of spices diffusing into her dress. 'I have grown, haven't I? Father noticed it, too!'

Chinthimani looked into her daughter's face, cupping it in her hands, unable to comprehend these fast foreign words that scattered from her own child's mouth. '*Kion, abghar chalain?*'

'Yes.' Mary nodded. 'I want to go home very much, *Maa*.'

Chinthimani released Mary's face and stood up, wiping the tears from her cheeks, looking around with concern. 'Serafina *kahan hai?*'

'She's here.' Mary turned, expecting to find Serafina directly behind her. Instead she saw her sister walking away, returning to their father. She took his hand and spoke to him. As she did so, James glanced towards the children's mother. He shook his head, and smiled at her sadly.

Shurika hummed to herself as she tended the vegetable garden, cropping the brinjals she had saved specially and setting them aside in a clay bowl on the ground before spreading mounds of dry grass over the new seedlings to protect them from the birds. The crows had taken all the strawberries, no matter what she did to conceal them, so she had given up on the soft fruits and added them to the cook's market list, if any could be found. From her lowered position, squatting on her haunches close to the earth, she could see Chinthimani pacing the courtyard slowly, one hand worrying at its fingers, the other fussing with the end of her sari. She was talking to herself again, mumbling as she walked, stopping sharply here and there to point at nothing and shake her head, shouting her refusal, arguing her victory over the imaginary opponent. There would be no reasoning with her today. No way to soothe her troubled mind.

Shurika placed the last handfuls of dry grass over the smallest shoots and collected up the bowl of brinjals. She would ask Cook to prepare some now for her mistress, hoping that she could tempt her into eating something before the children returned. The Sahib had sent for them for many days in a row now, each time with the promise of some grand entertainment. Shurika wondered if he knew. She had often caught Shiva glancing at her mistress suspiciously, and there had been times when he had questioned Shurika about the marks that appeared on her face and arms. But Shurika did not betray one word. There was nothing else she could do, except to pray every day for her mistress and her children. It was better that they were not here to see her like this. Each year when they returned home for the holidays, it had become harder for Shurika to conceal their mother's weaknesses. They were growing up, and there comes a time when a child will view the world with unclouded eyes.

They were no longer the barefooted children who once ran through the courtyard, chasing the animals and dodging between the drying sheets, reaching for each other's pigtails. They spoke English now, instruction in their mother's tongue having been deemed unnecessary. It was a miracle that Mary spoke any Hindi at all, and it was only that which she had learned from the cook. She was not supposed to go anywhere near the cookhouse, yet the moment she was home, she spent much of her time there, and was constantly getting into trouble for it.

Shurika rose from the vegetable patch, stretching the ache from her spine, and made her way to the cookhouse.

Serafina sat, posture-perfect, in a wide wicker chair on the verandah, reading the few carefully selected pages James had given her from his newspaper. Their father encouraged them to practise small talk of current events, although his efforts seemed to be entirely wasted on Mary, for whom any information appeared to go in one ear and straight out of the other. *It is probably just as well*, James thought, keeping the bulk of the newspapers to himself, their pages filled with bleak reports of historic cities lying in ruins in the wake of German bombs and Allied reprisals. It all seemed so far removed, the ripples in the pond long-dispersed before reaching these hills.

Every now and then, he glanced up from his article to regard his daughter's serious expression with fond amusement. Serafina pretended not to notice him looking at her and concentrated hard on the open page, barely moving a muscle, determined to absorb the complexities of each piece she read.

James cleared his throat lightly. 'Have you found anything interesting in your newspaper today, Serafina?'

'Yes, Papa,' she replied without hesitation, delighted that he had at last asked the question that she knew would come eventually. 'There's a new cartoon film in America and nobody likes it.'

'Really?' James nodded his approval. 'What's it called?'

Serafina trawled her memory, knowing that she had read the information somewhere, not wanting to have to glance at her newspaper to remind herself. For a moment she was plunged into self-doubt, frustrated at not being able to summon the answer at once. James sat patiently and gave her an encouraging smile, his head cocked in mock anticipation.

She remembered suddenly with a triumphant smile. '*Fantasia!*'

'Very good indeed.' James raised an eyebrow at her. 'Heaven knows, right now the world could certainly do with a little light-hearted entertainment.' He tutted and returned to his paper. 'There are evil forces at work, Serafina,' he said quietly, almost without thinking. 'Some men will not rest until they have forced the hand of Fate towards catastrophe yet again. We must all pray very hard and hope that good sense will prevail.' Serafina sat to attention, eyes fixed on her father, trying to comprehend his change in demeanour. 'I sometimes wonder what would happen to us if our newspapers did not exist. Whether we would still be carried along with the rest of the world, or if we would continue to go about our daily business, living in ignorant bliss.'

Serafina watched her father's thoughts darken, leaving her far behind, confiscating his warmth. Sensing the distance that had suddenly opened between them, she wished that she could bring him back to the moment when he had first smiled at her and asked her about the newspaper.

On the brief lawn set neatly before the verandah, Mary played with her father's dog, a long-legged boxer with a daft temperament, throwing sticks for him then running to hide behind the clipped hibiscus each time he tried to bring them back to her, barking his impatience. Several of the shrubs had been rudely dishevelled where she had deliberately flung the stick to a place she thought he would not find it, only to see him bolt after it and launch himself right into the middle of the rhododendrons.

Shiva appeared from the house carrying a tray of lemonade from the kitchen, where James's cook was busy preparing their favourite sweets.

'Ah, thank you, Shiva.' James shook off the concern that had rumpled his face, set his newspaper down and gratefully accepted a glass from Shiva's silver tray. Serafina observed her father closely, noting his every move in minute detail, and deliberately folded her piece of newspaper in precisely the same way as he had before taking a glass for herself. James drank a little and watched Mary teasing the dog for a while, a slow smile coming over him that quickly stretched into a full, raucous laugh.

'Mary!' he called out to her. 'Let Buster rest for a while before the poor animal dies of exhaustion. It's wearing us all out just to look at you.'

'Papa!' Mary dropped the stick to the ground, ran up the steps to the verandah and leaped to her father's side, causing him to spill his drink, then supped down half her glass in one go. Serafina scowled at her disapprovingly and sipped her own lemonade politely in remonstration. Shiva smilingly handed his master the cloth from his tray to mop the mess from his drenched hand.

Mary watched him dab the lemonade from his lap. 'Why does Mother never come here?'

'Be quiet, Mary,' Serafina snapped.

James nodded at Shiva to refill their glasses, giving himself a moment to consider his response.

'Your mother is a very busy woman. She has many things to attend to. Why? Do you not like spending time up at the big house with me?' Clearly, he was teasing her. Shiva smiled and returned to the house with the empty tray. James sat up straight, pulling Mary into the crook of his arm. 'Besides,' he announced dramatically, 'I have a big surprise in store for you today.' He picked up his glass and took his time with a deliberately slow sip. 'I was going to keep it a secret, but judging by the state of your socks, young lady, I suppose I will have to give you a little notice.'

'What is it?' Mary pulled at his shirt. 'Tell us!'

Her head filled with vivid memories of the wonderful surprises he had arranged for them during the school holidays long past, and she and Serafina exchanged an excited glance and grinned at each other. Unable to contain herself, Mary buried her face in her hands to stifle her squeals. James basked in her delight and gave her knee a tweak.

'We have a very special guest coming to meet you today, so I want you to be on your best behaviour over tiffin, all right?' He wagged a playful finger at her. 'I assume that you're both old enough now to be introduced to polite company? Or do you think I should wait another year or two?'

'Who is it?' demanded Mary, beaming from ear to ear.

Serafina sat patiently and held on to her own curiosity, knowing that her unguarded sister would invariably ask the awkward questions that she herself would not dare to raise. It was sufficient for her that they were permitted to visit the big house more regularly now. The house that she had stolen so many yearning glances at for so long. The house that she had crept through the trees to spy upon ever since she was big enough to get away with a small, unwarranted absence from her mother's compound.

'You know those big cakes that you like so much?' Mary nodded at her father eagerly. 'And the enormous tins of Staffordshire butter?' She nodded again. This time, James turned towards Serafina. 'Well, your Aunty Dorothy is coming to visit this afternoon so that she can see for herself where all those food parcels have been disappearing to.' He gave a little roar and tickled Mary's tummy, Mary squirming in delight. Serafina, suddenly agitated, looked down into her drink, her mouth set into a slight rigidity that gave her away. James squinted at her playfully. 'And may I ask what you are looking so worried about?'

'I don't know.' She shrugged, unable to pinpoint the reason for her anxiety, yet saturated with its charge.

'Good. Now go and tidy your dresses and ask one of the boys to polish your shoes.'

## CHAPTER 7

DOROTHY'S NERVES RAN AWAY with her as she prepared in her suite of rooms at the clubhouse, her home-from-home for three months every winter. It was now part of her yearly routine, to take her leave of the plantation for the sake of appearances, sometimes travelling to England to remind herself of the reasons she had left, reasons that had worn thinner as her resentment grew. She had not argued with James about the arrangement, hearing his plea that it was the only sensible thing to do. She had not protested at the gathering of her belongings and the erasing of her presence to preserve the carefully orchestrated veneer created for the sake of his children. She had not issued a word of complaint in seven years. Nor had she found herself blessed with a child of her own, her heart heavy with her husband's concealment. She had known it the moment their marriage was consummated, that his love for her was grounded in sedate devotion rather than the passion she had so dreamed of. Melting into his arms, sweet orange blossom still clinging to her hair, she had found his love-making perfunctory, his ardour restrained, and the truth of their union came upon her like an unexpected blanket of cloud on a summer day. James had no intention of creating a child with her. He had learned to be cautious, to chasten his desires, and she, in turn, had been forced to learn the lesson of acceptance.

Dorothy dressed carefully, choosing a simple day dress in a deep shade of fawn and a pair of mid-heeled shoes with small buckles on the single strap. Such was her state of unease that her hands trembled as she fumbled with the fastenings. She was ready far too early, and fretfully paced her rooms for half an hour, the gin and tonic in her hand rather stronger than she would usually permit herself. Checking her wristwatch every few moments, she couldn't prevent her thoughts from wandering. Her heart contracted painfully each time she recalled the terrible scene on that mountainside in Mussoorie, and the moment that she had surrendered to her fate, pledging to James that she would share the responsibility he so steadfastly refused to give up. Had she known what she was saying, the sacrifices that would be expected of her, she would have conceded defeat there and then instead of taking his hand.

Little by little, her wounds had slowly healed, but the scars remained. She began to write to the children regularly, cheerful, shallow missives that told nothing of herself, designed merely to fill the gaps left by a father who spent too long meaning to write and not enough time putting his pen against paper, always signing herself Aunty Dorothy, as though it lent some regularity to her life. She asked James if she wouldn't be better suited to pick out the things they needed while they were away at school, particularly the occasional pretties for a growing girl, and busied herself with their requirements. It was, she had felt, the very least she could do, a penance of sorts, for the wrongdoings of the man she had chosen to love. Yet as the years slid by, it became the cruellest torture, the unspoken words wedged uncomfortably between them, the forbidden subject never permitted to surface. His secret children. His secret wife. No matter how she tried to contain her rancour, silencing herself at every turn, her efforts were never enough. She had finally insisted upon meeting them, if only to exorcise the spectres that haunted her every waking moment.

A gentle knock disturbed her faint heart, the voice behind the door imparting that her driver was ready and waiting.

The girls sat awkwardly in the parlour, Serafina concealing her nerves with hands folded neatly in her lap, Mary beside her on the settee, nudging and giggling much to her sister's annoyance. Serafina was determined to make a good impression. Perhaps, if the introductions went well, her aunt would invite her to stay with her in England when school was over. It was common enough for the older girls. She had frequently overheard detailed talk of their plans for finishing, of being sent to live with their most well-connected relatives, learning the finer points of the social graces required to get along. Several of Aunty Dorothy's letters had been postmarked from London, and Serafina imagined that she would like it there very well indeed.

The sound of a car and raised voices outside jolted her to attention. She sat up straight, knees pressed neatly together, and after what seemed like an eternity, the parlour door opened.

'Children?' They stood immediately at the sound of their father's voice. 'Your Aunty Dorothy is here.'

Dorothy stepped into the room, a slight hesitation in her manner, and smiled nervously. Both girls chorused, 'How do you do?' and dipped a small, much-practised curtsey.

Without warning, Dorothy felt herself suddenly beset with a shocking surge of emotion. Her hand rose to her mouth to stifle the sob rising in her throat and she found herself powerless against the unexpected onslaught of tears pricking at her eyes. In that very moment, every poisonous droplet of the hurt and humiliation she had held inside for so long evaporated like beads of water in the midday sun. James moved towards her, then stopped himself. Dorothy looked at him fleetingly, just long enough to see the concern on his face. She had promised him that she would not react badly or cause a fuss, but nothing had prepared her for this.

Here before her stood the truth of it—two girls, twelve and fourteen years old, innocent and free from sin, dressed in the ribbon-edged yellow smocks that she herself had picked out for them not more than six weeks ago. Even then, they had not existed. They were not real at all, these two ethereal figures who plagued her thoughts and haunted her dreams. She had done her duty and tried to be generous of spirit, all the while wishing them away, swallowing bitter tears when no one was looking. The shame washed over her in great, drowning waves. She removed the gloved hand from her mouth, her stinging eyes darting again to James, before taking her ravaged heart in hand and returning their greeting.

'How do *you* do?'

Before Serafina could deliver her rehearsed response, Mary broke rank and rushed to Dorothy's side, grabbing hold of her hand, her face lit up with a beaming smile. 'We've been dying to meet you! We're having stuffed roasted chicken for lunch! I watched Cook kill it and it ran around for simply ages! There was blood everywhere! Do you like roast chicken?'

'Why, yes!' Dorothy returned Mary's enthusiasm. 'It just so happens that I like roast chicken very much!'

Seated at the dining table she had become so familiar with, Dorothy scarcely knew what to think or what to say. Physically, they were not as she had imagined them at all. The elder of the two bore a striking resemblance to her father: the wave in her hair, the dusting of freckles across the apples of her high cheeks. There was a squareness to her jawline. An elegant symmetry to her shoulders. And she was tall, like him, with the same, slightly haughty expression. She could be Italian, Dorothy mused, Spanish perhaps, but not Indian. Definitely not Indian. The nose was all wrong. The bone structure. Almost as though nothing quite went together. Yet among all that, beneath the yellow ribbon-edged dress, her startling aesthetics could not be denied, the first traces of a great beauty waiting to bloom already quite visible. Dorothy tried to wipe from her mind the notion of the mother who could produce such a child. Her eyes wandered to Mary, smaller, darker, with a pretty, doll-like face and rose-bud lips, her whole demeanour less angular than her sister, less brooding, with a constant, trusting smile. Dorothy sensed James watching her closely, his vulnerability a new quality that she had not seen before.

'Where do you live?' asked Mary.

'Ah.' Dorothy stalled. 'Well, sometimes I live in—'

'London,' James interjected. 'Your Aunty Dorothy is a lady doctor, and that's where she did her studying.'

'Really?' Serafina said. 'Did it take you a very long time?'

'Yes,' said Dorothy. 'I had to study hard for years before they gave me my white coat, but I loved every moment of it.'

'Do you have one of those tubes?' Mary asked.

'Tubes?'

'Yes, you know.' Mary mimed having her chest listened to.

'Oh! You mean a stethoscope! Yes, as a matter of fact I do.'

'Did you bring it with you?'

'Why, yes, I think it may be—' Dorothy stopped suddenly, struggling to find a reason why her doctor's bag would be in the house. 'Oh, wait. I'm not so sure, come to think of it.'

Serafina stared at Dorothy, sensing her nervousness. 'What's London like?'

'Well,' Dorothy began. 'Let me see now. It's very busy, and jolly cold in the winter, with endless rain, and there are lots of people, and big red buses that drive everybody around.'

'And special trains that go under the ground,' James added.

'Under the ground?' Mary laughed. 'That's impossible!'

'I'd love to go to London one day,' Serafina hinted, sitting perfectly straight against her chair. 'Are you going back there soon?'

'Well . . .' Dorothy hid her hands beneath the table, conscious that they were fidgeting. Oh, if only they had talked this through properly. 'Yes.' She hesitated. 'I'm planning on staying here for a while, then back to London, then hopefully another visit here.'

'Are you married?' Mary piped up.

Dorothy, unable to remove the glass from her lips quickly enough, choked on her wine.

'Really!' James chided Mary good-naturedly. 'What a very personal question, Mary. Don't they teach you anything at that school of yours?'

'Sorry, Papa.' Mary looked at her plate. 'I didn't mean to be rude.'

'So,' Dorothy recovered and smiled brightly, 'how are you enjoying school?'

Serafina opened her mouth to speak, but was cut off instantly.

'I hate it,' complained Mary. 'The food's horrible and there's never enough to eat. We have to go to church all the time and it's freezing at night so I have to wrap myself up in an extra shawl that always gets tangled up in the bed with me. Jane Cavendish snores and wakes everyone up. We're not friends or anything. She's older than me, but even if she wasn't, I wouldn't want to be friends with someone who snores like that.'

Serafina glared at her sister, clearly outraged by her babbling. Dorothy was careful to include them both in the conversation.

'And you, Serafina?'

'It's a very good school, Aunty Dorothy. We realise how lucky we are to be there. Please don't take any notice of Mary. She's always complaining about something. She doesn't mean to sound ungrateful.' Mary scowled into her chicken. 'The parcels are lovely. And thank you for sending the cakes.' Serafina put down her cutlery noiselessly, demonstrating the benefits of their distant education. 'We always look forward to them very much, and to your letters.'

'And the butter!' Mary interrupted again. 'And the jam! I love—'

'Mary!' Serafina kicked her hard beneath the table. 'You're talking too much again. And take your elbow off the table.'

'No, I'm not! I'm just saying about—'

'Aunty Dorothy doesn't want to hear about your silly friends,' Serafina snapped.

'Nonsense,' said their father. 'In fact, I think I'd quite like to have a few silly friends myself.'

Dorothy flashed her eyes towards James. Her heart went out to him. Finally, after all these years, she understood.

In accordance with the routine that had formed over the years, it was Shiva who was charged with the task of returning the children to their mother's house. James would not go there now, the prospect of witnessing such unhappiness too much for him to bear. He had heard the stories of her condition. There were still times when he caught himself standing on the verandah at sundown, staring unthinkingly towards the western estate road, his feelings aroused in one way or another. This evening, he gazed in the same direction, watching his daughters leave under a softly setting sky.

It was quite a distance to the homestead when measured in a child's footsteps, so they rode in a small cart tethered to the mildest of the oxen, an ageing cow who knew the way well and never complained. They took their time in returning, Shiva pausing to point out the iridescent flash of a kingfisher, waiting awhile to see if another came along, allowing the ox to dawdle the route at her own pace without a flick of encouragement from his switch.

The cart pulled gently to a halt shortly before the wild thicket with the spreading banyan tree. The track was rough from here, lying pitted and unrepaired since the Sahib had stopped calling years ago. Instead, solemn deliveries were made regularly by one of the runners with messages passed formally from household to household through the layers of protocol set by the servants. Anything Chinthimani needed or wished for was taken to her without question, but little else crossed the impossible distance between one world and the other.

Shiva lifted the girls down from the cart. Better to walk the rest of the way and enjoy the fragrant frangipani flowers that fluttered to the ground each day. As they walked, Mary reached down here and there, gathering the fallen blooms, picking them up carefully, filling her hands with the pale, creamy petals and lifting them to her face to take in their sweet vanilla scent. Shiva watched her, approving of the joy the child found in her surroundings. He watched her skip ahead and wondered what her future would bring.

Still some small distance from the gates, the sounds of Chinthimani's anguish crept towards them. Serafina tensed, her head drooping earthwards as she felt the gaiety of the day seeping inexorably away. With each step that took her closer to this place they called home, her heart dulled just a little more. It was as though a sinister sense of loss hung over the courtyard, even when she and her sister were there. Cook no longer crashed around, instead silencing his pots to a respectful simmer. Their mother no longer smiled as she used to, the pride in her eyes now shadowed with the tamarind bitterness of her deep sorrow. They turned the final corner, finding the gates left wide open for their return.

Chinthimani stood in the courtyard shouting her suffering at Shurika, her high-pitched voice fuelled by the wrath that lived with her constantly, its fire never far from the surface. Shurika stood meekly, eyes downcast, and did nothing to retaliate. Neither woman noticed the children arriving with their father's faithful manservant. Chinthimani stumbled and raised a hand to hit Shurika, howling painfully about nothing and everything, slurring her words. Shurika bent like a reed, flinching in anticipation and lifting her arms quickly to protect herself from the rain of blows that would certainly follow.

Serafina wrenched her hand from Shiva's immediate grip and ran into the courtyard, swooping down to pick up a small branch fallen from the silver oak. As she flew towards the two women, she flailed the stick above her head defiantly and screamed at her mother. 'If you touch her, I will kill you! Do you hear me? Leave her alone!'

Serafina shook, her whole body caught up in the brutality of this wretched place, shaking from her head down to her feet, her face red with rage. The women, visibly shocked, froze in their positions as Serafina's outburst filled the courtyard with a storm of violence, then dreadful silence. Mary stood beside Shiva, wide-eyed and open-mouthed. He squeezed her hand, but said nothing.

**M**arch came and went. School had started weeks ago, but James, weakened by the constant pleading from his children to stay just a little while longer, had not the strength to deny them.

'You can't keep them here for ever.' Dorothy sympathised with him as they strolled the wide manicured lawns of the club together, her voice soft and understanding.

'I know,' he said.

'And I really can't stay here at the club indefinitely. People are beginning to talk.'

'They've been doing that for a long time, darling,' James conceded, nodding a brief hello to another couple passing them by. 'I wouldn't take any notice. If they're not talking about me, they'd only find some other poor beggar to persecute.'

'This is different,' Dorothy said. 'People stop speaking when I come into the room, then quickly change the subject. It's so obvious. They smile politely at me as though I'm some kind of fool who doesn't know what's going on. It's humiliating, James. No one wants to be made a laughing stock of. Least of all you and me.'

'Since when did you care what people said?'

'I don't!' The sudden rise in her pitch protested too much. 'But one servant goes talking to another, and the next thing we know, the whole world knows your business, and mine, too.'

'I'm sorry, darling. You shouldn't have to put up with that sort of thing. God knows, this has all been hard enough on you as it is.'

'Oh, James.' She touched his hand. 'Don't you have enough to worry about? You know Felix has done everything he can to keep the dogs off, but he's said that even he has his limits.'

'It's just so damned difficult,' James said.

'So you haven't told them yet?'

'How can I? This is the only home they have ever known, no matter how precarious it may seem. Take that away from them and what will they have?'

'They'll have a future, James.'

James peered up at the darkening sky threatening from above. He stopped and paused, glancing back to the clubhouse. 'Come on,' he said casually, as if hoping to change the subject. 'It looks like we could be in for a soaking. I think we had better make our way back.' Dorothy ignored the rumble from above and stood her ground.

'Listen to me, James.' She took both his hands in hers. 'You have to face facts sooner or later. There's trouble brewing everywhere and we both know it, and I'm not just talking about the children. Look at what's happening in Europe, for heaven's sake. The newspapers are full of all kinds of terrible stories. And if what they're saying is true, this war is coming our way, no matter how much we all try to pretend it isn't.'

'The newspapers exaggerate, darling. They always do.'

'Don't treat me like a child.' Dorothy glared at him. 'Any idiot can see that there's just as much trouble in the east, and we're stuck right in the middle of it. It could spill over these borders and into our lives before anyone has a chance to even think about it.' She shuddered involuntarily against the damp, humid air. 'God only knows what might happen then.'

'No doubt the self-rule revolutionaries will have a heyday,' James replied. 'Nothing is what it used to be. And I have a feeling that this is just the beginning.'

'Then you know you can't wait indefinitely.' Dorothy linked her arm through his and together they began to walk back towards the clubhouse. 'You have to make proper arrangements. What if something should happen to you?'

A sudden shower fell from the clouds, engulfing the gardens in a curtain of warm water. James quickly pulled off his jacket and threw it across their heads as they rushed for the cover of the nearest tree. Beneath the protection of its branches, he shook the rain from his jacket and placed it round Dorothy's shoulders.

'Thank you,' she said, pulling it close, feeling the remnants of his warmth within its soft lining.

James put his arm round her. 'I'm sorry for getting you caught up in this mess. You deserved better.'

'I didn't want better. I wanted you.'

'And children.'

Dorothy averted her face. 'We promised each other we wouldn't talk of that any more.'

'I couldn't,' he said. 'I just—'

'Please.' The old, familiar ache began, just behind her eyes, pulling their lids tight shut. 'Let's not do this. Not now. I don't think I could bear it.' James swallowed, nodding towards the ground. 'Your first responsibility is to those girls. Don't shy away from it, James.'

'You're right,' he said. 'I'll take the children back at the end of the week. But don't ask me to tell them before they go. I just can't do it.'

'What about the woman?' Still, after all this time, Dorothy was unable to allow Chinthimani's name to pass her lips.

'That will have to wait, too, at least until the children have gone. Who knows what she might go and do? Probably run away into the jungle with them. I wouldn't even put it past her to take a knife to them all. She's losing her mind, you know.' His face clouded. 'The more I hear, the more I see that there's no other way, but it doesn't make it any easier.'

'Think of the children.' Dorothy pulled at his arm, willing him to make his resolve. 'As hard as it may be, you know it's the right thing to do.'

The train waited in the station, idling with a lazy hiss from the exhausted engine. The children sat in the carriage beside their father; Mary, mistrustful of the hired chaperone, staring dutifully out of the window at the teeming life on the platform edge.

Chinthimani had stayed behind this time, as she often did, her headaches rendering her unfit for the journey. Serafina had said nothing about it, barely able to give her mother so much as a glance. Mary sulked her disappointment but knew it would do no good to argue. She hated being stuck with a chaperone. They always behaved charmingly enough in front of her father, but the smile usually faded the moment he had retired to the first-class gentlemen's carriage, and they rarely offered much in the way of conversation. Mary chattered incessantly to her father, who humoured her kindly and tried to keep their spirits up, despite Serafina's glum expression.

'I expect you'll be looking forward to seeing all your friends again.'

'I'd rather stay at home.' Mary pulled a face.

'And what would you learn if you stayed at home all the time? You would never be able to find your way in this world, and that would be no good at all, would it?'

'You could teach us yourself,' Mary decided. 'Then we could live with you up at the big house. We wouldn't be any trouble.'

At that moment, the train began to pull out.

'Papa!' Serafina shouted. 'We're moving!'

Through Mary's busy conversation they had missed the stationmaster's final whistle. James got up quickly, thought briefly about making a dash for it, but saw that the engine was already picking up speed, the platform edge sliding past, taking the waving spectators with it. He sighed and sat back down.

'Papa! You are in the wrong carriage!' Mary's delighted face lit up. 'What are you going to do?'

He smiled and put a finger to his lips. 'I won't tell if you won't. Let's just hope that the guard doesn't come along and make a big performance about it. I'll change over at the next stop.'

Mary moved along the seat and snuggled in close beside him, resting her head against his arm, smelling the fabric of his clothes, feeling for the tie tucked in her pocket, a brown silk one with cream polka dots. James had taken her to his dressing room the previous day and had opened his closet doors then told her that she might choose one of his ties to take back to school with her as a reminder of the holiday. A keepsake from him.

Serafina remained quiet and stared out of the window at the changing landscape. She detested every long mile of it, reminding her that she belonged nowhere, passed like an unwanted consignment from one place to another.

Eventually, James broke the silence.

'I will miss you girls when you are gone,' he said sadly. 'We had a wonderful holiday together but—'

All at once, there came a terrible commotion. A tremendous sharp noise crashed against the carriage, followed by a succession of desperate scrabbling sounds that seemed to scrape against the inside of the walls.

The chaperone looked up from her book, her face white with alarm. 'What on earth?'

James became alert in an instant, his whole body tensing as he realised what was happening. Outside, two men had leaped onto the train from their hiding place within the dense trees and now gripped the moving carriage. Crude weapons in hand, they banged menacingly on the roof of the carriage, then slid down and began wrenching at the door handle, trying to get in. Terrified, the children grasped hold of their father, their screams deafening his senses. James jumped up from his seat, thrusting them roughly towards the shocked figure of the chaperone.

'Don't just sit there, woman!' he shouted at her. 'Take them!'

She immediately encircled them in her arms, hiding their faces in her chest, telling them to be quiet, drawing them into the seat with her.

James pressed himself against the carriage wall, quickly stole a glance out of the window, then pulled back.

'Bandits!' He shouted a helpless warning to his cowering children, then swore under his breath, wishing more than anything else at that moment that he had with him the small pistol that he kept in the teak case above his dresser. It had never seen the light of day, fool that he was. In his regimented comfort on the plantation, it was all too easy for James to forget that this was lawless territory and that these incidents had become increasingly commonplace as the world's troubles grew.

His anger at himself—for this and a thousand other things—rose in a sudden storm of fury. He reached for his cane and pushed the window down, thrusting the full armoury of his strapping frame outwards and flailing violently at the two men, shouting, *Chale jao! Chale jao!*' in the same commanding tone he used when there was trouble afoot in the coolie huts. The robbers, shocked to find a broadly built Englishman in the first-class ladies' carriage, glanced at each other, wide-eyed and bewildered.

Seeing his chance, James pushed himself out as far as he could and thrashed his cane at the leg of the nearest assailant. It hit its mark with savage accuracy, causing the man to cry out in pain and grasp down towards his injured knee. His accomplice, waving a long, broad knife, lurched towards James, screaming a stream of abuse, the confusion of the situation opening before him sending him into a deadly panic. With one hand holding on to the outside rail, the man swung himself out from the moving carriage, using the speed of the train to aid his swift movement, and flew directly towards James, knife outstretched. James ducked back quickly, throwing himself against the inside wall, the blade crashing against the window frame, lodging itself into the wood at the very point where his head had been just seconds before.

As the robber tried to recover his balance and retrieve his knife, James rushed forward once more and slammed his cane into the man's neck. The chaperone screamed in horror as James hit him again, this time full on the head, the scalp splitting and spilling crimson blood. The man lost his grip instantly, falling to the moving ground far below. The second assailant howled down at his friend's disappearing body, released his grip and dropped harmlessly to the ground. James watched as he rolled down the escarpment, the train quickly distancing the frustrated men from their intended victims.

With pounding temples and trembling hands, James pulled himself back into the compartment, gathering every ounce of his self-control to keep his head and conceal the sickening rush that had overwhelmed him.

'They've gone,' he said with a hollow smile, smoothing his dishevelled hair, trying to banish the flashing images of his bloody, murdered children from his mind's eye. 'I don't think they'll be back again.' He retook his seat, dabbing the sweat from his brow with a handkerchief. Serafina sat rigid, then threw herself towards him and held on tightly. 'It's all right,' he told her. 'We're all perfectly safe. They would never have managed to get in anyway. These carriages are stronger than the Tower of London.' Mary lifted her head from the chaperone's lap, her eyes wide with fear, cheeks wet with tears. 'Are you all right?' He tried to smile. Mary shook her head and started to cry again.

'Dear Lord.' The chaperone crossed herself. Her voice rose as her own panic set in. 'This is the last time I risk using the train like this—'

'That's quite enough.' James silenced her with a ferocious glare. 'You were never in any danger,' he insisted, the sharpness of his tongue declaring her talk to be out of place in front of his children. 'But perhaps I had better stay here with you for the rest of the way.'

James returned home the following evening to find Felix waiting for him, he and Dorothy sitting out on the verandah, watching the storm clouds gathering overhead.

'Good God, James.' Felix took one look at his friend's exhausted face.

'Whatever's the matter? You look as though you've seen a ghost, man.'

Dorothy stood the moment she saw him. 'Are you all right, darling?'

'What?' James seemed unaware of his unusually disordered appearance, the tear in the elbow of his jacket not quite visible from his viewpoint. 'Yes,' he said. 'Yes, I'm fine.' He accepted Dorothy's kiss. 'Get me a drink, would you, darling?'

'Yes, of course,' she said, skimming Felix a quizzical look before leaving them together.

James dropped himself into her vacant chair. 'What are you doing here?' Fatigued, he reached for a cigarette from the box on the table and struck a match.

'I've been asking myself that very same question for years,' Felix replied. 'You know I've always done my best for you, don't you, James?'

James drew on his cigarette long and hard. 'That I cannot deny,' he said. 'But if you've come here to give me another one of your lectures, you might as well save your breath.'

'I'm afraid not.' Felix spoke levelly. 'It's all a bit late for that now.'

Hearing the resignation in his friend's voice, James found himself for the first time genuinely concerned by Felix's disquiet.

'There's been a whole lot of brouhaha at the Calcutta office, James. Penderghast has been under pressure from the bigwigs in London. All this political nonsense going on.'

Dorothy stepped out of the door with James's drink and placed it on the low table in front of him. Just as she was about to take a seat, Felix half stood from his own.

'Dorothy? I don't suppose I could ask you to leave us two chaps alone for a few minutes, could I?'

'Well, I . . .' Dorothy looked embarrassed. 'Of course.'

'Just the usual dull business talk,' Felix explained diplomatically. 'We wouldn't want to bore you with it.'

She smiled understandingly. 'Come in when you're ready to eat.'

James waited until her footsteps faded before challenging his friend. 'All right, Felix. What the hell's going on? I leave the place for two days and come back to find you looking like an executioner waiting on my doorstep. Let's have it.'

'It's a mess, James,' Felix said. 'And if it isn't now, it soon will be. The company has demanded detailed inventories from each of the regional managers. And this isn't just about money; there are all sorts of other rumblings going on. They're not prepared to turn a blind eye any longer.' James felt the whisky burning his dry throat. 'It's not just you. They're making a clean sweep under these ridiculous new rules of constitution.

'It's been decided that there's quite enough trouble for the company to deal with without having the added complication of a load of illegitimate half-castes running around the countryside. It causes a lot of bad feeling, you know.' He leaned back in his chair and released a plume of smoke into the dense air above him. 'They can't allow anything to jeopardise future diplomatic relations. It's all just one headache after another.'

'So,' James said wryly. 'The British are finally discovering that their once faithful and subservient colony has had enough. I wonder what took them so long.'

'"Quit India", indeed,' Felix huffed. 'Can you imagine these peasants trying to rule themselves? They mean to take control of everything that we British have toiled so long to achieve and throw us out on our ears.'

'It was only ever a matter of time,' James said.

'Well, let them do what they want.' Felix threw back the rest of his whisky. 'Let them have their wish and may the whole bloody lot come tumbling down around their ears.'

'Don't let it get to you, Felix. It'll blow over, you wait and see.'

'Blow over?' Felix banged his fist against the arm of his chair. 'Are you mad? The whole world's in turmoil! First Europe, now north Africa, and it won't stop there, either. You just mark my words.'

James sat calmly and allowed his eyes to roam the far terraces, patterning the hillsides in an undulating cushion of jade. 'The writing has been on the wall for a long time, Felix. We were going to have to deal with it at some point, so you might as well get used to it. We'll all have to make adjustments, one way or another.' He waited for Felix to launch into another tirade, but instead of coming back at him with his usual bluster, Felix just sat there in silence. Then he put his empty glass down on the table quietly and sighed.

'You're to be moved on,' he said, without looking up.

The words hit James like iced water. In that moment, the whole world stood still. He felt his mouth open and close, his fingers flexing against the cool of his whisky glass. His throat tightened, strangling his reply.

'What?'

'Moved on. Shipped out. Whatever you want to call it. I'm sorry, James. I did everything I could to persuade Penderghast against the decision, but it fell on deaf ears. He knows all about your predicament. For heaven's sake,' Felix let out a small, ridiculous laugh, 'I don't know who doesn't, the way you've carried on.'

'But I've been here for over fifteen years! I can't just—'

'A damned sight longer than you should have been, if you ask me.'

'But what about—' He stopped himself.

'Forget it, James. You should have thought about all that a long time ago.' James sat, speechless. 'I'll take care of the place myself until the new chap arrives.'

'You'll let her stay where she is?' James heard the impotence of his words. 'It's out of the way. They wouldn't be in anyone's—'

'Oh, just give it up, will you?' Felix said irritably. 'Haven't you had enough yet?'

A hollow surge rammed through James's stomach. So this was it. The end. The end that he could never envisage, no matter how often he had tried to force himself towards it.

'Where will you send her?'

'What the hell do you care?'

'*Care?*' James jerked from his seat, throwing his arms into the air. 'Of course I bloody care. What the hell do you think I've been doing all these years? Where do you think I've been these last two days?'

'I know,' Felix said, finding his compassion. 'Dorothy told me. You've done the most honourable thing a man in your position could have.'

'Then why do I feel like such a heel?'

'She'll be paid off, just like the others. Where she goes will be up to her, James. There is nothing more that you can do. They're sending you west.'

Deeply shaken, James sank back into his seat. 'Where?'

'That I don't know yet, but your time here is done.'

'Have you told Dorothy any of this?'

'Of course not. I'm afraid that will be down to you.'

'I see,' said James.

'I expect she'll be bloody grateful and more than a little relieved if you ask me,' Felix said. 'I don't know how she's put up with your preposterous arrangements for this long. You should count yourself lucky that she hasn't upped and left you. It's probably a blessing in disguise, James.'

Shurika regarded her mistress's wan reflection in the cracked mirror of the dressing table. The once rosebud lips had given up their bloom long ago and seemed lost in the grey pallor of her sunken complexion. Teasing the tangles from her hair with slow ritual, Shurika sat behind her, working gently, beginning at the ends of its length, moving gradually upwards with practised fingers, massaging Chinthimani's scalp with perfumed oil.

Chinthimani did not move, hearing nothing, feeling nothing. Setting down the dish, Shurika ran the sandalwood comb through her mistress's glorious mane, the shining ribbon of jet-black hair holding the light and casting it back like polished onyx. She finished the task, set the comb into her lap, dropped her head and wept.

'Weep for us both,' Chinthimani said to the mirror, her voice dull. 'For I have no more tears.'

'I will never leave you, mistress. My place is with you. It is my purpose.'

'Your purpose,' Chinthimani said, drawing the words out in a slow chant. 'My purpose. Your purpose. My curse. Your curse. I want no more from this incarnation. I could wake no more and be content. There is no life inside me now.'

'We must make a new life for ourselves,' Shurika said. 'A new life far away from here.'

Shurika had chosen what to take, selecting only small objects of value, some clothes, sufficient food to sustain them on their journey for a while. They would have to manage the bullock cart on their own, the cook and his helper having upped and left almost the instant Shiva took his leave of them. Her brother had gone too, disappearing into the night after promising with empty words that he would stay and protect them. Shurika had left a few coins, her mistress's gold nose ring and some trinkets on the table deliberately, knowing that he would steal whatever he could and flee. She had listened intently as he had picked his way around in the darkness when he had thought them asleep, her heart racing at the thought of the money she had sewn into the folds of her sari. The rest of their valuables she had hidden in the earth by the vegetables that grew in her mistress's garden. It was all still there, undisturbed, when the sun rose and her brother was long gone. Shurika had then walked to the gatehouse, to leave one final message, before returning to the courtyard and waiting for a response.

'They have all left us,' she had said. 'What should we do?'

'I cannot help you,' Shiva replied.

'Please, tell me! We cannot stay here. It will be too dangerous for us.'

'It will be dangerous for you anywhere. Take this.' He had handed her a small envelope. 'It is a letter of introduction, vouching for your good character. It is the only protection I can offer you. Do not lose it.'

'Where should we go?'

'I don't know.' He saw hopelessness in her eyes. 'South,' he told her. 'There is talk of much trouble in the north. Go south. Or west. There are more people there. Find somewhere to disappear, where you will not be noticed. A town, or a city where you will become invisible. You must become invisible and hope that the gods are kind to you.'

Shurika sat quietly behind her mistress and dried her tears. They had a long day ahead of them, the bundles she had prepared ready and waiting. She wiped the oil from the sandalwood comb and rested it in her lap. Chinthimani watched her closely in the mirror, took the drink from the table and swallowed it.

'Now finish the job you started,' she said, holding her head up proudly.

'Yes, mistress,' Shurika said. 'It is my honour to serve you.'

Piece by piece, Chinthimani's hair fell to the ground, the floor around them becoming a silken carpet of one woman's life. With the work of her scissors done, Shurika took up the sharpened razor, dipped it into her bowl of oil and passed it gently across her mistress's head, carving the silhouette of a widow, the outcast of outcasts.

# CHAPTER 8

SIX MONTHS PASSED. The Angelus bell rang out from the chapel of St Agnes. All around, everyone halted, no matter where they were. The pupils stood and quietened, ready to recite the Angelus so embedded in all of them. It was Mary's favourite. She liked that it was a prayer to Mary, and the way her name sounded when sung in Latin. The ritual soon passed, and the small world of the convent reawakened and continued to go about the daily business of life.

In the quiet of the empty convent house, Serafina sat calmly in one of the two chairs set before the mother superior's desk. A small fire had been laid in the hearth, the single crackling log sufficient to warm the day's slight chill from the room. Hands folded neatly in her lap, Serafina sat quietly while the mother superior busied herself, uttering pleasantries about the sunshine outside while returning a leather-bound book to the shelf before taking her seat. She removed her half-moon spectacles and regarded Serafina with compassion.

'Serafina,' she said. 'I expect you will be wondering why I asked you to stay behind this afternoon.'

'Yes, Mother Superior.'

'You know that we can never be sure what the Lord has in store for us, Serafina. Sometimes we do not understand why certain things happen . . .' Serafina felt her blood run cold. She stared at the mother superior, empty-eyed, placing an invisible wall of protection between herself and the one piece of news she had always dreaded hearing. 'There is going to be no easy way to explain this to you.' The mother superior indicated a folded letter on the desk in front of her. 'I'm afraid that you and your sister will not be going home for the holidays.'

Serafina looked her straight in the eye and asked her outright. 'Have we been dropped?'

'No! Oh, dear child! Of course not! Your father is devoted to both you and your sister. He made that perfectly clear to us from the beginning. But he has moved to another job hundreds of miles away, so it isn't possible for him to have you home for the holidays.'

'What about our mother? Has she moved with him?'

'I—' The mother superior flushed. 'I don't know. But that isn't the—'

'Then we could go and stay with her as we always do,' Serafina said.

'I'm afraid that won't be possible, Serafina. Your father has left us strict instructions. You are to stay here with your sister.'

'I see.' Serafina remained perfectly composed, her eyes coming to rest on the desk. 'May I be permitted to read the letter for myself?'

'It is not addressed to you, child.'

'I'm fifteen. I am not a child any more.' An awkward silence settled between them before the mother superior took up the letter and handed it to her. 'This is much against my better judgment, Serafina.'

With the pale blue slip of paper in her hand, Serafina sat motionless and made no move to open it. The mother superior rose from her seat with a sigh. She stepped out of the room but remained close by, pacing the corridor slowly. A few moments passed in silence, then came the unmistakable sound of grief seeping through the closed door. Reaching for the handle, the mother superior found the door to be locked from the inside and fought to suppress the wave of panic that descended upon her.

'Serafina?' She pulled at the doorknob, rattling it hard.

Serafina slid down into the chair, turning to liquid, arms curled over her head, suffocating beneath the avalanche of shame that crashed down upon her, her skin crawling with the humiliation of her father's disgrace, the sheer degradation of it all plucking out her insides.

'Serafina! Open this door immediately!' Giving up on the handle, the mother superior rapped urgently on the door. 'Serafina! Open up this instant or I shall have someone come and break it down!'

Serafina felt the walls close in around her. She knew that she had deceived herself all along, that love had had nothing to do with it, that she had been no more than a burden of duty from the very beginning. Her stomach flinched at her blind adoration of a father who wasn't even fit to show his face in polite company, her shame over the mother she knew to be nothing more than the dirt on his shoes. It was loathsome. Detestable. The nausea came over her in an instant. She closed her eyes and breathed deeply until it passed, shutting it out, renouncing every last shred of their reprehensible behaviour and her own despicable situation.

It was some minutes before the mother superior heard the release of the lock. She took a deep breath, then entered the room to find Serafina sitting precisely where she had left her, as though she had not moved at all, the only indication of her anguish the rawness still visible in her eyes. Serafina spoke before the mother superior could seat herself or properly gather her own thoughts.

'Mother Superior, I would like to ask that this news be kept from Mary,' she said dispassionately. 'There's no point in telling her now. It will only upset her.'

'Of course,' the mother superior replied. 'I think that would be sensible.'

Serafina then fixed upon her a gaze of pure rage. 'And this letter is to be destroyed. Mary must never know what was in it, and I don't want anyone else to know either.' Before the mother superior could answer, Serafina held up the fist into which she had crushed the letter. In one swift movement, she threw it into the flames of the open fire, the mother superior watching on, speechless, as the thin blue paper combusted, the licking yellow flames reflected in Serafina's black eyes.

Serafina sat alone at the piano in the empty refectory, softly playing a simple piece of Chopin from the volume of preludes Father Lazarus had presented to her for her birthday last year. Her heart sagged under the weight of its melancholia. All around her the convent was bustling with activity, the corridors choked with luggage, everyone toing and froing. The girls scurried around in readiness for their departure, saying their goodbyes to each other, hugging one another excitedly and talking with great animation about where they were going and who they would see.

The door to the refectory opened quietly. Father Lazarus entered the room silently so as not to disturb Serafina's concentration, returning the heavy latch with his fingertips. He said nothing and quietly took a seat beside her, perching his weight unobtrusively on the edge of the black duet stool, watching with an occasional nod of approval before reaching out to turn the page for her. Serafina made no acknowledgment of his presence and continued to play, her mouth set into a hard line across her increasingly beautiful face. Through the open window drifted the shrill noises of excitement, the pupils shouting their final goodbyes and waving to the gathered smiling staff as they left one by one for the holidays.

Inside the mother superior's office, Mary sat wailing, great long, angry sobs filling the wood-panelled room, bouncing from the walls and ringing back at her, the mother superior and Sister Margaret trying hopelessly to console her.

'Why can't we go home? I don't see what could be so important that we should have to stay here for the holidays. It's not fair! I want to go home!'

The nuns looked at each other. They had said that her father had been called away, sent to work on a big plantation in Chandigarh in Himachal Pradesh, and that their mother was unable to take them for the holidays due to some trouble on the homestead. It was thought better than telling her the whole truth: that it had been said that their mother had gone mad and had been sent away, that she was not to be trusted with them, that she was to be turned away should she ever come looking for them, that their father's house was now lived in by another man, that they would never be sent for again.

Sister Margaret leaned over the sobbing Mary, shaking her head sadly. She had come to love this immature girl with her silly ways and her ready smile. She prayed for her every night and pleaded with the Lord to keep her and protect her.

In the refectory, Serafina finished the piece and sat paralysed. She waited until the last note died away, then dropped her head into her hands and cried bitterly. Father Lazarus wrapped his huge arms round her and brought her into his chest.

'Shh, my child. Hush now.'

He stroked her head and looked to the open window.

'Not that one,' Shurika said, eyeing the bruised brinjal. The vegetable seller cast her an irritable frown, muttering under his breath before returning the brinjal to the back of the basket and reluctantly taking up another. *It is a meagre specimen*, Shurika thought, comparing it to the plump fruits she had once nurtured in her own garden in another life, far from there. She inspected the goods and paid the man before tucking the brinjals into her bundle with the rest of her provisions.

Shurika held on to her bundle tightly, the jostling crowds in the cramped, noisy street harbouring more than their rightful share of thieves, particularly at this time of year as the population swelled. She had learned this, and much else besides, the hard way, having found her money stolen more often than she cared to recall in the early days before they finally found their feet and learned to live in this suffocating place.

Moving patiently along the crowded street, Shurika was carried along by the tide of humanity until she came to the narrow path that led away from the bazaar. It was no wider than a rough, cramped corridor, flanked on either side by ancient buildings in various stages of decay, each one housing its own populace, spilling out noise and waste in equal measure.

Relaxing her grip on the bundle, Shurika drew her breath deeply in relief, grateful to be away from the swarming masses. In the last week, it seemed that every person in India, whether able-bodied or not, had chosen to descend upon Vrindavan, filling every available space, rendering the whole town ripe with the cloying odour of congested living.

Shurika made her way quickly through the winding maze of unmarked alleyways, then disappeared into the narrow, doorless aperture that led to the tightly squeezed dwellings hemmed in behind. She did not stop to speak to her neighbours, and they did not speak to her, merely glancing up from their chores to convey their general disdain: she had brought bad luck upon them all by subjecting them to the presence of a widow. But Shurika had taken care to negotiate some degree of security from the landlord, handing him the slip of paper Shiva had given to her before they had left the homestead. The man had looked at it, pulling at his bottom lip thoughtfully with his fingers, copied down its contents and returned it to Shurika with another small document that she did not understand. She had paid him the money he'd asked for, being the greater part of all they had, and he had told her not to scrimp on the cost of a decent lock for the door.

Ignoring her neighbours' sideways glances, Shurika crept invisibly past the first few shabby houses before slipping unseen through the door to their tiny dwelling at the end of the alleyway. Light from the one small window showed Chinthimani lying in a corner, bound in a shawl, curled up with a blanket wrapped round her feet.

'Where have you been?' she grumbled, her voice still rasping with the sickness that had plagued her chest for months. 'You said you would not be long. I have been lying here suffering for hours. My throat is on fire.'

'I brought you some medicine.' Shurika put the bundle down on the floor by the stove and knelt down beside her, feeling her forehead.

'I don't want medicine,' Chinthimani mumbled. 'Give me a little whisky. It helps to ease my pain.'

'Mistress, you should not—'

'Don't tell me what to do!' Chinthimani snapped irritably as Shurika helped her into a more comfortable position.

'I will give you whisky if you promise to take some medicine and eat a little food.'

'Hmph,' Chinthimani conceded, screwing up her face in distaste as the bitter tincture was forced upon her. Reluctantly Shurika poured a small measure from the whisky bottle. Without it, her mistress would sicken, as she had done before when Shurika had returned from the back-street liquor seller empty-handed, claiming that she could not find him. Chinthimani had become agitated, clawing at her skin, shaking and descending into fits of anger, then confusion. After just one night of watching the demons take hold, Chinthimani lying on the floor, drenched in perspiration, Shurika had abandoned all hope of a cure and gone in search of the merchant. It had become her daily medicine, essential to her existence. Chinthimani snatched the drink without thanks and tipped it into her mouth as though it were water.

Shurika ignored her mistress's irascible manner: it was still too early in the day to expect anything else of her. 'Tonight is the night of the full moon,' she said, pouring some water into the small cooking pot and setting it down on the stove, persuading heat from the smouldering clod of solid fuel. She added a green cardamom pod to the pot, a pinch of sweet herbs and one dried tea leaf, picked carefully from the battered tin. 'The whole place is teeming with pilgrims. I think that more have come this year than ever before.'

'You should go to the festival,' Chinthimani said with a small, distasteful sniff. 'I've seen you smiling to yourself, watching our neighbours' preparations. Just because I have no joy left does not mean that you have to sit here like a corpse. It is not my fault that you would not go and make a life of your own. I have no reason to keep living,' she repeated matter-of-factly, as she always did. 'So I sit, and I wait.'

'I have no wish to see the festival, mistress. Besides, they will be making a commotion for a week. There will be no avoiding it.'

Suddenly Chinthimani was overcome by a coughing fit, racking her bones, her face streaming with the uncontrollable onslaught. After a while, it subsided, Chinthimani catching her breath and closing her eyes, exhausted by the severity of the attack. She wiped the blood from her mouth with a cloth and gave it to Shurika.

'Just go out and leave me here.' Chinthimani lowered herself to the floor. 'How can I be expected to die when you are always watching me?'

Evening closed in, the acrid smell of bonfires rising and hanging over the town, signalling the ritual burning of the effigy of Holika, the devil-minded sister of the demon King Hiranyakashyap, and the lighting of fires at the wealthier homes. Chinthimani lay sleeping on the mat, the shadowy outline of her bones quietened by the medicinal herbs and the whisky she had insisted on imbibing through the afternoon. Shurika stretched up onto her toes and peered out of the window. Perhaps she could step outside for a little while. Her mistress was asleep and would not wake for hours. Surely she would not be missed if she slipped away just long enough to watch the neighbourhood children shouting excitable insults at the burning figures and playing pranks on their parents?

Outside, beyond the deserted alleyways, the streets groaned under the strain of the revellers, hordes of them all heading in the same direction, moving slowly like one enormous cacophonous entity. All around her faces glowed with excitement at the symbolic slaying of evil, the assured triumph of goodness, the prospect of all that was corrupt and damnable being engulfed by the leaping flames of the raging fires.

An hour later, having taken her modest fill, it was with a heavy heart that Shurika tore herself away from the scene. She would have to satisfy herself with imagining the rest of the celebrations, so that she might recount the tales over many days and nights to her beloved mistress.

Finding her passage blocked by the thronging crowds moving in their single, determined flow, Shurika turned away from the main thorough-fare, choosing to thread her way home through the warren of side streets and alleyways instead.

The commotion was upon her almost the moment she heard it rounding the corner. A deafening ruckus of shouting voices. Metal pans clattering as they spilled to the ground. As she tried to untangle the images from the cover of blackness, a huge Brahmin bull, bucking and running amok, charged towards her, its panicked eyes glaring white, nostrils flaring. A thin group of barefooted men shouted after it, screeching hysterically, wielding sticks to no avail, the animal wild and unseeing.

The bull thundered down upon Shurika like an earthquake, the force of the impact sending her spinning. She howled, shafts of bright colours splintering before her eyes.

**M**ary lifted the mosquito net tucked round her bunk and crept to the end of the dormitory, where Serafina lay reading quietly.

'Can I get in with you?'

Reluctantly Serafina pulled the net aside to let her sister in and continued reading.

'Did you hear about the baby?' The story of an unwanted girl baby from the village being killed with opium had been circulating in the convent all afternoon.

'Yes.' Serafina did not take her eyes from the book.

'Who would do such a thing? How could anyone want to kill a baby?'

'It happens all the time. I don't know why they didn't feed us opium, too.' Serafina's voice was flat. Matter-of-fact.

Mary sat upright and stared down at her. 'What do you mean?'

'God, you're so stupid. They kill girls all the time,' Serafina said. 'They throw them into wells or leave them outside to die of exposure. Nobody wants them. At least the Indians are honest about it.' Mary stared at her. 'What are you looking at me like that for? I'm only telling you the truth.' Serafina glared back at her, her voice adjusted to sound like dispassionate boredom. 'You don't think that we were actually wanted, do you?' She laughed. 'That's why we ended up here. It's only one step down from the orphanage, and I suppose we are expected to feel grateful for that.'

'That's not true.' Mary's voice wavered. 'You know very well it's not true.'

'Whatever suits you.' Serafina began to talk to the ceiling, her voice a mere shadow. 'I can't wait to get away from this place. I'm sick to death of being kept here, hidden from the whole world like I don't exist. Just a few more days, then I swear I shall never look back. Not for a single moment.'

Mary started to cry. 'I don't want you to go. I don't want you to leave me here on my own.'

Serafina ignored Mary's small sobs, her own thoughts now thoroughly consumed by speculation about the endless possibilities that lay ahead of her. 'I'm going to leave everything behind and start again as though none of this ever happened,' she breathed. 'I'm going to find myself a wealthy husband and have the most wonderful life.' She moved her head to face her sister across the pillow and whispered sternly, 'You must never tell anyone where we came from. You must never mention the tea plantation or our mother and father. And never talk about this place. You are not to say a single word about any of it. Not for as long as we both shall live.'

'Why not?' Mary turned over, uncomfortable with the sinister under-current travelling the invisible cord that bonded the two of them together.

'Don't you understand anything? A halfling is a nobody. No one will ever want you. You'll never be accepted anywhere if people know what you are. Why do you think we were sent here? Why do you think we've been left to rot like this in the middle of nowhere? You must never breathe a word to anybody once you leave here, or we shall both be ruined.' Serafina grasped her sister's wrist. 'You must promise me you will never speak so much as a single word of it to anyone. Never.'

Mary's wrist started to hurt, the skin burning under Serafina's vice-like grip. 'All right.'

'Say promise.'

'I promise.'

Serafina let go of Mary's arm. They lay there together in silence for a while, both staring up at the ceiling. Mary could sense her sister's anger, her frustration. Where it came from she didn't know, this unreachable place, this grim detachment from everything and everyone around her. How she longed to feel her sister's embrace, her sister's love. That was how sisters should be. There should be something between them. Love. Warmth. Anything but this deathly void. If Mary reached out a hand to touch her, Serafina would move away. If she told her that she loved her, Serafina would scoff at her sentiment. If she whispered to her that she was afraid, Serafina would snap at her to toughen up. Mary lay there quietly, keeping herself small, willing herself not to intrude so much on her sister's bed that she would eject her and send her back to her own bunk. She hoped, too, in some small way, that her presence might give Serafina a little comfort. She knew her sister well enough to be able to feel those long, dark silences and to recognise that there was nothing to be said.

Serafina's dress, pale mustard yellow with a neat matching jacket resting just above her slender waist, erased the last vestiges of childhood from her womanly form. Mary stole small glances at her, unable to connect this elegance with the pinafored girl she had seen yesterday, as if needing to re-acclimatise gradually to the sight of her own flesh and blood.

Father Lazarus stood beside Serafina, hands folded in front of his cassock, his towering height like a guardian angel before her.

'May God go with you, Serafina.' He smiled down at her. 'Your gifts are many. Take care to use them well.'

'I will, Father.'

'Keep up with your playing,' he told her. 'What we will do without you in the chapel I really don't know.' Serafina nodded, knowing she would never lift a finger to play again. She would cut out anything and everything that reminded her of this place, including every note that had ever been drummed into her. 'You will always be in my thoughts and prayers.'

'Thank you, Father,' Serafina answered graciously. 'Thank you for everything.' Father Lazarus turned away and blew his nose.

Mary readied a smile for Serafina, as best she could.

'I like your dress,' she said self-consciously. 'You look so grown up.'

Serafina refused to acknowledge Mary's tear-stained face and swollen eyes, and spoke to her as if she were merely running an errand instead of leaving for good. 'I'll write to you as soon as I get to Bangalore.' Mary looked at the ground, still uncomfortable with Serafina's sudden air of maturity. 'Well? Aren't you going to wish me luck and kiss me goodbye?'

Mary snivelled loudly and tried to put her arms round her sister.

'Be careful of my clothes!' Serafina backed away quickly. 'You'll be fine. It will all be over before you know it.' In a moment of contrition, she hugged Mary back, softened her voice and whispered in her sister's ear. 'Always remember your promise.' Mary nodded silently into her shoulder. 'Maybe one day you'll understand.' She kissed Mary on the cheek, a small, slight kiss that barely touched her skin. 'Take care of yourself.'

And with that, Serafina climbed into the waiting cart and was gone.

Shurika stirred, half opened her eyes and listened for the ragged sound of her mistress's breathing. Her head felt thick, as though it were gripped within a tight metal band. She tried to sit up, then felt a hand upon her forearm.

'Do not move,' came a disembodied voice. It was soft, like butter melting on the warmth of her skin. Shurika tried to speak, but no sound came. She thought that she must be dreaming still, her motionless body refusing her, her senses dulled by the strange removal of her consciousness.

The ghostly presence left her side and moved away, the voice now distanced. 'Pramod! Come quickly! She has woken!'

Shurika opened her eyes and saw the faint outline of a woman peering at her closely. The woman smelled sweet, like cloves and jasmine.

'You are awake.' She smiled. The figure of a man appeared behind her in the doorway, his features blurred. Shurika blinked at them both, her mind a mire of confusion. 'Do not be alarmed,' said the woman. 'You were involved in an accident. My son was passing and saw what happened. At first everyone thought you were dead.'

Although Shurika heard the words, they made no sense.

'My son, Pramod. He is a fisherman but thinks he is a poet,' the woman clucked. 'I told him, we cannot eat your poems.'

Shurika felt strong arms lift her and some cushions eased behind her.

'Here,' said Pramod, offering a cup of water to her lips. 'You must drink. Take small sips.' Shurika felt powerless to resist, the few droplets of water moistening her parched mouth, freeing her tongue. 'Good,' he encouraged her. 'A little more. Then we will see about some food.'

When the cup was empty, Shurika finally managed a thin, cracked, 'Thank you.' Suddenly something began to stir. 'Oh!' she cried, pain splitting her head, the cup falling from her hands. 'My mistress!' The mother and son looked at each other. 'Please! I must go to her! She needs me!' Shurika sank back, the room swimming around her.

'Who is your mistress?' Pramod asked.

Shurika felt herself unable to breathe, as though a great weight had descended upon her. 'How long have I been here?' she wailed.

'Three days,' said the mother. 'Three days and four nights.'

'Help me!' Shurika raised a feeble arm. 'Please! I must return to her at once! She is sick!'

'You cannot go anywhere,' Pramod said. 'You are not well enough.'

'But I . . .' Shurika's head began to spin. 'I . . .'

'She must lie down,' insisted the mother, taking hold of Shurika's hand.

'Tell me where she lives,' Pramod whispered, lowering Shurika to the bed. 'I promise I will find her myself and tell her what has happened.'

Chinthimani fevered through unfathomable hours, the demons coming upon her repeatedly, tormenting her spirit, forcing pitiful pleas from her that disturbed the darkness of the nights, eliciting sharp-tongued calls from her neighbours. And then, after the seemingly endless hours, feeling the warmth of the eternal light, she cast herself adrift, as though floating through the air, a tiny seed attached to a gossamer umbrella caught on the skyward breeze. It had come to her at last, the release she had yearned for. She had dreamed of it so many times, imagining how it would be to leave her body far behind, to detach from this life and to have her atman, her very essence, set free into the endless heavens, yielding to the cycle of rebirth. At last, Shurika had left her to die in peace. She reached for death's mercy and asked it to hurry, for she could wait no longer.

Seeing he had come to a dead end, Pramod glanced around the clutch of tightly packed houses, each one no bigger than one room, perhaps two.

'Namaste.' He greeted some women with a small nod of deference.

'Forgive me for disturbing your work, but I am looking for the woman called Chinthimani.' They ignored him. 'I would be most grateful if you could tell me where she lives.'

Children's faces appeared at doorways, peering out curiously.

'There is no one here by that name,' one of the women said.

'You have come to the wrong place.'

Pramod stood for a moment, running through in his mind the landmarks he had passed. All was as Shurika had told him, including the coven of unfriendly women who pored over their rice with sullen hands.

'No.' He shook his head decidedly. 'I am certain that this is right.'

'You are mistaken,' said the eldest woman, adjusting her weight pointedly. 'I have lived here all my life and I have never heard that name.'

'Please.' Pramod frowned his frustration. 'It is very important that I find this woman. She is sick and needs to be cared for. Are you certain that there is no one else living in these houses?'

'Perhaps he means the widow,' whispered the youngest of the women, her swollen belly heavy with child. 'The woman who looks after her has gone. I am sure of it.'

'Who is this person you whisper about?' Pramod asked.

The women did not look up, bunching tightly together round their pans, turning their backs on him. Pramod looked around again. Every aperture in the hovels had been left wide open in the hope of dispelling some of the sweltering heat from the tiny living spaces and his eyes came to rest on the farthest house, its door sealed. There could be no mistaking it. He glanced at the pregnant woman, seeing that she had followed his gaze. She covered her head and looked quickly away.

Pramod walked over and knocked on the door. There was no answer. He knocked again, harder this time. 'Please open the door,' he shouted. 'My name is Pramod. It is very important that I speak to you. There has been an accident.' He peered up at the window. It was not so high that he could not reach it with the tips of his fingers. He stepped back and jumped up, grasping the rough sill and hauling himself up, just able to peer inside.

There was little light in the room, and it took a moment for his eyes to adjust to the gloom. There on the floor lay a woman, unmoving, the jagged outline of her pelvis thinly veiled beneath the worn cotton of a white sari. Pramod dropped down from the window and rushed at the door, ramming it with his shoulder again and again until the wood splintered and the door gave way. The stench that flew out to greet him tore the breath from his body.

The mother superior sat at her desk talking amiably with the well-dressed couple seated before her, the difficult business of the day now sealed in the envelopes she set aside, face down, in the drawer of the cabinet beside her. After the briefest of knocks, the door to her office opened.

'I have a little something here for you.' Sister Margaret stepped aside gladly, allowing Mary full view of the comfortable room. Her eyes widened, her mouth opening in surprise.

'Papa!' Mary rushed in.

James rose from his chair immediately, opening his arms to the youthful woman who ran to him, his expression visibly shocked by the sudden evidence of his long absence. 'My goodness!' He forced himself to look at her, shaken by the strong, spectral echo she carried of her mother. The pretty heart-shaped face. The rosebud lips. The delicate structure of her slight body. 'Who is this strange young lady in front of me?' Mary twisted with embarrassment and flapped him away, suddenly conscious of her shape beneath her pinafore.

'Do you have one of those for me?' Dorothy asked.

'Aunty Dorothy!' Mary found her voice and hugged her, too. 'When did you come?' Mary was suddenly overcome with confusion and a thousand unanswered questions. 'Why didn't you tell me? How long are you staying for? Am I coming home with you?'

The mother superior smiled sympathetically and brought Mary to order. 'Now, Mary,' she said. 'All in good time.'

Mary stood and stared at her father, uncertain if this was real or just another of her waking dreams. His face seemed different, deep lines etched into his brow, creasing the skin around his eyes. His hair, once raven black, showed flecks of grey at the temples. There were other differences too, in some small way that Mary could not pinpoint no matter how hard she looked.

The mother superior's voice floated into her reeling head. 'You may go out and have lunch with your father and aunt, but then he has a long trip to make, so you must save your questions and not be a nuisance.'

Mary smiled so hard she felt as though her face might split in two. 'Oh,

Papa!' She held on to him again and pressed her head into his chest. 'I don't care what anyone else says, I always knew you wouldn't leave me here. I have prayed every day that you would come for me.'

James caught Dorothy's eye, her grim expression speaking for them all.

The dining room of the little hotel in Haflong was remarkably busy for such a remote place. Most tables were occupied: some men in uniform in one corner; a group of Westerners of varying ages dining together. Mary's initial exuberance at the sight of her father soon waned as the conversation turned to her future. James tried to jolly her along.

'Oh, come on! It won't be so bad, and it's not until next autumn anyway, so you'll have plenty of time to get used to the idea. We all have to finish school sometime and then take our place in the world, don't we? It will be a very exciting time for you. Just you wait and see.'

Mary sulked into her plate. James looked to Dorothy for support. She smiled softly and raised her eyes to the ceiling.

'Who said I wanted to be a nurse? Serafina says it's completely revolting. All those sick people everywhere.' Mary grimaced. 'I'll probably catch leprosy in the first week. Why can't I choose for myself?'

'And do what?' her father said. 'This is the next part of your education, Mary. It has all been planned and arranged, just as it was for your sister, and that's that. It might seem like a long way away right now, but you will have to earn your living one day. Stand on your own two feet and make a life for yourself. That means that you have to be properly qualified.'

'I know, Papa, but there must be something else—'

'Mary, listen to me.' James reached out and grasped her hand. 'What would happen to you if I were no longer around?' Mary's face dropped. 'I don't mean to frighten you, but every parent knows that they cannot look after their child for ever. What if something were to happen to me?'

'But nothing's going to happen to you, Papa,' Mary insisted, rejecting his words.

'I'm sorry, Mary, but the decision has already been made and we'll hear no more about it. Do you want to end up a common shop girl?' The sudden stress in James's voice silenced any further argument.

'Your father's right, dear.' Dorothy leaned across the table and patted Mary's hand. 'Before you know it you'll be all grown up. You need a proper profession behind you. That's why I became a doctor, so that I could make my own way and look after myself if ever I had to. You're a young woman, with your whole life ahead of you. The decisions you make now will affect you for the rest of your life. And Serafina will be there. At least for your first year of training. You'll have a lovely time together. Just you wait and see.'

Mary managed a small, defeated smile. 'I suppose so.'

'That's my girl,' said James with some relief. 'Now eat all of that up and we'll see about some pudding, skinny legs.'

**O**utside the convent gates, Sister Margaret stood next to the mother superior, the pair of them keeping a respectful distance from the waiting car while James and Dorothy spent a last few minutes with Mary.

'I can hardly bear to watch.' Sister Margaret spoke quietly. 'Poor Mary.'

'Try not to be too harsh in your judgment, Sister. They are good people by any standards. At least he's taken the trouble to put his affairs in order and to make the proper arrangements for those poor girls of his.'

'When is he leaving?'

'I expect he'll be putting his uniform back on and heading up to the northeast frontier before the week is out. If the Japanese keep pushing through Burma at this rate, we're going to need every man we can get.'

'Dear heavens.' Sister Margaret shook her head. 'I can't even begin to imagine what hell awaits those men there.'

The threat hung over them like a dark, sombre cloud, and they watched as James ushered Dorothy into the back seat of the car, then put his arm round Mary and took her aside.

'Do well in your studies, Mary.'

'I will, Papa.'

'I want you to know that I shall always be thinking of you, no matter where I am.' James fought to control the slight tremor in his voice. 'You are very dear to me.'

'And I am always thinking of you too, Papa,' Mary said, her tone trying to convey more than the small words that sounded so empty.

James took something from his pocket, small and wrapped in a piece of homespun cotton, and gave it to Mary. She glanced down, untied the tiny bundle and took out the object inside: a carved wooden elephant, trunk pointing upwards for luck, fashioned from a piece of precious sandalwood. Its rich perfume filled her nostrils.

'It is from Shiva,' James told her softly. 'He made it for you a long time ago and asked me to keep it until I saw you again.' He leaned down and kissed her on the cheek. 'Goodbye, my darling.' He turned to leave.

Mary grabbed him and held on tightly, her eyes welling with tears. He squeezed her back, just briefly, then pulled himself free and got into the car. His command to the driver to move along was immediate, the car pulling away before Mary could shout her farewell. She ran for a few steps, grit flying into her face and hair, then stood and stared in disbelief at the disappearing car shrouded in red dust, waving furiously yet unable to see for her tears.

She would never see her father again.

# CHAPTER 9

*Dearest Mary,*

*Your father received your lovely letter. He is so very proud of you. Sister Margaret wrote to him just two weeks ago to say how well you are doing in your studies.*

Mary sat crosslegged on the dry grass. She had carried the letter in the pocket of her pinafore for three weeks, savouring it each time she read it, looking for something deeper, some hidden meaning.

*Your father has been posted to Imphal. His train will go through Haflong but will not be able to stop. He said that he will ask the train driver to blow his whistle when he passes the nearest point to school. Listen out for it.*

*If there is anything you need, you must ask the mother superior and she will send word or place an order with the department store in Calcutta.*

Mary heard a rustle from the pathway behind her and looked round with an immediate sense of alarm before waving in relief at the reassuring sight of Sister Margaret's approach.

*Do your best. Your father sends you all his love and will write to you as soon as he can.*

*With fondest love, Aunty D.*

Sister Margaret reached Mary's side, hitched up her habit, flashing a glimpse of grey-stockinged leg, and sat heavily on the grass next to her.

'I'm not disturbing you, am I?' she asked.

'Of course not.' Mary folded the letter and tucked it away in the front pocket of her pinafore. 'It's an old letter, anyway.'

'From your sister?'

'No,' Mary replied. Serafina's letters were few and far between, and rarely more than a few sentences. 'It's from my Aunty Dorothy. My father has been posted to Imphal.'

'Ah.' Sister Margaret nodded. 'It takes a very brave man to do what your father has done. He could quite easily have stepped aside and remained comfortably out of the way.'

'Will he have to fight?'

'Who knows, child. Let's hope not.'

The pair of them sat together for a while, quite comfortably, without exchanging a word. Mary leaned back, stretched out on the grass, and stared up at the cloudless sky.

'Why is the sky so blue?' she wondered aloud.

'There is something about the deep blue of the sky against the green hills here that reminds me of home.' Sister Margaret's lilting voice had lost none of the thickness of her soft Irish brogue. Her eyes quickly skimmed the perimeter, checking for any sign of her sisters. Seeing none, she flattened herself on the grass and gazed up at the heavens, too. They lay there together, contemplating the endless lapis above.

News of the evacuation spread through the convent like wildfire. The initial reports and warnings sent down to the mother superior from the governor escalated quickly, leaving no time for protracted arrangements. The Japanese had come right up and were now sitting on their very doorstep. The only certainty was that they would breach the Indian border any day. Telegrams were dispatched at once. All those girls who could be sent home left immediately under the escort of chaperones. Parents were sent for and came as quickly as they could from their scattered positions. This time the packing was done hastily and in silence, the trunks fetched quickly without ceremony or celebration. Soon, all had departed except the handful of pupils with nowhere else to go.

'Isn't this exciting, girls?' Sister Margaret's grey habit sailed behind her as she strode in front of the dozen or so evacuees, leading them to the crowded, idling train.

The girls clambered into the carriage, along with the six nuns and novices who had remained at St Agnes's, and settled in for the journey to the safe convent house at Shillong, in neighbouring Meghalaya. Sister Margaret wore her most courageous expression, and had a cheerful smile and a soft Irish lullaby at the ready for any girl who should need it. She kept the youngest of the waifs close to her skirts and encouraged the others to admire the scenery that passed the windows of the train.

'Keep your eyes open, girls. You might be lucky enough to spot a tiger in the trees.'

'Do the tigers know whose side they're on?' Roley asked.

'Now there's an interesting question,' Sister Margaret replied with a smile. 'Even if they did, I think it would take an awful lot of tigers to eat us out of trouble this time.'

The sweet perfume of jasmine and cloves did little to relieve the oppressive heat. The house was cooler than most, being close to the brown, muddied river, set in an elevated position at the quieter end of the row where the buildings petered out and the trees began. Pramod and his mother occupied the first floor, the relatively spacious luxury of its three airy rooms having passed from father to son for four generations.

The heat of the high season did not suit Pramod's mother at all. It disturbed her sleep at night, the temperature barely dipping, making her irritable, tempting her to vent her usually silent frustrations.

'How are we supposed to survive when the British government is commandeering so much food for the war effort?' she said crossly. 'Prices are so high that people are dying in the streets because they cannot afford to eat. And it is not just our food they are taking. What about our sons? Why should they give their lives for a ruler who takes the bread from their children's mouths? Every day, another mother mourns. You can barely get to the shrines for all the flames burning. What is a community to do without its sons? I thank the gods that you have been spared.'

'I would rather have fought.' Pramod stood by the open door, looking out into the deserted, sun-baked street, half listening to his mother's grumblings, his mind on another matter, as always.

'You are not a fighter, you are a fisherman. It is your job to keep our bodies fed. You should see the rice that came back from the market yesterday,' she complained. 'All dust and stones, hidden in the bag.' She shook her head. 'Those crooks in the bazaar are worse thieves than the street rats who rob from your pockets. They must think me stupid.'

Pramod allowed himself a small smile. Of the many things that his mother might be, stupid was not one of them. As a child, she had been taught to read and write by an educated father of modest means who thought himself scholarly and did not believe in the subjugation of women. As far as he was concerned, every man, woman and child in this noble country had already been enslaved by the British, and until such time as they understood the value of liberty, no matter what their gender, India would have no hope of regaining its autonomy. Pramod looked at his mother affectionately.

'You, stupid? Only a fool would think such a thing.'

'We have all been fools,' she said tetchily. 'This is not a war. This will go down in history as the lawless murder of millions of Indians who were too blind to see a hand in front of their own face. What do they think they are fighting for? For the British?' She gave a distasteful cluck. 'They treat us as though we are nothing, as though they have the right to send us to our deaths, like feeding worms to a hungry bird.'

'There have always been wars,' Pramod said. 'At least this time we are fighting together like brothers and not pitted against each other.'

'Your heart is blinded by romance, my fine son. When blood is spilled on the battleground, who is to know the colour of the body from which it came? Is Indian blood not as red as British blood? Do our wounds not run as deeply?' She flicked a hand in the air dismissively. 'Had your father lived, he would have been out there with Gandhi, fighting for the freedom of his country, not for the jailers who stole it from under our noses.'

Pramod still leaned against the frame of the open door, looking outwards, his back to his mother. She did not need to ask to know that he was watching out for Shurika's return.

Meek and subservient, she had been with them for almost a year now, becoming part of their daily landscape. She had not spoken for three months after the death of her mistress, the shock of the news having sent her into a grief so profound that it might have consumed her whole had it not been for their patience and perseverance. It was as though she had become an empty husk, devoid of all feeling. Pramod's mother had never seen her son so deeply moved by the plight of another.

'What is it about this woman that fascinates you?' she asked him.

'She is like a poem filled with sadness,' Pramod replied.

'She is not for you, my son.'

'So you have told me many times, Mother.'

'She is damaged. I can see it in her eyes. And she is too old to be taught new ways.' Pramod said nothing. 'You are a man of great sensibilities, my son. When you are ready to take a wife, I will find the perfect girl for you. Someone who will lift that sombre heart of yours and make you happy.'

'I never asked you to find me a wife,' Pramod murmured.

'You do not have to. A mother knows when her son is ready. He becomes restless, like a tiger in a cage.'

Pramod moved to the window and peered out across the shallow verandah, to the view across the sprawling town, shimmering in the hot pink haze. 'I don't understand why any woman would have put herself through such misery,' he said. 'Why pretend to be a poor widow when you know it will bring nothing but shame and sorrow?'

'That is surely a mystery,' his mother agreed. Her son spoke of this often, so astounded was he at the thought of someone doing such a thing.

'It is criminal that her neighbours should have left her as they did.' Pramod's mother shook her head in despair. 'How are women to survive when they themselves are such ignorant creatures? Perhaps in another hundred years we will learn to be more civilised to each other.'

'It is not their fault,' Pramod said. 'It is written in the holy scriptures.'

'Holy scriptures?' She clicked her tongue. 'What is holy about the choices a woman is given? To burn in the flames with her husband, to marry his younger brother, or to live in filth and penury for the rest of her life? And what if every widow in the land were to be subjected to that supposedly holy law until the ends of time?' She bucked her head in irritation and dared to question the divine doctrine. 'The scriptures were written by men who were fearful of losing their servants.

'Still. I am not sure that I believe her story,' Pramod's mother continued. 'She told us nothing of how they came to be here or where they had come from.'

'She does not remember,' Pramod said.

'Maybe. Or maybe she chooses not to remember. Perhaps that was more convenient for her.'

Although she tried to be charitable—after all, Shurika was a hard worker with a gentle heart who cooked and cleaned and mended for them tirelessly, despite their protestation that she owed them nothing—she could not bear to see her son's anguish, and secretly blamed Shurika for having stolen his silent attentions. As Shurika recovered, he had sat for hours just watching her, reciting poems for her while she slept to calm her fitful dreams, praying that her mind might be released from its unknown afflictions.

Pramod's mother had watched her son through the passing seasons, hoping that it was just a short phase of fascination brought about merely by enforced proximity. Yet as the months slid by, she knew in her heart of hearts that he was truly lost, and that there was nothing she could do.

Pramod turned his face briefly to his mother. 'She is not lying. Her heart is pure, and I doubt that she has ever told a lie in her life.'

'Be careful, my son. Do not lose your heart to an unworthy woman.'

'Unworthy.' Pramod laughed to himself. 'Oh, Mother,' he said fondly. 'I don't think any woman would ever be worthy of your precious son.'

'That is not true,' she snapped at him crossly, although the truth of it was real enough to cause her to turn on him defensively. 'I am only thinking of your future happiness.'

'And what if I have already found its source? What then? Must I deny it, just because it has come from an unexpected quarter?'

Pramod's mother bowed her head slightly, shamed by the sight of her son's torment. 'I have seen the way you look at her,' she said to him softly. 'The way that you wait for her when she goes to the shrine to pray. Why do you want to waste your life away like this? Her heart is already spent, my son. She cares nothing for you. Not in the way you want her to.'

'You cannot know that.'

'You must stop thinking of her,' she pleaded.

'I cannot,' he said, leaning his head wearily against the door frame. 'I am always thinking of her.'

Pramod's mother felt her son's pain and cursed herself inwardly. It was no use. She had tried her best but she had failed him. Failed her own son. Perhaps those people who had criticised her father had been right. That to educate a woman was to interfere with the very nature of all things. Perhaps then she would have betrothed her beloved son while he was still in his infancy, rather than shunning the ancient traditions and allowing him to grow up in his own time. She saw that she had been misguided, and she would have to pay the price for her folly. She nodded in defeat.

'Then you must tell her, my son,' she conceded. 'And I will give you my blessing.'

Shurika lit two sticks of incense, dipping their tips into one of the flames left to burn there, and placed them carefully before the carved figure of Krishna, alongside many others. She knelt before the shrine, bowing her head to the floor, sweeping her hand round her face, chanting her prayer to the gods, thanking them for restoring her, as she did every day, and begging for their forgiveness. Her bones had healed well enough, she had been skilfully nursed and her scars were no more than a few faint traces.

From the folds of her sari, Shurika took the piece of cloth in which she had wrapped the sweet *laddu* she had saved, left beside her while she was sleeping. She had gone to Pramod and thanked him for it, bowing her head in deference. He had seemed a little disappointed, as though he had wanted to witness her consume it, to watch her succumb to its sweetness. But she could not eat it. She did not deserve the pleasure of such a delicacy. Had it not been for her selfishness, her thoughtlessness, her mistress would not have died. Had she not run off into the night like a spoilt child looking for a moment's thrill, her mistress would have recovered and lived long.

She had often seen Pramod looking at her covertly when he thought himself concealed. Shurika knew that he had heard the spirit voices whispering her guilt, but that his heart was too kind to tell her. It pained her deeply, for he was a good man, sensitive to the needs of others. As time passed, she had wanted him to think well of her, although she now knew this to be impossible. And then there was his mother, without whom she would surely have perished. At first, she had treated Shurika like a daughter, with a touch so tender that it made Shurika's heart ache for the mother she had once known, the memory of her now so faint, like the farthest-flung stars in the cold night sky. But then, gradually, she had begun to change, distancing herself from Shurika's gratitude, whispering to her son when she thought Shurika was asleep. Perhaps she, too, had heard the voices, and knew that Shurika's heart was filled with darkness.

She placed the sweet *laddu* before the shrine, bowed her head to the floor and recited her mantras. Bringing herself to her feet, she offered her final devotions and moved away, another woman taking her place immediately, pouring out her grief, begging the gods to hear her suffering.

As she neared the house, Shurika saw Pramod standing on the narrow verandah, watching for her as he always did. Upon seeing her, he lifted his hand in a wave and smiled. Shurika nodded briefly and looked away, unworthy of his kindness. She slipped in through the doorway and up the stairs, her bare feet pressing silently against the old wooden boards.

At the rear of the house, in the room in which they kept the provisions and prepared food, the room in which Shurika also lived and slept, she swept the floor, although it was already clean, then made Pramod's mother a sweet *nimbu pani* and took it to her. Upon entering the room, she bowed and placed the cup of lemon-flavoured drink gently on the floor beside the mother's mat.

'Shurika,' Pramod's mother said, her voice as soft as it had been when Shurika had first opened her eyes and seen her, sari awash with colour, the sweet scent of cloves and jasmine in her hair.

'Yes, *mataji*.' Shurika kept her eyes respectfully downcast.

'Shurika, do you love my son?'

Shurika's eyes darted to Pramod. He was gazing back at her, his smile now more than just the simplicity of happiness. It told her of a thousand things she could never explain, a rare magic that few could understand. Inside, her spirit stirred, then began to sing the songs that she had banished from her heart long ago.

'Yes, *mataji*.'

Pramod's mother placed her hand upon Shurika's head and said, 'Then it is settled.' She took a sweet *laddu* from the dish beside her and offered it to Shurika's lips.

The population of the safe convent house in Shillong swelled to bursting point as it opened its doors to offer shelter to those who had journeyed from the nearby states to escape the perils of the far north. They were crammed in like sardines, every inch of the living quarters put to best use to accommodate the sudden deluge of pupils, sisters and priests who had come upon them.

'I don't think I can live like this for much longer,' Amelia complained tearfully. 'They promised us we'd only be here for a few weeks. Yet it's been almost three months and we don't even have proper beds to sleep in, and now I've gone and lost my book.' She began to weep.

'Please don't cry.' Mary tried to put her arm round Amelia's shoulders, but Amelia shrugged her off and threw herself onto the tiny bunk, burying her face in the pillow. Mary lifted her head to the sound of a slight knocking from the open door.

Sister Margaret raised her finger to her lips silently and motioned with a small tilt of her head. Reluctantly, Mary got up and followed her.

'She's lost her book,' Mary explained as they walked. 'It's the only thing she brought with her and—'

Sister Margaret placed a solemn hand on Mary's arm. 'It's not about the book, Mary,' she said, slowing to a halt by a wooden bench under the shade of some trees, taking a seat amid the soft petals. 'We received several wires this morning. They had been sent to Haflong, so heaven only knows how long it took for them to be relayed to us here.' Mary sat beside her. 'I have never seen such terrible news in one day.' Sister Margaret bowed her head. 'I don't even know how to say this. Amelia's father has been taken prisoner. He was one of the men who volunteered to stay behind in Burma and help destroy the oil wells when the Japs invaded.' Mary pressed her hand to her mouth, and shook her head. 'Father Lazarus spoke to her this morning. At least we know her father's alive.'

'Oh, Amelia,' said Mary, almost to herself. 'Why didn't she say anything?'

'There is something else I have to tell you, Mary,' Sister Margaret said, pausing for a while to gird herself. 'There have been a number of reports coming out of Imphal. It would seem that the city has been surrounded by the Japanese.'

'Imphal?' Mary's face became ashen. 'That's where my father is.'

'Yes, child, I know.' Sister Margaret grasped her arm. 'But don't you panic,' she said sternly. 'God looks after his own.' Tears cascaded from Mary's eyes. Sister Margaret pressed a handkerchief into her hands. 'Now stop that crying. I have no doubt that God will keep your father safe and well while he's doing his bit. And as for those Japs,' she tightened her jaw in anger, 'I wouldn't fancy their chances against our troops. We're not giving an inch, you know, and I'd bet you our boys will take down every last one of them.' Sister Margaret's hands balled into hard fists. 'Everyone is suffering, one way or another. You and I need to pray harder than ever, because your father will need your prayers, as will Amelia's.'

Mary nodded, sobbing into the handkerchief for a moment longer, then with an effort pulled herself together.

'Come on, now.' Sister Margaret hugged Mary hard, then stood up. 'There are others to think of. We have things to do. Important things.'

'Like what?' Mary swallowed her tears and took a deep breath of determination, standing ready for Sister Margaret's instructions.

'Like finding your friend's book, for a start.'

The ferocious fighting stretched on for three more weeks then, at last, the news came that the worst of the bloodshed was over; the broken Japanese forces, every gun and tank lost, beaten back from the Burma front and forced to retreat across the Chindwin River as the Allies pushed on towards Mandalay. Stories soon began to pass from mouth to mouth of Japanese soldiers chained to trees by their commanding officers, bound to fight on to the death despite the hopelessness of their situation, many of them without so much as a single bullet.

The girls received the announcement placidly, unable to bring themselves to show any sense of celebration, the price of victory already far too great.

Although the region remained perilous, the decision was taken that they should return to Haflong, to try to restore some sense of normality to their lives. The group prepared to go back to their abandoned convent, sending a cable ahead to the staff, in the assumption that at least some of them had stayed on. The relief of leaving the overcrowded safe house was clouded by a sense of trepidation over what they might find waiting for them.

They found the convent just as they had left it, peaceful and undisturbed, the gardens a little overgrown perhaps, the schoolrooms and dormitory slightly musty, in need of a few days' fresh air. No enemy had laid a footstep there, the dusty lock on the gate untried, the supplies in the cookhouse untouched. If any trouble had passed that way, it had not stopped to defile this consecrated place. They were silently grateful, all of them, to find their home spared the shame of an invading army of plundering men. Yet everything had changed and nobody felt the same, the fragility of life having been so clearly demonstrated to them all through the indiscriminate vagaries of war.

# CHAPTER 10

JAMES SAT ON THE VERANDAH, the late morning sun shimmering over the wide horizon and warming his weary face. Gone were the valleys and the hills with their high, whispering trees. There were no tea gardens here; no slender women picking their way along the high terraces, black eyes hidden beneath the wide canopies of their bright saris. Just the open African plains, and more heat than most men could imagine.

There had been much talk among the officers as the war came to an end. With the sun setting on the Empire's finest jewel, most were preparing to re-acclimatise to the distant shores of Britain or to seek out new fortunes elsewhere. But there were many who found themselves reluctant to leave their self-made princedoms: James knew very well that he would rather do almost anything than find himself tending an English garden and living a colourless life behind a clipped privet hedge.

'If they think things were bad in Delhi, they should have seen the chaos here in Calcutta!' James had found himself stuck with a talkative brigadier while awaiting news of transportation. 'All this bloody "Quit India" business. Nobody wants out of this hellhole more than the British Tommy, eh?' James had nodded politely from his chair at the next table in the officers' mess. 'And what about you, old chap? What dump have you been stuck in?'

'Burma,' James had replied.

'Burma, eh? Bloody awful show over Singapore. I saw some of those poor buggers who escaped and came over the border on foot. It was a sorry sight, I can tell you. They were so full of disease that all anyone could offer them was a clean bed to die in. It's a bad business. What were you doing up there?'

'Engineer.'

'Jolly good, jolly good.' The brigadier had rolled the whisky around in his glass, wondering whether to continue pressing this man for a bit of conversation. Perhaps he was one of the tricky ones whose nerves had been shot and was best left alone.

James had noticed the tremor in the man's hand then, and had taken pity on the stranger and engaged him despite his own overwhelming fatigue. 'Making your way back to England?'

The brigadier had looked surprised. 'Good God, no. Whatever for, man? An old chum of mine says that now this place has gone up the Swanee, it's time to move on to a younger colony where the natives don't make so much ruddy trouble!' Then he had touched his nose at James confidentially, as if disclosing a great secret. 'Southern Rhodesia, old boy. He's growing the big cash crops and hauling in a tidy fortune by the sounds of it. That's where I shall be heading. You mark my words. It's the next big thing.'

Somehow the brigadier's words had stuck.

But before he could leave India, an invisible thread had drawn James back to the hills of Assam, breaking open the fresh wounds of everything that he had loved when he was a more youthful man. The flash of a sunbird, the smell of the rain on the thick, shiny leaves, the call of the mahouts and the sounds of his children at play.

He and Dorothy had been welcomed at the big house like old friends and generously entertained. Yet James had felt displaced and ill at ease from the moment he arrived, despite Shiva's obvious joy at seeing him. He had noticed that the new master had the staff wear the uniforms he had dispensed with long ago.

Felix, however, seemed to approve of the changes and had come to share one last *burra-peg* with his friend. 'Best of luck, James.'

'Thank you, Felix.'

As they said goodbye, Dorothy had leaned forwards and kissed Felix on his ruddy cheek. 'We'll miss you,' she'd said. Felix had enlarged his cheerfulness at the sight of her watery eyes, uncomfortable with the formality of this final parting. He was glad to see his old friend well settled with a suitable woman, and relieved that he had seen sense and moved on.

Shiva had waited patiently beside the car and opened the doors for the master he had once known so well. To his surprised delight, James had ignored his bowed head and clasped palms and insisted that they shake hands. Shiva's arm had moved awkwardly, unused to the gesture, and he had smiled like a boy.

'Thank you, Shiva,' James had said. 'You have been a loyal servant and a good friend. I shall always remember you.'

'Thank you, Sahib. You have been very good to me. I shall always remember you, too.'

When James had left the estate a handful of years before, he had fulfilled a long-held tradition. A devoted servant knew that the small wage he received throughout his service would be handsomely supplemented at the end of his working life with the gift of a pension. This amount, decided upon by his employer, was intended to keep him through his old age. If his employer was generous, he might look forward to a comfortable retirement. Without it, he could expect only years of hand-to-mouth living. James had been generous indeed, in case the new master was not.

'I wish you would change your mind and come with us.'

Shiva had lifted his hand to his breast and shaken his head. 'This is my home, Sahib. And, besides, our elephants are much prettier.'

James and Dorothy had then slipped into the car. Shiva closed the door and moved aside for Felix. James had wound the window full down.

'Don't you stand any nonsense from those bloody Africans.' Felix had slapped his hand on the roof of the car as the driver pulled away.

Dorothy had looked over her shoulder, leaning on the back of the seat and waving. James remained facing front. She noticed his poignant expression. 'Not wanting to take one last long look, darling?'

'No,' he said, unable to voice the subtle torment of the ghosts that plagued him still, following him day and night. He yearned to find peace, to be able to rest his troubled mind. Dorothy had taken his hand and squeezed it.

Suddenly James had leaned forward and spoken to the driver. 'Take the western estate road.'

At the point where the ground roughened to become impassable, he halted the driver and left Dorothy in the car, walking the rest of the distance alone to the small enclave set among the trees. The moment he entered the rusting gates, he knew that he should not have come back.

Chinthimani's quarters lay empty and neglected, the courtyard over-grown with towering weeds and the creeping tendrils of untended plants. So quiet all around. James wandered bleakly among the ramshackle buildings. As he passed across the foundations for the building of a new storeroom that had never been finished, he noticed two small handprints set into the concrete at an awkward angle. He bent down and swept the loose leaves aside, slowly tracing their image with the tip of his finger, caressing the indelible marks of the children who had left them there, before covering one with his own palm, holding its hand.

The bitter smell of smoke from the supper fires burning in the distance had pricked his eyes and dried his throat. Whatever life had lived there had long since flown.

James's enquiries in the village as they passed through had been met with suspicion and silence. If anyone had any notion as to what had become of the woman and her companion, they kept it to themselves. It was as though she had simply vanished.

And so began the exodus as the British planters pulled out. There had once been more than a hundred of them across the region, often descended from the pioneering families who had come here a century before, growing indigo, then sugar cane and rice before the tea gardens arrived. Yet as India's tide turned, they feared that freedom would prejudice all against them, and that once the British officials were gone, there would be no one around to prevent them all being murdered in their beds.

James had the big old Riley motor car, a parting gift from Felix, shipped to Africa, and they ran it into the ground searching for the new lands on which they would establish a farm to raise tobacco. With the help of a hundred reluctant, slow-working men, a new house was built, the land cleared and irrigated, and a curing barn constructed of burnt brick. To carve a new life into a foreign landscape was not beyond him, no matter how trying the conditions. He knew how things worked, how to build machines that would stand the test of time, and the structures in which to house them. Dorothy stood by his side and devoted herself to the country that they would now call home. She could never have imagined how different this place would be.

James rose from his chair and moved to the verandah, leaning on the brick-built balustrade in the full glare of the Rhodesian sunshine, staring out across the veld. Faint columns of smoke rose towards the horizon, lifting from the distant compound where the workers lived in a rambling hotchpotch of rough, mud-built houses. It seemed desolate to him, this difficult place. Colourless, despite the dull green of the few flat-topped trees that remained and the changing hues of the light skimming against the koppies, the rough, jumbled outlines of rocky outcrops standing proud of the high grasses, immovable.

James folded the letter from the mother superior telling formally of Mary's progress and the passing of her exams, and slid it back into his shirt pocket. It was old news now, of course. It could take a long time for a letter to cross the ocean and reach the farm.

Dorothy appeared from the house and noticed how much he seemed to have aged these last few years. She walked to his side and put her arm through his.

'Penny for your thoughts?'

He smiled down at her and patted her hand. 'I wish it would rain.'

'You must promise to write to me always. Until we both die. I just can't bear the thought of you going.' Roley sighed heavily.

Mary grimaced at her plate. 'At least I'll never be forced to eat anything this awful again.'

'I have to wait a whole extra fortnight before I can leave. My arrangements couldn't be made any earlier.' Roley leaned a forbidden elbow on the refectory table, sulkily dropping her chin to her hand, rumpling her rosy cheek.

'It'll pass in no time. You'll be in England before you know it.'

Roley pursed her lips. 'But what if my aunt doesn't like me? That would be just my luck. I hope she's not a complete witch.'

Mary pushed boiled potatoes round her plate. 'Your father would never have arranged to send you there if she was. You know how much he adores you.'

Roley sighed. 'I do wish that Mama hadn't gone and died like that.' Mary smiled tenderly, nodding her sympathy. 'I'd much prefer to go back to Father, but he's been moved to another temporary post in Delhi and is adamant that I can't stay here because of all the trouble that's going on. He said that if they thought the war was bad, they haven't seen anything yet.' Roley took a gulp of water and set about her lunch.

'I wish I could come with you.' Mary sighed. 'You'll get to sail on a big ship and see half the world before you get there. Just think how exciting it will be.'

'Exciting? I can't think of anything worse. I'm going to train as a school teacher, then I intend to come straight back to India before my aunt can marry me off to some distant cousin. That's why my father's sending me there. I just know it is. He wants me off his hands.'

'Don't be silly.'

'I'm not. I can always tell when people are scheming about me.'

What if he's telling the truth about the trouble?'

'He is. The nuns missed a bit of newspaper in my last parcel. There was one page with a picture of the viceroy saying that we had all better put our tin hats on, but I had it confiscated.' Roley stopped eating and lowered her voice. 'It said that it's only a matter of time before they all start killing each other, but better that than they start killing us.'

'Really?' Mary said, trying not to sound as scared as she felt.

Roley nodded solemnly. 'It's all Gandhi's fault. He's got the whole country complaining about one thing and another and the viceroy doesn't know what to do with him.'

Mary forced herself to manage a piece of cold potato, the two girls mulling over the great politics of the day with little or no understanding of their meaning. They were not permitted to see newspapers. She changed the subject.

'I saved you my birthday cake.'

'Really? Is it one of the big fruit cakes with the sugar crystals on top?'

Mary nodded. Roley rubbed her ample tummy, eyes bulging, knowing how it made Mary laugh.

A nun's arm suddenly appeared between them, the palm landing heavily on the dining table. 'Quiet!' a voice snapped sternly, the girls jolted rudely into silence.

**M**ary felt strangely out of place, sitting in the office with Sister Margaret, eyes gritty through lack of sleep. Last night she had tossed and turned for hours, staring into the darkness until the dawn lifted its soft light to the small windows. Poised neatly on the edge of her seat, she was unsure of what to do with the hands that fiddled with the handkerchief she held in her fingers.

Feeling awkward, Mary did her best to ignore her self-consciousness and determined not to fidget. Her pinafores, along with almost everything else familiar to her, had been discarded yesterday evening, taken away by one of the sisters with the breezy comment that she wouldn't be needing them. She sat instead in a cotton dress of blue and white seersucker, the sleeves cut just above the elbows and trimmed with a pretty border of broderie anglaise, and tried not to stare at her shoes—soft leather courts with a neat heel and a stylish bow at the front. Her black steamer trunk, secured and waiting beside the gates, lay packed with the things that had appeared as if by magic, like a simple trousseau sent to replace her childhood.

'All your arrangements have been made,' Sister Margaret said. 'Your father has left provision for your further education and said that you are to write to us if there is anything else you need.'

With the boundary between adult and child imperceptibly lifted, Sister Margaret and Mary sat together in the window seat overlooking the gardens, pondering the places that Mary would soon see and the homes they had each left behind.

'You know, Mary, you have led a very sheltered life here. We keep ourselves locked away from the outside world for good reason. Even though the war is over, there is still much trouble to come.' Sister Margaret sighed. 'There are some things that you should know, for your own safety.'

'Like what?'

'Well, for one thing, the British are pulling out of India.' Mary felt her insides turn over. So the rumours were true. 'India is to be restored to her own people, but it won't be easy. The battles have already started.' She sighed. 'Try not to let the reports frighten you. It's just the same old story of men squabbling over power, which is usually where all the trouble starts. They are going to split India in half.'

Mary stared at her incredulously. 'How can you possibly split a country in half?'

'Ah.' Sister Margaret sucked her teeth. 'And therein lies the question that nobody wants to answer. You must promise me that you will be very careful, Mary. Watch what is going on around you and stay well away from trouble.'

'I will,' Mary said.

Sister Margaret noted the shadow of apprehension that had settled on Mary's face and sought to lighten the mood. 'Ah, Mary child. You're a sweet girl. I will surely miss our little chats.' She nudged Mary affectionately. 'I hope you find a nice boy one day. Somebody who will take care of that silly nature of yours and love you with all his heart.' Mary blushed a little. 'What's all this? There's no need to be embarrassed now!' Sister Margaret feigned surprise. 'It's what the good Lord put you here for! To fall in love with a fine man, to get married and raise a family together! Oh, yes, you may think it's all very daft now, but just wait and see.' She tapped her nose. 'It'll happen to you one day, you mark my words, and that's a promise made.' Her smile faded. 'I only hope he'll be worthy of you, Mary. You're a precious child. I don't mind telling you that.' She turned away, lifting her sleeve to her eyes for the briefest of moments.

The two of them sat in quiet affection, looking out of the open window towards the gardens in which they had strolled so often side by side. They were quiet now. Pensive. It was almost time. Sister Margaret took Mary's hand and clasped it hard, staring at Mary's soft brown fingers sandwiched between her own pale palms.

'Mary, child.' She hesitated for a moment, then drew a deep breath and started again. 'Mary, child. Do you know who your Aunty Dorothy is?'

Mary smiled directly at Sister Margaret and appeared somewhat baffled.

'Why, yes, of course I do! She's my father's sister!'

Sister Margaret's sigh hung heavily on the flower-scented air. She met Mary's puzzled gaze with a small, sympathetic smile. 'No, child. She is not your father's sister. She is your father's wife.'

**M**ary got into the carriage with a smartly dressed woman she had never met before. The chaperone would escort her on the long and arduous journey to Bangalore in the south.

Mary had promised herself that she would not cry, despite the waves of fear tearing at her insides. It was as though the world had turned upside down, leaving her unable to get a fix on what was real and what was not. There were no answers, just endless questions that seemed to make no sense. Serafina must have known, but had said nothing. The sense of betrayal filled Mary with a terrible uncertainty; that she could have been so gullible, so trusting, while all around her nothing was as it seemed, her whole life little more than a paper-thin veneer.

A burst of steam rose from beneath the carriages, the whistles and shouts indicating the imminent roll of the big engine. Sister Margaret perched precariously on the step, pressed halfway through the window, leaning her bulk in towards Mary, handkerchief in hand, calling her love and good luck. A passing porter tried to encourage her away, but she shooed him aside crossly, reached in and grasped Mary's hand.

'You be careful now, you hear me?' she shouted, afraid that her warnings would be lost amid the noise from the strain of the engine and the whistle that blew. The train groaned with effort. 'And mind that you write every week to tell me how well you're doing!'

The train began to pull out of the station, but Sister Margaret refused to let go, first walking with it, then forced to break into a faster, uncomfortable pace. Within moments, her hefty frame was unable to keep up with the movement of the carriage. She finally wrenched herself from Mary's grip, her handkerchief coming free in Mary's hands, and pressed her empty hands to her bosom as she stood and watched the train slide away through the whorls of steam.

Mary waved madly out of the window until the station curved out of sight, taking Sister Margaret's hazy figure with it. As the heat rushed to her cheeks, she recognised at once the sharp pain gnawing at her flesh. She felt utterly abandoned, bereft as the day she and her sister had been left at the convent, wailing as their father walked away. A huge, involuntary sob rose from her body as she crumpled into the seat beside her chaperone. Bringing Sister Margaret's handkerchief to her eyes, the sweet smell of sugar touched her nostrils, a jelly baby dropping silently into her lap.

## Part Three

### *Bombay 1953*

## CHAPTER 11

DOROTHY'S PREDICTION TURNED OUT to be right. Mary eventually became used to the grim realities of her prescribed profession, the memory of her dispatch from the convent having gradually ceased to cause the sickening anguish she carried with her for so long afterwards. By the time she had arrived in Bangalore, exhausted, disorientated and impossibly unprepared, the only thought that had kept her from falling apart was the certain knowledge that her sister would be waiting for her.

Only it was not like that at all.

During the preceding two years, Serafina had diligently made her own mark, choosing her acquaintances carefully, and was nearing the end of her training. If Mary had hoped that she would find protection and companionship with her sister, she was soon to be disappointed. Serafina had plans of her own. She would be leaving Bangalore the moment she qualified to take up a post at the King Edward Memorial Hospital in Bombay, a burgeoning, cosmopolitan city with a great deal more to offer than Bangalore's fabled greenery and glorious gardens. She told Mary in no uncertain terms that she would have to settle in with the rest of the new intake and fend for herself, just as she had done. Any onlooker would have thought that Mary's arrival was nothing but an irritation and that Serafina might have preferred to sever all connections with her. But Mary knew better. It was just her way.

Mary had found herself roomed with two other newcomers, Florence and Ruby, both of whom seemed to be just as at sea. They quickly realised that all three of them must have been born of similar circumstances, and that none of them had had much of a say in the matter of their onward paths. Not that it was ever discussed. Serafina made no pretence of her disapproval of Mary's friends, to the extent that Ruby and Florence were quite glad to see the back of her when she finally left a few months later.

Mary's new life had begun at the Lady Curzon Hospital in Bangalore, a sprawling, low-slung building with pretty blue latticed porches. After just two weeks spent in a constant state of distress, enduring the most menial of tasks meted out by unsmiling matrons and their ill-tempered sisters, Mary had begun to wonder what on earth she had done to deserve such cruel punishment. The routine, untouchable duties of her lowly status made her stomach churn and her lungs ache for the fresh air of the hills.

She had considered running away, but could think of nowhere to go.

In that moment, she had accepted her fate, and worked like a slave for three long years towards the shining clover-leafed pin that now sat proudly above the breast pocket of her uniform.

Terrible events had come to pass over the last eight years. No sooner had Mary left Haflong than the troubles had begun to escalate, as the inevitable power struggles gathered momentum and India tore itself apart while pressing to reinstate its identity after years of subjugation. In the absence of an agreement for a single, united land, everything was divided in a tragedy of epic proportions: twenty million people were displaced, causing untold misery and setting in motion the wheels of catastrophe. To the east and west there were massacres on the bloodiest scale. Hospitals were overrun with the sick and injured. Hundreds of thousands took to the roads searching for safety, Muslims travelling one way, Sikhs and Hindus the other. Two million people died, slaughtered merely because they were in the wrong place. Trains were ambushed and arrived at their destinations filled with nothing but dead bodies. Only the drivers were spared, so that they might bring the train back to tell the tale of their triumphant assailants.

**M**ary's soft white shoes moved noiselessly along the polished hardwood corridor. Her starched uniform had long since become a daily familiarity, its angular handkerchief veil no longer the nuisance it once was during the early days, when she could never get it to stay in place.

'Nurse! Where do you think you're going?'

Mary looked down at the cloth-covered bedpan in her hands. 'To empty this, Matron.'

'Well? Get on with it! And I expect you to be back here to deal with Mr Johnson in less than two minutes. Do I make myself clear?'

'Yes, Matron.'

Matron Kemp turned abruptly and marched away, leaving Mary smarting as she returned to the duty at hand. Before she could take another step, however, a faint whisper came from a side room.

'Hey! Psst! Nurse!'

The hushed tones belonged to the young ex-army officer still in traction after two torturous months. Mary took a step backwards, craning her head to peer into the room. 'Sounds like the old dragon's got it in for you again today.' He tried to pull himself up a little. Mary returned his smile and rolled her eyes. 'Don't take any notice,' he said. 'And if she keeps giving you trouble, you just let me know.'

'Thank you, Colonel Spencer.' Mary couldn't help but flirt a little. Despite the scar that ran the length of his right cheek—still an ugly red welt not yet healed to a less shocking hue—Colonel Spencer was a fine-looking man with more than his fair share of charisma. Mary paused at his door. 'But I can assure you that I'm well used to it.'

'For the hundredth time, it's Eddie,' he said with a wink.

'We like calling you Colonel,' Mary confided. 'It's romantic.'

'What's a nice young girl like you doing in a place like this, anyway?'

'I'm not so young.'

'Twenty? Twenty-one?'

'Now, Colonel, you know better than to ask a lady's age. I'm twenty-four.'

'And not yet married off by your family?'

'No fear.'

'Really? Well, that's done it.'

'What?'

'If a girl isn't married by the age of twenty-four, she is officially on the shelf, which means that you have no choice other than to accept the next proposal that comes along.'

'I'm far too busy looking after the likes of you.' Mary laughed a little.

'And emptying bedpans.' He grimaced at the vessel in her hands.

'It's my profession,' Mary said. 'I can take perfectly good care of myself. What on earth do I need a husband for?' Mary's cheerful smile belied the brief flurry that stirred her insides. She had come to see for herself just how deeply most people's social prejudices ran. She had heard what people said, usually beginning, 'Girls like those . . .' That they, and their corrupted parents, were disgraced. That few had a family who would defend their honour. That as a consequence, many were open to easy seduction in the desperate hope of snaring a doltish man. Behind her uniform Mary could hide herself away, one nurse among many, preserving at least some small sense of self-worth in an unforgiving world that placed such high stock in matters of birth and rank.

'What time do you get off today?'

'And what business is that of yours?'

'I'm bored senseless. Thought you and I might go out and paint the town red tonight. Then I'll ask you to marry me. What do you say?'

It was good to see the colonel in cheery spirits, and thinking about getting up and out. It was the ones who lay back and surrendered to their injuries who worried her.

'I'll come and pick you up for dinner at eight, then we'll go dancing and stay out until dawn. Put on your raciest frock.' A sudden surge of pain jolted his face into a tense grimace. Mary's smile disappeared.

'Pain again?' she asked. He was barely able to say yes, and began to lower himself back on to the bed, grappling awkwardly with the support handle. Mary deposited the bedpan on the floor and quickly came to his aid, carefully holding his head, turning and moving the pillows to receive him. 'In your legs?' He nodded sharply. 'How about the lower back?'

The colonel sighed angrily in response. 'This damned thing. I didn't survive a war only to be half killed by a bloody horse.' He stopped, shook his head in despair and leaned back gratefully on the pillows.

'You mustn't think like that,' Mary said softly, smoothing his sheets and checking the traction lines. 'Just rest and concentrate on getting well.'

He closed his eyes and smiled a bitter half-smile. 'All this for the sake of a chukka I was too drunk to play,' he said wearily. 'You should have seen me when I was younger. I used to run cross-country for my college. There wasn't a single chap who could catch me once that pistol went off. Set a new record and broke it twice myself. I had more cups and medals than you could—' He stopped mid-sentence and turned away.

Mary looked down at him, watching his face closely, trying to assess the extent of his discomfort. Picking up the charts hooked over the bottom of his bed, she glanced at her watch, calculating, then frowned.

'Has nobody brought you an injection?'

'I told them I didn't want any more.' He grimaced. 'I was getting to like it too much.'

'All right.' Mary sighed her understanding, took a pen from her breast pocket and wrote a prominent note on his chart, *Patient has refused further morphine*, tutting to herself at the previous nurse's oversight.

'Is it easing off a little?' she asked, returning to the colonel's side, checking his pulse. He nodded, eyes still closed, refusing to turn towards her. 'Do you want me to send for the doctor?' He shook his head, then reached out a hand. She took it immediately and felt his fingers squeeze hers hard, perhaps to help him endure the pain, perhaps to reassure himself that there were still such things in this world as kindness, love, beauty. The wave took hold of him again, urging him away from consciousness. Mary leaned down and whispered softly to him, 'Try to rest now. I'll come back in a little while to check on you.' She tenderly returned his hand to the cool sheet beside his broken body, before taking up the bedpan and quietly leaving the room. She had not gone more than three paces when the matron appeared in front of her.

'Nurse!' She pointed furiously at the cloth-covered pan. 'Are you still standing around here with that same bedpan?'

Mary looked at the evidence in her hands, and sighed.

'**I** knew we should never have left Bangalore,' said Florence. 'Now we're having to work twice as hard and live in a space half the size.'

'You didn't have to come,' Mary said. She was slumped miserably on the edge of her bed in the nurses' quarters, soaking her aching feet in a basin of hot water. 'And I do wish you'd stop going on as though this is all my fault. You were just as fed up as I was.'

'No, I wasn't,' said Florence.

'I was,' Ruby said. 'Bombay is much more exciting than Bangalore and the men here are so much more cosmopolitan. I shall find myself a rich husband in no time at all. Just you wait and see.'

'A husband? Dressed like that?' Florence looked her up and down. 'The only thing you'll get yourself is a bad name.'

'Oh, here we go again,' Mary sighed. 'Can't you two stop arguing for five minutes? My head is pounding.' She closed her eyes to blot out the bickering.

It had seemed like such an exciting plan last summer, that she would up sticks and follow in her sister's footsteps, just as she had always done. She had pined for Serafina awfully, feeling deep down as though a part of her was missing; the only part that felt that it had ever really belonged. Yet before she knew it, her plan had escalated to include all of them, a seemingly natural progression between three friends with no one else to cling to, friends who had become inseparable.

Mary looked down at her crumpled toes and wiggled them in the steaming water. 'Just look at the size of my feet,' she moaned. 'I doubt I shall ever be able to get my shoes back on. Maybe I'll pretend to be sick tomorrow. Kemp's on duty again and I don't think I could stand another of her roastings this week.'

'Don't take it personally.' Ruby handed Mary a small towel. 'She despises everyone, except her precious Mr Browning.' Patting the sides of her hair, Ruby gave a small impersonation of Matron Kemp's simpering manner whenever Mr Browning passed on his rounds. 'Just because he's married doesn't mean to say they're not—'

'Ruby!' snapped Florence. 'Stop this instant! That's precisely the kind of talk that starts trouble. We are not to forget ourselves nor our circumstances. There are plenty of unscrupulous men out there eager to prey on a young woman who seems free of the usual family constraints. What on earth would a man think if he were to hear you talking about such things?'

'You're such a prude,' Ruby said.

'Just because we work for our living does not mean to say that we are not of good stock.' Florence stamped her foot. 'Were it not for me, I have no doubt that the two of you would have fallen by the wayside long ago.'

'Do you have any idea what this could do to your reputation? To *my* reputation?' Seated in the far corner of the cheap, clattering restaurant, Serafina seemed to tower over Mary, her astonishing beauty drowning her sister out with its constant, immutable presence. Mary continued to stare into her lime water, refusing to look up. 'You can't just go gallivanting around with any Tom, Dick or Harry, you know. For goodness sake, Mary, don't you realise that by hanging around with these women, women of no pedigree at all, you risk being tarred with the same brush?' It was just too much.

Right from the beginning, Serafina had resolutely refused to share a room in the nurses' quarters, preferring instead to keep her own company and preserve her privacy despite the additional strain on her modest income. This existence was nothing more than a stepping stone: a barely tolerable way to hold body and soul together while she waited for the life she believed she was due. She despised the whole set-up: having to deal with the sick and the injured; being lumped in with these working women. She was not like them, and nor would she have anyone make such a comparison.

'All we did was go to the beach,' said Mary quietly.

'And who exactly was that man you were with?'

'He's a friend of Ruby's.'

'Give me strength,' Serafina muttered. 'What on earth does she think she's doing wearing a bikini, for heaven's sake? Goodness knows how many people saw her. And you! Out with her like that for all to see!'

'I did tell her it wasn't suitable.' Mary tried hopelessly to defend herself.

'And what is a man supposed to think if a woman goes out on a date with him half-naked?' Mary hung her head. 'Men have expectations, Mary. Especially from women who behave like Ruby. You have to stop fraternising with people like that. I won't stand for it, do you hear me?'

Upon her arrival in Bangalore ten years earlier, Serafina had realised immediately that she was not the only one who had been forced into a life of degradation and servitude. It was easy to spot those who had been sent away, out of sight, out of mind. She could tell just by looking at them.

These half-breeds. She would have nothing to do with them. She settled a reprimanding glare upon her sister.

Mary finally raised her head, tiring of the constant criticism. 'What is it that you're so ashamed of? Or have you told so many lies that you're having trouble keeping up with yourself? I don't know why you bother to speak to me at all sometimes. All I ever seem to do is annoy you.'

'You know exactly what I'm talking about,' Serafina whispered furiously. 'You have to stop making a spectacle of yourself. And I suppose everybody knows your business?'

'What is that supposed to mean?'

'I doubt that any of your friends would even know the meaning of the word discretion.' The disdain in Serafina's voice scorched Mary's delicate skin. 'For heaven's sake, Mary. How could you be so careless? I swear I just don't know what to do with you sometimes. Why couldn't you have stayed in Bangalore if you wanted to carry on like that? I had everything set up here just nicely, then you had to come bowling along with your ridiculous friends, determined to wreck my life. How dare you draw such attention to yourself? To *us*. If you refuse to behave in a sensible manner for your own sake, then you should at least consider the effect it will have on me. You should be thoroughly ashamed of yourself.'

How heavily these reproaches weighed on Mary's heart. 'You don't need to worry about my saying anything. I don't have anyone to tell, anyway.' She hoped that this would bring the matter to an end, that they would be able to make up and talk instead of more pleasant things, but Serafina had not yet finished with her.

'Are you deliberately refusing to hear my concerns? Don't you under-stand that I am the only person who will look out for you? It's not just my future that I'm concerned about. It's yours, too. If you don't find a suitable man and settle soon, what do you think will happen? You'll be ruined. Then we'll both be unstuck.'

'I refuse to pretend to be something that I'm not.'

'Don't be an idiot.' Serafina struggled to remove the strain from her voice. 'Do you understand why it is so important?' Mary nodded and Serafina sighed. 'I'm not going to suffer for the rest of my life as a punishment for a crime I never committed. I have plans for my life. Big plans. And you're not going to spoil them for me.' She wrung her napkin unthinkingly. 'No one is.'

Together they sat in frustrated silence, staring blankly at the table, Mary's face flushed with humiliation, her loyalties torn this way and that. She examined her conscience and reached for Serafina's hand.

'I'm sorry,' she said. 'Sera?' Mary gave her hand a little shake. 'Is something the matter?'

Serafina slipped her hand from beneath Mary's and reached for her handbag, settling it into her lap and taking out a small enamelled compact to check her reflection. She snapped it quickly shut, returned it to her bag and emerged composed.

'No,' she said. 'There's nothing the matter.'

Mary knew instantly.

'You've met someone.'

'Perhaps I have,' Serafina said.

'Oh, Sera!'

'Shhh!' Serafina cast her eyes around the room.

'I'm sorry,' Mary whispered. 'What's his name?'

'Joseph Carlisle.' Serafina flushed at the very mention of it. 'We met two months ago. It was one of those drinks gatherings to welcome a new arrival from England.' Serafina took a cool sip of her drink. 'He sent me flowers and asked me to have dinner with him.'

'Gosh.' Mary's stomach turned somersaults. 'Where did he take you?'

'Don't be silly! I didn't accept, you ninny. Whatever do you take me for? I sent a note back declining his kind invitation, saying that perhaps we would run into one another again at a future social engagement. So he sent me more flowers, this time with an apology.' She lifted her eyes to Mary in amusement. 'It was quite funny really, and terribly sweet.'

Their lunch arrived, spooned from the enormous cooking pots bubbling away on the open stove. Mary waited for Serafina to settle her napkin. 'I really mustn't get any marks on this dress,' she said absently.

'It's lovely.' Mary admired the flower-print cotton. 'I just don't understand how you manage to dress the way you do on our meagre wages.'

'Good housekeeping,' Serafina replied. 'And a matter of priorities. You like to squander your money on silly holidays and going to the pictures; I prefer to spend mine on clothes.'

'Well, make sure that you pay your bills.' This time it was Mary's turn to admonish her sister. 'The last time I went to visit Mr Chagdar, he almost threw me out of the shop because of your unpaid account.'

'Do you expect me to walk around in rags?'

'Of course not.' Mary smiled at the notion of Serafina, always immaculate, in rags. 'And stop trying to change the subject. I want to hear more about your Joseph, so tell me,' she tapped on the table, 'what happened next?'

'I kept putting him off until he practically begged me to put him out of his misery, so I finally agreed to have lunch with him.'

'Where did he take you?'

'The Taj Mahal Palace.' Serafina smiled proudly.

'Really? Golly. I've always wanted to go there. What was it like?'

'Wonderful.' Serafina sighed. 'In fact, it was a perfect day. You know, his family has very long connections with India. I would imagine he's on just about every wealthy family's list of prospective husbands.'

Mary's movements slowed as she listened. 'I'm assuming he's—'

'British,' Serafina said, without looking up from her plate. 'Of course.'

'And does he know about . . .'

Serafina shot Mary one of her looks. 'I thought we had already discussed my position on that,' she snapped.

'But you must have told him something? How can you have been seeing this man without him asking you a single question about your own circumstances?'

'I told him the truth. That our father left India after the war . . .' She faltered for a moment. 'And that our mother is dead.'

'What?' Mary gasped. 'She's not dead! How could you say such a terrible thing?'

'Then where is she? And what good has she ever been to us?'

Mary sat in silence, her upset profound. She could not bear to think of any of it. 'Don't you ever wonder what happened to her?' Mary's posture drooped, her sudden sadness all-consuming.

'No,' Serafina said resolutely, 'I don't. And nor do I want to.'

Serafina endured the discomfort of the soaring temperature inside the car and refused the driver's request to remove his hat after her insistence that the windows remain firmly closed for the duration of the short journey. To open the window would bring nothing but dust and insects, and Serafina, wearing a dress of the palest cornflower-blue, was determined that it must remain spotless despite its impracticalities. The car slowed to a halt, pulling up to the kerb just outside the hotel terrace.

Seeing his car arrive, Joseph sprang to his feet, waving at Serafina the moment she alighted; her sudden, dazzling smile directed only at him, despite the attention she drew from all quarters. Joseph took the steps in easy strides, greeting her proudly before guiding her inside. Every head she passed turned to stare.

Joseph dismissed the boy standing by to seat them and settled Serafina into the chair himself. 'Hungry, darling?' He placed a small kiss on her cheek before taking his seat.

'Famished,' she breathed, having eaten nothing since lunchtime the previous day; the discipline demanded by her slender waistline far more important to her than her body's need for breakfast or supper.

Joseph motioned to the waiter. 'Two gin slings, and bring us the lunch menu, will you?' He took a flat gold case from his inside pocket, flipped it open and offered her a cigarette, waiting patiently while she searched her handbag for the tortoiseshell holder he had given her as a token of his affection shortly after they had first met. She would never dream of putting a cigarette to her lips without one.

'Did you manage to convince the sourpuss about Saturday evening?'

'I'm afraid not,' she said. 'Although I haven't given up hope. Perhaps I can find someone to take my shift.' She leaned forward to accept the flame he offered her. 'I'm sure that she deliberately puts us on the weekend rota when she knows very well that we'd rather be at the pictures.'

'We're not going to the pictures.' Joseph began to peruse the menu, adding nothing more and encouraging a sense of mystery into his playful air. He knew very well that Serafina's curiosity would be burning, but that she would not permit herself to ask. It was a game he never tired of.

'Oh?' Serafina masked her intrigue, picking up her menu and making some pretence of examining each description.

'The fish looks rather good,' Joseph suggested. 'They brought out a tray of silver pomfret to show the couple over there. Would you like to share one with me?'

'If you like.'

'Good. That's settled, then.'

Joseph waved his menu at the boy, relayed their order, then sat back and relaxed with his cocktail. 'You're looking particularly lovely today, I must say. That's a very pretty colour.'

'Thank you.' Serafina glanced down at her dress, then looked up at him questioningly. He sipped his drink a little, then gave in. It would be cruel to keep her waiting too long. She was not a woman to be toyed with.

'I'm taking you to the company dance on Saturday evening.' The drop in Serafina's expression betrayed her alarm instantly. Joseph feigned normality, but allowed a small smile to pass across his handsome face. 'It will probably be dreadfully stuffy, but I thought you might like to come along and meet a few of the chaps and their wives.' Serafina's insides began to churn. 'If it's too awful, we can skip off and have a late dinner here instead. Richard Patterson will be there. He's a good chap. It's about time the two of you got acquainted.' He winked at her. 'Wear something wonderful.'

Clothes lay everywhere, draped across every available surface in the cramped single room in the nurses' quarters, hanging from the spartan furniture, strewn across the bed amid piles of mess and the occasional odd shoe. Serafina stood, breath drawn, clutching the back of the chair, utterly panic-stricken.

'Hold still, will you!' Mary struggled to fasten the fiddly row of hooks and eyes.

'I am! Pull it harder or you'll never get them done.'

'I'll be surprised if you're still able to breathe. Shouldn't you wear the blue one instead? What if you go and faint?'

'Don't be so ridiculous.'

'I don't know why you have to have your things made so tight on the waist. You'll be impossibly uncomfortable and you won't be able to eat.'

'I have absolutely no intention of eating, and it's perfectly comfortable. You just have to set it right once it's on.'

As the last of the fastenings were pulled into place, Mary collapsed dramatically to the bed. Serafina regarded her own reflection in the inadequate mirror, turning side on, approving of the effect that such unforgiving tailoring had on a figure of her splendour. She was tall, with the graceful elegance of her father, her tiny middle rising to a full and luscious bosom; her legs, long and athletic, tapering to fine ankles and pretty feet.

'This is the one,' she said, twisting this way and that, examining her image. 'I have been saving it for a special occasion.'

'Thank goodness. I don't think my fingers could stand any more.'

'What do you think?' Serafina swayed gently from side to side, her many-layered skirts rustling like autumn leaves.

'It's beautiful. Really it is.' Mary marvelled at the raw silk gown with the intricate embroidery curling round its bodice, the honey-cream skin of her sister's shoulders accenting the sculptured line of her collarbones.

Serafina leaned towards the mirror and fastened her earrings.

'All these clothes.' Mary gasped at the mess in the room. 'I don't understand how you can have the gall to overspend the way you do, and don't deny it. Mr Chagdar told me to remind you that you still owe him for five new summer dresses. Five! He was very cross.'

'So? He should be grateful for my custom. He'll be paid eventually, just like he always is.' Serafina continued to appreciate herself in the mirror, holding up a succession of shawls to see which one suited best. 'The man's a thief, anyway.'

'That's all very well for you to say. You should pay your dues and not expect me to put up with getting a telling-off on your behalf. Don't wear that one. It doesn't look right.'

'Which, then?' Serafina flung the shawl back to the floor and sighed.

'The green and gold one.' Mary got up from the bed and found it for her, then began to arrange the gilded shawl while Serafina watched. 'Here. Drape it round your shoulders.' She placed the fine silk organza round her sister, just so, and kissed her powdered cheek before answering the gentle tap at the door to find Florence, hovering self-consciously in full uniform, holding a white enamel tray covered with a muslin cloth.

'Drink this, she said, quickly lifting the cloth aside to reveal two china cups. 'It's for your nerves. It's gin and soda. We couldn't find any tonic water.' Florence stared down at the cups, the guilt of their contents creeping up at her. 'For goodness sake hurry up! I've been gone from the ward for nearly twenty minutes and Matron's bound to be on the war path.'

Mary took the cups and thrust one at Serafina, who took an uncharacteristically enormous gulp, shuddered at the bitter taste and sat heavily on the bed. Florence couldn't help but stare at her.

'What a heavenly dress,' she whispered. 'And your hair! You look like a film star.'

Serafina glanced up at her and smiled anxiously. 'Thank you, Florence. And for taking my shift.' In a rare move, she reached out and took Mary's hand. 'Thank you, both of you. I would have been stuck without you.'

But Florence had already fled, her footsteps dashing along the corridor.

Serafina went over to stand by the window. Staring out at the evening closing in, she settled herself with a few deep breaths of the city's thick air.

'Is it terribly important, this evening?' Mary said quietly.

'Yes.'

'Do you . . .' Mary wondered if she was prying. 'I mean, are you in love with him?'

At this, Serafina smiled. 'He's the man I'm going to marry.'

'Are you sure? Oh, my goodness.' Mary knotted her brow and chewed on her lip. So this was what all the fuss was about. 'Won't that cause difficulties? I mean, does he—'

'Mary, please.' Serafina returned to the mirror and began pulling at the bones in her dress, setting it correctly on her waist. 'Can't you see that I'm in quite enough of a state as it is?'

'I'm sorry. Of course, you must be.'

Mary hushed herself, having already sensed her sister's dark mood. Serafina was withdrawn, pensive, as if plagued by a constant uneasiness. Mary watched her nervous reflection in the mirror but couldn't think of anything to say to make her feel better.

The company's clubhouse echoed the grand colonial style introduced by the Empire more than a century before, its gables draping generously from the roof with a wide verandah passing all the way round the outer wall, edged by a shining teak handrail on carved balustrades. A chattering menagerie of women in shimmering dresses and men with starched white collars greeted each other with confident handshakes and wide smiles, exchanging well-worn pleasantries among themselves. The sweet scent of evening jasmine blossom clung to every corner of the night, while droves of staff, dressed in formal uniform with golden cockades terribly unsuited to the overbearing heat, aided the spectacle of a dying splendour.

There was a certain amount of nudging as a shining American car slid up to the marker posts—a Chrysler, gleaming red, drew admiring glances and whispers of approval. Two valets reached eagerly to open its doors. From the back seat, Serafina emerged beneath a cloud of emerald silk and gazed up at the sprawling building. Without warning, she froze as she found herself suddenly caught up in a fleeting memory. This aspect. This sprawling elevation. It reminded her of a place she no longer thought of for it tore her heart in two. A big house she once knew so well, with green-tiled gables that spread their shade far beyond the verandah. It came upon her all at once, a vivid picture of such rich detail that it engulfed her completely.

Joseph was by her side, offering his arm. 'Serafina? Are you all right?' The concern in his voice was apparent as he searched her wounded face.

The vision in her head disappeared as quickly as it had come. 'Yes. I'm fine. Really.' She allowed him to walk her up the steps to the entrance, through the hallway and into an opulent room hung with sparkling chandeliers. Guests gazed at her as she passed. Men forgot what they were saying mid-sentence, to the consternation of their female companions.

Sensing her nerves, Joseph murmured soft words of encouragement into her ear. 'Didn't I tell you that you would be the most beautiful woman here? Just be yourself.' He felt some of her stiffness disappear through the lessened grip on his arm. She nodded and smiled at him.

From the far corner of the room, the company chairman noticed Joseph making his way through the crowd, and prepared his small entourage for the dreadful embarrassment they were about to endure.

'Oh, dear,' he breathed. 'I've just spotted Carlisle. I suppose this is where we all have to save our colleague's blushes while he makes a complete fool of himself. I told him outright, "You can do what you bloody well like in your private life, but we don't bring junglies to the clubhouse." I expect she's one of those deluded sorts who tries to pass herself off as a European.

'And he didn't give me much choice about it,' the chairman continued. 'Came marching into my office a week ago and virtually demanded that I break the sporting rules and allow him to bring his floozy with him this evening. Why he can't manage to observe the usual discretion, I really don't know.' Heads nodded their agreement around him. 'When I turned him down, the bloody idiot threatened to resign on the spot!'

'So I heard.' Richard Patterson rolled the drink in his glass. 'Sounds to me like he's thinking with his trousers.'

'Well, he wouldn't be the first, Patterson, would he now? I seem to recall that you've had one or two colourful liaisons yourself.'

Richard Patterson smiled defiantly. 'Maybe I have. I don't see anything wrong with a man availing himself of a little local culture, but I wouldn't go bragging about it,' he added slyly.

'I'm surprised you don't already know this creature he's taken up with. I thought you and Carlisle were quite the pair around town.'

'We were,' Richard said. 'Then the poor chap suddenly took leave of his senses and refused to play any more. I did try to warn him off as soon as I got wind of it. She's something of an ice queen, apparently, though quite a looker if the rumours are to be believed. In fact, I might have been tempted to have a go there myself had he not gone and pipped me to the post.' He took a long swig of his drink.

The chairman cleared his throat and stood upright, warning his company of Joseph's approach.

'Charles.' Joseph stepped into the gathering and shook the chairman's hand. 'May I present Miss Serafina Macdonald?'

Serafina stood valiant, her eyes locked on the chairman. Her gaze refused to give way despite what she saw in the stupefied eyes of the man before her. She did not falter, not for one second, and in that moment remembered what it was to feel taller than the trees and braver than a lion. With every shred of her fear well hidden, her indestructible beauty rendered the group all but speechless.

Richard Patterson offered her his outstretched hand. She lifted hers in graceful acceptance. 'We were just saying,' he said, as he placed a kiss on the back of her hand, 'it's about time Joseph stopped keeping you all to himself. Everyone's been dying to meet his mystery woman. Now I understand what all the fuss was about. Richard Patterson, at your service.'

## CHAPTER 12

MARY PAUSED AT THE DOOR of the colonel's room, listening for his breathing, hoping that she would find it deep and regular, filled with sleep. Instead she saw him lying there, staring restlessly towards the window, where the smile of a new moon split a bright white crescent into the blackened sky.

'Still awake?' she whispered. He looked at her and nodded. She slipped into the room and pulled the door closed behind her. 'Why don't I go and find you a sleeping pill? You need your rest.'

'No, thanks,' he said. 'But I'd kill for a cigarette.'

'Shhh! You're not supposed to smoke in here. Kemp's on duty this evening and you know what she's like with her precious rules.'

'What's she going to do about it; string me up?' He pulled softly at his traction lines with a smile. 'Come on, Nurse Mary. Where's your sense of adventure? Open the window and pass me a smoke. She'll never know it was you. Promise. I won't say a word.'

Mary went back to the door to check the empty corridor, before pulling it properly closed. Quietly sliding open the window nearest to his bed, she stuck her head out. 'The stars are shining,' she said, stretching herself out up to her waist, taking a few deep breaths. She watched for a while, listening to the song of the night-time, forgetting herself.

The colonel gazed longingly at Mary, his eyes free to stare for as long as she chose to lean out of his window admiring the moon and stars. Her uniform glowed in the half-light, its white cotton skimming the slight curve of her slender hips, the gentle round of her behind, her hem pulled up by her stretched position just enough to expose the fragility of her legs. She looked as though she would waft up and flutter away if he blew just one breath hard enough.

'Yes,' he said. 'A beautiful sight, indeed.'

Mary bobbed her head back into the room. 'In here?' she asked, opening the draw of his bedside locker. She found him a cigarette and lit it with a match, puffing incompetently and trying not to cough and splutter before handing it to him.

'Thanks.' He smiled, amused by the face she pulled at the bitter taste of the tobacco. 'Will you have one yourself?'

'No, thank you.'

'Don't smoke?'

'Of course I do,' Mary said indignantly, making a mental note to buy some and practise. 'But I'm on duty, so I'm not allowed.'

She took the small kidney bowl from the shelf by the washbasin and perched herself on the edge of his bed, holding it for him as an ashtray. 'You mustn't worry, Eddie. Mr Browning is the finest of surgeons and his team know exactly what they're doing. They'll have you out of this lot in no time.' She glanced around at the tangle of weights and pulleys. 'I know it's going to be strange and you'll have all the physio to come, but you'll be all right. I just know you will.'

He patted her hand and took another long drag on his cigarette. 'I won't hold you to that,' he said.

'Well, you jolly well ought to. You'll be on your way back to England before you can say Jack Robinson.'

'Not if I have anything to do with it.' He flicked his ash into the bowl. 'I have a cushy number set up with one of the big petrochem firms once I'm out of here. An ex-officer with two dialects tucked under his belt? They almost bit my hand off.' He allowed himself a smile. 'I have absolutely no intention of going back to that bloody awful life. Think of England like the food it dishes up—boiled beef with carrots and puddings made out of suet. Trust me, you can't possibly imagine how stodgy the place is.' He puffed away for a while, thoughts elsewhere. 'Have you ever been?'

'No,' Mary said. 'But I'd like to.'

'Don't bother. It's a miserable, grey country full of miserable, grey people. It's no place for an exotic little bird of paradise like you.'

'Well, thank you for that insight, Colonel. Now I'm even more curious than ever.' Mary took the cigarette from his fingers and extinguished it in the kidney bowl before throwing the butt out of the window. She moved around the darkened room, flapping her arms in a hopeless attempt to disperse the smoke and get rid of the pungent smell. 'I want you to close your eyes now and try to get some rest. And if you're not asleep in half an hour, I'm going to bring you that pill whether you want it or not.'

'Yes, sir.' He gave her a small salute as she crept out and closed the door.

'Make it a little tighter on the waist.' Serafina scrutinised her reflection as Mr Chagdar pinched the surplus sliver of fabric from the small of her back and pinned it tight.

'I should refuse to do this until you pay your account,' he grumbled.

'I'll pay you some today if you promise me you'll have this one finished by tomorrow.'

'You have the cheek of the devil, Miss Macdonald.'

'And you have more customers than you know what to do with. Everybody asks me who my dressmaker is. Perhaps it is you who should be paying me?' She laughed lightly.

'Is that tight enough?' Mr Chagdar stood back and watched the dress. Serafina moved slightly, breathing deeply.

'Yes,' she said. 'That's much better.'

'All right.' Mr Chagdar shrugged his charmed defeat. 'I'll have it ready for you by twelve o'clock tomorrow, but you must bring me proper payment this time, not an empty promise and a bold smile.'

Outside on the blazing street, behind the dark green lenses of her sunglasses, Serafina's eyes shone. It was only a matter of time before Joseph offered her a marriage proposal. She was sure of it. He had taken on a more sober manner this last week or so, kissing her hand solemnly while gazing into her eyes, leaving certain sentences unfinished. Content to bide her time, Serafina had kept herself to herself and spoken not a word of her suspicions to anyone. It would do no good to tempt Fate.

'Miss Macdonald?' Serafina turned towards the voice, the man's outline silhouetted against the bright sun. For a moment she did not recognise him. 'It's Richard Patterson. Remember?'

'Of course!' Serafina relaxed. 'With the sun behind you like that . . .'

'I know. It's a blinder today, isn't it?'

'Yes.'

'Have you been to see your tailor?'

'How on earth would you . . .'

'Spotted you coming out of the shop.' Richard thumbed casually over his shoulder with a warm smile. 'Can I offer you a lift somewhere?'

'Oh! Thank you.' They began to walk together. 'What a coincidence, us running into each other like this. What were you doing here? It's rather out of the way from your neck of the woods, isn't it?'

'I was looking for a bookshop somebody told me about.'

'A bookshop?' Serafina frowned. 'I've never noticed a bookshop around here before. Did you write down the address?'

'Never mind.' He shrugged it off. 'I no doubt misheard and came to the wrong place. Still, look what I stumbled across instead!' His smile broadened. 'In fact, why don't we go and have tea somewhere? Now that the bookshop sortie is off, I suppose I find myself at something of a loose end.' Reaching his car, Richard opening the door for her.

'Well,' Serafina said hesitantly as she got in, her careful sense of etiquette ruffled by this unexpected turn. The last thing she wanted was to offend him, yet his wolfish grin had made the suggestion of tea feel somehow improper. 'I'm afraid I already have plans for the afternoon. Perhaps I should . . .'

'Nonsense!' Richard insisted, shutting the door on her before getting in himself. 'We may not be running the country any more, but teatime is sacrosanct to the British way of life and I simply won't take no for an answer.' He turned the engine over. 'I'll have you back in an hour. Scout's honour.'

'All right.' Serafina submitted to her seat.

'So,' Richard said after a while, 'it looks like you have the great Joseph Carlisle utterly smitten.' Serafina smiled demurely. 'Can't say I blame him. Tell you what, why don't we take a little detour since we're out and about? They're finishing some new houses for the company not far from Malabar Hill. We could go and have a look if you like. I expect the company wives will be fighting each other over them tooth and nail.'

'Well, I don't . . .'

'Oh, come on!' he chided her. 'Aren't you even a little curious to see?'

'All right.' Serafina said with a smile. 'Why not?'

The car soon found its way to a quiet residential district, the new houses cordoned off behind high walls, Serafina barely noticing as they drove through open gates, the car pulling to a halt beside a seemingly deserted house.

'Want to take a look inside?' Richard switched the engine off and got out of the car, Serafina following as he strolled casually to the door.

'Is it open?'

'Don't worry.' He produced a key from his pocket and gave her a conspiratorial smile before unlocking the door and pushing it wide.

'Are you sure it's all right for us to be here?' Serafina stepped in tentatively, a small gasp escaping her lips as her eyes came to rest on the grand interior, not quite finished.

'Of course.' Richard encouraged her. 'In fact, I should come right out and confess that I'm tempted to nab this one for myself. Quite a place, isn't it?'

'Where are the workmen?'

'Finished for the afternoon,' he said. 'They'll be back later this evening once it's cooled down.'

Serafina wandered into the main salon, noting the floor-to-ceiling cream silk damask curtains, some furniture still in packing cases.

'I expect Joseph would have been earmarked for one of these, especially if he was about to take a wife.'

Serafina felt herself seduced by the splendour of her surroundings, a smile rising to her lips. This was what she had been waiting for her whole life. She ran her fingertip along the deep shine of a cherrywood table.

'It's a shame about his career, though. I say that a man should be able to follow his heart and marry whoever he likes, don't you?'

'I'm sorry?' Serafina turned sharply.

'The company.' Richard lit a cigarette. 'They can get a bit sniffy about their senior men taking up with, shall we say, unsuitable wives.'

Serafina felt herself stiffen.

'If a man like Joseph expects to marry a girl like you, he will have to take it up with the board and get their permission, otherwise there'll be all hell to pay.' Serafina's eyes widened at this surprise humiliation. 'Now, now,' Richard said softly. 'You're a big girl. There's no need to take offence. Let's not pretend, shall we? After all, we're all friends. There are a thousand men like that who used to be thought of as having great potential, yet ended up pushing pieces of paper around in windowless offices. Still. Who needs a place like this? Love conquers all, eh?' Serafina felt a sudden hotness in her cheeks. 'I'm sorry, has he not discussed any of this with you?'

'I . . .' Serafina floundered. 'No.'

'Mmm,' Richard said thoughtfully. 'So he hasn't proposed to you, then?'

'That's really none of your business.'

'I see.' He paused. 'Perhaps they headed him off at the pass and he's changed his mind. Looks like I've gone and let the cat out of the bag, doesn't it?'

'I'd like to go back now.' Serafina fought to calm herself.

'He's a stickler for rules, our chairman. He likes to do things the old-fashioned way.' Richard moved towards her, coming close, reaching for an ashtray on the table. 'Mind you, under the right circumstances, I've known him to be persuaded once or twice. I suppose that's one of the benefits of being related to him.' Serafina held her breath. 'Without his blessing, Joseph wouldn't have a hope in hell of progressing the way he ought to. Pity. He's a valuable man.'

'Richard, I really don't think you should be speaking to me like this. I'm not comfortable with . . .'

He stubbed out his cigarette. 'What if I were to tell you that I could straighten all this out for you with a few choice words to the right people?' He smiled, touching her arm. 'Assuming, of course, that I get a little something in exchange?'

'I'm leaving.' Serafina turned away and headed smartly for the door. Richard was fast on his feet, catching her by the hand, wrenching her back. 'What's your hurry?'

'Get away from me!' She snatched her hand away, breaking into a run, just for the second until he caught up with her, his arm round her waist, hand clamped to her mouth.

'There's nobody here,' he whispered in her ear. 'Nobody here except you and me.' Serafina crushed her eyes closed and fought to free herself, kicking out wildly, her delicate shoes flying from her feet as he picked her up and hauled her back into the ghostly, sun-drenched parlour. 'There's no point in fighting. Besides, it's not as though I'm asking you to give up anything you haven't already passed around, is it?' She felt his clammy breath on her neck, his lips, his tongue. She squirmed her head away as she heard him inhale her perfumed hair. At last he took his hand from her mouth, fumbling at his clothes, releasing her screams. 'Shhh!' He pushed her against the table, pressing her face to its shining surface, bearing his weight down upon her. 'Careful now.' She felt her skirts lifted, her thighs exposed. 'We wouldn't want to spoil this dress now, would we?'

Mirrored in the expensive, polished wood, Serafina saw the grotesque reflection of his face, and shut her eyes.

**D**orothy clutched the truck's jolting steering wheel, bracing herself as the vehicle pitched and rolled. The previous season's rains had made a mess of the three miles of gravel road that linked Nalla Farm with the tarmac highway, and they had all but given up with the soul-destroying annual ritual of trying to repair it. The scant labour they managed to retain was hard-pushed enough trying to maintain the fragile crops and coaxing the thin livestock through the harsh, drought-ridden summers.

Dorothy slowed as she neared the house, pulling up on the wide, cracked patch of ground she had once tried to cultivate in an attempt to create something resembling a garden. She brought the truck to a shuddering halt in the shelter of the one partially shady spot beneath two thorn trees, releasing a cloud of dust into the dry air. She jumped out, walked round the vehicle, opened the passenger door and pulled the box from the seat, casually checking the contents as she swung the door shut.

Balancing the box under one arm, she grappled with the tall gate set into the high chicken-wire fence. 'James!' she called. 'I picked up our mail from the station!' His seat on the verandah was empty, the dogs gone. Dorothy wandered into the house, the insect screen clattering sharply behind her. 'James?'

'He no here, missus,' Kapo said without looking up, bending past her, sweeping the dust messily out of the door onto the verandah. 'He at the farmers' meeting, missus.'

Dorothy clucked at her forgetfulness. She had meant to be back in time, but then she had stopped in on the nearby kraal to check on the worker who had burned himself badly while tackling a bush fire. There were those on the neighbouring farms who were speechless when they heard about Dorothy's close contact with the native workers and her misplaced concern for their welfare. For a white woman to touch black skin was, as far as they were concerned, about as shocking a thing as they could imagine. Still, it was not her concern. She had sworn, when she was still a young woman, to practise her art to the best of her ability. There had been nothing in the Hippocratic oath about the colour of a person's skin.

She started unpacking the box—a newspaper, various medical supplies she had sent for which had taken an age to arrive, a few provisions, a scant handful of mail. She looked at the blue aerogramme, neatly glued at the edges, postmarked from Bombay.

James let himself in through the gate, the dogs an excitable tangle around his legs. He banished them to their kennel with a commanding word and a click of his fingers, then made his way to the house, his heavy gait slowed by the devouring heat. By the time he reached the door, Dorothy had it open for him. She kissed him hello, then, unable to wait a moment longer: 'Serafina's getting married,' she said. 'There was a letter waiting for us at the post office. I'm so sorry I missed you. I really wanted to come to the farmers' meeting with you.'

James sat down, pulling off his hat. 'What does she say?'

'It was from Mary,' Dorothy said. James nodded. Of course it was from Mary. 'His name's Joseph Carlisle. Mary writes very highly of him. Says he's a lovely man and that Serafina is very happy.'

'That's good.'

'The wedding has been set for the twenty-fourth of next month.' James seemed to glaze over. 'In Bombay.' Dorothy offered him the letter.

James took it from her, glancing over Mary's familiar writing, then stood up and went to the sideboard where the drinks were kept locked up, the letter limp in his hand. He reached for the whisky and poured himself a short measure, sipping a while, staring out of the window to where the dogs lay napping in the yard, the three of them curled up on the scrubby ground in what few patches of shade they could find.

'We can't leave this place,' he said. 'Not now. There's too much at stake.'

'Just for a visit,' Dorothy said. 'We could find a way. Ask one of our neighbours to keep an eye on the farm for us, just for a few weeks.' He silenced her with the merest shift of his weight. 'I know,' Dorothy conceded. 'I just thought you might want to . . .' She trailed off.

'Like it or not, we belong here now,' James said. 'Although why I chose to pick here of all places is beyond me. It's a fool's game. You would have thought I might have learned my lesson after watching what happened in India.' He drank some more of the whisky. 'Maybe it won't be so bad.'

'Was there much talk at the farmers' meeting?'

'Of course.' James threw back the rest of his drink and put the glass down heavily. 'It's the same old thing.' He opened the door to the verandah and let out a whistle. The dogs jerked towards his voice, the younger two ripping themselves out of the dirt and bounding to the house.

'The Fitzpatricks are hauling out,' he called over his shoulder. 'I was thinking we might pick up a few of their cattle.' A rare curl of breeze through the open door flipped the letter up from the surface where it had been left. Dorothy caught it, folded it in two and watched James's unease. 'All right, boys,' he grumbled in a low voice, pushing the dogs away.

'James? Didn't you want to read Mary's letter?'

'Later.' He patted a dog's head. 'I'll read it later.'

'A transfer?' Joseph held the flame steady for Serafina's cigarette. 'Whatever for?'

'Aren't you a little tired of Bombay?' Serafina sighed, lifting her cigarette away with a casual puff.

'I hadn't really thought about it,' Joseph said.

'Don't you think it might be nice to have a change? For us to start off as a married couple somewhere new?'

'Ah.' Joseph smiled. 'Worried about running into jealous old girlfriends, are you?'

'Not at all,' Serafina said, circling the diamond round her finger.

'Or wanting to dismantle my bachelor lifestyle now that you've decided to make an honest man of me? I hear that some men are never seen or heard of again,' he joked with her. 'Are you drawing up a list of my most undesirable friends?'

'Perhaps.' Serafina's insides tightened, the parasite of that man eating into her flesh. She could feel it, taste it, smell it, like a bitter river of poison coursing through her veins. The sickness stirred within her again. She made certain to smile. 'Can you blame me for wanting to keep you all to myself once we're married? We'll make wonderful new friends together. Married friends,' she added with a deliberate hint of mischief, although the brightness she attempted felt brittle. It was all she could do to look him in the eye, the fear of what he might see setting her into a panic so deep that it shredded her insides.

'So, you'll think about the move?' she persisted.

'I suppose I could have a little word.' Joseph picked up his gin and tonic. 'They've been crying out to get some new blood up in the Chittagong office, from what I hear, but I'm not sure how you'd feel about it, though. The climate's rather unpredictable and there's still a bit of uproar going on with the Pakistani states. These things take a while to bed in, I suppose.'

'There, you see?' Serafina said, decisively. 'You're exactly the kind of person they would need. The very best of their crop. They would fall at your feet with gratitude if you so much as mentioned your interest.'

'Perhaps you're right.' Joseph considered it for a while. 'And I have no doubt that they'd be very generous.'

**M**ary returned from her night shift, eyes gritty with fatigue, to find Serafina waiting for her outside her quarters, pacing the path, smoking a cigarette. She looked tired and drawn, thinned out already by the heat of the morning sun.

'Where have you been?' Serafina threw the cigarette to the ground. 'I've been waiting here for an eternity.' With her faculties dulled by exhaustion, Mary just stared at her, wondering what she had done wrong this time, bracing herself for the rebuke. 'You have to come with me right now.'

Yearning for her bed, Mary obediently followed Serafina to her room.

Serafina closed the door quietly and leaned against it. Now that the moment was upon her, she felt herself numbed, her body no longer her own, her voice drifting in from elsewhere, hollow and unfamiliar. 'Mary,' she said. 'I'm pregnant.'

Mary pressed her palms to her cheeks. '*What?* I mean, are you sure?' It was impossible. Unthinkable. Serafina would never be that stupid.

'Yes. I'm sure.'

'Oh, Sera!' Mary's thoughts charged at a hundred miles an hour. 'Does Joseph know?'

'No.'

'Why ever not?' Mary was astounded. 'You have to tell him! You have to get married straight away!'

'I can't.'

'What do you mean, you can't? Don't be so ridiculous! You must tell him at once, before you start to show.'

'Mary!' Serafina shouted, tears springing to her eyes. 'I can't! Don't you understand?' She screwed up her face. 'I have to get rid of it!'

Mary froze, Serafina's expression unlike any she had seen before, halting her breath. 'Oh, my God.' Her hand came slowly to her mouth. 'Oh, my God, Sera. What have you done?'

'**B**angalore?' Florence looked up from her newspaper. 'Why on earth would you want to go back to Bangalore?'

'It was Serafina's suggestion. She thought it would be nice for us to take a break together.' Mary was not a natural liar and her stomach lurched.

'Really?' Florence said, perplexed. 'I thought she was too busy playing all high and mighty to bother with you.' Mary battled with her conscience, desperate to unburden herself of this terrible weight. 'I never wanted to leave Bangalore.' Florence sighed. 'It's so beautiful. All the gardens and flowers everywhere. Sometimes I yearn to go back.' She suddenly set the newspaper down on the bed. 'Why don't I come with you?'

'Oh!' Mary felt certain her face would give her away. 'I really think it would be better if you and I were to go another time, Florence. You know how Serafina can be when her plans are interfered with.'

'I see.' The offence in Florence's voice was not easily hidden. 'It has nothing to do with my company not being good enough for her, I suppose?'

Mary sat beside her and searched for a plausible reason to keep her in Bombay. 'Not at all. I know she can be a bit stand-offish, but she doesn't mean anything by it. Don't you see that someone has to stay behind and make sure that Ruby keeps out of trouble? Can you imagine what might happen if she were left to her own devices?'

'Goodness me,' Florence said. 'I hadn't thought of that.'

The journey to Bangalore and the appointment that awaited them took three interminable days. Travelling along avenues of blossoming trees as they headed away from the bustling station crammed into the back of the rickshaw, Mary was reminded of just how happy she had once been here. If only they had all stayed, perhaps this would never have happened.

Mary had known that there were doctors who would do these unthinkable things, but only for certain people, and always at a price. That Serafina should know where to find them had come as a shock. Mary didn't press the matter. Some things were better left unsaid.

The house in Marathahalli came as even more of a shock. Rusted gates creaked on broken hinges. Faded blue paint peeled in great swathes from the tatty outside walls. The woman who came to answer their tentative knock was plainly interested only in their money and demanded that payment be passed through the broken pane before letting them in. She stood, counting the notes in her hand, while the two of them stared incredulously at their surroundings. Every instinct told them to turn and walk out of there as quickly as they could and not to look back, but there was nowhere else to go. The woman poked her finger towards them, asking in jagged Kannada which one of them it was.

'So you, go,' she said to Mary coldly. 'She stay.' She pointed at Serafina. 'She stay here. You go now. Leave her. Doctor come tomorrow.'

Serafina, shocked into silence, seemed unable to speak.

'No.' Mary spoke up. 'We will both come back tomorrow morning, and I must be present when she undergoes the procedure.' The woman shook her head violently and waved them away, shouting, but Mary stood her ground, arguing with her sister's ferocity until the woman reluctantly agreed to admit them again the following morning.

They spent the long night in an unassuming guest house they had found along the way. Despite their exhaustion, neither slept, the pair of them tossing and turning uncomfortably on the pair of worn charpoys in the tiny kerosene-tainted back room.

'We shouldn't go tomorrow,' Mary whispered. 'It's asking for trouble. We should have gone straight to the railway station this evening and got on the first train back to Bombay. For heaven's sake, Sera, you could *die*.'

'Do you think I don't know that?' Serafina said bitterly. 'This is what happens when women get stupid ideas about love and romance. It's not a game. It's a tragedy.' Her caustic words reverberated round the thin walls. 'Men aren't interested in love. They want sex, ownership, possession. Women want security. That's what marriage is about. It's no more complicated than any other business transaction.' The lump in Mary's throat grew. She swallowed, but it would not go. 'Are you listening to me?'

'Yes,' Mary responded. Her sister's altered state was unfathomable to her. She no longer blushed and smiled at the mention of Joseph's name. Instead she looked away, as if ashamed of it, her breath coming sharply.

The pair of them lay on their bunks in silence, devoid of the energy to argue any further, the atmosphere between them thickened once more.

Mary turned it over and over in her head. Serafina would never have compromised herself. Of that much Mary was certain. There could be only one explanation. The thought of it cut her open and tore out her insides. For a moment she could not catch her breath, her lungs burning as though filled with the acid that rose into her throat.

'Serafina,' she whispered. 'Did something happen?'

'No.'

Mary turned onto her side and tried to make out her sister's features in the gloom. 'Sera,' she said, her voice shaking. 'Who did this to you?'

'It is none of your business,' Serafina said coldly.

'Of course it's my business!' Mary sat up. 'You're my sister! You have to tell me!'

'Just leave it alone, will you?' Serafina snapped. 'And don't you ever ask me again.'

Mary stared into the blackness, afraid to speak for fear of igniting the rage that smouldered in Serafina, afraid to disturb the very seat of her fury; this woman, born of a man's lust. She turned away, her tears spilling in silent torrents, willing her sister's agony to enter her instead.

They arrived at the house the next day to find a doctor in attendance, the sickly odour of alcohol on his breath, eyes stained ochre-yellow. Under the light of a single lamp, Mary watched as the woman who had taken their money held the mask to Serafina's face while the doctor worked, gas leaking into the room around them. Despite his shockingly unkempt appearance, the doctor carried out the task quickly, his hands working with the skill of someone who had done it hundreds of times before.

After briefly washing his hands in the cracked basin, he began to throw his things into his bag. 'I must go now,' he said.

'No,' Mary said sternly. 'Not until I have seen her awake and recovered.'

The doctor stared at her. 'I don't think you understand me,' he said. 'I must go. *Now*. So should you. The woman will stay here with your friend.'

'I think I should inform you that we are both nurses,' Mary said. 'I can see for myself what a mess she is in.'

'You expected this to be tidy?' The doctor looked up, his eyes settling on her coolly. 'You knew what the risks were before you came here. Women like you, with your fancy clothes and loose morals. You think this is how decent women behave?' He jerked his head at Serafina, still groaning beneath the anaesthesia, now fast wearing off. 'She was lucky. It was straightforward this time. Maybe next time she won't be so fortunate.' He picked up his bag distastefully. 'Woman like you should learn to keep your legs closed.'

**M**ary was unable to settle herself. She remained wakeful throughout her nights, tormented by bloodstained visions of twisted, dead infants, and the screams of the desperate women from whose bodies they had been torn. The change in her demeanour did not go unnoticed.

'I knew you should have let me come with you.' Florence felt Mary's forehead.

'Please, Florence. Stop fussing. I just need to get some rest.'

'Rest? You've hardly left your bed since you got back. If there's nothing wrong with you, you should go out and take some fresh air and exercise; otherwise I shall send for the doctor and have him take a look at you.'

There came a knock on the door, quickly followed by Ruby's head. 'Are we ready to go?'

'No,' Florence replied matter-of-factly. 'Mary still isn't feeling well, so I think we should all stay in.'

'What?' Ruby closed the door with a bang. 'But I've been looking forward to this all week.'

'I told you I'm fine.' Mary sat up. 'I'll be perfectly all right on my own.'

'See?' Ruby attended to her reflection in the mirror. 'Now hurry up or we'll be last in the queue.'

'I'm not going anywhere with you looking like that.' Florence pointed at Ruby's cleavage. 'Do those buttons up before somebody sees you.' Before Ruby could protest, Florence had hold of her sweater.

'What are you doing? Will you please stop pulling at my clothes!' Ruby swiped at Florence's hands. 'It's only the pictures, for heaven's sake!'

'So you won't need to be putting everything on show, will you?'

'Do your buttons up, Ruby.' Mary turned away, po-faced. 'What do you want people to think of you?'

'And since when did you become all holier-than-thou? I don't know what went on between you and that sister of yours while you were away, but I'm not sure that I like it one little bit.' Ruby checked her lipstick and pinched colour into her cheeks. 'You've been no fun at all lately. The Saturday matinee is bound to be brimming with handsome young men, and I have every intention of attracting at least one of them.'

'Oh, don't be so . . .' Serafina's word dropped spontaneously from Mary's mouth, '. . . *obtuse*.'

'Obtuse, am I? Well, that's a big word to come out of a mouse's mouth.'

'For heaven's sake!' Mary burst into tears and shouted at her friend. 'Just do them up!'

## CHAPTER 13

A THOUSAND FLICKERING CANDLES illuminated the cavernous interior of the Cathedral of the Holy Name, its high vaulted ceilings bathed in a soft golden radiance. The coolness of the air inside gave way the moment the party spilled out into the glorious sunshine on this fine morning, bride and groom flinching briefly with wide smiles under the sudden scattered shower of rice and orange blossom.

Serafina stood proudly on Joseph's arm, allowing Mary to fuss with her gown and adjust her veil in anticipation of the photographer's portrait. The dress, layer after layer of translucent white silk, had been chosen from the pages of a glossy magazine and sent for all the way from Europe. It could not have been more perfect. Mary had cried as they had lifted it from the box. Her own dress, also of white silk, had been made by Mr Chagdar. Although simple in its design, the cut was flawless, the needle-work sublime. Determined not to be outshone, Mr Chagdar had gone to great trouble, working the delicate fabric with his own experienced hands rather than giving the job to his apprentice. He had cheerfully given Mary his best attentions without mentioning a word of her sister's bill: it had been cleared in full two weeks earlier by a gentleman caller, who had also left an allowance in anticipation of the bridesmaid's dress for Mary.

'There.' Mary stepped back, happy with her final touches to Serafina's whispering veil. 'Perfect.'

Serafina seemed not to hear her, carried away by the sight of the world slowing around her. Passers-by dawdled, taking time to gaze upwards. People on bicycles and packed into rickshaws waved and smiled their congratulations. Standing at the top of the cathedral steps with Joseph by her side, Serafina found herself smiling back at them, feeling as if in a dream, grateful for the noise of the street. It was over, her tortured life. She would have nothing to fear now, her future safely entombed in the tiny weight of the golden ring on her finger. She caught her breath, held it there, and squeezed Joseph's arm.

'Happy, darling?' He placed his hand over hers.

'Yes,' she said. 'Happier than you could possibly imagine.'

The crowd took quite some organising, with much laughter and chang-ing of positions on the steps until everyone could be seen by the camera.

'Isn't this exciting?' Ruby jostled alongside Florence.

'It was so nice of Serafina to invite us.' Florence peered out from the low brim of her borrowed hat. 'Wasn't it a beautiful service?'

'Of course she invited us,' Ruby said curtly. 'And everyone else she ever met by the looks of it. She wanted to make sure the whole world knows she's done so well for herself.'

'Do I detect a note of jealousy?' Florence shuffled along in compliance with the photographer's wave. 'I wonder what our weddings will be like?'

'I don't care.' Ruby sighed. 'So long as he's filthy rich and able to keep me in the style in which I intend to become accustomed.'

The photographer held one hand high in the air, his head buried beneath the black cloth draped behind the camera. At his command, the gathering on the steps smiled and cheered. The shutter clicked, freeze-framing the moment.

Richard Patterson offered Joseph a hearty congratulatory handshake. Serafina forced herself to look at him, turning herself to stone so that he might see nothing in her eyes except the loathing that burned inside. He acted as though nothing had happened, smiling like a snake, tapping his cigarette lightly on the gold case before flipping it casually to his mouth and taking a match from his pocket. Serafina suppressed the savage ferocity that threatened to erupt from within and send her clawing his face. Her mouth dry, she willed herself to get through this one last, torturous encounter. After this day, she would see to it that they never saw him again.

He spoke through his snake-like smile. 'May I kiss the bride?'

'No,' Serafina said coolly, stepping back.

'But, darling,' Joseph said with a smile. 'It's traditional.'

'I said no,' Serafina repeated to Joseph. 'My kiss is for you, nobody else.'

'Well,' Joseph said sheepishly, taken aback by her sudden bellicose manner. 'You heard my wife.' He offered Richard an apologetic shrug. 'Looks like you missed your chance.'

'Women, eh?' Richard rolled his eyes before taking up his mantle as best man once more and urging the party to move along to the wedding breakfast. 'Anybody with a car,' he shouted, 'would you please take as many passengers as you can! We're rather short on transport by the looks of it, so a friendly game of sardines would be much appreciated. If you get lost, ask for directions and head for the Army and Navy. The Wayside is right opposite. Just follow the noise!'

'Do you want us to wait for you?' Ruby called to Mary while Florence dithered on the pavement, unsure of how to handle the offer of a strange gentleman's lap inside an already overcrowded vehicle.

'No.' She waved them on. 'We're getting a lift with Richard.'

Mary, still giddy with excitement, took the steps quickly, the skirt of her dress bouncing with her girlish movements.

'Feeling all right, Colonel?' she said, a little breathlessly.

'Yes.' Eddie smiled, his eyes adoring her. 'Although I'm not sure I would have got very far trying to cram in with that lot.'

Mary accepted the offer of his arm and slid her hand neatly into the crook of his elbow, glad to have his company. She squeezed Eddie's arm lightly. 'Any discomfort?'

'For the tenth time, no,' he said. 'In fact, I might even risk a turn on the dance floor a little later.'

'Good man!' Richard, coming up behind them, slapped Eddie bluntly on the back. 'We'll kill the pain with a few whiskies and throw your sticks out of the window, eh?'

'Any day now,' Eddie said with a rueful smile.

Mary was pleased that he and Richard had hit it off. When she had asked Serafina if she might bring a friend to the wedding, Serafina had reminded her stiffly that she had already sent an invitation to Ruby and Florence, much against her better judgment, and that it wasn't a free-for-all. Mary had blushed and said that it was an old patient of hers who could do with getting out and kicking his heels up. A few probing questions later, covering matters of background and propriety, and Serafina was sufficiently satisfied to offer her a breezy, 'Bring him along, by all means.'

Eddie clambered awkwardly into the front seat, refusing any assistance. Richard adjusted the rear-view mirror while Mary climbed into the back.

'Seems to me you're going to be rid of those things in no time.' He knocked one of Eddie's sticks with a knuckle. 'How long before you're shipshape again?'

'Oh.' Eddie shrugged. 'About a month, I suppose. Maybe more, maybe less. It depends on who you ask. To be frank, I stopped taking any notice of the doctors a long time ago, didn't I, Mary?'

'I always said you'd be fine,' Mary reminded him. 'Just keep up with your physio and do as the nurses tell you.' The two men exchanged a mildly salacious glance, and laughed.

**A** pleasant hubbub rose from the guests, who, at the tinkling of a glass, burst into a warm round of applause as the happy couple arrived and began to circulate among the guests.

'Gosh.' Eddie struggled to Mary's side. 'Quite a squash in here, isn't it?'

'Hello, Colonel!' Ruby thrust herself through the tangle of bodies, Florence following cautiously behind. 'Don't you think Mary looks wonderful in her dress? I was just saying to Florence, they should have made it a double wedding, seeing as she looked the part so well.'

'Ruby!' Mary felt herself flush, a cold rush of guilt creeping over her; her fondness for Eddie having remained little more than that despite his unmasked affection.

'Quite right,' Eddie replied. 'But she's already refused me three times, so I'm assuming it's these things that are putting her off.' He waved a stick a little, unable to give it sufficient room for further drama. 'We shall have to wait a while longer, then see if she comes round to the idea. Either that or I shall have to knock her out with a handful of painkillers and drag her up the aisle before she wakes up.'

Serafina supervised the last of the packing while Mary stood aside uneasily, taking in the emptiness as Serafina issued curt instructions to her servants. She placed her teacup on the mantelpiece, the clack of the porcelain saucer on the cold marble echoing around the room.

'I can't believe that you would deliberately set out to deceive him.' Mary sat precariously on one of the packing cases and shook her head. Serafina met her incredulity with a sigh of impatience.

'I've told you, Mary. That's the end of the matter, and you are never to discuss it with Joseph, no matter what he asks. Do you understand? What do you think would have happened if I had gone around broadcasting that I was the product of a tea planter's fling with a peasant? Joseph wouldn't have given me a second glance.'

'Don't speak about our parents like that.'

'What parents? In case it has escaped your notice, we don't have any.'

'And what about Papa?'

'What about him? You talk about him as though he matters. The last time I saw him, I was a child.' She laughed thinly. 'I doubt he even remembers.'

'Of course he does,' Mary said. 'It must have half killed him.'

'Huh! He never had any intention of seeing either of us again, and you're a fool if you think otherwise.'

'That's not true!'

'Of course it is.' Serafina took a sip of tea. 'Why else go to Africa?'

'You must write to him once you arrive at Chittagong and let him know where you are.'

'Why? So that he and Dorothy can keep their conscience clear with an occasional letter about their dogs?' Mary bowed her head. 'They talk about those animals as though they're the most important things on earth.'

'Will you send him a photograph of the wedding?'

'For him to display proudly on his mantelpiece?' Serafina put down her cup. 'Yes. Why not?' she scoffed sarcastically.

'And what am I to say if Joseph asks me?'

'He won't. Joseph is aware that our father is from a well-to-do family and that he is a farmer in Rhodesia. That's all he needs to know.'

'Oh, Sera.' Mary sighed. 'How can you begin your life as a married woman on nothing but a pack of lies?'

Serafina turned on her. 'And what exactly would you have me say? It is the truth. My truth. I'll decide what people should know about me, and you would do well to keep the whole messy business to yourself, unless you want to spend the rest of your life having people look down their noses at you. I'm married now. Joseph is the only family I have that matters.'

Mary drew a sharp breath. 'So where does that leave me?'

'You know what you have to do, Mary. Life is unfair. We both know that. It's up to you to do something about it. As for me, I'm finished with all that.' Serafina pressed her cigarette out on her saucer. 'I shall never set foot in this city again, nor in any place that reminds me of it. Now it's my turn to live.' She snapped open the clasp on the small vanity case set down by the door, leaned down and took out her passport. 'I'm British,' she declared, holding the deep blue cover firmly in front of Mary's face. 'And from now on, woe betide anyone who dares to suggest otherwise.'

The delicate edge of Mary's sari, woven from the soft silk of mulberry worms and printed with a bold black and purple design, fluttered around her feet, bright colours melting into the crowds teeming through the gargantuan Gothic structure of Bombay's Victoria Terminus.

'You take great care of yourself, Mary,' said Joseph. 'And if there is anything you need, just call the number on the card. I've asked Richard to keep an eye out for you and told him that if you get into any difficulties now that we're gone, I shall hold him personally accountable.'

'Thank you, but that won't be necessary.'

'Well, let's just say that it's for my peace of mind rather than yours. It doesn't do for a young woman to be without a champion in a place like this, although if he asks you to have dinner with him, run a mile!' He winked. Mary knew Richard's dangerous reputation well enough, and Serafina had made no secret of the fact that she couldn't stand the sight of the man. 'Seriously, Mary. You be careful now that you're on your own.'

'I will,' she said, warming under Joseph's kind smile and gentle voice. Her sister had chosen well, a good man with a tender heart, generous of spirit, charming of nature, capable of offering Serafina everything she had ever wished for. And he loved her. Oh, how he loved her. Mary could see it in his eyes whenever her sister came into view, his silent sigh of ecstasy as he surveyed the beauty of his prize. She yearned for a love like that, a love of her own to cherish her above all others.

'I expect we'll be staying in Chittagong for a good long time if things work out,' Joseph said. Mary looked down at the card he had given her and ran her thumb over its raised lettering. 'If you lose it,' Joseph said with a smile, 'the Bombay office will know where we can be contacted.'

'You're a good man, Joseph. Sera is lucky to have found you.'

'Nonsense. It's me who's the lucky fellow.' He touched her arm. 'I think she and I were hoping to see you at least somewhere near the altar before we left.'

'Not much chance of that.' Mary self-consciously adjusted the shoulder of her sari.

'Are you sure?' His voice teased her slightly then sobered. 'Your colonel friend appears to be quite taken with you. You could do a lot worse. He seems like a decent fellow with a good background. There's a lot to be said for that, you know. It goes a long way these days.'

'What's the big rush?' Mary looked away, pretending to be distracted by something in the distance. 'I've only known the man for six months and already everybody's trying to marry me off to him.'

The thought of accepting Eddie's proposal had left her stone cold and she didn't know why. Perhaps Serafina had been right, that to desire the burning ache of a passionate, undisciplined love, over and above the need for shelter, status and security, was nothing short of foolhardy.

'It's not such a difficult decision.' Joseph poked fun at her befuddled expression. 'All you have to do is say yes and hope for the best. You should think about it. I promised your sister that I would speak to you before we left, and that's all I'm saying.'

'Thank you, Joseph.' She accepted the sweet kiss he placed on her cheek and brushed his concerns aside, silencing the disquiet in her heart with a trite response. 'But I'm far too busy enjoying myself.'

'Be careful not to enjoy yourself too much, Mary. Serafina worries about you, and I think she's right. If you spend too much time with your head in the clouds, it can be hard to see where you're putting your feet. Think about your future, and try not to take too long about it.'

The stationmaster shouted and blew his whistle long and hard, sending a cold wind of bereavement through Mary's thin shadow.

'Do hurry, Joseph.' Serafina returned from the platform kiosk and busied herself arranging the stack of magazines she had bought in her bag. 'You know what these people are like. They'll pull out and leave us behind without a second thought.'

As Serafina fussed with her bag and brushed a stray hair from her husband's shoulder, the familiar spectre of emptiness opened its cloak to Mary as she prepared to separate from the one constant presence she had relied upon throughout a lifetime of uncertainty.

'I'll miss you.' Mary kissed her sister, determined in her cheerfulness. 'Write to me as soon as you arrive.'

'Of course.' Serafina glanced disapprovingly at Mary's clothes, whispering quietly, 'Couldn't you have worn something else?'

The clear waters of Nagin Lake ran deep and blue. Here lay a paradise, a Garden of Eden, set like a shining jewel. The *Rowallan*, carved from rich, dark teakwood, rocked gently on its moorings by the tree-lined shores. Delicate, fretworked wooden shutters patterned remnants of the low afternoon sun across the luxurious cabins: it was serene isolation after the chaos of the city.

Mary sat on the sun deck watching dragonflies dart above the lotus blossoms on the lake and brilliant blue kingfishers dive for fish. They had been ferried to the *Rowallan* two days before, reclining on seats scattered with plump pillows decorated with heavy embroidery. Children had run along the bank shouting '*Salaam! Salaam!*' until they were far from the shore.

'I miss the mountains,' Mary sighed, although she was not speaking loudly enough to address the rest of the party. She looked out over the silver lake. *Shikaras* were returning home, some of them with lanterns lit already, having finished their slow-paced daily business of fetching and carrying between the houseboats. She heard Eddie's footsteps slowing to her side, the trace of his once prominent limp now less noticeable.

'What did you say?'

The scar across his cheek had long given up most of its redness and faded into a pale pink crescent that pulled gently at the side of his mouth, cocking it into a permanent half-smile that lent the terrain of his features a certain charm.

'Oh, nothing of any importance. But I do wish the cook would hurry up. I'm half-starved to death.'

'I'm not surprised. You look as though you haven't eaten a square meal in a decade.' He took advantage of the legitimate reason to openly assess her elfin figure. 'There's nothing of you.'

Ruby overheard his remarks and called out from the salon, 'She has the skinniest ankles I've ever seen!'

'Better that than to have legs like an elephant!' Eddie called back.

'It is a beautiful country, this India.' Mary returned her gaze to the outline of the mountains fading into the darkening sky. 'I've always wanted to see Kashmir. We'd been planning this holiday for such a long time, but Florence kept putting us off, three women travelling alone.'

'You were right to be sensible. I wouldn't have let you risk it either, although I do wish you'd told me first instead of Richard.'

'Why?'

'Because then I could have had the three of you all to myself!' He leaned in and whispered to her, 'And frankly, the man's a bit of a boor.'

'Joseph made me promise that I'd tell Richard if I was planning on doing anything even remotely dangerous.' Her eyes skipped to the sky. 'I hardly expected him to insist that he come along to play chaperon.'

'Of course he did.' Eddie sighed at her naivety. 'And if you think he did it for your benefit, you're even more daft than you look. Do you really think I'd let you out of my sight with him around?' He nudged her arm playfully. 'Although I think he has enough distractions on his mind for now.'

'I know,' Mary whispered under a sharp intake of breath. 'I do wish that he would leave poor Ruby alone.'

'Oh, I wouldn't worry too much about Ruby. She seems to be enjoying herself well enough. I'd say she's positively glowing with all the attention.'

'That's what concerns me,' Mary said. A sudden flash of blue flew across the water, the kingfisher's iridescent wings catching the last of the sun's rays. 'Did you see that?' She pointed towards the tiny splash rippling out from a drifting patch of water hyacinths. 'I could happily stand here all day long just watching.'

Eddie slipped his arm round her waist. 'I could get a posting here if you wanted, then you need never leave. Once the Banihal Tunnel opens, there'll be rich pickings for whoever gets here first. It wasn't so long ago that the only way to transport anything in or out of here was to drag it on a bullock cart.' He came closer, Mary's skin sensing the heat of his breath. 'I have a feeling it could be a very comfortable life. What do you think?'

'It's just wonderful.' Mary broke away from him. 'I shall never forget it.'

'Mary?' She compelled herself to look at him. 'I mean every word I say. Here, there, another country. I would take you anywhere you wanted to go, and I mean anywhere, if it would make you happy.'

'What is all this whispering?' Ruby crept out to see what she could hear. Eddie released Mary from his gaze and excused himself to find another drink. Ruby smiled sweetly as he disappeared into the salon.

'He's crazy about you.'

'I know.'

'So what's the problem?'

'Keep your nose out of my business.' Mary's scornful manner was only half-serious. Her heart had already made up her mind, and there was nothing to be done. 'We are here for a holiday, Ruby, nothing more.'

Ruby flicked her eyes beyond the curlicued shutters towards Richard. 'He's wonderful, isn't he?' she enthused. 'And terribly clever.'

'Ruby,' Mary warned her. 'I hope you know what you're doing.'

'Of course I do,' Ruby replied. 'I fully intend to see to it that by the time we get back to Bombay, Richard is as mad about me as the colonel is about you.' She sidled up to Mary, leaning against the teak rail, sharing her view of the placid lake. 'What better place to melt a man's heart and get him to promise his undying love?'

'Just be careful,' Mary said. 'That's all I'm saying.'

Ruby brushed an early night insect from Mary's shawl. 'You're a fine one to talk. I've never known anyone so fickle.'

'I'm not fickle. I'm just waiting to fall head over heels in love.'

'You're going to turn him down again, aren't you?' Ruby ran her hand along the dark timber rail. 'Have you told him yet?'

'Not in so many words, but he knows, I'm sure. I just wish it were easier.'

The dining room, beyond the salon, was at once quaint and grand, with a polished oval table and a long sideboard complete with neatly arrayed glass and silverware.

'We must visit the gardens of Shalimar while we are here,' Florence said.

'The ones at Nishat Bagh are even more impressive,' added Richard, his eyes wandering to Ruby's breasts. 'The marble arches and formal lawns are perfectly symmetrical. We should take a picnic and go tomorrow.'

Eddie watched Mary from across the table. He drained his wineglass for a second time, put it down heavily and openly declared himself to her. 'Mary? I must insist that you marry me. There's not a single person at this table who doesn't approve, and I think you've kept me waiting for long enough. I love you. You've always known that I love you. And I want to marry you.'

The room became still, silent like a painting, all eyes upon Mary as she sat, open-mouthed, staring back at him. In her embarrassment, she answered hastily, before considering his feelings.

'Don't be so silly, Eddie!' She looked around the table for support, but found only discomfort.

'I'm not being silly. It's a perfectly reasonable offer.'

At Richard's guffaw, everyone laughed good-naturedly, except Eddie. 'I told you three months ago, there's only so many times a man can stand to be turned down. You could certainly do a lot worse. I'm not a bad-looking chap, despite this awkward decoration.' He indicated vaguely the welt on his cheek. 'In fact, I think I would make a rather good catch.'

'I know you are, Eddie.' Then, before she could stop herself, it was out. 'But I'm not in love with you.'

The table quietened, the nature of the man's passion so painfully laid bare in front of them all.

'So? There's a lot more to marriage than being besotted, you know. You could learn to love me over the years, and I promise I will take great care of you. You will want for nothing.'

'But what do I want for now? I have everything I could possibly need and the freedom to do whatever I choose.'

Eddie concentrated on his glass, in his frustration turning it round and round. Mary did not care to dampen the mood of the evening on such a special night and softened her judgment. 'I'll tell you what, why don't you ask me again in another three months?'

'I don't think I want to wait that long.'

Richard raised his glass towards Eddie, a wry smile on his face. 'I told you she'd turn you down flat.'

'You should be thoroughly ashamed of yourself,' Florence said the next evening, refilling Mary's teacup.

'Oh, do give it a rest, Florence.' Mary sighed. She had lain awake in her bed for most of the night, the shame of her insensitivity devouring her.

'Don't go on at her.' Ruby took a sip of tea. 'Of course we all assumed that he would lick his wounds for a day then brighten up and forget the whole thing. It's not as though it's the first time she's turned him down.'

Eddie had packed his bag and left the houseboat at first light, making his silent departure before anyone else had woken. It was only when he missed breakfast, then lunch, that Richard had gone looking for him and found his cabin empty. They had turned to the staff, who disclosed that the colonel had asked for a *shikara* to collect him at dawn, slipping away in the stillness, the boatman's paddle cutting silently through the water.

It was mid-afternoon before Mary discovered the note that had been slipped under her door, the envelope inadvertently pushed partially beneath the rug. It had said that he could not bear to stay, but that he would fulfil his promise of safe escort and would wait for them to send word to him when they were ready to leave. He had then given the name of another houseboat, *Morning Glory*, moored across the lake on the opposite shore. Mary's heart had sunk, and she had hidden the note away, wishing that he had just gone back to Bombay and been done with it: it would be impossible for her to avoid her conscience now, knowing that he was little more than a stone's throw away. As the day wore on, her mood had slumped to such depths that she was unable to raise a smile for anyone, and moped around until her friends reluctantly agreed to cut the trip short. She couldn't face Eddie. She would write him a note and arrange to have it delivered in the morning, a few hours after they left.

'I hope you're pleased with yourself,' Florence said, unleashing her frustration. 'This holiday has been an unmitigated disaster.'

Mary stood up, upsetting her teacup, and threw her hands into the air. 'That's enough!' she said. 'I'm tired of your picking at me! Just leave me alone!' She stamped out of the cabin, slamming the door behind her.

Mary stood forlornly on the deck and gathered her thoughts from the darkness. The lamps had been extinguished early, as nobody was in the mood to socialise that evening and the lights would serve only to attract night insects to the houseboat. She pulled her shawl round her shoulders.

'Not thinking of throwing yourself overboard, are you?' came Richard's voice. Mary started and turned to find him almost upon her, his shape barely visible in the darkness as the clouds shrouded the moon.

'Richard!' She grasped at her shawl in fright. 'How long have you been standing there?'

'About an hour before you came up. Trouble below?'

The sudden flare of a match lit up the deck, Richard's face glowing orange as he put the flame to his cigarette and drew on it. Sucking the smoke deep into his lungs, he flipped the match over the side. Darkness fell around them again, punctuated only by the burning end of his cigarette.

'Quite a show you gave us last night,' he said. 'Poor bastard. Not that I blame you, mind. No woman wants to find herself saddled with a cripple. What you need is a real man, who knows how to treat a woman.'

'I beg your pardon?' Mary gasped. 'Don't be so rude!'

'You should let me take you out some time,' Richard said coolly.

'I don't think so.' Mary felt a sudden uneasy sense of claustrophobia and tried to move away, stumbling in the darkness. Richard gave out a little laugh and took hold of her elbow for a moment to steady her.

'Are you sure about that? Or are you just pretending to be coy, like your little friend downstairs?' He drew on his cigarette again. 'I've seen you twisting that miserable sap around your fingers whenever it suits you, leaving him hanging on a thread like the weakling he is.' Mary stared at his shadowy outline, dumbfounded. 'A stronger man wouldn't let you get away with it.' She felt his hand upon her shawl, pulling her towards him. 'I could teach you a thing or two about love.'

'Leave me alone!' Mary wrenched herself away, the shawl unravelling from her shoulders.

'You girls are all the same,' Richard said sourly, stepping away from her just a fraction. 'Acting like butter wouldn't melt in your mouths.'

'Give me your matches!' Mary demanded, stranded in the dark, scarcely able to believe this sudden, grotesque behaviour.

'You don't know what you're missing,' he said, shaking the matchbox lightly, taunting her with it. 'Just ask that prissy sister of yours.'

'What?'

'Oh, yes.' The tip of Richard's cigarette glowed as he dragged on it again. 'She gave it up all right, after a little friendly persuasion, just like I knew she would.' Mary caught her breath sharply, her insides turning to liquid. Her head began to spin and she cursed herself for her ignorance before realising with a terrible sense of foreboding the unspeakable danger that she had so unwittingly exposed herself and her friends to. And now there was no one here to protect them. She brought her hand to her mouth, swallowing hard.

'So she told you, did she?' Richard tipped his head back and released a cloud of smoke into the night air, mocking her with a small self-satisfied sigh. 'That Joseph Carlisle's a lucky, lucky man.'

'You!' Mary reeled away from him in horror, then began to shout. '*Koi hai! Koi hai!*' A sudden shaft of light from the far end of the houseboat cast a bright reflection across the surface of the lake. '*Koi hai!*' she shouted again. 'Bring a light to the deck! *Jaldi karo!*'

She gripped the railing, too shocked to do anything else while she waited for her rescue. The pool of light travelled along the gunwale, exposing the deck as the cabin boy scurried towards them, a storm lamp swaying in each hand, confusion on his face. She snatched one of the lamps from him and held it high above her head, swinging it from side to side, signalling to the distant flickering lanterns on the lake. 'Call for a boatman!' she commanded the boy.

In the next instant, Florence appeared, clutching the neck of her dressing gown. 'What in heavens?' She took one look at Mary's ashen face.

'Get our bags!' Mary shouted at her. 'Now!'

Florence took one glance at Richard's thunderous expression before turning and running for the stairs.

The *shikara* slipped noiselessly through the water, dispersing the stars floating in its soft wake, melting them away, leaving the *Rowallan* far behind and, on its deck, Richard.

Florence and Ruby exchanged apprehensive glances, holding hands beneath the blanket set across their laps, while Mary sat away from them, her eyes fixed on the distant shore. Barely a word had passed between them other than Mary's frantic calls for them to hurry as they boarded the boat. She refused to say where they were going, telling the boatman to paddle hard, waiting until they were at a safe distance before asking him if he knew a houseboat called *Morning Glory* moored on the opposite bank. He had nodded his response, then, at her request, had extinguished the lanterns so their destination might not be traced by a curious eye.

'Mary?' Florence leaned forward, offering her a blanket. 'Put this round your shoulders. You'll freeze.' Mary looked at it absently. She had lost her shawl somewhere in the ruckus and sat shivering, even though she felt no cold. On Florence's insistence, she took the blanket and wrapped it about herself silently. She felt empty inside, and foolish beyond measure. She willed the boat to make speed, counting each slither of the heart-shaped paddle, breathing along with its steady movements.

After a thousand breaths or more, the boatman relit his lanterns and hung them up, then slipped his paddle deep into the water, sliding the *shikara* towards a row of houseboats moored closely together on the tree-less bank.

'*Salaam, Morning Glory!*' he called softly. '*Salaam!*'

A stick-thin man quickly appeared on the small deck at the stern, holding a lantern aloft, rubbing his eyes before peering into the darkness.

'*Salaam,*' he replied suspiciously, his face a picture of puzzlement as the *shikara* slowed, floating towards him, revealing its cargo. Without waiting to be invited, the boatman tied off and hauled the first of the bags onto the narrow landing platform. The thin man started to protest, demanding to know what the boatman thought he was doing, waving his hands in refusal, at which the boatman just shrugged his shoulders before unloading the next bag. The man shook his head in umbrage and scurried away through the salon.

'*Morning Glory,*' the boatman said to Mary, helping her out of the *shikara*. Mary felt her legs unsteady, her head giddy with the motion of the water, and held on tightly to the carved newel post. Ruby and Florence followed, Florence looking around nervously as Ruby paid the boatman.

'Mary?' she said. 'What are we doing here?' Before Mary could answer, light flooded the salon, confused voices coming towards them, bearing more lanterns.

'*Kiya aap mujhay bata—*' Eddie stopped the moment he saw them and stood, unmoving, in the salon's open doorway. 'Mary?' He stared at her in disbelief. For a moment he made to step towards her, then halted, as though unsure of himself, mistrustful of her. Mary tried to speak, but nothing came. Instead, her face contorted, a huge sob rising from her chest, releasing a deluge of tears as she folded in two. Eddie rushed forward and gathered her up in his arms. This time, she did not protest.

# CHAPTER 14

THE BLINDS WERE DRAWN in Mr Johnson's room, diluting the worst of the afternoon heat, diffusing the searing light. His cancer had spread quickly, creeping insidiously from one organ to another until it could no longer be denied. All Mary could do now was to keep him comfortable, feed him when he wanted food, keep him clean, and sit with him when he was lucid enough to need a little compassionate company, holding his hand while he spoke earnestly of his life, although such occasions had become fewer and farther between, before petering out altogether a few days ago. Mary had nursed him assiduously through his final weeks. As the cancer took hold, so the doctors gave up and lost interest, dropping by now and then just for the sake of appearances, writing him up for generous palliatives so that his pain might at least be kept at bay without further need for his nurse to refer to them.

Mary crept to Mr Johnson's side, threading the thermometer carefully into his pyjamas and under his armpit, and left it there while she examined his charts, although the papers blurred nonsensically, her determined mind unable to fix itself upon anything other than the terrible compulsion that had gripped her continuously for weeks, to the exclusion of all other thought. Her meticulous planning had finally come to fruition. Today was the day. And tomorrow, everything would change.

All her life, Mary had been uncertain, dithering at every turn, unable to make up her mind about anything of any importance. Not that it had mattered. Every decision had been made for her anyway: her upbringing, her schooling, her profession. And she had followed those paths benignly, as though she had no say, tossed around like a leaf on the breeze, never landing to ground herself for more than a moment. Yet all that had altered in the blink of an eye a month ago, on the deck of a houseboat, when a man she barely knew had cut out her heart. It was as though a cold hand had reached through her flesh and torn out her soul.

When the night-times drew in, Mary's dreams would take hold, the same visions, over and over. Serafina, reading stories to her in a chilly, narrow bunk while she clutched at her hand for comfort. Serafina, luminous in the beauty of the love she had finally found. Serafina, bathed in blood, the image burning itself so indelibly that it would not leave her all day, pressing itself into her mind's eye like a grisly talisman. At first, Mary had felt powerless, as useless to her sister as she had always been. She had done nothing for Serafina, except to unthinkingly cause her unnecessary anguish at every turn. Serafina was the one who had borne the brunt, the one who had had to deal with the unspeakable burden of responsibility with no one to turn to, not even in her darkest hour. Mary had torn herself to shreds after her encounter with Richard, weeping herself to sleep night after night, waking to a pallid reflection in the mirror until, with a sense of divine clarity, she had known what she must do. Her sacrifice would be small compared to those her sister had suffered.

Mr Johnson moaned, his sleeping face twisted with pain. Mary checked his pulse, one eye on her fob watch, then removed the thermometer and noted down the vitals, before bringing the enamel tray from the table and lifting the cloth aside. Using the small, serrated blade she kept in her pocket for that purpose, she filed the neck of the glass ampoule before snapping off the slender tip and drawing the full ten milligrams of morphine up into the syringe. Still sleeping, Mr Johnson wouldn't feel a thing, yet Mary was as gentle as she had always been, her touch tender and warm. Carefully, she slid his pyjamas down, exposing the top of his rump, and gave him the injection before depositing the syringe back on the tray and sliding the second ampoule into her pocket. It was all she needed. She already had the other nine.

'Well, well,' Richard said, running his eyes down Mary's figure without inhibition. She was wearing the dress she had ordered specially from Mr Chagdar, a bold red flower-print design on a sky-blue background, cut to reveal a glimpse of her modest cleavage and set wide on the shoulder, baring as much flesh as she could tolerate. She had felt self-conscious when she had tried it on in the tiny dressing room, and had forced herself to bear in mind that this was the kind of thing that Ruby would wear every day, given half an excuse.

Mary smiled at Richard and accepted the kiss he placed on the back of her hand before taking her seat and allowing him to order her a drink. Richard regarded her with a knowing smile.

'Had a little change of heart, have we?'

'I owe you an apology,' Mary said meekly. 'I acted like an idiot on the houseboat and ruined the holiday for everyone. Whatever must you think of me?'

'Women,' he laughed to himself, eyeing her up with interest.

'I know,' said Mary.

'Spencer's been like a dog with two tails since you went scurrying back to him. What did you say to the poor man?'

'You've seen him?' A small rush of anxiety shivered over her. Although Mary had alluded to some ungentlemanly conduct that night in Kashmir, she had kept the details of Richard's abomination to herself, begging Eddie to let it lie when he threatened to break the man's neck.

'No, but there are some very interesting rumours passing around the Wayside. I hear he's thrown in his job and is planning to move on. It's all very intriguing.'

'Oh.' Mary feigned ignorance.

'Want to know the funniest thing I heard? He actually thinks that you're in love with him!' Richard picked up his drink and tipped it towards her. 'I wonder what he would say if he knew you were sitting here with me, playing him for a fool?'

'That is funny.' Mary smiled demurely. 'But still, you didn't mention any of this to anyone, did you?' She had been as careful with Richard as she could be, refusing to leave messages, speaking to him directly on the telephone and pleading for his confidence. Although the risk was out of her control, she considered that he was unlikely to go boasting about a conquest as yet unmade, but she sought the reassurance anyway, if only to calm her agitation. 'Only I wouldn't want him to know that you and I were . . .' She picked up her drink, clinking her glass gently against his. 'You know.'

'Mum's the word. It'll be our little secret.' Richard tapped his nose. 'And this place is about as out-of-the-way as you can get.'

'So I was thinking,' Mary said, coyly. 'Perhaps we could have a few drinks here and then go somewhere private?'

'Oh, yes?' He raised a lewd eyebrow at her. 'And why is that?'

'I've never been with a man before.' She raised her eyes to his, a flush of colour coming to her cheeks. 'And seeing that you . . . offered to instruct me in the ways of love, I thought we might . . .' She affected an embarrassed cough.

Richard sat back in his chair, regarded his whisky thoughtfully and rattled the ice in his glass, enjoying Mary's blushes. Then he leaned towards her, resting his hand on her leg. 'What say we leave these and go to my place right now? I've got drinks there.'

'No rush.' Mary sipped her gin and tonic, her hand wandering to the sheath of folded paper she had slipped into the tiny pocket Mr Chagdar had sewn specially into the side seam of her dress at her request. 'I have all the time in the world. Do you have a cigarette?'

'Of course.' Richard took a slim gold case from his pocket, flipped it open and offered her one.

'Thank you.' Mary searched in her handbag, a frown of frustration settling on her face. 'Oh, blast.' She looked around. 'I've gone and dropped my cigarette holder somewhere. Perhaps it fell out in the car. Would you mind?'

Richard was already on his feet. 'Back in a jiffy,' he said, leaving her at the table alone.

Mary took the paper sheath from her pocket and opened it, tipping its contents into his drink.

**M**ary had often wondered what these houses might be like on the inside. She had seen them being built, passing the district as she did when they went for picnics on Malabar Hill. She cast her eyes around the room, taking in the luxurious surroundings, marvelling at the way some people lived without conscience.

'Drink?' Richard said, standing at the cabinet in the corner of the room.

'Gin, please,' said Mary. She watched him carefully, mindful of the time that had lapsed.

'Here you go.' He came to the table and pressed the cold glass into her hands.

'Shall we sit?' Mary wandered to the settee and arranged herself prettily at one end.

'If you like,' Richard said impassively, beginning to show his impatience, his smile all but gone as he came to join her. But, as he sat, the drink slipped from his hand, the full glass exploding with a loud pop against the marble floor. 'Damn!' he said, then looked at it as though suddenly confused. He closed his eyes for a moment and took a deep breath. 'I . . .' he said. 'I'm sorry. Just let me . . .' He shook his head slightly, then put his hands to his temples, leaning his elbows to his knees. 'Too much whisky,' he mumbled.

'Are you feeling all right?' Mary asked softly.

'Mmm?' He took a deep breath, looked up and tried to smile. 'Yes. Yes, I'm . . .' A small giggle escaped from him. 'I think I'm drunk!' he said.

'There, there.' Mary moved along the settee and touched his hand. 'Lean back. You'll feel fine in a minute.'

His eyes settled on her, his mouth curving into a smile. 'Come here,' he said, crooking an unsteady finger at her. Mary moved closer, steeling herself. Slowly, slowly she reached towards him, undoing the top buttons of his shirt, loosening it at the neck. His head fell back against the cushions and he murmured to himself, 'Hot in here.'

Mary did not move. Instead, she stroked his chest, soothing him with hushed words of comfort. His eyes closed again, his mouth cocked into a smile. 'Take off your dress.' His speech became slurred, his breath thick.

'Yes,' Mary whispered, reaching slowly for her handbag, sliding her hand within, feeling for her sister's vengeance. His head moved slightly, one eye half opening.

'Kiss me.'

'Yes.' She smiled back at him.

Leaning gently to his face, Mary placed her soft lips upon his, and pressed the needle into his thigh, waiting for his body to slacken.

'Is that everything?' Ruby asked quietly.

'Yes. I think so.' Mary arranged the last of her clothes in the trunk and brought the lid down, fastening the thick straps, her palms damp, heart pounding through her chest with every footstep she heard in the corridor. Florence watched mutely.

Mary had gone out alone that morning, as she often did, and they had thought nothing of it, assuming that she was merely running an unremarkable errand. It was only when she returned with a posy in her hand and a pensive smile that she disclosed to them the quietly momentous event that had taken place an hour ago in a small chapel on the edge of Chaupati district, where she had stood beside Eddie as they exchanged their wedding vows. Shocked into silence, Ruby and Florence had been scarcely able to believe their ears, before accepting her apology for keeping them in the dark and helping her to gather her things. Mary could not have borne for them to have been there. It had been hard enough as it was, to stand in the company of strangers and promise her life away, all the while thinking of the dead man she had left last night, wondering how long it would be before his body was discovered.

'But why go running off to England?' Florence sat heavily on Mary's bed, shaking her head. 'I've heard the stories. They treat foreigners like dirt. You'll just be another unwelcome immigrant. That's what they call us over there.'

Mary felt her stomach flip over and forced a smile. Their passage had been booked two weeks ago and she had steadfastly refused to ponder the prospect of the unknown life that awaited her in that far-off place. All she knew was that she could not stay in India, and that with every moment that passed, the danger grew.

Standing on the quayside, new passport in hand, staring up at the gargantuan white steel structure, Mary felt a weakening surge of insignificance in the presence of the enormous ocean liner towering above them.

'It's vast.' She gazed up in awe, steadying herself against Eddie's arm. 'I had no idea it would be so big.'

'Tickets! Tickets!' A man in a peaked cap pushed his way through the sea of people, waving a handful of checked tickets in the air and searching the crowds, his experienced eye picking out the passengers from the bystanders. 'Tickets this way! This way!'

'You had better go.' Ruby pulled her shawl closer round her shoulders and tried to smile, she and Florence loitering impotently, clinging to those final moments.

The ship's horn gave out one long, sonorous blast, then another, filling the docks with its deep resonance. Then Mary saw something she had never witnessed before: Florence started to cry. Tiny, soft shrugs that barely moved her at all, and rivers of tears. Mary shivered at the sight, her resolve deserting her as she realised what she had done, and what she was about to do. She couldn't for the life of her remember how she had come to be standing there, moments away from boarding a ship that would take her to the other side of the world. Her heart began to pound, a rush of fear swirling up to engulf her. She could shout out now, confess to her madness and say that she hadn't known what she was doing and she wanted to go home. *Home.* The word flew round her head like a panicked bird trapped in a tiny cage. *Home.* A place where she could finally belong without looking back. A place where a soul could settle and live a life without shame, finding its peace. The ship's horn called again.

'That's you,' said Ruby, her voice tight with strain. 'Now hurry up, because I don't think I can stand here like this for a moment longer.'

Mary's bag fell to the ground as she threw her arms round her.

'Ruby,' she murmured into the softness of her neck.

Ruby pulled away, wiped her eyes with the back of her hand, sniffing away the tears and adopting a brave smile for Eddie.

'You take good care of her,' she said to him.

'I will.' Eddie kissed them both, one last time, before turning tenderly to his wife. 'Ready, Mrs Spencer?'

Mary held on to her husband's arm tightly as they walked up the gang-plank. Making their way to their allocated deck, pressing through the excited huddles, colourful streamers flew by, thrown by the first-class passengers on the highest decks, fluttering downwards in cheerful spirals.

Finding a tight space against the railings. Mary looked down on the dock, searching the crowds on the quayside, desperate to catch one last glimpse of her friends. She scanned the diminutive figures for Ruby's distinctive shawl, bright red, chosen specially for the occasion. A fleet of tugs began to haul the mighty vessel from its moorings, its bulk sliding slowly from the dock, huge whirlpools rushing into the gaping chasm that opened up so quickly between it and the cumbersome shore.

'I love you,' Eddie whispered to her.

'I know,' she said.

'Everything's going to be all right.' He tucked her hand firmly into his arm. 'I promise.'

Mary looked up at him, and felt as though her heart would break. She breathed deeply, closing her eyes and snatching what last remnants she could of the thick, scented air, her spirit reaching out and stretching away from her, clinging to India's burning soil. She leaned her head on Eddie's shoulder and, like a passing cloud, they floated away with the tide, gliding towards the swelling sun as the ship moved towards the horizon, the smoke from its funnels threading a silver-grey ribbon in the sky.

# Epilogue

## *England, 2006*

SERAFINA'S DAUGHTER SEARCHED her dog-eared address book, picked up the telephone and dialled the number of her only aunt two hundred miles away, tucked in a tiny white cottage called The Limit.

'If you want to see her, come now,' she said.

Mary held strong for her sister's child, fighting the stone suddenly lodged in her throat. 'Is she very bad?'

Caitlin, unable to answer, clutched the telephone. There were no words to describe the shadow of life that remained. Mary's heart began to bleed.

'Hush, now,' she said softly. 'Try not to upset yourself. You have to preserve your strength. You will need it.'

'She's going to die and I don't even know her.' Caitlin's voice crackled.

Mary lifted the frayed edge of her shawl to mop her face, her thoughts hauled relentlessly towards her sister's plight and the damage she had done. People mistook Serafina's fearful silence for elegance. Her coolness for decorum. If only she had told her family, freed herself from the no-man's-land where nothing belonged. Mary felt herself shredded, her loyalties scattered to the four winds as she listened to her niece's jagged breaths.

'The decisions we make.' Mary tutted softly. 'Sometimes so young. Too young to understand anything at all. That is one of life's great lessons, Caitlin, that we should learn by our mistakes, even though by the time we are old enough to realise them, it's often too late to do anything about it.' She sighed to herself. 'The things that frighten us most lose something of their terrible lustre as the years pass by.' She stood up from her old, worn armchair and went to the window, pulling back the lace curtain, watching the snow cascading in slow circles. She ached for Serafina's child, and she thought of that solemn promise: *Not for as long as we both shall live.*

Caitlin's tears ran dry. 'There's nothing of her. I'm so sorry, Aunty.'

Mary had to end the call quickly, before she broke into a thousand pieces. 'I'll call you soon,' she managed, then hung up.

Taking a deep breath against the stale, imprisoned air, Mary followed the auxiliary, recognising the surly countenances of the occasional nurses who had long since desensitised themselves to the grim conveyor of this forgotten place for bygone people. Halfway along the bleak corridor, the auxiliary left Mary at an open door, motioning her towards the bed.

Mary entered the flowerless room and pulled a grey plastic chair up next to the bed. Seating herself quietly, she leaned in close to her sister, watching her faded, vacant eyes, searching for some glimmer of recognition amid the merciless disease that had taken her mind apart, piece by piece. Mary had sometimes wondered if this terrible illness had not been a small mercy sent by the gods; that her sister should be stripped of the memories that had tormented her so that she might live out her final years in peace.

Mary had seen little of her since leaving India. Serafina had stayed on in Chittagong for many years, living the high life. Such was Joseph's value that irresistible offers had been laid at his feet as his hair greyed, enticing him to postpone his retirement for one more year, then another. They had finally said their goodbyes amid a splendid send-off before boarding the Boeing to begin a new life in a house set beside the River Thames in Oxfordshire. Compared to the grand perquisite residence in Chittagong, with its dozen servants and endless social engagements, the Henley house was undeniably modest in size, and ghostly quiet. Serafina had borne her immediate loss of status tolerably, busying herself with a headful of plans for a long and peaceful descent into old age with her husband, only to discover that his health would not support him for much longer. Joseph ailed within months of their arrival, his once handsome frame shrinking to nothing while she watched on helplessly. He was laid to rest before the dawn of his sixty-third birthday. And, when he died, it was as though something inside her died, too. Then the Alzheimer's took hold.

'Serafina, do you remember the river?' Mary whispered. 'The rustle of the high grass? The chattering houseboys, sent ahead to search for snakes? The coolness of the water when we dangled our feet from the bank?'

Serafina stared blankly into space. Mary extended her hand, her once fine fingers now deeply wrinkled, joints twisted with arthritis. Desperate not to let her sister down with an outward rush of grief, her eyes ached with the effort of stifling the tears that burned behind them, her face blushing vermilion beneath her soft brown skin.

'Do you remember the fresh concrete that was laid down once at our mother's house? Something was being built next to the cowshed. Do you remember?' Mary urged her. 'We waited until Papa's coolies were gone then stuck our palms on it, and when we stood up, there were two perfect imprints.' She took up Serafina's limp hand. 'So you see, my darling, we have left our mark there.' Mary stroked her sister's unkempt hair, thin and white, like a ghostly halo circling her unrecognisable head.

When the end came, it came quietly, like the turning of a page.

**M**ary sat with her grief, cross-legged on the carpet before her old packing trunk. Wiping the dust from its surface, she opened the lid on what remained of her keepsakes. There on top, tied with a white ribbon, were the few letters from distant friends that had survived her many moves. Among them, held separately by a loose, half-perished rubber band, was the brief, intermittent correspondence she had received from Dorothy over the years, the once confident hand having become increasingly shaky before being replaced entirely by the neat, rounded lettering of the secretary at the nursing trust where she had spent her remaining months, driving the staff round the bend with her determined efforts at independence, despite being well over ninety and rather absent-minded.

Sifting deeper, she began searching for the two journals she had kept as a younger woman, and the envelope of old photographs and onion-skin aerogrammes she knew to be tucked between them somewhere. Finding the envelope concealed beneath a blue sari of Benares silk, she tipped out the contents.

Among the papers lay a faded black and white picture of a group of student nurses, barely out of their teens, beaming at the Box Brownie camera, arms slung carelessly round each other's shoulders. She and Serafina were barely recognisable, faces still carrying remnants of childhood, their attempts at modern hairstyles protruding stiffly from beneath their uniform white veils. Mary touched the picture tenderly before putting it with the others and setting them aside.

Retiring to her room, she sat at her dressing table and began to write a letter, starting at the beginning when the world was a different place, and ending in the small hours of the morning when she had nothing more to say. She placed the letter in an old stationery box with the photographs and journals, and wrote her niece's name on the outside.

The cold, persistent drizzle of the early English summer seemed fitting for such a tiny cloud of mourners. Mary walked alongside her niece, a nurse like her mother before her. They came to rest at a lone bench beneath an ancient yew and sat together beneath its spreading branches.

Caitlin, face spent with grief, struggled to speak, interrupted by the deep, involuntary sobs that rose from her chest. 'As I grow older, I feel such a yearning to know who my mother was. She said that her life was none of anyone else's business. I was never to speak to you about it. She said that we had no right to delve into the past. And now she's gone.'

'You poor child.' Mary reached up and stroked Caitlin's hair. 'Always be proud of who you are. Proud of where you came from. Without that, what do you have?'

'Will you tell me about her?'

Mary didn't reply, but instead dropped her soft leather handbag from her shoulder, unzipped it on her lap and took out an old handkerchief, wound protectively round something small. She handled it carefully, cupping it lovingly in her palms for a moment, then passed it to Caitlin.

'Open it,' she said. Caitlin unfurled the tiny bundle, revealing a carved wooden elephant, trunk pointing upwards for luck, its back darkened with the waxy patina of a thousand caresses from Mary's fingers over many, many years. Mary pressed Caitlin's hands round it closely. 'This little elephant was made for me by our father's manservant. His name was Shiva.' Caitlin lifted it to her nose, the faint scent of sandalwood anointing her hands. 'Come,' said Mary, indicating with a small movement of her frail arm that she wished to stand. 'Let us go and say goodbye to your mother. Then I will tell you all about him.'

Mary watched as her beloved sister was laid to rest on the verdant hillside, so far away from home. A lone crow swooped down, its melancholy caw piercing the sky, and landed beside the freshly dug grave. She closed her eyes in silent prayer and was transported to a life that once was. The hills that rise beneath the mountain mists. The elephants that weep above the emerald terraces. The silver bells that graced her mother's footsteps. And the world continued to turn.

## Alison McQueen

Everyone wants to know who they are, but for me the question was never simple. My mother, Mary, was born in India in 1928. I was born in London in 1964. My father was raised in a Barnardo's home so I could only turn to my mother for answers about my family. But my mother would never talk about her life. I used to ask about where she was born, to which she would say Assam, but nothing else. I knew I had a grandfather who lived on a farm in Africa and I had seen one lone photograph of him in an Indian Army officer's uniform. She never mentioned anything about her mother, ever, and I somehow knew not to ask.

Very occasionally I was allowed to look through her old photo album and my mother told me a little of the people and places in them—Bangalore, Kashmir, the Himalayas. There was a picture of my auntie Joan (who by then was living on an estate in White City, London) on the beach in Bombay, wearing a starlet's bathing costume. In the photograph, she was utterly beautiful, as was my mother and my mother's sister (my only real auntie, although we rarely saw her). I didn't understand how these beautiful young women could have come from those achingly scenic landscapes to the grey skies of Britain.

My questions drove my mother half mad, but, as I grew older, her answers just didn't add up. There were too many holes in her story, and she'd get cross sometimes, seething her frustration when I asked her again and again. We fought about it quite a lot because I knew she was not telling me the truth and she was angry at having found herself in such a hideous situation. I had no idea at that point that she and her sister were the illegitimate daughters of a British tea planter to his Indian concubine. It was unthinkable and the shame of it had followed her like a shadow her whole life.

My mother missed India a great deal, and even now I find it hard to imagine what she must have gone through, losing both parents as a child without the closure of death, living in a country that thought nothing of insulting her in the street. Once, and not even that long ago in the grand scale of things (she was retired by then), a bus conductor made her stand on the pavement in the rain while everybody else got on the bus before her. Even now, at eighty-three, she is not completely comfortable here. Yet she is not completely comfortable in India either, knowing that she belongs to neither place entirely.

There are parts of *The Secret Children* that I wrote over a decade ago. It has been like a compulsion, to give those scattered fragments some kind of cohesion in my mind, to fill in the gaps that my mother had left, either because she wouldn't tell me, or more often because she simply didn't know.

There came a point when I knew I would have to tell my mother what I was writing. This was some years ago now, and I remember that she wasn't happy about it at all, voicing her objection with an outright 'No'. But then a strange thing happened over the following months. She began to talk, unburdening herself of every memory, good or bad. Together, we pored over maps, trawled through old pictures and keepsakes and trudged around India. She gave me a box of letters and photographs that I had never seen before. I don't think anyone had, except her. She cried quite a lot, too, which was hard.

My mother imparted her stories to me over many, many years. She told me things that she had never told to anyone else—not just her secrets, but those of her friends, my 'aunties'. I came to know things that their own children didn't know, and probably still don't to this day. All my aunties are now dead, my mother the only survivor. My fear was always that I would forget her stories, because they were too important to be forgotten. Nobody talked about these things. They still don't. I have finally come to know who my mother is and why things had to be the way they were. We talk for hours about anything and everything. Any sense of shame about the past has long since fallen away. She has learned to be proud of who she is and where she came from. *The Secret Children* was written with her blessing, and is dedicated to her with my love.

# Welcome to
# Rosie Hopkins'
# Sweet Shop of Dreams

## Jenny Colgan

*Rosie Hopkins has had a sweet tooth all her life, so when her mother begs her to go to the aid of her great-aunt Lilian, who has owned a sweet shop in the quiet country town of Lipton for many years, Rosie agrees. Well, she's between nursing jobs and absence just might make her boyfriend's heart grow fonder and encourage him to put a ring on her finger. What she finds is a frail, but indomitable, old lady and a run-down shop bursting with the smells and colours of every sweet imaginable—her very own sweet shop of dreams . . .*

# Chapter One

**Soor Plooms**

*This is a Scots term that translates as sour plums, but in its original language imitates exactly the contortions of your mouth as soon as you pop one in. More of an endurance exercise than a treat, this is a hard candy of exquisite, roof-of-the-mouth-stripping bitter intensity; the occasional rush of sweetness comes as a blessed relief. Near-impossible to bite and still maintain an entire set of teeth, they are therefore the ideal purchase for the pocket-money-strapped child as they last for ever.*

ROSIE PUT THE VERY PECULIAR book down. She was sitting near the front of the bus, hopping up every now and again, anxiously, trying to peer through the grimy windows. Why was the countryside so *dark*?

Rosie, a city girl born and bred, wasn't used to it at all. How could anyone live amid so much dark? The few people who had joined the bus in Derby had got off ages ago. She'd asked the driver to tell her when they got to Lipton, but he'd grunted at her in a noncommittal way, which meant that now she was hopping up and down nervously every time they entered a village, trying to figure out whether it was this one or not.

Rosie stared at her reflection in the dark window of the bus. Her dark curly bob was held back with hair clips above a button nose full of freckles. Her large soft-grey eyes were probably her best feature, but now they looked worried, lost and anxious. A sturdy suitcase sat above her in the luggage rack, feeling irrevocably heavy, reminding her that there was no easy route back. People's lives, she thought to herself, were meant to be full of excitement, lightness and freedom. Hers was just baggage. She checked her phone to ring Gerard, but there was no signal.

It never really got that dark in East London, where she'd grown up. The streetlights, and the cars, and the hum of the traffic and the people . . . Then, when Mum had left for Australia, she'd moved to St Mary's, the hospital in Paddington, where you were never far away from sirens and people shouting, and thronged streets. She thrived on living in the city, had always adored London—its shiny side, and the dark side she stitched up on a regular basis when it came in through Accident and Emergency. She'd even liked the grotty nurses' lodgings she'd lived in, although buying her own place with Gerard had been . . .

Well, it was grown-up, she supposed. It wasn't quite what she'd expected—she hadn't remembered the meeting where she'd volunteered to do all the housework, but he did earn more money. Still, that was adult life, wasn't it? And she and Gerard were settled now. A bit too settled. She could, it was true, do without all her girlfriends telling her that if he didn't put a ring on her finger by their second anniversary, he wasn't serious and in it for the long term. She had closed her ears and chosen not to believe them—Gerard was cautious, and safe, and didn't make big decisions lightly, and that was one of the reasons why she liked him.

But still, when her mother had called, she couldn't deny that she felt cross and emotionally blackmailed—and a teeny, tiny part curious.

Their last night had been sweet and sad all at once.

'It's only six weeks or so,' she'd reminded Gerard.

'Yes, so you say,' he said. 'You'll be round-the-clock caring from now till the end of time. And I shall stay in London and waste away.'

Gerard rarely looked as if he was going to waste away. Round of head and tummy, he had a cheery countenance, as though he was always on the verge of a laugh or a joke. Or a sulk, but only Rosie got to see those.

Rosie sighed. 'I wish you'd come. Just for a bit. A long weekend?'

'We'll see, we'll see,' said Gerard. He hated any change to his routine.

They'd been together so long now she could barely remember when they'd first met. He'd been at her very first hospital, when she was just out of a nearly all-female nursing college and dizzy with excitement at having a little money and a job. She'd hardly noticed the small, jolly pharmacist, who turned up occasionally when drugs were late, or rare, or urgent, and always had a quip, although she saw he was kind to the patients. He'd make silly remarks to her and she'd dismiss them as standard banter, until one night he'd joined them on a work night out and made it clear that he was actually a bit more serious than that. At the end of the night, when he offered to walk her to her tube stop, then took her hand, she suddenly felt alive with possibility, excited that someone could be so clear about fancying her. She'd often found that kind of thing confusing before, crushing helplessly on men who were out of her league, ignoring chaps with whom she later realised she might have had a chance.

Rosie often felt that she'd missed a meeting every other girl in the world had had when they were about fourteen, in which they'd learned how the boyfriend-and-girlfriend thing actually worked. Maybe the PE teacher had taken everyone aside, like she did with the period-and-BO talk, and briefed them all. This is how to tell who fancies you. This is how to talk to a guy you like without making a complete idiot of yourself. It was all a bit of a mystery to Rosie, and everyone else seemed to find it so easy.

Meeting Gerard at twenty-three had seemed like the answer to her prayers—a real, proper boyfriend with a good job. At least it would get her mum off her back for once. And right from the start he'd been keen. She'd been a bit taken aback to learn he was twenty-eight and still lived with his mother, but hey, everyone knew how expensive London was. And she enjoyed, at least to begin with, having someone to look after; it made her feel grown-up to buy him shirts and to cook. When, after two years, he'd suggested they get a place together, she'd been absolutely delighted.

That had been six years ago. They'd bought a tiny, grotty flat that they both felt too tired to do up. And since then, nothing. They were, if she was honest, in something of a rut, and perhaps a little separation might just . . . She felt disloyal for even thinking it. Even if her best friend Mike was always rolling his eyes. But still. It might just shake them up a little bit.

**W**hen her mother had rung that evening, Rosie had been thinking about her job. She had absolutely loved working in A&E as an auxiliary nurse. It was busy and exhausting, but she was never bored and always challenged. She loved it. So of course they closed the unit. Only temporarily, then they were going to reopen it as a Minor Injuries Unit, and she was offered the chance either to stay on for that, which didn't sound very exciting, or to relocate, which would mean a longer commute. She'd suggested to Gerard that they move, but he wanted to be close to his own hospital, which was fair enough. Even though an extra bedroom, maybe a bit of outdoor space, might be . . . Gerard didn't like change, though.

So, in the meantime, she was doing agency work, filling in for sick or absent auxiliaries wherever she was required, often at only minutes' notice. It had a reputation for being easy money, but Rosie knew now that it was the opposite. It was a grind—everyone used the agency staff to do the absolutely crappiest jobs that they might ordinarily have had to do themselves. And every day was like the first day at school, when everyone else knew where things were and how everything worked, and you were left scrabbling in their wake, desperately trying to catch up.

Rosie's mother Angie—there was only twenty-two years between them, so sometimes she was Mum and sometimes she was Angie, depending on whether Rosie felt like the younger or the older person in the conversation—still, after two years, found it difficult sometimes to coordinate telephone calls from Australia.

When Rosie called, early in the morning was usually best, but sometimes she caught her mum and her younger brother Pip at the thin end of a long afternoon's barbecuing and beer-drinking in the sunshine, and Pip's three children would be yelling down the phone too. Rosie felt sorry for them—she'd only seen Shane, Kelly and Meridian once and they were constantly forced to make conversation with their auntie Rosie—and it was tricky to chat. But now, with Gerard having his pudding, a large bowl of Frosties, wasn't a bad time at all.

'Hi, Mum.'

Rosie had heard her family talk about the good life in Oz, the swimming pools in the gardens and the lovely weather and the fresh fish. Her mother, whose unflattering opinions on Gerard (not Gerard himself, he was perfectly pleasant, but his seeming unwillingness to marry, provide for and impregnate her only daughter) she rarely hesitated to share, was always trying to entice her down under for a year or so, but Rosie loved London. She had absolutely no desire to move halfway round the world.

'Darling, I have a proposition for you.'

Angie sounded excited. Rosie groaned mentally.

'I can't work down under, remember? I don't have the qualifications or the points or whatever it is,' she'd said.

'Oh, who cares about that,' said her mother, as if there was no connection between her dad leaving and her failing half her A levels that year. 'Anyway, it's not that, it's something else. It's not us, darling. It's Lilian.'

## 1942

*L*ilian Hopkins *charged over the meadow slightly nervously. She wasn't sure if Isitt's bull was in his shed or not, and didn't want anyone to see her running.*

*Her heart sank as she saw a familiar outline sitting on the stile smoking and openly staring at her, and she picked up her skirts crossly. He didn't put out an arm to help her up, which was annoying, because if he had she could have made a remark about his impertinence.*

*'Excuse me,' she said, lifting the pail. 'I need to get on.'*

*Henry didn't budge an inch. 'I think I'd like to watch you climb over the stile.'*

*'You will do nothing of the sort,' said Lilian, flushing.*

*'Why were you walking so strangely out there anyway?'*

*'I was not.'*

*'You was. I saw you.'*

*'Well, stop spying on folks then.'*

*'I don't spy on folks,' said Henry infuriatingly. 'Anyone walks that strangely over a field, half the place is going to notice. You're not scared of Isitt's bull?'*

*'No!'*

*Henry smiled, then his face changed to sudden shock. 'Oh here he comes now, right galloping fury.'*

*Lilian leaped up on to the stile and spilled half the contents of her pail. 'Where?'*

*But Henry had nearly toppled back off the stile with glee and, chuckling, headed off down the lane towards the village, leaving her in the empty field, muttering to herself about rude herd boys all the way to the shop.*

*H*e *was in on Saturday too, while she was serving. The children were in with their ration cards and tightly clutched tuppences. The young farm men would come in, scrubbed and shaved for the village dance, spending their wages on the velvet-trimmed heart-shaped boxes for their sweethearts. At sixteen, Lilian felt it was well past time for her to find a sweetheart. Not one of the village boys though. Hugo Stirling, the farmer's son, perhaps, when he came back from college. She smiled wryly. By the time he got back from York, it wasn't very likely he'd be looking for a shop girl. More likely Margaret Millar, whose father owned the next farm over. It would make much more sense to join up the land, even if Margaret had one eye that looked at you and one that looked at the floor.*

*'I was looking for some service,' came the teasing voice. 'But I can see I've come to the wrong place.' Henry was standing in front of her. He looked unusually nervous.*

'Uhm, half a pound of lemon drops?' he asked, as an old lady browsed beside him and two children bickered on the floor.

'Have you your coupon?'

Henry looked shifty. 'Uhm, no. Thought you might slip me a couple.'

'Of course not,' said Lilian. 'I would never do that.'

'No,' said Henry. 'Well, that's all right. I don't really like lemon drops.' He glanced around. The old lady had left, and the children were engrossed in their squabble. 'I wanted to ask . . . uhm, would you like to come to the dance tonight?'

Lilian was so taken aback she instantly felt her face pinken up. Henry's eyes darted around, seeing her confusion.

'Uh, no, of course. It doesn't matter,' he said. 'It's not . . .'

'But . . .' Lillian tried to find the words. 'My dad probably won't let me go.'

'You've left school, ain't you?' said Henry.

Lilian hesitated, and they looked at each other. Then the two bickering children leaped up from behind the counter.

'Treacle toffee!' shouted one triumphantly, waving his penny in the air. The other looked as if he'd been made to give in and stood sullenly to the side. Both watched very carefully as Lilian measured out the thick, sticky shards. The first child held the bag in triumph as they marched out of the shop. By the time Lilian had closed the cash register, Henry had gone.

Rosie picked up the book and turned another page. 'Sweets: A User's Manual by Lilian Hopkins' was inscribed on the front, along with the insignia of a small press. She glanced out of the window again as the bus creaked its way along the main street of a village.

The bus trundled to a stop, the driver ringing a bell and shouting loudly, 'End of the line! All change! All change, please!'

'It's OK,' said Rosie. 'It's just me on the bus.'

'Just checking,' said the man. 'I'll be back in three days. Pick you up?'

Rosie glanced out towards the pub and back towards the now-darkened shop. She swallowed, then braced herself and her heavy suitcase.

'Not sure,' she said, stepping off the bus and onto the pavement.

'Lilian?' It had taken Rosie a while even to think who Angie could mean.

'Great-aunt Lilian,' said Angie. 'You remember?'

Rosie squinted into her memory. 'The lady who smelled of Parma violets? With all the sweets?'

'Yes!' said her mother triumphantly. 'I know. She started you off.'

Rosie's love of sweets was a long-running family joke. Even now, she was rarely without a packet of Fruit Pastilles or rhubarb and custards about her person. She said it was for the patients, but the nurses all knew it was Rosie you went to for a quick pick-me-up in the middle of the afternoon.

'Oh goodness!' said Rosie. She did remember, from when she and Pip were children. An old lady—she had seemed very old to them then—who would occasionally visit, bringing mounds of slightly out-of-date sweets with her: Edinburgh rock and hard candies, and humbugs and gobstoppers. She and Pip would stuff themselves silly, then lie around groaning and feeling completely green.

'Wow! I do remember! Is she still alive?'

'Rosie!' said Angie reprovingly.

Lilian was Angie's aunt, the spinster sister of Mum's beloved dad Gordon, and she lived in the Derbyshire village her family came from.

'She must be a hundred,' said Rosie absently.

'Mid eighties,' said her mum. 'Definitely getting on a bit. Although she was always one of those spinstery women who look old from about forty. Not that you'll be like that,' she added, hastily. Rosie hadn't actually been thinking that, but it was nice of Angie to give her a complex about it.

Since Angie had moved to Australia she'd come over all Kath and Kim and got into aquarobics and bleaching her hair and wearing Lycra pastels and having a deep tan, which had the effect of making her look simultaneously much older and much younger than fifty-three.

'But she still writes. And she sends sweets for the monsters.'

Rosie started boiling the kettle. 'But why are you telling me this, Mum?'

'Well,' said her mother. She paused. 'The thing is, Rosie, she's in a spot of bother. And you're the only one in the family who . . .' Angie left the sentence unfinished.

Rosie felt instantly cross. 'Who what? Who doesn't have a job? Who doesn't have any children? Who doesn't have a husband to look after?' She knew what people thought about her. It was a very sensitive spot. Why did she always let her lovely mum wind her up?

'OK, calm down,' said Angie. 'Darling, you know I didn't mean it like that. But.'

'But what?' said Rosie, conscious that she sounded like a truculent teenager. So Angie explained.

'So of course you said no.'

Rosie had bought Gerard an ice cream straight away. It was only the promise of ice cream that could force Gerard out on a Grand Prix day, even a glorious summer Sunday like this one. He really wanted to stay inside with the curtains drawn and watch cars racing round a track, then play a computer game that involved cars racing round a track.

The more Angie had explained it to Rosie, the crosser and more hemmed-in Rosie had felt. The situation was this: Lilian, who had apparently been happily living a quiet life running a sweet shop in Lipton for several thousand years, had suffered a bad fall and needed a hip replacement. Whereupon it had turned out that there was almost no money left, that the shop wasn't even open, and that there was no one to look after her. As she hadn't any children, it fell on the rest of the family, which couldn't be Angie or Pip in Australia, or Angie's brothers who were retired or point-blank refused, and all their kids had families of their own. In short, Lilian needed to be cared for and put in a home, and her shop and house needed to be sorted out and sold to pay for the afore-mentioned home. And was there a single unemployed nurse in the family?

'I'm not single, I'm not unemployed and I'm not a nurse, I'm an auxiliary nurse,' Rosie had retorted. 'Apart from that, spot on.'

'Hasn't she got any kids of her own that can do it?' said Gerard. 'It's not very fair that it's you, you don't even know her.'

'I know, but.'

Rosie felt an idiotic wimp. Her mother was always telling her to be more assertive with Gerard (or the 'ring-dodger', as she liked to call him). Gerard was always telling her to be more assertive with her mother. Ironic, as he still called *his* mother Mummy at thirty-six and they had lunch there every Sunday because Rosie couldn't possibly make roast pork as well as his mother could.

'Well, I know, but she never got married or anything.'

'Oh. Lesbo,' said Gerard.

'No, I don't think so . . . well, maybe. But I think all the men went off to the war and got killed and then there was nobody left.'

'Did she get really fat and spotty on all those sweets?'

'I don't know,' said Rosie. 'I don't know anything about her. Except she needs help and I'm her—'

'Yeah, what are you?'

'I'm her great-niece,' said Rosie.

'Great-niece?' said Gerard, dobbing her on the nose with ice cream. Rosie laughed but wiped it off, still thinking.

'You never know,' said Gerard. 'Maybe she's got thousands in a box under the stairs and she'll make you her heir.'

'Ha,' said Rosie. 'That's right, someone in our family with money. Hilarious. Anyway, I know she hasn't, because that's why I'm going: she's had to run that old sweet shop for ages, years after she should have retired. I think if there was a big box stuffed with money she might have used some of it to get hold of a nurse and get herself into a decent home.'

'Mmm,' said Gerard. 'But how long for?'

Rosie shrugged. 'Well . . . I mean, I can apply for jobs, obviously, while I'm up there. But I need to get a buyer for the shop, find her a home, check she's all right then sign something with a lawyer, so the money from the shop goes straight to the nursing home. With a little bit for me for expenses, Angie says, to pay for my time. There's a house with the shop, so it should be a useful bit of cash if I can sort it all out.'

'That sounds like loads of work,' said Gerard, 'in the middle of bloody nowhere. With some old bag who doesn't know you from Adam.'

'I know, I know,' said Rosie, sighing. 'What could I do? You know what Angie's like. Will you come and visit me?'

'No chance! I'm allergic to the countryside, and they don't have KFC.'

'You're teasing.'

'I'm not. You'll see. You'll hate it up there. And you'll miss the rest of the summer! Sitting out in pubs and drinking pink wine and lovely evenings and loads of parties and fun.' Gerard pouted. 'Don't go.'

'But a little bit of money,' she said. 'If I got a couple of thousand from the sale of the house . . . I mean, we could even think about moving. Into a bigger place. Big enough for . . . I don't know . . . It'll be quiet.'

She found her heart beating faster even as she said it. Maybe she should go for the unselfish reasons. But a little bit of spare cash to punt them up the ladder . . . maybe it was the right time for the two of them. Together. When she got back from this stupid thing. To bite the bullet and go for it.

'I think they're making ice creams smaller,' said Gerard, looking unhappily at his cone. 'I'm sure of it. They whack the prices up and put less in on hot sunny days. Stands to reason.' He eyed her up. 'You've said yes already, haven't you?' And that was the end of that conversation.

# Chapter Two

### Licorish

*Modern language seems to think it can change things willynilly for no reason. Licorish is a perfectly adequate word that also manages to sum up onomatopoeically the consistency of a thick black sweet in your mouth. Liquorice is French, and we know where that ends up—in crème de marrons and macaroons and all sorts of other unpleasantnesses.*

*For those for whom the dark, complex flavourings of the fruit of the licorice root and aniseed flower are too overwhelming (not all sweet appreciators can be connoisseurs), it comes too in adulterated form, notably (see sub-section 41) the allsort, the bootlace and, possibly its crowning achievement for non-purists, the sherbet fountain.*

LILIAN HOPKINS HATED staying up late. It gave her more pain than she could let on, and it made the day seem so terribly long—and it didn't help her sleep any later in the morning. Her internal clock had been stuck at 6.30 a.m. for a very long time now. And they showed such rubbish on the television, so she normally listened to the radio—it was company—and read her magazines and wrote in her notebook and tried to ignore the aching in her hip until it was a reasonable hour to retire to bed and not think about how she was going to get through another day tomorrow.

But tonight was different, of course. Tonight the girl was coming. She'd always had a soft spot for little Angie, her brother's kid. She'd been so blonde and funny and spunky and full of life, and had ended up pregnant barely out of her teens, two babies, dad long gone, and she had rolled up her sleeves and got on with it. The two women had exchanged letters (Lilian always sent sweets) for years, and it was a sadness to both of them that Lilian hadn't managed to get to know Angie's children. It was hard to leave the shop, and between the kids being at school and

Angie working and all of them trying to keep their heads above water, the dreams they'd had of Hopkins holidays in Derbyshire had never quite materialised.

So to meet Rosie again after all this time . . . well, she wasn't quite sure what to expect. Angie had said she was nursing-trained, so maybe she could help her out with everything. Since the operation . . . there was no getting around it, she was finding life very difficult.

She hoped Rosie wasn't expecting too much. After all the bright lights and noise of London, she was going to find Lipton very quiet indeed. She looked at the clock. Another five minutes till the bus got in. She would say hello. And then perhaps this girl wouldn't mind helping her to bed.

You would have had to torture Lilian before she would let you know she'd been sleeping every night in her chair.

## 1942

*If it hadn't been for Ida Delia Fontayne, it seemed unlikely that Lilian would ever have given Henry a second thought. Although a young man asking her to a dance wasn't something that happened every day. Lilian was too thin for the current fashion, too pointy of nose and elbows to be considered one of the village beauties, like Ida Delia, whose blonde hair and blue eyes and soft high bosoms drew the eyes of every man in the village; and didn't Ida know it. Mind you, she'd been a general showbox since Miss Millet's school yard, always in charge of the games, elbowing out shy, caustic, wiry-haired Lilian. They'd been best friends when they were little; Lilian's father had thought Ida Delia adorable and would let her have an extra piece or two of fudge, and Ida Delia caught on to the wisdom of this arrangement and started inviting Lilian to her birthday parties, or to summer hangouts round the swimming hole.*

*At first, scrawny Lilian, with no mother and three big brothers and no knowledge of fashion or Hollywood film stars or lipstick, felt out of place and awkward. But as they grew older, Ida Delia took to Lilian's sharp, funny tongue and for a time they were close. Then adolescence had begun in earnest, like a winnowing of who the boys liked and who wasn't quite going to make the grade. Ida Delia had palled up with Felicity Hayward from the neighbouring farm, whose russet curls and bright-green eyes made cows out of boys all the way to Hartingford, and left Lilian with Margaret who didn't always look directly at you. Margaret was fun enough, but Lilian hated the idea of friendship being traded as a commodity, and could neither forgive nor forget.*

*Lilian liked to think that since she'd started working and living like a young lady, she was less bothered by the likes of Ida Delia Fontayne, or so she thought that summer until she saw her walk down the main street side by side with Henry Carr, laughing uproariously at one of his jokes. Lilian smiled at them politely, but inside her guts were twisting furiously. So, you ask someone to a dance one day and then the next you're up and down the street with the village flirt. Lilian was amazed to find how annoyed she was about someone she didn't even like. It was just bad manners, that was what was getting her riled.*

*'Miss Hopkins,' said Henry.*

*'Hello, Henry,' said Lilian, as coolly as she could muster.*

*Ida Delia obviously wanted to stop and show off her prize. 'It's a shame you missed the dance on Saturday—such fun!'*

*'I must get on,' Lilian murmured, and Ida Delia waved gaily. Just once, Lilian glanced back at Henry, and was shocked to find him also looking after her. There was something in his nut-brown eyes that, for once, wasn't mockery or teasing. Something that, however much she wanted to fight against it, suddenly seemed to make her heart jump and flutter on the wind.*

The first thing Rosie noticed about Lipton was that it was possibly the quietest place she had ever been. The main street of the village was completely deserted even though it wasn't long after eight o'clock. There were only a few street lamps, old-fashioned lanterns that lit up a pub, a large square stone house that looked as if it might be the doctor's surgery, a post office and a couple of small businesses Rosie couldn't identify. A huge fat harvest moon sat low in the sky, silvering the landscape. Somewhere, far away, Rosie could just make out the hoot of an owl.

After Paddington, with its brash neon and sirens and fast-food joints and late-night trains and street-thronging hordes, Rosie felt as if she'd been picked up and set down again a hundred years in the past. She turned round slowly and picked up her big suitcase. She had printed out a map from Google that showed her aunt's house, and it quickly became clear from the size of the place that she wouldn't have far to go.

The cottage was absolutely tiny, like something out of a fairy tale. It really did have a thatched roof with a dormer window, and smoke coming out of the chimney.

'Hello?' Rosie yelled nervously.

'All right, all right,' came a cross voice. 'I'm not deaf.'

There was a pause, then a shuffling noise, and then, after some wrestling with the doorknob, Lilian opened the door.

The two women regarded each other. Rosie had been expecting a very old lady; Lilian had been old when she had been a child. Instead she was greeted by a bowed but still slender figure, with a severely cut bob, wearing what seemed to be a maroon chiffon dress and full make-up.

Lilian in return had been expecting a young girl, not this curly-haired, rather weighed-down-looking fully grown woman with bags under her soft-grey eyes. She remembered little Rosie as a pretty, sparky thing.

'Hello,' said Rosie.

'You'd better come in then,' Lilian said.

Rosie followed her over the threshold, noticing as she did so the pained stiffness in her aunt's movements. Inside, the room smelled beautiful, of a warm, flowery beeswax. Through another doorway was a little sitting room, toasty warm with a wood-burning stove flickering away merrily in the grate. The mantelpiece was covered in framed photos. Rosie surmised they were of Lilian herself, and she had clearly been something of a glamour puss in her younger years. Rosie admired a beautiful fifties shot of her, framed in black and white.

'Is this you?' she asked.

'No,' said Lilian. 'I'm creepily obsessed with someone who looks a bit like me.' Rosie glanced at her to figure out if this was a joke. Lilian's face gave nothing away.

'So,' said Rosie, looking around. The living room was tiny. Lilian sat herself down carefully in her armchair, as if her bones were made of glass.

'Thanks for having me to stay!' said Rosie cheerfully, as if she was a house guest and not someone with her heart set on getting in, completing an unpleasant job and getting out as quickly as possible.

'I dare say you don't want to be here any more than I want you here.'

'No, I'm thrilled,' Rosie lied, squirming at her aunt's rudeness. 'It's like a holiday in the country.'

'What, forcing me out of my home?'

There was an awkward pause.

'Mum just said maybe you needed a bit of help,' said Rosie, gently.

Lilian sniffed. Rosie took this, correctly, to mean that Lilian did indeed need help but couldn't bear to admit it.

'Well, the local doctors are no use.'

'How did you break your hip?'

'Practising for the ice-dancing finals.'

Suddenly Rosie felt tired. It had been a long day. She looked around again at the cosy room. Lilian had been born in this cottage. Never married, just focused on the business and stayed in the same village all her life. It seemed so strange.

'Are you hungry?' Lilian asked.

Rosie wasn't, really. She'd eaten three enormous and vastly overpriced sandwiches on the train.

Lilian glanced back towards a door that obviously led to the kitchen. It occurred to Rosie that Lilian might be very hungry; if she wasn't mobile, it was a bit of a mystery as to how she was feeding herself. The house was very tidy; how did she manage that?

'You could make tea . . .' Lilian said. 'Only if you want some.'

Rosie turned to her. There was a lot less hostility in her aunt's tone. 'OK,' she said carefully. 'Yes, actually, I'm really hungry. While I'm in there, can I rustle you up something?'

'Oh, hardly anything for me . . . I eat like a bird,' said Lilian defensively, willing the girl to hurry up. She was desperate for a cup of tea; her arthritis meant she could no longer lift the kettle.

Rosie stood up and headed into the tiny, immaculate kitchen. Ornate old-fashioned tins were lined up on the white surfaces, labelled flour, sugar, tea. Unfortunately they were all empty. Next to the kettle—the old-fashioned kind, which stood on a gas hob—there was a half-empty box of loose tea, a kind of sieve and a flowery teapot covered in a knitted cosy.

Once she'd figured out how to light the gas she peered into the kitchen cupboards. They weren't empty. But what she found surprised her. Instead of bread, pasta and cans of beans, there were packets and packets of sweets. Rainbow stars and jelly fish and cola bottles and Black Jacks, Minstrels and Maltesers, Highland Toffee and jelly flumps, Wham Bars and chocolate eclairs and wrappers Rosie couldn't even identify.

No wonder her great-aunt's bones weren't healing well, Rosie realised. This stuff was pure poison.

She went back into the sitting room to find her aunt snoring tiny baby snores, head nodding onto her chest.

'Lilian,' she said, quietly at first, then more loudly. 'Lilian. *Lilian*. Come on. Let's get you to bed. We'll eat better in the morning.'

Leaning heavily on Rosie—she weighed about as much as a child—Lilian let herself be led into the neat, small bedroom at the back of the house. Once there, she pretended to be half asleep, and Rosie let her professional nursing training take over, as she efficiently found a nightgown and helped the old woman change and toilet. Rosie didn't get a thank you, but she decided on balance it might be best for both of them if it stayed that way. She looked at the tightly tucked white bedspread. It didn't look as though it had been pulled back for a while. There was nothing else for it. Carefully, Rosie bent down, picked up the old lady and tucked her into bed, as cosy as a child. She placed the tea on the side table, mixed with cold water in case of scalding.

Something came out of Lilian's mouth that might have been a thank you, or just a sigh of relief, but the comfort of lying down in her own bed for the first time in weeks was simply too much: Lilian was overtaken, almost immediately, by the first good sleep she'd had in a long time.

Rosie came back to the sitting room and looked around, wondering where she was to go. Suddenly, she felt mind-achingly tired. She checked her phone; there was almost no signal here, and she had no messages. She texted Gerard quickly to say good night, but the message took a long time to get through and he didn't reply. He was probably at the pub with his mates. She would have liked to say good night to him.

Opening random cupboard doors, she eventually found a pullout wooden ladder, fixed to a trap door above. Was there something else up there? Surely Lilian would have said if she didn't have a spare bed?

The fire was dying down behind her and the dim lights made it hard to see her way. She gave up looking for a light switch and tentatively felt her way up the ladder. At the top, the trap door opened into a space so dark she couldn't see a thing, except a dormer window with a clear view of a starry, starry night, and the omnipresent dark shadows of the hills beyond.

Gradually, as her eyes adjusted, she made out the shape of a double bed, just under the lowered eaves. Her whole body relaxed; sleeping on a sofa would have been a bit much. Nipping down, she extinguished the lights, popped into the loo and hauled her case upstairs. Unable to find her pyjamas, she just slipped off her trousers and top, snuck under the heavy counterpane and thick, crisp cotton sheets, glanced briefly at the moon through the open curtains and, just as she thought she must get up to close them, fell into a deep, deep sleep.

**R**osie slept late the next morning and awoke, not to a chiming alarm clock or to buses wheezily groaning to a stop outside her window but to a faint rustling, and birdsong. The room, with its open curtains, was bathed in soft golden light and she sat up to take in her surroundings for the first time. Wiping the sleep from her eyes, she breathed a sigh.

The room had a plain whitewashed wooden floor covered in thick, patterned rugs, with two walls a pale blue and the other two papered in a tiny blue flower print. Her large, antique sleigh bed had white wooden cabinets on either side. A small wooden door led to a compact white en suite bathroom and another to a built-in wardrobe.

A dormer window looked over the front of the house. Jumping up and peering through it, Rosie saw it pointed towards a field full of sheep, the green gorse of the hills beyond, and miles and miles of blue-washed sky. On the other side of the room, above the trap door, a single tiny window high in the wall looked over into Lilian's back garden. It was exquisite, neatly laid out, with hollyhocks and wisteria predominating. One corner was given over to vegetables, one to herbs and, at the very end, two huge apple trees growing intertwined to form a bower.

Rosie had never been anywhere like this before. She took a deep breath, inhaling the scent of the garden. Shaking her head, she washed and dressed, feeling a tiny hint of excited curiosity about what the day might bring.

Downstairs there was no sign of her great-aunt. Rosie peeped into the bedroom: the old lady was fine, just fast asleep. Sleep and good food— what Lilian needed more than anything, Rosie surmised.

She changed into a floral frock, a denim jacket and the patterned wellies she'd bought four years ago in an attempt to be hip and go to Glastonbury. She left a note for Lilian and the door on the latch, and stepped out into the morning.

First off, Rosie stopped at the little shop next door. The front of it was ancient, and the mullioned windows, which were of thick glass, could do with a proper scrubbing out. The wood frontage was painted a kind of fading burgundy but although the building was pretty, the paint was flaking, and the swinging striped sign outside, *Hopkins' Sweets and Confectionery*, was gilded but tired-looking. Through the glass, Rosie could just about make out jars of this and that, in a slightly higgledy-piggledy order. It didn't, she thought, look terribly appealing. In fact, to her horror, she realised that it clearly hadn't been open for a long, long time. Lilian had been fooling everyone for what looked like years.

Rosie winced. This job of hers was going to be even more of a pain in the arse than she had expected. She shook off her horrible sense of foreboding and decided to follow the flow and see where she ended up.

The cottage and shop sat at the western end of the main street of Lipton, a collection of thatched cottages, a doctor's surgery, lawyer's office, dentist, several food stores, and a clothing store that featured some extraordinary mother-of-the-bride outfits. The clothing shop next door sold jodhpurs, quilted jackets and waterproof trousers.

Rosie mentally ran through her wardrobe. Since she and Gerard had moved in together, she had just got so comfy. A perfect night for Rosie these days was a takeaway, a bottle of wine and a movie, her head tucked under Gerard's arm, lying on the sofa they'd bought in Ikea. OK, so Gerard teased her about wearing her old pyjama bottoms and slippers around the house and asked what had happened to the hot young thing he'd met at the hospital, but this was what contentment looked like. She thought about Lilian's smart appearance, though, and wondered for an instant if her own approach might just be complacency.

She wandered past a bank, the post office, a large Spar that looked as if it stocked just about everything in the world, an electrical store that proudly boasted that it still fixed toasters, a large old-fashioned pub called the Red Lion and, unexpectedly, a chic little restaurant with wooden benches and a chalkboard menu. Streets ran off the main road, all heading upwards out of the valley, with houses dotted more and more sparingly up the hills till you got to the farmland.

There was no doubt about it, Rosie thought, the place was definitely pretty. She popped into the bakery and said a cheery good morning to the woman behind the counter, who smiled back. There was a queue of men who looked like farm workers and labourers stocking up on pies and sandwiches for lunch. She chose a cheese and onion pasty, bought a cup of tea from the vending machine and took it outside. Next to the war memorial was a green wooden bench, and from there she had a good view of the village coming and going around her.

A dapper young man with a briefcase bounced up the steps of the doctor's surgery with a large set of keys; a rather chubby vicar emerged from the beautiful Norman church across the road. A postie wearing shorts and riding an ancient bicycle freewheeled down one of the hill roads. The Land Rovers—they seemed to be the only type of car allowed around here—nudged through the narrow road. By the pond, on a small patch of green outside the church, two geese honked loudly in response. By the time she saw the two large ladies on horseback, Rosie was half expecting Windy Miller to arrive from somewhere. She phoned Gerard.

'Hey?' he said. He sounded groggy.

'What are you doing?' said Rosie, in mock annoyance. 'I've been gone five minutes and you're already having big celebration nights out?'

'Course not,' said Gerard easily. 'Just me and the lads, you know. Friday night out. Plus I've got to eat somewhere. So, how's the old witch?'

'She's very run-down, a bit weak . . . and a grumpy old witch.' Rosie said this to make Gerard laugh, but it felt a bit disloyal. 'No. She's all right. Just lonely, I think.'

'What's it like?'

'Well,' said Rosie. 'Well. It's a bit weird. And there isn't a Starbucks.'

'*Oh. My. God*,' said Gerard. 'You won't last the week. Have you been arrested and charged with witchcraft yet?'

'No,' said Rosie. 'But nobody has met me yet. It's pretty. You'll like it. You should come visit.'

'I will, love, I will,' said Gerard, stifling a yawn. 'But first, I think I have to get to Starbucks.'

**H**er pasty finished, Rosie decided to explore. She knew she should be getting back, making plans with Lilian but this idea was not appealing. A quick walk around to familiarise herself with her surroundings, that was what she needed.

She passed by the tiny red-brick primary school with hopscotch drawn out in the playground. After the sign thanking people for driving slowly through Lipton came a long avenue of trees without a pavement. Rosie marched along the ditch side, remembering as she did so how uncomfortable wellingtons were to wear for any length of time. Then she turned in to a side road that was little more than a muddy path. It was harder to see the fields from out here, and as she continued down the long, solitary track Rosie began to feel her optimistic mood draining away, particularly as the wispy clouds she'd noticed earlier were now massing greyly above her head. But she trudged on, turning along smaller and smaller tracks.

After about half an hour, she reached the crest of a small hill but, turning round, realised she could hardly see back down; the clouds were closing in much more quickly than she'd expected. Just at that moment, the first drops started hitting her head, and she realised that a) she didn't have an umbrella with her, b) she couldn't remember which way she had come and now she couldn't see it either and c) she was wearing a denim jacket, which, while stylish, would prove completely useless if the rain got any heavier.

The rain got substantially heavier.

'*Bother!*' shouted Rosie out loud at the sky, hoping this would make her feel better. It did, but not for long. Where was she? Where the hell? She took out her phone. Of course there was no signal.

The sky was nearly completely black. Rivulets of rain had started to infiltrate the collar of her jacket and dribble down her back. Her wellingtons might be keeping her feet dry, but stray raindrops were still finding their way inside and wetting her socks. Rosie wondered if it might be possible to drown. Didn't cows drown if they looked at the sky or something?

She turned round. She had to guess a route, and it would have to be downhill. She'd come uphill, hadn't she? Hopefully, she'd be going down the same hill . . . and not, for example, the other side of a different one, that led into a crevasse or a ravine. She realised she was shivering now. She couldn't believe it had turned so very nasty so quickly.

Suddenly, in the distance, she caught sight of a set of headlights. Her heart leaped. She'd be saved! It must be the farmer! Maybe he'd caught sight of her out alone on the wild moors and was coming to rescue her! And he'd take her back to his lovely farmhouse kitchen and his rosy-cheeked wife would have a plate of scones and . . . She put her hand out to wave down the car as it swept down the muddy lane. Dazzled by the lights, she couldn't see who was at the wheel. The car, a Land Rover, failed to slow down, even as Rosie waved her hands wildly. The car spat out a fan of muddy water all over her dress and down her wellies, and continued on its way. Rosie had an impression of an angry-looking face at the wheel. 'You *arse!*' she yelled after it. 'You've left me here to *die*!!!'

She was so wet now, it didn't really matter at all. She marched out into the middle of the road. 'I hope toads eat through your electrical wiring and a *badger* gets in your bed. A toe-eating badger. And that your car suddenly explodes for no reason. Without you in it because I am a *good person* unlike *you*. But with *all your stuff in it*, but when you ring your insurance company they *don't believe you* because you are so *obviously a nobber*. In a *Land Rover*.'

Rosie was so absorbed in bringing down curses on the head of the vanished driver, she hardly noticed when two lights appeared behind her, and another Land Rover skittered to a sudden, horrified stop.

A late-middle-aged, very tall woman alighted.

'What the *hell* are you doing in the middle of my road?' she shouted.

Rosie wiped the rain out of her eyes. 'Uhm . . . well, I got lost.'

'Where are your clothes?' barked the woman, who was wearing a Barbour jacket and an enormous deerstalker hat.

'Uhm, I got wet.'

'You're going to get hypothermia. Where are you going?'

'Lipton.'

'Well, you're facing completely the wrong way . . . get *out* of my road!'

Rosie jumped to one side, completely intimidated.

'You're not . . . you're not a vet by any chance?'

Rosie shook her head. 'No.'

'No, of course not, what was I thinking, look at what you're wearing.' She shook her head. Rosie realised she was extremely distressed.

'Why, what's the matter?'

'Bloody . . . bloody vet's an hour away operating on a horse in the next valley. I'll need to get to the town over . . . It's my dog . . .'

Rosie peered into the back of the Land Rover, then clapped her hand to her mouth. Staring at her with wide, unblinking, terrified eyes was a large golden retriever. Sticking out of his abdomen—grotesquely, spread-eagling his paws away from it—was a huge coil of barbed wire.

'Christ,' said Rosie.

'Quite,' said the woman. 'So, if you could get out of my way—'

Rosie shook her head. 'How far is the town?'

'Forty miles.'

'That'll take too long,' she said.

'I know,' said the woman. 'That's why we're following the doctor. But I don't know if he can manage on his own.'

'The *doctor*?'

'Do you have any better ideas?'

Rosie shook her head. The idea of a doctor trying to help the poor beast in the back . . . It was crazy. On the other hand, she definitely, definitely needed a lift back into the village. 'Uhm, I'm a nursing auxiliary,' she said quickly.

'You're a nurse?'

'Auxiliary,' said Rosie, quietly. 'I might be able to help,' she said.

The woman revved the engine. 'Get in then,' she said brusquely, and took off with a squelch of brakes in the mud before Rosie had even closed the door.

**B**ack in the village, which turned out to be over a completely different hill from the one Rosie would have expected, the sky was dark and the streets were empty. The practice was locked up—but the white Land Rover that had sprayed her earlier was parked haphazardly up alongside the building, and a side door was open.

The woman was opening the boot and the two of them, as gently as possible, started to lug out the huge dog.

'What's his name?' asked Rosie.

'It's Bran,' said the woman, her voice choking. 'Oh Bran, darling.'

Holding open the door with his elbow, his newly sterilised hands in the air, was a tall man trying to wipe a large mass of hair off his forehead with his other elbow. It wasn't a very elegant manoeuvre.

'Hurry up,' he was shouting.

The women followed him in and he let the door clang behind him. 'If Hywel finds out about this, we're screwed,' he said as they followed him down a small passage to a sluice room at the back of the building. 'Did you stop to pick up a hitchhiker?' continued the man.

'She *says* she's a nurse,' said the woman.

The man looked impatient and unconvinced. '*Are* you?'

'I'm a nursing auxiliary,' said Rosie.

'Do you know what you're doing?' he said, shortly. Fortunately, Rosie had seen this kind of thing before in A&E, many times. It was just a stab wound, she told herself. To a dog.

'How much do you think he weighs?' she replied. The doctor was already trying to fill a syringe with anaesthetic.

'Twenty? Twenty-five?'

They both glanced at the woman, but the sight of Bran stretched out and whining piteously was too much for her, and she dissolved in tears.

'Let's say twenty-five,' said the man. 'We don't want him waking up and biting us.'

Rosie went round to the back of the dog's head and made soothing noises while she held his paws apart. The man looked very tentative indeed as he stood over the animal with his needle. Bran chose this moment to wake up and growl, writhing and howling and twisting his body in agony. As soon as the doctor tried to hold down one paw, another would wriggle free, and the dog wouldn't stay still long enough for him to get the injection in. The woman had gone to pieces completely.

Rosie, almost without thinking, clambered up onto the table and, as she had been taught to do with violent drunks and drug addicts, held down the dog's thrashing paws in a wrestler's hold, which allowed the doctor to seize the scruff of the dog's neck and send the needle deep into the vein. After a few seconds, the creature started to relax.

'Hetty, do you want to go and wait in the waiting room,' said the man. It was an instruction, not a question. 'You,' he said to Rosie. 'Get scrubbed in.'

Rosie boiled up catgut while the doctor selected the right fine instrument and crouched down, starting to coax out the wire carefully. She watched, breathlessly, as he extracted pieces of metal.

'Stupid old fence,' said the man. 'It's rusted to nearly nothing.'

'Will you be able to get it all?'

The damage, though painful, didn't seem to be too deep, as he drew out the last poking piece, spiked with blood. The man shrugged. 'He can have an X-ray at the veterinary hospital tomorrow. But we need to get this little lot sewn up. An infection in there could be very nasty.'

Once the stomach was stitched up, with a large amount of antibacterial powder, they could both relax a bit, and Rosie stood next to him as he made a very tidy job of the rest of the dog. 'You're good at that,' she observed at one point. 'I've worked with some right butchers.'

'I always liked it,' admitted the doctor. 'I miss a bit of the wet work in general practice.'

He let a smile cross his face. 'I'm Moray.'

'Like the eel?' Rosie said, then immediately felt like an idiot. 'Sorry.'

'Don't be,' said Moray. 'I use it as a diagnostic tool. If you don't say "like the eel" then you're obviously suffering from some form of mental distraction or injury.'

'Oh,' said Rosie, feeling herself go pink.

'So, what—a veterinary nurse just suddenly appeared at the right moment out of the sky?' said Moray.

'Oh, no,' said Rosie, pleased he thought that. 'No, no. I'm a real nurse. Well, not really. I'm a nursing auxiliary. Or at least, I was.'

Moray raised his eyebrows. 'Well, that was lucky. It got really hairy there. Don't know what we'd have done without you. Do you have a name, Nursing Auxiliary, or are you going to vanish on your magical raincloud?'

'I'm Rosie,' said Rosie. 'Do you do this kind of thing a lot?'

'Almost never,' said Moray. 'Actually, never. You?'

Rosie shook her head, and they smiled at each other.

'I don't know how I'm going to get all this hair out of here,' said Moray. 'It won't go down well.'

And sure enough, when Dr Hywel Evans, head of practice, rolled up forty minutes later, he was amazed to find a dog on the sluice-room table. His most junior partner and a total stranger were putting a bandage on it while a woman cried tears of relief in his waiting room.

Moray turned around just as he entered. 'I think we got it all,' he was calling through to the waiting room. 'But probably worth an X-ray and a checkup just in case.'

Rosie saw Dr Evans had a face like thunder. 'Hello?' she said tentatively.

'Who the hell are you?' demanded a corpulent man in tweed.

'Oh' she said, her face falling. After the adrenalin of their dash to the surgery, Rosie finally realised just how many illegal things she'd done in the past forty minutes.

'Oh,' she said again. 'Oh dear. Oh dear. I'm so sorry . . . it was just . . .'

Hywel looked from the dog to Rosie to Moray to the dog again. 'You . . . you brought a *dog* in here?'

'Nothing else to be done, sir,' said Moray respectfully. 'Jim Hodds is over the other side of the mountain in the middle of a tricky foaling. Perforated abdomen. The dog would have died, sir. And, fortunately, this young lady happened to be passing and proved the most excellent nurse.'

'That is *absolutely* and *categorically* not *allowed*,' Hywel spluttered.

Rosie moved back towards the table and tentatively rested her hand on the dog's head. To her astonishment, Bran lifted his head a tiny amount, and gently licked her hand. She was delighted. 'Hey, boy,' she said softly, her voice trembling.

Moray smiled. 'Hey, old fellow!' he said. 'Look at that, Hye.'

'Well, I can't believe this,' said Hywel. 'Do I need to call the police?'

'Do you need to call the *what?*' came a loud, imperious voice, and the dog's owner strode into the room.

'He's stirring,' said Rosie.

The woman rushed over and put her hand to the dog's muzzle, and he tried another tentative lick. 'Bran,' said the woman. 'Oh, Bran.' She buried her face in the animal's neck. Dr Evans watched in disbelief.

Then she turned to him. 'Hye Evans,' she said. 'Your young doctor and this strange girl just saved my dog's life. They were *magnificent*.'

There was a long pause. 'Lady . . . Lady Lipton,' stammered Dr Evans.

A lady! Well, that was a stupid reaction, obviously. But even so. Maybe that's why she had kept insisting that it was 'her' road. Because it was.

'Amazing,' Lady Lipton said. 'I'll pay for the medicines, of course. Without these young people it would have been a very different outcome indeed.'

'You'll still need to get him X-rayed,' warned Moray.

'I certainly will,' said Lady Lipton. 'Well done, Hye. Nice to see you take on somebody competent for a change.'

Hye spluttered.

'I'll send Mrs Flynn down to clean up. Now, please, Moray, could you help me lift my darling boy back into the car?'

# Chapter Three

'In 1932 the Milky Way appeared in the US, followed by Mr Mars junior's invention, the Mars Bar, in the UK in 1933. 1935, the Aero, 1936 Maltesers, and in 1937 the Kit Kat, Rolos and Smarties. In music the equivalent would be the golden age of Bach, Mozart and Beethoven.

'Never mind about 1066 William the Conqueror, 1087 William the Second. Such things are not going to affect one's life . . . but 1933 the

*Mars Bar and 1936 Maltesers and 1937 the Kit Kat—these dates are milestones in history and should be seared into the memory of every child in the country.'*

*So said none other than Roald Dahl, and he should know and in fact gets the last word on just about every single sweet-related issue out there.*

*So take that, you smarty-pants 'one square of 90% cocoa dark chocolate with chilli taken with a glass of Château Pétrus 1978' brigade, and naff right off. Here are the facts: the more rarefied and bitter you take your chocolate, the less you TRULY like and appreciate the stuff. The chocolate you grew up with—mass-produced, high in fat and sugar, low in cocoa—is one of the many, many things that made Britain great.*

IT TOOK THE ADRENALIN wearing off for Rosie to realise how wet she was. That, and stepping out into an afternoon as clear and blue as the morning she'd left Lipton. What on earth had the weather done? As she dripped up the road towards Lilian's house it seemed unfair that so many faces turned towards her to stare. Didn't they know they lived in a mad climate?

Lilian was pottering about in the house looking worried when she arrived, but desperately trying not to show it too much. 'What happened to you?' she said. 'I thought you'd turned around and gone home.' Lilian wondered if she'd been too hard on the girl before.

'There was a storm! I got drenched!'

'Well, this is Derbyshire, darling, not the Balearics. Run yourself a bath and get a proper coat.'

Rosie put the kettle on and ran her fingers through her hair. Without wanting to drop anyone in it about treating a dog in a doctor's surgery, she mentioned in passing that she'd met the local doctor.

'Hye Evans? That fat old fool,' said Lilian. 'That man couldn't diagnose a nail sticking out of your leg if you turned up with a nail sticking out of your leg, saying, "Doctor, I just accidentally hammered a nail into my leg." And trust me, I should know.'

'Uhm, no, the other one.'

Lilian's eyebrows went up. 'Were you quite so damp at the time?'

'What do you mean?' said Rosie.

Lilian glanced briefly at the glamorous portraits of herself as a younger woman but didn't say anything.

Rosie sniffed and marched upstairs to run the bath, trying not to glance in the bathroom mirror. Her hair had widened to twice its normal size, like a loaf of bread proving by a stove.

'I have a boyfriend, you know.'

'Boyfriends, schmoyfriends,' said Lilian. 'I don't see him here.'

'**O**K,' Rosie said, coming down warm and dry forty-five minutes later. She had only one jumper. That, she probably needed to rectify. Lilian was sitting in her armchair listening to Radio 4 and staring into the fire.

Rosie heated up the vegetable soup she'd grabbed from the Spar.

'Eat this. And the bread.'

'This is *oozing* with butter,' said Lilian, looking disgusted.

'It is,' said Rosie. 'And if you don't want me to make you eat two slices, I'd get on with it. Unless you want me to dissolve it in milk.'

Lilian made a face, but started in on the soup. As she did so, she felt a little spurt of worry; how long had it been since she'd had hot food? Hetty popped in and warmed something up now and again but even she complained about her not having one of those new oven things that heated up things so fast. Lilian didn't trust the idea of them, and anyway, she'd always got along fine without.

'We need to get you a microwave,' said Rosie. 'You know. If you want to keep living here.'

'Ugly things,' murmured Lilian. 'So many modern things are so ugly.'

Rosie tried not to take this as a personal slight, but didn't quite know how to respond. 'Have you lived in Lipton all your life?' she asked.

'Well, I've travelled,' said Lilian crossly. It was none of this girl's business. 'I've been to York . . . Scarborough of course . . . Scotland once.'

'London?'

'I have no idea why the entire world seems so fixated on London,' said Lilian. 'I thought it was absolutely crammed full of unspeakable people, incredibly noisy and totally filthy.'

Rosie grinned. 'It is,' she said. 'All of those things. That's what makes it so amazing.'

'Well, if you like hooligans, I suppose.'

'Didn't you ever want to travel further?' said Rosie. 'New York? Paris?'

'Not particularly,' sniffed Lilian. 'I knew what I liked. And I had the shop. And I might go, still.'

A silence descended, and the atmosphere grew stiff. Neither of them could quite say it. That there was no 'still'. That what Rosie was here to do was not going to result in any trips to Paris.

Afterwards, Rosie insisted on examining her aunt's hip. Lilian would have liked to refuse, but realised she was in no position to do so.

Sure enough, the wound was a little nasty and sticky round the edges, but nothing Rosie couldn't sort out. Lilian, for her part, was a bit more impressed than she let on at Rosie's cool hands and efficient manner as she changed the dressing. After that, Rosie figured there was no point in pussyfooting around any longer.

'Let's have a look at the business then.'

Lilian looked guilty. 'Well, since I hurt my hip . . .'

'It's fine,' said Rosie. 'Honestly. I've seen it. Can I have the keys?'

With some difficulty Lilian picked up the large set of ancient brass keys from the mantelpiece.

'Come on then,' said Rosie. 'Let's go and have a look.'

The key twisted reluctantly in the old lock on the red-painted wooden door. With a horrible squeak Rosie managed to click it round.

Rosie pushed over the stacked mail on the mat. 'I can't believe this has been going on for so long,' she said. She moved into the middle of the tiny shop and turned round 360 degrees. 'Wow,' was all she could say.

First off, there was no denying it, the place was filthy. There were cobwebs in the corners. The windows were covered in grime. The antique till still had shillings and pence on its ancient keys. The scales, burnished and at an awkward angle, stood there as if the past seven decades had hardly touched them. It was a museum.

And inside, every square inch of the little shop was covered—in sweets, in posters, in things Rosie hadn't seen for years. There were little tins of travel sweets and jujubes, neatly piled up in pyramids, great glass bowls full of striped candy canes tied with bows, huge slabs of dark-red Bournville chocolate and neatly stacked alternating boxes of Dairy Milk and Black Magic. On the very highest shelves were the most enormous, elaborate boxes of chocolates, in red-velvet heart-shaped boxes with huge ribbons, completely covered in dust.

An old ladder was attached to sliding rails, as at a library, to allow the higher sweets to be removed from the shelves. The back three walls were lined with shelves that held glass jars filled with every imaginable sweet:

slabs of peanut brittle, bright-green gobstoppers, chocolate frogs and lady-birds, dolly mixtures and rainbow drops and fat pastel marshmallows. And tucked neatly by the black pop-up till, the classics, in neat rows: Mars Bar. Kit Kat. Aero. Fry's Chocolate Cream. Crunchie. Twix.

'But this is—I mean, it's obviously once been absolutely amazing in here,' said Rosie. 'It's fantastic.'

'Shows what you know,' said Lilian. 'It's all finished now. Anyway, it's not what kids want these days. They don't want gobstoppers any more. They want great big bars of Dairy Milk that you buy in six-packs from the supermarket. They want family packs and supersharers and litres of cola and hot dogs and nachos, whatever they are. Sweets are boring, and old-fashioned. No one is interested any more.'

Rosie looked around. 'I can't believe that's true. Lilian, why didn't you throw away all this stock?'

Her aunt looked cross but stoic. 'Sweets keep for a long time. I'm coming back to the shop.'

'Mmm,' said Rosie. This wasn't just from Lilian's operation. The shop had obviously been like this for a long, long time, and Lilian had been unable or unwilling to tell anyone that she could no longer cope.

'I was still getting some tourist trade,' Lilian was saying. 'Some chocolates round Valentine's day. But the children have moved on.'

'But this could be . . . I mean the fact that it's all unchanged . . .'

'Well, nothing much good happens in the world of sweets. Everything they invent now actually tastes worse than the old stuff. It's the children I feel sorry for,' grumped Lilian. 'So I saw no reason to change.'

Rosie looked at the ancient cash register. 'How did you use this?'

'Well, you just got used to it,' said Lilian. 'Decimalisation was terrible for the children though. It made their sweets more expensive. It was an awful thing. I definitely think they should go back. Idiot politicians.'

'I'm not sure that's going to happen,' said Rosie. 'But keeping the till may have been a smart move. This kind of thing is really fashionable.'

Lilian looked almost flattered. 'Well, good things never go out of style.'

Suddenly there was a ting, as the little brass bell above the shop rang.

It was the woman with the dog. Lady Lipton.

'Coo-eee! Lils, *darling*. You have to hear about this extraordinary new girl in the village, you won't *believe* what she did with Bran . . .'

'Oh, who is it?' said Lilian eagerly. 'Is she awful?'

'Hard to say,' said Lady Lipton, then finally realised who else was in the room. Completely unperturbed, she held out her hand.

'And here she is. Hello. Have you bought a proper coat yet? We're predicted four days of rain by the way. Which either means nine, or none at all. Lils, I stuck the groceries in your kitchen. Now, let me tell you the whole story.'

So Rosie had to stand by as Lady Lipton recounted the entire event to Lilian, laying it on quite thickly about Rosie careering around in the rain wearing a bikini. 'And that terribly smart young doctor managed to take out all the wire, wasn't that wonderful?'

Rosie was fascinated. She'd never met anyone with a title before.

'Do you live in a big house?' she asked, not realising how rude it sounded till it had come out of her mouth, almost like an accusation. Lilian laughed in a way that sounded as if she was trying to excuse her gauche London scruff of a niece.

'Well, that very much depends on what you think of as big,' said Lady Lipton. Rosie correctly interpreted this to mean 'yes, ginormous'.

'Doesn't it get freezing?'

Both women stared for a moment. Then Lilian burst out laughing.

'It certainly does,' she said. 'That's why Hets is down here all the time.'

'It most certainly is not,' said Lady Lipton. 'I'm being charitable.'

Lilian snorted. 'You're being cosy. Look at her,' she ordered Rosie, and lifted the edge of the woman's Barbour jacket with her stick. Underneath was a gigantic man's pullover, patently ancient, and the holes in the wool showed evidence of another underneath. 'And it's still summer,' cackled Lilian. 'You wait till November, she'll be camping out in her front room.'

'You overheat your house,' said Lady Lipton. 'It's not good for you.'

'She's strong as an ox,' interjected Rosie, who'd witnessed Lilian hurling logs onto the fire already that afternoon.

'Apparently I'm as strong as an ox,' said Lilian. 'And she's a nurse, she ought to know.'

'Auxiliary nurse,' said Lady Lipton and Rosie made a quick note not to underestimate her. 'And what exactly is an ox?' she added.

'It's a gigantic cow. A boy cow,' Rosie said, flushing, with a sudden stab of panic in case it was the one where you cross a donkey and a horse.

The two women laughed.

'Well, enjoy your stay,' said Lady Lipton, sweeping out.

'Well,' Rosie said. 'After I saved her dog and everything.'

Lilian chuckled. 'Oh, that's just Hetty's way.'

'Ugh,' said Rosie. 'I hate it when people say, "Oh, they're just like that." If someone is rude, they shouldn't be like that. Everyone else shouldn't have to make allowances just because they're Lady Snot-a-Lot.'

## 1942

*Lilian's father looked at her with a quizzical expression on his face. 'So, just a night out with your friend, is it?' he asked, poking at his bacon and eggs.*

*Lilian looked again at the little pot of rouge Margaret had given her. She wasn't exactly sure what to do with it. Sometimes she thought life had dealt her an unfair hand, not just in losing her mother but in having three big brothers and no big sisters, meaning there was no one to give her the merest hint of feminine insight.*

*Her friend Margaret tried to help, but Margaret was daft as a brush and boy-mad and only wanted to get married, and Lilian was never quite sure whether to follow her advice or not. She dabbed a little rouge on her cheeks.*

*'Ah, now you look like you've been hauling in the fields all day,' said her father, realising as he did so that it was exactly the wrong thing to say to his only daughter, sharp, clever Lilian, whom he loved dearly but didn't understand.*

*Lilian sniffed, and pulled down last year's sprigged cotton dress. Its sleeves now looked dated, and the waist was dropped too low to show off her pretty figure; she looked like a stick, she thought, all up and down.*

*She couldn't deny the truth: that since last week, she had thought of little else but Henry Carr. Suddenly, everything she had found irritating about him—the teasing, the hanging around the shop—now it had stopped, she found she missed it beyond reason. The idea of him walking out with Ida Delia filled her with horror.*

*Margaret arrived, clattering along on her bicycle, her hair tightly lacquered and her dress as tight as modesty allowed, almost disguising the slight cast of her eye. Margaret never mentioned her eye, but hated her front snaggletooth and would often spend the entire evening with her hand positioned directly in front of it. Despite this, she was funny and loyal and daft and Lilian loved her.*

*'Well, you look like you're going to kill them fellas tonight,' said Lilian's father. Margaret giggled.*

*Her father, as if on a whim, took out the bottle of Johnson the butcher's home-made rhubarb wine he kept for special occasions.*

*'Come on,' he said. 'Let's have a glass. Celebrate two lovely girls going out to have a good time.'*

*Her father poured them all a small glass of wine. 'And no messing about, you understand? If you have to dance with a chap, I want it to be someone nice, local, good family. None of that Derby mob.'*

*The girls blushed bright red, and Margaret let out a peal of laughter. A large group of young men were down for the harvest, hence the dance. Lilian rolled her eyes as if to indicate that all that was beneath her, trying her best not to betray that she did, indeed, have her heart set on finding a nice young man. A very specific one, that was all.*

*Her father knew other fathers worried about their daughters, but if anything he wished he could worry more about Lilian. And with three sons in the war— they'd said Gordon didn't have to go, could stay and mind the shop, but his headstrong youngest son was having none of it—he had enough to worry about. But he knew it wasn't easy for her, the one left behind, and the only girl. When the boys came back on leave and told their stories of the big cities and the shows and the lights, he felt sad for Lilian, stuck here with the shop. But what else could they do? A living was a living, even in wartime. Still, she could do with a bit of fun and he'd like her to meet a decent chap.*

*Feeling warm and jolly, Lilian and Margaret rattled off on their bicycles towards the village hall, Lilian's heart thumping in her chest, her eyes sparkling. The late-summer air was warm for once, clear and gentle, the stars just starting to come out overhead. Lilian felt as close as she ever had to beautiful.*

**R**osie was determined to start the next day afresh. She smiled at her aunt, who was coming to the table and trying not to look over-curious about the porridge with wild honey, full cream and fresh blueberries Rosie had made for her.

Lilian sat herself down. 'What's this?'

'It's to . . .' Rosie nearly said 'fatten you up' before realising that was unlikely to go down well. 'It's the fashion breakfast,' she said. 'It's what the models eat.'

Lilian sniffed. Today she was wearing a cerise shift dress with a bright-red scarf tied at the neck. It could have looked a bit peculiar, but with her silver hair nicely done at the back, it was actually rather chic.

'Where did you get the cream?' said Lilian.

'Uhm, the Spar,' said Rosie.

'Well, don't. The Isitts have a perfectly good dairy farm down the road. It's two miles out the village, turn left, down the hill. Milk too. Take the empty bottles back.'

'You want me to walk two miles with empty milk bottles?'

Lilian raised her eyebrows. 'No, of course not. You can take the bike.'

'Hmm,' said Rosie. 'Well, there's a problem with that.'

After breakfast, Lilian made her step out into the bright golden morning. Rosie followed her great-aunt out behind the little cottage and into the garden.

'In there,' said Lilian, indicating a small shed.

'Seriously?'

Lilian nodded her head towards the door, and Rosie finally did as she was bid, heaving and straining just to open the rusty bolts. Inside was a huge black metal spider of a thing, a ton weight. Rosie popped her head back out.

'You're not serious,' she yelled.

'Are you here to help me or not?'

Rosie hauled it out. It was the size of a small tank. She leaned it against the wall. They both stared at it.

'What is it?' Rosie asked, finally.

'That's my bike! I'm going to let you use it.'

The bike was very old, solid, with a huge basket on the front.

'Yes, well, I can't ride a bike.'

Lilian's substantial eyebrows shot up. 'You *can't*?'

'Well, of course I can . . . I mean, I did when I was younger. Obviously.'

Her mother had occasionally taken her and Pip to the park and sat having a flask of tea and a fag while they wheeled their bikes around, then dumped them to play on the climbing frames. Rosie wasn't sure this really counted. You couldn't ride a bike on the roads where she had grown up—well, some kids were allowed, but not them—and you couldn't ride them to school or they'd get nicked, so Rosie had never really got into the habit.

'You know,' said Lilian, 'you're in luck; I'll get Jake Randall round. He fixes bikes for the kids in the village. He'll fix it up for you pronto. He'll do anything for some Highland Toffee.'

Rosie sighed and headed back indoors again. 'I'm supposed to be looking after *you*,' she said as a parting shot.

'You will be,' retorted Lilian, 'when you pick up the milk and cream. And do notice which of us is wearing pyjamas in the street . . . Hello, vicar!' she called out to the man passing in a dark suit. Rosie scarpered up the stairs.

There wasn't even any point, Rosie thought, in getting dressed up today, given the horrible job of emptying out the shop, so she was steeled for the arched eyebrows by the time she came back downstairs in her old jeans and a fleece, her bouncing black curls forced up in a floral scarf. Lilian glanced over.

'Angie says you have kind of a boyfriend?' she enquired, as Rosie filled a large bucket with soapy water.

'Why did I ever think you were a quiet, frail old lady when you used to visit us? You're actually really nosy.'

'Because,' said Lilian dramatically, 'I only ever came to your house in London when I was recovering. From adventures.'

'What sort of adventures?'

'I'm not just an old lady who runs a sweet shop, you know.'

'Well,' said Rosie. 'Tell me about them.'

'I'm afraid not,' said Lilian, picking up the empty breakfast bowls. Rosie noticed Lilian's had been scraped clean. 'It's nearly time for *The Archers*.'

'Well, I won't have time to tell you about Gerard then.'

'Gerard? What kind of a name is that? Sounds very modern.'

'Yes, amazingly the man I'm going out with isn't a hundred years old.'

Lilian looked expectant.

'Well,' said Rosie. 'He's little and cute . . .'

'Sounds like a squirrel,' sniffed Lilian.

'He's a pharmacist,' said Rosie.

'Not a doctor then?'

'No, it's completely different,' said Rosie, not revealing that Gerard had never quite got over applying and failing to get into medical school. 'It's a very responsible job, he's really good at it.'

'Putting bum cream in paper bags?' said Lilian.

'If you're going to be rude we don't have to talk at all,' said Rosie. 'In fact, I want to get started anyway.'

'Get started on what?'

'One of the things I came here to do,' said Rosie in a tone that, on the wards, would brook no arguments. Her mild-mannered mother and brother had always wondered aloud where she'd got it from. Rosie was beginning to figure out the answer. 'Sort out your shop.'

Lilian had a radio in the shop, and Rosie retuned it from Radio 4 to Radio 1, and hauled out a roll of huge black bin bags. There wasn't a dishwasher in the cottage, so she was going to have to wash out all the glass jars by hand, and they weighed a ton. She started at the top and worked down, lining up all the glass jars, sampling everything and checking for sell-by dates. Any chocolate with white spots was binned instantly.

She washed the dusty old shelves till they smelled and looked fresh, blew the dust off the top of the huge red-velvet boxes of chocolates and decided that although their contents were past saving, she would clean up the boxes and keep them for display purposes. Likewise the tins of travel sweets with images of exotic places printed on the lids, of the Côte d'Azur and the Alps. They would make a lovely display, and in case someone actually did want some travel sweets, she would order some in.

After all, she was meant to be selling this place as a going concern. But, actually, the previous night a thought had struck her. Rather than get rid of everything and sell on a soulless shell, what if—what if—she returned *Hopkins' Sweets and Confectionery* to its glory days *just as it was*, almost like a museum, with the original fixtures and fittings?

Rosie had been so excited by this idea she'd called Gerard from the top of the house (if you leaned out of the window you could just about get a signal). When he said he was at his mum's watching *Midsomer Murders* and could they talk tomorrow, Rosie called Angie, who said to do what she liked as long as she sorted it all out.

Before she got started on the windows, she took a packet of chocolate caramels and a glass of water, and sat down on the large grey stone step outside the shop, to polish up the original brass scales and watch the world go by. A couple of smart-looking ladies clopped by on horses with shopping bags in their hands. She watched as they continued on their way.

'What's this?' The voice was snappy, with a heavy local accent. It did not sound happy. Rosie looked up, squinting in the sunlight. It was hard to make out the silhouette of the man standing over her, but from what she could see he was bald and exceptionally thin.

'Hello,' she said, scrambling up. 'I'm Lilian Hopkins' niece. I'm here to help her out with the shop.'

The man took a step back. He wore little round glasses and had peculiarly red lips, which he licked, quickly and nervously, displaying extremely white teeth that glinted obtrusively. Rosie wondered if they were false.

'What do you mean, help her out with it? You mean you're going to reopen it?'

'I haven't decided,' said Rosie, staring at him. 'We'll see.'

'Well, I don't like that,' said the man. 'Best thing that happened to this town, that place closing down.'

What kind of weirdo is happy when a sweet shop closes down? wondered Rosie.

'Roy Blaine,' said the man. 'Town dentist.'

'Oh,' said Rosie, understanding. 'Ah. Hah. Well.'

The man peered in the windows, unsmiling.

'Actually, I would have thought a sweet shop would be good for business.' Rosie risked a joke, but the man didn't smile.

'It's a bloody disgrace,' he said.

'Uhm, it's only sweets,' said Rosie. 'I think you'll find the Spar sells the same stuff. Except they sell lots of fizzy drinks too. Which are *far* worse.'

'It's a bad business,' he said. 'A damn bad business.'

'We'll promote good dental hygiene,' promised Rosie suddenly. 'We'll put signs up reminding children to brush their teeth after eating a sweetie. And we sell small portions. And we'll sell chewing gum!' Then she suddenly remembered that one of the chapters in her aunt's book was entitled '*Why Chewing Gum is Death*'. 'Well, maybe not chewing gum. But we'll be responsible!'

She realised as she said this that she wasn't actually meant to be opening the shop up again the way she wanted it, just readying it to be sold.

Roy Blaine sniffed. 'Nobody cares,' he said. 'Nobody cares about the infants with rotting mouths howling and dying in agony. From *sweets*.' He hissed the last word, as if it pained him even to say it. And he walked off down the road, muttering.

Rosie returned to her polishing rather crossly after that. She wasn't here to make enemies, and really, how passionately could one fight against a sweet shop? They weren't pretending to be healthy. It was a place for treats, for somewhere to come excitedly clutching your pocket money, to look forward to. They sold honest-to-goodness, up-front sweets, wrapped in pink and green paper bags . . .

Rosie realised suddenly that she'd taken on the shop's identity as her own. She was just here to help out for a little bit. Set her great-aunt up. Obviously Lilian would never again be up for a whole day serving behind the counter, but clearly all her marbles were there; if the shop could pay its way and make a little extra, that could mean a bit of care for her aunt and someone to run the business, and then everyone would be happy.

'Penny for 'em,' came a gruff voice. She looked up, squinting in the sun, and was greeted by a friendly smile, showing off strong white teeth.

'You Lilian's girl?' he said, his accent made thicker by a deep voice.

Rosie scrambled up, suddenly wishing she wasn't wearing crappy old trousers and a fleece, of all things. Maybe she could take off the fleece. Then she remembered that underneath it she'd pulled on her faded Race for Life T-shirt, which had breast cancer written all over it. Maybe not.

'I'm Jake,' he said, holding out a strong, calloused hand. His hair was the colour of straw, some bits lightened by the sun, his face a walnut brown, the kind of brown that came from working outside all day. Round his eyes were creases, but his eyes shone out of them, a very bright blue.

'Something about fixing a bike?'

**B**y the shed, Rosie watched him work. He had the bike upside-down and was gripping the front wheel between his legs as he did something to the gears. She wondered if she could pop off and put some lipstick on. 'Want a cup of tea?' she asked.

'No, you're all right, duck,' said Jake.

Rosie didn't notice her arriving, but suddenly Lilian was at her elbow. 'Enjoying the view?' said Lilian, chuckling to herself.

'Did you do this on purpose?' said Rosie.

'Yes,' said Lilian. 'But I thought you'd have washed your hair.'

'I know,' groaned Rosie. 'Oh well, I'm sure he's horrible.'

'Jake's a pussy cat,' said Lilian firmly. 'He does all the . . . I mean he *very occasionally* helps me out with the heavy lifting.'

'All right, Miss Hopkins?' said Jake, glancing up. 'Don't you ever oil this thing? It's as stiff as a badger's gate.'

'What does that mean?' asked Rosie.

Lilian told her to be quiet. 'Thanks so much for fitting us in,' she said in a nice voice Rosie hadn't encountered before. 'We'll sort you out with some peppermint ice. I know you're very busy.'

Jake rolled his eyes. 'Tell me about it.'

'Bad as ever?' Lilian asked.

'She's a . . . she's a . . .'

Jake looked like he was about to say something harsh. Then, as if realising he was in the presence of two ladies, he checked himself.

'OK. Here you go. Good as new.' He righted the bike and held it up by the saddle.

## 1942

*The village hall was wreathed in smoke under the lights, and perfume mixed with a hint of illicit alcohol and sweat, and was absolutely packed with people, young boys and giggling young girls. These were the boys down to work the harvest, along with the land girls, whom the local girls roundly shunned, seeing them as competition for the few remaining menfolk. Soldiers home on leave had come from all the towns around. There was an overheated atmosphere engendered by the warm night and the transient population; Lilian felt the excitement of being young and free, not tied down—although, of course, she was, in so many ways. With all the seventeen-year-old confidence she could muster, she thought that this just might be the most important night of her life.*

*Margaret was in flirt overload as they parked up their bikes and sidled in. The noise level was overwhelming. On the raised platform at the end the band were perspiring in their cheap shirts to keep up with the dancers, who seemed hell-bent on squeezing as much fun out of the night as they could.*

*Lilian paid the small ticket price on the door and left her cardigan on her bicycle. She might not be wearing the most fashionable dress, she noted, but it was light, and cool in the hot sticky room. She was almost too scared to scan the room, just in case he wasn't there, and kept her head down as she followed Margaret to the fruit-punch stand.*

*Clutching their paper cups nervously, Margaret and Lilian smiled at each other—which was about all that was possible through the noise—and looked around. The uniformed men were sitting down, looking handsome, with a couple of girls nearby. On the opposite wall, eyeing them up, were the harvest boys: those too young to enlist, the travelling groups who fought for no one, the farmers' boys too important to go off to war. They were sunburnt, not smartly dressed in uniforms, and looked awkward. There were no girls hovering around them. Lilian sensed there might be trouble later.*

*Out on the dance floor the girls' dresses shone like parachute silk; there was not much around, but they had made the best of what they had. Cyan blue, primrose yellow, the girls flashed and twirled around the floor to the enthusiastic farmers' band—who were doing their very best Glenn Miller with a double bass, a banjo, an oil drum, two trumpets and a harmonica—laughing over-exuberantly as the boys threw them about the floor, showing off their moves.*

*Lilian wasn't interested in being whisked off by a navy man from Scarborough, or toyed with by a slumming-it officer down from Harrogate. There was only one boy, one mop of unruly nut-brown hair, one pair of laughing nut-brown eyes, that was of the faintest interest to her.*

*Suddenly, she saw him at the other end of the hall.*

**R**osie looked at Jake the bicycle fixer, and did her best to smile at him. She didn't want a bicycle as good as new. She didn't want a bicycle at all.

'I've replaced the tyres, fixed the brakes and raised the saddle.'

'Well, thank you,' Rosie said, hoping Jake would simply leave the bike against the shed and stay for a cup of tea. Then, when they needed some of her aunt's precious milk supply, she would just call a taxi.

Jake was still standing there. 'Well, let's be having you then, I haven't got all day.'

'Oh, well, I'm going to . . . in a minute . . .'

'Come on, I need to see if the seat is the right height.' He shook the bike in what was obviously meant to be an encouraging fashion.

Her heart in her throat, Rosie slowly stepped forward. This bike was huge, and weighed a ton. She held it up to herself, tentatively. 'Well, this seems *fine*,' she said brightly. 'Thank you so much.'

'Come on, lass,' said Jake again. 'Let's be having you.'

With a sigh, Rosie threw up her leg, and tried to mount as if she was getting on a horse, all the while conscious of his eyes on her. Once in the saddle, her feet only just touching the ground, she set a foot to one of the pedals, telling herself fiercely that no one ever forgot how to ride a bicycle. Obviously this motto was invented on the assumption that you'd properly learned how to ride one in the first place, but still. Taking a deep breath, Rosie pushed the pedal forward.

In her defence, she nearly made it. She pitched and wobbled, and almost, almost got going. As it was, she did a graceless soar across the right-hand side of the handlebars, straight into the flowerbed, hitting her right shoulder before landing, winded, on her back.

There was a long silence.

'Miss, would you like a hand?' Jake's friendly face loomed over her, but actually, for the moment, Rosie felt she was almost more comfortable lying in the flowerbed.

'All right,' she said finally, standing up and shaking herself like a dog. 'Sorry about your lovely flowers,' she said sadly, twisting her shoulder round to check for pain, but it was more her pride that was hurt.

Lilian sniffed. 'I don't know what Angie was thinking of, not teaching you to ride a bicycle.'

'She was mostly thinking of us not being squashed flat beneath the wheels of a truck,' said Rosie, conscious of being very pink in the face. 'I'll just go call a taxi,' she mumbled.

Jake and Lilian looked at each other and burst out laughing.

'That's right, darling,' said Lilian. 'You'll find it just beside Fortnum & Mason, opposite Le Caprice and near the National Gallery. There's a whole rank of them. And some unicorns.'

Jake smiled uncertainly and glanced at his watch.

'Look,' said Lilian, 'Jake has to get back. Go cycling with him, he'll help you out.'

Rosie rolled her eyes, but allowed herself to be led back to the bicycle. Jake held the end patiently, disregarded her complaints and made her go a little way, then a little farther, until finally Rosie turned her head and realised that she was moving and he wasn't holding on at all! And it felt amazing; the wind blew in her hair as she started to pick up speed.

'Easy now,' yelled Jake, but Rosie couldn't believe she'd never wanted to do this. Riding a bike was *great*! Confidently she took the alleyway at the side of the house. She hadn't, though, realised it was on a downward slope so the bike moved very quickly. Before she knew it she was charging out into the street, completely unable to help herself.

Thankfully there wasn't any traffic at that moment. Instead, marching down the street was the young doctor from the day before. Rosie attempted an insouciant wave and smile as she sailed past, but that made her wobble alarmingly and a concerned look crossed Moray's face.

Still watching him, Rosie didn't realise the bike was continuing to move, and she was about to hit an enormous rut on the other side of the road. Swerving to avoid it, she managed to get back on to another road that led downhill via a rutted track towards something marked Isitt's Farm, past fields of cows who gazed at her as she passed by . . . Faster, Rosie realised, then faster still, as the inexorable slope made the bike pick up speed, with brakes that seemed to be doing nothing, until all she could see in front of her was a gigantic barn and a grey stone farmhouse.

Rosie twisted the handlebar to the left, heading round the side of the house, through, to her utter horror, a perfectly maintained vegetable patch, then swerving again, now losing speed on the level, until she ended up behind the barn, managed to turn a 180-degree semicircle and inelegantly let herself fall sideways, breathless, into a gigantic pile of straw in the middle of the Isitts' farmyard.

Staring at her from the side of the house were a stern-looking old woman and an old man leaning heavily on a walking frame. Rosie tried to smile politely, as if crashing into someone's farm was something she did every day. Her head hurt, and she felt a bit stunned, and her elbow had really taken a knock. Suddenly, Rosie was overwhelmed with the desire to burst into tears. Instead, she half smiled and said, 'Hello.'

The woman did not smile. 'What the 'eck are you doing?' she said, folding her arms and looking down at Rosie.

Rosie was so fed up she was on the point of saying, 'I'm from MI5 checking for sniper activity,' when she heard two sets of running footsteps pounding round the side of the barn. She squinted and raised her head, and suddenly thought how much, however embarrassing a time she was having, she suddenly didn't feel like an almost-engaged cohabiting type of person at all. Instead she felt a bit squeaky and slightly giggly. Because there, both looking concerned and out of breath, stood Jake and Moray.

Rosie sat up as carefully as she was able, checking herself for broken bones. She realised she was under the scrutiny of four people, and a cow. 'Uhm, two pints of semiskimmed?' she said shakily, picking a piece of straw out of her hair.

'Din you *see* what she did to Pa's vegetable patch?' shouted the woman.

The man didn't look as upset as his wife. In fact, he didn't seem too put out at all. He scratched his head.

'I'm really sorry,' said Rosie. 'The bike . . . must have malfunctioned.'

Moray crouched down. 'Well, you're certainly making an impression,' he muttered, as he peered into her eyes with a tiny flashlight. 'How many fingers am I holding up?' he asked her, and Rosie realised that she was quite dazed because she wasn't actually focusing on his fingers at all, she was reflecting on how his eyes were a very unusual mix of blue and green, which probably meant she was concussed.

'Uhm. Four,' she said, snapping back. 'Definitely.'

'And are you drunk or under the influence of any substances . . .' he asked, with a slight moue of amusement around his mouth.

'Is that an offer?' Rosie found herself saying before clutching her head in horror. 'Sorry. Sorry. It's been a big couple of days.'

'So can I take that as a no?' asked Moray, helping her to her feet.

'It is indeed a no,' said Rosie, brushing herself down. She smiled at Jake, who was looking anxious. 'You are the worst cycling teacher ever,' she said.

'Why didn't you brake?' he asked.

'Well, I couldn't brake, could I? I'd just have gone arse over tit.'

'Into our vegetable patch,' said Mrs Isitt fiercely.

'I am very sorry about that,' said Rosie. 'I really am. I'm new here.'

Mrs Isitt flared her nostrils with a harrumph that made Rosie wonder if a horse had wandered into the barn.

'While I'm here,' said Moray, 'Peter, let me take a look at that hip.'

'It's fine,' said Mrs Isitt.

'Yes, well, I'd still like to take a look. In passing,' said Moray. 'Seeing as we have no further casualties.'

Rosie was still blushing from saying something so stupid to Moray, but Jake came up beside her, kindly asking, 'Would you like me to get you the cream?'

Rosie smiled gratefully. 'I wouldn't want to face Lilian without it.'

Jake steered her towards the barn door.

'You've got that silage to move,' said Mrs Isitt huffily as he left.

'Yes, Mrs Isitt,' said Jake. 'I'll just sort this out.'

Rosie followed him obediently. 'You work for them?'

Jake shrugged. 'Times are hard,' he said, in a tone of voice that indicated he didn't want to talk about it any more. Rosie followed him quietly out into the dairy, a large, bare concrete area.

He picked up two plastic-capped water bottles, went to a large silver-metal vat and ladled them full of dense, freshly churned cream.

'No charge today,' he said. 'But bring back those plastic bottles or else Mrs Isitt will have my guts for garters. And she will too.'

Rosie nodded. 'But how do I get back up the hill?' she asked.

Jake laughed. 'Get a pedal on, girl,' he said.

'That is simply not possible,' said Rosie severely. 'You are kidding.'

'Fine,' said Jake. 'I'll send the helicopter.'

'*Jacob!*' came a shrill voice from outside the barn. 'Are you getting on with that silage?'

'I have to go,' said Jake. 'Bye now!'

And he left Rosie standing there with her bottles of cream, feeling more than a little dazed by the country life she'd expected to find so dull.

The bike was absolutely fine, and someone had picked it up and propped it on the side of the barn. There was no one to be seen. Rosie looked longingly at the Land Rover parked outside the austere-looking farmhouse, but there seemed to be nothing else for it. She started to push the heavy machine up the steep muddy track.

It took for ever. She was boiling hot, and incredibly thirsty and seriously pissed off and sick of being a laughing stock, and . . .

She hardly heard the Land Rover pull up beside her, till it honked loudly.

'OK, OK,' she said, trying to pull the bike off the muddy ruts to the side of the road. 'I'm moving! I'm moving! Bloody hell.'

Moray leaned out of the window. 'Need a lift?'

Rosie shook her head. 'I have this gigantic bike,' she said.

'Yes, uhm, I can see that,' said Moray. 'Sling it in the back.'

Sure enough, the Land Rover was about the size of a truck. Rosie tried to fling it in casually, but the damn bike swung round and knocked her on the shin. Muttering darkly, she manhandled it in upside-down.

'Tell me,' said Moray when she clambered into the front seat, 'are you always either soaking wet or covered in straw?'

'Have you always lived in a world of rain and mud, even when everyone else followed the industrial revolution and moved?' said Rosie. 'Look, it's clouding over again.' This was true. Ominous black clouds had appeared out of nowhere. 'How do they even do that?' Rosie complained.

Moray glanced at her as they continued bumping up the pitted track.

'Why are you here?' he asked. 'Is it some kind of alternative to prison?'

'Yes,' said Rosie. 'Well, I think so. It's not easy coming to stay somewhere new. Everyone thinks I'm some kind of city type that knows nothing about country ways.'

'Is that mud on your nose?'

'I don't care,' said Rosie crossly, looking to change the subject. 'How's that old man's hip? He didn't look too happy.'

'Week five,' said Moray.

Rosie squinted. 'He should be moving better than that. He's mobile, but he's obviously wincing.'

Moray glanced at her again. 'I agree. I think that old witch . . . I mean, his wife . . . is forcing him back into stuff he's not ready for. Jake helps out, but I think she's pushing it too far. A little exercise is good but I think she's got him on full-time hoofing, and it's not doing him any favours.'

'No,' said Rosie. 'Maybe if you drew up a plan? On official-looking paper, which mentions the word "insurance"? Those are always handy. And have a word with Jake, see if there's some way Mr Isitt could *look* as though he was working without actually having to move the wrong way?'

'That might work.' Moray was pulling up in front of Lilian's house.

'Hmm,' said Rosie. 'Thanks for the lift.'

She got out of the car. Moray helped her with the bicycle. 'Thank you,' said Rosie. 'Now I shall take it into the garden and ceremoniously burn it.'

Moray smiled. 'Actually,' he said, 'if you like . . . it's always useful to have a nurse's eye around the place. We have a district nurse, but she's quite frightening and marches about looking for things to vaccinate . . . Well, anyway, if you like, I could take you out on my rounds tomorrow. Show you around a little bit. To say thanks for your help yesterday. And for, well, inadvertently getting me to check in on Peter Isitt. He wouldn't come to the surgery in a million years.'

Rosie thought about it. 'OK,' she said. 'Will I get absolutely soaking and mucky?'

'Not normally,' said Moray. 'But seeing as it's you, I expect so.'

'What's this?' Lilian said, pushing at her soup with her spoon.

'It's more vegetable soup,' said Rosie firmly. 'With plenty of cream.'

'I would rather,' said Lilian, in a dignified fashion, 'have a tutti frutti.'

'Well, you can't,' said Rosie. 'You have to build up your strength. I think we need to get back to work on the shop. Formulate your way ahead for when I go back to London.'

'Hmm,' said Lilian. 'And when are we starting? Tomorrow?'

'Uh, no, not exactly,' said Rosie. 'Actually, uhm, the local doctor asked me out tomorrow. To, er, show me around. Show me how nice it is here.'

Lilian's eyebrows shot up. 'That young whippersnapper. Hmm.'

'What?' said Rosie. 'It's nothing. He's just being friendly. He's not after me. It's just friendliness, that's all. And I have a boyfriend.'

'So you say,' said Lilian. Rosie chose to ignore her. 'You'll get yourself a reputation in the village,' said Lilian.

'I think I'm doing that already,' said Rosie.

'I think you are too,' said Lilian primly. Then they lapsed into silence once more.

# Chapter Four

*You would have to be very ill indeed to consider a lozenge any kind of a treat.*

## 1942

THE CENTRE OF THE HALL *was, if anything, even hotter, and at first, among the excited faces and sparkling eyes, Lilian hadn't been sure she'd be able to spot him. Margaret was waving and smiling at people she even vaguely recognised, sipping her punch and whispering that she thought some of the hay boys had brewed their own beer, and should she try and get some for them. But Lilian said nothing, and had gone stock still, for there, in the far corner, engaged in what was clearly a serious chat, were two heads, one curly and brown, one blonde.*

*Lilian felt a furious flush start at her chest and climb up her neck, to the very tips of her ears. At that exact moment, Henry Carr looked up and saw her stricken face. No expert in the moods of women, he wondered what was wrong with her. Then, when he tried a cheery smile and received nothing in return, he wondered if it might be something else.*

'I'm just going out to get a breath of air,' Lilian managed to gasp to Margaret, who was already entertaining the affections of a young, very short soldier.

Ida Delia marched up to the party. 'Lilian,' she said, 'are you all right? You look very high-coloured.' Her voice was dripping with fake concern. 'It's not Henry, is it?'

At that moment Lilian knew that Ida Delia had set her cap at Henry precisely because she knew Lilian liked him. And what Ida Delia wanted—with her lovely green print dress with its tiny bird motif—Ida Delia got.

'I mean, there's nothing wrong? It's just every time you see us together you seem to go all queer!' She laughed a little tinkly laugh. 'Henry! Come and say hello to Lilian.' Ida Delia waved in a way that implied that Henry was her devoted slave, following solely at her whim.

'I'm just going out to get some air,' Lilian managed to choke out again.

Henry grinned at her optimistically. 'One dance?' he said.

Just then the ramshackle band struck up a fast-moving jitterbug.

'Oh no, I can't,' said Lilian, covered in humiliation. She had waited for him, was expecting him . . . but there was Ida Delia. She barely disguised the look she gave Lilian as Henry asked her to dance.

'Yes, you should dance with him,' she said to Lilian in a superior manner. 'He's a very good dancer. Could teach you a thing or two.'

Almost unable to say no, she let Henry take her by the hand and lead her to a tiny uncongested spot on the busy dance floor. Young red-faced soldiers still in heavy tweed trousers were jitterbugging furiously, trying to chat up ladies who were enjoying the unusual situation of being outnumbered.

Instead of attempting all the new moves, Henry simply took her in a dance hold and led her around, nimbly keeping to the rhythm. Lilian gradually found her body relaxing, as she let him lead her wherever he wanted to go.

Emboldened, he attempted a spin or two; she flunked the first one but managed the second, and suddenly felt herself swept up in the music; they hit every beat, and as Henry bent her back, both of them laughing into each other's eyes, she forgot, for possibly the first time in her life, to be self-conscious. She didn't worry about who was watching, didn't think about anything other than the person regarding her, twirling her around the floor. The brash bare bulbs overhead dissolved to shimmering chandeliers; the plank walls seemed hung with tapestries and thick plush curtains, her skimpy, dull dress a full, swinging gown. And her partner the handsomest, kindest, most charming prince she had ever imagined.

As the dance ended, their hands lingered, unwilling to let go.

Ida Delia of course was there, clucking over them like a mother hen. 'Well, there you go,' she said to Lilian. 'Did you enjoy that? I told you he was a good dancer.' She slipped her hand through Henry's arm like she owned him. 'Now come on, get me a drink,' she whispered to him.

Henry looked at Lilian askance.

Lilian was confused. After the way they'd danced . . . he wasn't going to let Ida Delia drag him off, was he?

**H**enry was confused too. This girl was all over him. All he wanted to do was dance more with Lilian. But even as he looked at her, she was retreating, with that anxious face again. When they'd danced, she had glowed; she had looked straight at him and it had felt . . . well, it had felt like nothing he'd ever felt before. But now she looked awkward, uncomfortable, as if she didn't want to be there with him at all. Even now, she reversed into a table full of half-discarded cups—and suddenly upended it, without realising.

Ida Delia erupted into high-pitched peals of laughter. Henry leaped forward to clean up the mess, and hush the expostulations of the soldiers who'd been sitting there. But Lilian, horror-struck, looked at the catastrophe, turned around and fled.

**O**utside, in the quiet and the coolness of the air, Lilian marched to the end of the field, past the already paired-off couples, until she reached the fence at the far end. When the music of the band had fallen behind her, she grabbed on to the wire and waited for her heart to slow down. She felt, for the first time, unbelievably and dramatically stupid.

The mess, the fuss. He must think she was such a fathead. Going all gooey over one dance, then making an idiot of herself. Looking at the huge stars dripping from the sky above her, she cursed herself over and over.

Then, even though she hated herself for doing it, she turned round. Just in case. Just in case he had seen her, and understood, and come after her. Like David Niven would have done.

There was nobody there. Not even Margaret.

Lilian rubbed furiously at the ridiculous rouge she had painted on her face, vowed never to come to a dance again, and went to find her bike.

By the time Henry had calmed everyone down, finished clearing up the spilt punch and gone into the field to find her, she was gone.

Rosie presented herself for inspection, her bouncy dark curls washed and hanging loose around her face, mascara, a touch of blusher to give her the pretty pink glow she was still waiting for the countryside to bestow on her, a black sprigged skirt and a black jumper.

'Can't you girls wear a bit of colour?' sniffed Lilian. 'So much more flattering to the skin. Look at me, for instance.'

It was true; today Lilian was wearing a lilac top underneath a very pale pink pinafore with heavy silver jewellery. It should, Rosie reflected, make her look like a four-year-old. Instead, the effect was charming.

'You look lovely,' said Rosie. 'Not sure it would suit me, though.'

Lilian harrumphed, as a hearty voice yelled out, 'Halloooo!' It was Hetty.

'Oh good, you're up,' she announced, taking off her gloves.

'How cold was it last night?' asked Lilian.

'A three-dogger,' said Hetty, incomprehensibly to Rosie's ears. 'Stick the kettle on, will you, toots?'

Rosie belatedly realised this meant her and jumped next door.

'Rosie has been getting up Roy's nose,' said Lilian.

'Oh good,' said Hetty. 'I don't hold with dentists anyway. Ridiculous bourgeois convention. When are you opening?'

'Well, our Rosie has got herself a date today, so she can't work,' said Lilian mischievously.

'I have *not*,' said Rosie, feeling her face go hot as she waited for the kettle to boil. 'And you're not having tea, by the way, you're having Bovril. And a peanut butter and banana sandwich.'

'I don't eat American things,' said Lilian. 'They were too late entering the war.' Rosie rolled her eyes and ignored her.

'It's that young Dr Moray,' said Lilian to Hetty. 'Taking her out in his car.'

'And you accepted?' said Hetty, looking amused.

'Yes!' said Rosie, suddenly cross. 'Because it's not 1895, and because I'm not fourteen. So you can mind your own business!'

Hetty and Lilian exchanged another look.

'Obviously you are not even vaguely like a fourteen-year-old,' said Hetty. Rosie stomped back into the kitchen to finish making the tea.

'Of course,' said Lilian, her voice carrying effortlessly through the cottage's thick stone walls, 'you know why he's asking her?'

'Oh yes,' said Hetty cryptically. 'Well, I wish them luck with that. But— and I know she's your niece—but. Really. I don't think so.'

'Why not?' demanded Rosie, furiously pink, as she set down the tray.

'Talking to us again, are you?' said Lilian.

'Oh, you'll find out,' said Hetty, as they heard a car horn honk outside.

'Tell me!' said Rosie, cutting Lilian's sandwich into small pieces.

'Well, I shall just wish you good luck,' said Hetty. 'I wonder if you can succeed where so many others have failed.'

'Are you going out like that?' demanded Lilian. 'You'll catch your death.'

Rosie was wearing a large cardigan. 'It's lovely outside! It's summer!'

Hetty sighed. 'You are never going to get the hang of this, are you?' She shook her head, then picked up her huge waterproof mackintosh with the flaps that came off the shoulders and made her look like a particularly hefty ruddy-cheeked velociraptor. 'Here, take this. It'll be pouring by eleven.'

Rosie stared at it. 'I can't take that.'

'Course you can,' said Lilian.

'I need a new coat,' muttered Rosie to herself.

'Yes, you do,' said Hetty. 'But until then, this will be perfectly adequate.'

'No!' said Rosie, struggling, but Hetty forced her into the enormous overcoat, which smelled of hay and dog. Rosie caught a glimpse of herself in the mirror above the fireplace. She looked like a murderous fisherman.

'I'm sure I'm . . .'

'Not a word,' said Hetty in a regal voice that brooked no argument. 'Off you go now!'

'And tell us everything when you get back!' pealed Lilian, who was obviously finding all of this hilarious, and the arrival of Rosie clearly some huge entertainment package on a par with Sky Plus.

**M**oray stared at the figure emerging from the cottage with that same twitch of amusement around his mouth.

'I'm sorry,' he said, leaning against his Land Rover with his arms folded. 'I was looking for a new girl. You, it is clear, have been here for generations.'

'Shut up,' said Rosie. 'It was Lady Lipton's fault.'

'That's her coat?' said Moray. 'She *is* grateful we saved Bran.'

'It's a loan. Can I take it off and put it in the back?'

'If you like,' said Moray. 'But it's going to hose it down in about forty minutes. You may want to keep it close by.'

'So, what's this in aid of?' Rosie said.

'Well, I thought you might like to ride along,' said Moray carefully. 'Show you a bit of the area and so on.'

'So you won't be needing my professional opinion?' said Rosie, smiling. 'What happens round here anyway? Goat bites?'

Moray raised his eyebrows. 'Well, let's get the morning calls out of the way first.'

They popped in on a heavily pregnant young woman who demanded to know if Rosie had children. When Rosie said she didn't, she ignored her. Then they went to see Anton Swinley, who had hurt his back in a lorry-driving accident six years before and since then had made it his life's ambition to become Britain's fattest man. He had fallen well short of that, but he still had various medical conditions, not least a skin fungus that was a lot easier to cope with when two people were attending to it.

Moray looked at Rosie, a tad guiltily.

'I've brought you lunch for later,' he said.

Rosie looked back at him. 'I hope it's not pork scratchings,' she said quietly, but readily put the rubber gloves on.

'Ooh,' Anton was saying, in a wheezy voice. Next to his bed was a large respirator that helped him sleep. 'You're going to reopen that sweet shop! I really love Lilian's sweet shop. Chocolate caramels . . . fudge squares.'

'Hmm,' said Rosie, scrubbing away. She didn't at all mind the unpleasant jobs—they were part of life. She did, though, slightly mind the hunky doctor having to see her in such unromantic circumstances. She wasn't looking for a man. Obviously not, she had a perfectly lovely man waiting at home. On the other hand, it would be nice to know that a man might perceive her as an attractive woman, as someone you might want to take out on a date. When she'd seen Moray—tall, handsome, humorous—leaning on his car that morning, her heart, however much she tried to deny it, had skipped. Just a tiny bit. Just because she was taken, she told herself, didn't mean she was dead.

Plus, also, it hardly mattered. It seemed more than likely that if you fancied someone, you wouldn't take them on a first date to scrub down a morbidly obese man's fungal skin folds. Yes. Pretty improbable. So. Nothing to worry about at all. She should try to stop sneaking peeks at his eyes, to see if they really were that amazing mix of blue and green.

'Doesn't your health visitor have a word with you about how many sweets you can eat?' Rosie asked.

Anton and Anton's wife, a surprisingly petite woman, both shook their heads. The fact that she was petite was slightly less surprising than that he had a wife at all, thought Rosie. Maybe the man shortage was even worse than she'd realised.

'Well,' said the wife tentatively, 'we watch those fat TV shows, don't we?'

'Yes,' said Anton, nodding his head. 'Yeah, we do. All of them.'

'But you don't think to do any of the things they say?' said Rosie.

'Oh yes,' said Anton.

'Yes,' said his wife. 'We're going to fill in the forms. They come and give you a haircut and all sorts of things.'

'Well,' said Rosie, 'even if you don't actually appear on the shows, I'm sure there's plenty of useful tips you could take from them.'

'Oh, I'll get on the show,' said Anton proudly. 'I had four bacon butties this morning. Four! That should do it.'

Rosie shot a look at Moray, whose face betrayed nothing. 'But if you followed what they say about fruit and vegetables and exercise, you wouldn't need to go on the show! You could move around much more easily instead!'

Anton looked confused, then glanced at his wife and back at Rosie again. 'Are you going to have violet creams when you reopen your shop?'

Rosie looked surprised. 'I hadn't thought of it. Do you think there's much call? Violet creams are a bit out of fashion these days.'

'Not with me,' said Anton. 'I love my creams, don't I, love?' His wife beamed proudly. 'Violets are the best, but I'm not that fussy really. Coffee. Raspberry.'

'I bet you do well at Christmas,' said Rosie. 'Loads of people hate them.'

'I know,' said Anton. 'It's my party trick.'

'What is?'

'I can tell you which Revel is which . . . without even touching them!'

'Wow,' said Rosie. 'Maybe we could get you down to the shop to do that!'

'Hmm,' said Anton.

'I'm serious . . . if you manage to get yourself together and walk down, we'll have a display event and people can bet against you. It'll be great.'

Anton's eyes lit up. 'That *would* be great. I could hustle them a bit, just to get them started. Mix up a peanut and a raisin.'

'Which is a rube's error,' said Rosie seriously.

'Right . . .'

Moray harrumphed and, as they finished up, handed over large bottles of emollients, with instructions to Anton's wife on how to apply them. 'This is the only cream I want you anywhere near,' he said, pointedly. 'Is it worth giving you this for the bath?' He was looking critically at a big white bottle of bath salts. The woman shook her head.

'Me in a bath?' said Anton. 'They'd never get me out again!'

He and his wife started to chuckle. They were still giggling as Moray and Rosie left the house, which did indeed smell of bacon.

Moray took the hilltop road. 'So we see one patient who's eating himself to death and you suggest he eats more?'

'I did not, in fact, suggest anything of the sort,' said Rosie. 'I dangled a carrot. OK, a carrot made of icing, but nonetheless. I have tempted him with something that involves getting out of the house. And getting out of the house is the first step in this. Trust me. I've worked on bariatrics. I've cleaned stuff out of crevices I thought was starting a new civilisation.'

Moray shot her a look. 'OK,' he said. 'Maybe you can *occasionally* be useful when I'm not digging you out of ditches.'

As they rose higher and higher the Land Rover clung to the road, effortlessly cresting the switchbacks and steep gradients. Now the clouds had cleared away, Rosie could take a proper look around at where she'd ended up. At the very top of the crags, Moray stopped. The road was deserted.

'Spot of lunch?' asked Moray, and they both got out of the car.

There was no denying it: it was stunning up here. The grey sky was broken with weak beams of sun; shadow and light passed through the valleys and over the softly rolling moors, all divvied up by ancient stone walls so it looked like a gently shaded eiderdown, with the oranges and greens and browns merging into one another.

Sheep were dotted around, but all Rosie could hear was the caw of a circling bird; in fact, she felt as if she were seeing the landscape the way a bird would see it, without human concerns. Except that over in the far corner, tucked under the next set of hills, was a magnificent mansion. It stood four-square, with a tower on each corner, as if just waiting for Mr Darcy to roll up. It was extraordinary.

Sitting down on a boulder, Rosie felt all the stresses of the morning slowly melt away. Silently, Moray held out a bottle of water and a package of waxed paper. Inside was thick white crusty bread, filled with rare cold roast beef and a smear of mustard, with sliced tomatoes on the side.

'I picked it up in the village,' he murmured.

Rosie thanked him, bit into a sandwich and stared out at the view. 'This is gorgeous.'

'Well, say what you like about Phyllis, she does make a good sandwich,' said Moray.

'No, I mean, this . . . all this.'

Rosie indicated the brown and green and gold of the world beneath her feet and pointed to the mansion. 'Is that . . . is that Hetty's place?'

'Do you mean Lady Lipton?' said Moray, sounding amused.

'Uhm, yes. I probably will go back to calling her that now I've seen it. How could you *live* there? There's like a million rooms.'

Moray smiled. 'I think she only lives in a little bit of it. Rents the rest out for weddings and film shoots and so on. She opens it up from time to time, especially the gardens. She has to, I think. It must cost a fortune to run. She's probably skinter than you.'

'I'm not sure that's possible,' said Rosie, heaving a sigh.

'What?'

'Oh, nothing. I just need to get it together to sell the shop. Quickly.'

'Well, that'll be good, won't it?'

'Yes,' said Rosie. 'Yes it will.' She looked at the big house again. 'Wow. Is it just her?'

There was a long pause. Then Moray changed the subject. 'I wonder, can I ask you something of a favour? My next patient.' For the first time, Moray looked slightly unsure of himself. 'My next patient. He's proving a little . . . intractable.'

'I don't know what that means,' said Rosie. 'Has he got a gun?'

'I don't think so,' said Moray, then looked worried, as if this possibility had never occurred to him. 'I hope not. God. No. No, definitely not. He's just . . . he keeps refusing treatment. And all three of us from the surgery have been up there and he hasn't really wanted to see any of us. So I wondered if . . . possibly . . . a fresh face might clear the way a bit.'

'What's wrong with him?'

'Actually,' said Moray, 'why don't you tell me what you think? Once you're inside, just tell him we're going to take a look at it, then call me.'

'There's no mobile phone signal up here,' said Rosie.

'No, *call* me. "MORAY!" You know.'

Rosie swallowed. 'I'm not sure about this. Is he violent?'

'No!' said Moray. 'No, no, nothing like that. I'm sure. No. No. And you're very brave, I saw that with Bran.'

'Am I in more or less danger of being bitten?'

'It's just five minutes,' said Moray. 'Till I can get through the door. I wouldn't ask if we weren't . . . a bit desperate.'

They got back in the car. There was a long drive down a heavily wooded track, where the trees blocked out much of the light. When the Land Rover emerged into the open, Rosie found herself looking at a road that led to the edge of a cliff. At the end, perched right at the top, and absolutely deserving of its name, was Peak House.

At first glance, Rosie thought it was indeed from a fairy tale: the giant's castle. It was a flat-fronted edifice of grey local stone; its forbidding aspect stopped it from being beautiful. It was a little too large, with rows of sash windows, unlit, facing into the late afternoon, where the sun was already leaving and a chill wind had begun to blow. Rosie stepped out of the car. 'You just stay there and enjoy yourself,' she said.

'You just get us inside,' said Moray, 'with your exceptional charm. I'll be, uh, right behind you.'

Rosie stuck her tongue out at him and trudged towards the huge front door. There was a bell, a proper old-fashioned clanging one, by the door. She couldn't be meant to pull that, could she? Tentatively, she knocked. There was no answer. He could be very deaf of course.

'Hello?' She tried cautiously, then louder. 'Hello?'

No response. There was nothing for it. She gave the bell pull a tug. The ringing erupted; in the silence of the high hills, it was deafening.

Still no reply. Rosie started to worry. This did happen on the job, of course—sometimes old people, left alone too much, with no friends or relatives living close by, simply fell asleep in their armchairs and never woke up again. The older nurses who came to give lectures would tell them horror stories—of bodies fused to sofas, of terrible decomposition. It couldn't happen to her, though; Moray wouldn't let it. Surely?

Telling herself not to be so stupid, Rosie pushed at the door. Sure enough, it wasn't locked. She sniffed, tentatively. No scent in the air apart from a little dust. Well, that was something. Unless, of course, there was already a skeleton.

'Get a *grip*,' she said to herself, out loud. 'HELLO! HELLO!'

Nothing. Rosie took a step into the building. 'HELLO!'

The first door on her right revealed a large sitting room with two high-backed chairs around an empty fireplace, but apart from that, no signs of human habitation at all. She closed the door and reversed back into the hall. She marched forward, past the staircase and on towards the back of the house. Rosie pushed open the door. Facing away from her was the silhouette of a man, sitting stock still. All the breath went out of her body. As she gasped, staring at the form in front of her, suddenly it twisted round and let out a high-pitched yelp of its own.

'GRRRAAAAARGH!'

For a second, they stared at each other, paralysed with fear. Finally, some oxygen made its way to Rosie's brain, and she understood that she was looking at a) a person, b) a living person, c) quite a young person, not entirely ugly, as it happened, and d) it was wearing headphones.

As her brain computed this, the man, looking shaken, took the headphones out of his ears.

'Who are you?' he said, incredibly loudly. 'And what the *hell* are you doing in my kitchen?'

Rosie was shaken up. She gave him a Paddington Bear hard stare, but it had absolutely no effect at all; he was still staring at her furiously.

'Oh,' he said finally, his eyes on her bag. 'What are you? Some nurse?'

'I'm not some nurse,' Rosie said, trying to recover herself. 'I'm here to help. And I stood outside for half an hour ringing your bell, actually.'

He glared at her. 'Why didn't you come round the back door?' he said, indicating a glass half-door at the back of the kitchen.

'Because I'm not looking for a job as an under-housemaid,' Rosie said. 'I didn't know where your back door was.'

'You're very grumpy for a nurse,' said the man.

'Auxiliary nurse,' said Rosie.

'Oh well, that explains it,' said the man sarcastically.

'*And* you yelled at me,' Rosie said.

The man rolled his eyes. 'I reserve the right to yell at anyone who materialises in my kitchen. You're lucky I didn't throw a golf club at you.'

'Yes, that's what I feel right now,' Rosie said. 'Really, really lucky.' They looked at each other. 'I'll just go get the doctor.'

'That spiv?' said the man. 'Get lost.'

Rosie raised her eyebrows, and stuck Moray's bag up on the scrubbed kitchen table. She'd brought it in for him just in case.

'OK,' Rosie said, 'let's take a look at you. Stephen . . . can I call you Stephen?'

'As opposed to what—Patricia?'

Rosie looked up at him. He hadn't moved out of the chair to greet her. Behind him, leaning up against a kitchen range that was blazing merrily, was a walking stick. He had very broad shoulders and a large head, with a thick brush of black hair. His eyes were a surprisingly bright blue, given the blackness of his hair. He was sitting upright, and she noticed that his left leg was set out at a stiff angle, held away from the rest of him.

'So, it's your leg,' Rosie said, taking out her blood pressure gear.

'Good work, Sherlock,' said Stephen. 'Actually, it's fine. Don't worry about it. I don't need anyone to come in any more.'

'Really?' Rosie said. 'What happened to you then?'

Stephen snorted. 'You can tell *you're* new around here.'

'How are you finding getting around?'

'I'm entering the Olympic gymnastics,' said Stephen. 'Honestly, I'm fine. Tell that horse's arse Moray he can stop these visits.'

Rosie gave him a look.

'Could you make me a cup of tea please?'

'No,' said Stephen rudely.

'Well, could you get me a glass of water please?'

'The glasses are in the cupboard behind you.'

Rosie stared him out. With a heavy sigh, eventually Stephen pulled himself out of his seat. Rosie watched him closely. His arms were heavily muscled. It was patently obvious how he was getting around, and it wasn't by using his leg. One leg was significantly thinner than the other. Stephen lugged himself to the cupboard.

'It's all right, I've changed my mind,' Rosie said. Stephen looked at her crossly, but it was with clear relief that he dropped back into the chair.

'Are you going to let me take a look at it?'

'No.'

Rosie made some rapid notes on a piece of paper.

'What are you writing down?'

'Well, I'll need to tell Moray to set up a plan for when they have to do the amputation.'

'What are you talking about?' said Stephen. 'It's fine. It's OK. I'm OK.'

'You're nowhere near OK,' she said. 'You won't even let me see it, you won't put weight on it, I see no evidence that you're doing your exercises, and you're clearly depressed.'

'I am not depressed.'

Rosie snatched up his iPod. 'Leonard Cohen? This Mortal Coil?'

'So is that what they teach you at nursing university? Diagnosis by pop music?'

Rosie looked around. The kitchen was clean and tidy, at least, and a lingering scent of toast hung in the air.

'Who's feeding you?'

Stephen shrugged. 'Mrs Laird comes in.'

'And apart from that you're here all alone?'

'I like it. Look, nursey, I don't mean to be rude, but could you go now, please?'

'I am *at least* going to check your blood pressure.'

Rosie came round and took his left arm, which was extremely muscular. She fumbled a little as she did it, nervous around his truculence and aware that she was off her turf. Stephen said nothing, sitting as still as a statue. Rosie was peculiarly aware of him so close up.

She checked the dial: ninety over sixty. Low.

'Well, that's fine.'

'Thank you, nurse,' said Stephen.

'What about physio?'

'Yeah, yeah, yeah.'

'Sleep?'

For the first time, when he paused, Rosie glimpsed a crack in his armour. His voice, which before had sounded confident, faltered a little.

'Uh. I . . . I never sleep at all.'

Rosie looked at him, then made a few more notes on her pad.

'What's that for?'

'You'll see,' Rosie said. She packed her kit away.

'You're going now?'

'Yes. But I'm coming back.'

'Don't.'

'Well, either I'm coming back or the ambulance is, when they have to take that leg off after all because of neglect.'

Stephen looked her straight in the face. 'Nurse . . .'

'Rosie,' she said firmly.

'*Rosie*,' said Stephen. 'You know nothing about neglect. Believe me.'

Then he picked up his iPod again, clicking it round and round like a sullen teenager and refusing to look at her.

Rosie felt in her pocket and withdrew a large pink-striped paper bag of cola cubes she'd brought with her from the shop in case she met any recalcitrant children. Clearly, she had. She left it sitting on the table.

Moray was hovering anxiously outside the car. 'Can I come in?'

'Uhm, probably not,' said Rosie.

'You were in there for ages!' said Moray. 'You've done better than anyone else has. Better than me, better than Hywel.'

'I didn't really get anywhere,' said Rosie. 'His blood pressure is low though. Unhappily so.'

'He let you take his blood pressure?'

'Sorry, I know I shouldn't have.'

'No, no, that's fine. That's great.'

Moray lapsed into silence as they bumped down the hill and Rosie reflected on what she'd just seen. This Stephen Lakeman was obviously in all kinds of pain, only about 20 per cent of it physical, she reckoned, but the most crucial thing was getting someone in to take a look at that leg.

He couldn't be up there all by himself, could he? Who lived like that? Where were his family? His siblings? His girlfriend? 'What *happened* to him?' she asked out loud.

'God knows,' said Moray. 'Turned up with an injured leg, missing notes and an absolutely furious refusal to engage with anyone anywhere who might possibly be able to help him. Something about a military hospital.'

'So?'

'If you ask me,' said Moray, 'I reckon the silly bugger blew himself up by accident and is too embarrassed to tell anyone.'

Rosie couldn't shake it, lying in bed that night. It was as if her not-a-date with Moray had sent her head bursting, because now, ludicrously, she found she couldn't stop thinking about Stephen Lakeman. She wondered if his behaviour was just what people did up here. Where life was more old-fashioned, maybe they had more of the stiff upper lip. Look at her

252 | Jenny Colgan

great-aunt. So bottled up, so cross. Obviously a bit of a beauty in her day, there was no way she hadn't had intrigues, hadn't had romance in her life. But did she ever mention it? Never. It was all locked up and she had thrown the key away decades ago, and if this boy didn't sort himself out, the exact same thing might happen to him.

There was still no mobile signal. Rosie cursed, then remembered that there was a telephone next to her bed. It was a lovely old thing, and she'd assumed it was just an ornament, but as she picked it up she could hear the hum. How, she wondered, had people ever been able to dial all these numbers? It took half an hour; her fingers kept slipping off the keys. Eventually she got through and it rang. And rang. And rang.

She tried another number.

'Yes?' said Mike. She could tell straight away this wasn't a good time. His partner Giuseppe was muttering crossly in the background.

'Don't tell him it's me,' she said quickly. 'He hates me.'

Mike snorted. 'He hates everyone. Because you hate yourself! *Perche mi odio!*' he hollered away from the phone. The flood of invective continued, only slightly muffled. 'Uhm, yes?' he said.

'Never mind,' said Rosie quickly. 'Just . . . have you seen Gerard about?'

There was a tiny pause.

'Well, yes,' said Mike eventually.

'Oh,' said Rosie. 'How's he looking?'

'You really want to know?' said Mike warily.

'Yes,' said Rosie, suddenly feeling fearful. 'What is it?'

'Well, OK,' said Mike. 'He was looking . . .' Mike searched for the words carefully. 'He was looking . . . ironed.'

There was a long silence.

Rosie sighed. 'Oh,' she said.

'I know,' said Mike, to the accompaniment of a door slamming.

'I can't . . . I mean, I really thought . . .'

'I know.'

'I can't believe he's moved back in with his mum. *I just left.*'

'She's got him tucking his shirts back in.'

They were both quiet. Mike loved Rosie and didn't want to rub it in by talking about it.

'Sometimes,' said Rosie, 'sometimes I wonder . . . if he can't look after himself, he's never going to want to look after me, is he? Or . . .'

'I'm sure he was just hungry,' said Mike, optimistically.

'Yes, for fish fingers and beans done just the way he likes them with lots of ketchup in front of Formula 1,' said Rosie. 'Bollocks.'

Mike started to get a bit twitchy. 'Listen, I'd better go after Giuseppe . . . you know what he's like.'

'He's crazy,' said Rosie. 'But at least he doesn't live with his mother.'

'She's even worse,' said Mike. 'Chin up, sweets.'

The next morning, still cross, Rosie took to scrubbing with a gusto that would have surprised Angie very much if she'd seen it: taking apart the glass cabinets and washing them, removing every sticky smudge and trace, until they were restored to a pristine condition. She threw away boxes and boxes of sweets that were past their best.

The hard manual labour, accompanied by the radio, actually worked a little to up her mood; the day was warm and fine and about lunch time she was considering trying to figure out where Moray had bought that sandwich, when she heard a noise and turned round. Coming up the road into the village was a large party of people, starting with a coach pulled by horses and a huge crowd around it. Rosie stood up to get a better look.

It was a wedding party, most of them on foot, surrounding the coach and horses. In it sat a girl, her dress long and elegant, like a thirties tea dress, and long blonde hair tied back simply with flowers. She was very, very young to Rosie's eyes—early twenties. She sat between her parents: the father bald and wearing a ridiculous top hat, his face one huge smile, and the mother, anxious in fuchsia. Behind, Rosie could now see, was a smart Rolls-Royce, containing grandparents and older members of the party.

People came out of their houses to watch and shout good wishes, car horns honked, and the bells of the church started to ring out.

Lilian emerged too, slowly and stiffly, leaning on a stick. Rosie was delighted to see the stick. Accepting that she needed help was Lilian's worst problem.

'Look at this,' said Rosie.

Lilian looked at the procession, but her dark eyes seemed misty and unfocused. 'Yes, well, weddings. Overrated. Waste of time usually.'

'What do you mean?' said Rosie.

'Nothing,' said Lilian petulantly. 'Waste of time, that's all.'

**1943**

They all got their call-up papers in the end, all except the eldest sons, the ones who'd own the land. They got to stay, though many of them didn't want to, managing the land girls, the elderly workers, the itinerants. But nearly everyone else was off, one by one, household by household.

Margaret too was off to Derby, going to build munitions in a factory, boy-crazy and half mad with excitement. 'You should come,' she begged Lilian. 'You must! You know, there are bands playing every night of the week, and the Forces boys through all the time. It'll be parties and dancing, and we'll be earning our own money too.'

Lilian couldn't admit she was tempted. With the harvest over, the village had simply seemed to shut down, to get smaller and quieter as the pickers moved on and the men all left to go to war, and it was as if she was there by herself, tending what felt very much, at the age of seventeen, like a broken heart.

She'd seen Henry and Ida Delia together, of course. That was how it seemed to be now; the girl wouldn't let him alone for a minute. She'd pasted on a cheery smile when she'd seen him, and he'd looked confused, then been dragged away. He didn't come in the shop for sweets any more, she noticed. She missed him hanging around and teasing her. Still. That was then.

Yes, she was tempted. So she told Margaret she'd think about it, which Margaret immediately took as a yes, and started planning how they would room together, and find her a job at the same factory. And with the resilience of youth, Lilian found that she did have something to look forward to after all.

That was before the telegram.

When Tom, the wireless boy from the post office, was going through the village on his bicycle, hardly anyone could look at him, waiting till he had passed before they turned their heads to see in which direction he was headed, sighing in relief when it was not their road or track.

Lilian hadn't even noticed him stop by. She popped over at lunch time to have some dinner with her da, to find him, unusually, sitting at the kitchen table. He wasn't moving, or smoking, which was most unlike him. He didn't even turn his head when she entered.

'Da?' she said. When he didn't respond, even at the third time of asking, a cold grip of fear clutched at her, and she realised there was a feeling worse than seeing Henry Carr with Ida Delia at the dance. Far worse.

She spotted it immediately without quite realising what it signified—the ripped envelope, the typewritten sheet. Taking a deep breath, she felt herself go *suddenly faint and, conscious she was wobbling, grabbed on to the back of a chair, then sat herself down, feeling her vision narrow and her head grow dazed.*

*'Da,' she said again, but he still hadn't heard her. There was only one thing left to know: which? But she didn't even have to read the telegram. She knew. It wouldn't be Terence junior, so steady and thoughtful like her father. And it wouldn't be Gordon, the youngest, who was a rascal, a troublemaker, who always managed to get himself out of any sticky situation with a bright grin.*

*'Ned,' she said, as sure as she'd ever been of anything. Sweet, dreamy, easygoing Ned, with a smile and a kind word for everyone. It could only be Ned.*

*And sure enough, it was. Blown up by a mine on a road. They found out later from a man in the same platoon that he'd stopped to pick everyone some apples. So typical. So like him.*

*Everything in Lilian's life came before and after the telegram.*

*It amazed her constantly, later, that something as ridiculous as worrying what another girl thought about her could ever have caused her pain. She would never again care what anyone else thought, what anyone else saw. Because when you knew what life really was, what pain and tragedy could do to a person, then all the pettiness fell away and no one could tell you what to do, not really. Because anyone could go, anyone could die, anytime.*

*Lilian and her father never spoke of her moving to the city again. By contrast, neither Terence, who took advantage of soldier's tickets after the war and went back to college and became a successful accountant, nor Gordon, who moved to London and wheeled and dealed and eventually fathered four children, including his beloved youngest daughter Angela, could ever face living in Lipton again, with the constant echo of the boy who did not come home.*

Lilian seemed to come back to herself. 'It's Farmer Blowan's daughter. Taking up with a Romany man. He wasn't happy about that to start with, but he seems to have got over it now.'

Rosie watched, fascinated, as one of the children ran up to the coach with a huge knotted wreath of corn. The horses were stopped as the bride took it with grateful thanks, queen for a day.

'She hardly looks old enough to be getting married,' said Rosie, striving to keep the bitterness out of her voice.

Lilian shot her a look. 'What about you?' she asked her. 'Are you and your chap going to tie the knot?'

'Hmm,' said Rosie. 'We like things just how they are, I think.'

'Do you?'

'Yes,' said Rosie. 'We have a lovely time. Not tied down . . . we've got our freedom.'

'Oh yes? What do you do with all your lovely freedom?'

'Well, we go to the pub,' said Rosie, feeling a bit uncomfortable. 'And, you know. Out. To the cinema. But mostly we just like being at home and being together,' she said. 'You'll meet him soon. You'll like him.'

She hoped this was true. Lilian didn't seem to like a lot of people.

'Hmm,' said Lilian. 'Well. Anyway. She's twenty-two.'

'*What!*' said Rosie. 'Twenty-two is ridiculously young to be getting married. Good luck!' she called to the bride as she passed.

Impetuously, Rosie turned back into the shop and grabbed a box of cherry lips that weren't past their sell-by date. Running back out, she threw handfuls of the sweets into the crowd, and watched people laugh as the children dived and pounced on them, happy shrieks rending the air.

'Thank you,' mouthed the bride, and Rosie couldn't help but smile back, as the coach moved on. Lilian was giving her an old-fashioned look but she ignored it. 'It's marketing,' she hissed out of the corner of her mouth. 'That's right, opening up again soon!' she said bouncily out loud.

Rosie watched them go, her thoughts far away, until she became aware of a presence at about waist height. She looked down, into a very serious face with an old-fashioned haircut and steel-rimmed spectacles.

'I think you should know,' said the small boy, 'I didn't get any sweets.'

'Well, you weren't fast enough then, were you?' said Lilian. 'You'll know better next time.'

The boy and Rosie regarded each other. 'I can't bend down in case I lose my glasses,' explained the boy carefully. 'Well, Mummy thinks I lose them. Actually sometimes they are knocked off. On purpose. By bad boys.'

'That sounds terrible,' said Rosie, meaning it.

'Yes,' said the boy. 'Yes, it is.'

'Well,' said Rosie, 'here is a sweetie for you. And do you have any brothers or sisters?'

The boy shook his head.

'Oh. That's a shame. Well, would you like a spare one to give a friend?'

'My friend isn't allowed sweets,' said the boy. Rosie had an idea of what the boy and his friend might be like.

'OK,' she said. 'Just the one then.'

'Yes,' said the boy hesitantly. 'I think that would be best. Thank you very much for having me. Goodbye.'

He scampered off down the road.

'What a peculiar chap,' said Rosie.

'Some academic and his hippy wife,' said Lilian scornfully. 'They've pampered the bloody life out of him. He has a terrible time of it.'

'That's awful,' said Rosie. 'Well, I like him. What's his name?'

'Edison,' said Lilian, 'short for Edison, have you ever heard anything more ridiculous?'

'Ooh, I rather like it,' said Rosie.

Lilian peered through the shop door. 'Scrubbing up, are you?' Her tone was less peevish and sarcastic than usual.

'Yup,' said Rosie proudly. 'And I'm doing a stocktake.'

'What's that?' said Lilian, turning to go back indoors.

'It's . . . never mind,' said Rosie. 'And I'm going to need to see your accounts!' she yelled after the elegantly departing figure, who did nothing apart from wave a bony hand in response.

Several hours later, with Lilian napping again and the shop clean as a whistle, Rosie looked around her with some satisfaction as her mobile rang. She squinted at the unfamiliar number. 'Hello?'

'Nurse Rosie?' came the amused-sounding tones.

'Moray!' she said, pleased. 'What are you doing? If it's catheterisation, I'm really incredibly busy.'

'Nothing *quite* that exciting,' said Moray. 'Actually I was going to ask you another one of those special favours.'

The little road to Peak House looked more fairy tale than ever, with the first leaves littering the pathway leading up to the grey stone building. Moray drove round the side, honking the horn loudly.

'That'll sort him out if he's got headphones on,' he said. 'Now, use the kitchen door.'

'Why is everyone so frightened of this guy?' Rosie took the pills Moray had prescribed, as well as the page of written instructions.

'I'm not *frightened* of him,' said Moray. 'Apart from the fact that he shouts a lot and has a gun.'

Rosie raised an eyebrow at him.

'I'm not, honestly,' said Moray, laughing. 'Trust me. I did my training in Glasgow. Very little scares me.' His face turned serious. 'He's one of my patients and I'd like him to get well. And it seemed the other day that you might have been getting through to him. That is, he spoke to you.'

'Rudely,' added Rosie.

'Yes, but that's more than anyone else has had in a long time. I just wanted to borrow your skills.'

'You're a flatterer.'

'Plus, I think it was a good move with the sweets.'

Rosie smiled. She had a box of little fruit salads with her and she'd only chewed four so far, Moray two.

'Fine,' she said, 'if you swing by later and see Lilian. I know she won't make appointments, but she really does need checking out.'

Moray shook his head. 'It's amazing, you know. I become a doctor to help people and not one solitary bugger wants me anywhere near them.'

'OK,' Rosie said. 'I'm going in. And I'm armed.' She held up the sweets.

Moray smiled. 'You're a brick.'

'Just what girls love to hear. Keep the engine running.'

**R**osie went straight up to the kitchen door and hammered loudly.

'SWAT strike!' she yelled, then realised that shouting something like that was at best tasteless and at worst dangerous for someone who proba-bly used to be in the services, so she simply tried the handle. 'Stephen? We're here to check up on you.'

She needn't have worried about the noise. At first she got a shock. A man was lying with his head on the table. Rosie started forward.

'*Stephen?*' she repeated, and the head lifted from the table.

'Gah?' came out. Clearly disorientated, he stared at her through blood-shot eyes. His face was bleary and unshaven, and a half-empty whisky bottle and a dirty glass sat next to him on the wooden kitchen table.

'Now, now,' said Rosie, suddenly overcome by a wave of sympathy for this young wreck of a man. 'What's this?'

Rosie filled a glass of water at the sink and handed it to him. He drank it in one gulp and his eyes gradually began to focus.

'Stephen Lakeman,' said Rosie. 'This is getting out of hand.'

'Oh *God*. What do I have to do to get people to leave me alone?'

'Your physiotherapy exercises?' said Rosie tartly.

Stephen looked at her. 'Are you the one who's just turned up in the village, can't ride a bike and is flirting with all the local men?'

'I have no idea why they say the countryside is a hotbed of gossip,' said Rosie, huffing. 'And I am *not* flirting with all the local men.'

'Maybe that's why you're in my kitchen,' said Stephen wonderingly.

'No, it is not. I'm in your kitchen because I have some antibiotics for you and I need to make sure you take them.'

'How will that work then?'

Rosie took a look at the whisky bottle. 'How often is that going on?' she said softly.

Stephen gave her a challenging stare.

'Why? Planning on what to haul me off for first—leg rehab or booze?'

'I'm sure I can find somewhere that'll do both,' said Rosie.

Stephen held her gaze for a long time. His eyes were very blue and direct. Rosie looked around. Once again, the kitchen was tidy, with one plate in the sink and only the empty glass out.

'Mrs Laird looks after you,' she said. 'So obviously *some* help is OK.'

'Why are you here again?' said Stephen. 'Is this some volunteer programme for nosy people who like to be annoying?'

'What would you care?' said Rosie. 'Just drink another bottle of whisky; that will make it all go away.'

Stephen breathed a heavy sigh and glanced longingly at the kettle.

'Would you like a cup of tea?'

'Are you going to make me make it?'

Rosie weighed up the options. Ideally, he ought to make it. Anything that got him moving around was a good thing. On the other hand, the chance to talk to him a little, find out what was going on, might be better.

'I'll make it,' she said finally.

In fact, Stephen had to get up to go to the loo. She pretended to be busying herself at the sink, but watched him out of the corner of her eye. He was very thin, even though his frame was big. His navy T-shirt was hanging off him, his flat stomach visible as it flapped up. But though his torso looked young and taut, his gait was an old man's. It was pitiful to see.

Ten minutes later, with the tea brewing in a brown pot, Rosie had found fresh milk, a box of eggs and an unopened packet of bacon in the fridge. She lit the range, located a frying pan and started to cook up what she decided to call brunch. Stephen came back to find the kitchen warm and smelling good; Rosie turned round to see him scrubbed and looking a lot better, in a clean T-shirt, with wet hair.

'What on earth are you doing?' he asked.

'I was hungry,' said Rosie. 'I'm eating your food. You are quite at liberty to attempt to perform a citizen's arrest.'

Stephen sniffed. 'And is that all for you? Is that how you keep your sweet-shop-based figure?'

'Can we keep the personal remarks to your health please?'

'Sorry,' said Stephen, looking a bit sheepish, as if he'd overstepped the mark and knew it. 'There's nothing wrong with your figure. In fact . . .'

'*Ahem*,' said Rosie.

There was a silence while Rosie dished up two platefuls. The bacon smelled heavenly. She set down two huge earthenware mugs filled with strong tea. She saw Stephen look at it, weighing up his need to be ornery and difficult against his obvious hunger and a bit of a hangover.

'It's all right,' she said. 'I won't tell anyone that you lowered yourself to actually eating. I'll tell them you wouldn't talk to me and turned away and went boohoo in a corner.'

'Is that meant to shock me out of my latent depression?' said Stephen lazily. 'Congratulations. You're clearly an eminent psychiatrist. Why didn't I think of that?'

'No, it's meant to get you to eat your breakfast,' said Rosie.

Sighing heavily, Stephen sat down, carefully favouring his injured leg. He was being so stupid and bloody-minded, as if ignoring the problem would make it go away. She wondered idly if this was what having children was like, as she put her hand on his fork.

'But first,' she said, handing over the antibiotic.

'More pills?' groaned Stephen. 'You came all this way just to give me more pills?'

'No,' said Rosie. 'I came for your wit, charm and conversation. Now, do I have to make my arm into an aeroplane?'

Stephen looked longingly at his breakfast. 'No,' he said.

'Are you sure?' said Rosie. 'Bbbbbrrrrmmmm . . . bbrrm . . .'

'Stop it! Shut up!'

At first Rosie thought he was joking with her, then she realised, somehow, that he was genuinely distressed.

'Could you stop that noise please?' He pulled himself together, then quickly swallowed the pill and started to eat his breakfast.

Rosie sat back, staring at him. There had been genuine anger—no, fear, of course. Anger was just fear made loud. About what, her pretending to be an aeroplane? That was daft. And serious too. He needed help.

They sat in silence, eating. Stephen cleared his plate at rapid speed, then sat back swallowing his tea. No words were spoken till Rosie said, 'Thank you, Rosie, for the delicious breakfast.'

'Thanks,' mumbled Stephen. Rosie picked up the pills.

'One three times a day with meals,' she said. 'And you have to finish the packet,' she said. 'If you don't, it's pointless, and it makes antibiotics weaker and less likely to work. That means, now you've started the course, that you have to finish it, or you're basically killing future generations with invisible bugs.'

'Is that so?' said Stephen, with a twinge of his former sarcasm.

'Yes,' said Rosie. 'And also, it takes five seconds for infections to take hold in poor-healing wounds, of which you undoubtedly have one. And you don't want an infected wound. Because you will be spending months lying in a bed surrounded by old men telling you their prostate problems and coughing all night every night. I just don't think you would like it.'

Stephen sat still, and Rosie put the plates in the dishwasher. Then she picked up her bag. She got the feeling that, although he couldn't possibly articulate it, he would rather she didn't go—better a bossy, judgmental presence in his kitchen than no one at all.

Rosie turned towards him, just at the same moment as he turned towards her, and they found themselves in awkward proximity. It had looked like Stephen was about to say something, but instead Rosie took a step back and he stopped himself. So she leaned towards him instead.

'This . . . hiding up here,' she said, softly but clearly. 'It won't make it go away, you know. There are ways to make it go away, and I can help you with them, but you're going to have to reach out to somebody. At some point.'

Even as she said it, she didn't quite know why; after all, she'd be gone in a few weeks. Lilian was looking better already. Gerard needed her . . . Well, maybe not needed her exactly, but missed her. She missed her home. She needed to go home, not waste time here.

Anyway, it hardly mattered, as Stephen didn't bother to reply.

# Chapter Five

*There is no doubt about it, with the possible exception of rock, which is unpleasant in any case: peanut brittle is the worst killer as far as teeth are concerned. Which would be all right, if it wasn't such an average slice of confectionery. Its continued existence in a world of Reese's Peanut Butter Cups, possibly the only good invention to come out of America since the potato, remains a mystery. The crunchiness of the toffee is liable to send shards into the gums, while the peanuts root in between the teeth, attracting bacteria like a coral reef. Peanut brittle, as well as being slightly unpleasant, is probably responsible for more dental visits than any other sweet, with the possible exception of the molar-cracking gobstopper. Still, what is life without a little danger?*

## 1943

THREE DAYS AFTER THE TELEGRAM, the shop was still shut. The people of Lipton had been by, leaving pies and cabbages on their doorstep; letters and notes of condolence were arriving. Alerting Gordon and Terence was a horrible task made worse by an army bureaucracy that endeavoured to make it as difficult as possible. Finally, from the private phone box at the post office, she spoke to a kindly woman who promised to link her message through to Tripoli, where Gordon was stationed with a tank unit, but had less luck with Terence, shepherding the merchant fleet on the Atlantic, impossible to contact in any way.

After an hour, Lilian stumbled out into the street, shocked, suddenly, to find it the same as always: the same villagers going about their business, when she had been trying to connect to an entire world, a whole world in torment and disarray. Of course Lipton was affected by the war. They all were. But until now, it had been possible to carry on, to think about normal, everyday events.

Until now. Now everything was rotten and stupid and changed and no one appeared to be paying the least bit of attention. Didn't they know? Didn't they *know there was a war on and anyone could die and anything could happen, and everything was awful? Suddenly, in the middle of the street, without thinking how it would look, Lilian burst into heart-rending sobs.*

*Henry was the first to notice. He had seen her in the post office and had hovered, to see her when she came out. Ned and he had been in the same class at school. Henry had liked him without knowing him very well; he couldn't imagine how Lilian, who had already lost a parent, could cope with his loss.*

*And there she was, sinking to her knees in the middle of the square, passers-by looking uncomfortable at the sight of a young woman displaying emotion so publicly. Henry rushed forward, appalled that no one was looking after the girl.*

*'Darling,' he said, leading her away. 'Darling. Hush.'*

*Lilian barely knew who had picked her up or where they were going, till she found herself behind the churchyard, where the village shaded into the woods. She found herself on a shady knoll, underneath a huge spreading oak, away from the main street and the post office and the kindly but distant women doing their best on the far end of a telegraphic wire, and guns and mortars and sweet boys who got out of trucks at the wrong moment. She threw herself into Henry's strong arms, and wept and wept and wept.*

'So where have you been, fannying about all day?' said Lilian.

'Did you say fannying?'

'It's a perfectly normal word, thank you, been around for donkeys.'

Rosie boiled up the pasta and started grating the Parmesan cheese. Lilian was to get the larger portion. It seemed a bit unfair that her job at the moment seemed to be feeding everyone else up. And what had Stephen meant about her sweet-shop figure? Rosie knew she wasn't a supermodel, but men had always complimented her curvy hips and little waist, and liked the fact that she was short, even though she hated it.

So, anyway. Less pasta for her, more for everyone else. She hoped Lilian appreciated it, as she led the old lady to the table.

'Actually I've been seeing *yet another man*. All on his own! In his house!' said Rosie in mock-shocked tones. 'I am going to get a name for myself as the village tart. You will have to call the vicar in to give me a talking-to.'

Lilian snorted. 'He makes you look like Julie Andrews. Liberal vicars.'

'Why, what's he done?'

'What hasn't he done? Oh, it's all right, do this, disbelieve that, divorce that, marry your farmyard animal of choice.'

Rosie let her chunter on, as she served up the bolognese.

'Foreign food now, is it?' said Lilian.

Rosie was so astonished that someone would think pasta was foreign food that at first she couldn't figure out what her aunt meant. 'Hmm,' she said. 'Do you not really like foreign food then?'

Lilian sniffed. 'I have never,' she announced, in a tone that suggested she was about to discuss her Nobel prize, 'bought garlic in my life!'

'Well done,' said Rosie. 'Doesn't it grow out in your garden? Wild garlic is just amazing.'

'Oh yes, there's some. I usually throw it away.'

Lilian had already scarfed up half of her spag bol. Rosie, watching her, realised for the first time how difficult life must be when you couldn't even lift a pan of boiling water. How, even when Lilian was being rude to her, it was a million times better than having no one to talk to at all.

'So it's not *so* bad I'm here, is it?' she ventured.

'Well, as long as you're happy,' sniffed Lilian, letting Rosie inwardly roll her eyes and remind herself that Lilian pretending she was here for her own good was all part of her getting better.

Suddenly, out of the blue, the telephone rang. It was an old-fashioned ringer, and made a noise like a fire alarm going off. Rosie jumped six feet.

'Christ,' she said when she came down.

'Must be one of your admirers,' said Lilian. 'Darling, I know Angie didn't raise you in a barn. Where are the napkins?'

She leaned over and picked up the telephone.

'Lipton 453? Hello, Angela darling. We were just talking about you.'

Rosie picked up some napkins from Lilian's very tidy linen cupboard, eavesdropping shamelessly on the conversation with her mother.

'Yes, well, she seems to be doing all right,' said Lilian. 'She is slacking it up a little around the village, I will say. But young girls don't mind getting a reputation these days, do they? Positively welcome it.'

Rosie harrumphed loudly. Lilian affected not to have heard.

'So, all in all she's getting some colour back in her cheeks . . . It's obviously doing her good to get away.'

Rosie stopped short. What on earth did Lilian mean? As soon as she could, she wrested the phone away from her aunt.

'*Mu-um?*' she said.

'What?' said Angie.

'Did you tell Lilian I needed to get away from London?'

'Well, darling, I had to get her to accept some help, and—'

'But did you think I needed to get away from London?'

There was, suddenly, a tiny fraction of a pause. Rosie felt wobbly.

'No, no,' said her mother. 'It was just that Lilian needed someone. And you were between jobs. That was all it was. Definitely. That's all.'

'Are you sure?'

'Definitely,' said her mum.

'I mean, you like Gerard, don't you?'

Gerard and her mother had met many times over the years. He had been cute and flirtatious and delightful with her, just like he was with everyone. Everyone liked Gerard. Although Angie had seemed immune.

'This is a very bad line,' said her mother. 'Darling, Meridian needs me. I have to go now.'

True enough, a loud scream was making its presence felt.

Rosie handed the phone back to Lilian without complaint.

'OK,' she said. 'Bye.'

Sitting in the living room, trying to tune the ancient television, Rosie wondered what her mother had meant. Surely it was just a sop to Lilian, to let the proud old bird stand on her own two feet, think she was taking care of her rather than vice versa. That must be it. It must be. On the other hand, Rosie vowed, she was going to get Gerard to come and visit sooner rather than later. Then they could be back together, and still in love, and she wouldn't have to worry about a thing. Not that she was worried. Definitely not.

Distracted, Rosie hardly noticed the rap on the door. She got up, wondering if it was Hetty but, to her surprise, it was Jake.

'There you are,' he said.

'Well, where else would I be?' said Rosie.

Jake smiled. 'I've just finished work. So, come on. Saddle up.'

'I am *not* getting on that bicycle again,' said Rosie. 'No way.'

'You need milk for the morning, don't you?'

'No. I'll get it from the Spar. I do *not* want to run across Mrs Isitt again.'

'Oh, she's not so bad,' said Jake. Then he reflected. 'OK. She is very, very bad. But she's had a hard life.'

'Sitting in her big house drinking milk,' said Rosie. 'Yes. I see it.'

'No, more than that . . .' Jake's voice tailed off. 'Anyway, don't worry about that. You have to come with me now. We have stuff to do.'

'I'll get my coat,' said Rosie, resignedly.

Jake went easy on her to begin with—he was completely amazed to find out she'd never had a 'backie' before—and rode up and down the streets a few times to get her used to it. Rosie sat on the saddle, the wind in her hair, the sensation of travelling quickly exciting and new. She found herself starting to giggle, then laugh out loud as Jake went faster and faster, then taking the slope down to the Isitts' farm, gathering even more pace. Rosie tilted her head back and let out a happy yelp, amazed at herself— she certainly wouldn't have done this at home—war-whooping down the rutted track.

Jake dismounted safely at the bottom, grinning widely.

'Are you always that noisy?' he said. Then he looked embarrassed, as if he'd asked something cheeky. Which of course he had. Rosie was saved from answering by the line of garden instruments up against the wall.

'What are those for?'

'For us,' said Jake. 'You hammered Peter's vegetable garden. We have to put it back together. Or rather you do, but I figured if I left it to you you'd try sowing packets of crisps and chocolate cake and things.'

'Ooh, a crisp tree,' said Rosie. 'That's a wonderful idea.'

Jake didn't say anything, but handed her a hoe and gave her instructions on what to do with it. Together, in the fading sun of the day, they worked over the patch, raking it and setting it into tidy rows, whereupon Jake let her pop the seeds in—for cabbages, potatoes and purple sprouting broccoli—at regular intervals. After an hour, the entire patch looked much better than it had before.

As the two of them stepped back to admire their handiwork, the last rays of the setting sun alighted on a heavyset woman who was carrying out a tray from the house as if she held a grudge against it.

Mrs Isitt looked at the new vegetable patch, sniffed, then, without a word, set down the tray and turned back indoors. Jake inspected it. 'I think,' he said, 'that's her way of saying thanks.'

On the tray sat two foaming mugs of beer, and two plates with gigantic slices of buttered fruit-cake alongside a large pale-yellow hunk of cheese. Jake and Rosie sat down side by side on the edge of the grass.

'I don't think I'm going to like this,' said Rosie, picking up the tankard. 'I'm not really a beer drinker. More rosé.'

'More rosé,' he mimicked. 'Well, I am sorry, your majesty. I'll have yours.'

But then Rosie tried the beer—dark, not too fizzy, not too cold—and found it bitter and peculiar at first; by the third sip she was a convert.

'This is *gorgeous*,' she said.

'And about the same proof as a bottle of wine,' said Jake. 'Go easy on it.'

Rosie stuck her tongue out at him, took another long draught, giggled and sank her teeth into the melting, tangy fruit-cake.

'Oh God,' she sighed. 'I am going to get as fat as Mrs Isitt if I hang around here. This is amazing.'

Jake smiled and munched on his cheese. 'Maybe it's being outdoors.'

'Who eats cheese with fruit-cake?' wondered Rosie, then took another bite of cake, followed by another bite of cheese and a slug of the beer. 'Oh,' she said. 'Oh, wow.'

Jake took a long look at her.

'I think I'd better get you home,' he said. 'Before you start blundering around and muck up that bloody veg patch again.'

Up the hill, Rosie found pushing the bike hilarious for some reason, and when Jake dropped her off at the house she found herself inadvertently leaning on him.

'Whoops!' she said. Then she leaned in. 'But I have . . . I have a boyfriend, you know. He's not got as many muscles as you though.'

Jake moved away as if he'd been scalded.

'I didn't know you had a lad,' he said, scowling slightly. Then he looked at her. 'Why did you move here without your lad?'

'Uhm, it's only . . .' Rosie suddenly sobered up as she realised that what she had taken for daft flirting might have meant something more. 'Uhm, I'm not . . . I'm not here for very long.'

'Oh no?' said Jake. 'Well, maybe we can still have some fun then.'

'Oh . . . Oh.' Rosie was mortified. She hadn't expected her silliness to mean anything.

Jake was looking at her with a definite spark of interest in his eye. And there was no doubt, she thought regretfully, no doubt at all that he was absolutely gorgeous, blue-eyed and straw-haired and firm of muscles. If she took him to London he'd be snapped up by some long-limbed blonde-haired Chelsea clothes horse in about ten seconds flat. She was so used to there being no men around, or at least none she particularly liked or who liked her. She'd been single for two years before she met Gerard. She was out of practice. She smiled anxiously.

To her complete and utter horror, Jake reached out one thickly muscled arm and touched her face, gently drawing her towards him.

'What are you doing?' she spluttered. 'I have a boyfriend! I just told you about him!'

'Yes, in *London*,' said Jake, in the same way you might say 'in *Mars*'. 'Come on, lass, you're in the country now.'

'I very much am *not*!' said Rosie, scrambling backwards.

'Oh well,' he said. 'Worth a shot.' He winked at her.

Rosie's feelings changed from indignant to slightly peeved. 'And that was it? That was your shot?'

Jake shrugged. 'Well, I'm not going to kiss a girl who don't want kissing, am I?'

'It wasn't exactly romantic,' complained Rosie. 'You could show a bit of dedication.'

Jake smiled at her. 'Well, you know where to find me,' he said.

## 1943

*When there was no one, Lilian felt, to hold on to that autumn—the shop, all but closed, her father, sitting at the scrubbed kitchen table, staring into space— the house was a dismal place. And they had no body for burying, nor would they ever have, and no brothers home to mourn him.*

*Henry came away as often as he could from the farm, at lunch or in the evening, and let her lie there, her head on his shoulder or sometimes by his knees like a child, and weep till it was out. Then she could get on, and make supper, and try to get her father to eat, and sometimes—not often, but some- times—get some sleep.*

*One morning, just before the dawn, as she lay there trying not to think about Ned, sleepless, she heard the rattle of a little stone against her window.*

*As she jumped up, heart pounding, and went towards the front dormer, she saw in the early light a figure wearing brown canvas trousers held up with braces and a collarless shirt. His throwing hand held the back of his sunburnt neck, the other supporting his bike. Nothing else stirred in the village, except far away over the hills, where a kite circled lazily.*

He looked up at her with that heart-meltingly shy smile, and put his finger to his lips to shush her, then beckoned her down.

She dressed in an instant, throwing water from the ewer over her face and rinsing out her mouth, then put on her plain, old-fashioned day dress. She crept downstairs through the silent house.

Henry refused to accept her demurral, insisting, all the time in silence, that she get on the bike seat. Worried that someone would see her creeping out of the house, Lilian couldn't do much else but spring on.

He pedalled off in the direction of his farm. The early-morning mists of the dew ascending turned the village and the fields beyond into something out of a dream, as if they were moving through the clouds. As the bike picked up speed downhill Lilian exhaled and felt the tension leave her, if only for a moment.

'All right now,' said Henry, as they clattered to a halt. 'Here. I have to pen them this morning, they need marking. But I have a problem.'

Lilian looked at him, uncomprehending.

Henry whistled, and Parr, his dog, shot out of one of the distant outbuildings like a black and white flash.

'Come by, Parr,' said Henry. With another two short whistles, Parr bounded off to do his duty, Henry about to follow him.

'Why do you need me?' asked Lilian, timidly.

Henry took a bottle of frothy warm milk from his pocket. 'We've got one . . . She was very late,' he said. 'Her mother got caught on the wire. Bloody stupid buggers, sheep. Tore her own bloody throat open. And the little one . . . she's not adapting well. Needs a bit o' help.'

Sure enough, Lilian could see, just up the hill, that as the sheep trotted along in unison to Parr's practised manoeuvres, there was one lamb, small for the time of year, trailing behind, its nose practically on the ground. Lilian nodded. 'All right.'

'It will take all day to round them up otherwise,' said Henry.

But he didn't need to explain himself. Lilian understood, as she picked up the little lamb. She sat on a rock in the corner of the field and waggled the teat of the bottle under the lamb's nose. At first it struggled, anxious and frightened. Then it caught the scent of the milk, and sniffed, nervously. Its little body felt heavy and warm in Lilian's arms, its white fleece still soft. Finally, the lamb figured out what to do, and she felt its entire body relax as it grabbed hold of the teat and started sucking vigorously, and Lilian held it close as the sun came up, and the lamb drank the bottle, and Henry and Parr got on with their day's work up the valley, and she felt, if not happy, then a tiny modicum of peace.

**R**osie was whistling. She couldn't help it. She'd woken up bright and early, and it was a glorious day. But more than that, yesterday she'd had her first delivery for the shop. And today she was unpacking it all. The smell was light and rosy, with tinges of mint and lavender, fruit and sweet caramel escaping through the shop. With the freshly cleaned windows, the sun shone straight in on the new, brightly polished jars, ready to be filled with humbugs and jujubes and cola cubes. There were long red liquorice laces, to be pulled out two at a time, and striped candy canes, even though they were a bit Christmassy. Rosie felt strongly that you couldn't call yourself a sweet shop if you didn't have striped candy canes.

'**A**nd,' Angie had been relentless, 'you've got to have a business brain. Any buyer is going to want to see profit-and-loss accounts, all of that.'

Rosie had shaken her head in disbelief.

'*Angie!* You sent me up here for, and I quote, "a couple of weeks looking after the old lady". Now you're telling me I need to apply for *Dragon's Den*.'

'There is not a man on *Dragon's Den* I don't fancy,' said Angie dreamily for a minute. 'Anyway, think about it. Of course you have to know how the business works.'

And she had explained, rather well, in fact, how the business should run: what percentage Rosie should spend on stock, what the difference was between turnover and profit, how much stock to hold. Rosie ended up grudgingly taking notes. At last it started to make a bit of sense.

'Angie,' asked Rosie finally, after she'd been listening for an hour. 'You know when you were working your head off when me and Pip were little and we didn't have much money and stuff . . .'

'You never went short,' said Angie.

'I know! You were amazing! I didn't even realise at the time! I liked getting toothbrushes for Christmas. Anyway. All I wanted to ask is, Lilian here . . . I mean, she doesn't really have anyone to spend money on. Did she ever . . . I mean, well, I suppose she was busy and everything, but . . .'

'Did she ever help us out? Is that what you're asking?'

Rosie shrugged. 'I mean, it doesn't matter, I mean, everyone's busy.'

'Of course she did,' said Angie, softly. 'We'd never have made it through without her, and your granpa. All the Hopkinses. That sweet shop kept us afloat for years.'

Now Rosie looked around approvingly. There was Edinburgh rock in its pretty pastel dustiness, and Turkish delight by the pound set out in the glass display cabinet next to the violet creams and chocolate truffles. Rosie had started off very small on the expensive handmade chocolates though, and had bought some tiny boxes in case people just wanted to try one or two. She wasn't sure how big the market would be here. Whereas who didn't want rainbow drops? Or raisin fudge, or cream-whipped caramel chews? She kept whistling, happily, as she donned her new apron.

She'd persuaded Lilian it was an essential shop purchase, after Lilian had offered her a clean, soft, but obviously very old white one. This apron was chic, stripy and brand new, and Rosie kept admiring it.

Humming cheerfully, she tidied the boxes away neatly, making final alterations so that all the jars stood equidistant in a row, their labels facing outwards. She'd kept Lilian's original scales, polishing them up with Brasso till they absolutely gleamed. She'd kept the antique till too but had also found a cheap electronic one secondhand. She'd hidden it behind the counter, hoping to keep the illusion of the original sweet shop intact. At last, she'd done as much as she could do. The whole place was gleaming and it looked like a set from a period drama, or something out of *Harry Potter*. It was, to her eyes, utterly beautiful. She sighed with satisfaction.

'Lilian?' She knocked on the cottage door before she went in. 'Lilian? Do you want to come and see something?'

Lilian was dozing, slightly irritably, in her blanket. Rosie didn't want to wake her up, but she was stirring.

'What? Why are you always shouting at me?' Lilian squinted.

'Come on. Give me your arm.'

Grumbling and reluctant, Lilian got up. She leaned on Rosie heavily as she left the house. Rosie had borrowed a stick from Moray but was having almost no joy in getting her to use it.

Rosie led her next door. She had refurbished the bell that hung above the door, scrubbing and polishing it with Brasso, and now it dinged out cheerfully. When she heard it, Lilian exclaimed despite herself. Then as she walked forward into the new, shiny sweet shop, she stopped dead.

'*Oh*,' she said, hands grasping a shelf to keep herself upright. '*Oh*.'

Rosie watched the colour drain from her great-aunt's face and redoubled her efforts to support her.

'What . . . what's the matter?' she said. But all Lilian could do was point around her.

'But,' she said, gasping for breath and leaning perilously, 'this is . . . this is just how it was then. Just how it was.'

When Rosie had got her back, as fast as she could, and into bed, and made her some restorative tea with three sugars, she found Lilian sitting up, staring into space.

She sat down on the edge of the covers. 'Are you all right?'

Lilian's eyes seemed a thousand miles away.

'It hasn't . . .' Her voice was tight and high. 'It hasn't looked like that . . . in a long time.' She shook her head. 'Just . . . just seeing it again. I haven't really seen it . . . I haven't really been there for . . . maybe a while.'

'Yes, I'd gathered that,' said Rosie.

'It brought a lot of things back,' said Lilian. She had been thinking of a hot summer's day, with clean, gleaming windows, when the bell had dinged and in had walked a mop of brown curly hair. 'Someone I know,' Lilian said, 'who used to come into the shop. And when he did, the bell would ring.'

'Ooh,' said Rosie. 'Intrigue! A man! Tell me everything!'

But Lilian just looked tired. 'I think,' she said, 'I had better have a rest.'

'All right,' said Rosie, 'but I am waking you up very shortly. You can't snooze the day away. It makes the nights too long.'

'My nights,' said Lilian as Rosie closed the door, 'are always too long.'

Rosie wondered about Lilian all that afternoon, as she handmade traditional leaflets to distribute round the village, advertising the reopening of the shop and 20 per cent off all first-day purchases. After all, Lilian had kept the fact that the shop was closed a secret from all of them for years. How many other secrets did she have? And it was mad to think you could get as old as Lilian and not have had at least some intrigue. She had obviously been quite glamorous. Never left the village, so there must have been someone there.

Aha, she thought, smiling at the sight of the doctor's surgery. The door to the large house was opened by a distracted-looking receptionist. 'Can I ask you to put a few leaflets out?'

Hearing her voice, a mop head popped round one of the surgery doors.

'I thought that was you,' said Moray.

'Hello!' said Rosie.

'Have you come to join the surgery?' asked the receptionist.

'Oh no,' said Rosie. 'I'm perfectly healthy.' Moray raised an eyebrow. 'And I'm not staying. I just wanted to put out a few of these leaflets.'

Moray took them. Rosie's spinster calligraphy teacher of long ago would have been delighted to know that he was actually quite impressed.

*Come to the grand reopening of*
*Hopkins' Sweets and Confectionery*
*. . . no request too small . . .*
*20% off on our grand reopening day!*

There followed a list of sweets, and the promise that everything would be served with a smile, and a special gift for the first fifty customers.

Moray looked at Rosie sternly. 'Rosalind,' he said.

'It's Rosemary actually,' said Rosie.

'Really? I prefer Rosalind.'

'OK, Morgan.'

Moray gestured round the waiting room, which held lots of old toys and magazines and, on the walls, many bossy posters.

'What do these say?'

Rosie glumly looked at a poster of an apple and an orange wearing training shoes, bearing the slogan *We love fresh stuff.* Next to it was a picture of a child lying on the sofa playing computer games with the caption *Choose an early death—do nothing.*

'Cor,' said Rosie, 'it's very perky round here. No wonder everyone is miserable and sick, staring at those half the morning.'

'Hmm,' said Moray. 'So you don't think there'd be any conflict of interest in us stocking your leaflets?'

'But these are just sweeties!' said Rosie. 'They're not made of scary trans fats. We don't have to give away free toys to get the kids coming back. They're just sweets! A treat, not their bloomin' breakfast! Look,' said Rosie, taking out her pen. 'What about this?'

On the bottom of a leaflet she quickly scribbled, *And don't forget to eat your five fruit and veg a day too!*

'That's like people who tell you to drink whisky responsibly,' said Moray. 'You do have to wonder if someone isn't taking the piss.'

'Well, I think you're very not helpful towards a local enterprise,' said Rosie. '*And*, you know, if the business works well it will be good for the village economically and, as everyone knows, the better off everyone is, the better their health is. So actually it would be making Lipton healthier.'

'You're wasted in sweets,' said Moray, 'when you should really be in epidemiology.'

'Yeah,' said Rosie.

'Well,' said Moray. 'I might take a few, with your fruit and veg waiver, thank you. If you do something for me.'

'Is it what I think it is?' said Rosie, with a twitch of an eyebrow.

'No,' said Moray. 'It's to go and see Stephen Lakeman again. You're the only one who seems to be able to get any sense into him.'

'That is *exactly* what I thought it was,' said Rosie.

'Oh, was it?' said Moray, looking guilty. 'Uhm, yes. I mean. Obviously.'

**R**osie cycled up the hill to Peak House by herself. She figured it would be just what she needed to counteract the effects of the stodgy meals—including roast pork with crackling and apple sauce, which she had guessed, correctly, that Lilian would be unable to resist.

Roads that zipped by in a Land Rover went on for bloody ages at ridiculously steep angles. Her rucksack weighed a ton on her back, she got a stone in her shoe and was cursing for once not the rain but a hot summer day that made her striped T-shirt cling to her back.

Finally, and in a thoroughly grumpy mood, she dismounted, stiff and saddlesore, outside the back door. Maybe, she thought. Maybe this time he'd be pleased to see her. Drop the hostility.

Rosie rapped loudly on the kitchen door, then marched in.

'Meals on Wheels,' she announced. There he was, still in that same seat at that same table. 'Are you *still* here?' she asked, trying to keep the horror out of her voice.

'No,' came the clipped tones. 'Obviously I took some time off to test-drive my new rocket. And I spent a pretty wild weekend in Ibiza.'

'You're becoming one of those shut-ins,' said Rosie. 'Next time I come here you'll have sixty-seven cats.'

'Next time,' said Stephen. 'Be still, my overexcited heart.'

But she could see him eyeing her bag.

'What's in there?' he said.

'Nothing,' said Rosie, unpacking pork chops, half-roasted potatoes, homemade apple sauce and red cabbage on the table between them, as well as half a pound of butter fudge. They regarded each other.

'The NHS is a lot more caring than I remember it,' said Stephen.

'This isn't about the NHS,' said Rosie. 'This is about me trying to bribe people to come to my sweet shop.'

Stephen looked completely bemused as Rosie turned on the oven.

'Oh yes?'

'My lovely sweet shop . . . I mean, Great-aunt Lilian's lovely sweet shop is having its grand reopening ceremony . . . tomorrow.' She showed Stephen her leaflets. 'Why don't you come?'

Stephen grimaced. 'Thanks for that. Afterwards, maybe I could do some basket weaving and art therapy?'

'No. You could eat a lolly, like normal people.'

'Thank you for lumping me in with the normal people,' said Stephen.

'Ha, you'd *hate* that. You'd hate being one of the normal people.'

'That's not fair,' said Stephen mildly, but with real hurt in his voice. Rosie loaded up the surprisingly clean grill pan, and set the potatoes in the oven to finish cooking. Already they smelled wonderful.

'To what do I owe this munificence?' said Stephen. 'Is Moray trying to poison me?'

'No,' said Rosie. 'Maybe yes. No, I don't think so. But there is a snag.'

'I thought there might be.'

'You have to let me change the dressing.'

The light went out of Stephen's eyes. 'No,' he said. 'I do that myself.'

'God,' said Rosie, 'I'm surprised you're not dead of blood poisoning.'

'It's fine,' said Stephen.

'If it were fine,' said Rosie, 'you'd be out in the garden, or climbing the stairs, or going to the gym, or seeing your friends or chatting up some girl or boy or going back to work . . . Stephen, where's your *family?*'

Stephen scowled. 'Can't you just keep out of my business?'

'No,' said Rosie. 'I'm involved now. If I just wander off I'll have to live with the hideous image of you still sitting at your kitchen table, or being eaten by ladybirds or something.'

'Ladybirds?'

'The amount you move about, it could happen.'

'Seriously, ladybirds?'

'I've herbed the pork chops,' said Rosie, as a heavenly aroma started to fill the kitchen.

Stephen looked torn, and so sad Rosie suddenly felt overwhelmed. What on earth had he gone through to make him like this?

'If we start now, the food will be ready by the time we're finished.'

'Rosie,' said Stephen. 'It's horrible, you know. Horrible.'

'I've seen worse,' said Rosie stoically. 'Come on.'

Gently yet firmly, Rosie took his elbow and steered him into what she guessed, correctly, was the bathroom, old-fashioned but clean.

'Take your trousers off,' she said, turning to scrub her hands. 'I'm not looking. Let me know if you need me to help you.'

He insisted he didn't, but she could tell by his careful movements that it wasn't easy for him.

'Are you looking in the mirror?'

'Yes,' said Rosie. 'Looking, and giving you marks out of ten. Get on with it please.'

When she turned round, he was perched anxiously on the side of the bath, running his hands through his hair.

He wore white boxers, and his right leg was extremely long, muscled, still brown and firm. His left, though, was white and hairless, and almost wasted away. Rosie knelt down and, without speaking, because she knew it would hurt, quickly and expertly unravelled the bandage. Although he didn't make a sound, Rosie could tell by the tensing of his muscles how painful it was, and his fingers gripped the side of the bath.

Ready for something much worse, she looked carefully at the wound: a great jagged rent down the inside of his thigh. It did not look particularly nice—it still gaped—but it was clean; it didn't smell and there was no sign of degradation in the wound. Rosie looked up at him.

'This is clean,' she said, her face furrowing.

'Hmm,' he said. 'I'm not a complete idiot.'

'Well, apart from the fact that you are,' said Rosie, who could see clearly where the stitches had dissolved before they'd done their job properly, 'you've been cleaning this. Or someone has.'

'No,' said Stephen. 'Mrs Laird is nifty, but she's not a nurse.'

Rosie followed his eyes to the medicine cabinet above the sink. On top of it was a huge, half-empty brown bottle of surgical spirit.

'Jesus,' she said. 'That must hurt like crazy.'

'The whisky helps,' said Stephen. 'I like to feel I'm doing the job from inside and out.'

'But can't you see it doesn't matter?' said Rosie. 'It doesn't matter how much of that stuff you pour in; if you don't get it restitched it's never going to get better. It can't.'

Stephen didn't say anything as she set about cleaning the area—gently, using an anaesthetic cream. Then he said, 'Could you do it? The stitches?'

'No,' said Rosie. 'I shouldn't even be doing this really.'

'You mean I'm going to have to go and see that prick Moray?'

'What's your problem with Moray?'

Stephen shrugged. 'Thinks he knows it all. Likes to stick his nose in everyone's business. Goes to all the trouble of getting a medical degree, then spunks it sitting on his bum looking up old ladies' arses.'

'Well,' she said. 'What about going to the nearest hospital? A&E could stitch that right up for you. I could probably drive you there.'

'On your bicycle?'

'I'll figure something out.'

Stephen said nothing, just sat and sighed. Then finally he looked up. 'Can you get out while I put my trousers on?'

Rosie packed up her bag and turned to leave the room. 'I'm taking that as a yes!' she yelled cheerily.

## 1943

*Life returned to normal, or as normal as wartime life could be. Pure unrelenting grief, Lilian found, was too heavy to keep up. Little by little the real world returned; she would find her attention distracted by a programme on the radio, or the touch of the warm sun on her skin would make her feel happy, for a moment, before she would remember all over again. And although it seemed that her father's jaunty, energetic sense of humour might have gone for good, he could still make a comment, over supper, about how good the soup was, or how takings were up, or down, in the shop. And after the lamb, which they'd christened Daisy, was on to grass, she and Henry had more time to chat, and found they wanted to talk about almost everything, not just her loss—about how he wanted to go to technical college in Chester.*

*And Lilian found she enjoyed talking about his life, his plans and dreams; and gradually, little by little over those stolen hours, sometimes sharing a bottle of cider as Lilian stared at his sunburnt neck and curly hair, she wondered how for the life of her she could ever have found him annoying, how she could ever, for a second, have found him anything but the most wonderful, kind, amazing man she had ever known. Gradually, growing more and more bold, she laid her head on his shoulder, let him take her hand as they lay and talked in the meadow and, slowly, their plans, their ideas for life, started to include both of them, started to twist together like two plants growing side by side.*

*Before the war, Lilian reflected, as they walked home late, this would have been absolutely disallowed; the scandal could have affected everything. Now, it seemed, the rules had changed; so many young men had gone, or left the village, or been killed. They were crossing the cobbled main street when, biting her lip, she reached out her hand and, without even breaking stride, Henry reached out his strong fingers to meet it as they walked down the darkening road.*

*Despite the fact that she knew deep down it was only a matter of time before he got his call-up papers, that Henry must leave shortly, despite the loss of Ned, and the fact that her two brothers were still at war, despite all of this, she would look back on this for ever as one of the happiest moments of her life.*

# Chapter Six

**Younger children often disdain boiled sweets in favour of a more instant hit, and they are quite right to do so; the boiled sweet is the sweet of the older connoisseur, one who knows that it releases its pleasures slowly. Boiled sweets—particularly boiled butter sweets—are a sweet of contemplation, the relaxed pleasure of the cigar, as against a quick rush that doesn't last and needs to be immediately replicated. So keep the originals, the gobstoppers, the pineapple chunks and the red hots for your slower, more fruitful years. They will repay you in kind.**

'TA-DAH!' ROSIE STOOD at the bottom of the stairs. Even though it was only just past 7 a.m., she hadn't been able to sleep for excitement, and had heard her aunt moving restlessly downstairs, and helped her wash and dress, before making scrambled eggs and nipping upstairs to get dressed. 'What do you think? Too much?'

Lilian looked up from perusing the local paper.

Rosie was wearing a Get Cutie dress, which suited her very nicely. It had a sweetheart neckline and three-quarter-length sleeves and a pattern of nesting birds, and was protected by her candy-striped apron. A mobcap covered her dark curls. 'It's the cap, isn't it?' she said. 'The cap's too much.'

'I wouldn't say the cap was too much,' said Lilian, a ghost of a smile hovering round her lips. 'Although it does look a little bit like the themed catering staff Hetty gets in at the big house round Christmas time.'

Rosie snatched it off. 'It was just an idea,' she said hastily. 'Plus I need to wear it when I'm handling the chocolate.'

Lilian snorted. 'Political correctness gone mad.'

'So, are you coming? I'm going to have free lollipops! And balloons!'

'*Free?*' said Lilian.

'It's called marketing,' said Rosie. 'And if you wanted to come . . . Moray has a spare wheelchair in the surgery I thought he might lend me.'

'Absolutely not,' said Lilian. 'I'm not going to sit out there like one of those awful war-wounded old . . . I mean one of those awful old crones.'

'Just a thought,' said Rosie. 'I'm hoping . . . well, I'm hoping we get some people. Jake said he'd bring along some farm boys and I've handed out lots of leaflets and . . .'

'No,' said Lilian. 'Lipton people don't fall for things like that, I think you're just going to have to face it, Rosie. These shops . . . they're dying. Like everything else. Like me, and everyone I've ever bloody known.' Lilian attempted a wry smile. 'We're done. It's nice of you to come here, and it's nice of you to look after me, and if we can sell the sweet shop as a going concern, well, that will be jolly wonderful for me, I suppose. I can find a home, and sit in a corner and watch television all day with drool hanging out of my mouth. I know what you're up to.'

'We're not "up to" anything,' said Rosie. 'I thought it was wrong you being left to cope on your own. I still think that. And I'm trying to do the best I can for you and for the shop. And I think we can do that.'

Lilian snorted. 'I was fine, you know.'

'I know,' lied Rosie for the nine hundredth time. 'I know you were, Aunt Lil. We're just trying to help. I'm only trying to help.'

'People shouldn't help until they're asked.'

Rosie thought of someone else. 'Some people can't bear to ask,' she said. 'Maybe that's where I come in.'

It was another lovely day. The village was full of itinerant labourers, a few late holidaymakers and the first groups of children. By eight thirty, Rosie had already mastered the helium canister for the balloons (quickly passing over a small pang of loneliness that Gerard wasn't there to hear her funny voice) and stuck them up outside. Listening to the happy tinkle of the bell, she turned quickly to see a small boy looking up at her solemnly. She recognised him from before.

'Hello, Edison,' she said.

'I'm here early,' said the boy. 'I thought if I got here early I might be able to put away some of the sweets before the big boys take them off me.'

'Tell the big boys not to do that!' said Rosie. 'Or punch them.'

'I can't do that,' said the boy. 'I'm a pacific.'

'A what?'

'A pacific. It means I don't fight back, as it's morly wrong.'

'Are you a pacifist, Edison?'

'Yes,' said Edison. 'That's what I said.'

Rosie took out the big dish of old-fashioned lollipops—strawberries and cream, lemon and lime, and blackcurrant and vanilla.

'Well, one way of looking at it,' said Rosie, 'is that you never start a fight, but if you get into one, make sure you fight back.'

'Yes, but the thing is,' he said, sounding like a very small professor, 'my glasses cost one hundred and fifty-nine pounds, you see? I have stig-mis-ma. Mummy says it will make me very clever.'

Rosie arched her eyebrows, then glanced outside. A woman with a severe haircut and no make-up gave her a tight smile, then glanced deliberately at her watch.

'Would you like to take one for your friend who isn't allowed to eat sweets?' said Rosie.

'Reuben?'

'Yes, Reuben.'

'But would that be morly wrong?'

'No,' said Rosie. 'Not if mean people are going to try and take your lollipop. You can offer up Reuben's, if he wasn't going to eat it anyway.'

Edison's brow furrowed as he followed the ramifications of this. Finally, he smiled and popped his head back up. 'OK!' he said. 'Can I have strawberries and cream and *Reuben* would like lemon and lime.'

Rosie popped the sweets in a bag for him.

'Congratulations!' she said. 'You are officially our first customer.'

Rosie propped the door open, to find several rubberneckers, passers-by and curious children had gathered round.

'I now pronounce this sweet shop . . . open!' said Rosie, with a big smile.

In poured quite a river of people. Rosie looked among the little boys and girls to see if she could work out exactly which ones were making Edison's life such a misery, but they all looked identically rosy-cheeked and adorable.

'I'm going to get the *biggest bag ever in the world* and buy every sweet in this shop,' announced one tow-headed chap.

'I am going to bring all my birthday money, it's a lot, it was ten pounds, yes and I am going to buy *all the chocolate in the shop*,' said another.

'You will not,' said a mother's voice, and when Rosie looked up she realised it was Maeve Skitcherd, the receptionist from the doctor's surgery.

'Hello!' she said.

'Hello,' said Maeve. 'I couldn't resist. When I was little Miss Lilian always used to have . . . I don't suppose they make them any more . . .'

Rosie cocked her head, keeping her fingers crossed. This was the crux of it; this was where the shop could rise again. Not from the pennies and birthday money of the children, but from the memories of the adults.

'. . . I don't suppose you have any mint creams?'

Rosie nearly punched the air with pleasure. They did. She had restocked as much of Lilian's originals as she could track down.

'Why yes,' she said, 'of course. Would you like a big bag or a small bag?' She was selling small, medium and large bags at one, two or three pounds. You could choose all of one kind or, for medium and large bags, mix up two or three scoops together.

'Ooh, large,' said Maeve, colouring with pleasure.

And while Lavender, her daughter, unwrapped her strawberry lolly, Rosie filled a large bag with mint creams.

People requested the oddest things: rhubarb and custards with pineapple chunks, barley sugar and eucalyptus, sweets that sometimes Rosie had never heard of but often, thanks to Lilian's little book, she found she did have.

She weighed and twisted until she got the hang of it. One huge box of heart-shaped chocolates was borne away by a newly married young man to his bride, seeing as, he admitted somewhat shamefacedly to Rosie, they had had to spend their honeymoon on the harvest even though she'd wanted to go to Malaga. This charming gesture immediately made her knock five pounds off the price.

To be honest, she hadn't really expected to sell much. But here they were, inundated. It must be the novelty factor. Everyone would pop in for a couple of days, then it would go back to normal. Which meant, Rosie thought, measuring out a small bag of Parma violets, which immediately filled the shop with their sharp, slightly astringent odour and made two small children ask for the same thing, that she should probably get it on the market as soon as possible. That would be the right thing to do.

Rosie bent down and offered a small purple sweet to each of the children. They looked up at her, wide-eyed, then glanced at the woman standing by the door, who nodded indulgently.

'I *like* your shop,' said the little boy.

'I'm glad,' said Rosie.

'Wass your name?'

'I'm Rosie,' said Rosie, smiling.

'*Heyo Miss Rosie. Mah name is Kent.*'

'Hello, Kent,' said Rosie. 'And what about you?'

But the little girl, obviously Kent's sister, was struck dumb with awe and stared at Rosie with her eyes and mouth wide open.

'She's very shy,' said the woman in the doorway. She was slender, young and, incongruously in Lipton apart from Lilian, beautifully dressed, in yummy-mummy style, in a soft pink cashmere pullover and expensive-looking draped trousers. 'But I think she likes your shop. This is Emily.'

'That's great,' said Rosie.

'I like it too,' said the woman, peering in. 'You've done a lovely job. It looks just like a proper old-fashioned place.'

'Oh well, it is,' said Rosie. 'This is all genuine. I didn't change a thing, just polished it up a bit.'

The woman smiled. 'Well, I like it. I hope it does really well. I'm Tina, by the way. Tina Ferrers.'

'Hi,' said Rosie. 'I'm Rosie Hopkins.'

'Oh, I know who you are. The whole village knows who you are.'

'Hmm,' said Rosie. 'Is that good or bad?'

'Oh, they all know me too,' said Tina, rolling her eyes. 'It's the country. It's just how it is. Come on, Kent, come on, Emily. We should have coffee some time and you can tell me about this place,' she said to Rosie as they dinged their way out of the shop, and Rosie tried to pretend she wasn't pleased that someone was being friendly without her having to save a dog first. And Tina seemed interested in the shop. That could be useful.

## 1943

*There was no denying that it helped. Gordon had a week's leave from the North African front and had fought his way home over seventy-two hours, hitching rides on supply boats and trucks and, finally, had pootled over the hills from Derby in a slow-moving bus, in time for Saturday lunch. Lilian could see it in her father's eyes: the first spark that had been there for a long time. She reflected, briefly, on the fact that she hadn't been the one to put it there.*

*The two men did not hug—they didn't do that in their family—but her da held Gordon's hand for a long time, and clasped his shoulder, with water in his eyes. Gordon seemed older, more grown-up, but he still had a look of mischief about him.*

*The men sat in near-silence at the table as Lilian served up two weeks' meat ration of chops; but she could tell that, although they merely muttered and made remarks about army food, both of them were happier than they had felt in a long time. And so, inside, was she. Every time she thought about Henry, her insides lit up with a nervous, excited kind of joy.*

*Gordon told them funny stories about his commanding officers, and how clueless they were, and how their equipment broke down, but when Da asked him about any skirmishes he went quiet for a while. Lilian thought about Ned. But Gordon couldn't keep his natural ebullience down for long. After a pause he looked up and remarked, 'Da, I was scared out of my bally wits.'*

*Lilian's dad let out a huge guffaw, the first she had heard from him in months. 'Ha,' he said. 'Ha. Yes. It's exactly like that.' And he laughed so hard he had to wipe a tear from his eye. 'You are a tonic, son,' he said. 'It's good to see you.'*

*Lilian had never heard anything so effusive from her dad before.*

*'Come on,' said Gordon, after he'd had a bath and a nap. 'We might as well go to the Red Lion. I'll take you to the lounge bar.'*

*Lilian snuck a glance at her father, who just waved his hand. 'Aye, on you go, young 'uns,' he said. 'I'll see you in the morn. Behave yourselves.'*

*L*ilian didn't quite know how to tell Gordon, but in the end she didn't have to. As they walked down the blacked-out road together he quite naturally asked her, 'Got a fella?' And when she paused for the briefest of moments, he laughed and nudged her.

'Anyone decent?' he said. Lilian bit her lip.

'It's . . . it's Henry Carr,' she said quietly.

Gordon let out a guffaw. 'Carr! 'E managed it at last. By gum, I thought he'd never get round to it.'

'What do you mean?' said Lilian, completely surprised.

''E always had a soft spot for you, didn't he? Terence warned him off often enough. Well, there you go. Good on 'im.'

'But he was always really horrible to me.'

Gordon gave her a sideways glance. 'You know, I'd have thought having three brothers would have taught you a little bit more about chaps, sure enough.'

Lilian felt the blush steal up her face. Was it true? Had he always cared for her, all this time?

The pub wasn't lit, but slits of warm light could just be seen at the windows, poking out of the blackout curtains. Lilian felt excited and a little bold, but mostly nervous.

Then, to her relief, she saw Margaret home from Derby, heading over from the opposite direction with a gormless big chap in a naval uniform. Seeing Lilian she shrieked and waved mightily.

'You're out of the widow weeds!' she yelled, tactlessly, then gave her a hug.

'This is George,' said Margaret proudly, pushing forward the lanky chap with bright red hair, who muttered something so quietly she could barely hear it. 'I brought him down to meet Ma and Pa.' With this she winked massively at Lilian, in a slightly confusing way, obviously intended to be confiding.

It took Lilian a minute or two to realise the message she was trying to convey. 'Are you . . . are you two . . . ?'

'Yes!' said Margaret. 'Isn't it the most romantic thing ever! I have to tell you the whole story!'

George did not, at that moment, look like the world's most romantic man— but Margaret linked her arm and they headed inside.

Gordon was on her other side. 'Now I have no regrets about missing out on the lovely Margaret,' he said to her, sotto voce, 'but there's someone over there I always hoped I might take a crack at one of these days.'

For there, in a cosy corner table by the fireplace in the ladies' lounge bar, *nursing a port and lemon and deep in what appeared to be a very intense conversation, was Ida Delia Fontayne with Henry Carr, once again only a heartbeat away from one another.*

'Hello, Anton!' Rosie said, delighted. 'You're out of the house!'

Anton smiled shyly, setting his walker down heavily in front of him. 'You recognised me!'

Rosie swallowed a giggle. 'Yes, Anton, I recognised you. And well done for getting out of the house! That's brilliant!'

Anton beamed. 'Yeah, well, Chrissie said . . . she said it might be about time. She also said if I manage to get up and down the high street she'll take me to McDonald's.'

'Isn't that one step forward, two steps back?'

'Oh no,' said Anton. 'I already eat lots of McDonald's. I'm just really excited by the idea that I might get to eat a hot one. By the time they reach Lipton they're always cold.'

'Everyone needs a dream,' said Rosie. 'And look, this is mine. What do you think?'

Anton looked around. 'I think,' he pronounced carefully, 'I think it is one of the nicest places I've ever been to. It hasn't changed at all.'

'I know,' she said. 'Where's Chrissie?'

'She's driving the car down to the other end of the street. She said it'll make me walk.' He looked around again. 'It's a shame you don't have a chair. I could stay all day.' Rosie made a private note not to bring out a chair.

Anton's eyes rose up the shelves. 'Oh wow,' he said. 'I don't know what to have.'

'Tell you what,' Rosie said. 'Just for you—and I wouldn't do this for anyone else—how about I give you a small selection? One of each, in a little bag.'

'I was thinking,' said Anton, 'about maybe two pounds of butter fudge. And a pound of tablet. And—'

'But with this,' said Rosie persuasively, 'you get to try a little taster of absolutely everything. Without overdoing it. Just a tiny delicious taste, like pick 'n' mix. For after your tea.'

Anton looked unconvinced, and gave a hopeful glance towards the Turkish delight tray. 'And some of that,' he said.

'A tiny, teeny taste,' said Rosie.

286 | Jenny Colgan

The door clanged and Moray walked in. Rosie smiled at him, then remembered she'd put the mobcap back on again when she was dishing out chocolate and snatched it off her head. Moray grinned.

'I like the way you dress,' he observed. 'Every day is an adventure.' He glanced around. 'Morning, Anton.'

'Miss Rosie was just saying I could have any sweets I wanted from the whole shop,' said Anton.

'*Was* she?' said Moray with a querying look.

'Not *quite* like that,' said Rosie. 'We're just going to have a little taste, aren't we, Anton?'

'I suppose so,' said Anton, who hated conflict of any kind.

'I thought I'd pop in to say congratulations,' said Moray, gazing at the shelves. 'Are those . . .' His face suddenly looked disarmingly young. 'Are those bubble-gum *Golf Balls*?'

'They certainly are,' said Rosie.

'I haven't seen those for . . . well, for a long time.'

'Would you like one?'

Moray was still shaking his head. 'We used to share them at school. And fight like mad if there was an uneven number.'

'Who's we?' asked Rosie, but Moray was caught in a flood of reminiscence. Then he snapped himself out of it. 'Doesn't matter. No one important.'

'But would you like some?'

Moray shrugged. 'All right, I'll take two.'

Rosie grinned, and made up two bags, one with a smattering of every-thing for Anton, and one with some Golf Balls, which Rosie handed over with a smile, then put out her hand for the shiny pound coins.

'Thanks,' said Anton, making to turn his body round.

'No problem,' said Rosie. 'And Anton, please don't finish them before . . .'

But the doorbell had already tinged, and Anton had his big paw inside the incongruously small-looking bag.

'Oh well,' said Rosie. 'It's a start.'

## 1943

'Ang on,' said Gordon, 'Isn't that the man you're stepping out with?'

*Lilian couldn't say anything. The breath was sticking in her throat. Margaret clasped her arm and said loudly, 'Henry sodding Carr? That eejit?'*

*At the sound of his name, Henry's head flicked to the side, and once again he* took on that terrible guilty look Lilian had seen at the dance. She couldn't believe it. He was a two-timing, woman-baiting idiot, a dame teaser, and she couldn't believe she'd fallen for it again.

For once, Lilian didn't care. She didn't care what was right and proper, whether people would talk in the village; what Ida Delia would think. She looked straight at Henry's stricken face, turned round and stormed out.

At first, caught up in the drama of the thing, she worried that no one would come after her. Then, the gravity of the situation—what a fool she was, all the private hopes and dreams she hadn't dared to admit even to herself—came bubbling up, and erupted, not in tears but in fury, an absolute rage at the universe, the enormous unfairness of falling in love. She wanted to scream, to howl. Her eyes blinked in frustration, as she found herself making her way to the churchyard, hardly even noticing what she was doing.

Footsteps pattered to a halt behind her, but she didn't turn round.

He didn't even say her name. She felt, instead, a strong, tentative touch on her shoulders. He gave a sharp intake of breath then slowly, as if against her will, she allowed herself to be turned round. Only then did he say her name.

'Lily.' His face was a mask of misery and desperation. 'Lily, I . . .'

But then, like the last gasp of a drowning man, he reached for her, and she let him grab her shoulders and hold her, as she gave herself up entirely to his fierce, devastating kiss. Then she didn't think at all; she channelled her anger and her rage into passion, a huge and long-pent-up passion for him that she felt, once it had burst its banks, would never stop flowing. But eventually, gasping for breath, his whole body, it seemed, straining towards her, Henry pulled himself away. Lilian baulked; was she doing it wrong? Had she done something lewd or awful? Inside she started to panic. But it was far, far worse than that.

Rosie was flushed with success cashing up that evening; she put all the money neatly into the smart little bags she'd got from the bank and put the figures into her laptop with a little sigh of satisfaction. It was far more than she'd expected. She was secretly rather proud of herself.

'Don't you think that was amazing?' she said to Lilian, hoping to elicit a word of praise. 'I do,' Rosie said to herself. 'I think I'm amazing. Let's order in a curry.' She thought about it. 'Is that even possible? Is there Indian food here?'

'Is there *what*?' asked Lilian, as if Rosie had asked her if there was any chance of getting an elephant burger-to-go.

'What about pizza?'

In fact, it turned out, there was pizza, a little van that parked up at the side of the school, and Rosie wandered down, feeling curiously content. The sun was sinking gradually over the top of the distant hills, turning them purple and pink and sending huge shadows shooting out for miles against the undulating fields. It was exquisitely beautiful.

'Wow,' said Rosie, as her mobile rang, and she didn't even notice for a second, or realise till she heard it that it hadn't rung in days.

She snapped back when she heard it ring a second time; it was Gerard. 'Hello?' she said, tentatively, then more fondly, 'Hello, sweetie.'

'Where have you been?' came the voice, sounding cross. 'Every time I call your phone is switched off.'

'It's not switched off!' said Rosie. 'It's just really hard to get a signal up here. Middle of nowhere and all that.'

'Hmm,' said Gerard.

'How are you, sweetie? It's amazing here, the most gorgeous sunset.'

'Sounds like you're loving it up there,' said Gerard, an edge to his voice.

'No, it's not that,' said Rosie. 'No. No. There's nothing to do.'

As if in mockery, suddenly Jake and his friends passed by, shouting and laughing and nut-brown from the sun.

'Hey, Rosie!' they called out. 'Coming for pizza?'

'I'm all right!' She waved quickly.

'Who's taking you out for pizza? I thought you were in the middle of nowhere, not Pizza bloody Express.'

'It's nothing,' said Rosie. 'Just a van they have here some days.'

'You didn't phone yesterday.'

'Well, lots of times when I called you were out, or on your way out.'

Gerard's voice was sullen. 'Well, I was just enjoying . . . you know, first few days of freedom and all that.'

'Freedom? What kind of freedom?'

'Nothing like that. I mean, just going out with the lads and that. Then back to Mum's.'

'Well, that sounds reassuring.'

His voice changed. 'But, you know, I miss you, Rosie. I really do.'

'Now you're tired of being on the booze and have run out of socks?' Rosie teased gently.

'No! Yes! Maybe. A bit.'

Rosie smiled. 'I miss you too,' she said. 'All the time. I mean, well, I have been really, really busy and everything, but . . .'

Rosie paused. Something struck her. She'd been working, making friends, seeing the countryside, making an idiot of herself. And Gerard had been going out, seeing his mates, dossing at his mum's. It hit her forcibly that someone really ought to have been missing somebody else a bit more in this scenario.

'So,' said Gerard finally, 'so I thought I'd come up this weekend!'

'Oh yes!' said Rosie, relieved. 'It's market day! They have a fête! Apparently it's great, everyone brings their cows and stuff and there's a fair and it's going to be amazing, and brilliant for the shop.'

'OK, whatever,' said Gerard. 'You know this is only a temporary job, this shop thing. It's just a favour to your family, you have to get rid of it.'

'I know, I know,' said Rosie.

'Well, have you advertised it yet?'

'Uhm, no, not exactly. I've been really busy.'

'And what about your career? Have you seen anything in *Nursing Times*? Have you spoken to your agency?'

Rosie had to admit that she hadn't done any of them, but she was close to perfecting her recipe for cauliflower cheese, as Lilian loved it so much.

'Well, I'll drive up on Friday night,' said Gerard.

'OK!' said Rosie. 'Hang on, I'd better ask Lilian.'

'Ask her what, if it's all right for unmarried people to spend the night under her roof?' Gerard let out an incredulous guffaw.

'Yes!' said Rosie. 'It *is* her roof. It's only polite.'

'Yeah, whatever,' said Gerard, and they rang off. It was hard, Rosie reflected, to get your meaning across properly on the phone. She was sure all they needed was a proper cuddle and they'd be fine.

Jake smiled at her from over by the pizza stand and introduced her to some of the lads who worked with him, or were down for the fair. All of them were friendly and chatty, and Rosie ordered a large ham and mushroom with extra pepperoni and cheese for her and Lilian. She passed a pleasant ten minutes with the lads and then went home to the cottage.

To her horror, she had almost forgotten about Gerard coming till she and Lilian were halfway through dinner. 'Uhm,' she said, 'my boyfriend was thinking of coming up this weekend . . .'

Suddenly, she wasn't sure if she wanted Gerard and Lilian to meet.

Lilian was regarding her with an intense, beady look. 'Is he going to marry you?'

Rosie shrugged, twisting slightly. 'Ha. Well, you know, we haven't really discussed it!'

'How long have you been a couple?'

'Eight years.'

'Hmm,' said Lilian, with feeling.

Rosie shifted in her seat. She thought it was too long, too.

'And how old are you?' Lilian kept her bright bird eyes fixed on her.

'I'm thirty-one,' said Rosie. 'That's nothing these days.'

'Well, you're hardly a couple of kids,' said Lilian.

'No,' said Rosie slowly. 'But I think we're fine as we are, thanks.'

She started to clear away the dishes. Lilian looked at her, uncomprehending. Young people . . . didn't she realise? That if it wasn't the real thing, if it wasn't proper, true love then she was wasting her time. She was wasting her life.

'People always believe,' said Lilian, 'that they have plenty of time.'

The weather held into the weekend, and Rosie waited with anticipation for Gerard to arrive on Friday. The roar of his cool Alfa Romeo lit the quiet high street just after five o'clock. Rosie was in the shop—it had been another good day, with children popping in all ready for the weekend with pocket money to spend.

The door opened with its traditional ting, and Gerard walked in. Something surged in Rosie's heart. Gerard was looking delighted. But it wasn't at her. He was scanning the shelves and the tins and bars with a cheerful, hungry look on his face.

'Hello!' said Rosie.

'Hello!' said Gerard. 'Wow, look at this place! You've got *everything*!'

'And it's lovely to see you, Rosie.'

'And it's lovely to . . . Have you got liquorice torpedoes?'

'I have,' said Rosie.

'Wow. Can I have some?'

'You can, for a pound.'

Gerard stuck out his lip. 'I don't get free sweets?'

She reached up to the high shelf and got the liquorice torpedoes. A real boy's sweet. Classic Gerard.

'A pound please,' she said, holding out her hand.

Gerard grimaced, then handed over a pound.

'Thank you,' said Rosie. 'We are, of course, a going concern.'

'Yeah, yeah, yeah,' said Gerard. He looked, Rosie thought, a bit wobbly; he'd put on some weight and his jowls were beginning to show. Too much of his mum's indulgent cooking, or takeaways, she imagined.

'I've missed you,' said Gerard.

'I've missed you too,' said Rosie, remembering back to those first chilly evenings. 'Come here.' She gave him a hug, smelled his familiar scent—aftershave, crisps—and smiled.

'OK,' said Gerard, greedily attacking his torpedoes. 'What are you making for supper? I'm starving. Or sex first. Sex then supper? Or after supper? Or both? What about now? In the back room? I like the apron.'

Rosie grinned. 'No, darling! I've got to lock up and cash up.'

'Well, hurry up,' said Gerard. 'Come on. Can't you do it all tomorrow? It's not really your shop.'

'No,' said Rosie. 'But right now it's my job. It won't take long.'

Gerard looked pouty. 'But please. I've come all this way.'

'And I'll be ten minutes. Wait here, then we can go and I'll introduce you to Lilian. Or you can take yourself off to the pub down the road and have a pint if you like and I'll meet you in a minute.'

Rosie hadn't meant the last one seriously, but to her disgruntlement his face immediately perked up and he asked her for directions.

'OK. Great. See you down there, yeah?'

Rosie turned back towards the till and started putting things away.

'I really won't be long,' she protested.

'Great,' said Gerard, leaving her to it. 'I'll order you a gin and tonic.'

Rosie was so cross she dawdled doing the books, then nipped back next door to get changed.

'Isn't your young man coming?' asked Lilian by the door. She had dressed up and was wearing a lavender coat dress and matching lipstick.

'Uhm . . . he's . . . I'm meeting him at the pub.'

'At the *pub*?' said Lilian, as if she'd said 'at the brothel'.

'Yes, it's all right. Here, I have pie and beans for you, I'm just going to heat it up in the microwave.'

With her first week's profits, Rosie had bought Lilian a microwave.

'Sorry, I know it's nothing fancy, but it's delicious and full of calories.'

'He's at the pub?' asked Lilian again as if she hadn't heard her. 'He didn't come to say good evening?'

Rosie tried to tell herself that Lilian was just an old fuddy-duddy caught up in old-fashioned ideas. That was it. But even so, doubt crept in. It was terribly rude, wasn't it? Not to greet someone who was putting a roof over your head for the night? Classic Gerard.

'He was really exhausted after driving up here,' she said.

'So he can't stay off the sauce?' said Lilian acidly.

'No,' said Rosie. 'I'll . . . I'll go meet him. We'll see you later.'

'I don't like that pub,' said Lilian. 'Never set foot in it again.'

'Again what?' said Rosie, but Lilian didn't answer. 'Are you all right?' asked Rosie, taking her dinner out of the microwave.

Lilian waved her away. 'You have fun,' she said.

'OK,' said Rosie. 'Don't wait up.'

Lilian smiled. And for the first time, spontaneously, Rosie leaned over and kissed her great-aunt on the cheek before she left.

The Red Lion was lively-looking on a Friday night. Rosie had never been in there before and felt tentative at the entrance, the busy noise spilling out on to the pavement with the warm light and the smokers.

She pushed open the door. Inside, the fire was burning to stave off the autumnal chill; big oblong tables were positioned around the room, with horse brasses on the walls. And there he sat, slightly awkward-looking, his boyish face and pink cheeks out of place among the tanned agricultural labourers. In front of him was a nearly empty pint of cider and three empty crisp packets. This was her man, she thought. For the first time since she'd been so wrapped up in the giddiness of moving in together, planning their future, she looked at him, hard. Here he was. Not perfect. Well, she wasn't perfect. And he was her bloke. Her face broke into a smile.

'Hey!' she said. 'Where's that gin and tonic?'

Two hours later, Rosie was well into the swing of things, although Gerard did talk a little bit about how great it was to be back at his mum's and suggested, after his third pint, perhaps a little too loudly, that they should nip into the bathrooms and have sex. Jake and his friends, the vicar and Malik from the Spar were all within earshot.

'How do you know everyone already?' said Gerard. Rosie considered telling him it was because she'd ruined Mr Isitt's vegetable garden and as a consequence was considered by half the village to be sleeping with the other half, but she shrugged and said, 'Oh, you know, villages.'

'I don't,' said Gerard. 'It's weird. Did you say that guy runs the Spar?'

Rosie smiled and nodded over at Malik, who was, it had to be said, quite sanguine about their opening, and had merely remarked that as long as she stayed out of booze, fags and lottery tickets they would get along fine. They had a quick chat about how they expected to do on market day. Then Jake came over to say hi, and gave Gerard such a blatant up-and-down look that Rosie found herself blushing.

'Who's this?' said Jake.

'This is . . . this is Gerard,' said Rosie. 'Uhm, my, my boyfriend.'

Gerard wiped some crisp dust off his fingers and didn't get up.

'Hello,' he said amiably, 'you're a big fella.'

Jake gave Rosie a questioning look. She ignored him.

'We need to go and do some more gardening,' he said. Behind him, his friends were nudging each other.

'What, now?' said Rosie.

Jake stuck out his bottom lip. Rosie suspected he probably found it quite easy to get women. She was just the new thing in town.

'Soon,' he said.

'Yes, all right,' said Rosie. 'Soon.'

She took a long slug of her gin and tonic, waving politely to Hye and Moray over in the far corner, already well into some bottles of wine. Typical doctor behaviour, she thought.

'What is this, *The Waltons*?' said Gerard, turning his head. 'You've been here five minutes and you know half the town.'

'Well, I run the local sweet shop,' said Rosie. 'Of course I'm going to meet a few people. And everyone knows Lilian.'

'Yes, but . . .'

'And I don't know everyone, anyway. There's loads of people I don't know, like them, for example.'

Rosie gestured at a random couple by the window, then realised she'd seen the woman before. The woman got up and came over.

'Hello,' she said. 'I'm Edison's mum.'

'Oh, hello, nice to meet you.'

The woman had naturally grey hair and wire-rimmed spectacles. She wasn't wearing a scrap of make-up, and was very thin. Potentially, thought Rosie, she could look amazing.

'Actually,' said Rosie, 'I did want to ask you something.' She stood up. 'Edison talks about his friend who isn't allowed any sweets? I realise mothers do take quite a firm line on this kind of thing, but we sell fruit drops and raisins, and . . .'

Edison's mother smiled in a slightly superior kind of way.

'Oh gosh, no,' she said. 'There's no Reuben! Reuben is his imaginary friend!' she added cheerfully. 'Edison's terribly imaginative! It's a sign of very high intelligence.'

Rosie stifled the unkind thought that if his mother bought Edison a pair of normal trainers then he might not have to make imaginary friends and could make a real one.

'You know,' confided his mother as if this were a badge of honour, 'we've taken him to all these child psychologists and they just don't know what to do with him.'

'Loads of children have imaginary friends though, don't they?' said Rosie, stunned they would send such a small boy to see a shrink. 'Maybe they think it's perfectly normal.'

Edison's mum let out a little laugh. 'Oh no, you would never call our Edison anything like normal! There's nothing average about our Edison! You see, he's particularly intelligent. So really it is something of a worry for us.'

She didn't look like it was a worry, thought Rosie. She looked absolutely delighted that she was turning her own child into the village weirdo. 'Oh,' she said, 'well, he's welcome any time. And his "friend".'

Edison's mother smiled. 'Oh, it's *so* nice to have someone a little broad-minded around town,' she said, loudly, and Rosie smiled her goodbyes as politely as she could and sat down again.

'So,' said Gerard, 'what about selling the shop then? Have you got it on the market? Have you had any viewings? What are you selling it for?'

'Uhm,' said Rosie. 'Well, you know, I've been very busy getting it up and running.'

'Getting it up and running?' said Gerard. 'You've been here four weeks. It was only meant to be for six. You've got a career waiting for you.'

For the first time, oddly, Rosie found the idea of going back to a big hospital—which she normally found buzzy, and exciting, and endlessly interesting, so unlike here, she supposed—unappealing. Instead of being anxious to get back she found herself in no hurry at all.

'Yes, yes, I know,' she said. 'I know, you're right.'

'Well, if you know I'm right, why don't you just do it?' grumbled Gerard. 'Don't just nod your head and say yeah yeah yeah.'

'Mmm,' said Rosie. 'No, I will, definitely.'

'Because I don't want to keep living at my mum's.'

'You don't have to live at your mum's!' said Rosie suddenly in exasperation. 'Why don't you live in our home like a normal adult human being?'

'What, ha, and do my own laundry and buy my own food when I can get it all done for me for free?' scoffed Gerard. 'Yeah, right, that sounds like a great idea, Rosie. Yes, brilliant.'

'But don't you enjoy your independence?'

Gerard shrugged. 'Why should I? My mum didn't move to Australia.'

'Oh, that is very unfair,' said Rosie, incredibly annoyed that, suddenly, they seemed to be skidding towards a fight. She was also conscious that, around her, people were watching them. This was a definite disadvantage, she thought, of knowing everyone in the village.

She took a deep breath. She was going to make an effort. They could try again. 'Hey,' she said. 'Why don't we have another drink?'

Gerard smiled, his pique forgotten.

'Pint of Magners please! And some crisps! Then I'm going to have the scampi! Can I have the scampi?'

Rosie wondered if he'd always been so young. Well, it was endearing, of course. It was just . . . well, Jake wouldn't bother asking her if he could have scampi. Moray wouldn't eat it. And Stephen . . . well. Anyway.

'I don't mind what you have,' she said, sounding slightly sharper than she'd intended. 'Eat what you like.'

'It's just I thought, crisps *and* chips . . .'

'Yes, they're a terrible combination.'

His face fell. 'But I really like scampi.'

'Well, have that and I'll eat the chips.'

Gerard's face relaxed. 'OK!'

Sighing slightly, she got up out of her seat and was heading to the bar again, pinkly conscious of all the faces in the room following her, when the door of the lounge bar crashed open and all eyes turned.

**1943**

'No, no, it's not you.' Henry looked half crazed, completely wild-eyed, as they stood, heart to heart, both of them breathless and panting. 'It's not you. It's never you. It's always been you.'

Henry was holding her shoulders now, though Lilian felt that if she didn't kiss him again, right now, she was going to explode. She could barely breathe. What was he saying to her? She couldn't take it in at all.

'Kiss me again,' she said, suddenly emboldened by the smell of him, and the feel of being wrapped so tightly in his arms; she had to feel it again, she had to.

Instead, Henry wrenched himself free, with a huge effort of will, and gradually lowered her arms, holding her thin wrists in his huge hands.

'I don't . . .' Lilian's voice sounded strange, even to herself, like a child talking. She couldn't keep the wobble out of it. 'I don't understand.'

Henry turned his head away. Lilian wanted to force him to look at her.

'What is it?'

'It's Ida,' he muttered. 'From months back. She's only up the bloody pole.'

Lilian had forced her arms from his as if they were on fire.

'What?' she said, thinking it was possible she'd misunderstood.

Henry had a look on his face that Lilian recognised from her brothers when they'd received their call-up papers, that of condemned men.

'I . . . I,' he started. 'Me and Ida . . . that night at the dance. I came looking for you and I couldn't find you and . . . oh, I were so stupid, but she was all over me and I thought that would be it, you know. I mean, I wanted to see you so badly and I thought . . . I've messed up, Lilian. I've messed up, right badly.'

Lilian thought about Gertie Fanshawe last year, who'd been spirited away from the village and came back about five months later. Her mother insisted it had been a bad bout of influenza and she'd been on a rest cure. Nobody said anything about it, of course they didn't. But Lilian remembered Gertie at school: wild, and funny, smart as a whip, but she only really loved her horses down at the Fanshawe place. Lilian remembered seeing her, flying across hedgerows whenever she got five minutes off from working the farm—which wasn't often.

When she returned, she didn't ride any more. She was hardly seen. When Lilian saw her she was shocked at how thin she'd become, how meek. It was as if something vital inside her had vanished; something had died.

Six weeks after she had returned to her family, Gertie Fanshawe had left without a word and no one had ever seen her again.

'I . . . I have to marry her,' stuttered Henry. 'I have to. Remember . . .'

*Lilian nodded. 'I do. I do remember.'*

*'I can't . . . I can't let that happen to Ida. It's inhuman. She'd be ruined.'*

*Lilian shook her head. Her hands were still shaking, but she was, she knew, practical, sensible Lilian. That's what everybody thought. What she felt inside was, get me pregnant too then. Get me pregnant too.*

*'Henry?' a familiar voice screeched down the road. It sounded exasperated. 'Henry? Darling? Where are you? Where are you?'*

*'I'll go,' said Lilian quickly, her mind working. This didn't need to be any worse than it already was. Henry looked at her with desperate eyes.*

*'I don't . . . I don't want you to go,' he said, furious with himself—bitter, and ashamed, and choked up with emotion. 'I never ever wanted to let you go. Ever.'*

*'If only . . .' Lilian wasn't going to say that sentence, although she would dwell on it for a long, long time. If only she had let her feelings be known earlier. If only she had swallowed her stupid pride when he'd asked her to the dance. If only she'd been bolder, stronger, more of a woman. If only, if only, if only.*

*The voice was getting closer. Henry stiffened, and stood up to his full height, trying to look stoic in the face of what lay ahead. Then, quick as a flash, Lilian turned and took the back way through the woods, running until she felt as if her heart would burst, running because she wanted her heart to burst, wanted it to burst its very banks, and carry her away, and let her drown in it all.*

The door to the pub banged back and everyone turned to look. Standing silhouetted against the dark street, white as a piece of paper, was Stephen. Rosie leaped forward, and Moray jumped up from the far table.

Stephen looked straight at Rosie and managed to say, 'I think . . . I think I need . . .' before his head started to loll to the side.

'*Quick*, someone help me!' shouted Rosie, rushing to his side. Gerard stayed put, but Moray was already there and they helped Stephen to a chair. His left leg was an absolute waterfall of red. Moray and Rosie looked at each other with worried expressions, and Les, the landlord, indicated they could carry him into the back room. Even as thin as he was, his large frame was heavy to manhandle and the landlord had to help.

Stephen was looking around him blearily as Rosie fetched a glass of water. He was still bleeding, and Moray rushed off to fetch his medical kit. The landlord made himself scarce once he'd worked out there was nothing more he could do to help.

Stephen and Rosie were alone.

'What the hell did you do?' said Rosie, close to his ear. She tied together two bar towels to make a tourniquet.

Stephen shook his head. 'Nothing. Nothing. Accident.'

'What kind of an accident?'

Stephen gulped down more water. His face was very white indeed. 'Stupid bloody step . . . Tripped.'

'You are *bleeding out*, for goodness' sake,' said Rosie. 'I'm calling an ambulance.'

'Take too long,' said Stephen. 'Durn't matter.' His breathing was shallow, and his eyes were having trouble focusing.

'Why didn't you call us?'

'Forgot to pay the bloody land-line bill. And no mobile reception.'

Rosie shook her head. 'Ah, this *bloody* countryside.'

'I am very cold,' announced Stephen quietly. Rosie covered him in a tablecloth, the nearest thing to hand, and checked her tourniquet. It was holding it, but he was in a very bad way indeed. Rosie knelt close to try and keep him conscious.

'It's all right, it's going to be all right,' she said. Where was Moray? She clasped Stephen's freezing fingers between her own. 'Just hold on.'

His eyes were drooping.

'How . . . how did you get down the hill in the dark?' asked Rosie.

'Mm?' said Stephen. 'Oh. Oh, they left . . . they left some stupid old thing . . . stupid really. Stupid.'

At that moment, the door burst open and Moray came in with a large black bag, and the landlord close behind him carrying what looked like a quadruple brandy.

'There's no time for that now,' scolded Rosie.

'Not for me, for him,' said Moray.

'You don't keep a full medicine cabinet?'

'*Someone* never sorted it out after the dog thing,' panted Moray, glancing back into the bar. Hye hadn't bothered to come through to see what was going on.

Rosie knelt down, holding Stephen's hands as Moray scrubbed up at the sink.

'Listen,' she said, turning his face so he could see her. 'Moray is going to stitch you up, and the landlord's called the ambulance. You need a blood transfusion really, really quickly. What type are you?'

Stephen couldn't answer.

'OK, well, fine, I'll make sure they bring whatever they have. But listen. Moray's going to stitch you now. But I'm afraid there's no anaesthetic. There's just . . .'

Moray was holding up a packet of Nurofen.

'Oh, for Christ's sake,' said Rosie. She took the brandy off the barman. 'Drink this,' she said.

Together, they managed to get most of it down his neck, along with a couple of tablets. Then Moray ripped off the last of Stephen's trouser leg. The wound was a horrible, livid thing against the stark white of his leg.

'OK,' said Moray, breathing out.

'So, Stephen,' said Rosie, 'you have to trust me. You have to trust me, OK?' She turned quickly to Moray. 'Do you think the tourniquet would hold till the ambulance arrived?'

'I don't know when that might be,' said Moray. 'So, no.'

Rosie nodded. 'Just keep looking at me,' she said, and moved to the side to let Moray work.

Stephen's eyes didn't waver from hers for a moment, although they closed, briefly, when the needle went in for the first time.

'It hurts,' he breathed, quietly, his grip on Rosie's hands strengthening.

'I know,' said Rosie. 'You're being very brave.'

'Oh, Rosie.'

'I know. I know. You doof, if you hadn't been such a stubborn arse, you'd have had this done under a lovely local anaesthetic.'

The shadows under his eyes gave him a haunted look as he winced.

'Christ.'

'I know, I know.' Rosie glanced at Moray, urging him to work faster, but he was making a careful job of it.

Rosie concentrated on Stephen. Later, he would remember very little of it. Nothing but a tight hold on his hands that did not falter, even when he was gripping them in agony as if his life depended on it, and a pair of grey eyes that refused to let him look away.

In reality, stitching Stephen's leg took just over ten minutes. To everyone in the room it felt like a million years. Stephen fell silent, the only sign he was conscious a tear he could not prevent falling from the corner of his eye. Rosie tried to focus on breathing, taking deep breaths, holding them and exhorting Stephen to do the same, to breathe in time with her to relieve the pain, to keep the oxygen moving, until their breath was going in and out at the same time and Rosie, briefly, had the oddest sensation of being unable to tell quite where Stephen ended and she began.

Moray worked away accurately and intently, the only sign of pressure a bead of sweat on his forehead. The landlord brought in another brandy and announced that there was no sign of the ambulance yet, and that everyone was worried. Rosie concentrated on trying somehow to propel herself into Stephen's body, to keep him with her, stop him nodding off, or his blood pressure dropping too far.

Finally Moray straightened up. 'Fine,' he said. 'That'll hold it. But he needs blood. And he needs to be in hospital now.' He eyed Stephen harshly. 'If you'd got over yourself three months ago, we wouldn't have had all that little drama, would we?'

He went over to the sink and washed his hands.

Rosie found she couldn't put Stephen's hands down. She was cramped, but barely felt it. It was as if the entire universe had contracted to the dark blue of his eyes, fringed with black and his shallow breathing.

At last, the ambulance siren sounded, and as soon as the medics arrived everything exploded into noisy colour and action.

'Did you find out his blood group?' shouted a stout paramedic at Rosie.

'O-neg,' said Stephen suddenly. 'I'm O-neg.'

A gurney was brought in through the back door of the pub; someone set up a drip, someone else checked the wound area. There was a lot of yelling and noise and the ambulance lights lit up the quiet street, attracting large numbers of curious onlookers. The entire pub was out on the road. In the back room, the stout paramedic turned to Rosie.

'OK, you can go now, duck,' she said. At first Rosie didn't realise. Then she worked out that her left and Stephen's right hand were still intertwined.

Stephen looked at her. 'Can you come with me?'

Rosie suddenly remembered that she was in a pub, that she was meant to be here with her boyfriend whom she hadn't seen for four weeks, that the hospital was an hour away over the dales and she didn't even have her wallet. All of those things dissipated in a millisecond.

'Of course,' she found herself saying, as the pub door banged open again.

There stood Lady Lipton.

# Chapter Seven

## Free Games with Sweets

*First, we shall have a naming of parts. Anything that is more than 70 per cent small plastic wheels is not confectionery. It is a choking hazard, a losing hazard, an absolute cast-iron guaranteed tantrum generator and, frankly, an abomination in any self-respecting sweet shop.*

*I have absolutely no idea when it came to pass that one treat was not considered enough for a child, that on being offered chocolate, they would instantly expect to receive something else as well. Therefore I shall oppose the creeping invasion of plastic and nasty cheap choc-o-like items whenever I see fit and for as long as it is within my power to do so. The real thing is out there. If you really want to be kind to your children, let them discover it.*

## 1943

'DOWN BY THE SALLEY GARDENS,' Lilian was humming repetitively to herself in her bedroom, finishing up the accounts for the shop. She found the singing distracted her. Since that awful night in the woods, she had decided to put everything behind her. Gordon had gone back to his regiment; Margaret, after begging her to come to Derby with her for the last time, had gone back to her life with her young man.

Lilian had thrown herself into the shop and was teaching herself double-entry bookkeeping as a way of taking some of the burden from her father. Gordon had signalled that after the war he was never coming back to Lipton; now he'd seen a bit of the world, he wanted to make his way in it. Terence was so far away it made the mind boggle even to think of it. And her Neddy was never coming home again. So she would have to shoulder the burden. She realised, even at seventeen years old, this was how it was going to be. Carefully, day by day, swallowed tear by swallowed tear, she built a carapace over her heart. When the banns went up for Ida Delia and Henry, she smiled politely at *everyone gossiping about it and maintained her composure. When she heard on the grapevine that Henry had received his call-up papers, she simply nodded, even though inside she was riven. There was a bit of her that thought, that hoped, that he would realise the error of his ways at the last minute.*

*And now he had his papers. It felt as if, somehow, while she could still see him there was still hope. He didn't come into the sweet shop, of course, he avoided her as assiduously as she avoided him, but she had seen him—at church, standing next to his in-laws to be, or being tugged up and down the high street by Ida Delia, wearing a too-large dress and pretending to all and sundry that there was nothing in there and they were madly in love, that was all.*

*Glimpses, as he rushed past, head bowed . . . they were nothing. There wasn't a note, nothing. It seemed that Henry, once he had given his word, was a man of it. The fact that, as far as Lilian was concerned, he had given it to the worst person she could possibly imagine didn't detract from his commitment.*

*The wedding was sparsely attended. Henry had started basic training and was wearing an ill-fitting uniform in rough wool. Lilian stayed upstairs in her room all day, but couldn't resist a glimpse outside to see the procession go past. Ida Delia, wearing a rose-pink suit dress, and a pink netted hat on her lavish golden curls, looked glorious: happy and radiant, her face beaming in triumph. Henry looked tall, different, with his newly shorn hair and his awkward worsted uniform. Lilian decided there and then that she hated weddings.*

*At around six, when the procession was long past, her dad knocked on Lilian's door. That she wasn't crying was the worst bit. Instead, she sat, perched on the edge of the single bed with its floral counterpane, not looking, not making a sound, but completely and utterly blank.*

*Not knowing what else to do, he took her in his arms and sat her on his knee as if she was a child again and waited, till gradually her rigid body bent a little towards him, and she turned, and buried her head in his shoulder, and made small, mewling animal noises of pain. Terence senior stared out of the window and felt her heart break.*

'She was,' remarked Moray quietly, 'a lot quicker with the damn dog.'

Rosie gazed at Lady Lipton, not understanding.

Stephen had allowed his eyes to close briefly. 'Ah,' he said. 'Mother.'

Rosie stared at him in consternation, then looked at Lady Lipton. Sure enough, the resemblance, though slight, was there. But this didn't make any sense at all. She'd been over at the big house all the time? Knowing her injured son was stuck in that cold house all by himself? Why hadn't she been looking after him?

Rosie shook her head in disbelief. 'Why . . .' she began. She looked from one to the other.

Lady Lipton turned on her, ferociously.

'This is all your fault,' she spat at Rosie. 'Up there pestering the life out of him since the day you arrived. Don't think I didn't spot what you were up to. Mrs Laird tells me everything, you know. He'd have come back to his family in his own time. But now . . . now . . .' Her voice cracked.

'Rosie,' came a weak voice from the gurney, but they were already wheeling him away, and Rosie's head was reeling. She took a couple of steps back and watched, as the ambulance took off for Ashby.

Shaken to the core, Rosie tried to wash her hands in the tiny pub sink. Moray was right beside her, packing up his equipment.

'What the hell?' said Rosie. Moray looked at her curiously.

'Didn't you know?'

'How would I have known? I've only been here five minutes. Why didn't you tell me?'

'I thought he'd have told you!'

'What happened?' But at that moment, Gerard burst through the doors at the back of the pub.

'Where the hell have you been?' he said. He was clearly a bit pissed, and had crisp crumbs all round his mouth. 'There wasn't any food! And you just disappeared when that guy fell over. And I had to sit there by myself for ages! And everyone was talking about that guy. And you. And I had to sit there and listen to it! That scary woman reckons you're sleeping with him.'

'Of course I'm not!'

His lower lip was wobbling. Rosie genuinely feared he might cry.

'I'm sorry,' she said. 'He was sick. He needed help.'

'Well, *he's* a doctor, isn't he?' said Gerard. Moray tried to make himself scarce.

'Yes, but I needed to help.'

'I thought you ran a sweet shop now,' said Gerard stubbornly. 'You made me sit out there all by myself feeling an idiot.'

'I have no relationship with him except he's injured!'

Gerard harrumphed furiously, then turned to Moray and put out a pudgy hand. 'I guess I don't need to introduce myself?'

Moray didn't bother to hide his bewilderment. 'Uhm . . .'

Gerard looked at Rosie then. 'You've told him my name?'

'Uhm. . .'

'Unbelievable,' said Gerard. 'I'm Gerard, her boyfriend. Which she hasn't seen fit to mention, apparently. Fine. What a great trip this is turning out to be. I'm missing Formula One for this.' He looked round. 'I'd storm out, but there's nowhere in this godforsaken backwater to actually go.'

'We could go home,' said Rosie quietly. After the adrenalin burst of the past hour, she suddenly found she was exhausted.

'It's only nine o'clock,' whined Gerard.

'We'll get a bottle of wine,' said Rosie. 'And I'll make you something in the house.'

'Can you make scampi?'

'Of course I can't make scampi, Gerard.'

Moray was keeping his head down, but Rosie felt herself go pink at the thought of him overhearing this ridiculous conversation.

'Can I call you tomorrow?' she said as they were leaving. 'Continue what . . . what we were talking about?'

'Of course,' said Moray.

'What's that?' said Gerard as they were leaving. 'What were you talking about? Me?'

'No,' said Rosie, in exasperation. She'd had enough. The last thing she needed right now was Gerard making it all about himself. Especially when she suspected there was a grain of truth in what he was saying.

OK, so she and Gerard didn't have a massive spark in their relationship. Who did? Everyone got annoying sooner or later, right? And she was hardly the catch of the century.

'No. About the boy . . . the man who was hurt. Anyway, it doesn't matter. Just village gossip, I expect.'

'Well, no point in finding out then, you'll be gone in a couple of weeks.'

'Mmm,' said Rosie. There was a very good chippie open halfway up the main street; she'd take him there for fish and chips.

Out in the street the crowd had dispersed; Les was having a truly fantastic night. Out of the corner of her eye, halfway up the alley that led to the back of the pub, Rosie spied something. Going closer, she confirmed her suspicions as to exactly what it was.

'Well, I'll be darned,' she breathed. It had to be four miles up to Peak

House. Stephen might be an awkward so-and-so but anyone that sent themselves hurtling down a road in a standard-issue military hospital wheelchair most definitely had balls.

**R**osie was half expecting Lilian to be asleep already. It was past her bed-time, but she'd underestimated the old lady's curiosity, and there she was, in her chair, her eyes bright as a bird's. She looked Gerard up and down. Pink and smelling of cider and fish and chips, slightly sweating from the walk up the hill, Rosie had to admit that he didn't look the most appealing prospect. Well, maybe his charm would kick in.

But Gerard looked down in the mouth, not his usual ebullient self at all. It was as if all the bounce had gone out of him.

'Hello, Miss Hopkins,' he murmured. 'How are you?'

Lilian gave him a long look, then glanced quickly at Rosie. This made Rosie even crosser. It was none of Lilian's bloody business.

'It's nice to be here,' mumbled Gerard.

'What were the sirens for?' demanded Lilian, as Rosie went into the kitchen to put the kettle on.

'Uhm, it was Stephen Lakeman. His leg took a turn for the worse.'

'Oh, Hetty's boy. He is no end of trouble.'

Rosie marched out waving the sieve. 'Why didn't you tell me he was Hetty's son? Why does no one tell me anything? Her name is Lipton!'

Lilian shrugged. 'I assumed you knew. Not much of a son he's been anyway. And she's Lady Lipton, that's her title. Lakeman is her name.'

'Right,' said Rosie. 'This is ridiculous. Once and for all, I have to know.'

Gerard sighed. 'I'll just sit down over here, shall I?'

Rosie came out bearing a tray and sat next to her great-aunt.

'How?' she said. 'How could Lady Lipton just abandon him like that?'

'And how,' said Lilian simply, 'could you ever believe that she hadn't tried to help?'

**I**t was Felix's fault of course,' said Lilian. 'Stephen's father,' she added. 'He was obsessed with his regiment and everything to do with the military. And so when they had a boy after Jessica, he was over the moon. Had that boy drilling before he was five, little uniforms and everything.'

Jessica, it transpired, had joined the diplomatic corps and now worked in Malaysia.

'So he didn't want to join the army?'

'He did not,' said Lilian. 'Of course it's common as coppers, children who don't want to do what you want them to do. Any sensible man would have just ignored it. But have you ever met a sensible aristocrat?'

'No,' said Rosie, honestly.

'So there were fights, and threats, and will rewritings and all of that. Big scandal. Stephen was such a sensitive child.'

'He still is,' said Rosie.

'Wanted to do English literature at university. Felix wouldn't hear of it. No son of his doing some namby-pamby subject, not on his money, etc.'

'No, really?' said Rosie. 'That's just daft these days.'

'Well, them lot don't necessarily live in these days,' pointed out Lilian. 'There's an inheritance, a big house to maintain. It takes hard work and duty. A lot of people rely on the estate for their livelihoods. You can't just swan off and read poetry.'

'Why can't the sister do it?'

Lilian rolled her eyes. 'Oh yes, well done, you are very modern.'

'So, what happened?'

'Well,' said Lilian, 'finally . . . finally they came to an agreement. He could do his college course if he did army training at the weekends. Felix thought it was the only way to learn discipline and restraint for when he inherited, rather than all the drug-taking and loose living you need to get an arts degree, apparently.'

'Then what?'

'He took himself off to Africa without telling his dad. Gave up his course to go run a village school in Namibia. He owed the army time too.'

'He went AWOL?'

'Not exactly, you're allowed to defer, but Felix was utterly furious. Sent his blood pressure sky-high.'

'What happened?'

Lilian half smiled. 'Well, I believe you might call it ironic . . . Stephen was hit by a blast from a land mine. A piece of shrapnel got stuck in his leg. He ended up being airlifted to a military hospital.'

'Whereas if he'd joined the army . . .'

'If he'd joined the army, he could have been part of a land-mine clearing team. Yes. Could have made things better. And of course, while he was convalescing in Namibia . . .'

'His dad?' said Rosie, sadly.

Lilian nodded. 'Heart attack. He was getting on.'

Rosie sipped her tea. 'But Stephen didn't help.'

'Your only son getting his leg half blown off in Africa? No, I doubt it.'

'Oh God,' said Rosie. 'What a stupid bloody mess.'

'People carry on,' said Lilian, 'but Hetty and Stephen . . . found it very difficult. She wanted to look after him . . . I think he just wanted to wallow in the guilt. She wanted to hand over the estate. Well, you can imagine.'

'Hadn't he been disinherited?'

'No,' said Lilian. 'It was all bluster and nonsense. Felix was stubborn as a mule too, but he wasn't daft, and he loved his boy. Poor Hetty, she does such a good job of carrying on, but she needs him.'

'I think he's depressed.'

'He owns half of Derbyshire,' said Lilian sharply. 'He ought to get over it.'

They both glanced over at Gerard suddenly. He had fallen asleep and let out a surprised, jerking snore.

'I think you'd better get Jemima Puddleduck to bed,' said Lilian.

'Lilian!' said Rosie. 'Don't be rude.' She gently shook Gerard awake.

Gerard stumbled clumsily up the stairs. Rosie took the teacups back into the kitchen to wash and drain them. Lilian carefully and gently, but nonetheless on her own, got up and started to make preparations for bed.

As Rosie went to head upstairs Lilian asked, gently, 'Do you love him?'

And for the tiniest split second, Rosie didn't have the faintest idea who she meant.

## 1943

*Life went on. It had to. Lilian hurled herself into her work at the sweet shop, trying to balance the books. And the long hot Indian summer finally passed, and when she saw Ida Delia in the street she would quickly look the other way, and so would Ida, so that suited them both well—although Lilian couldn't quite quell a pang every time she saw Ida's swelling stomach. All the while she thought to herself, it could have been me.*

'Bacon sandwich?'

Rosie vehemently hoped that Gerard's favourite sandwich would make up for the night before. They'd just got out of the habit of being together, she decided.

She sat down and looked at him stirring awake, struggling to remember where he was. It was so like him. Suddenly, she realised she had to know.

'Darling,' she said, very quietly. 'Can we talk?'

'That's odd,' came a sleepy voice from the pillow. 'Because at first I thought I heard someone asking me if I'd like a bacon sandwich.' Gerard opened his eyes. 'What time is it?'

'Seven thirty,' said Rosie. 'It's a lovely day outside.'

'Seven thirty?' said Gerard. 'On a *Saturday*? You've changed.'

'Hmm,' said Rosie.

Gerard turned over. 'I'm going back to sleep,' he said. 'I never get up before eleven on Saturdays. You know that.'

'Yes, but this is different . . .'

Watching him, seeing how completely oblivious he was to her own plans, how uninterested in anything other than when she would come back to cook his dinner and take care of their flat, Rosie realised something. Something, she supposed, she'd known for a long time. As quietly as she could, she withdrew into the bathroom, sat down on the seat and, painfully, silently, burst into tears.

It wasn't Gerard's fault—his easy-going, laissez-faire approach to life had charmed her once. But what she'd taken as his likeable good humour concealed, instead, simple laziness; it was easy to find someone like Rosie to look after him and take the place of his mother. But to grow up, to take on the responsibilities of the things she wanted—a nice home, a family, nothing too ambitious, surely?—these were beyond him.

She felt such an idiot. Eight years of her life, *eight years*. Eight years when everyone else had been settling down and building a home and starting a life together. She didn't even know how much Gerard earned. The only reason they'd got a mortgage together was that apart they wouldn't have been allowed one. Oh God, there was so much to untangle. And she would have to sit and listen, over and over again, to everyone— including her bloody great-aunt, it looked like—telling her how they'd known all along, and how was she going to find someone else now . . .

Rosie stared out of the window. What a stupid mess. She'd come up here to stop Lilian getting into trouble, and all that had happened was that she'd got herself, irrevocably, into trouble.

Suddenly the bathroom door banged open, and Rosie jerked up, guiltily. Gerard was still half asleep.

'Need a wazz,' he mumbled, his hand ferreting inside his boxer shorts, his paunch protruding. Then, rubbing the sleep from his eyes, he finally cottoned on to her tear-stained face. 'Hey, what's the matter?' he asked.

Of course that made it worse. Sweet to the end. Rosie found she was no longer capable of crying silently, and instead let the whole lot come out in unsightly choking sobs. Gerard sat down on the side of the bath.

'What's wrong? Do you really hate it here?'

'No! No, it's not that. Gerard. I don't . . . I don't . . .' She sighed. 'Gerard, you have to tell me. Are we going anywhere?'

Gerard furrowed his brow. 'I thought you were working.'

'You and me, Ger. You and me.'

There was a long pause where, for the final time, Rosie thought he might have suddenly revealed himself, gone down on one knee, whipped out a ring, declared undying love. Rosie worried. Had she not been clear? 'I mean, I don't expect fireworks and flowers, but . . .'

Gerard's face had taken on a rather frosty look. 'It sounds like you do.'

'We only get one life, Gerard. Is this it?'

'What do you mean? Why do girls always want to know what we're doing and what's coming next? We're boyfriend and girlfriend, aren't we?'

'Yes, but . . .'

'But what? You're up here surrounded by all these blokes and you've decided I'm a bit boring for you? Not good enough? Maybe I can't chop up a sheep? Which I can do, by the way. I've done dissection.'

'No, Gerard, it's not that.'

'So, what is it? The second we're not living under the same roof you want to go out and do your own thing? Screw half the local pub?'

'Of course not! Stop being childish!'

Rosie couldn't believe what she was hearing. She didn't expect him to be delighted but she hadn't thought he'd be spiteful.

'Ooh, ooh, let me go see that man! With that other man! I'll just leave my silly old boyfriend in the pub, will I? He won't care. All he does is look after me and hang out with me and put up with me all the time.'

Rosie's eyes were wide. 'I didn't think that . . . I never did. I promise.'

'You changed the second you got here,' said Gerard.

'No,' said Rosie. 'No.' But she knew she owed him the truth. 'I think I started changing a long time ago.' Rosie blinked in sadness.

'Oh well,' said Gerard. 'Mum'll be pleased.'

'Really? Didn't she like me?' said Rosie, genuinely surprised.

'She liked you fine, but she always said you wouldn't hang about. And she was right.'

'I wish you'd listened to her five years ago!'

'Plus she didn't even know you were a tart.'

'That is out of order, Gerard, and you know it.'

Gerard shrugged. 'Yeah, whatever.'

There was a long awkward pause, while they both stared in different directions. Finally Gerard looked up. 'Uhm, I still really need a wazz.'

And oddly, as though they hadn't peed in front of each other a thousand times, Rosie left the room to give him some privacy.

Gerard emerged from the bathroom standing a little straighter. Now he looked at her, the picture of wounded male pride.

She felt, suddenly, as if she was waiting for the off. It was like being at the top of a roller coaster, the second before it plummeted.

'When do you want to collect your stuff?' he asked.

Rosie bit her lip. Of course. All of that. 'We'll need to figure it out.'

'That's right,' said Gerard. 'Because you haven't only messed up my personal life, you're going to mess up where I live as well.'

She couldn't deny it. She had thrown a big bomb into his life.

'I . . . I haven't quite thought about it,' she said. 'I might . . . I can maybe buy you out, or you could buy me out, own the whole thing outright.'

She crossed her fingers at the awful lie. Skint and unemployed . . . surely she'd think of something?

'Oh great,' said Gerard. 'You leave me and charge me thousands of pounds for the privilege.' He glanced at his watch. 'If I leave now I can get back to Mum's before the Arsenal friendly. I wouldn't want to hang around this hole anyway.'

Rosie smiled apologetically.

Gerard shook his head. 'Well,' he said.

'I'm sorry,' said Rosie. It sounded so pathetic and weak.

Gerard started getting his stuff together and she sat on the bed and watched him. Rosie suddenly felt panicked. Eight years couldn't just vanish like this, could it? Not just get thrown away so fast?

'Can I ask one thing?' said Rosie. 'Just so as I know?'

Gerard shrugged.

Rosie took a deep breath. 'Were you ever going to pop the question?'

He shrugged again. 'Dunno,' he said. 'I'd never really thought about it.'

'Really?' said Rosie, wondering if this was bravado. 'What, all those weddings we went to and you never once thought about it?'

'I liked things as they were,' said Gerard. 'I didn't have a problem with it. I thought you were cool too.'

'So did I,' said Rosie. It had never even crossed his mind. 'So did I.'

They gazed at each other in mutual incomprehension.

They even managed an awkward, difficult embrace as he left, a little, social kind of kiss that Gerard tried to turn into something else.

'I can't believe I didn't even get a farewell shag,' he said, which Rosie thought was encouraging. That was the thing about Gerard: his irrepressible cheerfulness. She didn't think he'd be down for too long. But for now it was undeniable, as she heard him gently closing the bedroom door, then the front door, which squeaked, and heard the thrum of his beloved Alfa Romeo start up, however much she might regret it later, even if Gerard was her very, very last chance, she could still feel it. Relief.

'That was an awful lot of door-banging,' observed Lilian at breakfast, pained to see how pale Rosie looked. She had that slightly drained skin she'd had when she arrived, which a few weeks of outdoor living, early nights and good food had put paid to. She tried to remind herself that this was the evil family stranger who was here to take all her money and dump her in a home, but she couldn't help being concerned for the girl.

'I don't want to talk about it,' said Rosie, dourly frying up eggs.

Lilian raised her eyebrows. 'Well, better get ready for a busy day then.'

### 1944

*You couldn't ever really dislike a child, Lilian knew. It wasn't right or fair. But still it did seem incredible that any offspring of two such attractive specimens as Henry Carr and Ida Delia Fontayne could be so badly favoured. Dorothy was a difficult birth, Lilian had heard, with Henry advancing with the Allies through Italy, and Ida Delia in labour for three days yelling like a stuck pig. Dorothy had been undersized and bright red, slightly boiled-looking. She always appeared irritated when pushed about in the perambulator, uncomfortably trussed up in several layers of bright yellow wool that gave her a jaundiced look, and a howl or a scowl on her little features.*

Lilian hadn't oversold market day. The entire village was absolutely thronged; there seemed to be as many horses as cars, and cows were lowing as they were driven through in large trucks on their way to the Stirlings' field where the market would be held. Rosie took a deep breath and tied on her apron.

Outside the door of the shop her first customer was already waiting.

'Does your mother know you're here, Edison?' asked Rosie, seeing no one behind him.

Edison nodded seriously. 'Yup. She said it was the best place for me. Encourage self-safishsee.'

'Really?' said Rosie, slightly peeved. 'Why's that then?'

'I am most terribly afraid of animals,' he said.

'What, all animals?' said Rosie, turning the heavy key.

'Yes,' said Edison. 'And some plants. That's why it's best if I keep myself out of the way. Hester said I should make myself useful.'

'Who's Hester?'

'My mother.'

'Of course she is,' said Rosie. She called her mum Angie sometimes, but it didn't seem quite the same.

'She thinks I would be a good help to you.'

'Does she now. Why doesn't she take you to see the animals so you could find out they're not scary?'

'Hester thinks it's wrong that animals get killed for us,' mumbled Edison. 'She doesn't really prove.'

At that moment Hester appeared, grey hair glinting.

'Hello,' she said coolly. 'Now. Listen. I have to go distribute these vegan leaflets at the market. Can I leave Edison with you for a little while? He'll be a huge help, I'm sure.'

Rosie was taken aback. 'Well,' she stuttered, 'well, I suppose so.'

'Fantastic! Wonderful!' said Hester, barely breaking stride.

Rosie and Edison watched her disappear down the high street. Then Rosie turned towards the skinny little boy.

'The thing is,' said Rosie, 'everyone's entitled to their own opinion. But I'm going down later to see all the animals.'

Edison looked at her, his eyes blinking anxiously. 'Oh,' he said.

'You could come with me if you like,' said Rosie. 'I promise to protect you from them.'

Edison considered. 'OK,' he said.

'OK,' said Rosie. 'Now, I need you to fold up these boxes very small and put them in this larger box for cardboard recycling.'

'Can I draw on them first?'

'You can,' said Rosie, 'as long as you keep out of my way. Now, let's open up, shall we?' she said.

The next person to arrive was Roy Blaine, the dentist. He was holding a local newspaper in his hands.

'I have notice of an advert here,' he said.

Rosie squinted. What was he talking about?

'About the forthcoming sale of a going concern . . .'

'Oh, but I only advertised in the Derby paper,' Rosie said.

'We share advertising.' Roy marched round the shop. 'So,' he said, looking around, 'it's not exactly a *going* concern, is it?'

'Are you interested?'

'I might be,' said Mr Blaine. 'This might make a rather good site for my new dental practice. Brand new veneers, perfect smiles, superfast whitening, expensive fillings.' He was practically rubbing his hands together. 'Everyone wants that perfect smile nowadays.'

Personally Rosie thought that his hyper-straight, neon-white Hollywood teeth were creepy and weird, like a direct view of a skull picked clean by birds. But she didn't want to say so.

'Yes, it's all new techniques in dentistry these days. A quaint little place like this might work rather well.'

'So you wouldn't be selling sweets?'

'No!' said Roy. 'I'd be selling top-of-the-range teeth whiteners at four hundred pounds a pop. So what do you think about that, Snaggle Mouth?'

'Did you just call me Snaggle Mouth?' said Rosie.

'Affectionately of course,' said Roy. He looked around greedily a little longer then checked his expensive watch. 'Well, I'd better get on. Time is teeth, and teeth are money,' he said, with a final flash of his luminous grin. He left the shop, making the bell ring abruptly.

The idea of Roy Blaine taking over Lilian's beloved shop and turning it into some high-tech tooth emporium made her feel absolutely miserable. He'd rip out all the shelves and the counter and the fixtures and . . . She didn't want this. She didn't want to sell it like this.

The shop filled up quickly. Many people who had come into Lipton from the surrounding villages exclaimed with delight at the restoration of their beloved sweet shop, missing from so many market days past. Tentatively they asked for their favourites, asked after Lilian, exclaimed as to how much Rosie resembled her, and beamed when Rosie deftly twirled and passed the little striped paper bags full of memories out into the crowd.

The morning flew past, the door and the till ringing busily. Things were going so well that Rosie almost forgot about her terrible start to the day. She persuaded Anton that four sugar mice were more than enough to get him through the next half-hour as he waited for his wife to get back from the fête. Chrissie admired the shop when she popped in to fetch him.

'Oh,' she said. 'And I'm on the organising committee for the tombola. I never thought, we could have touched you for a donation.'

'Of course you can,' said Rosie. 'What about a big box of chocs?'

'You're a darling!' The two women looked at each other. Anton's wife had her hands full of shopping, and a steadying arm on Anton.

'Why don't I bring them down later?' said Rosie.

'That would be fantastic,' said Chrissie.

'You know,' said Rosie to the pair of them, 'you could run this sweet shop.'

There was a ringing of the door right behind her. Rosie didn't even have to turn round.

'What are you doing now, Hopkins?' said Moray, sighing. 'I wish you'd stop trying to kill all my patients.'

'I *meant*,' said Rosie, 'when he's slim enough to get behind the counter. Like a challenge. What do you think, Anton?'

Anton looked thrilled. 'I would like to run a sweet shop,' he said.

'No!' said Moray. 'Out of here.'

'I only sold him four sugar mice,' said Rosie defiantly after Anton had heaved his vast bulk out of the shop. 'I talked him down from nineteen.'

Moray checked his watch. 'Well, we've been in the same space for almost four minutes and nothing has turned up bleeding to death. A record for us, wouldn't you say?'

Rosie smiled. 'What can I get you?'

'Just some mints. I'm judging the baking and some of those old ladies get a tad overenthusiastic when they win.'

'I bet they do,' said Rosie. Moray was looking dapper in his tweed jacket and checked shirt. She was less sure about his mustard-coloured trousers.

'Are you looking at my trousers?' asked Moray.

'Yes, but I'll stop before I go blind.'

'They're *country*,' said Moray. 'Anyway, you are in no position to be making sartorial comments.' Which was the exact moment when, in a blinding flash, Rosie realised—it wasn't like her to be slow; after all, she'd been surrounded by male nurses—that Moray hadn't been asking her out on dates.

'They are a little bit country and a little bit rock 'n' roll,' said Rosie, grinning at him with sudden—what? Relief? Disappointment? 'How's Stephen?'

'I thought you were going to go with the ambulance,' said Moray.

'Yup,' said Rosie. 'But once that old bag was on the scene . . .'

'She's all right, Hetty,' said Moray. 'Her life is just a bit different from ours, that's all. Remember, she lost her husband only last year.'

Rosie instantly felt a bit guilty. It was true, she'd only ever seen one side of the story. 'Anyway?'

'Anyway,' said Moray. 'I called the hospital this morning. They got plenty of blood into him. He was very weak, but they put him on a drip. He was malnourished too. Then as soon as they'd checked him out—I did a beautiful stitching job by all accounts—'

'Helped by me,' said Rosie.

'By my glamorous assistant, yes. Anyway, as soon as they'd patched him up, he insisted on discharging himself. Doesn't like hospitals apparently.'

Rosie tried to think of him alone in a military field hospital in Africa. She wasn't at all surprised.

'So. Just goes to show he should have done this months ago. Bloody stubborn idiot,' said Moray.

'Sounds as if you rather like the bloody stubborn idiot.'

'Oh, Stephen was always different. Always his own man,' said Moray. He picked up his bag of sweets. 'And some Golf Balls,' he said. 'I'll drop them off at Peak House.'

'Were you guys good friends?' asked Rosie.

Moray nodded. 'We were, actually. Till he went off on his do-gooder jobs in Africa. Couldn't believe I didn't want to go with him.'

'Why not?'

Moray snorted. 'Would you? Anyway, I believe my sort isn't exactly welcome over there. No. Seriously, I'd have been rubbish, no help at all.'

I like my home comforts too much. Just too selfish. Anyway, of course he pulled a classic Stephen, stormed off and I didn't hear from him . . . I didn't even know where he got his injury, I only found that out the other day. I figured he'd been bitten by a stoat or something and was just too embarrassed to tell anyone. Or a tiger.'

'You don't get tigers in Africa,' piped up Edison.

'Hi, Edison,' he said to the small figure crouched behind the counter.

'Well, when you see him . . .' said Rosie. Then she couldn't think what to say. 'Oh, nothing. Just say hello from me. And that he's an idiot.'

'Will do,' said Moray. 'Are you coming down later?'

'Yes, in a bit. Keep some cake for me.'

'Is that really what you feel like after a morning surrounded by fudge?'

'It's for Lilian,' said Rosie strictly. 'Don't you start. I've already had Blaine in.'

'Ugh. Dentist cooties,' he said, and winked and turned to go.

Rosie watched him leave, shaking her head in disbelief. The country air had clearly made her gaydar go on the blink. She was pleased too, though kicked herself for feeling that it would have been strange for such a good-looking man to fancy her. It wouldn't have been strange, she told herself, trying to make herself believe it. She still couldn't get her head round it; after being in a relationship for eight years, she was single. Single at thirty-one. It was terrifying and upsetting and oddly liberating.

'*I wan egg wi present!*' a child was screeching on the floor, as the mother rotated anxiously, her hands fluttering like butterflies.

'I'm so sorry,' said Rosie, for the tenth time. 'We just don't have any.'

'*I want an egg!*'

'Now, Nathan, they don't have any,' the mother was saying anxiously.

'*Want it now!*'

'Come now, little man,' said Rosie, gently. 'Would you like to try our bird's eggs? They have a candy shell, then chocolate, then inside a little candy bird. What do you think?'

'*Shut up!*' shouted the boy. Rosie smiled apologetically at the queue, who were rolling their eyes. Nobody really liked to buy sweets while someone was screaming, and people quickly grabbed chocolate bars or just left altogether. Edison popped his head out from behind the counter.

'That's Nathan,' he hissed to Rosie. 'He's the mean kid who took my lollipop,' whispered Edison.

'Him?' said Rosie, surprised. 'That little squirt?' Edison nodded. He touched her knee, obviously frightened.

'But he's pathetic,' said Rosie. 'Go and take a look at him.'

Edison shook his head frantically. 'He's mean.'

'He's rubbish,' said Rosie. 'Come on, let's have a look.'

Gently, she coaxed Edison out to the front of the shop, where Nathan was rolling from side to side on the floor, shouting about how it wasn't fair. As soon as Nathan felt them looking at him, he turned. When he saw it was Edison his eyes widened. He clearly became conscious of how he was lying prostrate on the floor. The two boys regarded each other for a long time. Edison pushed his glasses up on his nose.

'Hello, Nathan,' he managed, his voice quavering. There was a pause.

'Is this your sweet shop?' came the voice from the floor. Rosie nodded her head.

'Yes,' said Edison. 'Kind of.'

Casually, Nathan picked himself up off the floor.

'You've got a whole sweet shop?'

Edison shrugged. 'Whatever.'

Rosie looked at him. 'Did you just say "whatever"?'

Edison got up on tiptoes to whisper in her ear. 'I don't know what it means. It's something you're meant to say.'

'OK then,' Rosie whispered back.

Nathan was now rubbing the back of his shaved head.

'Iss all right,' he said.

'Did you want anything?' said Rosie, as if she and Edison were partners.

Nathan shrugged. 'Chocolate eggs please.'

Nathan's mother was practically sobbing with gratitude as she handed over the money.

'Thank you so much . . . He's just tired, aren't you, Nathan?' she said, nervously caressing her son's shoulders.

Nathan pushed her hand away. 'Whatever,' he said.

'See?' whispered Edison.

Nathan took the chocolate bag without a thank you. Then, turning to go, he looked back. 'Wan one?'

Edison's eyes popped behind his spectacles. Hardly daring to believe it wasn't a trick, he stepped forward very shyly and carefully. Rosie reckoned Nathan was buying his silence.

Tentatively Edison reached out his hand towards the bag. Then, suddenly, he stopped himself.

'Neh,' he said. 'It's my shop. I can have anything I want. Can't be bothered.'

There was a moment's silence, as Nathan reassessed the boy standing in front of him as though through totally new eyes. Then he nodded.

'Awright,' he said. 'Maybe see you down the fête later?'

'Maybe,' said Edison, nonchalantly.

'Edison,' Rosie said, after they had left, 'I could kiss you.'

'Please don't do that,' said Edison. 'It would be Inpropreet Behaviour.'

Rosie smiled. 'I would not like to inflict inpropreet behaviour on you,' she said. 'But well done.'

Edison shrugged and went back to playing with the boxes.

'Some of them are quite a handful, aren't they?' came a voice, nodding down the road at Nathan. Rosie looked up; she hadn't even noticed the nice woman from before, Tina Ferrers, quietly browsing the powdered sugar sweets with the twins, Kent and Emily.

'Not yours,' said Rosie. 'Yours are angels.'

Tina laughed. 'Ha, right. Yeah. They do show an amazing turn of being angels when promised a visit to your sweet shop though, I will say that.'

Rosie smiled. 'I wish all of them did.'

Tina looked around. 'I love what you've done here. It's brilliant. Imagine, having your own business. I'm totally in awe of that.'

'Oh, it's not mine,' said Rosie. 'I'm only caretaking for my aunt. In fact, it's going up for sale.'

'Really?' Tina ran her hands down one of the shelves, and sighed.

'What?' said Rosie.

'Oh, nothing. Just a silly idea . . .'

Rosie smiled. She liked this woman. 'What, about this place?'

'I mean, there's no reason why you couldn't sell more things here. Little souvenirs maybe. Nothing tacky, just things to add on for holidaymakers to remember their time here.'

Rosie smiled. 'It sounds like you have lots of ideas,' she said.

Tina smiled. 'Well, you know. Once Kent and Emily are at school I have a bit of time on my hands. And I have my divorce settlement . . .'

'You're divorced?' Rosie said. Tina was so pretty, so obviously nice, with such nice children. Could it really happen to just about anyone?

Tina looked sad. 'Well, let's just say he preferred the bottle to me,' she said. 'Open secret round these parts, like bloody everything. That's why I took a final settlement in the divorce. In case he drinks everything else away.'

She tried a half-smile but Rosie could feel pain beneath the words.

'If you like,' she said, 'you could come round one night and I'll take you through the books.'

'Really?' said Tina. 'But . . . well, I don't know. I'd have to employ some-one to help.'

'Oh, it can't be done alone,' said Rosie. 'I'm going half crazy here. Have to shut the shop if I'm to do anything else at all.'

'But you're not shutting up today?'

'Well, I know it sounds a bit daft, but I wanted to see the market-day fair. I won't be here for it next year, and so it's probably my only chance.'

Tina's brow furrowed. 'But this is one of your busiest days of the year! You can't just shut it up and go!'

'But it's my shop! And I want to take Edison.'

Tina grinned. 'OK, how about I mind the shop for you for an hour?'

Rosie was taken aback. But she considered it from all angles. Tina seemed absolutely nice and decent. She was interested in the shop. If the worst happened and she ran away with the cash box, well, Moray would know where she lived. This was a village. Nothing bad would happen.

She made up her mind. 'OK!' she said, joyfully taking off her apron.

She watched Tina serve a couple of customers—of course she knew nearly all of them, and had a friendly word for each one. This could, Rosie thought to herself, just possibly work.

The main street was empty; everyone was up past the churchyard, in Farmer Stirling's large pasture. Over in the next field, teenagers in neon vests pointed out parking, and tinny music played through a sound system. Edison's grip on Rosie's hand grew a little tighter. Over the PA a man was talking about a pony parade and a cucumber competition. The place was thronged with people—all of them, Rosie noticed, wearing waxed jackets and wellingtons. She glanced down glumly. She was wear-ing wedges. They were pretty, comfortable and good for the shop. Now, she was in severe danger of lurching into a bog. She never got it right.

There were wooden walkways, thankfully, round the perimeter of the field, and Rosie stuck to those, looking for the tombola stand. Plenty of people nodded at her as she passed and she smiled back politely and tried to say hello to everyone. She peered into tents—there was one full of different types of jam, one with huge vegetables that looked like they were on steroids, a baking tent, where she would have liked to spend a little bit more time, till she overheard the PA bellow that the tombola draw was about to take place in Tent A. Tent A was, of course, all the way back round the field again, but Rosie decided not to risk cutting through the parade of lambs in her silly shoes, and walked the entire circumference.

When she passed Mrs Isitt, the woman simply looked at her feet and made a loud harrumphing noise, as if you couldn't expect anything else from a townie like her. Just after her came Mr Isitt, walking so much better he was like a different person.

Finally, they made it to the right tent, and she crashed in, holding up the enormous box of chocolates, just as the tub was beginning to spin.

'Here it is!' she yelled. 'Don't start without us!'

The entire room turned to look at her. Of course, standing up on the stage, wearing her magnificently large coat and with a rather haughty expression on her face was Hetty. Lady Lipton herself.

Rosie immediately glanced around for Stephen. Hetty saw her do it, and smirked. Chrissie, Anton's wife, approached her and took the large red-velvet box off her with sincere thanks.

Rosie hauled out the raffle tickets Lilian had made her buy earlier and handed them to Edison to watch for her, but as the prizes came and went— a ginger cake, an hour of free gardening, a fishing rod—she realised she wasn't about to get lucky. Finally it came to the large box of chocolates, and a roar of applause went up as the winner was found to be Anton.

'Now,' said Lady Lipton, 'I'm afraid Anton can't have his prize, as his wife is on the committee.'

'Everyone's wife is on the committee,' said Anton in shock.

'And,' said Lady Lipton, 'we'd like you here next year to play again. Do I have your permission to donate these to the local children's home?'

'No,' said Anton.

'Yes!' said his wife, and jumped up on stage before he could stir himself. She shook Hetty firmly by the hand.

'Thank you,' she whispered.

'And finally,' said Hetty, 'our top prize.'

The tombola twirled round, but Rosie barely paid attention; she was busy thanking Anton, who looked pink, but not pleased, at being complimented for his generosity. So when Hetty called out the number Rosie missed it completely, and Hetty was required to repeat herself.

'Yellow 197! Yellow 197!'

Gradually Rosie became aware of a tugging at her sleeve. 'What is it, Edison?' she asked.

'Look! Look!' He waved the ticket in the air. It was yellow, number 197.

'There it is!' shouted one of the farmers behind her. 'She's got it!'

There was a general outburst of clapping, and much chat. Rosie glanced around, looking confused.

'Up you go,' said Chrissie. 'Go and collect it. I'll keep the boy.'

'Go and collect what?' said Rosie, as Hetty beckoned her up on stage. The man from the local paper crouched down in front of her to take a photo, and the room applauded as Rosie, feeling extremely confused, was handed a very small, very pink, very curious-looking piglet.

'What . . . what's *this*?' she said as the camera flashed.

'It's your pig. First prize in the raffle,' said Hetty. 'Congratulations.'

'A pig.'

'Yes.'

As Rosie held the pig, it started to pee on the straw and mud floor of the marquee. It didn't stop for quite a while. There was much guffawing, particularly when the pee began to flood her already-muddy wedges.

Rosie decided just to stand still and pretend it wasn't happening. Hetty was laughing her head off.

'What am I supposed to do with a pig?' she hissed.

'Bacon sandwich?' said Hetty, clasping her hands round Rosie's shoulders so the photographers could get another shot. After that the crowd drifted away, leaving Hetty, Rosie, Edison and the pig.

Edison was absolutely fascinated with the creature. He would approach within a few centimetres of her and they would go nose to nose and regard each other seriously, then he would back off again.

'What am I meant to do with this?' said Rosie.

'That's a very valuable animal,' said Lady Lipton. 'I'd hold on to it if I were you.'

Rosie looked at it mulishly. The pig looked back and made a small grunting noise. It was, she supposed, rather cute.

Lady Lipton let out a sigh. 'So. It appears that my son. And the, ahem, the entire village. Thinks I owe you an apology.'

Rosie looked at her. 'But you don't.'

Lady Lipton shrugged. 'I was . . . I was upset. It appears that . . . yes. Without you . . . well. He is up. And about. And outside. So. Thank you. Thank you for what you did for Stephen.'

'And Bran,' reminded Rosie, with a slight twitch of the lips. 'So how's—'

'Bran's fine, thanks,' said Hetty.

Rosie smiled to herself. She had walked into that.

'My son? Well, he's fine. He's going to be all right,' said Hetty.

Rosie bit her lip. 'But why weren't . . . Sorry, but I have to ask.'

'Why wasn't I looking after my only son?' said Hetty. There was no one else in the tent now except the two of them and Edison.

'You don't have children, do you?' Hetty said. 'Until you do, you can't know. You can't know how much you love them.'

'Hmm,' Rosie said.

'And when you're a family . . . you just try as hard as you can to hold it all together. I lost my husband. And my son. Even though I bounced between them for years trying to make it right. Even though I tried everything. You have no right to march in here with your big city ways and think you know about us. No right at all.'

Rosie felt ashamed, as Hetty's face manifested how deep was her grief.

'I'm sorry you lost your husband,' she said. 'So sorry. But that night . . . I still can't get my head round how quickly you came running when it was your dog and how late you were when it was your son.'

Hetty turned on her, suddenly furious once more.

'Bran loves me back,' she said, imperious. 'And don't you ever think I stopped trying,' Hetty added. 'Not for a second.'

She turned and stormed out of the tent in her wellingtons. Rosie watched her leave, feeling awful.

**R**osie went out in search of lunch and someone to give the pig to. The fête was in full swing; dogs were showing off their prowess at jumping obstacles round a miniature race course; people walked about proudly wearing large rosettes that they'd won for different competitions.

She found him—and realised instantly it wasn't really lunch she'd been looking for—in the corner of the flower tent. It was practically deserted, and a shocking display of incredibly vulgar dahlias had taken first place. But on the floor was possibly the most even surface in the entire place: green Astroturf. Stephen was crossly, and painfully, inching his way up and down it with a large stick.

'Nice stick,' she said. Stephen's back stiffened, then he turned.

'Nice pig,' he said. Then he sniffed. 'Can I smell . . .?'

'It's the pig,' said Rosie.

'Well, that's good.'

'There's flowers everywhere. That should mask it.'

As if in response to this, the piglet leaned over and started eating one of the more gaudy arrangements.

'So, how are you?' Rosie asked.

'I'm fine, I'm fine. I'm pretending I'm Charlie Chaplin. Plus, they gave me good drugs.'

'Well, that's nice,' said Rosie. Even so, she saw him wince and look around for a chair. 'I saw Hetty,' she added.

Stephen winced again. 'Oh yes? Did she tell you all about her hideous ungrateful son who killed his own father? I kind of liked it better when you didn't know who I was.' He sat down. 'Is that really your pig or did you put a magic spell on my mother? And it's true,' he said, 'I did like it when you didn't know. You can't imagine what it's like around here, everybody knowing everyone else's business. And now the news is out, ooh, Stephen's OK again. The jags will be out in force.'

'What are jags?'

Stephen looked at her wryly. 'You don't know? Uhm, they're like wags. But for chaps they think have big houses.'

'Really?' said Rosie. 'I've never heard of them.'

'You're lucky,' said Stephen. 'Neither side tends to come out of it well.'

'I can imagine,' she said.

'Sometimes it's easier to have secrets,' Stephen mused. 'I mean, you might have disliked me because I was an oaf, but you didn't dislike me because I killed my dad.'

'It was definitely the oaf thing,' said Rosie. 'But you didn't kill your dad.'

'She thinks I did. So I imagine half the village thinks I did. And look at me now, still not facing up to my responsibilities.' He bit his lip.

'Did you love him?' she asked.

'Of course I did!' said Stephen. 'I loved him however he was.

Unfortunately, he didn't extend the same courtesy to his son. You can't make people be how you want them to be! And she backed him all the way.' Stephen smiled, cynically. 'Just because they were right doesn't mean I'm not still pissed off about it.'

'How were they right?'

'Because if I'd been clearing land mines it could have saved my leg and . . . and . . . ' His voice trailed off.

'Did you like it in Africa?' Rosie asked him gently.

'Some of it,' he said thoughtfully. 'Well, I stayed eight years. I loved the people and building the school, and the children were so amazing. They didn't care that they didn't have big houses or computer games or liberal arts degrees . . . All they wanted to do was learn, and play, and be kids. I didn't want to stay there for ever. But yes, I was happy. I didn't want to think about bloody Lipton and bloody Lipton Hall and all the dreary day-to-day penny-pinching *stuff* of it. Paintings and rugs and roofs and taxes and all of that. Out there we hardly had anything, but it was real life, you know?'

In a funny way, even though their experiences couldn't have been more different, Rosie did know. To leave everything behind: your home, your friends, your job. It was something she knew a bit about too.

'I would have come back one day,' said Stephen. 'You must think I'm such a child.'

'Families are families,' said Rosie. 'Always complicated, no matter how old you are.'

'But to get stretchered back here in disgrace, without Dad.' Stephen stared at the floor. 'I think anyone would have found it difficult.'

'I agree,' said Rosie.

The fête was quietening down outside. Stephen looked miles away. 'Akibo,' he said, 'and his brother, Jabo. Akibo was really serious, all the time. Had a million questions about all sorts of things. Was obsessed with Manchester United. There was one TV in the village, but it didn't show the football of course. But sometimes I could get up to town and go to an Internet caff, and I'd check out the scores for him. He was delighted. Once a charity sent us some clothes, and I looked the shirt out for him. It was like I'd got the whole team to stop by and do a kickabout with him.'

'Probably better,' said Rosie. 'They're not that nice.'

'And Jabo was the most beautiful child ever. So cute. All he wanted to do was whatever Akibo was doing. He'd sit with a piece of paper and a stone and pretend he was writing letters. And you'd say, "Are you doing your sums, Jabo?" and he'd say, *"Yessuh! Nine! Seven! Sixty!"'*

Rosie smiled.

'Akibo wanted to come with me to get a frog. I was going to dissect it with them. I wasn't meant to, but I thought it would be a useful exercise. Akibo came to help because he was useful for that kind of thing, knew a lot. And Jabo came because . . . because Jabo did whatever Akibo did.' He stuttered. 'There wasn't . . . I don't know. But I don't think there would have been enough left for their mother to bury.'

Rosie went back to the house. Peter Isitt, thank God, had offered to look after the pig for her, and Rosie had seen a spark in Mrs Isitt's eye that made her think the pig must be worth something. She crept back through what was now substantial rainfall and early dusk, with a lovely set of lamb chops she had felt only momentarily squeamish about buying from the butcher's tent—perhaps she was turning into a country girl after all—and some new potatoes, green beans and fresh mint from the produce stands, the potatoes still covered in earth.

Tina had helped the sweet shop have its best day ever, and cashed up. Rosie insisted on paying her. Tina looked at the money.

'Wow,' she said. 'It's like having a real job again.'

Rosie looked around. Tina had moved the chocolate teddies right to the very front, near the till. It was a good strategy. Few small hands could resist a chocolate teddy, and few grandparents could resist buying one.

'You know,' said Rosie, 'there have been expressions of interest . . .' She thought again of Roy Blaine's terrifying image of rows of gleaming gnashers. 'But why don't you see . . . talk to the bank or someone? If anyone has to take it over, I'd really like it to be you.'

The second she walked in the house, unlocked as ever, she knew. Not a light was on; neither was the perpetually-tuned-to-Radio-4 wireless. The fire wasn't lit and there was an odd smell in the air.

Rosie rushed to the bedroom, cursing herself for being absent for so long. Her great-aunt was sitting up, shaking and staring straight ahead. There was something wrong with the left side of her face, Rosie saw with a sinking heart. And there wasn't a second to lose.

# Chapter Eight

### Barley Sugar

*Barley sugar is nature's way of making sure you don't feel too guilty when you are unwell and want to eat sweets. The concept of barley as a healthful, life-giving cereal, albeit found in confectionery as more of a trace element, should help lift your mood. And under the circumstances, when you're feeling poorly, the best possible remedy is to improve your mental attitude, which means that eating a sweet which feels on some level as if it might be good for you is surely the way forward.*

*Plus as long as you suck and don't bite, the barley sugar will release a comforting sweetness that will raise your spirits, make you feel cosy and safe and set you on the road to health again. Frankly they should prescribe it with aspirin.*

'SO YOU'RE HER CARER?' the snappy nurse had asked, not very kindly. Rosie couldn't blame her. She knew that when someone had a stroke—or a mini-stroke, as seemed likely; Lilian had come round and although a little confused seemed basically all right—speed was of the essence. Moray had helped her give Lilian aspirin, then had driven them to the hospital, and now Lilian was being eased into a robe. Rosie had packed her aunt's favourite nightgowns and a dressing gown. She didn't want Lilian confused and frightened, in a strange place with her bum hanging out.

'Yes,' said Rosie. 'But I have to look after her business as well.' She was feeling horribly guilty, knowing she had taken the afternoon off. If she hadn't, if she'd been just next door . . . Maybe that would have made a difference. Maybe not. She'd tried to interest Lilian in a mobile phone, but Lilian had looked at her as if she'd suggested she started carrying a shark in her pocket, so she hadn't insisted.

'She needs someone watching her all the time,' scolded the nurse. 'If you can't look after her, she should be in a place where people can.'

Rosie nodded. The fact that she knew this was coming—it was, she supposed, inevitable—didn't make up for the fact that she couldn't bear, suddenly, to have to tell Lilian that she'd need to move. Move out of the house, indeed, she'd been born in, the high attic room, and the garden. Her beautiful, beautiful garden. How could she tell her to give that up?

Oh God, why were things so complicated? Rosie rushed into the little side ward. Lilian was sitting up, looking around her.

'Rosie,' she said. 'What kind of a hellhole is this?'

'Uhm, it's the hospital,' said Rosie.

'It's horrible. Can I go home? I'm hungry.'

'Well, that's a good sign,' said Rosie. Behind her the nurse was shaking her head crossly. 'You can't go home quite yet, though. They have to check you over. But I'll stay with you. We'll play Scrabble, it'll be good.'

Lilian's face looked perturbed.

'But who's going to mind the shop tomorrow?' she asked.

'Uhm,' Rosie said, 'I might have someone in mind.'

Tina was absolutely delighted. And as soon as they got Lilian home, and comfortably ensconced, Rosie offered her a job. Rosie knew it was only a temporary solution, but she had placed a baby monitor next to Lilian, taken the other end into the shop, and scared Lilian half out of her wits by talking into it every so often to check she was OK. Lilian got her revenge by listening to Rosie advising customers on their sweet choice, and then vigorously advising them some other way. It took a bit of getting used to, not least for the children who were startled by the disembodied voice, but after a while it became obvious to Rosie that Lilian was loving her involvement in the life of the shop.

Tina dropped Kent and Emily at school, then worked a long lunch so Rosie could sit with Lilian, organise her prescriptions and run any errands, while Tina served the lunch-time rush and helped with stock control, product suggestions and some gentle marketing tips. Then she would leave at three and Rosie could finish up the day and make supper for Lilian, who, while technically recovered, was still rather wobbly.

So life continued, the year moving deeper and deeper into autumn. Every morning now, as Rosie looked out of her window, she would see a mist curling off the grass, the precipitation of the night before turning to frost, then gradually melting under an occasional autumn sun. Some mornings, the skies ouside her window were black as pitch, and the rain and the wind howled down the vale. Even the locals talked of it as a shocker for the time of year, cold beyond memory. Which was how Rosie found herself, one lunch time, outside Lipton's clothes shop.

She stared in the window. This was the place, on her first day here, she'd sworn never to enter. But she had been here a lot longer than expected, and hadn't even heard from Gerard. For all she knew, he'd made a bonfire of her clothes on their tiny balcony. On a whim, she took out her mobile and called Mike, her best mate back at the hospital.

'*Rose-oh!*' Mike yelled. 'Where the *hell* have you been? You've just totally disappeared off the face of the planet.'

'Off the face of London you mean,' said Rosie.

'Yes,' said Mike. 'The planet. Like I said. When are you coming home, love? We heard about you and Gerard.'

'What did he say?'

'Oh, nothing. He said you'd gone a bit mental in the country. And that he thought maybe the sugar had gone to your head. And that you're living with a mad old spinster lady and turning into her.' Mike said the last bit in a rush, as if he were trying to get it all out.

'OK, OK, that's enough,' said Rosie crossly. 'How is he?'

Mike paused. Rosie didn't really like the pause.

'Uhm. You are totally over him, right?'

'Well . . . you know, we've only been broken up—what, a month?'

Mike sighed. 'Well,' he said. 'I did see him at the Bears.' That was the local hospital pub. 'With his arm round the neck of Yolande Harris.'

Rosie was so surprised she nearly tripped up. She couldn't believe what a strong reaction she was having. After all, she'd dumped him, hadn't she? But really, how had he managed to get over her that fast?

Rosie realised she wasn't thinking about Gerard, specifically. It wasn't him. It wasn't him she was missing. It was the horrifying realisation that eight years, *eight years*, could be wiped out in a flash. And everything she had told herself—that he had loved her really, that they'd been in love and it just hadn't worked out, instantly became meaningless in her eyes.

'Yolande Harris?' she gasped. 'How does he even get up there?' Yolande Harris was about six foot of gorgeous, imperious attitude. Rosie was amazed she'd even look at a squit like Gerard.

'Oh, you know what he's like,' said Mike. 'He's been doing all the running. I think he just wore her down in the end.'

Rosie did know what he was like. When he turned on the charm full beam, when he brought out the romantic gestures and the love poems and the . . . well. It was a long time ago now.

'She'll eat him for breakfast,' said Mike.

'I hope she'll make him breakfast,' said Rosie, a little stutter in her voice. 'Otherwise he'll starve to death.'

'Darling, I'm sorry,' said Mike.

'No, it's all right,' said Rosie, meaning it. 'It's good that . . . it's good I know. It means I can stop worrying about him.'

'You think? You know Yolande though, right? If anything, this is just the start of his problems.'

Rosie blinked as she hung up. She hadn't thought about Gerard, not really, not with Stephen's injury and her aunt getting ill and all the work of the shop. But it was obvious that he had been not-thinking-about-her a lot more than she'd been not-thinking-about-him, and that hurt her terribly. Other people were getting on with their lives. She couldn't hide away up here for ever. Otherwise her life was going to slip through her fingers.

**H**ow are you doing, Lil?' Rosie said, sitting next to the old lady on the bed, sharing the freshest baps from the baker's. Lilian had deliberately requested corned beef, which Rosie privately thought was disgusting.

'You know,' Rosie said, 'Tina might buy the shop. What would you think about that?'

'Hmm,' said Lilian, feigning lack of interest. 'And don't call me Lil.'

'The thing is,' said Rosie, 'I have to go back to London. At some point. I do. I have a whole life there . . . well, I don't really. I have the ruins of a life there. But the thing is I need to go home. At some point. Some time.'

Lilian looked at her. 'Well, people do leave,' she said, faintly.

'I wouldn't be "leaving" leaving,' said Rosie. 'I wouldn't want to do that. I'd want to come up and make sure you were OK, and pop in and check on the sweet shop and that.'

Lilian fixed her with a gimlet eye. 'Mmm-hmm.'

Rosie took a bite of her bap and chewed thoughtfully. 'I mean, I can't stay here for ever. You need proper care. I thought I might hire a car, and maybe we could look at some . . . some old people's homes.'

'My body is a bit rubbish,' said Lilian. 'But I'm not *old* old.'

'You're eighty-seven.'

'Not old in my head,' said Lilian defiantly.

'How old are you in your head?' said Rosie, genuinely curious.

Lilian stared out of the window. In her head, for ever, she was seventeen. With a handsome young man coming down the lane at the end of the day.

'I feel . . . I feel young,' she said. 'Just like everyone else.'

'I see,' said Rosie. They sat in silence for a while.

'The thing is,' said Rosie, not sure how she could broach this. 'The problem is, well . . . Lilian, you need someone to look after you. And I know this is selfish, and I do . . . I am really, really fond of you . . .'

'It's all right,' said Lilian. 'I know. You're young. You really are.'

'I don't feel it,' said Rosie.

'Can I take it that that young . . . gentleman was not the man for you?'

Rosie smiled ruefully. 'Yes. You can take it like that. Yes. And . . . I kind of feel, at *some* point, that I need to get back to London. Sort my life out a bit. I sometimes feel that everyone else is moving on miles ahead of me, that they all know what they're doing while I'm just floundering on in the slipstream. Do you ever feel like that?'

'All my bloody life,' Lilian said. She sat up to be more comfortable. 'I know,' she said suddenly. 'I'm being selfish, you can't stay and devote your life to a silly old woman. You have to go. I realise that. I'll go . . . wherever you like. I don't suppose it matters.'

Rosie felt awful.

'I won't . . . I mean, we'll get the best price possible. Even if I have to sell to that dentist arsehole,' she vowed. 'And you'll go to the nicest room in the nicest place with the nicest people . . . or if you like you can come down to London and I'll find a lovely home there and I can come and see you all the time and . . .'

Lilian patted her hand. 'Don't worry about me,' she said. 'You find your own life, and live it.'

'But it's in London,' said Rosie.

'London, London, London,' said Lilian. 'Now darling, if I have a little midafternoon nap do you promise not to call an ambulance?'

'If you nap now you'll get grumpy tonight when you can't sleep.'

'Then I shall listen to the shipping forecast,' said Lilian. 'Everyone needs a hobby.'

Rosie kissed her soft white cheek. 'Sleep well then. And if you feel the least bit strange . . .'

Lilian patted the panic button on her chest.

Rosie turned out the light.

'Oh,' said Lilian. 'I almost forgot. The postman came for you.'

The large cream-coloured envelope was lying on a little table by the entrance to the sitting room that normally bore keys; Rosie realised she must have been very deep in thought coming in to miss it. It was made of thick paper, properly stiff. It was addressed to 'Miss Rosemary Hopkins, The Sweet Shop Cottage, Lipton'. That was all.

It was the most beautiful envelope Rosie had ever received. Carefully, she unstuck the back and pulled out a stiff cream card. At the top was a little golden crest and a coat of arms. Rosie gave herself a stern talking-to about how ridiculous it was to be impressed by this kind of thing. Nonetheless she couldn't help it; it was pretty impressive.

*Lady Henrietta Lipton*
*invites you to the Lipton Hunt Ball*
*Saturday, 27th October 8 p.m.*
*Lipton Hall*
*Carriages: 1 a.m.*
*Dress: black or regimental tie; hunting colours*

Ooh, thought Rosie. It was the first thing that had perked her up all day.

The harvests were gathered in, great bales of corn sheathed in fields, just as the rains came tearing down the mountains from across the Irish Sea, freezing and soaking anyone unwise enough to step out of doors. Rosie sensed the encroaching dark, the wheel of the year turning. The first new season in such a long time that she was alone, she thought, wondering what stars her mother and brother saw on the other side of the world.

The one thing that kept her cheered was the sweet shop. It was small enough that with a little heating it became very cosy in there. She and Tina got on well, and it was lovely to have a friend. She was always hopping up and down the ladder to the topmost jars. Jake had come in once and repeated his request for mint toffees, which were kept on the highest shelf.

'Are you doing this to see up my skirt?' she'd finally managed to ask.

Jake had smiled, utterly unembarrassed. 'Come on, love,' he said. 'What else am I meant to do for fun round here?'

Tina had chuckled.

'That's not funny,' said Rosie. 'That's harassment.'

'You're the one in the short skirt.'

Rosie rolled her eyes. 'No more mint toffee for you.'

'I'll have some sweetie bananas.'

'*Jake!*'

'Also your gorgeous assistant.' He bowed. 'Hello. I'm Jake.'

'How come she gets bowed to like you're a highwayman and I get leered at like I'm Barbara Windsor in 1965?' grumbled Rosie, marching up the steps in an awkward sideways movement so as not to reveal a snatch of thigh.

'Because Tina's a lady who doesn't throw it about,' came the voice over the baby monitor.

'Thanks, Lilian,' said Rosie.

'Maybe that's because I never get the chance,' said Tina. 'Children and an evil ex and a mortgage I can barely pay.'

'Don't be daft, you're still young and gorgeous,' said Rosie. 'And, as soon as you hear from the bank, you'll become an entrepreneur.'

Tina smiled. 'Oh, yes. I hope they hurry up with that. It's a big ask.'

'You'll do it though,' said Rosie.

Jake was looking at Tina, with a little smile on his face. 'You and that doof finally broken up then?'

Tina looked a little pink and shrugged.

'You're coming to the pub this weekend, aren't you, Rosie?' Jake said. 'Why don't you bring Tina?'

Tina started stuttering. 'Oh, I . . . I mean, I'd have to find a baby sitter . . .'

'Couldn't your mum do it?'

'Yes, I suppose . . .'

'Amazing, how everyone knows everyone's business,' said Rosie.

'And useful too, sometimes,' mused Tina. She did, though, still look terrified.

Rosie decided to take over. 'She'll call you,' she said, practically. 'Or send a badger or whatever it is you country folks do to communicate.'

Jake smiled his slow, handsome Brad Pitt smile, and held up his sweets. 'Well, give me an answer quickly before I turn into Anton.'

Rosie grinned as the doorbell tinged and he left.

Tina turned, cheeks pink. 'Well!' she said.

'I think,' said Rosie gently, 'without wanting to be a killjoy, and you know you are completely gorgeous, but I will say that when I arrived . . .'

Tina grinned. 'Oh, you don't need to tell me. I was at school with Jake Randall. Always got through the womenfolk.' She shook her head. 'I was a bit older than him. Never thought he'd get round to me.' Tina bit her lip. 'Do you think I should go?'

'Of course!' said Rosie. 'Go out and get back on the horse.'

'The horse you didn't want?' said Tina mischievously.

'Well, I was in a relationship then.'

'Ha! I'm still married. Technically.'

'He's all yours,' said Rosie. 'I saw the way he was looking at you.'

'Honestly?'

'Honestly.'

'Just get over yourselves and step out with him,' came the wobbly but opinionated voice over the intercom. 'You girls don't know you're born. There's no point messing about with these things.'

'Would you like a shot at him, Lilian?' said Rosie into the speaker.

'Be quiet,' came the voice. 'I'm listening to *The World at One*.'

That Saturday, Tina came over to Rosie's to get ready, oohing and aahing at how sweet the cottage was. She lived in a modern house behind the main street. The first thing she jumped on was the invite.

'*Ooh!*' she said.

Lilian had propped it up on the mantelpiece, even though Rosie had wanted to stick it in a drawer somewhere. She was sitting by the fireplace. Rosie had insisted on getting her a DVD player, although she couldn't work it. Then Rosie had ordered a cheap job lot of DVDs off eBay with names she'd heard of only distantly: Errol Flynn, Rita Hayworth, Esther Williams, Joan Crawford. Rosie had pretended she wanted to watch them, and sure enough Lilian had come round, sometimes gasping in recognition of something she hadn't seen for half a century.

Rosie had originally done it to help her aunt, but soon realised she had selfish reasons for losing herself in these wonderful old black and white movies . . . *It Happened One Night*, *The Philadelphia Story*. By the time they got to *Brief Encounter*, both of them sniffling quietly by the fire, she was completely hooked on the dramatic romances. Part of her knew that hiding herself away here, immersing herself in other people's romances, was not exactly consistent with the vow she'd made to get on with her life. But as she waited for Tina to work out the details of purchasing the shop, well, she knew what she should be doing. She should be sorting out a new place in London. Finding a home for Lilian. Making sure all the paperwork for the shop was in order. Preparing to leave. Not making herself comfortable by the fire. It was as if there was a whole new life clamouring at her door, but she wasn't quite able to open it up yet.

Lilian, if even more restricted in her movements, didn't seem much worse in the head following her stroke.

Now, she turned round as Tina entered the sitting room. 'A woman?' she said loudly. 'Have you managed to make a female friend, Rosemary? I thought it was just every boy in the village you were touting yourself around.'

'This is my great-aunt,' said Rosie.

'Yes, we've spoken on the intercom,' said Tina. 'Hello. I've always loved your shop. When I was little I used to hang about for ages before I could decide what to buy.'

Lilian took off her glasses.

'I never forget a child,' she said, and peered at Tina closely. Then she sat back. 'Christina Fletcher,' she said with evident satisfaction. 'Candy shrimps and gobstoppers.'

'That's amazing,' said Rosie. 'Your mind is like a steel trap.'

'You were such a quiet little thing, Christina,' she said. 'Not like Drew, that brother of yours that liked the fizz bombs.'

Tina nodded. 'I know. He went off to York, got into finance. He's done really well for himself. I suppose . . . I didn't know what I wanted, not really. I just kind of bobbed along, played it safe. Married the first guy that came along. Mind you, he gave me Kent and Emily. I'm happy about that.'

'And they like sweets?'

'Of course. Emily is just like me. She gets Hello Kitty flumps and a Chupa Chups lolly so she has a bit of everything. Kent wants to try whatever is the latest thing.'

'Funny,' mused Lilian. Then, catching Rosie glancing at her watch, she said, 'All right, all right.'

Upstairs in the bedroom, Tina opened the bag she'd brought with her.

'Oh my God!' said Rosie, her eyes hungrily taking in the logos—Zara, Topshop, even Reiss. 'Look at all your amazing clothes!'

'My amazing clothes I *never wear*,' said Tina. 'Since I had the twins I dress exactly like them. Jeans, T-shirt, flat shoes.'

'You always look immaculate though,' said Rosie loyally.

'I'm a mother, not a slipper-wearing invalid,' said Tina, smiling. 'OK. Dive in!'

'Nothing you have will fit me!'

'Of course it will,' said Tina. 'Well, the tops will.'

'OK, OK.'

Tina came back to the invite. 'But look at this!' She'd carried it upstairs.

Rosie shrugged. 'I just assumed everyone got invited.'

'Everyone does *not* get invited. Why do you think Lilian has it on the mantelpiece to impress people? Lady Lipton's ball is the talk of the county.'

'The whole county?'

'Yeah, yeah, very sarcastic. But it's like all the landowners and aristocracy from all around, and she does the place up and makes it all fancy . . .' Tina's voice trailed off. 'I kind of hoped . . . well, it's silly. But last year when I broke up with Todd, I wanted to go so badly.'

'Maybe Jake will be going.'

Tina snorted. 'Yeah, to park the cars maybe.'

'Really?' said Rosie. 'Well, actually it sounds a bit naff now, the way you're talking about it. I'm not going.'

Tina gave her a knowing look. 'Not even to see your patient?'

'I haven't heard hide nor hair of my ex-patient in weeks,' said Rosie, realising as she said it how irritating this was. She had thought they were becoming . . . well, maybe not close. Stephen didn't seem to do close. Intense, and often irritating, he could manage. But not a line, not a phone call, not even a proper thank you. It stiffened her resolve. 'I don't think I want to go to some poshos-throwing-themselves-about thing,' she said. 'Plus I won't know anyone except Stephen, and she's not inviting any of my friends and anyway she's rude to me all the time.'

'She's only rude to people she likes,' said Tina. 'Everyone else she's just kind of distractedly polite. You should be flattered.'

'And yet I'm not,' said Rosie. '*Argh!*' She was trying to do up a dusty-pink party dress at the back. It was beautiful, but clearly wasn't going to fit.

'Bum, this is annoying. Running a sweet shop is doing nothing for me.'

'It's still pretty,' said Tina. 'Try this.'

And she handed over a top in the same colour, which did fit, and made Rosie's dark hair and pale skin look like Snow White. She shrugged on a dark red bolero over the ruched pink top.

'Ooh,' she said. 'What do you think? Too much of the sexy señorita?'

'I think what Lipton needs is a sexy señorita,' said Tina. 'That is the *only* thing lacking in this village.'

'**A**ll right, girls,' said Les as they pushed open the door of the Red Lion. 'Ooh, look at you two, going somewhere fancy?'

Tina started to sigh, but Rosie said, 'Of course! Here! For you, Les!' Amazingly, this made him smile, and the normal residents grin. One of the farmers came forward and asked to buy them their first gin and tonic and from then on they were happily ensconced by the fire.

'This,' said Rosie, 'is because of my terrible reputation.'

But it wasn't Rosie who was getting all the attention—it was Tina.

'We never thought we'd see you out again after Todd left,' said Jim Hodds, the vet, who was enjoying a rare and well-deserved night off.

Tina smiled. 'Well, you know, it's been hard.'

The farmers were good company, cheeky and funny and flirtatious over the course of the next few hours.

When she got up to go to the loo, Rosie realised that she was drunk. Oh well, they were having fun. And it was nice to see Tina happy. She wobbled slightly coming out of the toilet. Then she blinked, and blinked again, just in case her eyes were deceiving her. Sitting in the corner with his back to her, his stick on the floor, was Stephen Lakeman.

Had she not had some vodkas, and gin and tonics, Rosie would probably have thought twice about what she did next. Instead, emboldened and in a rash mood, she marched straight up to him.

'Hey!' she yelled. 'Not a phone call? Not a word? What kind of a grateful ex are you?' She meant, of course, ex-patient. But it came out wrong. Stephen, startled, turned round hastily, and Rosie noticed that the other person at his table was a girl. A long-haired, very slender, wide-eyed blonde girl, with a flick to her hair. She flicked it now, then glanced up at Stephen. It was not a friendly glance. It was a 'Who the hell is this?' glance.

'Hello?' she said enquiringly. She wasn't local, Rosie noticed. She was from the south, just like her. It came to her suddenly. She must be a jag!

Stephen looked uncomfortable. 'Uhm,' he said. 'Hi. Hello.'

Rosie felt like she was intruding. And worse: she realised, in a horrible, blinding flash, that whatever she'd told herself she believed, she did have feelings for Stephen. Real feelings. Real feelings that were being whipped into a frenzy of jealousy by this woman here with the flicky hair.

'Uhm,' said Stephen again. Rosie wondered about this too. He was obviously uncomfortable. But why? If she was just a nurse to him, he wouldn't feel embarrassed, would he? The fact that it was awkward . . . A tiny pilot light lit inside her. If he . . . if he . . .

'This is Rosie,' said Stephen. 'She was my nurse.'

The light inside Rosie sputtered and died. His *what*?

'Uhm, Rosie, this is CeeCee.'

*CeeCee?* The girl gave her a tight social smile that basically said, back off, I am chatting up the hot young aristocrat. She reminded Rosie of the girls you saw on TV at Formula 1. All blonde and skinny and identical— and *desperate* to hang around the rich boys.

'Nice to meet you,' drawled CeeCee in the most languid way imaginable, before picking up her iPhone.

CeeCee looked as out of place in the cosy confines of the Red Lion as a tropical fish in a goldfish bowl. Her shoes had red soles. She was talking loudly on her iPhone.

'Who's that?' said Rosie bluntly.

'Uhm, she's an old friend of mine . . .'

'Oh, it was so nice of her to spend so much time with you when you were poorly,' said Rosie. 'Still, now you're on the mend and set to inherit, it's lovely she's made the trip.' Stephen gave her a sharp look. 'I'd better go,' she said.

'Maybe you had,' he said. 'You're not being very nice.'

'Maybe I'm not very nice.'

Stephen half smiled. 'Well, neither am I.'

'I bet she isn't either,' said Rosie, knowing she'd gone too far. There was tension in the air as they looked at one another. Then Stephen laughed. 'Are you coming to the ball?'

'No,' said Rosie. 'I won't know a single person there. There's not one single nice person I like from the village going. It'll be full of people like CeeCee and your mum treats me horribly. But thanks for asking.'

**T**he fun had gone out of the night, and they all knew it. Tina wanted to head home anyway; the twins would be up at seven. Rosie trailed up to bed alone, taking off the pink ruched top—what had she been thinking, she looked like she was dolled up for flamenco fancy dress. Stephen and CeeCee were probably chuckling about it right now. Rosie groaned in embarrassment. Oh God. Did he know? Of course he knew. She must have made it so obvious. But how hadn't *she* known?

She had of course. A bolt of electricity had shot through her when she saw him there. She couldn't help it. And he was going to think of her as such an idiot, a chunky little curly-haired London girl against a slender, lissom creature like CeeCee. It probably happened to him all the time before he cut his leg open. Handsome aid worker, posh family, big house . . . God, what an idiot she must seem to him.

And she realised something worse: that when she had ditched Gerard, a perfectly nice man, she had obviously, on one level, hoped there might be a chance with Stephen. What a totally stupid thing that had been. Of course now he was on the mend he'd have bees round the honey pot.

'Bother,' said Rosie, out loud, her voice resounding in the silent room.

**'I**'m not going, so stop it.'

It was 4 p.m. on Saturday, 27 October. The shop had been overrun with customers all day, buying Hallowe'en lollipops, white chocolate skeletons with raspberry icing, gum balls that looked like eyeballs and gobstoppers with teeth. Tina had suggested making up special Hallowe'en bags with a few sweets in, to be handed out easily, and these had proved highly popular.

'*Yes you are*,' came the voice over the loudspeaker. 'Tina, you tell her.'

'I would love to go,' said Tina. 'Jake and I supposedly have a date and I can't seem to get further than the bloody Red Lion!'

Rosie stuck her lip out. 'It is going to be full of bloody nobbers, all of whom will look down their noses at me and go "*Hwa hwa hwa*" when they laugh and dance with swords and talk about horses. Of course I'm not going.'

'Did you ever go to those balls, Miss Hopkins?' asked Tina.

Lilian was silent for a while. Then, 'Not at first. Of course, she was the girl of the big house, I was just the sweet-shop lady. But then the world changed, and lots of new people moved into the village, and it suddenly didn't seem to matter quite so much exactly who your parents were, and then we somehow . . . we became friends. We'd had a lot of people in common growing up. But it was too late for me by then!'

'Too late for what?' said Rosie.

'To really enjoy the dancing of course. And the beautiful gowns, and the champagne, and the romance of it all, the men so handsome.'

The bell tinged, and Lady Lipton breezed in, imperious as ever.

'Ah!' she said. 'It's the little scarecrow. How are you?' She eyed Rosie. 'Still not got any clothes sent up for the winter?' She was looking at Rosie's floral frock. It was freezing outside now, incredible given that it wasn't even November. The ground was frosted over every morning.

'I'm fine, thanks.'

'But what are you wearing tonight?'

'Uhm,' said Rosie.

'Well, come on, spit it out. Also, you.' She meant Tina. 'I need all the eyeball gobstoppers you have. I think it will be *hilarious* for my guests.'

Tina jumped to it. Rosie couldn't bear the rudeness.

'I'm not coming,' she said quietly, but she knew she could be heard.

'What's that?' Lady Lipton looked like she couldn't believe her ears.

'I'm not coming. Tonight.'

'Why ever not?'

Rosie was on the brink of making up a good excuse when the voice squawked again from the baby monitor.

'Because she's a bloody idiot!'

Hetty looked all around her in surprise and consternation; it did sound like Lilian was booming out of nowhere.

'Lilian? Where are you?'

'She's on the monitor,' said Tina shyly.

'*Why* isn't she coming?' continued Hetty.

'Ask her yourself,' said Lilian.

Because I fancy your son and he thinks I'm a servant and you think I'm a gold-digger, thought Rosie bleakly.

'Why not?' demanded Hetty, red in the face.

'Because I have nothing to wear and I won't know anyone there.'

'What *nonsense*,' said Lady Lipton. 'Invite some friends; we always get some people passing out from drink before dinner. What about you?'

Tina looked delighted and barely stopped short of clapping her hands.

'Ooh, yes please!'

'And you can bring that dirty Isitt labourer if you must,' sniffed Hetty. 'A bit of what I believe you call "eye candy". Not quite so broken-veined as the rest. And I've invited that poofy doctor. Isn't that enough chums?'

Rosie felt her face flame.

'And I'll lend you a dress!' Hetty boomed. 'I have a full-length kilt I'm sure will look splendid on you. Of course Bran used it as a blanket, but it's absolutely fine.'

'I'm sure I can find something for her,' pleaded Tina.

'Jolly good!' said Hetty, handing over a twenty for the huge bag of sweets. 'See you at eight, trippety trip.'

And the bell clanged and she was gone.

'Eek!' said Tina, hugging Rosie. 'Now it'll be great! What's up?'

'Nothing,' said Rosie.

'What?' said Tina. 'What's up?'

'It's stupid,' said Rosie. She was torn. On the one hand, she couldn't bear to reveal what an idiot she'd been. On the other, if she didn't tell someone she thought she was going to burst.

'What?'

'It's Stephen,' she said. 'I fancy him.'

Tina stared at her for a few seconds, then burst into peals of laughter.

'What? Why's that funny?' Rosie was stung.

'Oh no, it's not, it's not, it's just . . . Oh,' said Tina, 'back when we were at school . . . he didn't go to our school of course.'

'Of course,' said Rosie.

'He was sent away. But when he came back in the holidays . . . oh wow. *Everyone* fancied him.'

'You don't say.'

'He was always slouching round the village with a book of poetry, in a furious mood because he'd just had another big fight with his dad.'

'Oh yeah? Did anyone ever pull him?'

'Oh God, no. What, him mess with the likes of us?' Tina grinned. 'It wasn't for want of trying though.'

'OK, OK, I get the message,' said Rosie.

'Then he went all weird of course . . .' Tina suddenly looked stricken. 'I mean . . . There's no reason he wouldn't fancy you back, none at all!'

'There are a million reasons he wouldn't fancy me back,' said Rosie, starting to clear up. 'All of them tall and blonde and rich and posh.'

There was a silence.

'Well,' said Tina, 'Just because you fancy someone is absolutely no reason not to let me go to the party of the year. It wouldn't be fair. I'm going to text Jake and Moray right now and order them to come and pick us up, and we will go, and get squiffed again and ignore all the stupid posh folk and have a brilliant time, the four of us. It'll be great. And that big stupid pouty Stephen won't know what he's missing.'

'I can't say no, can I?' said Rosie. 'I'd be ruining everyone's night out.'

'Exactly,' said Tina. '*Free champagne.*'

There was a happy snuffle from the baby monitor.

'*Lilian!*' said Rosie warningly.

'I am pleased you are going to the dance, that's all,' said Lilian.

## 1944

*The news seemed to be getting slightly better; even Terence, on his leave, had seemed more cheerful. The tide was turning, everybody said. The Germans were in retreat. The war was going to finish.*

*Gordon came home one spring evening. Henry had now been away for one year and four months. Lilian assumed Ida Delia was getting word of him; she never heard and was far too proud to ask. She hoped he wasn't scared out there. She hoped he wasn't seeing terrible things. She had seen him, once, on leave. The family was walking down the high street. Ida was obviously displeased at something; she was shouting at Henry, who had lost weight and gained muscle, and looked tall and rangy and somehow older in his army suit. He wasn't saying anything. Lilian had hidden behind her bedroom curtains until he'd gone away.*

*But now, she told herself, all she cared about was that he was safe. That he came home safe. When the war finished. If it ever did.*

*'Look what I have for you,' said Gordon, ebullient as ever, dragging his huge heavy kitbag over the kitchen floor. Their da looked up from his ledger.*

*'What's this then, son?'*

*Gordon flashed his cheeky grin. He drew two bottles out of his kitbag, and their da wolf-whistled. 'Is that . . .'*

*'Certainly is,' said Gordon. 'It's pure champagne.'*

*'I've never even seen it,' said Da, shaking his head. He picked the bottles up very carefully. 'You carted these back all the way?'*

*'Slept on them like a pillow,' said Gordon. "Case anyone nicked 'em. I've been*

*doing a bit of, well, nod-nod-wink-wink on the side for the men, like. Making sure they get some decent grub. And these came my way. Thought I might need 'em for a bribe coming home, but I forgot what a straight old place England still is. So here they are!'*

*Da sent Lilian down to the dairy for an ice block. Then he insisted they laid a bottle in it for an hour to get cool. Mostly, they sat around and watched it.*

*'Put the other one away in the larder,' said Da. 'We'll keep it for a special occasion.' Lilian tucked it right at the back of the top shelf. For when Henry comes home, she said to herself.*

'**W**hen did you ever need a cocktail dress?' said Rosie.

Tina had brought half the contents of her wardrobe over, and they tried on everything.

'Well, you never know,' said Tina. Rosie raised her eyebrows.

'OK, OK,' said Tina. 'So when Todd was going through his worst phase I maybe became a bit . . . shopaholicky. Apparently it was my way of getting him back for his illness. So his counsellor told me.'

'Revenge cocktail dresses,' marvelled Rosie, pulling them out. They really were beautiful. But however many they tried on Rosie none of them was quite right. Most of them fitted OK as Rosie's bust and small waist worked very well in a frock, but none was really *her*.

'Oh well,' said Rosie, coming and going for the sixth time. 'The black one with the lace at the top—that's probably the best we're going to get.'

Lilian sighed. 'The black is no good. It works on Tina, but it's no good for you. You need something to make you stand out. Make him notice you.'

'Yes,' agreed Tina.

Rosie felt herself grow uncomfortably hot. She'd forgotten Lilian would have overheard the conversation she and Tina had had about Stephen. 'Well, he won't,' she said.

'Why not?' said Lilian. 'Stranger things have happened. Sometimes the handsomest man in the village *does* notice the girl with the dark hair.'

'Not if it's me,' said Rosie.

'I think Jake's the handsomest man in the village,' said Tina.

'Yes,' said Rosie. 'Closely followed by Moray.'

'If Hetty thinks her son is too good for my great-niece, she's got another think coming,' said Lilian. 'Go into my bedroom. The large armoire.'

'The what?'

'What do they teach you at school these days? The wardrobe. Tch!'

Rosie did as she was bid. It was a huge old thing. Inside the clothes were packed so closely together it was hard to see what was in there.

'Count six from the far right side,' said Lilian. 'No. Seven.'

Everything was in dry-cleaning bags, immaculately ironed and hung. Rosie gasped as she started to leaf through them. There were beaded gowns in jewel shades, bright hot fuchsias, a jacket with a proper fox trim. Tina came charging in and her eyes widened.

'Oh my God, *look* at this stuff.' She popped her head back into the sitting room. 'No wonder you always look so immaculate. This is a treasure trove in here.'

Lilian shrugged and tried not to look pleased. 'Well, everyone needs a hobby,' she said.

Tina pulled out things here and there but it was the dress seventh from the end that drew the eye. Lilian had been absolutely right.

Rosie pulled the cool green silk over her head. It shimmered, almost iridescent. It wasn't a forest green, or a racing green, more of a dark emerald, but the material itself was so light it seemed to dance before the eyes. Rosie was convinced it would be too small, but there was ruching along the back, cleverly concealed at the waist.

'It's to allow room for dancing,' grumbled Lilian when she saw her. 'Of course you stretch it out.'

'You were bigger then though,' argued Rosie.

'I was,' said Lilian. 'You'd think you'd be happy that being terribly old helps you lose weight. I assure you, you won't be.'

Finally, however, Rosie wriggled and shrugged and felt the material flow over her hips with a soft swooshing sound. She could tell by the way Lilian and Tina had gone silent that they approved.

'What?' she said. Lilian, suddenly, quickly, found herself wanting to look away. Rosie was a softer-looking girl than she had been, not so angular. But something in the long, dark curling hair and the wide pink mouth caught and tugged hard on Lilian's memory: the memory of a hopeful young woman in front of a full-length mirror, waiting, and waiting, until there was no point in waiting any more.

'You look *amazing*,' said Tina. 'That colour is gorgeous on you!'

Rosie dashed off to the full-length mirror over the bath. She couldn't help smiling at what she saw there. Odd, really, but a few months of staying off the late nights, and getting a bit of fresh air, and not eating takeaways; it had changed her. She could see it. Her skin looked soft and creamy, with a pink blush in her cheeks that she identified, correctly, as excitement. Her grey eyes were clear, and the green in the beautiful silk dress made them shine. She felt . . . Well. Beautiful would be silly, she told herself. But really, this was as good as it was going to get.

She went back into the sitting room, grinning.

'All right, all right,' said Tina. 'Look at you, cat who's got the cream. OK, so you look lovely.'

'Sorry,' said Rosie. 'I will go back to being my normal grumpy self immediately.' She caught sight of her great-aunt's stricken face.

'Lilian,' she said, darting forward. 'Are you all right? Are you feeling all right?' She turned back to Tina. 'I'll have to stay behind, I can't go.'

'Stop being daft,' said Lilian. 'I was just thinking how nice you look. Now, go into the larder and look behind the mustard box on the highest shelf. Carefully.'

**T**hey put the ancient, dusty, exquisite bottle of champagne into the freezer, on Tina's advice.

'Probably ruin it,' she said with a nervous giggle.

'It was probably ruined a long time ago,' said Lilian. 'It'll be the most undrinkable muck, probably.'

'Stop being such a pessimist,' said Rosie. 'I can't believe you've had that there all this time. It could be worth a fortune. Can't you sell it?'

Lilian shrugged. 'It won't be worth that much. Anyway, sell it so you can pack me off to a home? Not bloody likely.'

'Actually I was thinking we could use the money to hire a nurse for a bit, *so there*,' said Rosie.

'Well, that is my bottle of champagne. Your granpa Gordon liberated it during the war and brought it all the way back to Derbyshire. He brought two actually. We drank the first one to celebrate Gordon being home—he said it would be like drinking stars. I thought he was talking rubbish myself. But by his second glass, my da was singing a stupid song about blackbirds I hadn't heard since my ma died. We spent the whole after- noon just laughing, and talking about Neddy—that was my middle brother, he died in the war—and, well. It was the first time I'd been happy in a long time. And then we were going to keep the second one for

Terence coming home, but then we weren't all there together, and he was always so low-key anyway, hated any fuss. So we never drank it. Then your granpa went off to London and that was the end of that branch of the family, till a few months ago.'

'Sorry,' said Rosie, listening intently.

'And, well, me and my da kept waiting for some great occasion to drink it on, and it just never arrived. And then after Da died, well. I never thought to have it after that, I never was much for the drink.'

Tina and Rosie swapped glances. Rosie squeezed Lilian's hand.

'Thank you,' said Lilian.

'That's all right,' said Rosie gently. Then she jumped up and went to get the glasses and fetch the bottle out of the freezer.

Tina peeled back the ancient, brittle foil and untwisted the wire.

'Oh God,' she said. 'I can't pop this. If it all goes wrong, I'll be a mess.'

Rosie took it from her. 'I will now try to look like I do this every day of the week,' she said, smiling. 'OK, everyone cover their eyes.'

And she very carefully and very slowly twisted the old cork out of the bottle. It eased itself out with a gentle pop, no great crack at all, and the women held their breath in case it had gone flat. But it smelled good, a deep, viney scent, and when Rosie poured it into Lilian's heavy crystal glasses, it made a satisfyingly fizzy noise. It was darker than the champagne Rosie had drunk before, but when she took her first sip from the thick-edged glass, it still burst on to her tongue.

'Not so fast!' commanded Lilian, as if she drank champagne every night and this was a terrible breach of etiquette on Rosie's part. 'This is special, and we must have a toast.'

Tina giggled nervously. 'Oh yes! To . . . to . . . hmm. Baby sitters! And big posh nights out! And . . .'

Lilian raised an eyebrow. 'I'll make the toast. To exciting nights out, where anything could happen. How when you're young and in a pretty dress you should always say yes to a ball.'

Rosie rolled her eyes.

'This is pretty much what I said,' whispered Tina.

'To grabbing what you want, Rosemary. As quickly as you can. And to love and to family,' concluded Lilian. And then they chinked the glasses.

Rosie smiled. 'That was a lovely toast,' she said. And Lilian had been right about something else: it was like drinking stars.

# Chapter Nine

### Turkish Delight

*Turkish delight has had a bad reputation since that man C.S. Lewis—a genius in other ways—linked it for ever with one of the most terrifying creations in literature, the White Witch of Narnia, and that naughty, sticky, traitorous Edmund. But with the sensuous pleasure imbued in its melting, gelatinous texture and, when made in the proper way, delicately perfumed with rose petals, flavoured with oils and dusted with sugar, it reclaims its power as a sweet as seductive as Arabian nights.*

'WHO ARE THESE PEOPLE?' said Rosie, still nervous and exhilarated from the champagne and their drive up the hill. The weather had turned, suddenly, vicious: colder and colder, and there were mutterings that it might snow.

The place was thronged. Up close, and floodlit from below, Lipton Hall was truly imposing: built in the Queen Anne style, with red sandstone, gargoyles on the upper reaches. The rows of windows were brilliantly lit with chandeliers, and loud voices and rowdy laughter poured out.

'How does she pay for all this?' Rosie wondered aloud. 'I thought they were broke.'

'Oh, she is, completely,' said Moray. 'People pay a fortune to come.'

'They *pay?*' said Rosie. 'Do we have to pay?'

'We do *not* have to pay,' said Moray. 'We are Lady Lipton's guests. But you'll see big tables full of the rotary club and the masons and all sorts.'

'But why do they want to pay?' said Rosie, completely confused.

'To rub shoulders with the toffs of course,' said Moray.

'They pay to do that?' said Rosie.

'Could you just get inside, before I take you home? And if you start singing "The Red Flag" you'll be in serious trouble.'

Inside was a seething mass of people, all hailing one another and looking slightly pink in the face. Rosie walked up the long flight of steps, then over the threshold. The main hall was enormous, panelled, with large animal heads attached to the walls. A huge grandfather clock, just like in Peak House, stood at the end. Teenagers in white shirts and black trousers were taking coats, or scuttling about with drinks.

'I always wanted to do that job,' whispered Tina.

'Why didn't you?' said Rosie.

'Oh, it's notorious,' said Tina, as Jake sniggered. 'They drink all the left-overs and get into *terrible* trouble later on. Getting off with guests, getting off with each other. My father wouldn't hear of it.'

Jake smiled again.

'You did it though?' said Rosie.

'Oh yes,' said Jake.

Tina grinned. 'Course 'e did.'

'And was it as bad as what her dad thinks?' said Rosie.

'Well, let's put it this way,' said Jake. 'With the exception of us four, those kids in the black and white are going to have the best time out of anyone at this party tonight. *And* they're the only ones getting paid.'

They moved to the left, where, opening off the great hall, was a ball-room, not panelled but with a parquet floor, pastel-coloured walls and, at the far end, large sets of French windows leading out on to a balcony overlooking a sunken garden. Despite the cold outside, the heat in the room was immense, and the doors were open. People stood just outside, smoking cigarettes, watching as the first flakes of snow began to fall.

Tina wanted to see everywhere and everything and she scuttled off to explore, Jake close behind her. It made Rosie smile. Tina deserved a good man. Moray was waylaid immediately they entered the room by dozens of people he knew, and, with his affable manner, fell into conversation.

Rosie wandered alone out to the balcony beyond the French windows. The cold had driven most people indoors and the hubbub dimmed behind her as she gazed out at the garden. It was almost incandescently beautiful, watching the snow fall on the knot garden beneath the shadow of the house, on the hedges and the neatly trimmed borders and tumbling down the ridge of the land below.

She felt, suddenly, as if she were being watched, and turned, swiftly. Just inside the doors, in the corner of the ballroom, was a dark area filled with sofas and chairs. She had barely registered that a large group had moved there, but she saw it now, and was just in time to catch Stephen's eyes on her. He glanced away quickly, as she gave a slightly awkward smile through the open door. He was surrounded. CeeCee was there, looking unbelievable in a cutting-edge metallic silver dress. There were other girls there, many blonde, or with thick sheets of straight hair that covered their eyes, and dresses in pale nudes or sheer fabrics or plain unadorned black. Suddenly Rosie felt silly wearing green, like a little girl in her party frock.

And there were other young men, Stephen's age, obviously his friends, laughing and drinking and flirting with the girls and teasing each other. One was wearing the most ludicrous pair of tartan trousers.

Where were they? Rosie found herself thinking. Where were they when he was sitting by himself in the kitchen, pouring whisky down his throat?

She composed herself to give the coolest, most distantly polite hello she knew how—it was, she knew, the only way. She risked another look, but of course his attention was elsewhere. How foolish, she thought, remembering how she'd looked at herself in the mirror. As if she compared to these model girls. But she was not going to be downhearted.

To her delight, Moray came towards her, waving madly. 'Dinner!' he said. 'You have to be quick, these country types enjoy their grub and they don't hang about.'

'Excellent,' she said, proffering her arm. He might be the only gay in the village, but Stephen's stuck-up chums weren't to know that. 'Hello,' she said to Stephen politely as she passed by.

'Hi,' said Stephen shortly.

'Hi, CeeCee,' she said. CeeCee looked up from a conversation and did nothing to disguise the fact that she had not the faintest idea whether she'd ever met Rosie before.

'Oh yeah, hi,' she said, then turned back to her friend.

'That's CeeCee,' said Rosie to Moray, loud enough for Stephen to hear. 'She's very special.' Stephen didn't react. 'Well, it was nice of your mother to invite your nurse,' said Rosie.

'I don't . . .' Stephen started but then couldn't go on.

'What?'

'I don't think of you as my nurse,' he said.

'You just call me your nurse.'

'No. No.'

'*Lippy!*' came a loud voice. An enormous pack of rugger buggers was crossing the floor. '*You utter weapon!*'

Stephen looked crestfallen. 'Oh God.'

'*Dinner!*' said Moray.

Stephen was engulfed, as Moray walked her across the ballroom and in to dinner.

'Well, well,' he said.

'What?' said Rosie.

'How long have you had a little soft spot for our lord of the manor?'

'I do *not* . . .' Rosie felt herself turn pink. 'Never mind. I know everyone fancies him.'

'Christ, yes,' said Moray. 'Oh well.'

The dining room was more of a dining hall, with round tables set up with autumnal leaf arrangements. Most people were already seated and they found their table was full of other fun young people from the village, the farmers and their wives. Rosie could see that they were determined to enjoy their night to the full, and they heckled the speeches and imitated the hunting horns that were blown to announce each course: mulligatawny soup, roast pheasant with autumn vegetables and game chips, and a splendid rhubarb crumble made with rhubarb from the gardens.

'There is *not*,' announced Rosie, 'enough ruching in this dress.'

Tina and Jake were nowhere to be seen. Someone said that they'd spotted them in the orangery and Rosie decided to leave them to it. She couldn't even see Stephen, and did her best to forget all about him, helped by the tremendous food, and a story about pig insemination she suspected she wouldn't be able to forget even if she tried.

The noise in the great rooms grew louder and louder as dinner finally ended and everyone repaired next door. One room was to have disco dancing, the other proper reeling. Rosie wanted to stay in the disco room, but Moray was adamant.

'No way,' he said. 'How many times are you going to come to a thing like this if you piss off back to London?'

'Are you sure you don't want to come to London with me?' said Rosie. 'I think you'd like it.'

Moray gave her a look. 'I do better here in Lipton than you will ever know, love. These farmers play a good macho game, but . . .'

Rosie laughed as she let him lead her back to the ballroom, where a band with a fiddle player, an accordionist and a bodhrán drummer was ready.

'Good God, what is going on?' she said, as several men including the one in tartan trews, all took to the floor.

'It's easy,' said Moray. 'You fold your arms behind your neck like this.'

'How is *this* easy?'

'Now take your partners for the Gay Gordons,' the leader of the band announced.

'Oh well, I see why you like it,' grumbled Rosie. Moray ignored her and lined her up with everyone else, as the band leader walked them through it. And, sure enough, once she'd done it a few times, she got the hang of it, and found herself enjoying the skirl of the music. Moray was a skilled partner, his hands always there to catch her as she twirled. And the green silk dress twirled beautifully. It was made for it. Made to be danced in, on a dark night in early winter, where the snow whirled in front of the great window panes of the big house.

After the first dance, Rosie found she wanted to dance another, and another, and she found no shortage of partners. Gasping with thirst, she drank plenty of water but plenty of champagne too, then allowed herself to be carried off into a dance that involved two partners: Jake, who had reappeared, and Frankie, one of his farmer friends. Her head spinning, she danced between them, lighter and more graceful, she knew, thanks to the green dress, than she had ever been in her life.

Traversing the room, floating in a huge bubble of champagne, she barely noticed when Frankie spun her round, then deposited her not two feet from where Stephen was sitting, perched awkwardly on the sofa. She gave an involuntary gasp of surprise to find herself so close to him, especially so flushed; her hair had escaped from the clasp Tina had found for it, and her curls were tumbled round her face, her eyes shining.

'Oh,' she said.

Stephen's face was like stone. 'Oh,' he repeated. 'Is there anyone in this village you *don't* let yourself get manhandled by?' he barked suddenly.

'*What?*' said Rosie, unable to believe what she'd just heard.

But Stephen didn't repeat himself. Instead, he hauled himself up and started pushing his way through the hordes of people dancing to the door.

The spell of the dance broken, all Rosie could do was stand there, staring after him, mouth open in fury.

There were mumblings nearby, but not for long, as the band played on and people restarted the dance.

Rosie stormed across the dance floor after him. Outside the snow was thick and still buffeting it down, but Rosie didn't feel a thing. Without thinking twice, seeing one car roar away into the distance, she jumped into Moray's Land Rover. As usual he'd left the keys in the ignition. Regardless of the weather, she turned the key.

She was going to tell him a thing or two. About rudeness, and how just having a bit of a gammy leg was no excuse for behaving like a total arse-hole, and how what he really needed was therapy.

It was utterly freezing when she got out of the car. Rosie pushed open the door to Peak House without knocking. He was sitting upright in the chair, stick to one side. She could see his jaw twitching with the tension. His eyes darted to her when she walked in, but he gave no other signal that he was aware of her presence in the room.

Rosie stopped short. She thought, suddenly, of how many times she had waited for things to happen in her life: how she had waited for a man to grab her, then settled for Gerard, how she had waited for a job to consume her, then settled for agency work. Before the sweet shop. Waiting for life wasn't enough any longer. Anything she wanted now, she was going to take with both hands. And, if she was being totally honest, she didn't want to tell him a thing or two. That, she realised, wasn't why she was here.

Rosie stepped forward into the dim light, towards him. He was gazing into the fire, hand clutching an empty whisky glass.

'Stephen,' she said. He didn't answer. She wasn't a hundred per cent sure if she wanted to kiss him or slap him. 'What the hell was that you said?'

He wouldn't meet her eyes. 'I'm sorry,' he said. 'I was feeling stupid and useless and jealous. It was dumb. I'm sorry.'

'But . . . but.' Jealous?

Rosie decided, right then, that she didn't want to talk any more. Fortified by the champagne, she was almost unable to believe she was being so bold. Almost.

Without saying a word, she knelt before him and carefully, decisively, unzipped his black trousers. He didn't move a muscle to stop her. Agonisingly slowly, she manoeuvred them downwards. Carefully, without pulling, she drew as much of his trousers as she could down his left leg.

The light from the lamp shone upon the white and puckered skin, the scar disappearing down his long leg into the shadows. The leg was plainly paler and thinner than the other one, and the long seam was hairless and shiny. Yet it was not at all repellent. It was cleanly healed, simply a mark on the man, nothing more, nothing less. If she was to love this man, she would love all of him, and that was that.

Slowly, she lowered her head and, gently but firmly, kissed the very top of the scar, halfway up the warm inside of his thigh—once, twice.

For a moment, there was silence. Then, above her, she heard a very low groan. She kissed the scar once more, then rose up. Stephen's eyes were closed now, his expression completely unreadable.

Rosie felt her heart pound, felt the adrenalin course through her body. Was he trying to think of a polite way to tell her to get the hell out? Had she just made a terrible, terrible error?

Stephen's eyes snapped open, and before she could respond, he grabbed her upper arms and pulled her towards him, kissing her fiercely and fearlessly. The clumsiness of their position—he already had his trousers halfway down—meant Rosie threw caution to the wind, lifted up the silken layers of her skirt and clambered onto the chair, both of them still kissing passionately. Instantly, as she wrapped her legs tightly around his waist, she could feel that her instincts had been the correct ones.

'Christ,' said Stephen. 'It's been . . . it's been so long.'

'Well, it is now,' said Rosie, trying to lighten the mood. 'Sssh. Ssh.'

Stephen held her face between his hands and gazed fiercely into her eyes. 'And so hard,' he said finally, a spark of mischief flickering across his face. They stared at each other for a second longer, then suddenly he was unzipping her bodice, with the excitement of a man coming back to life; and she was pulling up his white shirt, desperate to put her hands and mouth on the flat stomach and muscled chest she'd been dreaming of.

Neither wanted to mention whether he would be capable of moving them both to the bed; Rosie didn't want to move too much, in case it caused him pain; so instead they stayed exactly where they were, pressed tightly into the high-backed chair, the dim light in the kitchen, the fire blazing, then eventually dying, as the heat from two bodies rose and fell and rose again. The motion was made more delicious by its necessary slowness. Finally Stephen could stand it no longer and, all thoughts of pain forgotten, he pulled down hard on her shoulders, pressing her tightly into him until she felt they were one person. When she came to herself, she found to her astonishment that she was crying.

Later, Rosie could never remember how long they had stayed, afterwards, her curled up, both of them staring into the fire. 'I thought you thought I was a prick,' whispered Stephen into her hair.

'To be fair,' said Rosie, 'that was only after you'd been a complete prick. I have to ask though. That night in the pub.'

'Where you were completely trollied.'

'For the first time in about sixty-five years!' said Rosie. 'I'm a very cheap date. *Don't* say it.'

Instead, Stephen gave her a kiss, which started getting a little out of control, until he winced. 'Maybe we could . . . move?'

'Yes,' said Rosie. 'But why did you tell that blonde girl I was your nurse?'

Stephen bit his lip. 'Honestly?'

Rosie nodded. 'Yes! You made me feel like some awful below-stairs . . . Well, I don't know.'

'Because I didn't know where I stood with you,' said Stephen. 'Well, I did. You were always giving me grief and telling me off for things.'

'Oh,' said Rosie, stung. 'I was trying to help.'

Stephen stared deep into her eyes. 'You think you weren't helping?'

'No.'

'But I thought . . . I thought I was just a kind of project for you. Professional boundaries and all that.'

'Is that why you never phoned me or asked me out for a coffee or anything?' said Rosie, still slightly disgruntled.

'Can't we just say I'm out of practice?'

'Oh, I don't know,' said Rosie, still pink. 'What about all those people who are suddenly hanging around all the time?'

'Well, word went round that I was back . . . The jag grapevine moves pretty fast.'

'Where were they before?'

Stephen looked uncomfortable. 'This is a lot of questions. I thought we were going to bed.'

Rosie tried to bite down her concern. It wasn't attractive, she reminded herself, to show off her insecurities. She looked at his gorgeous, stern head and lean, pale physique and decided to count her blessings instead. 'Let's,' she said, and stood up, feeling confident in the gentle light coming from the fire, her hair tumbling down her back.

Stephen smiled. 'Cor,' he said. 'You are *lush*.'

It was such an unlikely thing to hear him say that Rosie burst out laughing. He laughed too, and pushed himself up and out of his chair.

'I think I can still outrun you,' said Rosie.

'Not for long,' said Stephen with a wolfish look on his face, lurching for her. She screamed—and then screamed again as suddenly she was blinded by enormous beams of light shooting straight through the kitchen window. It was another car coming back. She could hear voices and barks of laughter in the air and understood, to her utter horror, that it was all of Stephen's friends, arriving home from the ball.

It probably wouldn't have been so bad if Stephen hadn't found it so funny, as she scurried about the kitchen, desperately trying to find something to cover herself with, giving up on the idea of shrugging herself back into Lilian's tight green gown. When she came up with Mrs Laird's flowery apron, she thought he was about to bust a gut.

'Stop laughing and *help* me,' she said, conscious of the sounds of feet crunching on gravel and people making a lot of noise.

'But you don't need anything! You look incredibly beautiful as you are.'

'*Piss off!*'

'Sorry, sorry,' said Stephen, hurling her his jacket.

'I'm going to run away upstairs,' she said.

'Don't!' he said. 'You look lovely. And I thought you wanted to be introduced properly.'

'Stop it,' she said. 'I'm going.'

But it was too late. First to come in were two red-faced rugby-playing gents. 'Way hey!' they leered. 'Sorry, mate, should have knocked.'

'Yeah, whatever,' said Stephen. He could see Rosie was desperate to get away, and pulled her close to him, holding her hand. Rosie thought this was even worse, like she was some undignified doxy, half covered up.

'This is Rosie,' he managed. 'We weren't expecting you back so soon.'

'Obviously!' said the taller of the rugger buggers. They didn't bother introducing themselves, simply turned round, looking for wine. There was a bottle of claret open on the big kitchen table and they grabbed that.

Then in through the door walked CeeCee. What would it take, Rosie wondered, to jerk her out of her near-unconscious levels of coolness?

'Oh yeah, hi,' she said, sweeping Rosie with a glance that implied that she, Rosie, was still below notice. 'Stephen, *darling*. I can't believe you deserted us.'

'Uh . . .' Stephen stuttered again.

Rosie shook her head. 'Well.'

CeeCee accepted a glass of wine from one of the rugby boys. 'Not to worry. I see you were having a spot of local fun.' Venom dripped from her voice.

Rosie had had enough. She looked around the room to see if there was a way to reclaim her dignity. There wasn't.

'I'm going,' she said to Stephen, whispering in his ear.

'Please don't. You can stick on my pyjamas, they're in my room.'

Rosie shook her head. 'Uhm, no. I need to get Moray's car back. Truly.'

Stephen blinked. He wondered if she were already regretting it.

'OK . . . sorry, this lot are staying here tonight . . .'

The other three sipped their wine, completely unperturbed. Stephen saw her to the door, Rosie fully aware that she was wearing a ridiculous apron and a too-short dinner jacket. She found she wanted to cry again, but for very different reasons.

'Don't you want to get dressed?' he said.

'No,' said Rosie, her face flaming. She wanted to get as far away as fast as she could.

'I wish you could stay,' said Stephen. 'I know there's guests, but . . .'

'No thank you,' said Rosie.

'OK. OK, then I'll call you.'

Rosie shrugged. 'If you get a signal.'

'Uhm . . .' CeeCee paused. 'Don't you want to take your knickers?'

Burning with frustration and embarrassment, Rosie didn't answer, just tried her hardest not to give her the Vs on her way out.

Stephen stood in the doorway, his untucked shirt hanging out of his black trousers, looking at her car for a long time as she drove away down the long steep road. Rosie didn't even notice him; she was looking at the other three, outlined in the kitchen windows, laughing their heads off.

Fully sober now, she caught up with her friends as they marched down from a darkened Lipton Hall.

'Hurrah!' said Moray. 'I thought it had been nicked.'

Rosie opened the Land Rover doors. 'Do not say anything,' she ordered as they all got in, Moray taking over the driving and Jake with his arm tightly around Tina's shoulders. They were all giggly and happy and loved up.

'But,' said Tina. 'You've got your dress on back to front.'

'Stop it.'

Moray and Tina exchanged worried glances. Jake tried to hide a smirk and failed.

'*No smirking,*' said Rosie. 'Otherwise I will cry, and I mean it.'

There was a long silence. 'So,' said Moray finally. 'You pulled him then.'

The rest of the car collapsed in laughter.

'It's not funny,' said Rosie, just before she started to cry.

'Don't worry, girl,' Moray said. 'Don't worry. He's just some posh nutjob with a hole in his leg. He's an idiot.'

'He let them laugh at me,' sobbed Rosie. 'Like I was some stupid tart he'd picked up somewhere.'

'Did he really?' said Tina. 'That sounds horrid.'

'Arsehole,' said Jake. 'Would you like me to punch him for you?'

'I would like that,' said Rosie. 'On his leg.'

Her sniffs turned to hiccups. 'Oh God. He'll be having such a laugh about it with his mates. We never even had a cup of coffee. Not a date or anything. Nothing. I'm just some slutty nurse who went round his house and did him. They'll all be pissing themselves.'

'No they won't,' said Tina, unconvincingly. 'Or OK, even if they are. That means they are all pathetic idiots. So it doesn't matter.'

'No,' sniffed Rosie. 'It doesn't matter.'

**T**hings are meant to look better in the morning, grumbled Rosie to herself, as she woke up to a world where the snow was already turning grey and melting, and the lane looked dreary.

At breakfast, Lilian glanced at Rosie quickly and declined to ask. This was a mistake.

'So has the news reached you?' said Rosie.

'No,' said Lilian pleasantly, and sipped her tea.

'Well, good,' said Rosie. 'Never mind then.'

And they spent the day like that. Except Rosie couldn't help it. She spent a lot of time up by the highest front window of the cottage. If she leaned her arm out at a dangerous angle, she could just about get a mobile phone signal. Once, the idea swept over her that CeeCee and her friends would drive by, see her arm and know immediately what she was doing and piss themselves all over again, and she broke out in a cold sweat, but she stayed where she was. All the while thinking, he wasn't like them, was he? Was he?

Had she known it was the exact same position Lilian had sat in nearly seventy years before, she would have been horrified.

Just after four, she heard a bang downstairs. At first, she thought it might be the door, and Stephen striding manfully through it . . . Of course not. That was ridiculous, a completely stupid thought. Then, panic hit her and she couldn't believe she'd been so selfish.

'Lil!' she yelled, charging down the stairs. 'LIL!'

Lilian was lying there with her ankle at a strange angle.

'What the hell . . . what on earth were you doing?' she said.

Lilian blinked up at her, confused. 'I . . . I . . .' She looked down, to where she had urinated on the floor. 'Oh,' she said.

'Don't worry about that,' said Rosie. 'Don't worry about that for a second. Come on, let me get you to a chair.'

She still weighed little more than a child, even after all of Rosie's feeding up.

Lilian was tearful. 'I just . . . I just wanted to get to the bathroom.'

'I know, I know,' said Rosie. 'Why didn't you call me?'

'Because,' said Lilian. 'Because it is utterly ridiculous I can't make it to my own bathroom.'

'I know,' said Rosie. 'I know it's ridiculous. Doesn't make it any less true. I had the monitor upstairs.'

'I hate . . . I hate being a stupid old woman,' said Lilian. 'I hate it.'

'I know,' said Rosie. 'I hate it too.'

'I'm all covered in pee and I can't garden and I can't cook and I can't run my shop and I can't do anything. *Anything*,' she said fiercely.

'I'm here,' said Rosie. But they were empty words, and they both knew it.

'You can't stay here,' said Lilian. 'I won't let you.'

'I don't have much else going on,' said Rosie, ruefully.

'Don't you ever say that,' said Lilian. 'Don't you dare ever say that to me.'

Moray came, clutching his head and looking very under the weather. Rosie had cleaned up Lilian, and together they ascertained that it was a sprain rather than a break, but that she needed to be careful.

'I need to be somewhere with soft walls,' said Lilian, sulking. Rosie let her eat a packet of caramels for supper, while Moray handed her a leaflet.

'It's time,' he said. 'You know it's time.'

'But she's so sharp in herself!'

Moray shrugged. 'I'm sorry, Rosie. Old age is an absolute bitch.'

'Is that your professional opinion?' said Rosie.

'As a doctor, yes. I believe it is accepted fairly widely among the medical profession.'

'An absolute bitch,' said Rosie. 'Yes.'

# Chapter Ten

*Please let me clear this up once and for all: 'Life is like a box of choco-lates. You never know what you're going to get' is a quotation of the high-est nonsense. Every box of chocolates comes with a handy and clear picto-gram relating the shape of the chocolate to its flavour. Also a box of chocolates is always welcome. Life is in fact like a bag of Revels. You never know what you're going to get, and half of it you won't like.*

MONDAY MORNING had grey lowering skies that perfectly suited Rosie's mood. She checked her phone (inside and outside to make sure she was getting a signal). Nothing. Nothing at all. What kind of a prick was he? Presumably just because she turned up there, offering herself on a plate . . . She gulped. That was it. She was a cheap date, that was all. Probably happened to him all the time. She sighed, mightily. Stupid girl.

'Rosie,' said Tina, when she came crashing in at ten thirty.

'What's wrong?' Rosie said. 'What's the matter? Is it Jake?'

Tina's face cleared. 'Oh. Oh, no, it's not Jake. No. God. He's amazing.'

'Oh well, that's good,' Rosie said. 'It's not . . . it's not Kent and Emily, is it? There's nothing wrong with the twins?'

'Oh, no,' said Tina. 'No, thank God. No. Touch wood. No. But oh, oh, Rosie.' She dissolved in floods of tears. 'It's the shop.'

Once they had sat down with a cup of tea, Tina could choke out the story. It turned out, in fact, that her credit rating was nowhere near good enough to take out a business loan. She had tried to raise the money to buy Lilian out, but . . .

'But we gave them all the books and projections and everything!' wailed Rosie. 'It's so obvious you're doing great things for this place! And turning it into a real business!'

'It was always a real business,' croaked Lilian over the baby monitor. Rosie had placed her on the sofa with her ankle raised. Moray had popped by with a walking frame. Lilian didn't mind her stick so much, but there was absolutely no way, she warned them, she would be seen dead with that awful thing, and Rosie didn't want to press the issue. Still, they had appointments made for that afternoon and that was that. Now this was throwing a spanner right in the works.

'There's no one else?' said Rosie. 'Your ex? Could your parents help?'

'I haven't heard from the ex in months,' snorted Tina. 'And my parents run a strawberry farm. What do you think?'

'Oh Tina,' said Rosie. 'Oh, I am so sorry.'

Tina shook her head, unable to hide her disappointment. 'Those stupid bloody cocktail dresses,' she said bitterly. 'What was I thinking?'

'You were thinking, one day I want to wear beautiful dresses to look lovely for my hunk of a boyfriend,' said Rosie, trying to be encouraging. But she hadn't had a sniff of other interest. Nothing at all. Except for . . .

As if reading her thoughts, the little bell rang and the two women turned round, to see Roy Blaine standing there.

He smiled unpleasantly, his ridiculous teeth glinting in the subtle lighting.

'So,' he said, seeing them both there, 'I heard the news.'

'How did you hear about it?' said Rosie crossly.

'His brother's the bank manager,' said Tina.

'No way! Small bloody communities!' howled Rosie. 'Is that why he turned down the loan? That's totally illegal.'

'No,' said Tina. 'They hate each other. It really was just the computer saying no. Because of my "bad credit history".'

'Well, I,' said Roy, 'have a perfect credit history. There's a reason dentists pay very, very low car insurance.'

'They're too stupid to drive?' asked Rosie.

Roy's lip curled. 'Well, you have my offer,' he said. 'Valid till the end of the week. Then I'll go elsewhere. Had lots of other interest?' He paused. 'Thought not. Well, up to you.'

And he was gone.

'He didn't really mean that end-of-the-week stuff,' Tina said. 'It's not like he's going to go anywhere else. Nobody likes him.'

Rosie shrugged. 'He's right, though. Apart from you and him, no one else has shown the least bit of interest.'

**M**oray had come up trumps with the Land Rover, thankfully. After squinting at the map, Rosie settled Lilian in carefully, propping her up on cushions, otherwise she was barely large enough to see out through the windscreen. She looked tiny in Moray's huge car.

In fact, as it turned out, the map was almost unnecessary. Lilian knew everywhere they were going: the home that had once been a cottage hospital where half the babies in the area had been born, the old hotel, the army training centre. Every home that once had a heart and a reason for existence had been turned into a holding pen for the elderly.

'No wonder Hetty doesn't want to convert Lipton Hall,' said Rosie, after their third visit. The first two were absolutely horrible, degrading places that smelled heavily of disinfectant and sadness. In one, a woman with almost no hair sat in the front room by herself, tears coursing down her cheeks, like a child abandoned by her parents. The woman showing them round didn't even notice. In the second, the rooms they saw were tiny dark cupboards; even though the building was set in the countryside, there were no views from any of them. The next two homes were similar, and Rosie felt herself beginning to panic.

The last place on her list, Honeysuckle House, had had a very bare web site. All the others were full of jaunty promises they hadn't even looked close to being able to fulfil. But as they drove up towards this one, the gardens were tended, and there were even a few people out in the greenhouses—old people, not staff. Rosie snuck a look at her great-aunt, who was affecting not to have noticed them.

A tired but pleasant-faced woman met them at the door.

'Hello,' she said. 'Come on in.'

As they walked—slowly, of course—the lady, whose name was Marie, didn't stop doing other things for a second—checking a light bulb, answering queries from a junior, straightening a painting, smiling at everyone she passed, pulling up a cleaner about her uniform. Rosie recognised the style immediately. It was the style of the most successful hospital matrons, those for whom nothing escaped their gimlet eye. The house, once a barracks, was unfashionably furnished, but its parquet flooring gleamed, and although there was a faint trace of disinfectant, it was almost entirely overpowered by the scent of beeswax and the bonfire smells coming through the open windows. Lilian was very quiet as the tour continued; the rooms were simple but comfortable.

'This is the first place I've seen,' said Lilian, when Rosie asked her what she was thinking, 'that has the windows open.'

The residents were having lunch. Rosie sniffed. 'Is that . . .'

Marie checked the schedule. 'Coq au vin,' she said. 'The residents complain something awful. A lot of them don't like foreign muck,' she said, 'but they still clean their plates. Sometimes people like to have things to complain about. And I don't blame them. But we do try our best.'

She didn't have to say it. It was obvious. Honeysuckle House was far and away the nicest place they'd seen. And far and away the most expensive. And it was only affordable on Roy Blaine's money. That was that.

The tour complete, Rosie and Lilian paused by the front door; on the left was a large and pleasant day room, without the enormous blaring televisions they'd seen elsewhere. Televisions were kept in rooms and used with headphones, Marie had explained carefully, for the comfort of all residents. Here they encouraged reading, talking, a daily crossword competition and board games, although if you wanted to stay in your room and watch television and eat Caramac, that was also fine.

Inside were a small group of residents playing what looked like bridge, as well as, by the window, a woman sitting quietly. Her hair was bright white, and while very thin, the woman still wore it long, curled round the nape of her neck. She was dressed in a pale pink dress with a ruffle on the front, and she sat perfectly still, an abandoned magazine on the table in front of her.

Lilian froze.

Rosie immediately felt for her aunt's left hand. But Lilian was many miles and many years away, her vision fixed.

'Lil!' shouted Rosie desperately. '*Lilian!*'

Eventually, Lilian seemed to come back to them. Marie was anxious that she should come and sit down in the office and be checked over by a doctor, but Lilian point-blank refused. 'Let's go,' she said. 'Rosemary. Take me home. Now. Now.'

As they left, Rosie got another shock: leaving their car in their usual order, with her stomping up front and Peter trailing behind, were the Isitts. Peter stopped to say hello; Mrs Isitt marched straight past with barely a sniff in their direction.

'There's Mrs Isitt,' said Rosie in surprise.

Lilian looked at her furiously. 'Well aye,' she said. 'It would be.'

'What do you mean?' said Rosie.

'Well, her mum's in there,' said Lilian. At the window, the woman sitting there began to move as she saw her daughter.

'Ida Delia Fontayne. She's Dorothy Isitt's mother.'

**T**ina shut up the shop. Rosie made macaroni cheese. Lilian had stared out of the window the entire way home and refused to discuss things. Rosie was determined to get it out of her. Macaroni cheese—and some violet creams for dessert—was the only method she knew.

She bent over carefully and lit the fire. Lilian was sitting back in her chair, but her fingers were wavering lightly on the arms, as if they wanted to say something. Rosie concentrated on taking the dish out of the oven, then set it down with salad and a large glass of water.

At last they were both sitting at the table. Lilian pushed her dinner round the plate and sighed like a grounded teenager. After five minutes of this, Rosie could take it no longer.

'OK,' she said. 'Who was that woman?'

Lilian heaved a great sigh. But she did, she realised, want to tell the story. And it was important that Rosie knew. That Rosie didn't let things go by her like she had. It seemed to her that Rosie was at a crossroads. If Lilian could have had her time again, she wouldn't have taken the same path. Not by a long chalk.

She sighed again. It was hard, to talk about this. Everyone who knew her—who had known her for a long time—knew the story. They would probably have been surprised to discover she ever thought of it at all; it was so very long ago, and she had been only a girl.

The fire blazed as the darkness crept around the tiny cottage and Lilian told Rosie about Henry, and how much she had loved him. And how she didn't grab her chance while she had it.

'What happened to him?' asked Rosie quietly at the end, their tea cold.

Lilian shrugged. 'Oh, the same thing that happened to all of them. All the good ones. It was in Italy. They didn't . . . there was nothing to send home. His dust is Italian now. Has been for a long time. He was such a boy of the soil, always in the fields . . .' She smiled to remember it. 'Always grubby. But in a good way, you know. Well, I liked it anyway.'

Rosie blinked several times and reached for her aunt's hand.

'Oh,' said Lilian, 'I know what you must think. That it was so very long ago. How can I still be thinking about it now? But it doesn't feel long ago to me. It feels like yesterday. And Henry and I had so little time together.'

'That probably made it worse,' said Rosie, thinking of Gerard. 'Maybe if you'd had a few years washing out his dirty socks, it wouldn't have been so awful.'

'Maybe,' said Lilian. 'Or maybe we'd have settled into this little house and worked hard and raised our children and we'd have been looking after one another right now. And he would still look as young and handsome to me as he did then. Maybe it would have been that.'

They both fell silent for a moment.

'But after . . .' said Rosie.

'Oh, there was a big fuss,' said Lilian. 'Ida Delia was in such a state. I'm sure they'd give it a name now: call it postnatal depression, get her sorted out in a hospital. You were just left to get on with it then. Poor Dorothy.'

'I can't believe she was Henry's daughter,' said Rosie.

'There wasn't much of Henry in her,' said Lilian. 'And the raising of her was a mess, a terrible shame. Her mother blamed her and she blamed her mother and they both blamed Henry for dying and . . . I'm amazed,' said Lilian, her eyes watering. 'I'm truly amazed. I had no idea Ida Delia was still alive. She moved out of the village when Dorothy left home.'

'And for you there was never anyone else . . .'

Lilian gazed into the fire.

'Well, first off, a lot of men didn't come home. And the ones that did, they couldn't stomach village life; they couldn't believe we'd been here quiet and safe all the time after what they'd been through. Like your granpa. He had it figured out. Life was short, and he was going to make the most of it. So a lot of them never came home, for one reason or another. And then of course I had to help Dad, and he was getting older.'

She paused. 'And, you know, it wouldn't have been fair. I had this big lake of unhappiness inside me. Anyone else would have been second best. It would have been unfair on some poor sod if I'd hurled myself at him.'

'And did you never regret that?'

Lilian shook her head. 'I only had one bad year,' she said, 'It was 1969. The year of the new divorce act. I couldn't help thinking . . . I don't think they'd have stuck it out, those two. Not in the end. Not with Ida so highly strung and him so . . . so decent. I reckon she'd have pushed him too far. So. That was hard. Apart from that . . .'

She gave a half-smile. 'I haven't been idle, if that's what you're asking.'

'I don't think I need to know the details,' said Rosie.

'I took Felix off Hetty's hands for a few years. Oh, don't look so shocked,' Lilian said, seeing Rosie's face. 'It was the sixties. Everyone was at it. Hetty didn't mind a bit, she was getting tupped by the gardener.'

'If you tell me you are really Stephen's mother I am going to kill you,' said Rosie.

'Oh goodness *gracious* no, don't be absurd,' said Lilian. 'No, no. I was just helping Hetty out. Felix was so terribly demanding.'

'You *are* good friends,' said Rosie. 'Please don't tell any more.'

'And there was . . .'

'OK, OK. I get it.' Rosie looked at her. 'When I was little I thought you were just some old lady who sent us cough drops,' she said.

'Did you now,' said Lilian.

'This has been a good life,' said Lilian later. It was getting late, but it was so cosy in front of the fire.

Rosie had poured them both a sherry. She looked around at the lovely sitting room with the fire still crackling away merrily. 'I meant to ask you,' she said, 'how do you keep this place so nice? You can hardly move and I'm out all day and the garden is immaculate and the logs are always chopped. I know Hetty comes in, but . . .'

Lilian smiled. 'Ah, my elves.'

Rosie raised an eyebrow.

'Pretty much everyone comes by once in a while,' Lilian said. 'When you've served every child in the village, they don't forget. And they drop in. A bit of wood-chopping here, a bit of cleaning there.'

Rosie looked at her straight on. 'Amazing.'

'Well, there are some benefits to living in the same place for a long time,' said Lilian. 'Don't pity me, please.'

Rosie shook her head. 'Not in a million years,' she said.

'I've had a happy life here,' said Lilian. 'I have a lot of friends. A lot of people who help take care of me. A good job. I never lost a son to war, or a man to the bottle, or a baby. I've never been rich, but I've paid my way—well, almost.' She laughed, ruefully. 'And I've had some adventures and kept safe and sound, and lived in a beautiful place and enjoyed every season of it. This has been a good life.'

Rosie let out a great sigh. It did sound like a good life. 'I know. I know. But me—I've made such a fool of myself.'

'Oh, you've been making a fool of yourself since you arrived,' said Lilian. 'Why stop now, I say.'

Rosie bit her lip. 'Bed,' she said.

Next morning was bleak, a grey Tuesday morning for Rosie, after a sleepless night thinking of everything Lilian had been through. She made a decision. It was the right thing to do, she was sure of it. She needed, she knew, to make a call. It was just that the very idea of it made her feel sick.

Lilian, conversely, slept well and woke up feeling rested and calm, as if something had been decided for her. Which in a sense it had. Angie had rung in the dead of night Australian time, when she knew Rosie would be at the shop, and had let the phone ring till Lilian had picked it up.

'Aunt Lily,' Angie had said, in her no-nonsense tone with its new Australian twang. 'You know what you have to do.'

'Of course I do,' Lilian had grumbled.

'She's a good girl, you know. She's my good girl.'

'She is, she is.'

'But there are limits, you know?'

'I know,' said Lilian, crossly.

'Will you miss her?'

Lilian sat up straight on the bed. 'I do not for the life of me know how you can bear to be apart from her,' she said in a tight voice.

Angie smiled ruefully. 'Me neither. Listen, don't tell her, I'm going to come back for a bit. I want to visit, come and see you all. It sounds like you've been getting up to all sorts.'

'We've been doing nothing of the kind,' said Lilian stiffly.

'Ah, you would say that, wouldn't you? Always been a dark horse.'

And Lilian's mind was made up.

**I** think,' she said at breakfast, 'I think I might like to visit Ida Delia.'

Rosie looked at her, bleary-eyed. She knew this was coming. She knew what it meant. 'Sure,' she said. Carefully.

Lilian smiled. 'She's probably doolally,' she said, almost to herself. 'Probably won't remember me at all.'

'Maybe,' said Rosie. 'Maybe not.' Something else struck her. 'How could you have been getting milk from Mrs Isitt all these years and never ever asked after her mother?'

Lilian shrugged. 'Well, you know. We respect privacy around here.'

'Ha!' said Rosie. 'Anyway.' She had decided in the night. She was going to do it. She was going to make the call. 'I have to use the phone.'

Lilian raised her eyebrows. Rosie would not be drawn, but instead went upstairs and crouched by the window, the only place with a signal.

Her heart quaking in her chest, she scrolled through her address book and pressed the button. She tried to imagine what he'd be doing right now, and found, somewhat to her surprise, that she couldn't. However, he answered on the second ring. Rosie felt her heart leap in her chest.

'Hello?' came the voice. He sounded busy and preoccupied.

'Hello,' said Rosie, finding herself shaking. 'Hello, Gerard.'

**A**fter breaking the news to Lilian, Rosie decided to walk down the high street even though the weather was horrid. She layered up her cardigans and borrowed Lilian's umbrella, which was a ridiculous lavender frou-frou number, but it did the job. Even the lowering clouds that touched the top of the hills, and the sucking mud that had sunk in by the side of the road, could not daunt her spirits. Halfway down, she caught sight of Edison, kicking his away along the road by himself as usual.

'Hello!' he said cheerily when she caught up with him.

'What are you doing?' she asked, looking around for his mother. As usual, she was nowhere to be seen. Ghastly woman.

'I'm mingering,' said Edison proudly.

'You're what?'

'*Min-ger-ring*. It's when something bad has to happen but you don't want it to happen so you walk about going hum-hum-hum, hoping it will happen later.'

'Malingering?' said Rosie.

'What I said,' said Edison.

'I'm not sure that's quite right,' said Rosie.

'Yes it is,' said Edison. 'I am very smart and have a huge cablary.'

Not for the first time, Rosie wanted to wring his mother's neck. 'OK,' she said. 'What are you mingering about?'

'I have to see Dr Roy. For my teeth.'

'He's not a real doctor.'

'He likes to be called Dr Roy,' said Edison. 'He thinks it's friendlier.'

'I think it's fraudulent,' said Rosie. 'Hmmm.'

'He will say, "No sweets",' said Edison sadly.

'Well, do you have any sore teeth?'

Edison shook his head.

'Open your mouth.'

Rosie looked around thoroughly. A healthier set of straight white teeth and pink gums was hard to imagine.

'Dr Roy said he was sure he'd find lots of cavays because he sees me in the sweet shop,' said Edison mournfully.

'Where's your mother?' asked Rosie.

'She sent me by myself. She says she needs to do her meditates and that I am a big boy and she will be over in ten minutes.'

'Well,' said Rosie, 'as it happens I'm going that way and I'll take you.'

She marched up with him into the dentist's, absolutely furious.

'Ah, the young sugar addict,' said Roy, his sparkling gnashers on display. 'Your mother said she'd be in in five minutes.'

'She's doing her meditates,' said Edison.

'Very good, very good,' said Roy.

'I'm here though,' said Rosie.

Roy looked at her. 'Here to accept my offer?'

Edison jumped up on the dentist's chair.

'I am going into space,' he announced loudly. 'Hello, space. Countdown is progressing. We are OK to go.'

'I'm going to stay for Edison's examination,' said Rosie.

Roy's face fell immediately.

'Just to make sure he doesn't have any unnecessary work done.' Rosie was staring him straight in the face. 'You hear a lot about that with dentists these days,' she said. 'Of course you would never do that.'

'I'll be a lot happier when you're no longer around here making trouble, Miss Hopkins.'

'Well, I don't know about that,' said Rosie, as he picked up his mirror and tiny pointed probe. 'You see, I've had a little stroke of luck. My ex is selling our flat and moving in with his new girlfriend. And he's giving me my share of the proceeds. Very fairly in fact. He didn't have to.'

Gerard's grace, in the end, had overwhelmed her. She knew it had a lot to do with him not wanting confrontation, and wanting to get on with moving in with Yolande. It turned out she had a proper little house with a garden in Bow, and cooked a mean chilli con carne and his mother absolutely loved her. She had been happy for him. But for him to give Rosie a share of the profits, rather than just what she'd put in, was more than kind. It was charming. And just like him. All the good things, she'd remembered, not just his annoying habits that had worn her down. She had been right to love him. She hadn't set her sights too low. Not at all.

'So I'm buying the shop. I'm buying the shop and running it and I'll rent half the cottage and that will be enough to cover it all and get Lilian into the nice home. If she wants to go. She doesn't know she wants to go, but she does really. So you can't have it.'

Roy looked at her, startled.

'*Blastoff*,' shouted Edison, spraying a whole load of spit over Roy's face. Rosie smiled at the boy.

'Get down,' barked Roy. 'There's nothing wrong with your teeth. Tell your mother I'll send her the bill.'

Edison jumped off and pretended he was in space, careering around in orbit.

'Careful!' she said to Edison. 'And you too,' she said with a backward glance at Roy as she left the surgery. 'There're a lot of overcharging dentists doing unnecessary work these days. I'll be telling everyone to keep an eye out for it.'

Rosie ran into Hester in the street outside. She was wearing her usual expression of smug calm.

'Sorry,' said Rosie. She pasted the biggest, brightest smile on her face so Edison, still careering up and down being in a spaceship, wouldn't realise what she was saying. 'I don't mean to be rude. But if you let your gorgeous, delightful six-year-old roam the streets alone one more time instead of behaving like a proper mother, I'm reporting you to social services.'

Hester took a step back, her mouth falling open. Rosie ruffled Edison's hair and marched on up the street.

'Come and visit me soon,' she hollered to Edison. 'We'll watch *Star Wars*.'

'What's *Star Wars*?'

'You'll like it.'

**U**p towards the turnoff, Rosie spied something that at first didn't make sense. It looked like two old men walking . . . It took a second for her to realise who it was. It was Peter Isitt, walking . . . with Stephen.

Rosie looked around. Either she could slow to a crawl, which would probably mean Roy coming out of his office to harangue her again, or run past them, which would be weird. So Rosie tried to keep up her normal pace, hoping she wouldn't get noticed.

'Hi, Rosie!' called Anton cheerily from the top of the high street. He held his belt open. 'Look! Look! I have space in my trousers!'

The two men turned to look as Rosie felt her face redden.

'I . . . I . . .' She hurried towards Anton. 'That's great news.'

Anton beamed. 'And it's down to you! I decided just to eat one of every-thing! So on Monday I have one fish and chips and on Tuesday I have one burger and chips and on Wednesday I have one chicken and chips and on Thursday I have one sausage and chips and . . .'

He was continuing, but Rosie hushed him.

'That's not exactly what I had in mind,' she began, but then, seeing his fallen face, consoled him. 'Well, if it's working for you, that's fantastic.'

'I know,' said Anton. 'Can I have some fudge?'

'When you're in trousers you can buy from a shop,' said Rosie. 'A real shop. Trousers with buttons.'

'I think I've forgotten how to do buttons,' said Anton sadly.

'I'm sure you've forgotten how to do a lot of things,' said Rosie, winking at him. 'But I suspect it's all about to come back to you.'

Anton was giggling smuttily when Peter and Stephen reached them.

'Hello,' said Rosie.

Anton smirked. 'Rosie and I were just discussing . . . *bedroom matters*,' he sputtered out and lumbered off in the direction of Malik's.

Stephen raised an eyebrow. 'All part of the service?' he said.

Rosie smiled tightly. 'Hello,' she said again. 'Glad to see you're both out and about. You both look much better.'

Peter smiled at her. How odd, she thought, that he had spent his entire life married to the daughter of Lilian's great love. Did he know? He must do. Was he happy?

'Well,' Peter said. 'I'd better get back. She'll be on the lookout for me.' He set off for the lane to his farm.

'So have your friends left?' she said, for want of something better to say.

'Yes,' said Stephen carefully. 'They have. They've gone back to London. But I've been thinking . . .'

He paused. Rosie couldn't help it. She couldn't help the little burst of excitement that leaped inside her now they were gone. It was stupid; he'd been awful and he hadn't contacted her or anything to apologise—it was all too embarrassing for words. She kept her eyes on the ground.

'I was thinking about what you said . . . You know, I do need something to do. Something practical to do with my life instead of sitting around moping. I see that now. So I've decided.'

At once Rosie knew what was coming. Unbelievable.

'You're going down to London,' she said, her voice sounding choked.

Stephen nodded. 'Get a change of scene. It'll be good, don't you think?' His voice betrayed a hint of nerves. Rosie felt herself go shaky too.

'Well, that's good,' she said, trying to sound cool and poised. 'I'm sure it will be great.'

Stephen looked at her questioningly.

'I'm staying here,' she announced, very quietly.

'You're what?' said Stephen.

'I'm staying here. I'm buying out my great-aunt, so she can get looked after properly. Well, buying the business. Renting half the cottage. I'll have to get a tenant as well. Then when Tina gets more together she can buy in too. I don't know if it will be for ever. And I don't know if I can make a go of it. And I don't know if it will make me happy. But . . .' She looked around her, the frosty fields white in the morning mists, the sun glinting off the icy tops of the hills. 'I . . . I like it here. I'm happy here. I have friends here. And family. I have family here, and I don't really have that anywhere else. So. I'm going to change. I'm going to stay.'

Stephen looked completely taken aback.

'Oh,' he said. 'That's a shame. That's . . . oh. I thought maybe, you know, you'd show me round London a bit.'

'I think the London I would show you and the London CeeCee will show you would be very different things.'

Stephen smiled. 'I thought I was meant to be the chippy one,' he said sadly. 'But I'd hoped . . .'

'What did you hope?' said Rosie, suddenly furious. 'That I'd do a naked dance in front of your chums? That I'd come up and give you a few handy shags before you got fully back in with your London set? That you could pick me up whenever I was of use to you and drop me afterwards?'

Stephen's brow furrowed. 'What are you talking about?' he said.

'You used me,' said Rosie. 'You used me when you were sick and you used me when you were getting better and I fell for it every bloody time. You're not worth it.' Rosie was furious. 'I wasted . . . oh. It doesn't matter.'

'Wasted what?' said Stephen, cross. 'Wasted what? Sorry, was I wasting your time as well as the rest of the village's? Oh God, how long do I have to limp around being sorry? You seemed quite happy at the time.'

'And now it's over,' said Rosie. 'Well, thanks very much. It's fine. I don't need you and I don't need anything. It is *very* unclassy not to call a girl. Very. Although I'm sure those tarts in London won't give a toss.'

Stephen looked at her in disbelief. 'Who uses a phone round here? Have you seen anyone use a phone round here? If you need something you go and get it.'

There was a silence.

'I have to be getting on,' said Rosie, stiffly.

'Fine,' said Stephen. He stomped off the other way, his limp pronounced but, oddly, rather suiting him.

Tears stinging her eyes, it took everything Rosie had not to run up the high street in hysterics. She had the awful, awful feeling that this was the last time they would ever speak. That she had blown it, if she'd ever had it in the first place. She couldn't think, now, of the night at the ball, how exciting it was and how much she'd wanted him. Still wanted him.

Well. He was going away. Good. Better to crush her hopes now than for things to run on indefinitely. Her heart, though, sank into her boots. Was this how Lilian had felt when Henry went away? Worse, she supposed, because Lilian knew she might never see him again. But something told Rosie she'd never see Stephen again. Not the real Stephen: the funny, cussed, brave Stephen she'd got to know. She might see a polite stranger, swishing past her in the pub or coming home at Christmas time, CeeCee tapping her foot impatiently till the family visits were out of the way. But seeing Stephen again? It seemed unlikely. She ran through the door of the cottage, the first sobs already on her lips.

'Lilian!' she howled. Lilian was sitting up on the sofa and, like a child, Rosie threw herself down next to her and burst into tears.

'There, there,' said Lilian. 'There, there.'

'He's going away,' howled Rosie. 'He's going away. I thought it wouldn't matter and I wouldn't care and I'd be all grown-up. But it does!'

It was only gradually that Rosie realised there was someone else in the room. Sniffing, she tilted up her head, horrified to see Lady Lipton standing in the shadow of the kitchen door, two cups of tea in her hands. Rosie didn't care, she was so red and damp and her face was a mess and the tears wouldn't stop dripping. Hetty would be pleased, presumably, that she wouldn't be going near her beloved son again.

'Oh, for goodness' sake,' said Hetty, looking her up and down. 'This has to stop. You must be freezing in that jacket.'

Rosie hadn't even noticed what she was wearing.

'If you're going to live here, you'd better get yourself sorted out once and for all.' She picked up a paper bag at her feet. 'Here,' she said. 'Lily told me your size. I thought you might like these.'

Inside were a pair of wellingtons. Round the top was a narrow stripe of material. And the motif on them was little wrapped sweets.

'Pulled in a favour from Hunter's,' sniffed Hetty. 'It really was getting beyond a joke.'

Rosie wanted to laugh and cry at the same time. Instead, she took Lilian's proffered cotton handkerchief and blew her nose.

'Here,' said Lilian. 'Have my tea.'

Hetty looked at her. 'And I suppose you'd better have these. They've been cluttering up my son's kitchen for days now while he's looked at them and hummed and hawed. I suppose they're for you. Well, he's never going to give them to you, so I suppose I'd better. I can't handle you *both* mooning around, it's bad for my angina.'

She handed over a box of sweets, something Rosie didn't recognise immediately. Then she cottoned on that they were Love Hearts. She opened the box with fumbling fingers. Instead of different messages, on every single one was a single word: *Rosie. Rosie, Rosie, Rosie, Rosie.*

Rosie gasped and looked up.

'I need to tell you something,' said Lilian. 'Last night, when we were talking, I lied. I have had a happy life, mostly.'

She took a deep breath. 'But if I had the chance to do it again, if things had been different . . .'

'Mmm?' Rosie couldn't take it all in. Hetty had turned her head away.

'I would never have left that bally dance,' said Lilian, proudly. 'And I would have grabbed his other arm. I wouldn't have walked backwards. I would have kept on walking forwards and kept on dancing, and I would have done everything in my power to make sure he didn't get near that other girl. And kept him on bloody farming duty while I was at it, and I wouldn't have cared tuppence for what anyone else said. I'd already sacrificed as much as anyone else in that damn war.'

Lilian gave one of her looks. 'Do you understand what I'm saying?'

Rosie squirmed. 'It's not like that,' she said. 'Henry chased you. It's nothing like that with Stephen.' Hetty harrumphed.

'I am not going to sit here and tell you that Stephen Lakeman isn't one of the awkwardest buggers ever to walk the face of the earth,' said Lilian. 'He's ridiculously proud and needlessly difficult. But he's a good boy,' she added. 'He's decent. And he's kind. And I think if you want him . . . I think if you want him you should go get him.'

'But he's supposed to do the chasing,' moaned Rosie.

'Men are meant to do all sorts of things,' said Lilian. 'Doesn't mean they ever bloody manage it.'

'Amen to that,' said Hetty. But already Rosie was on her feet and heading out the door.

'STOP!' said Hetty. 'I cannot bear you going out looking like a farm animal one more time. *Especially* if you are taking my son off my hands.' Her tone was crusty but her eyes were twinkly. 'Put on that dress!'

Hetty held her and brushed out her hair with thick strokes, and Lilian tried to apply some black mascara, and Rosie pulled on a thick jumper over the green dress that was ridiculously unsuitable for the middle of a winter's day, but finally they judged her ready. Rosie's heart was fit to burst and she was at screaming point before they let her go; for speed, she leaped on the bicycle and threw herself up the hill as fast as she could manage. Was she too late? Had her words hardened his heart? Maybe he had got into his car and headed south straight away. She pedalled harder and harder—till she spotted him, on the flat part of the road leading up to Peak House. He must be trying to walk it. To see him marching onwards with his stick distracted her for a second and, as she skidded round the corner, she realised suddenly she had absolutely no chance of stopping.

'Get out the way!' she screamed at him. The bicycle made almost no noise on the tarmacked road. 'MOVE!'

He tried to move aside but he was too late, and she saw his eyes widen as she remembered, at the very last minute, to jam on the brakes. Then, gracelessly, she felt herself, as if in the stretched-out timing of a dream, fly over the handlebars and crash headlong into his arms. They both fell flat, the stick clattering to the ground, and found themselves, caught in each other's arms, squelching deep into the soft, forgiving mud at the side of the track, Love Hearts scattered all around.

At first they stared at each other, shocked and appalled. Then, almost inexorably, Stephen, then Rosie, started to laugh. And finally, filthy with mud and wet with newly falling rain and fuelled by adrenalin and happiness, they kissed once again, as hungrily and passionately as the young of the village had kissed each other by the side of the harvest fields, witnessed only by cows, owls and deep-swooping birds, for hundreds of years.

# Coda

THE SNOW HAD FALLEN so thickly the cottage looked like something out of a Christmas-tree advert, the day they loaded up the Land Rover—Stephen's this time, not Moray's. Stephen and Moray had grudgingly made up, Stephen admitting it was hard to see his contemporary fit and well and swanning about when there was so much need in Africa; Moray sniffing loudly and saying he was probably also jealous of his good looks and how much everybody liked him, but Stephen had ignored that.

They had packed all of Lilian's photos, her cushions and as many of her dresses as Rosie could get in the car.

'Why will I need those?' Lilian had said, not displeased.

'Because there'll be a different social occasion every night,' Rosie had said. 'You'll be tea-danced off your feet.'

Lilian sniffed. 'Not with my hips.'

'Don't be daft, they've all got dicky hips. They play the music at thirty-three and a third. And you'll be by far the best-looking woman there.'

'Well, I can't deny that,' said Lilian. She was full of nerves about moving from the only home she'd ever known. But in a funny kind of way, she was excited too, excited to be doing something new, trying something different. The idea of room service and games nights and someone to play Scrabble with . . . well, she couldn't deny it sounded interesting. The presence of Ida Delia made her slightly nervous, though Ida Delia would have forgotten her long ago, gone doolally or something.

But the best news of all was Rosie. That Rosie would still be near—that she could visit the shop whenever she chose, come to the cottage or pick up the phone, that this was going to happen without ruining Rosie's life, that Rosie *wanted* to do this—made her feel safe and content inside.

Rosie looked at her, sitting like a queen with a blanket over her knees in the front seat. Stephen was driving. She still couldn't believe it. That he was there, and that he was hers. The past few weeks had been a blur. Gerard had been unimaginably decent; mind you, when she'd gone to see him his shirts were perfectly ironed and his hair had been cut.

'Yolande likes me to look my best,' he'd said when she mentioned it.

He looked even more well fed, if that were possible, but undoubtedly, in Rosie's eyes, happier. Gleeful, in fact. She was slightly sad—she was human after all—that after all those years it had been somebody else, but she couldn't deny it was right.

'I'm so glad,' she said. 'And your mum likes her?'

'She *loves* her,' said Gerard. 'Well, there are a *few* things she doesn't do quite right, but I'm sure Mum will sort her out.'

Rosie had given them the most enormous box of chocolates, which made Gerard light up with glee, just like a little boy.

'Thank you,' she said to Gerard from the bottom of her heart.

He shrugged. 'Mum said it was the right thing to do.'

'It was,' said Rosie. 'Even though I didn't deserve it. Thank you.'

And they hugged, tentatively and awkwardly.

'And if you're ever in . . .'

'The wilds of rural Derbyshire? I know, I know.'

'There's a big box of sugar mice with your name on it.'

Gerard smiled. 'I'll remember that.'

**S**he had had to tear herself away from Stephen to look after Lilian. It had been a struggle. Thankfully Tina had agreed to take on longer hours in the shop, but even so, Rosie found it incredibly difficult to leave Stephen's old cast-iron bed in the high, pale bedroom in Peak House, with its view of nothing but sheep all the way down the valley, the clouds so near it was as if you could touch them.

But life had to be planned; work had to be done; arrangements had to be made. Inch by inch, things started to take shape. The deeds were signed over in front of a sweet, quiet notary. Lilian insisted on giving power of attorney to Rosie. Rosie was on the point of looking for a tenant, when Stephen, with his head in her lap in front of the fire one evening, talked about how he was getting sick of Peak House, and his mother needed it back to rent as a holiday cottage before she went bust again. He'd been thinking for a while of moving to the hustle and bustle of the village, he said, and Rosie had teased him and asked about London.

'I hate London,' he said. 'I was only moving there because everyone here thought I was a dingwad. Correction: *you* thought I was a dingwad.'

'Yes, but I never said I don't *like* dingwads. Anyway, you'd have been a dingwad in London too. Just a posh one.'

'The worst kind,' said Stephen, rotating his leg out in front of him. 'But fair-weather friends were still better than none at all.'

Lilian woke up from the sofa where she'd been pretending to have a snooze. 'So what are you going to do, Lipton?'

Stephen shrugged. 'I'm not sure. I expect my mother will rope me into something or other, trying to make the estate pay its way. Which it cannot do and it'll be even worse when I get my paws on it.' He sighed. 'I just wish I could do something more useful.'

Lilian sniffed. 'You know they've just lost one of their teachers down at the school?' There was a silence.

'Was this about five minutes ago?' said Rosie. 'Lilian, really, you've practically invented Twitter all by yourself.'

'I would say it's imminent,' said Lilian. 'So, if you were looking for a job to annoy your mother and that makes even less money than a sweet-shop owner . . .'

Stephen thought about it for a while. 'Hmm,' he said. 'Hmm.' He glanced up at Rosie. 'Posh enough for you?'

'Perfect,' said Rosie, her heart brimming. 'Perfect.'

And now today was the day. Stephen drove slowly, being careful over the icy bumps and ruts, up the winding road to the home. As they crested the hill, Lilian let out a sigh. Rosie was leaning over from the back seat, holding tight to her hand.

'Don't worry about it,' she whispered. 'We're here.'

Lilian nodded. 'I know, my dear. I know.' But her voice quavered.

They spent an awkward hour settling her in and unpacking her things—it had seemed so much in the car, and it helped a lot to humanise the spotless, cosy but bare little room. Finally, Marie gently hinted that they should leave so she could introduce Lilian to the other residents.

Rosie turned towards her aunt. 'I . . .' Then she didn't know what to say.

Lilian shook her head. 'Don't . . .'

Both of them stood there for a moment. Then, for the first time, Lilian stepped forward and took Rosie in her arms, and they held each other in an embrace, Rosie enveloping Lilian's fragile frame.

'You've put on weight,' Rosie whispered.

'Shut up,' said Lilian. And then, very quietly, 'Thank you, my darling.'

'We'll see you in the shop next weekend,' said Rosie. 'And if you learn how to use that mobile phone you can put it on speaker and shout at us all day.'

Lilian indicated Stephen, who was lounging by the door. 'From one wounded bird to another then?'

'I heard that!' said Stephen. Rosie grinned and blushed.

'All right,' said Lilian. 'Off you go, the pair of you.' And Rosie kissed her.

Then they did go, hand in hand, walking gently through the falling snow, stopping, out of sight of the house, to have a quick snowball fight. Rosie screamed as Stephen chased her, her wellies full of snow, up to the avenue of trees.

'I can't believe you can finally outrun me,' she said, her face pink from the wind, her mouth laughing wide. He grinned full at her.

'Ah,' he said. 'I don't want to. In fact I faked the entire thing.'

'Piss off!'

'OK, OK. I didn't. I didn't, obviously. But Rosie—' His tone turned serious for a moment. 'I never . . . I never in a million years thought that out of something so awful would come . . . something so sweet.'

And Rosie thought of her life and how terrible she had thought it would be, to be buried alive in the country, looking after an elderly lady, and how selfish she had been.

'I got lucky,' she said. 'God, I got lucky.'

'So did I,' said Stephen fervently. And beneath the freezing grey sky, the cloud cover that wouldn't lift for another six months, they kissed until it got dark. Which wasn't very long. But they kissed on anyway.

Lilian was tired after being introduced to a long line of old women mostly, all of whom seemed nice. Ida Delia wasn't there, but after supper Lilian made her way, timidly, to the games room. Sure enough, sitting in the elegant salon, looking out into the darkness, was Ida Delia.

Lilian, taut with nerves, cleared her throat.

'Ahem,' she said. Ida Delia looked up.

'Lilian Hopkins,' she said. Then a pause. 'It is Hopkins, isn't it? You didn't get married and change it?'

Lilian felt a bolt of frustration shoot through her.

'No,' she said. 'I did not get married and change it.'

Ida Delia nodded. There was a long silence; much left unsaid went between them.

'Well,' said Ida Delia. 'I have a box of dominoes here, if you're interested.'

And after an equally long pause, Lilian shrugged.

'All right,' she said. And she sat down quietly, and they opened the box and began to play.

The letter was tear-stained and rain-stained and goodness knows what else; it was hard, after all this time, to make out anything on the yellowing paper that had come back with his watch and his medals. It said, in Henry's handwriting, just one thing—a note, perhaps for a letter never sent, or simply an affirmation. Ida had kept it all this time, almost convincing herself over the years. If she screwed up her eyes and pretended, or was telling people who had not known them both that the ink had run in the rain, or the sweat or the blood or whatever it was, that where it said, 'I will love you always, L,' that it was not an L but an I, an I caught in the rain. That was all. She had never shown it to anyone, not even Dorothy, who would snort at anything romantic anyway. She could never ever entertain the belief that it said L and not I. But maybe, just maybe, thought Ida Delia Fontayne, it was time.

'Are you a sweet shop or a book shop?' asked a curious Edison one frosty Saturday morning. 'I think you should be both. That would be good.'

Rosie looked up from where she was unpacking the box of Lilian's self-published books she'd found in the bottom of her wardrobe, propping the copies up beside the ancient cash till.

'No,' she said. 'Not a book shop. We've only got space for this one.'

*People think love should be popping candy: always surprising and exciting and fresh to the mouth. Or like dark chocolate: mysterious and adult and bitter. Or the tough candy shell of a Minstrel, waiting to be cracked, spiky as peanut brittle, as painful as a sharp shard of toffee. I think love is caramel. Sweet and fragrant, always welcome. It is the gentle golden colour of a setting harvest sun, the warmth of a squeezed embrace, the easy melting of two souls into one and a taste that lingers even when everything else has melted away. Once tasted, it is never forgotten.*

*And that is all I have to say about that.*

## Jenny Colgan

**With three children under seven to look after, how do you find the time to write?**

The same way I always have—employing a really fantastic housekeeper, without whom I couldn't possibly work. I'm very lucky to be able to do this, I realise. Another very lucky feature is that I write from home so I can easily be there if one of the kids is sick or something. I know I have such a great job.

**Where do you write? Do you have a strict regime?**

All writers have a strict writing regime otherwise you'd just mess about on the internet all the time and never get anything done. I go down to our local baker's, have a cup of coffee and a bun and sit there. They don't have Wi-Fi, which is extremely helpful.

**Your stories have moved from cup cakes to sweets. Do you have a sweet tooth?**

Not as much as I used too, but sweets were certainly a big part of my life growing up in Scotland. Spending your pocket money was very important.

**What sweets did you buy?**

I liked chocolate limes and sherbert dip dabs.

**Did you have a favourite sweetshop?**

Well, I grew up in a small town so there only was one—Mrs McCreadie's. She had a generous hand on the scales and was kind to children, so it was definitely a good one.

**What sweets, if any, do you have in your bag today?**

I have a Carambar from one of my children's party bags. It's not very nice and appears to have sand in it.

**What is the easiest, most delicious sweet to make?**

Coconut ice is incredibly easy, but I would say honeycomb. Not only is it easy—you just stir, really—but it's fun; you add the bicarbonate of soda and it all fizzes up into honeycomb. Anyone can make it.

**You live in France. Are the French good sweet makers?**

They are dreadful sweet makers, they don't see the point. There's no sweet shop culture in France, instead you have patisseries everywhere. What they're really good at are *tartes* and pastries.

**What do you love most about living there? What do you miss about Britain?**

I love the weather here, being near the sea, having a big garden, the food, the schools for the children are amazing too and I love that they are growing up bilingual, it's such a gift. It sounds mundane but I miss Boots—you can't even buy an aspirin in a supermarket here—and bacon. And Cheddar cheese!

**Countryside or town? Lipton or London?**

I'm a townie, I love London. I'm wildly allergic to loads of animals and I get dreadful hay fever so the countryside and I are never destined to be friends.

**Unlike Rosie, can you ride a bike?**

I can and I do. We lived in the Netherlands for two years so I'm a fully-fledged obsessive. I had a baby seat on the front for all the children that took them from six months. It's a great way to get about and helps stop me getting too fat from all the cakes and sweets!

**Did you plan to tell Lilian's story in flashback from the beginning or did it come to you while you were writing Rosie's story?**

Lilian's story came more gradually and I wasn't quite sure what to do with it, whether she should tell Rosie or whether it should be told separately. But Lilian didn't seem to me the confiding sort, she dreads being pitied, so I put it in flashback.

**You are writing for the *Dr Who* series. How did this come about? Are you a big fan?**

I'm a huge fan. I pestered the BBC and they were a bit dubious about it because of the other books I do but I managed to talk them round in the end and I think (fingers crossed) everyone's really pleased and excited about it.

**Who is your favourite Dr Who?**

Oh, that changes all the time. I grew up with Tom Baker. But David Tennant was very marvellous indeed. As a Scot, I'll need to go for him.

**What's next for Jenny Colgan?**

If I am very good and very lucky, more of exactly the same.

# THE
# BUNGALOW

## Sarah Jio

*In the summer of 1942, Anne Calloway's life seems perfectly predictable—until she suddenly sets off to serve as an army nurse on the Pacific island of Bora-Bora. On this idyllic tropical island at the edge of World War II, nothing is predictable. Who would think that in the middle of the fighting a young woman could find the love of her life? And get trapped in a mystery that will haunt her for the rest of her days?*

*Tuck a slip of paper into a flimsy envelope, seal it with a swipe of the tongue, then send it on its way. That letter might be handled by dozens of people and journey a thousand miles before reaching the intended mailbox, where it nestles anonymously between pages twenty-nine and thirty of some unwanted catalogue, lying in wait for its unsuspecting recipient,who tosses the catalogue, with its treasure tucked inside, into the recycle bin with a flick of the wrist. There, next to poorly rinsed milk cartons, an empty wine bottle and yesterday's newspaper, a life-changing piece of mail quietly awaits.*

*That letter was for me.*

# PROLOGUE

'Hello?'

Startled, I opened my eyes at the sound of a familiar voice—pleasant, but sorely out of place. Jennifer, yes, my granddaughter. *But where am I? Or rather, why was she here?* I blinked a few times, disorientated. I had been dreaming of sandy beaches and coconut palms—the place my unconscious mind always tries to visit, but this time I was lucky enough to find it in the archives of my memories.

He was there, of course—in uniform, shyly smiling at me as the waves fell into the shore. I could hear them—their violent crash, followed by the fizz of a million bubbles kissing the sand. Closing my eyes tighter, I found him again, standing there amid the fog of sleep that was lifting, too quickly. *Don't go,* my heart pleaded. *Stay. Please stay.* And he obediently appeared again with that beckoning grin, those arms outstretched *to me.* I felt the familiar flutter in my heart, the longing.

And then, in an instant, he was gone.

I sighed and looked at my watch. *Half past three.* I must have dozed off while reading. Again. Spontaneous sleepiness was the curse of the elderly. I sat up in my lounge chair, a bit embarrassed, and retrieved the novel I'd been reading before the exhaustion hit.

Jennifer walked out onto the terrace. 'Oh, there you are,' she said, smiling at me with her eyes, smoky brown, like her grandfather's. She wore jeans and a black sweater with a light green belt round her slim waist. Her blonde hair, cut to her chin, reflected the sun's rays. Jennifer didn't know how beautiful she was.

'Hi, honey,' I said, reaching my hand out to her. I looked around the terrace at the pale blue pansies in their simple terracotta pots. They were pretty enough, peeking their heads out of the dirt like shy, repentant children who'd been caught playing in the mud. The view of Lake Washington and the Seattle skyline in the distance was beautiful, yes, but cold and stiff, like a painting in a dentist's office. I frowned. How had I come to live here, in this tiny apartment with its stark white walls and a telephone in the bathroom with a red emergency call button beside the toilet?

'I found something,' Jennifer said, her voice prising me from my thoughts, 'in the recycle bin.'

I smoothed my white, wispy hair. 'What is it, dear?'

'A letter. It must have got mixed in with the junk mail.'

'Just leave it on the table. I'll look at it later.' I walked inside and sat down on the sofa, turning my gaze to the reflection in the window. *An old lady.* I saw her every day, this woman, but her reflection never ceased to surprise me. *When did I become her?* My hands traced the wrinkles on my face.

Jennifer sat down next to me. 'Has your day been any better than mine?' In her last year of graduate school at the University of Washington, she had chosen an unusual subject for a class-assigned article: an obscure work of art on campus. Donated in 1964 by an anonymous artist, the bronze sculpture of a young couple had a placard that read simply, *Pride and Promises*. Jennifer hoped to profile the artist and learn the story behind the work, yet an entire quarter's worth of research had turned up very little.

'Any luck with your research today, dear?'

'Nada,' she said, frowning. 'I hate to admit it, but I think the trail's gone cold.'

I knew something about being haunted by art. Jennifer didn't know it, but I'd spent the majority of my life searching in vain for a painting that I'd held in my hands a very long time ago. My heart ached to see it again, and yet after a lifetime of working with art dealers and collectors, the canvas eluded me. 'I know it's hard to let go, honey. Some stories aren't meant to be told.'

Jennifer nodded. 'You may be right, Grandma. But I'm not ready to let it go. Not yet. The inscription on the placard—it has to mean something. And the box the man holds in his hands, it's locked, and the people in the archives don't have a key.' She smiled. 'There may be something inside.'

'Well, I admire your spirit, sweetheart,' I said, clutching the gold chain round my neck, the one that held the locket I'd worn and kept safe for so many years. Only one other soul knew what was tucked inside beyond the protective guard of the clasp.

Jennifer walked to the table. 'Now, don't forget this letter,' she said, holding up an envelope. 'Look at this gorgeous stamp. It's from'—she paused, reading the postmark— '*Tahiti*. Grandma, *who* do you know in Tahiti?'

My heart rate quickened. 'Let me see it,' I said.

I scanned the simple white envelope. No, I did not recognise the handwriting, or the return address. *Who would be writing to me from Tahiti? And why? Why now?*

'Aren't you going to open it?' Jennifer said.

My hands trembled a little as I ran my fingers along the exotic stamp, which depicted a Tahitian girl in a yellow dress. I swallowed hard, trying to purge the memories that were seeping into my mind like rising flood water, but mere mental sandbags could not keep them out. Then, powerless to resist, I opened the envelope with one swift tear.

*Dear Mrs Godfrey,*

*Forgive me for my intrusion. It has taken me many years to find you. I understand that you were an army nurse stationed in Bora-Bora during the war. If you are indeed the woman I seek, I urgently need to speak with you. I was raised in the Tahitian islands, but have only now returned, with a mission to solve a mystery that has troubled me since girlhood. A murder occurred on a quiet stretch of beach on Bora-Bora one evening in 1943. I am haunted by the tragedy, so much so that I am writing a book about the preceding events.*

*I was able to locate army employment records and noticed that you were blocked out on leave that day, the day of the tragedy. Could you, by chance, remember something or someone on the beach that night? Even a small detail may help. I pray that you will consider my request and get in touch. And, if you ever plan to visit the island again, there is something of yours I found here, something you might like to see again. I would love nothing more than to show it to you.*

*Yours truly,*

*Genevieve Thorpe*


Genevieve Thorpe. I did not know this woman. And here she was, stirring up trouble. Too many years had passed. How could I go back to those days? I closed my eyes tightly, willing the memories away. I could throw the envelope into the garbage can and be done with it. But then I remembered the last few lines of the letter. 'If you ever plan to visit the island again, there is something of yours I found here, something you might like to see again.' My heart, already in poor condition, raced at the thought. *Visit the island again? Me? At my age?*

'Grandma, are you all right?' Jennifer leaned in and wrapped her arm round my shoulder.

'I'm fine,' I said, composing myself.

'Do you want to talk about it?'

I shook my head and tucked the letter safely inside the book of crossword puzzles on the coffee table.

Jennifer reached for her bag and retrieved a large manila envelope, wrinkled and worn. 'I want to show you something,' she said. 'I was going to wait until later, but I think it's time.'

'What is this?'

She handed me the envelope. 'Look inside,' she said.

I pulled out a stack of black-and-white photos, instantly recognising the one on top. 'That's me!' I cried, pointing to the young woman dressed in white nurse's garb, with a coconut tree in the distance. 'Where did you find these?'

'Dad found them. He was going through some old boxes and these were tucked inside.'

I flipped to the next photograph—of Kitty, my childhood friend, sitting on an overturned canoe on the beach, her feet kicked out like a movie star's. Kitty *could* have been a movie star. I felt the familiar pain in my heart when I thought of her, pain that time hadn't healed.

There were several more in the stack, many of them scenes of the beach, the mountains, lush with flora, but when I reached the last photograph, I froze. *Westry. My Westry.* There he was in his uniform, his head tilted slightly, with the bungalow's woven palm wall in the background. *Our bungalow.* I remembered everything about the snapshot, the way the air had smelled that evening—of seawater and freesia, blooming in the moonlight. I could recall the feeling I had in my heart, too, when my eyes met his through the lens.

'You loved him, didn't you, Grandma?' Jennifer's voice was so sweet, so disarming, that I felt my resolve weaken.

'I did,' I said.

'Do you think of him now?'

I nodded. 'Yes. I have always thought of him.'

Her eyes widened. 'Grandma, what happened in Tahiti? What happened with this man? And the letter—why did it affect you the way it did?' She reached for my hand. 'Please tell me.'

I nodded again. *What would be the harm in telling her?* I was an old woman. There wouldn't be many consequences now, and if there were, I could weather them. And how I longed to set these secrets free. 'All right, dear. But I must warn you, don't expect a fairy tale.'

Jennifer sat down in the chair beside me. 'Good,' she said, smiling. 'I've never liked fairy tales.'

'And there are dark parts,' I said, doubting my decision.

'But is there a happy ending?'

'I'm not sure,' I said. I held the photo of Westry up to the light. 'The story isn't over yet.'

# CHAPTER 1

**August 1942**

'KITTY MORGAN, you did not just say that!' I set my goblet of mint iced tea down with enough force to crack the glass. Mother would be happy to know that I hadn't spoilt her set of Venetian crystal.

'I most certainly did,' Kitty said, smirking victoriously.

Kitty, with her heart-shaped face and wiry, untamable blonde ringlets springing out of the hairpins she'd been so meticulous about fastening, hardly provoked anger. But on this subject I held my ground. 'Mr Gelfman is *married*.'

'James,' she said, 'is impossibly unhappy. His wife disappears for weeks at a time. She doesn't even tell him where she's going.'

I sighed, leaning back into the bench swing that hung from the enormous walnut tree in my parents' garden. Kitty sat beside me. I looked up at the leaves tinged with a touch of yellow, hinting that autumn was imminent. It seemed like only yesterday that Kitty and I were two schoolgirls, walking home arm in arm, setting our books down on the kitchen table and making a dash to the swing, where we'd tell secrets until dinner time. Now, at twenty-one, we were two grown women on the verge of—well, something.

'Kitty,' I said, turning to face her. 'Don't you understand?'

'Understand what?'

She looked like a rose petal, sitting there in her dress brimming with pink ruffles. *Does she not know his reputation?* Certainly she remembered the hordes of girls who had flaunted themselves at Mr Gelfman in high school, where he had been Lakeside's most dashing teacher. Every girl in English Lit had hoped to make eye contact with him as Elizabeth Barrett Browning's 'How Do I Love Thee?' crossed his lips. That was all girlish fun, but had Kitty forgotten about Kathleen Mansfield? Kathleen—shy, big-breasted, terribly dim-witted—had fallen under Mr Gelfman's spell. she hovered near the teachers' lounge at lunch, and waited for him after school. Everybody wondered about them, especially when one of our girlfriends spotted Kathleen in the park with Mr Gelfman after dusk. Then, suddenly, Kathleen stopped coming to school. Her older brother said she'd gone to live with her grandmother in Iowa. We all knew the reason why. 'Kitty, men like Mr Gelfman have only one objective, and I think we both know what that is.'

Kitty's cheeks flushed to a deeper shade of pink. 'Anne Calloway! How dare you suggest that James would be anything but—'

'I'm not *suggesting* anything. It's just that I love you. You're my best friend, and I don't want to see you get hurt.'

Kitty kicked her legs despondently as we swung for a few minutes in silence. 'You're just jealous,' she finally said, still smug.

'Nonsense,' I retorted. The sun, high in the summer sky, caught the diamond ring on my left hand, producing a brilliant sparkle. 'I'm marrying Gerard in less than a month. I couldn't be happier.'

Kitty frowned. 'Don't you want to do something with your life before you become Mrs Gerard Godfrey?'

I shook my head in protest. 'Marriage, my dear, is not suicide.'

Kitty looked away from me, her gaze burrowing into a rosebush in the garden. 'It might as well be,' she murmured under her breath.

I heard footsteps on the lawn, and I looked over to find Maxine, our housekeeper, approaching. In heels, she walked steadily across the lawn, requiring only a single hand to bear a laden silver platter. 'May I fetch you girls anything?' she asked in her beautiful, heavily accented voice. She was petite, with soft features and great big sparkling green eyes. Her hair was pulled into a tidy chignon. She wore a starched white apron cinched round her small waist. Lots of families in the neighbourhood had servants, but we were the only household that employed a *French* housekeeper, a fact Mother was quick to point out at bridge parties.

'We're fine, Maxine. Thank you,' I said.

'There is something,' Kitty said conspiratorially. 'You can convince Anne not to marry Gerard. She doesn't love him.'

'Is this true, Antoinette?' Maxine asked. I was five years old the day she came to work in our home, and after a quick once-over, she said declaratively, 'You do not have the face of an Anne. I shall call you Antoinette.' I had felt very fancy.

'Of course it's not true. Kitty is just in one of her *moods*.' I gave her a sideways glance of disapproval. 'I'm the luckiest girl in Seattle.'

And I *was* lucky. Gerard was tall and impossibly handsome, with his strong jaw and dark brown hair and eyes to match. He was quite wealthy, too, not that it mattered to me. Mother reminded me that at twenty-seven he was the youngest vice-president at First Marine Bank, a title that meant he would come into a fortune when he took over for his father. You'd have to be a foolish woman to turn down a proposal from Gerard Godfrey, and when he asked for my hand, under this very walnut tree, I nodded without a moment's hesitation.

Mother had been giddy upon hearing the news. She and Mrs Godfrey had planned the union since I was in infancy, of course. Calloways would marry Godfreys. It was as natural as coffee and cream.

Maxine picked up a pitcher of iced tea and refilled our goblets. 'Antoinette, have I ever told you the story of my sister, Jeanette? She loved a peasant boy from Lyons. But our father and mother pushed her towards another man, a man who made a decent wage in the factories. So she parted with her farm boy and married the factory worker. And she was miserable.'

I smoothed my dress, blue crepe with a delicate belt on the bodice. Mother had brought it home from one of her European shopping trips. 'Well, that's very sad, and I'm sorry for Jeanette. But this does not have any application to my life. You see, I *love* Gerard. There is no one else.'

'Of course you love Gerard,' said Maxine. 'You've grown up with the boy. He is like a brother to you. Dear, it is your life and your heart. You say there is no one else. I'm simply saying that maybe you haven't given yourself enough time to find him.'

'Him?'

'Your one true love,' she said.

I felt a chill come over me. 'I don't believe in knights in shining armour. I believe that love is a choice. You meet someone. You like them. You decide to love them. It's that simple.'

Kitty rolled her eyes. 'How horribly *unromantic*,' she groaned.

'Maxine,' I said, 'what about you? Were you ever in love?'

'Yes,' she said, running a cloth along the tray to wipe up the rings our goblets had left. 'He was married to someone else.'

We all looked up when we heard Papa's footsteps on the terrace. Puffing on a cigar, he crossed the grass towards the three of us. 'Hi, kid,' he said, smiling at me through his thick grey moustache. 'I didn't think you were coming home until Tuesday.'

I returned his smile. 'Kitty talked me into taking an earlier train.'

I had finished my college courses at Portland State University in the spring, but Kitty and I had stayed on for two months to obtain our nursing licences. What we'd do with these credentials was of great concern to our parents. Heaven forbid we actually use them. Our mothers didn't work, nor did any of the women we knew.

In truth, I didn't know what I wanted to do. I'd chosen nursing because it stood in stark contrast to everything I'd grown to detest about the lives of the women I knew—Mother, who devoted herself to luncheons and the current state of ladies' hemlines; and my school friends, who had spent months luxuriating in Paris or Venice upon high-school graduation, with nary a worry, save finding a rich husband. Nursing, in all its gritty rawness, promised to fulfil a part of me that longed to help others in a way that had nothing to do with money.

Maxine cleared her throat. 'I was just leaving,' she said to Papa, picking up the tray. 'Can I get you anything, Mr Calloway?'

'No, Maxine,' he said. 'I'm just fine. Thank you.'

She nodded and made her way across the lawn to the house.

Kitty looked up at Papa with concerned eyes. 'Mr Calloway? I heard about another wave of men being drafted for the war. Do you know if any from Seattle have been notified?'

'It's still very early, but I think we'll see a great deal of men going off to fight. The Larson twins are shipping out on Thursday.'

I felt a tightness creep up in my chest. 'Terry and Larry?'

Papa nodded solemnly.

The twins were going off to war. *War.* Wasn't it only yesterday that they were tugging at my pigtails in grade school? I wondered if they'd be allowed to stand next to each other on the battlefield. I closed my eyes as if to try to suppress the thought, but it lingered. *Battlefield.*

Papa read my mind. 'If you're worried about Gerard shipping out, don't,' he said.

Gerard was as strong and gallant as any man I knew, but as hard as I tried, I couldn't imagine him anywhere but in a suit at the bank. Yet, as much as I wanted him spared from fighting, a secret part of me longed to see him in uniform, to see him stand for something other than dollars and cents.

'His family's position in the community is too important,' he continued. 'George Godfrey will see that he isn't drafted.'

I hated the conflict brewing inside my heart—the fact that I took comfort in Gerard's protected position and detested it at the same time. It wasn't right that men from poor families had to fight a nation's war while a privileged few dodged the draft for frivolous reasons. Sure, George Godfrey, a bank mogul now in failing health, was a former senator, and Gerard was the next in line to fulfil his duties at the bank. But even so, it was unsettling to imagine the Larson twins fighting in a European bunker in the dead of winter while Gerard rested comfortably in a heated office with a leather chair that swivelled.

Papa could read the anxiety in my eyes. 'Don't let it worry you. I hate to see you worry.'

Kitty stared at her hands in her lap. I wondered if she was thinking of Mr Gelfman. *Will he join the war?* The ill tidings of conflict hovered, creeping in and spoiling even the most perfect summer afternoon.

'Mother's eating in the city tonight,' Papa said. 'Will I have the privilege of dining with you ladies this evening?'

Kitty shook her head. 'I have an engagement,' she said vaguely.

'Sorry, Papa, I'm having dinner with Gerard.'

He nodded, suddenly looking sentimental. 'Look at you two, all grown up, with big plans of your own. It seems like only a moment ago that you girls were out here with your dolls.'

Truth be told, I longed for those easy, uncomplicated days that revolved around paper dolls, dressing up, and tea parties on the terrace. I buttoned my cardigan against the wind on my skin—winds of change. 'Let's go inside,' I said, reaching for Kitty's hand.

'OK,' she said sweetly. And just like that, we were Kitty and Anne again.

**M**y eyes burned from the haze of cigarette smoke hovering like a low cloud over our table. The lights were dim in the Cabaña Club, the place everyone in Seattle went dancing on Saturday nights.

Kitty pushed a box wrapped in blue paper towards me. I eyed the gold ribbon. 'What's this?'

'Something for you,' she said, grinning.

I looked at her quizzically, and carefully untied the ribbon before peeling off the wrapping. I lifted the lid of a white jewellery box and pushed aside the cotton lining to reveal a sparkling object inside.

'It's a friendship pin. Remember those little rings we had as children? I thought we needed a grown-up version.' She pulled a lock of hair away from her shoulder to reveal a matching pin on her dress. 'See? I have one too.'

I eyed the silver bauble, dotted with tiny blue stones that formed the shape of a rose. I flipped it over: *To Anne, with love, Kitty.* 'It's perfectly beautiful,' I said, pinning the piece to my dress.

'I hope it will be a symbol of our friendship, a reminder to us both that we'll never keep secrets from one another, that we'll not let time or circumstances change things between us.'

I nodded in agreement. 'I'll wear it always.'

'Me, too.'

We sipped our sodas and scanned the bustling club, where friends, schoolmates and acquaintances revelled in what could be the very last Saturday night before whatever waited in the wings scooped them up. War. Marriage. The unknown.

'Look at Ethel with David Barton,' Kitty whispered in my ear. She pointed to the two of them huddled together at the bar. 'His hands are all over her,' she said, staring a little too long.

'She ought to be ashamed of herself. She's engaged to Henry. Isn't he away at school?'

Kitty nodded. But instead of mirroring my disapproving gaze, her face told a different story. 'Don't you wish someone could love you *that* much?' she said wistfully.

I scrunched my nose. 'That, my dear, is not love.'

We watched the couple saunter hand in hand out to the dance floor. Kitty shrugged. 'Well, they have passion.'

I retrieved the pressed powder from my bag and dabbed my nose. Gerard would be here soon. 'Passion is for fools,' I said, snapping the compact closed.

'Maybe. But just the same, I'll take my chances with it.'

'Kitty! Don't talk like that!'

'Like what?'

'Like a *loose* woman.'

Kitty giggled, just as Gerard arrived at our table with his friend Max, a colleague from the bank—short, with a plain, honest face, and eyes for Kitty.

'Do share your joke, Kitty,' Gerard said, grinning. I loved his smile, so charming, so confident. He towered over the table in his grey suit, adjusting a loose cuff link.

'You tell him, Anne,' Kitty said, daring me with her smirk.

I smiled deviously. 'Yes, Kitty was just saying that she and Max made a better dance duo than the two of us. Can you believe that?'

Gerard grinned. 'We can't have her carrying on like that, can we, dear?' He looked towards the dance floor and held out his hand. 'Shall we?'

The band began playing, and Max grinned from ear to ear. Kitty rolled her eyes at me as she took Max's outstretched hand.

Gerard clasped his arms round my waist, smoothly, elegantly. I loved his firm grasp. 'Gerard?' I whispered in his ear.

'What is it, sweetheart?' He was an excellent dancer—precise in the same way he was about finances.

'Do you feel . . . do you feel *passionate* about me?'

'Passionate?' he said, stifling a laugh. 'You funny thing, you. Of course I do.' He squeezed me a little tighter. 'Anne, you must know by now that I love you more than anything on earth.'

I nodded, and closed my eyes. I nestled closer to Gerard, so close I could feel the beat of his heart, and I was sure he could feel mine. With each step, I assured myself that we had *it*. Of course we did. Gerard was head over heels for me, and I for him. What nonsense these feelings of uncertainty were. I blamed Kitty for planting them. I glanced over at her, dancing unhappily with Max, when, out of nowhere, Mr Gelfman appeared on the dance floor. He walked straight towards her, said something to Max, and took her into his arms as Max, crestfallen, scurried away.

'What is Kitty doing with *James Gelfman*?' Gerard frowned.

'I don't like it,' I said, watching Mr Gelfman twirl her round the room like a doll. 'Let's go. I don't feel like dancing any more.'

'So soon?' he asked. 'Is it Kitty?'

I nodded. I'd be damned if I was going to watch my best friend give away her heart to a man who wasn't worthy of her. But there was something more my mind wouldn't acknowledge: I envied her. I wanted to *feel* what she was feeling. And I feared I never would.

On the drive home, Gerard wanted to talk about real estate. Would we buy an apartment in the city or something in Windermere, the opulent neighbourhood of our youth, near our parents? The apartment would be closer to the bank. And how gay it would be to live on Fifth Avenue, he crooned. But the Buskirks would be selling their home this fall, the big Tudor with the four dormers in front. We could buy it and renovate; build a new wing for the help and a nursery for the baby. For the *baby*.

Gerard droned on and suddenly the air in the car felt too warm. The road blurred in front of me and the streetlights multiplied. What was wrong with me? *Why can't I breathe?* Dizzy, I clenched the door handle to steady myself.

'Are you all right, darling?'

'I think I just need a little air,' I said, rolling the window down.

He patted my arm. 'Sorry, honey, am I overwhelming you?'

'A little,' I replied. 'It's just that there are so many decisions to make. Can we take them one at a time?'

'Of course,' he said. 'No more talk of homes for now.'

He turned the car into Windermere, passing the stately, lit columns flanking the entrance. Within was a well-tended sanctuary, where gardeners spent hours manicuring lawns and grooming flowerbeds, not a petal askew, and governesses tended to children in a similar fashion. We passed Gerard's parents' grey gable mansion on Gilmore Avenue, and the Larsons' white colonial, with the clipped boxwood hedges and stone urns shipped from Italy. *What is wrong with me?* Here was a man who loved me, who wanted to give me a beautiful, comfortable life, a life I was accustomed to, I scolded myself.

Gerard parked the car in my parents' driveway, and we walked into the house and straight to the darkened kitchen. 'Maxine's probably gone to bed,' I said, looking at the clock. Half past nine. Maxine always retired to her downstairs quarters at nine. 'Would you like a sandwich?' I offered.

'No, I'm fine,' Gerard said.

We both looked up when we heard footsteps.

'Papa?' I said, peering round the corner, where I detected a female form coming down the stairs in the darkness.

'I was just stocking your bathroom with towels,' Maxine said. 'Francesca wasn't here today, and I wanted you to have some for the morning.'

'Oh, Maxine,' I said. 'Look at you worrying about my towels at this late hour. I will not hear of it! Please, get some rest. You work far too hard.'

'I think I shall say good night,' she said. 'Unless you need anything.'

'No,' I said. 'No, we're fine. Sweet dreams, Maxine.' I wrapped my arms round her neck the way I had done as a girl.

After she'd left, Gerard kissed me, gently, quickly. *Why can't he kiss me longer?* 'I suppose I should be on my way too.'

'Do you have to go?' I said, pulling him towards me, eyeing the couch in the living room with other intentions.

'We need our rest. Tomorrow's going to be a big day.'

'A big day?'

'The party. Have you forgot?'

Until that moment, I had. Gerard's parents were hosting an engagement party for us at their home, on their enormous lawn. There would be a band, croquet, ice sculptures, and platters of tiny sandwiches served by white-gloved waiters.

'Just put on a pretty dress.' He grinned. 'And be there by two.'

'**M**axine!'

I opened my eyes, blinking, trying in my deep state of grogginess to place the voice—loud, shrill, a bit angry, but mostly annoyed. Mother.

'I told you Anne would wear the blue dress today—why isn't it pressed?' The voice was nearer now, right outside my bedroom door.

I pushed the quilt aside and sat up, reaching for my robe before setting my feet down reluctantly on the cool hardwood floor. *Poor Maxine.* She didn't deserve to be shouted at. Again.

I opened the door and walked slowly into the hallway. 'Mother,' I said cautiously. 'I thought today I'd wear the red one you bought in Paris.'

She smiled. 'Oh, good morning, dear,' she said, walking towards me. 'I didn't know you were up.' She cradled my face in her hands. 'You look tired, love. Were you out late last night? With Gerard?'

I shook my head. 'No. It was an early night.'

She pointed to my eyes. 'Then why the dark circles?'

'I couldn't sleep,' I said.

Maxine approached timidly, with a dress on a hanger. 'Antoinette, is this the one?'

I nodded.

'I wish you wouldn't call her that, Maxine,' Mother snapped. 'She's not a girl any more. She's a woman, and about to be married.'

'Mother, I *like* to be called Antoinette.'

Mother shrugged. A new pair of diamond earrings swung from her lobes. 'Well, I suppose it doesn't matter now. Next month you'll be Mrs Gerard Godfrey, the most important name of all.'

I felt a prickly sensation in my underarms. My eyes met Maxine's, and we shared a knowing look.

'Must you wear the red dress?' Mother continued. She was a beautiful woman, far prettier than I would ever be. 'I'm not sure it's your colour.'

Maxine looked Mother straight in the eyes, something she didn't do often. 'I think it's perfect on her, Mrs Calloway,' she said.

Mother shrugged again. 'Well then, wear whatever you wish, but we need to leave for the Godfreys' in two hours. You had better start getting ready.' She was halfway down the hall when she turned back. 'And put your hair up, dear. Your profile looks so much more becoming that way.'

I nodded in compliance. Mother subscribed to all the fashion magazines and attended the runway shows in New York and Paris each year. She cared a great deal about appearances—always designer dresses, perfect hairdos, the latest accessories. And for what? Papa hardly noticed. And the more clothes she amassed, the unhappier she seemed.

Maxine handed me the dress. Her eyes told me she was still smarting from Mother's dismissive tone. We walked to my rooms, and I shut the door.

I draped the dress against my body. 'Are you sure this one will look all right on me?'

'What's bothering you, Antoinette?' Maxine asked.

'I don't know,' I said, hesitating. 'I worry that it's all happening so fast.'

Maxine nodded. 'You mean the engagement?'

'Yes,' I said. 'I love him; I really do. He's such a good man.'

'He is a good man,' she said simply, leaving room for me to continue.

I sat down on the bed and leaned my weary head against the headboard. 'I just wish some things were different. I want to feel passionate about him. Kitty thinks we don't have enough passion.'

'Well,' Maxine said expectantly, 'do you?'

'I don't know,' I replied. 'Listen to me going on like this. What a terrible fiancée I am even to speak this way. Gerard is a dream come true. It's time I start playing the part.'

Maxine's eyes met mine. 'You must *never* talk that way, Antoinette. You can never play a part in life, especially not in love.' She wrapped her arm round my shoulders the way she'd done when I was a child, nuzzling her cheek against mine. 'Never ignore what your heart is telling you, even when it hurts, even when following it will be very difficult or untidy.'

I sighed and buried my face against her shoulder. 'Maxine, why are you telling me this? Why now?'

'Because I didn't follow my heart. And I wish I had.'

Gerard's mother, Grace Godfrey, was a formidable woman in appearance. Her dark eyes and sharp features, which looked so handsome on Gerard, manifested in the female form as alarming, jarring. But when she smiled, the edges softened. As a child, I often wished Mother could be more like Mrs Godfrey—practical, down-to-earth, despite her wealth and her position. In a time when women in her class offloaded much of the child-rearing to hired help, Mrs Godfrey did not. During their childhood, if one of the Godfrey boys skinned their knees, she'd shoo the nanny away and swoop in to bandage it herself.

As my parents and I walked across the Godfreys' lawn that afternoon, Grace could be seen assisting the waiters in carrying an ice sculpture—a large duck with three ducklings—from the terrace to a table on the lawn.

'Let me help you with that,' Papa called out from behind me.

'Thank you.' Mrs Godfrey relinquished her hold on the duck and turned to Mother. 'Hello, Luellen, Anne. Isn't it a lovely day for a party?'

'Yes,' I replied, peering up at the blue sky, a single fluffy white cloud its only resident. Tables covered the expansive lawn, and in every vase atop the lilac-coloured table linens were five stems of purple hydrangeas. 'It's all so beautiful.'

'I'm glad you like it,' Mrs Godfrey said, entwining her substantial arm in mine. 'Gerard's on the terrace waiting for you, dear.'

I could see him in the distance, stretched out on a chaise longue, puffing on a cigar with his father. When he saw me, he stood up quickly and snuffed the celebratory smoke. 'Anne,' he called, waving, 'I'll be right down.'

Maxine's words rang in my ears: 'You can never play a part in life, especially not in love.' But everyone plays a part, don't they?

Moments later I felt Gerard's arms round my waist. 'You,' he said, 'are the most beautiful woman I have ever laid eyes on.'

I blushed. 'Do you really think so?'

'I know so. Where did you get that dress? You are a vision.'

'I wore it for you,' I said. 'I wanted you to—'

'Wait, is that Ethan Waggoner?' He squinted at the entrance to the garden. 'Sorry to interrupt, sweetheart, but it's an old friend from college. Let me introduce you.'

The afternoon was so filled with introductions and how-do-you-dos that I hardly saw Gerard, except for an occasional wave from across the terrace or a kiss on the cheek in passing. Engagement parties were not for the engaged.

I didn't see Kitty all afternoon. Throughout dinner, her spot at the head table next to Gerard and me remained empty. When the band started to play the first song of the night, 'You Go to My Head', I began to worry.

'Gerard,' I whispered in his ear as we swayed on the dance floor, feeling what seemed to be a thousand pairs of eyes staring at us through the warm night air. 'Kitty hasn't shown up.'

'She's probably just running behind schedule. You know Kitty.'

I rested my head on his lapel as he led me round the dance floor in perfect form. True, Kitty was often late, but *five hours* late? My thoughts were interrupted by motion, detected in the corner of my eye, at the entrance to the garden. Someone was waving, trying to get my attention. The lights from the dance floor blurred the periphery, but I squinted hard to bring the person into focus. *Kitty.* There she was, standing behind the garden gate. She dabbed a handkerchief to her eye.

The song ended and several couples joined us on the dance floor. I leaned in close to Gerard. 'Do you mind sitting this one out?'

He gave me a confused smile, but nodded, before I raced through the gate, where I found Kitty seated on the sidewalk, slumped over, head buried against her knees.

'You must think I'm a terrible, terrible friend,' she sobbed.

I smoothed her hair, tucking stray locks back into her hairpins. Her curls were dishevelled in a way I'd never seen before. 'Of course I don't. What's wrong? Tell me.'

'I'm so sorry for standing you up like I have. I am a miserable, unworthy friend.' More sobbing ensued.

'You are not an unworthy friend. You are my dearest friend.'

Kitty looked up at me with frightfully grief-stricken eyes. Her gaze telegraphed sadness, but also a glint of desperation. 'I arrived hours ago, but I just couldn't come in.'

'Why on earth not?'

'Because I can't bear to see you off.'

'But I'm not going anywhere, Kitty.'

'You are. You're getting married. I should be happy for you, but all I can think of is how I'm losing you.'

'Oh, Kitty,' I said. 'You'll never *lose* me!'

'But I will. And it's the way it has to be. I just haven't got used to it yet. I'm so sorry, Anne.'

I reached for her hand. 'No,' I said firmly. 'You mustn't apologise.' I used the hem of my dress to blot a tear from her cheek.

'Anne,' she said, a little distantly. 'There's something I need to tell you.'

I let go of her hand. 'What?'

'I've made a big decision. You're moving on, and so must I.' She took a deep, calming breath. 'You remember the pact we made when we signed up for nursing school together?'

I nodded. 'Yes. We swore we wouldn't end up like our mothers.'

'Exactly,' she said, staring straight ahead. 'And that we wanted a different life, a more meaningful life.'

I frowned. 'Kitty, if you're implying that by me marrying Gerard I'm—'

'No,' she said quickly. 'I don't mean that at all. I'm just saying that it occurred to me that there is something *I* can do with my life, with my skills. I'm going away, far away—to the South Pacific. I'm joining the Army Nurse Corps to assist with the war efforts. I was downtown today at the volunteer registration centre. Anne, they're desperate for trained nurses. This could be a chance for me to do something of value.'

My heart surged with emotion. 'Are you sure?'

'Yes,' she said softly. 'Listen, everyone's getting married, or going to school, or going somewhere. I won't sit and watch while everything changes. I want to be a part of the change.'

Yes, change was happening, whether we wanted to participate or not. The closer we came to it, the more painful it felt. And now that we were staring it in the eye, it produced an ache in my heart that I could not ignore.

'Mother hates the idea, of course,' Kitty continued, 'of me running off to an untamed island, to mingle with *savages*, to live among army men, but I don't care. I don't care what anyone thinks, except you.'

I couldn't bear to think of Kitty out there either, but not because of the 'savages' or the men. No, I couldn't stand it that Kitty was leaving, flinging herself to another part of the world—without me.

I thought about the wedding, just weeks away. All the little details ran through my mind. My dress, French silk. The blue garter. A five-tier cake, with fondant. Doilies. Bridesmaid bouquets. White peonies and lavender roses. I shuddered. How can I get married without Kitty by my side?

'I'm going with you,' I said matter-of-factly.

'Anne! You can't mean that. What about the wedding? We'd have to leave in a week. The commitment is at least nine months.'

I shrugged. 'They need nurses, don't they?' My heart pounded—with excitement and with fear. 'What kind of friend would I be if I let you set off on the adventure of your life without me?'

Kitty threw her arms round me, and we sat there on the sidewalk together for the next song, and another. The music from the party sounded as if it might be a world away, and in some ways it was.

'Gerard will never forgive me,' Kitty said, 'for stealing his fiancée away on the eve of his wedding.'

I shook my head. 'That's nonsense. You're not taking me prisoner. I'm going because I want to.'

I looked over my shoulder at the party behind us. My decision would come with consequences; I knew that. Mother would be beside herself. Papa would warn against it. And Gerard . . . *Gerard*. I sighed. He would find this hard to take—his fiancée going off to a battle zone while he stayed comfortably at home. He'd also be hurt, which is what worried me most. But I couldn't think about that, not now. If he loved me, he would wait.

# CHAPTER 2

KITTY JABBED AN ELBOW into my side, and I groaned, opening my heavy eyelids. 'Look out of your window,' she said. 'We're almost there!'

It had been a forty-five-minute flight from an island to the north, where we'd arrived by ship. I'd been seasick for four days and longed to be on land again. I looked around the cabin of the small plane, so grey and mechanical. A place for men. Yet, other than the pilots in the cockpit and a single soldier on his way back from an extended medical leave, the plane was filled to capacity with nurses.

'Look!' Kitty exclaimed, holding her hand to her heart. 'Have you ever seen anything more beautiful?'

I leaned over to the tiny window and gasped at the scene below—the impossibly light blue water against white sand, the lush, emerald-green hillside. Newspaper articles from home told a different story, one of an unrelenting tropical heat, squalor and misery. And yet the view from the window didn't seem to fit that description.

My thoughts turned to Gerard and the concerned look on his face when I told him I was going. Of course, he tried to talk me out of it, but eventually he said, 'I'll be here for you when you return. Nothing will change that.' We decided to postpone our wedding a year. Mother was devastated. Papa's eyes glimmered as he said he wished he had my courage.

Constance Hildebrand, the charge nurse who was now our superior, stood up in the front of the plane. She was a portly woman with grey hair tucked under a nurse's cap clipped so tightly it looked painful. 'We are almost to the island,' she said. 'Don't be fooled by its beauty; it isn't a place of luxury. You will work harder than you can imagine. The heat is harsh. The humidity is suffocating. And if the mosquitoes don't get you, the natives will. The ones close to the shoreline are friendly, but cannibal colonies still exist not far from the base.'

Nurse Hildebrand cleared her throat. 'I know you are tired, but there is work to be done. You will find your quarters, wash, and meet me in the infirmary at fourteen hundred hours. And a word of warning: there will be a great many men watching your arrival, men who haven't seen women in a very long time, aside from the *wahine*. Do not oblige them with eye contact. They must be made to behave like gentlemen.'

One of the girls in the row in front of us whipped out her compact, dusting her nose with a bit of powder before applying fresh lipstick.

Kitty leaned in towards me with a grin. 'There are two thousand men on the island,' she whispered. 'And forty-five of us.'

I frowned. How could she let her mind turn to men when all I could think of were Nurse Hildebrand's chilling warnings? 'Do you really think there are *cannibals*?'

'Nah. She's just trying to scare us.'

The plane began to shudder and jolt. Kitty and I held hands as we touched down with a thud, speeding down a runway that appeared dangerously close to the ocean. A few moments later, I filed in with the other women to exit the plane.

I felt Kitty's hand on my shoulder behind me. 'Thank you for coming,' she whispered. 'You'll be glad you did, I promise.'

One by one, we walked down the stairs. The breeze hit my face—warm and humid, and when I took a breath, I could almost feel steam rising in my lungs. I looked across the airstrip and saw that Nurse Hildebrand was correct—about the men, at least. A sea of dark green uniforms swarmed like hornets. The bold ones whistled; others just leaned up against trucks behind lit cigarettes, staring.

'You'd think they had never seen women before,' Kitty whispered, batting her eyes at a soldier in the front of the crowd.

Nurse Hildebrand faced us. 'Ladies, allow me to present Colonel Donahue,' she said, turning towards a man in uniform decorated with at least a dozen medals. As he crossed the tarmac, his men moved into formation. The nurses watched in fascination as he approached. The colonel was about forty, with golden skin, dark hair with specks of grey, and striking eyes. He looked powerful, and a little frightening.

'Nurse Hildebrand, ladies,' he said, with a tip of his hat. 'I would like to formally welcome you to Bora-Bora. We are grateful for the service you are bestowing on the country, and I can assure you that your work will not go without heartfelt thanks from the men stationed on this island, myself included.' He turned to the men and shouted, 'At ease,' and they erupted in applause.

'What a perfect gentleman,' Kitty said in a whisper.

I shrugged. The sun felt hotter now, its rays pelting us with an intensity I hadn't noticed when we first stepped off the airplane. It radiated off the tarmac, causing heat to swirl around us, unrelenting. Kitty's body swayed slowly next to mine. When I turned to her, I could see that her cheeks had gone white and her arms limp. 'Kitty, are you all right?'

Her eyes fluttered just as her legs buckled. I was able to catch her as she fell, but her bag, overstuffed with dresses, was the real saving grace, cushioning her head. She lay in a crumpled heap on the hot tarmac. 'Kitty!' I screamed.

'Smelling salts!' Nurse Hildebrand ordered, pushing through the circle of hovering women. She produced a green glass vial and held it under Kitty's nose. 'The sun has got to her.'

Colonel Donahue appeared at Nurse Hildebrand's side. 'Get her a stretcher!' he shouted to a man near the airplane. 'And quick.'

'Colonel Donahue,' Nurse Hildebrand said, 'we're dealing with a simple case of heat stroke. She'll be fine, this one.'

He eyed Kitty. 'Just the same, I'd like to make sure she's comfortable.'

Two men appeared moments later with a stretcher and lifted Kitty, now conscious but groggy, onto it. 'Anne,' she said, 'what happened?'

Colonel Donahue swooped in by her side before I could respond. 'It's always the prettiest ones who faint in the tropics,' he said with a grin.

Kitty beamed. 'How terribly embarrassing. Was I out long?'

The colonel smiled in return. 'Just long enough to miss the news that we're having a dance tonight in honour of your arrival.'

Kitty smiled much too flirtatiously. 'A dance?' she said weakly.

'Yes, a dance, tonight at twenty hundred.'

'Thank you,' Kitty said, unable to stop smiling.

'My pleasure. I just ask one favour: that you save a dance for me.'

'I'd love to,' she replied dreamily as the men wheeled her away.

Kitty always knew how to make an entrance.

The rest of the crowd began moving. I looked down at my suitcase and Kitty's enormous bag and groaned. The men had scattered, and now I was left to carry both.

'Can you believe that?' a woman said from behind me.

I turned to find one of the new nurses. Her soft auburn waves resembled Rita Hayworth's. 'I'm sorry?' I said, unsure of her meaning.

'Your friend pulled quite a stunt there to get the colonel's attention,' she said, smirking. A second nurse, with shiny dark hair and a meek smile, appeared at her side with a look of agreement.

'Oh no, no,' I said. 'You're not implying that Kitty fainted intentionally, are you?'

'It's exactly what I'm saying,' the auburn-haired nurse replied. 'Scenes like that don't happen *spontaneously*. She staged it.'

'She most certainly did not,' I said in protest.

She shrugged. 'I'm Stella, and this is Liz. You'll thank us someday for warning you of what your little friend is capable of,' she said. 'I wouldn't trust that one as far as I could throw her around any man of mine.'

**O**ur quarters in the nurses' barracks were meagre at best, just two crudely constructed beds, a dressing table, and one closet for the two of us to share. The flimsy cotton drapes seemed inadequate to block the light or the men's line of vision. I arrived to find Kitty standing on one of the beds, hammering a nail into the wall. 'What do you think of this spot for a picture?' she asked. 'I was thinking of hanging a photo of Mama and Papa.'

I set her bag down with a thud and wiped my brow. 'I think it's fine,' I said blankly. 'You're feeling better, I see.'

'Yes, thanks, dear,' she said.

Kitty flitted like a spring bird around our little first-storey room, chattering on about how we'd fix the place up. A sheet would make a perfect valance, she crooned, and we'd certainly be able to locate a coffee table somewhere. *Certainly.* And the walls, weren't they such a lovely, soothing colour? *Yes, infirmary beige—very soothing.*

In my view, the room was dank and strange. The striped mattresses were speckled with visible stains. Stacks of threadbare linens sat folded in neat little piles atop each. I longed for Maxine, even though the thought made me feel childish. She'd have jumped in and made the beds, settling each of us with a calming cup of tea.

I was on my own now.

'Anne, can you believe there's going to be a dance tonight? A dance! And Colonel Donahue wants to dance with *me!*'

I thought of Gerard and twisted my engagement ring round my finger, which was swollen from the heat. 'Yes, won't that be fun?' I chimed in, working hard to sound cheerful.

'I'm going to wear my yellow dress,' Kitty said, running to her bag. She looked great in yellow, especially in the dress she held up for my approval. I'd seen her wear it a half-dozen times—on the last occasion with Mr Gelfman's arms wrapped tightly round the bodice. Funny, she'd been so heartbroken about the man when we left Seattle, but the island seemed to have erased her memory.

Kitty looked in the mirror, pressing the dress to her body. 'I don't know. The blue one is a bit more conservative, I guess.'

I shook my head. 'No,' I said. 'Wear the yellow one. You look stunning in it.'

Kitty would be the most beautiful woman at the dance. She'd have the time of her life. And I'd be happy for her.

The infirmary, a white building with a red cross painted above the entryway, smelt of soap and ipecac, with a touch of rubbing alcohol thrown in for good measure. Kitty and I, the last to arrive that afternoon, nestled into the circle of women watching Nurse Hildebrand as she demonstrated, on a nurse's arm, the art of wound care in the tropics. Bandages were to be wrapped, she said, counterclockwise, not too tight, but snug enough to stop the bleeding. 'Too much or too little air, and you get infection,' she said. 'Especially in this godforsaken place.'

We spent the rest of the session rolling bandages into tight little bundles, then tucking them away in crates pulled off the plane. I laid out the big bolts of taupe linen on the table, trying not to dwell on the wounds they would one day cling to. Kitty took one end, and I another. After an hour, my fingers ached.

We worked in silence. But when Nurse Hildebrand left to attend a matter in the mess hall, the women began to find their voices.

'She's a tough one, that Nurse Hildebrand,' said a woman to our left. A few years older than Kitty and me, she had hair the colour of straw, freckles dotting her nose, and large, friendly eyes. Her smile revealed crooked teeth, which she tried, unsuccessfully, to keep hidden behind pursed lips.

'She is,' I said in agreement.

'I wouldn't want to be caught on her bad side.' The woman nodded to Kitty and me. 'I'm Mary.'

'I'm Anne.'

'And I'm Kitty.'

Mary tucked another bandage into the crate on the table. 'What brings you here?'

'Service to our country,' I said simply.

Mary smirked. 'Isn't that what we all say? No, why are you *really* here? We're all running from or searching for something.' She looked down at my engagement ring.

'Anne is engaged,' Kitty said, 'but she delayed the wedding to come with me.' She nuzzled her shoulder against mine. 'I was in a horrible romantic mess before we left. I felt I needed to escape.'

'Me, too.' Mary held up her bare left hand. 'My fiancé broke off our engagement. He said, "Darling, I love you but I am not in love with you." If that wasn't enough, he then announced that he was going to marry my best friend. Girls, it almost sent me to the loony bin. When I was coherent enough to think about my next move, I knew I had to leave town. I wanted to go to the farthest corner of the world to dull the pain.' She sighed. 'Our wedding was going to be in the fall, at the Cartwright Hotel in San Francisco. It was going to be grand.'

'I'm so sorry,' I said.

'Thank you,' she replied. 'I don't mind talking about it now, not really.' She began working on another bandage roll. 'We were going to move to Paris,' she continued. 'He was—well, is—joining the Foreign Service.' she shook her head wistfully. 'I should never have fallen in love with Edward. Mother was right. He was much too good-looking for me.' She shrugged, replacing the hurt in her eyes with practicality. 'And now I'm here. And you?' She looked at me. 'Do you love the man you're going to marry?'

'Of course,' I said, a little more defensively than I had planned.

'Then why are you here and not at home with him?'

*Why am I here and not at home with him?* 'Because my friend needed me,' I said, squeezing Kitty's hand.

'That's sweet,' Mary said. 'You're lucky, you know—to have each other. I don't have a friend like that.'

Kitty, ever the generous spirit, smiled warmly at Mary. 'You can have us.'

'I'd like that,' she said, tucking another bandage into the crate. We'd rolled at least a hundred—a small feat, yes, but I was proud of it. A mountain of bandages on our first day on Bora-Bora. We were *doing something*. We were really living.

The nurses had two designated tables in the mess hall, a building with long cafeteria tables packed in rows. We were not to eat with the men, said Nurse Hildebrand. Even so, we were aware of their every move. Their eyes bored into us as we ate—Spam and beans.

'This food is *awful*,' Mary said, stabbing a green bean with her fork. 'Look, this thing is petrified.'

'We'll come home perfectly thin,' Kitty said, ever the optimist.

Stella and Liz sat across from us, but after their comments about Kitty earlier in the day, I dismissed their presence. 'Well, well,' Stella said with dramatic flair, pointing to a corner table where three men sat. 'Get a load of that!'

Mary and Kitty, unaware of my grudge, turned to see what the fuss was about. 'He's the spitting image of Clark Gable,' Kitty said.

'His name's Elliot,' Stella said. 'The corporal who carried my bag today introduced us. Isn't he dreamy?'

'Very,' Mary said, swallowing a bite of Spam with a strained gulp.

'It's too bad, though. Word is that he spends his leave holed up in his bunk writing in his journal, brooding about a woman back home.'

'How romantic,' Kitty said dreamily.

I took another look at the table, where this man, Elliot, sat. He did resemble Clark Gable. Handsome, with dark eyes and thick ebony hair. Yet my eyes were drawn to another man, seated to his left. Tall, but not nearly as well built, with lighter, wispier hair and sun-kissed skin with a dusting of freckles. His left hand shovelled food into his mouth while his right cradled a book. As he turned the page, he looked up. His eyes immediately met mine, and the creases of his mouth formed a smile.

I snapped my head back round, instantly regretting the breach of decorum. *What has got into me?* Stella had seen the exchange, and she shot me a mocking glance.

Tropical nights were better than tropical days, I decided, even if there were mosquitoes. The break from the sun made the air more agreeable. And then there was the cool mist wafting off the sea, and the stars, those luminous stars, so close you could almost reach out and pluck one from the indigo sky.

Kitty and I walked arm in arm along the gravel path to the centre of camp to join in the evening festivities, she in her yellow dress and I in my red one. It wasn't much of a walk, maybe the equivalent of five city blocks, but it felt like a great distance in heels. We passed the infirmary and noticed an interior light shining. *Is Nurse Hildebrand inside?* We scurried past swiftly. As we neared the men's barracks, we pretended not to hear the whistles from the men smoking outside.

A safe distance past, Kitty tugged at my arm. 'Look.' She pointed to a large shrub erupting in the most breathtaking blossoms.

'They're beautiful,' I said. 'What are they?'

She picked a red bloom. 'Hibiscus,' she said, tucking the flower behind her right ear, before offering one to me. 'In French Polynesia, when your heart is taken, you wear the flower in your left ear. When it's not, you wear it in your right.'

'How do you know that?'

Kitty grinned. 'I just do.'

I stared at the enormous bloom in my hands; its crinkly petals were a brilliant shade of crimson. 'Then I must wear it in my left,' I said, dutifully tucking the flower behind my ear.

'How lovely,' Kitty said, pointing to a makeshift dance floor in the distance. It had been cobbled together from plywood. 'Fairy lights.'

Strands of tiny white lights hung above, crisscrossing the rafters constructed of palm fronds. Men huddled on the sidelines as a group of nurses made their way across the lawn.

'I would like to welcome the corps of nurses to our little island,' an announcer said. 'Let's show them a good time, lads.'

There was a round of cheering and applause before the band started, and for a moment, no one moved. Stella and Liz ventured forward a few steps, and two men asked them to dance.

'Look at them,' I said to Kitty. 'So fast.'

Kitty was too distracted to hear me. I knew she was looking for the Clark Gable lookalike. Suddenly, though, a man approached her. 'I saw your flower,' he said, bowing in an exaggerated way. Men did strange things around Kitty. 'I'm Lance,' he said, extending his hand, and she relinquished hers, allowing him to lay a mock kiss upon it.

I rolled my eyes. He was tall and athletic, with hair a forgettable shade of brown, sharp features, and a coy smile that made me distrust him instantly.

'I'm Kitty,' she said, clearly flattered.

Lance grinned. 'Would you like to dance?'

Kitty nodded, and he whisked her off to the dance floor, leaving me alone on the sidelines. I tapped my foot to the music. It was a fine band— for the middle of nowhere. I felt prickles on my arm when I heard a clarinet play the introductory lines to 'A String of Pearls'. I'd last heard the Glenn Miller tune on the Godfreys' lawn. At our engagement party. I sighed, suddenly feeling lonely. Out of place. *Where is Mary?* I looked around, but saw only strange men staring at me. *Thank God for the flower.*

But oblivious to the ring on my finger or the code of the flower, a man approached me. I could smell alcohol on his breath. 'Care to dance?'

'Thank you,' I said politely, 'but no. I think I'll sit this one out.'

'You're much too pretty to be a wallflower,' he protested. 'Besides, I'm tired of *wahine*. I want to dance with a real American woman.' He prised my hand from my side and led me to the dance floor.

'I think I'd better not,' I said, startled by his bravado.

'Nonsense.' He pressed his cheek against mine. The band struck up a melody. His hands were hot and moist, and his embrace suffocating, yet I willed myself to endure to the end of the song.

But, to my horror, the song ended and another man approached, presumably a friend, and as the tempo hastened, I found myself caught between them. One twirled me by the arm, spinning me to the other. I bobbled back and forth, looking desperately for Kitty. She was tucked in the arms of Lance. *Don't cause a scene.* I felt a hand brush my breasts. I froze, even though my legs were still moving. My eyes darted from left to right, and another hand cinched my waist, this one firmer. The room began to spin. Men were all around me. Hot, sweaty. Then there was scuffling and a loud thud. Someone fell to the ground. My original dancing partner was out cold. Blood trickled from his nose.

I pushed my way through the crowd off the dance floor, feeling guilty, even though I'd done nothing wrong. I darted for the path back to the barracks, quickening my pace to a light jog when I passed the men's barracks. I felt tears welling up in my eyes as the wind whistled through the palms, a lonely sound, so foreign. I missed the walnut tree. I missed Seattle.

Spooked by a sound in the bushes, I instinctively turned to the infirmary. A light shone inside, and I expected to find Nurse Hildebrand at her desk. Seated there instead was a man, the very man I'd seen in the mess hall at dinner.

He smiled, and I offered a startled smile in return.

'Hello,' he said from across the room. 'Don't let me frighten you. I'm just looking for a bandage. I thought I could find one in here, but you all must have the place soldier-proofed.'

His hand was bleeding. I ran over to the bandages I'd rolled that afternoon. 'Here,' I said, pulling one out, 'let me help you.'

I told myself not to be embarrassed. I was a nurse. He was a patient. There was no reason to feel odd about the interaction.

'What happened?' I asked, dabbing his wound with gauze I'd soaked in rubbing alcohol.

He winced. 'You didn't see? I couldn't bear to watch Randy Connors have his way with you on the dance floor. It's why I punched him.'

'Oh,' I said. 'It was you. Well, then I owe you my gratitude.'

'You'll have to forgive the men,' he said. 'They haven't seen women like you all in months, some longer.'

I nodded. 'Well, I don't care if these men have been away from women for a century. It's no excuse for barbarism.'

'It's not. Which is why I avoid most of them. The tropics bring out the savage in all of us. The island dulls your inhibitions. It changes you. You'll see.'

'Well,' I said, wrapping his knuckles in just the way Nurse Hildebrand had instructed, 'I don't believe that something can change you unless you *want* to be changed. Have you heard of free will?'

'Sure.' He looked very amused. 'I'm just saying that this place has a way of revealing the truth about people.'

I fastened the bandage with an aluminium bracket, and exhaled. 'Well, I'm not sure about that,' I said. 'But you're all fixed up.'

'I'm Westry.' He extended his bandaged hand. 'Westry Green.'

'Anne Calloway,' I replied, shaking his hand gently.

'See you around.' He headed to the door.

'See you around,' I said, catching a glimpse of red in his left hand. As the door clicked closed behind him, I reached up to my ear. The hibiscus was gone.

# CHAPTER 3

'WHAT TIME DID YOU come in last night?' I asked Kitty the next morning from my bed. I'd been awake reading for two hours.

She took one look at the clock, then pressed her head back into her pillow. 'Late,' she said, her voice muffled by down stuffing.

'It's nearly nine,' I said, remembering our good fortune to have arrived on the island on a Friday. Saturday was our day of leave. 'I won't let you sleep away our only day off. Come on, let's get dressed!'

She yawned and sat up. 'I can't believe it's nine already.'

'Yes, sleepyhead,' I said, walking to the closet. I wanted to explore the beach today and I'd need to wear something light.

Kitty stood up quickly. 'I have to hurry,' she said. 'Lance is taking me into town for the day.'

My heart sank, and Kitty could tell.

'You can come too,' she offered. 'He invited you.'

'And be the third wheel? No, thanks. You go on your own.'

Kitty shook her head, unbuttoning her nightgown and letting it fall to the floor. 'You're coming with us. Lance is taking a jeep. Elliot's coming, and Stella.'

'What?' I said. 'How did she wrangle him into going?'

'She didn't,' Kitty said. 'Lance did.'

'Is anyone else coming?' I thought of Westry.

'I think that's it,' Kitty said, looking into the closet. 'Wait, is there someone you were thinking of?' There was a hint of teasing in her voice.

I shook my head. 'I was only thinking of Mary.'

Kitty didn't look up from the closet.

'I didn't see her last night, did you?'

'No,' she said, pulling out a powder-blue dress. 'What do you think of this one?'

'It's fine,' I said, less concerned about Kitty's wardrobe than the safety of our new friend. 'Don't you think we ought to check with Nurse Hildebrand to see if Mary's all right?'

Kitty shrugged, holding up a pair of tan heels for inspection. 'Yes or no?'

'No,' I said. 'Wear the blue ones. Your feet will thank me later.'

She clasped her bra and stepped into a white silk slip, before putting on the dress.

'Tell me about Lance,' I said a little cautiously, zipping her up. 'Do you like him?'

'Yes,' Kitty said, though I thought I detected a note of hesitation in her voice. 'He's great.'

'Did you ever dance with the colonel last night?' I asked, selecting a glaringly simple tan dress from the closet.

'I did,' she said smiling. 'And it was divine. Lance wasn't too happy, but he could hardly challenge his superior.'

I took a look at myself in the oval mirror on the wall. My cheeks were flushed from the morning heat, and my hair looked limp.

'Ready?' Kitty said, grabbing her handbag.

I stared back at her. Her cheeks were rosy, not ruddy like mine. Her hair, curlier than ever, looked alluring the way she wore it, pinned to the side.

The tropics became her.

'Ready,' I said, following her out of the door.

Lance drove much too fast. Kitty was unaffected, however, looking gay in the front seat while Stella, Elliot and I were squeezed into the back. The dust was thick. The pothole-littered gravel road that encircled the island wasn't for the faint of heart.

'First to town centre,' Lance said. 'Next, to the beach.'

Kitty let out a little cheer, and Stella eyed Elliot, whose gaze remained on the road ahead. 'Do you get into town much?' she asked him sweetly.

He looked at her. 'Not often,' he said, before turning his gaze back to the road.

The air smelt of dirt right after a rain, mingled with a sweet, floral scent. Makeshift homes, constructed of scrap lumber, dotted the roadside, tucked in under the lush palms. Occasionally we'd spot a chicken pecking about. I was curious to see some of the natives.

The jeep wound round the north side of the island and past a small turquoise cove. Lance pulled over. 'Here we are,' he said.

I stepped onto the dusty ground and turned my gaze to the busy scene. There were rows of tables cluttered with exotic fruits and vegetables, handmade necklaces, cigarettes, and bottles of Coca-Cola. The scantily dressed shopkeepers, with their olive skin and enigmatic eyes, sat looking vaguely bored as soldiers buzzed about spending hard-earned cash on whatever trinket caught their eye.

'Look.' Stella pointed to a native woman walking towards us. Bare-breasted, she wore her hair twisted in a single braid that rested between her breasts. A swath of green fabric hung round her waist, tied loosely, dangerously so. I noticed the flower in her left ear as she walked right up to us as if she knew us.

'Mr Lance,' the woman said, setting down the bag she had been carrying. Her thickly accented voice was sweet and soft. She was maybe eighteen. Her breasts swayed as she bent down to the bag and produced a pack of Lucky Strikes. 'Your cigarettes,' she said.

*How does Lance know this woman, or rather, woman-child?*

'Thank you,' Lance said. Kitty eyed him as he tucked the pack into his shirt pocket. 'Atea is the only shopkeeper who can track down my Lucky Strikes. She saves a pack for me every Thursday.'

Atea looked proud standing there, not the least bit modest. Her eyes sparkled at Lance. 'Are you coming today?'

'Not today, Atea,' he said. 'Be a good girl and rustle up some more. I'll be back in a few days.' He tucked a coin in her hand and then reached for Kitty's arm. 'Now, let's go see the rest of the market.'

'That was strange,' Stella said, leaning in to me moments later.

It *was* strange, but I wasn't going to discuss it with her, not when Kitty might overhear. 'What's strange about buying cigarettes?'

Stella smirked and continued on, stopping at a table of brightly coloured beads.

'You OK?' I said to Kitty when Lance was a safe distance away.

'Of course,' she said. 'Why?'

'Oh, I just wanted to make sure the heat wasn't getting to you.'

She took a deep breath of the humid island air and smiled. 'I'm having the time of my life,' she said gleefully.

Stella laid a blanket out on the beach, careful to secure a spot next to Elliot, but he leaned back against a large piece of driftwood, snuffing out all conversation by pulling his hat over his eyes.

We'd driven round to the other side of the island, close to base. Though we selected a spot beneath the shade of a palm for our picnic, the white sand still radiated heat. I shifted my legs uncomfortably as Kitty set out a loaf of bread, a cheerful bunch of miniature bananas, four bottles of Coca-Cola, and a wedge of cheese—our improvised lunch cobbled together at the market.

We ate in silence, watching the waves crash onto the shore. Then Kitty said what we all felt: 'It's hard to believe there's a war happening. This corner of the world is too beautiful for destruction.'

I helped myself to a banana. 'But there is,' I said practically.

'Yesterday the Japs shot down three of our planes,' Lance added.

Stella looked worried. 'Do you think we'll see fighting here?'

'I think we might,' Lance said gravely. 'Colonel Donahue doesn't see it that way, though. He's a fool. I tell you, we'll be all asleep in our bunks when the Japs fly over, bombarding us when we least expect it.'

Kitty shook her head. 'Colonel Donahue will protect this island.'

Lance smirked. 'I could run this operation better blindfolded.'

Kitty must have been unaffected by his arrogance, because she laid her head lightly in his lap. I could tell by his smile that he liked it.

Elliot began to snore. Stella brooded.

'I think I'll take a walk.' I said, standing. Kitty's eyes were closed in pretend slumber as I adjusted the brim of my hat and kicked off my shoes. 'I'll be back,' I said, though I don't think anyone looked up.

I walked down the beach, stopping occasionally to examine a rock or a shell, or to marvel at the palms reaching out to sea in horizontal fashion. Years of wind and tropical storms had sculpted their trunks. The deserted beach seemed to stretch towards infinity. I walked close to the water, relishing the feeling of the cool sand on my feet.

A sea bird squawked on a rock a few feet away, which is where I noticed another set of footprints, fainter but still fresh. Farther down the beach, beyond the bend, the footprints stopped at a crumpled beige blanket, anchored to the sand by a book. I had the same standard military-issue on my bed in the barracks.

I turned quickly when I heard a rustling sound in the thick brush behind the palms at the edge of the beach. 'Hello there.' A man appeared out of nowhere carrying a large palm frond. It was Westry Green. 'Are you following me?' he said teasingly.

I felt foolish, then irritated. 'Of course not! I was merely taking a walk—which reminds me, my friends are expecting me.'

Westry smiled. 'Oh, don't go,' he said, pushing the base of the palm branch into the sand and sitting under it. 'Look, the perfect shade. Won't you sit down? Just for a minute?'

His smile was impossible to resist. I felt the corners of my mouth turn upwards, without my permission. 'All right. Just for a minute.'

'Nice day,' he said, leaning back on his elbows.

'Quite,' I said, pulling the hem of my dress lower on my legs.

'What brings you to my beach?'

'*Your* beach?'

'Yes,' he said matter-of-factly. 'I discovered it.'

I let out a little laugh. 'You're really something.'

'It's all virgin coastline, you know. Of course, the natives have been here for ever, and it will always be theirs. But the rest of the world isn't onto it. For now, this little slice of heaven is mine.' He looked at me. 'Well, ours. I'll let you have half.'

'That's awfully generous of you,' I said.

'After the war's over, I'm going to buy this stretch of beach,' he said earnestly. 'As much as I can afford. I'm going to build a house and raise a family, right here. My wife and I, we'll watch the sun rise every morning from our porch and listen to the surf crash onto the shore at night.'

'You'd actually want to live here after'—I pointed to the Pacific, where Japanese warships may have been taking up residence at that very moment—'after all this? After the war?'

Westry nodded. 'Sure,' he said. 'It's paradise.'

It *was* paradise. 'But don't you have a life waiting for you at home?'

'No,' he said, without hesitating. 'But *you* do.'

He'd seen the ring on my finger. 'I do,' I said honestly.

'Do you love him?'

'What kind of question is that?'

'A simple one,' he said. 'So, what's the verdict?'

'Of course I love him,' I said, looking away.

The waves crept in closer to the blanket. Westry stood, and I followed. 'We'd better shift camp, or Old Man Sea will swallow us up.'

'I really should get back.'

Westry nodded. 'I'll walk you.'

The shoreline looked different in reverse, perhaps because I was seeing it through Westry's eyes. I imagined his life on the island years from now, with a house and a wife, and two or three barefoot children, and smiled to myself. 'How's your hand?'

He held it up. 'I think I'm going to pull through,' he said.

Moments later he gestured towards something in the brush line, where palms grew thick. We walked closer and stopped, just as the beach ended and vegetation began. Birds sang and animals howled under the cover of shady green plants with gargantuan leaves, just as I'd always imagined a jungle.

'Do you see that?'

I shook my head. 'What?'

'Look closer,' he said.

'No,' I whispered. 'I don't see anything.'

I followed him a few paces beyond the beach, which is when I finally saw what he did: a thatched-roof hut, just beyond the thicket. Though constructed in as makeshift a manner as the homes along the roadside, this one had a charm all its own. The exterior was built of bamboo canes, into which someone had painstakingly cut holes to approximate ocean-facing windows. A small door dangled from a single hinge, creaking in the afternoon breeze.

'I don't know if we should be here,' I whispered.

'Why not?' he said, grinning mischievously. 'Now that we've found it, we have to see what's inside.' Before I could protest, Westry set foot on the steps. He lifted the door off its hinge and set it down on the sand, peering inside before turning to me with a wink. 'All clear.'

We surveyed the place in silence. The interior walls, made of woven palm branches weathered to a light shade of caramel, had been beautifully strung together in a V-shaped pattern. They provided a perfect backdrop to a dark mahogany chair paired with a small desk containing a single drawer. Westry reached for its handle and pulled out a book, some French coins and bills, and a yellowed piece of paper. 'Can you read French?'

I shook my head. 'I wish I'd paid more attention in school.'

'Me, too,' he said, slipping the paper back in the drawer.

The bed, big enough for just one person, looked tidy, even with a layer of dust on top, as if someone had woken up one morning and tucked the linens in place in anticipation of a return that never occurred. 'Who do you think lived here?'

He looked out at the sea. 'My best guess? A shipwrecked sailor.'

It sounded plausible enough. 'But what happened to the ship?'

'Maybe it sunk.'

'So how did he recover the paper and'—I opened the book with its dark brown leather cover—'and this book?'

Westry touched his index finger to his chin. 'Maybe he had a knapsack packed with a few rations.' He pointed to the lamp on the desk. 'A lantern, this book, a tin of biscuits. And he managed to find a piece of wood to drift on until he reached the island.'

'The book would have got wet,' I said.

'So it may have. But he let it dry in the sun.' Westry fanned the pages, and sure enough, they were covered in water stains. 'See?'

I nodded. 'But where was he heading? He was clearly French.'

'And poor,' Westry added, pointing to the small stash of coins.

'So he's a poor, shipwrecked, French sailor who likes to read. And appreciates art,' I said, pulling away a scrap of burlap that covered a painting over the bed. The canvas depicted an arresting scene: a bungalow just like the one we found ourselves in, nestled between impossibly blue water and a hibiscus bush flowering vibrant yellow. Two figures stood in the distance.

'My God,' Westry gasped. 'It's beautiful.' He stood on the bed to gaze at the painting. 'It looks *familiar* somehow.'

My artistic knowledge was woefully inadequate. 'Do you think the artist lived *here*?'

'Maybe,' Westry said. 'What year was that book printed?'

I thumbed the opening pages. 'Copyright 1877.'

'It might have been one of the master Impressionists.'

'You can't be serious,' I said, in awe.

'It's as possible as anything. I'm almost certain I've seen this one in books, or something similar.' His eyes were wild with excitement. 'You know what this means, don't you? We have to protect this place.'

I nodded. 'But how?'

'It will be our project, while we're here. We'll restore it.'

'It does need a good scrub.'

'And a new door,' Westry added.

'And the curtains are rags,' I said. 'I can make new ones.'

'So you're in?' He looked at me with slightly mischievous eyes.

*Why not? It will pass the hours Kitty spends with Lance.* 'I'm in. But how will we ever find the time, and how will we get here?'

'We'll walk,' he said simply. 'The base is less than a half-mile up shore. You can slip out and be back before anyone knows you've even left. A trail leads up to the road, so I'll bring the tools and the wood in a jeep. We'll figure it out.'

Westry turned to the door and a weak floorboard creaked. He knelt down and pulled it up, exposing the rickety subfloor and a small alcove just below the surface. 'Here,' he said. 'This will be our mailbox. I'll leave you letters when I'm here without you, and you can do the same.'

My heart leapt with excitement—for the bungalow, for the artist, for the prospect of letters tucked under floorboards, but especially for this man who held the key to it all.

Westry wrapped the painting in its burlap covering and carefully slid it under the bed for safekeeping. 'There's just one thing,' he said. 'We can't tell a soul about this place, not anyone.'

It pained me to think of keeping a find this marvellous from Kitty, and yet, I couldn't imagine her here in the bungalow, a place that already felt special to me, sacred, even after only a few minutes. I touched my hand to Kitty's pin, and felt a pang of guilt. We vowed not to keep secrets from each other.

'What do you say?' Westry continued.

I nodded. 'Cross my heart,' I said, convincing myself that Kitty didn't need to know—not yet, anyway. 'I won't tell a soul.'

'Good. Shall I walk you back?'

'Yes,' I said.

# CHAPTER 4

'WESTRY SEEMS NICE,' Kitty said as soon as we'd shut the door to our room later that day.

'He's all right,' I said vaguely. 'We only spoke for a moment. He was kind enough to walk me back. Seems like you and Lance are getting along fine,' I said, changing the subject.

'Yes,' Kitty replied. 'I do like him. Very much. It's just'—she paused—'it's just, well, I don't care for the way he speaks of Colonel Donahue. I suppose it's a small detail. Lance has so many standout qualities.'

*Like his philandering with the island women. His smug attitude.*

'Anne,' Kitty said, a little shyly, 'I haven't had a chance to tell you, but on the night of the dance, Colonel Donahue—'

We both looked up, startled, when we heard a loud, rapid knocking at the door.

'Yes,' I said, turning the knob.

Liz stood outside, panting and out of breath. 'It's Mary,' she said. 'In the infirmary. Come quick.'

We followed Liz down the stairs and out of the barracks door. The infirmary wasn't far. Inside, Nurse Hildebrand hovered over Mary's bed alongside Dr Livingston, a middle-aged physician with thinning hair and spectacles. Mary looked unnaturally pale. Her eyes were closed. 'Dear Lord,' I whispered. 'What happened?'

'One of the women found her in her room,' Nurse Hildebrand said, 'collapsed by the bed. Malaria.'

'The fever broke,' Dr Livingston said, 'but I'm afraid it weakened her heart. The only thing we can do now is wait.'

My hands trembled. 'But she's going to make it,' I said.

Dr Livingston looked away.

I thought of Mary, poor Mary. Tall, perhaps a little too tall. Teeth a bit crooked. Heart broken. Her fiancé had left her and she had felt alone; she'd told us so. *No, I will not let her die alone.*

'Kitty,' I said, 'will you run back to the barracks and fetch my reading glasses and anything you can find to read? Bring the damn *War Digest*, if that's all there is—whatever you can find.'

Kitty nodded.

'We're going to hold a vigil,' I said. 'May I pull up a bed and stay next to her tonight?' I asked Nurse Hildebrand.

She nodded in approval.

Kitty returned with two magazines, three books—two from Liz and another from Stella—a copy of the *War Digest*, and a nursing textbook.

'Good,' I said. 'We'll take shifts reading to her. We won't stop until she regains consciousness.'

Kitty reached for my hand. 'Anne, you can't save her if she's—'

'I won't let her die alone,' I said. 'Nobody deserves that.'

I picked up a copy of *Vogue*, turned to the first page, and began reading aloud. I read for four hours, every word on every page in front of me. Kitty read next, turning on a lamp when the sun set, then passing the torch back to me a few hours later after her voice became hoarse. We'd covered three magazines and three-quarters of a novel by the time the sun shone through the windows, which is when Mary's eyes began to flutter.

'Where am I?' she said weakly.

'In the infirmary,' I replied, choking back tears. 'You've been stricken with malaria, dear. But you're going to be fine.'

Nurse Hildebrand excused us from duty that day, and I slept until noon, when the sound of the lunch bell ringing from the mess hall woke me. My stomach growled. 'Kitty?' I said. 'Are you awake?'

I turned my head expecting to see her fast asleep, and instead found her coverlet pulled tightly up over her bed and the two pillows fluffed and neatly stacked against the headboard.

I sat up and stretched, then noticed a note on the dressing table.

*Anne,*
    *I didn't want to wake you. I left at 10 to go canoeing with Lance. I'll be back this afternoon.*
    *Love,*
    *Kitty*

Boating with Lance. A perfectly normal thing to do, yet I felt uneasy. *We were granted the day off only hours ago, so when did she have time to make plans with Lance?* I thought of the bungalow, and realised our little dormitory room was already thick with secrets.

The lunch bell rang a second time—the last call. If I dressed and ran quickly I could make it in time. But I saw an apple on the nightstand and thought of a better idea.

I slung over my shoulder a knapsack packed with the apple, a bit of bread Kitty had brought back from the mess hall, and a canteen filled with water. Then I snuck past the infirmary, briefly glancing through an open window to where Stella and Liz and a few of the other nurses hovered over a patient who looked as if he had nothing more than a skinned knee. This wasn't the wartime life I'd expected.

I made my way to the beach. Westry had said the bungalow was a half-mile north of the base. I hoped he was right. I walked fast, and looked over my shoulder more than a few times.

Just round the bend, I began to make out the thatched roof of the bungalow, nestled in the thicket, as we'd left it. As I grew nearer, I could hear the sound of a saw zigzagging.

My heart pounded in my chest. 'Hello,' I said, knocking ceremoniously on the place where the door had hung. 'Anyone home?'

Westry looked up, wiping his brow. 'Oh, hi,' he said. 'Are you real or a mirage? I've been here all morning without water, and I can't tell if I'm hallucinating or if there's really a beautiful woman standing in the doorway. Please tell me it's the latter.'

I grinned. 'You're not hallucinating,' I said, pulling the canteen out of my bag. 'Here, drink.'

Westry took a long gulp, then exhaled, handing the canteen back to me. 'I've almost got the door in working order,' he said. 'It didn't fit on the door frame. The weather must have warped it. I had to take an inch off the side. See? I rustled up some old hinges from the supply yard.' He held up the hardware as if it were treasure. 'Our bungalow needs a proper, working door.'

*Our bungalow.* I smiled and pulled a box of Borax and some rags from my bag. 'I thought I'd give the place a shine,' I said.

'Glad you could join the work party,' Westry said, turning back to his sawing.

By three, the floors were fit to eat from, and Westry had the door fastened in place. He plucked a scuffed brass doorknob from his knapsack and attached it.

'Our key,' he said, holding up a shiny piece of steel. 'Now, if we can just find the right hiding place for it.'

I pointed to the open-air windows. 'But anyone who wants in can just climb on through.'

Westry nodded. 'Sure. We'll get windows installed soon enough. But where to hide the key, that's the question.'

I followed him outside, and we looked around near the front step. 'How about here?' I pointed to a spot in the sand. 'We could bury it.'

'It's the first place someone would look. Like the welcome mat—every crook knows to go there first.' He paused. 'Wait.' He ran back inside and returned with a book from his bag. 'We'll use this.'

'A book?'

'Yeah,' he replied, pulling out the ribbon attached to the spine. Its purpose might have been to mark the page for a reader, but Westry had other plans. He tied the ribbon securely round the lip of the key, tucking it into the book. 'There.' He slid the book below the step. 'Our secret spot.'

The waves were crashing loudly now.

'The tide's coming in,' he said. 'Want to watch it with me?'

I hesitated. 'I probably should be thinking about walking back.'

'C'mon,' Westry said. 'You can stay a few more minutes.'

'All right,' I said. 'Just a few.'

'There,' he said, pointing to a piece of driftwood a few paces ahead on the beach. 'Our perch.'

We sat down together, mesmerised by the waves.

'I don't know anything about you,' I said, a little abruptly.

'And I don't know anything about you,' he retorted.

'You start.'

Westry nodded. 'I was born in Ohio. Mother died of scarlet fever, and I moved west with my father. He was an engineer on the railroads. I tagged along, attending a different school every month.'

'Far from a proper education,' I said.

'Better than most. I saw the country. I learned the way of the railways.'

'And now what? After all of this, you said you wanted to come back here, to the island, but surely you have other aspirations, other things to attend to first?'

Westry's eyes were big and full of life, full of possibility. 'I may go back to school, become an engineer, like Pop. Or go to France, and learn to paint like the great Impressionists. Or maybe I'll just stay here,' he said, motioning with his head towards the bungalow.

'Oh, you can't do that. What a lonely life that would be!'

'Why would you call it lonely? I'd have everything I could want. A roof over my head. The most beautiful scenery in the world.'

I thought about what he'd said about settling down and raising a family right there on the beach before us. 'But what about companionship?' I said a little shyly. 'What about . . . love?'

Westry grinned. 'I suppose I'll find her. Out there somewhere.'

'What if you don't?' I asked.

'I will.' He smiled confidently. 'Now, let's hear about *you*.'

I tugged at a loose thread on my bag. 'There isn't much to tell.'

'Sure there is. Everyone has a story.'

I shook my head. 'I was born in Seattle. I lived there all my life. I got my nursing licence, and now I'm here.'

'And there you have it. An entire lifetime in three sentences.'

I felt my cheeks get hot. 'Sorry. I guess my life isn't exciting.'

'I think you're bluffing.' He sized me up with his eyes. 'The man you're engaged to, why didn't you marry him before you left?'

'Because I . . .' My voice trailed off without an answer. I thought of the practical reasons, yet none were satisfactory.

Westry winked. 'See? You do have a story,' he said.

**K**itty wasn't in the room when I returned, so when the mess hall bell rang, announcing dinner, I walked out of the barracks alone, making a quick stop in the infirmary to check on Mary. I was happy to find her sitting up and sipping orange juice through a straw.

I walked back out to the path that led to the mess hall, passing the hibiscus bush where Kitty and I had plucked flowers that first night. I kept walking until I could see the recreation dock. Canoes bound by rope tethers bobbed on the water, and I spotted two figures climbing out of one. The tousled curls could have belonged to no other but Kitty, but the man helping her onto the dock wasn't Lance. I gasped when I saw instead the face of *Colonel Donahue*. She smiled sweetly at him as they walked together up to the lawn, where he bade her adieu, and Kitty hurried along the trail back to the women's barracks.

'**H**ow's Lance?' Stella coyly asked Kitty at breakfast.

'Fine,' Kitty said, picking at her scrambled eggs and grits, both the consistency of rubber. 'We're seeing each other tonight.'

Stella shook her head jealously, a gesture that I'd come to learn was merely Stella's way. 'My, do you have luck with men,' she said, before sighing in defeat. 'I've given up on Elliot. His head is much too tangled up with that woman from back home. Anyway, I met an airman last night. His name is Will, and he isn't half bad.'

Liz approached our table with a tray. 'Is Mary on the mend?'

'Yes, thank God,' I said. 'She's much stronger.'

Liz gazed at an envelope in her hand. 'This came for her today,' she said. 'Didn't she say her ex-fiancé's name was Edward?'

I nodded. 'Let me see it.' I held the envelope up to the light, unable to make out anything significant, just that the sender was indeed Edward. Edward Naughton, with a return address in Paris.

'Anne!' Kitty scolded. 'You shouldn't read her mail. Its private.'

'I will if I think it's going to compromise her recovery,' I said. 'Listen, if this man could leave her, almost at the altar, and send her into such a tailspin that she banished herself to a far-flung island on the other side of the world, imagine what a letter from him could do to her.'

The other women nodded in agreement.

'Look,' I said. 'I'm not going to read it; I'm merely tucking it away until she's ready. Her heart is weak. She needs to regain her strength first. I won't let this letter conflict with her recovery.'

'All right. But you really shouldn't meddle when it comes to love.' Kitty pushed her plate aside. 'Well, girls, I'm heading to work. Nurse Hildebrand says we've got a live one coming in today.'

The wounded pilot arrived at a quarter past ten. It was as serious a case as any of us could have imagined—shrapnel wounds to the head. Kitty worked alongside the doctor in the operating area, removing bits of blood-covered metal and piling them on a plate. Liz excused herself to vomit, yet Kitty didn't flinch. She handled the procedure with such skill and ease that the doctor requested she stay on for another hour to assist with the patient's care.

After our shift ended, I walked back to the barracks. I packed a little bag and tucked in scissors, a needle and thread, and a bolt of pale yellow fabric I'd found in a trash barrel outside the infirmary. Westry wasn't inside the bungalow when I arrived, so I retrieved the key from the book and unlocked the door, setting my bag on the old mahogany chair.

I immediately got to work on the curtains, measuring the windows and calculating the length and width of each panel. I laid out the fabric on the floor, shooing a baby lizard away as I did, and commenced cutting. I listened to the birds' songs as I hemmed. I thought of Westry, so spirited and spontaneous, so unlike Gerard and his consistent, measured ways. Concerns I had harboured in Seattle seemed to fester in the tropics. In particular, his ability to sidestep the war gnawed at my conscience.

I remembered the painting under the bed as I fitted a rod into the first set of curtains. I wondered about the subjects of the canvas, but mostly I wondered about the artist.

*Who lived here so long ago? A man like Westry, with adventure in his soul?* I pictured Westry spending the rest of his days on the island. Maybe he'd marry a native girl, like Atea, the one at the market. *Would that make him happy? Yes, happy in one way, certainly, but would they be on the same intellectual plane?* Passion fades, yet love lives on. It's what I wished Kitty would come to believe.

Darkness fell on the bungalow just then, and I looked out of the open-air window at grey, rain-soaked clouds looming in the sky. I scanned the beach, hoping I might see Westry bounding towards the bungalow, which is when I remembered the mailbox, or rather, the creaky floorboard in the corner. I walked over and lifted it, peering inside, and a white envelope caught my eye.

*Dear Mrs Cleo Hodge,*

*I suppose you're wondering who Mrs Cleo Hodge is. Why, my dear, she is you. We need code names in case we're found out. Let's not forget, we live in war times. So, you will be Cleo. I will be Grayson. What do you think? I considered the surname Quackenbush, but we'd fall to our knees in laughter every time we address each other and get nothing done. So, we shall be the Hodges, unless you have a better suggestion.*

*Yours,*

*Mr Hodge*

I giggled to myself, turned the letter over and wrote:

*Dear Mr Grayson Hodge,*

*Today, I have been hard at work on the drapes, which I hope you will find satisfactory. Do you think we need a rug? A nice Oriental? And how about a bookshelf and a place to sit, other than the bed? Perhaps, if we are lucky, a sofa will wash up on the shore.*

*Yours,*

*Mrs Hodge*

I tucked the note in the space below the floorboard, locked the door behind me, and hurried along the beach. The clouds overhead, now even darker, threatened rain. Not far from the bungalow in the brush, I heard a rustling sound, causing every muscle in my body to freeze. I worried that someone was following me.

I took a few steps towards the jungle line, taking cover behind a very large palm, and squinted. Two figures stood in the shadows of the lush jungle brush. I saw the telltale sleeve of an army dress shirt, and a bare female leg. I shrunk back behind the palm before tiptoeing again to the beach and quickening my pace.

Once inside the room, I was disappointed to see that Kitty wasn't there waiting.

# CHAPTER 5

'CAN YOU BELIEVE it's been two months since we arrived?' Mary marvelled, her cheeks tinged a rosy pink. It was good to see the life back in her face. She had insisted that Nurse Hildebrand let her work morning shifts instead of making her continue on bed rest.

'I know what you mean,' I said. 'It sometimes feels as if we arrived only yesterday.' I paused to count the vials of vaccine we'd be giving the men after breakfast. 'Yet, so much has happened already. I hardly feel like the same girl who stepped foot on that tarmac the first day.'

Mary nodded. 'Me, too. It's hard to imagine life back there.'

I sighed. 'I've almost forgot what Gerard's voice sounds like. Isn't that terrible?'

'Not really,' Mary said. 'You still love him.'

'Yes, of course,' I said with extra emphasis, feeling guilty for not yet taking the time to write to him.

'I've almost forgot Edward's voice,' Mary added, grinning. 'But that's definitely not terrible.'

I remembered the letter I'd been keeping from her. *Is she ready yet?* I listened to her hum as she unwrapped packages of vaccine and set them on trays. *That letter could spoil everything.*

'Where's Kitty?' Mary asked. 'I thought I saw her here earlier.'

'Oh, she's here,' I said. 'We walked down together.'

'No,' Nurse Hildebrand grumbled. 'She said she wasn't feeling well, so I sent her back to the barracks.'

Kitty had been behaving strangely, almost since the moment we'd arrived on the island—saying she was going somewhere and turning up in another place; promising to meet me at lunch only to disappear. She rarely spoke of Colonel Donahue, and I hadn't mentioned witnessing their boat trip. That ship seemed to have sunk, yet she spent far too much time with Lance.

'She must have caught the virus that's going round,' Mary said. 'A terrible stomach illness.'

I didn't believe that Kitty had a stomach illness. No, something else was going on. Our shifts in the infirmary didn't leave room for meaningful conversation, now that more wounded men were arriving from nearby islands, where the fighting was thick. They trickled in slowly, but the cases were grim. Knife wounds. Gunshots to the abdomen. A nearly severed leg. The sombre work consumed our days, and when our shifts ended, we'd scatter like mice to our favourite hiding places. But where was Kitty's? I snuck away to the bungalow. Sometimes Westry would be there, sometimes not, but I always hoped to find him.

'Mail's here!' one of the nurses cried from the front door of the infirmary.

I left Mary and ventured over to the wooden crate filled with letters and parcels. Mail deliveries had been sparse. But this was a mountain of mail. It spilled out on the floor when I pushed the crate closer to the table. I saw one addressed to me and felt a tugging at my heart when I recognised the handwriting. I opened it discreetly.

> *My love,*
>
> *The leaves are turning colours here, and I miss you so.*
>
> *Seattle is just as you left it, only it's lonelier without you. I suppose the war has something to do with the loneliness factor. It's all anyone can talk about. I worry about you. There will be great action in the Pacific. I pray that your island will be shielded from it.*
>
> *The war has taken the best of us. Every able-bodied man has joined up or been drafted, and even after all Father has done to protect me, I can't help but wonder if I should join too. The next wave of troops ships out on the 15th of October, and I'm thinking about going with them.*
>
> *Please do not worry about me. I will write often and dream of the day when we are reunited. I love you with all my heart and think of you more than you know.*
>
> *Yours,*
>
> *Gerard*

I held the letter to my heart and blinked hard. As much as I revelled in his burst of patriotism, I hated to think of him in danger.

'What's the matter, dear?' Mary asked softly.

'It's Gerard,' I said. 'I think he signed up.'

'What do you think it would be like to be a military wife?' Kitty asked me that night before bed. She sat in a pink cotton nightgown on her bunk, brushing her blonde curls and clearly feeling just fine.

'You can't be saying you're already thinking of marrying Lance, are you?'

Kitty didn't answer; she just continued brushing her hair. 'I suppose the lifestyle has its benefits. All the travelling and the excitement.'

'Kitty, but you've only just met him,' I said.

She set her brush down and climbed into her bed, pulling the coverlet up to her neck. 'Anne,' she said. Her voice was childlike, naive, tremulous. 'Did you always know that Gerard was the one?'

The question caught me off guard in a way it wouldn't have in Seattle. 'Well, yes, of course I did,' I said. 'I just knew.'

Kitty nodded. 'I think I have the same feeling,' she said, turning her head to the wall before I could question her. 'Good night.'

Westry had been away on a mission to another island for thirty days, and when he returned on November 27, I waited near the men's barracks, gathering hibiscus, in hopes of meeting him on the path. Twenty minutes of flower picking resulted in no Westry sighting, so I retreated to the barracks with a heavy heart.

'The mail came,' Kitty said, tossing an envelope on my bed. 'It's from your mother.'

I shrugged and tucked the envelope into my dress pocket.

'I got a letter from Father.' She tore the edge of the envelope and pulled the letter out. She read at first with a grin. But then a frown appeared, and a look of shock. Tears began a slow trickle down her cheeks.

'What is it?' I asked, running to her side. 'What does it say?'

She threw herself on the bed, burying her face in the pillow.

'Kitty,' I persisted, 'tell me.'

She didn't budge, so I picked up the pages of the letter that had fallen to the ground and read it myself. Mr Gelfman had left for war in September, to Europe, and had been killed.

I tucked the letter into her dressing table. 'Kitty, I'm so sorry.'

'Just let me be,' she said quietly.

'I'll bring dinner up for you,' I said, hearing the mess hall bell ring out.

'I'm not hungry,' she whimpered.

'I'll bring it anyway.'

**I** heaped a pile of mashed potatoes on my plate and got an extra plate for Kitty, followed by carrots and boiled ham that looked curled and dry under the warming lights.

Stella and Mary waved at me from the nurses' table, and I nodded and walked towards them. 'I'm just grabbing a tray for Kitty and myself, to take back to the room. Kitty got a letter from home today. A bad one.'

Mary frowned. 'I'm sorry to hear it.' she said. 'Can you sit for a minute, though? You can't juggle both of those trays on the path back. You'll trip. Why don't you eat first?'

I thought it over, then agreed, sitting down next to Mary.

'They say there was a fight in the barracks today,' Stella said in a hushed voice. 'This island's really wearing on the men.'

'It's wearing on all of us,' I replied, attempting to cut the tough slice of ham with a dull knife.

Stella nodded. 'I saw Lance at the market yesterday. He had his arm round that girl, that native.'

'You mean *Atea*,' I said. 'She has a name.' It irritated me that Stella held the island's indigenous population in such low regard.

'I guess that was her name. Lance sure has a thing for her.'

Mary looked doubtful. 'Oh, Stell. Just because he gets his cigarettes from her doesn't mean he's carrying on with her.'

Stella shrugged. 'I'm just telling you what I saw.'

'All right, girls,' I said. 'I'm off to deliver a meal.'

I waved flies from the tray as I followed the trail, pausing in front of the men's barracks, hoping, in vain, to find Westry gazing down from a window. Was his bunk on the first floor or the third? I scanned the first floor and my eyes stopped at an open window. There was rustling and movement inside. *A fight.* 'Yes, sir!' a voice rang out. 'Please, sir!' It was *Westry's* voice.

I set the tray down on a bench and walked to the entrance to the barracks. I had to help him. But how? Women weren't allowed inside. I stood on the steps in desperation, listening to the sound of flesh pounding flesh and furniture breaking.

A moment later, it stopped. A door slammed, then heavy footsteps pounded down the stairs. Colonel Donahue appeared at the entrance, clutching a bloodied hand. I shrank back against the hibiscus and watched as he walked to the infirmary.

My heart raced. 'Westry!' I called out, pitching my voice into the open window. 'Westry!'

There was only silence, and I feared the worst.

I ran to the mess hall, where many of the men were still eating, and found Elliot at a table near the entrance. I motioned for him to come over. 'Westry was beaten by Colonel Donahue,' I whispered. 'He's in his room. He may be unconscious.'

Elliot's eyes widened. 'I'll go,' he said, pushing through the double doors and sprinting out to the trail.

I waited outside the barracks for a long while, alternately pacing and peering up at the first-floor window. Then the door opened and Elliot stepped outside.

'He's been beaten pretty bad. A laceration on his forehead's going to need stitches,' he said.

'Why won't he come down, then?' I said.

'He won't talk about it. But something bad must have happened.'

'Can you stay with him? Try to get him to go to the infirmary?'

'I'll do my best.'

**K**itty's dinner tray was cold by the time I returned to the room, but it didn't matter. She still refused food.

'Can I do anything for you, dear?' I said, stroking her curls.

'No,' she said meekly. 'I just need to be alone.'

'Yes, I understand,' I replied softly, a little hurt. 'Kitty, I'm stepping out for a while. I'll be back soon.'

The wind blew stronger than it usually did, tousling my hair as I trudged along the sand towards the bungalow. When I arrived, I unlocked the door and lay down on the bed. The new quilt I'd brought last week, found on the top shelf of our bedroom closet, felt warm and comforting. I propped up the pillow behind my head and pulled out the letter from Mother that I'd tucked inside my pocket earlier.

*My dearest Anne,*

*I write with a heavy heart, for it is I who must relate the most terrible news to you. Believe me, I pondered, for a very long time, whether to write to you with this news or wait until you return. But, I feel you must know.*

*I am leaving your father. The circumstances are much too grave to discuss in a letter, but I will only say that, despite our separation, I will love you as much as I always have. I will explain everything when you come home.*

*May your marriage to Gerard be more love-filled than mine has been.*

*I love you dearly and I hope this news doesn't hurt too much.*

*With love,*

*Mother*

I felt the sting of salty tears in my eyes. *She's leaving Papa. Poor Papa. How could she?*

I heard a sound outside on the beach, followed by the slow creak of the bungalow door opening. My heart calmed when I saw Westry's face.

'I hoped you'd be here,' he said, grinning.

'Look at you!' I exclaimed, ignoring my inhibitions and running to his side, where I instinctively reached my hand out to caress his cheek. 'Why did Colonel Donahue hurt you?'

'Listen,' he said firmly, 'I need to make myself clear. You did not see Colonel Donahue today.'

'But I did—'

'No,' he said. 'You didn't.'

'But, Westry, why?'

He looked conflicted and pained. 'Please, don't ever mention it again. It has to be this way.'

His face caught the light, and I could see the severity of his wounds. 'You must let me take you to the infirmary.'

Westry flashed a devious smile. 'Now, why would I do that, when I have my very own nurse right here?'

I grinned. 'Well, I should have a first-aid kit.' I riffled through my bag until I found the little white case stocked with nursing essentials, then removed the suture set. I opened a packet, pulling out an alcohol-soaked square of gauze. 'This might sting a little.'

I took his hand, feeling the familiar flutter inside when our skin touched, and led him to the bed. 'Now,' I said when we were seated, 'hold still.'

Elliot had been right. The laceration on his forehead was deep. 'It looks bad,' I said nervously, dabbing the wound. 'We have a topical numbing cream at the infirmary. Let's go there.'

I began to stand, but he pulled me back. 'I want to stay here.'

I picked up the suture set. 'All right, but this may hurt.'

Westry stared at the wall ahead as I made one stitch and then two. A third was all I needed to close the gap. I tied it firmly, then snipped the edge. 'There,' I said. 'That wasn't too bad was it?'

'You're a natural, Cleo Hodge,' he said, gazing into my eyes. I smiled, then quickly turned away. 'You've been crying. Why?'

'Just some disturbing mail from home.'

'What did it say?'

I hesitated. Tears came again. 'My mother's leaving my father.'

He reached out and pulled me towards him; his arms wrapped round my back, and the side of my head nestled into his chest. I felt protected, encircled. 'I'm so sorry,' he said. Neither of us spoke again for a great while.

I looked up to face Westry. He was here. Present. Now. And in that moment, nothing else mattered.

His hands moved up along my shoulders to my neck and my cheeks, where they pulled my face towards his. I felt something new stir inside me. Westry pressed his lips against mine so delicately, so perfectly. He pulled me closer, weakening any lingering resistance.

He held me in his arms, cradling me. November 27. It was an insignificant date, just a blip on the calendar. But it was also a life-changing occasion. It was the day I started loving Westry.

# CHAPTER 6

THE SUN BEAT DOWN without reprieve, which seemed unfair, given that it was Christmas Eve. At home, Mother would be trimming an enormous fir tree in the entryway—but Mother had moved out of the house. Her most recent letter indicated that she'd taken an apartment in New York.

The mail had slowed, and I hadn't heard from Gerard. His silence had been welcome in some ways, leaving a place for my feelings for Westry to grow undisturbed. And yet, I worried about him every day, fighting on a cold foreign battlefield.

Kitty had grown to accept the death of Mr Gelfman, though she didn't talk about it. Instead, she seemed to invest every fibre of her being in Lance. She frequently slipped off to meet him and stayed out much too late. But who was I to judge?

I had time to head to the beach before the Christmas Eve service at the chapel. I was disappointed to find the bungalow empty. Westry had been on three missions in the past month, and I'd seen very little of him. I checked the mailbox under the floorboard, and found an envelope waiting for me.

> *My darling Cleo,*
>
> *Merry Christmas, my dear. I'm sorry we haven't seen much of each other lately. My commanding officer seems to have taken on all the qualities of a slave-driver. I had hoped to meet you here this morning, the only time I could break away, but no luck. So I will leave your Christmas present here for you to find. Maybe someday we'll have a real Christmas together.*
>
> *Yours,*
> *Grayson*

*Maybe someday we'll have a real Christmas together*. The idea was frightening and exciting at the same time. My fingers worked fast to untie the red ribbon from the little box below the floorboard, wrapped with tinfoil he must have stolen from the mess hall. I lifted the lid and found a gold, oval locket on a delicate chain. The inside was empty, but on the back, the inscription read: Grayson and Cleo.

I smiled, clasping the chain round my neck proudly, before producing a pen and a notebook from my bag.

> *My darling Grayson,*
>
> *Thank you for the necklace. I love it. Do you know that in my twenty-one years, I have never owned a locket? I don't think I shall ever take it off. My mind is filled with ideas about what to put inside. You'll have to help me decide.*
>
> *I miss you so much. Merry Christmas.*
> *With love,*
> *Cleo*

**T**he mail arrived that evening, just before the service. Mary handed me a pink envelope. I looked at the handwriting, so elegant, and the return address. *Maxine*. I tucked the envelope into the pocket of my dress.

Kitty had promised to go with me to the service that night, but she wasn't in the room when I got back. After fifteen minutes of waiting and no sign of a note of explanation, I gave up and went to the closet to find something to wear, which is when I noticed that her yellow dress was missing—the one that clung to her body a little too suggestively. *Where is she going in that dress?* I chose a simple blue frock for myself, then retrieved Maxine's letter.

*My dear Antoinette,*

*How are you, my dear? My, how I have missed you. The home isn't the same with you away. It's lonelier. It lacks life.*

*So much has changed since you left, and I'm afraid I don't know where to begin. But, we have always been honest with one another, so I will start with the truth. Bear with me, because the next few sentences may be very hard to take.*

*You must know, my dear, that I have loved your father for a very long time. It has been a love I have fought with all my might. For many years, I hid my feelings so efficiently that even I was fooled. And yet, when I learned that your father returns my love, it changed everything.*

*I do not know if you will ever speak to me again, but I pray that you will find it in your heart to forgive me. Your father and I want nothing more than your blessing.*

*With love,*

*Maxine*

Maxine and Papa. I crumpled the letter into a tight ball and tossed it into the wastebasket. I didn't want to read it again. And when I walked out to the hallway, I startled myself with the force with which I closed the door.

I made my way down to the foyer, but turned round upon hearing Stella's voice behind me. 'Are you going to the service?' she asked. Her face appeared softer in the dim light of the entryway.

'Yes,' I said. 'I was just coming back to get Kitty. We planned to walk over together.'

'Oh, I almost forgot to tell you,' she said.

'Tell me what?'

'Kitty asked me to pass along a message that she's terribly sorry, but Lance had some special Christmas date planned for her tonight and she won't be able to attend.'

'*A date? On Christmas Eve?*'

Stella shrugged. 'You know better than I would. Seems like those two are spending an awful lot of time together, doesn't it? Every time I pass Kitty in the hallway, she says she's off to see Lance. Lance this, Lance that. If you ask me, the man is dangerous.'

'Dangerous?'

'Yes. Everyone knows how he carries on with the native girls. Besides, that man has a temper the size of the USS *Missouri*.'

I remembered the way Atea had looked at him, and the instinct I'd had about him shortly after. But I hadn't seen his temper flare. 'Well,' I said, 'it's Kitty's prerogative.'

We walked outside and headed to the little chapel adjacent to the mess hall. Inside, the choir was warming up at the piano, and nearby stood a Douglas fir, adorned with red apples and tinsel finely cut from tinfoil. A Douglas fir, in the tropics. I gasped. Some of the women must have loaned out their hair ribbons, as there were at least two dozen white satin bows from top to bottom.

The choir, which was nothing more than a group of volunteer soldiers, began singing 'O Come, All Ye Faithful'. Men filed in, removing their hats at the door. Mary nestled in next to us, followed by Liz. Partway through the service, shortly after the candles were lit, I heard some commotion and turned towards the back.

'What's going on?' I whispered to Stella.

'That's what's going on,' she said smugly, pointing at the centre aisle.

There, walking towards us, was Atea—bare-breasted, beautiful Atea, with tears rolling down her face. She looked as striking as she had the day at the market.

'Where is he?' she screamed, looking from left to right, scanning the pews. 'Why he not here?'

One of the men stood up and took her arm. 'Don't you see that you're disturbing the service, miss.'

She wrenched her arm away from him. 'Don't touch me! Where is he? He lie. I tell everyone.'

The soldier regained his grip and attempted to pull her towards the door. Atea screamed.

'Stop!' I shouted, waving my arms. 'I know this woman. Let me speak to her.'

No one seemed to object, so I walked over to Atea and smiled warmly. Her big brown eyes, red from crying, searched my face. 'Would you like to talk outside?' I asked.

She nodded and followed me. We walked in silence along the gravel pathway that led to the beach. Atea led me to a log, and we both sat down.

'I am fear,' Atea said.

'You mean, you're *afraid*? What are you afraid of?'

'Him,' she said simply.

*Lance.* My cheeks burned with anger. 'What did he do to you?'

'He hurt me.' She pointed to a bruise on her wrist and another on her upper arm, purple and black.

'I'm so sorry,' I said. 'But why did you come here, to the chapel, tonight?'

Her eyes swelled with tears. 'I tell everyone what he did,' she said, 'then he no hurt me again.'

'Atea,' I said, 'you must leave this base. If he wants to harm you, he'll find a way. You must leave and stay far away.'

She looked confused. 'Where can I go?'

'Do you have someone you can stay with?'

Atea shook her head. 'No. I have no one, except Tita.'

'Who is Tita?'

'The oldest woman on Bora-Bora. She take care of all of us.' She looked unsettled. 'What I do when he comes? He will come.'

I patted her arm. 'See that white building in the distance, and the window on the corner of the first floor, just near the palm?'

'Yes,' she said meekly.

'That's my room. You call up to me when you're afraid. We always leave the window open. I'll hear you.'

She searched my face with trusting eyes. 'If you not there?'

'Then run down this beach,' I said, pointing my finger towards the shore. 'About a half-mile up there's a bungalow, a little hut a few steps into the thicket. The door is locked, but you'll find the key in a book beneath the step.'

'The artist's home? No one goes there. Tita say it's haunting.'

'*Haunted?* Do you believe it's haunted?' I asked.

Atea shrugged. 'Maybe, but I go there if I must.'

'Good. You're going to be fine. Everything will be fine.'

'Really?' She looked so beautiful, yet so innocent and afraid.

'Really.' I'd make sure Lance never hurt her again. 'If you see Lance, you mustn't tell him about our chat. It will only anger him.'

She looked confused, but nodded.

'Good night,' I said.

'*Taoto maitai*,' she said before disappearing into the moonlight.

'**C**an you imagine having a bright morning like this in Seattle—in January?' I said, turning to Kitty.

'No,' she answered in a flat voice. 'I'm tired of all this sun.'

'I don't know that I could ever tire of it,' I said, sitting up and reaching for my robe draped over the foot of the bed. 'Kitty? Can I confide in you? I'm worried.'

'Worried about what?' Her eyes looked tired, but not just because it was early. Deep exhaustion punctuated her face. We hadn't spoken of Lance since Christmas Day, when I'd told her what Atea had said. I'd warned her about Lance, and yet the news hardly fazed her. Things were over between them, or so it seemed. As each day passed, she grew quieter and more introspective, and I grew more concerned. Had Lance hurt her in the same way he'd hurt Atea?

'I'm worried that this island has changed us,' I said.

Instead of looking at me, Kitty looked *through* me, right on to the wall behind my back. 'It *has* changed us,' she said simply.

'Kitty, it's just that I—' I stopped when I heard a sudden knock at the door. 'Who is it?' I called out.

'It's me, Mary.'

I cinched the tie on my robe and opened the door to find Mary, rosy-cheeked and beaming. ''Morning, lovelies,' she said, poking her head into the room to catch Kitty's eye, with little success.

Mary had regained her strength after her bout with malaria, and she now hummed in the infirmary while the rest of us grumbled. Stella said Mary had been seeing a man named Lou, though Mary hadn't let on yet. I felt a pang in my heart. *Mary's letter.* I reached inside the shoebox under my bedside table, remembering that I'd hidden it there. Gerard's most recent letter fell out onto the floor. My cheeks flushed, and I hurriedly stowed it away. *How could Mary face her past if I couldn't even face mine?*

'I want to invite you to a little soiree tonight.' Mary's eyes sparkled. 'A group of us are getting together for a cookout. Stella, Liz, a few of the other nurses, and some of the men. We're piling into a truck at seven thirty for Leatra Beach. I think Westry's coming, Anne.'

She gave me a knowing look that I did not return. I hadn't spoken to Westry in three weeks, and I feared there was a silence growing between us. Sure, his commanding officer kept him busy. But I hardly found him in the bungalow any more, even when I knew he was off duty.

Leatra Beach was just a stone's throw from the bungalow. I felt my chest tighten. It wasn't too far off the beach, only loosely hidden by palm fronds. Anyone with an ounce of curiosity would see it on second glance. So why hadn't others found it? How had it gone unnoticed with an army base down the shore? These questions made me wonder if the bungalow was merely a mirage in the French Polynesian sun, custom-made for Westry and me.

'So,' Mary said expectantly, 'will you come?'

I glanced back at Kitty. She looked uninterested, distant. 'I'll go,' I said. 'But only if Kitty joins me.'

Kitty joined me, reluctantly. I took a good, long look at her before we left the room. What had changed about her? True, the colour had left her cheeks, and her hair was even wilder now, untamable. She didn't even stop to catch her reflection in the little oval mirror in our bedroom. And if she had, I wasn't certain that she'd even be able to see the change. It wasn't only her hair, but her figure. I'd heard Stella whispering to Liz in the mess hall about Kitty taking a second helping of mashed potatoes. 'She's going to go home fifteen pounds heavier,' she had said. Kitty did look plumper now, but her beauty still shone through the mussy hair, pale cheeks, and rounder appearance. Kitty would be beautiful no matter what.

'You look pretty,' I said as we walked out of the barracks.

'No, I don't,' she said. I didn't like the defeat in her voice.

'Stop it,' I chided her. 'I wish you'd snap out of this mood you're in. I miss my old friend.'

Kitty stopped suddenly on the trail. Colonel Donahue was approaching. He tipped his cap to us, but didn't say a word. A sick feeling came over me. The incident with Westry had made me despise him, but seeing the way he dismissed Kitty, without so much as a hello—especially after the interest he'd taken in her when we'd arrived months ago—well, it made me fume. He was rumoured to be seeing one of the other nurses—quiet, with dark hair and a figure rivalling a pin-up girl's.

'I've never liked that man,' I said when he was a safe distance away. Kitty looked sad. 'I didn't mean to—'

She reached for my hand and squeezed it tightly. 'It's all right, Anne. You don't need to apologise. It's just that . . .' She paused, as if to consider if anyone was listening. The men's barracks were nearing. 'It's nothing.'

'I wish you'd tell me. Are you sad about his new girlfriend? Or is it Lance? Kitty, did something happen? Did he hurt you?'

She shook her head. 'Anne, please don't.'

'All right,' I said, 'but will you tell me when you're ready?'

Kitty nodded, but I feared it was an empty promise.

Just ahead, I spotted some men and women piling into a truck. Stella was there, with Will, as was Liz, and Mary, with Lou.

Kitty and I climbed in. 'Hi,' I said, taking a seat next to Mary.

She beamed. 'I'm so glad you could come. Liz sweet-talked a mess hall cook into joining, and look at the loot!'

Mary pointed to a chest of ice with chicken and potato salad and corn for roasting. Another cooler held an enormous quantity of beer. There were many faces I didn't recognise, eager faces. Lance was there, seated next to a blonde nurse. I hoped Kitty didn't see the way he was flirting with her.

I searched the vehicle for Westry.

'Looks like he didn't make it,' Mary whispered. 'I'm sorry.'

I shrugged. 'Don't be,' I said, tugging at my engagement ring. 'There's nothing between us. Nothing at all.'

The truck sped along the bumpy road. Each pothole punctuated the shame I felt. *How did I, an engaged woman, let myself become involved with Westry? What has this island done to my judgment?*

The truck came to a stop. Mary led the procession onto the beach, telling the men where to set out the blankets and the fire for the cook. There were oohs and aahs when a lance corporal named Shawn pulled out a radio and extended its antenna. Even Kitty smiled. None of us were immune to the power of music.

'Now,' Mary said, 'if I can just get a signal.' She worked on the tuner for some time, stopping momentarily when she heard the faint sound of a man's voice—an Australian accent—relating war news. 'Japanese bombers stormed the north shore today, leaving a wake of death and destruction.' She turned the dial. After a few seconds, the static parted to reveal a crystal-clear signal. The melody was sweet, haunting. 'How strange,' she said. 'A French station.'

The words were foreign, the melody unfamiliar, and yet it entranced me, and everyone else who was huddled together on the beach. Stella leaned in closer to Will. Lou reached for Mary's hand. A few other nurses, even Liz, paired up with men I didn't recognise. And Kitty didn't object when a soldier sat down beside her. The melody aroused a longing in my heart that I tried to squelch, a longing for Westry. I turned my gaze towards the stretch of beach that led to the bungalow. It was getting dark now. *I shouldn't.* Besides, he wouldn't be there anyway. But the music played on.

I could no longer resist it. I stood up and walked quietly towards the beach. *No one would miss me.* I walked quickly, glancing back several times, just to be sure that no one followed. I slipped into the thicket and made my way to the bungalow. I knelt down and felt around under the step for the book and the key, but I heard the door creak open in front of me and there, standing in the dim light, was Westry.

A faint shadow punctuated his jawline, and his wet hair and unbuttoned shirt suggested that he'd just returned from a swim. He smiled. 'I was hoping you'd come tonight. Did you see that moon?'

I nodded, gazing up at the sky, where an orange-tinged full moon dangled on the horizon, so close it almost kissed the shore. 'I've never seen anything like it.'

'Come in.' He reached for my hand. 'I have something for you.'

He closed the door behind us, and I sat down on the bed. I felt the pulse, the electricity in the air. I knew he felt it too.

'Look.' He held up a radio. 'I got a signal.' He turned the dial and there was that sound again—that beautiful, haunting foreign melody. 'Listen,' he said. 'French. This song, do you know it?'

I listened intently for a few moments, then shook my head. 'No, I don't think I do.'

'It's *"La Vie en Rose"*.' He sat down next to me. Our arms brushed, and I could feel the warmth of his body.

'What does it mean?' I asked, feeling Westry's gaze on my face.

He took a breath. 'It means, *Hold me close and hold me fast / The magic spell you cast / This is la vie en rose / When you kiss me, heaven sighs / And though I close my eyes / I see la vie en rose / When you press me to your heart /*

*I'm in a world apart / A world where roses bloom / And when you speak /
Angels sing from above.'*

'It's beautiful,' I said, unable to look at him. My hands began to tremble.
I tucked them under my legs.

Westry stood up. 'Will you dance with me?'

I nodded, taking his hand.

As our bodies swayed to the music, he held me close, keeping his arms
low on my waist. I nestled my cheek into his chest.

'Westry,' I whispered.

'You mean Grayson?'

I smiled. 'My dear Grayson.'

'Yes, Cleo?'

'Well, that's just it. Are we only pretending? Is this *real*? Why is it that
when we're here, everything feels so right? But—'

'But when we're out there,' he said, 'it's different?'

'Yes.'

'Because it is. This is our paradise. Out there, it's complicated.'

'And that's just it,' I said. 'I almost didn't come tonight because I feared
that you were growing distant. That night with Colonel Donahue—why
haven't you spoken of it?'

'Would you believe me if I told you I was protecting you?'

'Protecting me? From what?'

'It's a crazy world out there, Anne. War. Lies. Betrayal. Sadness. It's all
around us.' He cradled my head in his hands. 'Next time you worry that I
am growing distant, come here. Come to the bungalow and you will feel
my love.'

Love. *Westry loves me.* I pressed my body closer to his and felt something
akin to hunger welling up inside, an unfamiliar longing I'd never felt with
Gerard. *Passion. Is this what Kitty meant?*

Westry took a step back. 'Look at you,' he said. 'You are a vision. I'm
going to take your photograph.' He retrieved a camera from his knapsack.
'Perfect,' he said after the flash went off.

I lifted the camera from his hands. 'Now I want one of you.' I stared at
his eyes through the lens, hoping to memorise the moment for ever,
before I clicked the button.

I set the camera down on the desk, and Westry lifted me in his arms
and laid me on the bed effortlessly. His lips touched mine, and my heart

rate quickened as I took in the familiar scent of his skin, breathing it in. I unbuttoned his shirt completely and ran my fingers along his chest. His muscles quivered a little, and he smiled. Something in me trembled too as he reached for the zipper of my dress.

'Westry,' I whispered. 'What will happen after all of this is over?'

'After the war? I wish I knew,' he said, kissing my forehead. 'You're thinking of him, aren't you?'

I sighed. 'It's all so complicated.'

'Not when love is so certain,' he said.

I loved this man with every ounce of my being. I kissed him softly and laid my head on his shoulder. We listened to the French songs on the radio, forgetting people, places, even time.

It may have been minutes or hours later, but I bolted out of bed when I heard the snap of a twig outside. I hurriedly dressed, fussing with the zipper on my dress as I peered out of the window, where I could see a shadowy form on the beach.

Westry quickly rose, slipping on his trousers and shirt before opening the door. I followed close behind. 'Who's there?' he called out to the figure in the distance.

'It's me,' said a familiar voice. 'Kitty.'

We pushed past the thicket, and the light from the moon revealed her face. I could see that she was frightened.

'Anne? Is that *you*? Oh,' she said when she noticed Westry beside me. 'I—I didn't mean to interrupt; it's just that we were getting ready to leave, and we couldn't find you.'

'I'm sorry. I must have lost track of time.' Kitty couldn't see the bungalow from where she was standing, and I was glad of it. I turned to Westry. 'Good night, Westry,' I said.

'Good night, Anne,' he replied, smiling a secret smile.

Kitty and I walked in silence up the beach, until she finally spoke. 'You love him, don't you?'

'Kitty!'

She nestled her hand in mine. 'It's OK,' she said. 'I don't care who you love. I just want to see you happy. Are you?'

I looked up at the moon overhead and then back towards the stretch of beach that led to the bungalow. 'Yes,' I said. 'I've never been happier in my entire life than at this moment.'

446 | Sarah Jio

# CHAPTER 7

'DID YOU HEAR?' Liz said at breakfast. 'The men are shipping out. Almost all of them. There's some big fight south of here.'

'Colonel Donahue is leading them out this evening,' Kitty said, with little emotion, as if she was reading the *War Digest* verbatim.

'Does anyone know who's going?' I asked, hoping the panic I felt wasn't evident in my voice.

'Yes,' Stella said. 'Go and look at the list.' She pointed to the bulletin board outside the mess hall. 'I saw Will's name on it earlier.'

I turned to Mary. 'Will you go and look with me?'

She nodded, and we walked to the board. There it was. His name, halfway down, in black ink. Westry Green. Lou's was there, too. Mary gasped, and we clutched each other tightly.

'We have to find them,' she said. 'We have to say goodbye before . . . Anne, I can't bear to lose him.'

'Let's be confident,' I said. 'Let's think positively. They need that from us.'

I'd already worked the early-morning shift in the infirmary, so I didn't feel guilty about sneaking out after breakfast to the men's barracks, where I gazed up at Westry's window. The room, or what I could see of it from standing on a bench outside, looked empty. *Has he already left?*

I walked quickly to the beach, and once I'd rounded the bend, I started to run. My shoes filled with sand as I rushed along—sand that had never felt so heavy.

I pushed through the brush to the bungalow. The morning sun shone on its palm walls, streaming light all around it. I reached for the doorknob, praying that Westry would be inside. Locked. I was too late.

I pulled out the key and let myself in anyway, sitting down in a heap of disappointment on the chair by the desk. The little room immediately comforted me. I could sense his presence, just as he'd said I would. I could feel his love. It enveloped me.

I lifted the floorboard and saw a letter inside.

*My darling Cleo,*

*I have to leave now, my dear. I am shipping out to Guadalcanal for what the CO calls 'serious combat'. The men don't know what to expect, nor do I. After all, we've been sitting pretty on this rock for so long, we were almost fooled into thinking we were on vacation. It's about time we fulfil our jobs, to do what we came here for. To fight.*

*I stopped by the infirmary this morning to say goodbye, but you were busy. I watched you work from the window. My, you are beautiful. The way you move. The way you talk. I have never loved as I love you.*

*I pray that you will hold the memory of last night in your heart, that you will think of me. For I will return, and we will be reunited. And when the war is done, we will never part.*

*Remember me, la vie en rose, my darling.*

*Yours for evermore,*

*Grayson*

I wiped away tears, then ran outside to the shore as a squadron of airplanes flew overhead in formation. I blew a kiss out into the sky.

He'd come back. He had to.

**T**he days passed with very little news from the war front.

The Allies were closing in on the Japanese in the Pacific, Liz had explained. Liz knew more about the war than any of us. She said the Japanese had planned to colonise New Zealand, to rape and kill. And while the Allies had taken Guadalcanal, pockets of enemy forces remained throughout the South Pacific. We had to win.

Every day more injured men were wheeled off airplanes. Some came in on stretchers, dazed and bloodied, mute, as if what they had seen had robbed them of their voices. Others had such severe injuries—severed legs, missing arms, shrapnel in the eyes—that they moaned for morphine, and we gave it to them as quickly as our hands could inject needles into their pain-ravaged skin.

The steady stream of men kept us busy in the infirmary. Nurse Hildebrand directed us with the force of a drill sergeant, and rightly so. As each man was wheeled in, the women crowded round to check for a familiar face. And on one morning in early April, a pilot brought in Stella's

Will. Blood covered his face and neck. I took him to the operating room. Twenty-three more men came in, and then nine more, and then another eleven. Three died. Rows of men waited for medicine, for a bandage, for surgery. Dr Wheeler said Will might not make it, and the tears streamed down Stella's face, but he regained consciousness and pulled through.

We worked until the shift change at 11 p.m. Even then, many of us didn't want to leave. Nurse Hildebrand forbade us to stay. 'You're too tired, and you're getting sloppy,' she said.

She was right. Beds, numbers, men—all blurred together, and when I closed my eyes, all I could see was a deep red shade of blood.

The mail had come, and I brought a letter from Gerard back to the barracks. Kitty went to bed and slept. I stood by the window so I could read in the moonlight without disturbing her.

> *My love,*
> *I haven't heard from you, and I hate to even mention it, but yesterday, I was overcome with fear. Are you safe? Please write and tell me.*
> *I am in France with the 101st Airborne Division. The conditions are tough, as they are everywhere, I imagine. Men are dying right and left. But I will come home to you, Anne. I promise.*
> *Yours,*
> *Gerard*

I wept, ashamed that I hadn't taken more time to write. I sat down to compose a letter, even if I didn't know what I'd say.

> *Dear Gerard,*
> *I wanted you to know that I am well and fine. The mail has been backed up, so I am only now receiving your letters.*

I paused, considering the lie. A white lie.

> *I'm so busy here, or else I'd have written more. When we're not working we're sleeping.*

Another lie.

> *I think of you often, and miss you.*
> *With love,*
> *Anne*

'We need a knitting circle,' Stella suggested at the mess hall one morning. 'All we do in the evening is listen for news on the radio.'

'Easy for you to say,' Mary snapped. 'Your Will is safe and sound. And you think *yarn* is what we need?'

Stella looked wounded.

'It's not a bad idea,' I chimed in.

'I'm sorry,' Mary said. 'I didn't mean that. I'm sure the natives could use blankets for the children. We could make them.'

Stella smiled. 'Good. I'll gather the supplies.'

Those next couple of weeks, it was yarn that sustained us. We made one blanket, and then two. By the third and fourth, we were already planning the fifth: green and yellow, with a palm motif. Nurse Hildebrand gave me permission to deliver them.

The market seemed quieter than usual, eerily so. Since most of the men had been deployed in the fight, fewer islanders turned up to sell their wares, but I hoped Atea would be there.

It had been months since I'd seen her, since that fateful Christmas Eve scene at the chapel, and I worried about her. 'Excuse me,' I said to a toothless woman holding an infant at a table stacked with bananas and a few clumps of dusty salad greens. 'Have you seen Atea?'

The woman eyed me sceptically. 'She no here,' she said.

'Oh.' I held out the blankets. 'I just wanted to give her these.'

My gesture changed the woman's demeanour. She softened, pointing to a nearby hill. 'She with Tita. Green house.'

I walked along the pathway that led to the hill. It was darker under the cloak of the tropical forest, and I almost didn't see the little green house. A bicycle leaned up against the side of the small one-room home, which appeared to be constructed of scrap wood and treasures that had washed up from the sea. An old woman appeared in the doorway, her grey hair fashioned into a single tidy braid.

'I'm here to see Atea,' I said meekly.

The woman nodded and muttered something in French, or maybe Tahitian. I heard footsteps from behind the door.

'Anne!' Atea poked her head round the old woman. 'You come!' She looked different, which might have been because she was wearing a dress, one that was about five sizes too big for her small frame. It appeared to

450 | Sarah Jio

have been plucked from the Sears Roebuck catalogue circa 1895.

'Yes,' I said. 'I'm sorry to intrude. I—I wanted to make sure you were safe. And I wanted to give you these blankets.'

Atea took them. 'They're beautiful. For me?'

'Yes. And for anyone else you think can use them. How have you been?'

She looked conflicted about answering the question. 'Come in,' she said instead. 'This is Tita.'

The old woman nodded.

'Pleased to meet you, Tita,' I said, smiling. 'I'm Anne.'

Atea directed me to a grass-woven chair, and I sat. Moments later Tita produced a mug containing something warm. 'Tea,' she said. 'For you.'

I thanked her and took a sip. The beverage was sweet and spicy at the same time.

'It's good,' I said. 'What is it?'

'Kava,' Atea said. 'It calm you.'

She was right. Each sip had a soothing, somewhat dizzying effect. Everything softened—the jagged window frame, the dirt floor.

Tita moved to the chair next to me. 'You are the one who found the artist's home.' She gave Atea a knowing look. 'There is something you must know about this bungalow. According to legend, whoever steps foot in it will face a lifetime of heartache.'

Her eyes were so arresting, I could not look away. 'I'm not sure I understand what you mean,' I said, setting the mug down on a little wooden table to my left.'

'Bad things happen there,' she said. 'Things too dark to speak of.' Tita cast her eyes to a crucifix that hung on the wall.

I shook my head. No, she had it all wrong. *Good* things happened there. It was our beloved hideaway, the place where I had grown to love Westry. I stood up abruptly and the room seemed to move. 'Well,' I said, steadying myself on the edge of the chair. 'Thank you for the tea. But I really must be going.' I turned to Atea. 'Please, remember my offer if you need assistance.'

She nodded and eyed Tita cautiously as I reached for the door handle.

'Wait,' I said, turning back round. 'You said the bungalow belonged to an artist. Do you happen to know who?'

Tita looked at Atea and then at me again. 'Yes,' she said with wistful eyes. 'His name was Paul. Paul Gauguin.'

The following night, Mary passed out yarn in the rec hall just as the onslaught began. A rush of men came through the door. 'Nurses, quick!' one shouted. 'It's a plane full of wounded men.'

I ran with the other women to the infirmary, where Nurse Hildebrand was shouting orders. We scattered to our stations.

It was like nothing we'd seen before. Mary and I worked the doors, admitting the men, many of whom shrieked and pleaded for help, some with such force that it was terrifying to witness. A young soldier with a head injury pulled my arm so hard he tore the sleeve of my dress. 'Mama! Where is Mama?' he screamed.

It was harrowing to witness. The blood and misery and pain, and especially seeing men reduced to children in their suffering. But we kept on. When our reserves of strength ran out, we found more.

It was two thirty in the morning when the last plane came in. Nine men were wheeled into the infirmary. I heard Mary scream at the doors. I ran to her side, and there on the stretcher lay Lou—limp, lifeless, and very badly burnt.

A soldier said, 'I'm sorry. This one died on the way over.'

'No!' Mary screamed, shaking her head violently. '*No!*' She fell to her knees. 'No, this can't be.' She stood up and laid her head on Lou's chest, sobbing into his blood-soaked shirt. 'Lou!' she cried. 'Lou. No.'

'Mary,' I said. 'Mary, stop.'

'I won't!' she screamed, pushing me away.

'Honey,' I said, taking her left arm. Liz came and took her right. 'We're going to take you to bed. Liz, grab the sedatives.'

'No,' Mary moaned.

Moments later, her body went limp on a nearby bed.

'Lou,' she muttered weakly before her eyes closed.

Kitty and I walked back to the barracks in silence. We fell into our beds and, for a long time, I prayed for Westry.

'Anne,' Kitty whispered. 'Are you still awake? I have to tell you something important.'

I sat up. 'What is it?'

She sighed, looking at me with eyes filled with sorrow, with hurt that I could not understand. 'I'm pregnant.'

I ran to her bed. 'Oh, Kitty!' I cried in disbelief.

452 | Sarah Jio

'I've been so afraid to tell you.' Her eyes welled up with tears. 'I knew it would disappoint you.'

'Disappoint *me*?' I ran my fingers through her curls. 'No, I'm only disappointed that you've had to carry this burden alone.'

Kitty pressed her face against my shoulder and wept so intensely her body shook with grief. 'I don't know what to do,' she cried. 'I've been hiding under girdles for months. Everyone will notice before long. The baby's coming in a month, maybe sooner.'

I gasped. 'We'll speak to Nurse Hildebrand,' I said.

'No!' Kitty pleaded. 'No, we can't go to her. Please, Anne.

'It's the only option. You can't be working such long hours in your condition, and the baby will be coming soon. We must plan for that.'

Kitty looked frightened and lost. 'All right,' she said. 'If you think it's best, tell her. But I can't bear to be there when you do.'

I kissed her forehead and smiled. 'You don't have to, dear,' I said. 'I'll take care of everything.'

The following day, I managed to run into Nurse Hildebrand in the storeroom. 'Nurse Hildebrand,' I said, quietly closing the door behind us. 'May I speak to you about something?'

'Yes, Anne,' she said without looking up from the crate she was unpacking. 'Quickly, please; I must get back.'

'Thank you,' I said. 'It's about Kitty.'

Nurse Hildebrand nodded. 'I already know,' she said simply. 'I've been a nurse for a very long time. I've delivered babies and had children of my own. I know.'

'She needs your help,' I said cautiously.

Nurse Hildebrand's face softened. 'Tell her not to worry about the work here. If the others ask, I'll say she has a bout of the fever going round, that she's been quarantined. You'll need to bring her meals up to her. Can you manage that?'

'Yes,' I said, smiling. 'Yes, of course.'

'And when the time comes, come to me. I know a missionary couple who will take the baby. They are good people.'

'Thank you, Nurse Hildebrand,' I said with such emotion, tears fell from my eyes. 'I didn't expect you to be so—'

'Enough,' she said. 'It's time to get back to work.'

The day Mary left the island was sad for all of us, particularly for Kitty, trapped in the barracks and unable to join the other nurses on the airstrip. The island had been hard on Mary, perhaps harder on her than on any of us. It had given her malaria and nearly taken her life, and then it broke her heart.

'Farewell, friend,' Stella said to Mary.

'We'll never forget you, dear,' Liz chimed in.

Mary looked like a shell of a woman standing there before the door of the plane, thinner than ever, with wrists bandaged from her self-inflicted wounds, wounds that had almost ended her life.

She retrieved a handkerchief from her bag and dabbed her bloodshot eyes. 'I'll miss you all so much,' she said. 'It doesn't feel right to leave. You've become my dearest friends, my sisters.'

I pulled the letter from Edward from my pocket and tucked it in her hand. 'This arrived,' I said, 'for you. I hope you will forgive me for keeping it from you.'

Her eyes brightened when she saw the return address.

'I wanted to protect you from any more pain. I'm so sorry.'

'No,' Mary said. 'Don't be. I understand. I do.'

And with that, Mary was gone from our lives. And the island was lonelier because of it.

For a long time it felt like Westry might never come back. The island was different without him, especially now that Mary had left and Kitty was bedridden. But then one morning in late May while working in the infirmary, we heard the loudspeaker at the centre of camp announcing that the men had returned.

'Go,' Nurse Hildebrand said to me.

I didn't stop to thank her; instead I ran out to the pathway and didn't pause until I'd reached the edge of the airstrip. Men trudged with heavy bags and even heavier hearts towards camp. Lance, Colonel Donahue, and other men I knew. *But where is Westry?* I noticed one of his bunkmates from the barracks. 'Ted,' I said. 'Have you seen Westry?'

He shook his head. 'Sorry. Not since yesterday.'

My heart raced. 'What do you mean?'

'He was on the front line, and . . . There's another plane tonight.' Ted tipped his cap at me. 'Let's pray he's on it.'

That night I walked along the beach, a foolish move given Kitty's state. She'd been having mild contractions for days now, but she assured me they weren't serious. I promised I'd only be gone an hour. I felt guilty about leaving, but I needed the comfort of the bungalow.

I unlocked the door and draped the quilt round me, listening for airplanes overhead. *Is he coming? Please, God, bring him home.*

But I could only hear rain—just a few drops at first and then a hundred, a thousand. The sky appeared to have opened up, dumping its contents right on the roof of the bungalow.

I opened the door, extending my hand to feel the raindrops, like firm kisses on my skin, beckoning me outside. I took another step, and looked up to the sky, letting the warm drops cover my face, my hair. Moments later my dress was soaked. And then, out of the corner of my eye, I saw a figure, faint and blurred in the distance. I walked closer, pushing my way through the rain, like a curtain of beads from the sky, until I could make out his face, thin from months of fighting, and hungry for the love I desperately wanted to give him.

Our bodies collided, fiting together perfectly as his bag dropped to the sand. 'Oh, Westry!' I cried.

'I came directly here,' he said.

Westry pulled me close, and I felt the intensity in his kiss. He lifted me in his arms and carried me to the bungalow.

An hour later, when the storm had passed, I lay tracing Westry's face with my finger as he gazed out of the window facing the beach. The stubble on his jaw was thick. I counted five scrapes on his face, if you counted the gash on his ear. 'What was it like out there?' I whispered.

'It was a living hell,' he said, sitting up against the pillows.

I sensed his hesitation. 'You don't want to talk about it, do you?'

'I'd rather enjoy this perfect moment,' he said before planting a soft kiss on my lips.

I thought of Kitty, and felt guilty for being gone so long.

'Our clothes,' I said, a little panicked. 'They must be soaked.'

Westry stood up, letting the blanket fall to the bed, and returned a moment later with my damp, wrinkled dress. I fitted it over my head, as he slid into his trousers.

'Can you stay for a while?' he asked, combing my hair with his fingers.

'I wish I could.' I wanted to tell him about Kitty, but I decided against it. 'But I said I'd be back hours ago.'

We both turned when we heard a faint knock on the door.

Westry opened the door cautiously, and I peered over his shoulder to see Kitty standing outside. She clutched her belly in agony. 'Anne!' she screamed. 'It's *time*.'

I didn't stop to think about how she found us. 'We need to get you to the infirmary,' I said, running to her side.

'No. The baby's coming *now*.'

Westry's mouth flung open as I helped her up the step into the bungalow, where she rested on the bed, moaning in such pain, it was heartbreaking to witness.

I tried to recall an ounce of what I'd learned about childbirth. Hot water. Forceps. Ether. I shuddered. I had nothing but my two hands.

**A** girl!' I cried. 'Kitty, it's a girl.'

Westry placed the baby in Kitty's arms. She clutched the newborn to her chest. He tucked Kitty under the quilt, and then carefully swaddled the baby in his ragged green army shirt.

Once they were settled, we walked outside together and sat down on the sand. I could no longer repress the emotion I felt.

'Don't cry,' Westry said softly. 'She's fine. You delivered that baby better than any doctor could have.'

I nodded. 'It's just not what I wanted for her. Lance should be court-martialled for leaving her in a position like this.'

He looked confused, but nodded. He stroked my hair softly. 'Anne, I hated being away from you. It was misery. The only thing that got me through it was knowing I'd return to you.'

I nestled my face into his chest. 'I don't know what I would have done if you hadn't made it home,' I said.

He held my hands in his, lifting up my left hand and touching the ring on my finger. 'I can't share you with him any more,' he whispered.

'I know,' I said, breathing in his breath. I slid the ring off my finger and let it drop into the pocket of my dress. 'You don't have to any more.'

**W**estry carried Kitty, wrapped in the quilt, back to the base. It was no small feat, even for a man of his strength. The baby slept in my arms. She looked just like her mother. She had Kitty's nose, for sure, and those high cheekbones.

It was 5 a.m. I directed Westry to a small room in the infirmary, where he set Kitty down gently on the bed. Kitty looked at him, running her hand along the stubble of his chin. 'How can I ever thank you?'

'No thanks necessary,' he said, smiling.

We all looked towards the door when we heard the knob turn. Nurse Hildebrand walked in. 'I can take it from here, soldier.'

Westry nodded. 'Good night, ladies.' He sent a grin my way.

'Good night,' I said. I couldn't help but notice something unsettled in Kitty's eyes as Westry walked out.

'Anne, Kitty, are you all right?' Nurse Hildebrand pulled a basin from the closet.

'Yes,' I said. 'And the baby is healthy.'

'Anne, you'll give the child her first bath. You can swaddle her in this spare sheet. The Mayhews have clothes and blankets for her at their home.'

Kitty shook her head. 'The Mayhews?'

'The couple who is taking your child,' Nurse Hildebrand replied.

Terror appeared on Kitty's face. 'But it's so soon. I—I . . .'

'It's what you wanted, Kitty. And it's what has to be done,' Nurse Hildebrand said without emotion. 'You can't keep a child here. This is the right choice for her, for you. The sooner you let go, the easier it will be.'

Kitty watched despondently as I bathed her little girl, lathering her tiny head with soap and gently wiping the suds with a facecloth. 'Her name is Adella,' she muttered.

'You can't name her, dear,' Nurse Hildebrand retorted. 'The Mayhews will have their own name.'

'I don't care!' Kitty snapped. 'To me she'll always be Adella.'

I rinsed the remaining soap bubbles off the child's delicate skin. Once she was dry, I swaddled her in the sheet, then tucked the tiny package into Kitty's arms.

'No,' she said, turning away. 'If I hold her, I won't be able to let her go. Can't you see that?' She began to cry, but it wasn't the same sort of cry I'd heard from her in years past. This was sorrow that emanated from some-place very deep.

I swallowed hard, trying to stay strong for Kitty's sake, and walked the baby outside the room. I waited there until a couple, maybe in their early thirties, appeared in the hallway. Kitty's muffled sobbing seeped through the closed door.

Nurse Hildebrand indicated the couple and nodded. 'John and Evelyn Mayhew.' She forced a smile. 'They'll take the baby now.'

The couple looked kind, and I could see by the woman's eager smile that she would welcome the child with love. 'Adella is her name,' I said quietly, on Kitty's behalf.

'It's a beautiful name,' she said. 'But we've chosen another. I will put it in her birth records, though, so it will always be a part of her history.'

I nodded and stepped back as the couple thanked Nurse Hildebrand and left, an instant family of three.

# CHAPTER 8

NURSE HILDEBRAND EXCUSED ME from my duties so I could care for Kitty in the days that followed. I kept her company, though I think she would have preferred to be alone. I brought her meals and tried to interest her in magazines, but Kitty just set them on her bed, preferring to stare at the wall.

I knew I couldn't fix things for her. She had to wade through this on her own, which is why I excused myself two days after the birth for a beach walk and a visit to the bungalow. I craved a change of scenery, and Kitty needed to be alone.

Westry was there, just as I'd hoped he'd be, napping on the bed as the afternoon sun streamed in.

'Hi,' I whispered, nestling my body beside him.

He opened his eyes and smiled warmly at me, pulling me closer.

'I bet you didn't know that you were sleeping in the presence of a masterpiece.' I reached for the painting under the bed. 'It's a *Gauguin*.'

Westry sat up quickly, looking at the canvas with fresh eyes. 'You're serious?'

I nodded.

He shook his head in disbelief. 'I always thought it had to have been done by a younger, lesser-known painter. Gauguin? How can you be sure?'

'An old woman on the island told me,' I said, smiling proudly.

'It's not signed.'

'Maybe he didn't sign his work early on.'

'You could be right about that. Monet did the same.'

'What will we do with it? We can't lave it here when the war's over, when we're gone. I couldn't bear to think of it swallowed up by a tidal wave.'

Westry agreed. 'Or deteriorating out here in the elements.'

I sighed. 'There's something else I need to tell you. The old woman, Tita, she warned me about this place. She said that all who step foot inside live with some sort of curse.'

Westry grinned. 'And you believed her voodoo?'

'Well, it frightened me, I will admit.'

'Anne, the first day we met, you told me you believed life is about free will.' He stroked my hair lightly. 'Your life will be rich and blessed and filled with love because of what you make it.'

I tucked my hand in his. 'You're right.'

'Besides,' he continued, 'look at all the good that has come from these four walls. Our love has grown. A baby has been born. And we may have discovered one of the greatest artistic finds in our century. Is that what the old woman calls a *curse*?'

We sat listening to the waves roll onto the shore. *God, please let him be right.*

**T**ime was growing scarce now; we all knew that. May had blown through like a fierce storm, and Kitty and I would be leaving the island in mid-June, at the same time that Westry and the other men would ship off for another tour of duty—this time in Europe. I could almost hear the tick-tock of a clock in the distance, a constant reminder that the world we'd come to know was hurtling towards an abrupt end.

I'd have to face Gerard. Kitty would have to leave her daughter's birth-place. How could we return to Seattle such changed women? How could we even pretend to resume our old roles in that foreign place we once called home?

'I think I'm going to stay,' Kitty announced one morning in the mess hall in early June. 'Nurse Hildebrand could use the help. Besides, no one's waiting for me in Seattle.'

I wondered about Kitty's motivation to stay. She had become a shell of her former self. Vacant. Distant. Lost. She devoted herself to work, and spent every spare minute in the infirmary.

'I don't understand,' I said between bites of boiled egg. 'Don't you miss home? Don't you want to leave after . . . everything?'

She forced a smile. 'I thought I'd want to. I'm just not ready.'

I nodded.

'These past months have sure turned out differently for us,' she said, her voice thick with regret. 'But you've met the most marvellous man. To think that you found him out here in the middle of a war.'

As if on cue, Westry waved from the other side of the mess hall. Then, in a breach of protocol, he approached our table. 'Well, if it isn't the two most lovely women on the island,' he said.

'I missed you in the bungalow this morning,' I said. It felt strange to speak openly about our secret, but it didn't matter now that Kitty had been there herself, and besides, there weren't any other diners at the table.

'Westry,' Kitty said, perking up. I didn't like how she batted her eyelashes at him. 'I found some stray floorboards in a closet in the infirmary. I thought they might work to fix that creak in the bungalow's floor.'

My cheeks burned. *How could Kitty think it's her place to talk to Westry about the bungalow? And how in heaven's name does she know, or remember, that the floorboards creak?*

'Thanks, Kitty,' Westry said. 'I'll take a look at them.'

'But—' I opened my mouth and then shut it again.

'What is it?' Westry asked.

'Nothing,' I muttered. 'I was just going to suggest that we meet at the bungalow this evening.'

'I'd love nothing more,' he said. 'I'm off at five thirty.'

'Good,' I said, instantly feeling better.

As Westry turned to leave, Kitty stood up. 'If you'd like to come by this afternoon, I'll be working until eight.' She looked at me awkwardly. 'I mean, if you want to see those floorboards.'

Westry nodded noncommittally and walked out of the building.

We ate in silence for a few minutes, until Kitty spoke again. 'So, as I was saying, I'll probably stay on for a few more months, and then who knows?' Her gaze drifted towards the window. 'Maybe I'll sign up for a post in Europe.'

I watched her mouth open and close and the words pass her lips. *Who is this woman before me?* I searched her eyes, but she looked away.

'**S**omething's wrong with Kitty,' I said that evening, kicking my shoes off as I walked into the bungalow and collapsed on the bed.

'Well, hello to you, too,' Westry said, grinning, tucking a bouquet of hibiscus in my hand.

'Sorry,' I said, marvelling at the blossoms, vibrant yellow—a stark contrast to the red hibiscus that grew like weeds around the base. As far as I knew, they were the only yellow hibiscus on the island, and they grew right here, mere feet from the bungalow. I set the flowers down on the chair and sighed, thinking of Kitty. 'It's just that I'm worried about her. She's changed so much in these past few months. I hardly know her any more.'

Westry pulled out his pocketknife and carefully sliced a red apple on the mahogany desk. 'She *has* changed,' he said. 'Anyone who's gone through what she's gone through would have to. Do you think you might be being too hard on her?'

I nodded. 'You're probably right,' I said, reaching for the slice of apple he held out to me.

'You're not upset about the comment she made about the floorboards, are you?'

'Well, maybe a little. Is it wrong that I feel possessive of this place?'

He grinned, sitting down next to me on the bed. 'No, but I'd rather you feel possessive of me.'

I gave him a playful shove. 'I do, which is why my next question is, did you go to see her at the infirmary today?'

'Yes,' he said, revelling in the discovery of my jealousy. 'And the floorboards were all wrong.'

'Good,' I said. 'I like our floorboards.'

He ran his finger along the nape of my neck. 'Me, too.'

'Besides, new floorboards would mean we'd lose our mailbox.'

'It's unanimous, then. The creaky floorboards stay.' He took the gold locket into his hands and carefully opened it. 'Still empty?'

'I know. I'm trying to think of the perfect thing to put inside.'

'It needs to be something that reminds you of here, of us, that will warm your heart with the memories of our love.'

I frowned, snatching the locket from his hands. 'Memories of our love? You talk as if our days are numbered, as if this is just a—'

'No,' he said, putting his hand to my lips. 'I intend to love you for the rest of my life, but I have another tour of duty ahead. While I'm in Europe, I want to know that you can find me, and this place, in your memories. It will help sustain you while we're apart.' He stood up and searched the room, running his hands along the desk, the woven walls. 'I've got it,' he said, crouching down, prising a tiny piece of wood from an edge of warped floorboard. 'A piece of the bungalow. You can carry it with you always, and with it, there I will be.'

My eyes welled up with tears as he opened the locket and placed the piece, just a mere splinter, inside. It was *perfect*.

**S**hortly after the sun set, Westry lit a candle on the desk. We huddled together just listening to the breeze and the crickets chirping in the moonlight, until a startling sound caught our attention.

A man's voice, angry and determined, followed by a woman's desperate scream deep in the jungle brush. I clutched Westry's arm. 'What do you think that is?'

'I don't know.' He stood up. 'I think she's in trouble. Stay here.'

'Be careful.' I didn't know what worried me more—Westry going out there by himself or me staying in the bungalow alone.

He slipped through the door. I stood up and swallowed hard, wishing I had some sort of weapon. I couldn't just stay in the bungalow and wait, I decided.

Quietly, I stepped outside. My heart pounded. I sensed danger lurking. Something evil was in our presence.

Another scream rang out, this one near the beach.

'No, no, please, please no hurt me, please!'

I knew that voice. *Atea*. Lance must have followed her. *Where is Westry?* I pushed through the brush to the clearing on the beach and saw the scene that would be burnt in my memory for ever.

In the shroud of darkness, it was difficult to make out faces, but he held her by a clump of her hair; I could see that. Then a flash of steel shone in the moonlight. God, no. A knife. He sliced the blade along her neck, and I watched, mute, as her small, limp body fell to the sand. *No, this can't be.*

The shadowy figure tossed the knife deep into the jungle, before pitching a jog down the beach. I ran to Atea, choking back tears.

'Atea, I'm so sorry, I'm so sorry.' I lifted her blood-soaked head onto my lap. She gurgled and choked for breath.

'He—he—' she sputtered.

'No, honey,' I whispered. 'Don't try to say anything.'

Blood pooled in her mouth. She gestured to her belly, swollen, round. *She's pregnant.* 'Westry!' I screamed.

I heard footsteps approach from the direction in which Lance had left, and I prayed he wasn't coming to finish the job. 'Westry!'

'I'm here,' he said. 'It's me.'

'Oh, Westry! Look at what he's done to her. And to her baby.'

Atea lifted her hand in the air, as if to reach for something.

'She's not going to make it,' he said.

Atea's breathing was reduced to sporadic gasps. 'Of course she's going to make it. She has to.'

Westry put his hand on my arm. 'Anne, her neck is half-severed. The best we can do for her is ease her pain, end her misery.'

Holding Atea's dying body in my arms, I knew it was the only choice. 'Go grab my bag under the desk,' I said. 'Hurry!'

He returned with my knapsack and pulled out the supply of morphine that every nurse kept on hand in wartime. There was enough to sedate a 280-pound man, or to send a 100-pound woman to the gates of heaven.

I kissed Atea's forehead, and injected the first dose in her arm, trying to be calm for her sake. 'There. The pain will be over soon.'

Her breathing slowed to shallow gurgles. When I injected the second dose, her eyes turned to the stars, then fluttered and shut. I checked her pulse, and then pressed my ear to her heart.

'She's gone,' I said, tears streaming down my face. Westry slid Atea's limp body onto the soft sand, and helped me to my feet. 'How could he do this to her?' I cried. 'We have to find him, Westry. We have to take him to the colonel. He needs to pay for what he did.'

Westry stroked my face. I felt tears on my cheeks, and he wiped them away. 'Listen to me,' he said softly. 'What we saw was tragic. But I need you to believe me when I tell you that we can never speak of what we saw—not to anyone.'

I shook my head. 'A murder was committed; we must report it. We can bring him to justice.'

'We can't.' His voice sounded strange, thick with defeat. 'For one, an assault was committed . . . We committed the murder.'

'No, that's not true.'

'It's how it would be viewed. And there's something far worse that could become of us, of those we love, if this secret gets out.'

*What does he know? What is he hiding?*

'This makes no sense,' I said. 'How can I go back to the base knowing there's a murderer on the loose?'

He searched my eyes. 'Will you trust me?'

I held up my hands in confusion. 'Westry, I just, I—'

'Promise you won't say anything. One day you'll understand.'

I looked at Westry's strong, steady face. No matter how uncertain his plan seemed, I trusted him. If he said this was the right course of action, I had to believe it. 'I won't say anything,' I said.

'Good,' he said, stroking my cheek. 'We'll have her buried by sunrise.'

# CHAPTER 9

IT WASN'T A GRAVE WORTHY of her short, beautiful life, but we laid Atea to rest forty feet behind the bungalow under a plumeria tree. Fortunately, we had a shovel, Westry had brought one over a week prior in hopes of resetting one of the bungalow's foundation beams. It took him an hour to dig the grave. I slipped away to the beach when I could no longer stomach the gritty sound of the shovel hitting the dirt again and again.

Once my feet hit the sand, I collapsed to my knees. Never in my life had I seen such horror. I replayed the scene in my mind over and over, hoping to find some clue, some frame I'd missed, which is when I remembered the knife.

Lance had thrown it into the brush. I remembered the flash of steel in the moonlight. If I could find the knife, I could at least secure proof that he did it.

I ran to the bungalow and retrieved the lantern, then cautiously walked to the edge of the jungle. Animals howled and snickered in the distance. The wind rustled the bushes. I considered turning back, but I found my strength. *Atea. Remember Atea.*

I nodded to myself and took one step forward, and then another. I shone the lantern farther down the path. A snake slithered by, too near for my liking. I looked back towards the beach and tried to mentally calculate the distance the knife may have travelled. I eyed a large palm to my left, moving my search there. It had to be near.

But after several more minutes I wondered if the jungle may have swallowed up the knife, a co-conspirator in the gruesome crime. I leaned against the palm and set the lantern down, and when I did, it made a little clinking sound.

I knelt down and immediately noticed a familiar shimmer of metal. My hands trembled as I pulled the bloodied knife from the soil, inching the lantern closer to read the inscription on the army-green handle: *Unit #432; Issue #098.*

'Anne? Anne, where are you?' Westry's voice filtered through the thicket. What would he think of me searching for the knife after I promised to trust him?

'Anne?' His voice was near now. I reached down to the edge of my dress and ripped off a piece of the blue linen. Quickly, I wrapped the knife, dug a deep crevice, and tucked the blade inside.

'Oh, there you are,' he said. 'I was worried. Come on. I know this has been a hard night, but we need to'—he paused to find the right words—'see it through.'

I nodded and followed Westry back to the makeshift grave, where I waited while he went to get Atea. He returned with her in his arms, and tears streamed down my face again at the sight.

He set her body in the hole, and we both stared in silence. After a few minutes, Westry reached for the shovel.

I pulled his arm back. 'Not yet.' I picked three pink plumeria blossoms from the tree, then knelt. 'She deserves flowers,' I said.

I scattered the blooms across Atea's body, then looked away as Westry began shovelling the earth over her.

The next night, after dinner, I spotted Westry on the other side of the mess hall, laughing with Ted and a few other men. *How can he be so jovial after what we went through just hours before?*

I carried my tray to the kitchen, and waited for him outside.

'Hi,' he said when his eyes met mine. We walked a few paces together, towards the marina. 'How are you doing?' he whispered when the other men were out of earshot.

'Not good,' I said. 'I keep having memories from last night and praying that it was only a nightmare. Westry, tell me it was all a nightmare.'

He pulled my head close to his. 'I wish I could.'

'Have you seen Lance?' I whispered.

'No,' he said, looking around uncomfortably. 'He shipped out this morning, on a special mission.'

'Sounds to me like he's running away,' I huffed.

'We can't talk about this any more. It's too dangerous.'

I nodded. 'Will I see you tonight at the bungalow?'

Westry rubbed his forehead. 'I wish I could, but I'm working late, and after last night . . . I guess I could use the solitude.'

*Solitude?* 'Oh,' I said, visibly hurt.

Westry tried to lighten the moment. 'I only mean that we're both operating on such little sleep, it would make sense to turn in early.'

'You're right,' I said, still smarting.

'Besides, are you really ready to go back there?'

Yes, horror had infiltrated our private world, but I couldn't shake the feeling that Westry was giving up on the bungalow, on us. 'I don't know. What we had there was beautiful, and I don't want to lose it.'

'Neither do I,' he said.

It was a week before I stepped foot in the bungalow, and I did so alone. Westry had joined some of the men on a construction project on the other side of the island. He'd been vague about when he'd return. But as the days ebbed on, I felt the bungalow drawing me back, and after a particularly long shift in the infirmary, which the women spent huddled over a tiny radio listening to the latest on the fight heating up again in the Pacific, I succumbed to its call.

It was dusk when I set out, and I clutched my locket as I made my way up the shore. I pushed past the brush, but took a step back when my eyes detected a figure sitting on the step of the bungalow. The figure stood and began to walk towards me. It was Tita.

'Anne,' she said.

My heart pounded. The old woman's face looked tired and anguished. 'Would you like to come in?' I said.

She looked at the hut with eyes that told me she'd been inside, perhaps a long time ago. She shook her head. 'Maybe you don't remember what I told you about this place,' she muttered. 'It's cursed.' She pointed to the beach and I followed, unsure of what was in store.

'Sit,' she said, gesturing at a spot not far from where Atea had clung to life. I was grateful the waves had washed away the bloodstained sand.

We sat in silence for a few minutes until Tita finally spoke.

'I know she is gone,' she said.

I looked out at the surf, letting the soothing ebb and flow of the waves numb my heartache.

'I warned you,' she said, scowling. 'This place is evil. It's no good. And now it took my Atea. She was special, you know.'

Tears seeped from my lids. 'Oh, Tita,' I cried. 'I'm so sorry.'

'Hush,' the old woman said, standing. 'What's done is done. Now it is your duty to make justice.'

I watched, bewildered, as she made her way towards the jungle. 'Tita. Please, wait. You're wrong. If you think that I, that we—'

'Justice,' she said, turning towards me a final time, 'is the only way you will ever break the curse.'

I watched her walk into the thicket until the jungle seemed to swallow her whole. I rose and walked to the bungalow, unlocking its door with the familiar motions, stowing the key back in the book. The air inside felt thick and suffocating.

I reached for a piece of paper and pen on the desk, and sat to write Westry a letter, my heart racing at what I was about to record:

*My dear Grayson,*

*I wish you were here now, to take me into your arms, to erase my memory of the horrors I have seen.*

*I have a plan. We've only spoken of the future in vague terms, but after the war, after this is all over, perhaps we can go to the military superiors and report the crime. Perhaps the hesitation you feel will be remedied by time. I*

*have evidence, something that will clear our names from any wrongdoing*
*when the time is right. My dear, please tell me when the time is right.*

*But, there's something else. By now you know of my love for you, and I*
*want you to know that there is nothing else I'd rather do than share my life,*
*share eternity, with you—right here on this island if that's what you want.*
*My love, I am yours, if you ask me to be.*

*Love, for ever and always,*

*Cleo*

Two days later, Kitty, seated on her bed, looked up, startled. 'Did you hear something hit the window?'

It was half past three. We'd all been ordered to the barracks after a Japanese warship was detected two miles offshore.

I shook my head. 'I didn't hear anything.'

One of the nurses said the ship was en route to another destination. Another said that a soldier had confirmed by its coordinates that it was heading dead on to Bora-Bora. War here? On our island? Our only option was to watch and wait.

'There's a cellar,' I said, 'below the barracks. Stella thinks we'll be moved down there in the event of—'

Kitty flinched. 'There,' she said, 'that sound. I heard it again.' She stood up and walked to the window. 'See?' She grinned. 'It's Westry. He must have been trying to get our attention.'

*Our attention?* I watched Kitty waving down at Westry.

'I'll go and see him,' I said possessively, walking out of the door and briskly down the stairs to the entrance.

'Hi,' I whispered once outside.

Westry grinned. 'Why the whisper?'

'Don't you know? The island may be under attack.'

Westry looked at me with an amused grin. 'I love your spirit, you know that? Come here, let me see you.'

I lingered in his embrace for longer than was proper for the base, but somehow decorum seemed insignificant now. 'You seem overly confident,' I sparred back.

He shrugged. 'After you've been through a fight like I've been through, a battleship on the horizon doesn't ruffle your feathers, I guess.' Westry caressed my chin, tracing my profile with his finger until tingles ran down my back. 'Let's go to the bungalow,' he whispered into my neck.

'We've been ordered to stay in the barracks,' I protested weakly.

Westry looked at me with his big hazel eyes. 'But it may be our last time in the bungalow together before . . .'

I squeezed his hand. 'OK,' I said. I frowned, remembering the beating Colonel Donahue had unleashed on Westry in the barracks, then hesitated. 'Will you get in trouble for this?'

'Probably,' he said, his eyes sparkling. 'But I don't care.'

I glanced up to the first floor, where Kitty lingered at the window. I gestured towards the beach and waved, hoping she'd understand. But she turned quickly without so much as a smile.

Westry unlocked the door to the bungalow, and we exhaled deeply once inside. 'I feel like we're fugitives,' I said.

'I suppose we are,' he replied, resting his hands on my waist.

'Westry, a few days ago Tita was here, the old woman Atea lived with. She seems to know about Atea.'

'How could she?'

'I don't know. But she warned me again about the bungalow's curse. She said justice was the only way to break the cycle of the curse.'

Westry frowned. 'What she and you don't realise is that with justice comes something far worse than the guilt we may carry with us.' He sat down on the old mahogany chair. For the first time, I detected the weight of the secret in his eyes. He didn't want to keep it any more than I did; yet he was holding to his convictions. 'How can I make you understand that we can't seek justice? Not the kind you want, anyway.'

I nodded, reaching for his hand. It felt wrong to argue on what could be our final night together. I poked my head out of the front window and could make out the battleship in the distance. 'It's still there,' I said.

He pulled me closer, and I remembered the letter I'd left, with my confessions about the future. *Does he want to spend a lifetime with me, too?* I sighed nervously. 'Did you get my letter?'

'No, my love. I haven't been here in days.' He began walking to the floorboard to retrieve his mail, but I pulled him back.

'Not yet,' I said. 'When we leave. I want you to read it alone.'

'Is it bad news?'

'No, no,' I said. 'Just wait. You'll see.'

He nodded, pulling my body tight against his. He flipped on the little radio on the desk, and the French station came through again, crystal clear. 'Let's not think about anything else but our love,' he said.

'OK,' I whispered, and for a moment, the bungalow was ours again, ours alone.

**W**estry kissed my cheek shortly after the sun went down. 'It's probably time we started back,' he said. I could sense his anxiety building, and it worried me. I didn't know whether it was the enemy in our midst that gave him pause or what we both knew and dreaded—that our time together was coming to an end.

'We probably should.' I smoothed my dress and refastened a pin in my hair. 'Don't forget your letter,' I said as he opened the door.

'Of course,' he replied, kneeling down to the floorboard and reaching inside. 'Wait, what letter? There's no letter here.'

'Silly,' I said, kneeling down next to him. 'Of course there is. Maybe I pushed it back too far.' I wedged my hand deeper behind the joists, but was horrified to find the space empty. 'My God. It's gone.'

'What do you mean? No one knows about our hiding place. Unless you told someone.'

'Of course I didn't,' I said, confused.

A light flashed in the ocean. 'We'll have to figure this out later,' Westry said. 'I need to get you back.'

The door creaked to a close, and Westry locked it ceremoniously. 'We'll head back through the trail in the jungle,' he said. 'It'll be safer.'

I nodded, taking his hand. As we walked through the thicket, I thought about the letter. *Who could have taken it, and why?* Now, with so little time left, I needed Westry to know my true feelings. But as he walked me to the women's barracks, something else haunted me. 'Westry,' I whispered, in a panic, 'we have to go back. We left the painting there.'

'We can get it later.'

'No, no. Whoever took the letter could take the painting.'

Westry looked concerned, then shook his head. 'No. Whoever may have taken the letter could have taken the painting, but they didn't.'

'I have a bad feeling about this,' I said. 'The painting belongs in a museum somewhere, where it can be admired and treasured.'

'And we'll make sure it gets there. Just as soon as this ship passes. I promise. I'll bring it back for you.'

'You promise?'

'Yes,' he said, kissing my nose.

I turned to the barracks. 'Be careful,' I said.

'There you are!' Nurse Hildebrand whispered in the hallway. 'I don't have time to hear your explanation, nor do I have time to discipline you, so I will just say that you are the last of the nurses to make it to the cellar. The Japanese are coming. The colonel gave orders for the women to go under. We must hurry.'

My heart raced. As I followed her, I patted the place on my dress where I'd fastened the blue rose pin Kitty gave me in Seattle. I'd worn it on a whim that morning and gasped when I realised it was gone. *How could I be so careless?* I imagined it lying on the beach. *Is it a sign of the end of our friendship?*

Nurse Hildebrand pulled up a rug and prised open a hinge in the floor. 'You first,' she said, pointing to a dark cavern below.

I descended a ladder into a shadowy space where a few lanterns flickered. When my feet hit the floor, I could make out Liz and Stella, and some of the others in the distance. 'Kitty?' I called out. 'Are you here?'

Only silence answered back. 'She's over there,' Nurse Hildebrand said, pointing to the light of a single lantern in the far right corner.

'Kitty,' I said, walking towards her until I could make out her small, frightened face, wayward curls springing out in disarray.

She sat against the wall, looking despondent. 'I was worried you weren't coming,' she said, wiping away a tear.

I sat down beside her and squeezed her hand. 'I'm here now.'

No one knew what was happening above. After two hours, or what felt like twelve, Nurse Hildebrand enlisted Stella to pass out rations, water, and beans in tin cans. Enough to last days, even weeks. I thought about the prospect of living in the dark, eating canned Spam, and I shuddered.

'Here,' said Stella, offering me a canteen. I took a swig and swallowed hard. It tasted of rust.

We all froze when we heard footsteps on the floor above.

'Nurses,' Nurse Hildebrand whispered, reaching for a rifle on the wall, 'put out your lanterns.'

We listened in the darkness as the footsteps grew closer, louder. There was a thud, and the creak of the trap door opening. I squeezed Kitty's hand harder. Dear Lord. The Japanese are here.

But instead of a foreign accent, a familiar voice rang out. 'Nurses, it's all clear. The ships turned west. You can come out.'

The women let out a cheer—all but Kitty, who just stared ahead. 'Come on, dear,' I said. 'It's over. We can go now.'

She turned on her lantern, and I could detect the familiar cloudiness in her eyes. The distance. 'Yes, of course,' she said.

'Can you believe we ship out tomorrow?' Liz marvelled at breakfast the next day.

*Tomorrow.* I'd been dreading this day since the moment I fell in love with Westry.

'The men ship out in the morning,' Stella added. She didn't like that Will was joining the fight in Europe any more than I liked that Westry was. 'If I went to serve in Europe, I'd at least be closer to him. In case—'

I shook my head. The war had taken its toll on Stella, who was now shockingly thin. She needed leave more than any of us. 'Going to Europe won't protect him. Go home. Wait for him there.'

She nodded. 'Can you believe Kitty? I hear she's heading to France, right in the middle of the action. She's joining a group headed for Normandy.'

My cheeks flushed. France? *Why didn't she tell me?*

'Well, speaking of the devil,' Stella said, pointing to the door.

Kitty walked in, smiling. Her cheeks looked rosy, the way they once had. She was holding a cluster of yellow hibiscus, and my cheeks burned at the sight.

''Morning, ladies. How are the rations today?'

'Fine,' Liz said, 'if you like rubberised eggs.'

Kitty set the flowers, tied in a white ribbon, on the table. 'Aren't they beautiful?' she said, admiring their yellow petals against the sterile beige tabletop. I knew them instantly—the hibiscus that grew near the bungalow. They had to be.

'Well, well,' Stella said. 'It looks like someone has an admirer.'

'Oh, Stell,' Kitty said, playing coy.

'Then where did you get them?' she said relentlessly. I wished she'd stop. I didn't want to know.

Kitty grinned and twirled round towards the buffet line, leaving us to our imaginations. I stood up abruptly and walked to the door.

Outside on the path to the barracks, my heart pounded as I thought of the way Kitty lit up whenever Westry appeared, the way she'd pulled back from me. *Of course she feels something for him.*

I froze for a moment. *Could he share her attraction?* My mind raced. *The letter. My God. He didn't seem at all concerned about someone taking it. Did he pretend it had been stolen so he wouldn't have to face my declaration of love, my hope for a future together?*

'That's it,' Kitty said the next morning after breakfast, sighing. She bent over to zip up her bag. 'My flight leaves in an hour. Nurse Hildebrand and I will meet up with a squadron flying into France tomorrow.'

*Kitty in France. All by herself.* I hated the thought of it, just like I had hated the thought of her coming here, to the South Pacific, alone. It didn't matter what I thought of her feelings for Westry. Somewhere, beyond the layers of emotional scars, resided my best friend. But this time I wouldn't insist on going with her.

'Oh, Kitty!' I cried, leaping to my feet. 'Why did things turn out the way they did for us?'

Kitty shrugged, reaching for her bag. She looked at me for a long moment. 'The island had its way, I guess,' she finally muttered.

'No, you have it wrong,' I said, hearing the panic in my voice. 'Kitty, I haven't changed. I'm still the same old Anne. And I'd wager that you're still the same old Kitty in your heart. I want nothing more than to go on being Anne and Kitty.'

She looked at me with eyes I didn't recognise. They were tired and older, hardened. 'I wish that, too. But I don't think we can now.'

I nodded, feeling tears spill out unbidden on my cheeks.

'Goodbye, Anne.' Kitty's tone was businesslike. I felt the urge to scream at her to stop, to end this charade, but I could only stand there, too stunned, too sad to open my mouth. 'I wish you the best of luck,' she said, reaching for the door handle. 'With everything.'

The door clicked closed, and the silence in the room pulsed. I fell to the floor, sobbing into my hands. *What right does she have to declare our friendship over? How could she behave so coldly?*

When the clock told me it was eleven, I willed myself to stand. I'd promised Westry a farewell on the tarmac, and his flight left in a half-hour, just after mine. I glanced in the mirror at my red, swollen eyes. I hardly recognised myself.

For a moment, I feared I wouldn't find him. I looked out at the thick and frenzied crowd of men, awash in army green. A small cohort would stay on the island, but the majority had been selected for new assignments. France. Great Britain. I squinted, scanning faces, and then towards the edge of the crowd, our eyes met.

Ignoring the orders over the loudspeaker for the nurses to begin boarding, I set my bag down by Stella and ran to Westry. He lifted me into his arms, and we kissed. 'Don't cry, my love,' he said, wiping a tear from my cheek. 'This isn't goodbye.'

'But we don't know what will happen out there.'

Westry pulled a nosegay of yellow hibiscus from his bag and tucked it into my hand. A white ribbon tied the blooms in place.

'These flowers,' I stammered. 'You gave the same ones to Kitty yesterday, didn't you?'

Westry looked confused, then nodded. 'Well, yes. I was—'

Another voice piped through the loudspeaker. 'All men proceed to board.'

'Westry,' I said, feeling panicked. 'Is there something you need to tell me? Something about Kitty?'

He looked to his feet momentarily and then back at me. 'It's nothing, but I should have told you. A few weeks ago, I found her weeping on the beach. I was on the way to the bungalow, and I invited her to join me.'

*Our bungalow? Alone, without me?* 'Why didn't you tell me?'

'I'm sorry, Anne. I really didn't think anything of it.'

I turned to glance at the plane that would take me home. Stella was standing beside it waving her arms frantically at me.

I took a final look at Westry. The wind had tousled his hair. I longed to run my hands through the sandy blond strands the way I'd done a hundred times in the bungalow, to take in the scent of his skin, to surrender myself to him. But something told me no.

'Goodbye,' I whispered in his ear, letting my cheek brush his a final time. I reached for his hand and placed the flowers in his palm before running towards the plane.

'Anne, wait!' he shouted. 'The painting. Did you get it?'

I froze. 'I thought you were going to get it.'

He threw his hands in the air. 'I'm sorry. There just wasn't time.'

His unit had boarded, and I could see his commanding officer walking towards him. My legs felt as though they'd been strapped with lead as I climbed the steps to the plane. Before the pilot's assistant pulled the hatch shut, my eyes met Westry's. I couldn't hear him over the airplane's engine, but I could read his lips.

'I'm so sorry,' he said. 'I'll come back. Please don't worry. I—'

The door slammed shut before I could interpret his last words. What did it matter, I reasoned, blotting my tears with a handkerchief. It was over. The magic we'd found in the bungalow was gone, and I could feel its spell lifting as the plane gained speed and altitude. I watched as the island grew smaller, until it appeared a mere dot on a map. A dot where so much had happened.

Stella leaned over to me. 'Will you miss it?'

I nodded. 'Yes,' I said honestly.

'Will and I have talked about returning for a visit. When the war's over.'

I looked out again, unable to take my eyes off the speck of emerald floating in the turquoise sea. 'I don't think I ever will.'

# CHAPTER 10

'WE MISSED YOU, KID,' Papa said as I climbed into the car, grateful not to see Maxine in the back seat. Even with months to process the affair that had destroyed my family, I still couldn't make sense of it.

I sighed, leaning back into the soft leather as Papa started the Buick. 'It's good to be home,' I said, taking in a deep breath of the temperate Seattle air.

'Gerard's home,' Papa said a little cautiously, testing the waters.

I looked at my hands in my lap, hands that had loved Westry, still loved Westry. Hands of betrayal. 'Does he want to see me?'

'Of course he does, sweetheart. Perhaps the real question is, do you want to see him?'

He could read my heart. He always could. 'I don't know, Papa,' I said, beginning to weep. 'I don't know what I want any more.'

'Come here, honey,' he said. I inched closer to him in the front seat, and he draped a firm arm round me, one that told me that despite everything, I would be fine. I only wished I could believe it.

**W**indermere looked untouched by time, by war. As we passed the familiar estates, however, I knew that appearances were deceiving. The Larson home still had its beautiful lawn with elaborate urns, yet heartache clung to every wall, every surface. The twins weren't coming home. Terry had died in a fight near Marseilles, Larry in a plane crash two days later.

The Godfrey mansion also kept up appearances. As we drove past, I held my breath, remembering the engagement party, Kitty's face, and how we'd sat on the kerb outside making plans for the future. The memories pierced, and I looked away quickly.

'He came home on Friday,' Papa said. 'Got sent home a bit early on medical leave.'

I stiffened. '*Medical* leave?'

'He took a bullet to the shoulder. He may never regain functionality in his left arm, but in the scheme of war wounds, that's no tragedy.'

Waves of emotion rolled through me. Papa was right. Boys were getting maimed, dying. Gerard's injury hardly compared, but for some reason the news made me grieve in a way I hadn't expected.

'Don't cry, dear. He's going to be fine. It's hard to take, I know.'

'This war,' I cried, 'it's changed everything, all of us.'

'It's true,' Papa said solemnly, pulling the car into the driveway.

Everything was the same, of course, just as I'd left it. But it wasn't; I knew that. And I could never get it back to the way it had been.

**I** heard a muffled knock on my bedroom door. I sat up and tried to get my bearings. The old lace curtains. The big trundle bed. Yes, I was home.

I pulled the blanket tighter round my body and ignored the knock that sounded again, this one a bit louder. I couldn't face Maxine. Not yet. Moments later, a slip of paper slid under the door. I tried to ignore it, but it seemed to pulse, to flash like a bright light.

*My dear Antoinette,*
  *I know you are hurting. Please let me comfort you.*
  *Maxine*

I slowly opened the door, far enough to see Maxine in the hallway outside, her hair pulled back in the usual fashion. An apron, pressed neatly, encircled her waist. She held a tray. A single pink rose rested inside a glass bud vase, and puffs of steam seeped from an ivory mug. I could smell the Earl Grey.

I released my grasp on the doorknob. 'Oh, Maxine!' I cried.

She set the tray down on my bedside table and took me into her arms. The tears erupted with volcanic power, first in little spurts, then in great big heaves, pouring out of my heart, my soul, with such ferocity, I wondered if they'd ever stop.

'Let it all out,' she whispered. 'Don't hold back.'

When the tears had subsided, Maxine handed me a handkerchief and the cup of tea, and I leaned against the headboard, tucking my knees to my chest under my pink cotton nightgown.

'You don't have to talk,' she said softly.

I looked into her eyes and could see anguish residing there.

'I'm so sorry,' she said, 'about the letter I sent. I should have let your father tell you. It wasn't my place.'

I reached for her hand. Her fingers felt cold. 'You have always been honest with me,' I said. 'You were right to send it.'

'Will you forgive me? Will you ever love me the way you once did?'

I took a deep breath. 'I never stopped loving you, Maxine.'

The next day, around two, I heard Gerard's car pull into the driveway, followed by the sound of his steps on the porch. Papa had said he was coming. I froze. *What will I say to him? How will I act?* I smoothed my hair and walked to the top of the stairs, composing myself.

*One step, and then two.* I could hear him in the parlour talking to Papa. *Three, four.* The voices stopped. *Five, six.* And there he was, standing at the base of the stairs, looking up at me with such love, such intensity, that I could not unlock my gaze. 'Anne!' he said.

'Gerard!' My voice cracked a little. His left arm rested in a sling.

'Well, are you going to just stand there or are you going to kiss this wounded soldier?'

I sailed down the final steps, welcoming his embrace before planting a light kiss on his cheek, operating on instincts, or muscle memory.

Gerard took my hand and led me to the sofa in the living room before closing the double doors with his good arm. 'I can't tell you how much I've missed you,' he said, sitting down beside me.

I'd forgot how handsome he was, shockingly so. 'I'm sorry I didn't write often,' I said, frowning.

'It's all right,' he replied lovingly. 'I knew you were busy.'

'Your arm.' I touched his shoulder gently, then retracted my hand in haste. 'Oh, Gerard. Papa says you may never use it again.'

He shrugged. 'I should have died out there,' he said. 'All the men around me were shot down. I can't make any sense out of why I was spared.' He reached for my hands, and then paused, holding up my left hand, bare without the engagement ring.

'Gerard, I—'

He shook his head. 'You don't need to explain,' he said. 'Just having you here, having you back is good enough for now.'

I let my head rest on his shoulder.

**September 1944**

'Can you believe I'm getting married?' I said, admiring the white silk gown Mother had shipped from France before the war broke out.

'You look beautiful, Antoinette,' Maxine said. 'We'll just have the seamstress take it in a bit. Have you been losing weight?'

I shrugged. 'It's nerves, that's all.' The phone rang in the kitchen. 'I'll get that,' I said. 'It's probably Gerard.'

When I said hello, static crackled over the line. 'Anne?' a familiar female voice spoke. 'Anne, is that you? It's me, Mary.'

I gasped. 'Mary! How are you?'

'I'm fine. I'm calling with some bad news, I'm afraid.'

The blood left my face. *Mary. Bad news.* 'What is it?'

'I'm in Paris. I'm here on account of Edward, but that's for another conversation. You've probably heard about the liberation of the city. What you need to know is that today at the army hospital I saw Kitty.'

I had thought of Kitty often, and now the mention of her inflamed the familiar wound in my heart. 'Mary, is she OK?'

'Yes,' she said. 'She's fine. But, Anne . . . Anne, it's Westry. He got hit. He was part of the 4th Infantry Division, the men who stormed the city. Most died. He held on, but it isn't good.'

'My God, Mary, how bad is it? Is he conscious?' The line began to crackle again. 'Mary, are you still there?'

'Yes,' she said. 'I'm here.' Her voice sounded garbled and more distant. 'You need to come. You need to see him, before—'

'But how?' I cried. 'Travel is restricted, especially to Europe.'

'I know a way. Do you have a pen and paper?'

I fumbled in a drawer and pulled out a notepad. 'I'm ready.'

'Take down this code,' she said. 'A5691G9NQ. It's a Foreign Service travel code. You can use it to board a ship leaving from New York to Paris in four days. And when you arrive, come to my apartment: 349 Saint Germain.'

I scrawled down the address. 'You really think this will work?'

'If you run into trouble, mention the name Edward Naughton.'

I clutched the receiver, trying to hold on to the connection. 'Thank you.' But the line had been swallowed up by static. Mary was gone.

'Gerard, I need to tell you something,' I said that night at dinner. I pushed my plate aside.

'You've hardly touched your food,' he said, frowning.

He looked dapper seated across the table from me in a grey suit. The war had rendered the Cabaña Club a ghost town without the buzz of people and the fog of cigarette smoke. A lone saxophonist played on the stage. I swallowed hard.

'What is it, my love?' He dabbed his mouth with a white napkin.

I took a deep breath. 'While I was in the South Pacific, there was a man. I—I . . .'

Gerard closed his eyes tightly. 'Don't tell me. Please don't.'

I nodded. 'I understand. But there's something I need to do, before the wedding. I need to go away. Just for a while.'

Gerard looked pained, but he didn't protest. 'When you return, will you be yourself again?'

I looked deep into his eyes. 'It's why I need to go. To find out.'

He looked away. My words had hurt him, and I hated that. 'Anne,' he said, his voice faltering. 'If this is what it takes. If there's a chance I can have your whole heart again, I will wait.'

It was late when the train pulled into Grand Central Terminal. The city lights glistened. It was hard to imagine Mother making her home in this big, bold place so unlike Seattle.

A taxi took me to 560 East 57th Street. My eyes blurred as I gazed out of the window. Lights flashed—green, red, pink, yellow. Sailors on leave in stark white uniforms clung to women—blondes, brunettes, tall ones, short ones. The war hadn't ended, but the tide had turned. You could feel it.

The cab stopped. I paid the fare, and the cabby pointed to a brick town house. I rang the doorbell, and moments later Mother appeared. It was almost eleven, but she stood in the doorway in full make-up and a red off-the-shoulder dress. A poorly balanced martini glass sloshed in her hand.

'Anne!' Mother cried, pulling me towards her. 'Let me look at you.' Her eyes pored over me, then she nodded in approval. 'The South Pacific was kind to you, dear. Why, you must have lost ten pounds.'

I smiled. 'Well, I—'

'Come in! Come in!' She turned, and her red dress swished ahead. I followed, lugging my bag. 'It's not Windermere,' she said, 'but it's home now. I've grown to love city life.' She led me into a small front room with parquet floors and a Victorian sofa. 'Of course, I'm having it all redone. Leon is helping me with that.'

'Leon?'

'My interior decorator,' she said, taking a long sip from her glass. I didn't remember Mother liking martinis in Seattle, nor did I remember her collarbones protruding from her chest. 'He's insisted on mauve for this room, but I rather fancy a shade of teal.'

'Teal might be a little bold for this room,' I said honestly.

'That's just the look I'm going for, dear,' she said, running her hand along a wall. 'Bold. Your father was so traditional.'

I nodded.

'Listen to me going on like this,' she said, reaching for a bell on a side table. 'You must be exhausted, dear. I'll ring for Minnie.'

She sounded the bell, and a small woman, no older than me, materialised moments later. 'Minnie, be a dear and show Anne to her room.' Mother caressed my cheek. 'Good night, my dearest. I know you can't stay long, but I have the morning packed with fun before your departure. Go get some rest, sweetheart.'

The sound of a horn outside my second-floor window woke me the next morning. I glanced at the clock; it was barely 6.40, but I got up and dressed anyway. I wanted to spend as much time with Mother as possible before I boarded the ship.

The light shone through the windows downstairs. 'Good morning, miss,' Minnie said shyly from the entrance to the kitchen. 'May I make you coffee or tea?'

'Tea would be lovely, Minnie, thank you,' I said, smiling.

Moments later she appeared with a cup of tea on a tray with a plate with fruit, a croissant, and a boiled egg.

I eyed the tray. 'Shouldn't I wait for Mother?'

Minnie looked conflicted. 'About that . . . It's just that, well . . . Mr Schwartz was here last night,' she said nervously.

'Minnie, do you mean Leon?'

'Yes, ma'am,' she said. 'He arrived after you turned in.'

'Oh. And is he still here?'

She looked at her feet. 'When he comes to stay, I often don't see her until after twelve, sometimes one.'

I nodded, trying my best not to show the disappointment I felt. 'Then I'll take my breakfast right here. Thank you.'

An hour later, I stepped onto the street. I had five hours before I needed to make my way to the dock to board the ship. I hailed a cab, unsure of my destination. 'Where to, miss?' the driver asked.

'I don't know,' I said. 'I only have a few hours in the city. Do you have any suggestions?'

He smiled, revealing a gold tooth. 'You like art?'

'Yes,' I said. 'I do.'

'Then I'll take you to the Metropolitan Museum of Art.'

Minutes later, I stood before the great stone building, with its enormous columns flanking the entrance. I climbed the steps to the double doors, walking inside to an information booth. Paintings by French artists were all upstairs on the east wing.

Aside from a security guard near the west wall, the floor was empty. I moved from painting to painting, reading the placards: Monet, Cézanne, and others whose names I didn't recognise. When I'd scoured the entire room, I sat down, defeated, on a bench.

'Excuse me, miss.' I looked up to see the security guard walking towards me. 'May I help you find something?'

I smiled. 'Oh, it's nothing. I had a silly idea that I'd find the work of a certain artist here. But I was wrong.'

He tilted his head. 'What artist?'

'Paul Gauguin.'

'Well, we do have some of his work.' The man pointed to a door. 'The wing is closed for maintenance, but, seeing how much you're interested, I might be able to open it up. I have the key.'

I beamed. 'Could you?'

I followed him to the door, where he slipped a brass key into the lock. 'Take all the time you need,' he said. 'I'll be right outside.'

I thanked him and let the door close behind me. The wing was small, but the walls were crowded with paintings. At first I didn't know where to begin, but then a canvas caught my eye. A beach scene on the far wall. It looked *familiar*, somehow. I walked closer.

The canvas revealed a yellow hibiscus bush near a thatched-roof bungalow. *Our bungalow.* The silhouette of an island woman lingered on the shore. It looked like a companion to the scene on the canvas in the bungalow—a photograph shot right before the other.

I took a step back, searching for a placard. The wall was blank.

I opened the door and leaned out. The guard walked towards me. 'Do you know if some of the placards have been removed?' I asked. 'There's one painting in particular I'd like to know about.'

The man smiled. 'Let me see if I can help.'

Inside, I pointed to the canvas. 'This is the one.'

'I know this painting,' he said. 'It's very special.'

'Whose is it?'

'Why, Paul Gauguin. The signature is right here.' He pointed to a spot on the lower left. The yellow paint he'd used to sign his name blended in with the hibiscus.

*Of course it was Gauguin. If only Westry were here.*

'And here's another,' the guard said, pointing to a larger canvas featuring a bare-breasted woman with a plumeria blossom in her hair. I gasped when I realised there was a resemblance. *Atea. She's the spitting image of Atea.*

'Do you know when he painted this?'

'It would have been during his time in Tahiti. The early 1890s.'

'Tahiti?'

'Yes, or thereabouts. It's rumoured that he spent time all over the nearby islands. Occasionally some of his work turns up from a ship captain who barters with a local. A priceless painting in exchange for cigarettes.' He shook his head. 'Can you imagine?'

'Do you know anything about his life on the islands?'

'Just that he was reclusive. He lived in little hideaways, mingling with women half his age and often coming into misfortune. He died alone of a syphilitic heart attack. Not a very happy life.'

I nodded, wishing I could transport myself back to the island and retrieve the painting Westry and I had left behind. I'd bring it to the museum and request that it be hung right here, by the other, completing the story one canvas began to tell and the other could finish.

The Foreign Service travel code worked just like Mary said. My hands had trembled at the dock, and a sceptical young soldier had looked me over suspiciously, but at the mention of Edward Naughton, he'd handed me my cabin assignment and waved me on.

On the final day of the voyage, green from seasickness, I began to wonder whether I was making the trip in vain. Even if I did get to see Westry, would he want to see me? It had been more than a year since our strained goodbye on Bora-Bora, and he hadn't called or written. Sure, it would have been difficult, given the intensity of fighting in Europe, but he didn't even try.

From the port of Le Havre, Paris was just a short train ride away. Soon I stood on Mary's street, Saint Germain, looking at a stately stone building. I wondered what kind of life she'd been living here, and I wondered about Edward. *Did the letter change everything? Did he take her back? Was it a happy ending?*

It was late, nearly ten. I proceeded inside, checking the apartment number before knocking. Moments later, I heard footsteps and the sound of a latch opening. 'Anne!' Mary cried. 'You came!'

My eyes filled with tears as I embraced my old friend. 'I have to pinch myself,' I said. 'It hardly seems possible that I *am* here.'

'You must be exhausted,' she said.

I took a deep breath. 'Have you seen Westry recently? Is he . . .'

'I haven't been to the hospital in a few days,' she said quietly. 'But,

Anne, his injuries are serious. He was shot multiple times.'

The air suddenly felt thick. 'I can't bear to lose him, Mary.'

My old friend wrapped her arm round me. 'Come, we'll get you comfortable,' she said. 'Save your tears for tomorrow.'

I followed her inside, where she motioned for me to sit with her on a sofa with gold-plated trim. All around were walls decorated in toile panels. 'It's a beautiful home,' I said, still thinking of Westry.

Mary shrugged. 'I won't be here much longer,' she said, offering no further details. 'Care for a sandwich? A croissant?' I looked at her left hand and noticed that her ring finger was bare. Instinctively, I covered the diamond solitaire on mine, remembering how I'd hidden it away on the island.

'I'm fine,' I said, 'thank you.' *What's different about Mary?* She wore her hair, the colour of tawny hay, in the same fashion. Her smile still hid crooked teeth. But her eyes . . . Deep sadness had taken up residence, and I longed to know the story. 'And Edward?' The second the name escaped my lips, I wished I could retract it.

'There is no Edward,' she said blankly. 'Not any more.' She pulled a handkerchief from the pocket of her dress. 'I'm sorry,' she said. 'I thought I could talk about this with you, but I'm afraid—I'm afraid it's all too painful.'

'Mary,' I said cautiously, 'how is it that you ended up here? Did you come because of . . . the letter I gave you before you left Bora-Bora?'

'If only the answer was that simple,' she said nostalgically. 'No, I was a fool to come here.'

I took her hand in mine, noticing the tiny pink scar on her wrist. Memories of Bora-Bora came rushing back. 'Will you go with me to the hospital tomorrow? I'm terribly nervous about seeing Westry after all this time.'

'Of course I will. You know, Stella's here too.'

'She is?'

'Yes,' she continued. 'She's been here since last month.'

'And Will?'

'He's here too. They're getting married in a month or so.'

'That's wonderful,' I said. 'I'd love to see her.'

'She and Will took a train down south for a few days,' she said. 'She'll be disappointed to have missed you.'

484 | Sarah Jio

'What time should we leave for the hospital in the morning?'

'Visiting hours begin at nine. We can catch a cab over first thing. Now, your room is down the hall—second door on the left. Go and get some rest.' She tried to smile, but her mouth seemed paralysed with grief. 'We'll catch a cab over first thing in the morning.'

I took a final look into the living room before turning down the mahogany-panelled hall towards the bedroom. Mary sat on the sofa, motionless, hands folded in her lap, looking out of the window at the Seine and the shimmer of a liberated Paris.

Something had happened here, inside these walls. Yes, something unspeakable. I could feel it.

The First US General Hospital was the largest in Paris. 'There's been nearly a thousand admits in the last two weeks, and we expect many more,' Mary said, pressing the elevator's eighth-floor button.

As we began our ascent, my mind reeled. 'Oh, Mary,' I said. 'I'm so frightened.'

'It's the right thing to do, coming here,' she said. 'No matter what, you'll have closure.'

I sighed. 'Have you been in touch with Kitty?'

Mary looked uncomfortable for a moment. 'About that,' she said nervously. 'Since I called you, there's been—' The elevator stopped on the fourth floor, and a doctor entered, silencing our conversation.

We stepped off on the eighth floor, and I gasped at the sight. Perhaps three hundred, maybe more, wounded men lay on cots with dark green wool blankets pulled over their limp bodies.

'This is a tough floor,' Mary said. 'A lot of serious cases.'

My heart pounded loudly inside my chest. 'Where is he?' I said.

A nurse approached Mary. 'I thought you were off today.'

'I am,' Mary said. 'I'm here with my friend. She'd like to visit Mr Green.'

The nurse looked at me and then back at Mary. '*Westry* Green?'

'Yes,' Mary said, '*Westry* Green.'

The nurse turned to me. 'And you are?'

'Anne,' I muttered. 'Anne Calloway.'

'Well, I'm not sure that . . .' She sighed. 'I'll check.'

When she was out of earshot, I turned to Mary. 'I don't understand. Why did she act so strange?'

Mary looked anywhere but at my face. 'Let's sit down,' she said, leading me to a bench. 'When I called you, I didn't have all the information. I didn't know that Westry—'

We both looked up when we heard footsteps. My eyes widened. 'Kitty!' I cried, leaping to my feet. Despite the past, I found myself unable to resist the urge to run into the arms of my old friend. But I stopped quickly when my eyes met Kitty's, the eyes of a stranger.

'Hello,' she said stiffly.

Mary rose and stood by my side. 'Kitty,' she said, 'Anne has travelled a great distance to see Westry. I'm hoping we can take her to him.'

Kitty frowned. 'I'm afraid that won't be possible.'

'Why, Kitty?' I cried. 'Is he hurt badly? Is he unconscious?'

Kitty looked at my engagement ring. 'I'm sorry, Anne,' Kitty said coldly. 'I'm afraid the fact of the matter is that Westry doesn't want to see you.'

The room began to spin. 'I don't understand. I—'

'Again, I'm sorry.' Kitty walked away. 'I wish you all the best.'

I watched her disappear behind a curtain. 'Let's go, Anne,' Mary whispered. 'I'm so sorry, dear. It was wrong of me to bring you. I should have explained—'

'Explained what?' I cried. 'That I would be barred from seeing the only man I've ever loved by my best friend?' I listened to my words echoing in the air, surprised by their raw honesty. Gerard may have had my hand, but Westry would always have my heart.

I pushed past Mary and into the room of injured men. Sounds that had been muffled near the elevator now amplified to reveal moaning, babbling, crying. I walked fast through the rows of beds, scanning face after face, praying that just round the corner I'd see his familiar hazel eyes. I combed every aisle.

I looked around the floor frantically, then remembered Kitty slipping behind a curtained area in the distance. I walked across the room, stopping in front of the grey-and-white-striped curtain. My hands trembled as I lifted the edge of the fabric. Four hospital beds lay inside. I gasped when I made out the face of the man in the bed farthest away. *Westry.*

My legs weakened when I saw his face—thinner now, with a shadow of stubble around his chin, but just as handsome, just as perfect. Kitty ran a wet towel over his face, lightly, lovingly, before caressing his forehead. He gazed up at her with a smile that made my cheeks burn.

I heard Mary's voice. 'Anne, don't do this to yourself.'

'But Westry, my Westry!' I cried, releasing the curtain and burying my head against her shoulder. 'How could she, Mary?'

Mary lifted my chin and dabbed my cheeks with a handkerchief. 'I'm so sorry, honey,' she said. 'Let's go.'

I followed her to the elevator, then stopped, reaching into my bag for a scrap of paper and pen. Moments later, I handed her a folded slip of paper. 'Tomorrow, will you give this to Westry?'

Mary took the paper in her hands and looked at it sceptically. 'Are you sure you want to say anything more to him?'

I nodded. 'I need him to read this.'

'Then I'll make sure he gets it,' she said, but I could hear a strain in her voice that worried me. 'I work the morning shift tomorrow. I can try to give it to him then.'

'Promise?' I said, searching her face for the assurance I needed.

'Yes,' she said softly. 'I'll do my best.'

Seattle did little to take my mind off Westry. More than a month had passed since that dark day in Paris, and even with the wedding just weeks away, I couldn't get him out of my mind, or my heart. I jumped every time the phone rang, and sat by the window each morning, awaiting the mail. Surely after he read the note Mary had delivered, he'd write, or call?

Then, on a quiet Tuesday morning, the doorbell rang. I opened the front door to find a postman standing outside. He handed me a small envelope. 'A telegraph for you. From Paris.'

My heart lightened as I ran up the stairs to my bedroom. I ripped open the envelope and held the yellow paper to the light.

> Came home early from trip STOP
> Mary is dead STOP
> Hung herself the morning of September 18 STOP
> Edward broke her heart, irreparably STOP
> Sending love and well wishes from Europe, Stella STOP

I stared at the paper for a long time, until the haze of shock lifted. *No! Not you, Mary.* I remembered the sadness in her eyes, the hesitation. Tears trickled down my cheeks as I crumpled the paper and threw it to the floor.

Moments later, my pulse raced. I retrieved the scrap of paper. September 18. No. No, this can't be.

I stared at the wall in horror. Mary never made it to her shift the day after we'd visited the hospital. She died before she had a chance to deliver my note to Westry.

'**A**re you ready?' Gerard stood in the doorway on the morning of our wedding, two weeks later. Spurning tradition, he had insisted upon picking me up and taking me to the church, maybe because he was worried I wouldn't come any other way.

I looked at him, dashing in a tux, with a perfect white rose pinned proudly to his lapel. *He loves me. He will always love me. That will be enough for a lifetime.*

'Yes,' I said, gulping back the hurt, the pain, the ghosts of my past and weaving my hand in his. 'I'm ready.'

As I stood, my gold locket dangled from my neck, before settling itself once again over my heart.

# CHAPTER 11

'So you married Grandpa,' Jennifer said, her voice pulling me back to the present. The sun had set, leaving just a line of pink on the horizon outside the window.

I smiled. 'Of course I married Grandpa. And aren't you glad I did? After all, you wouldn't have been here any other way.'

She looked dissatisfied. 'I owe my existence to your heartache?'

'Nonsense. I loved your grandfather.'

'But not in the same way you loved Westry.'

I nodded. 'There are all sorts of love. I've come to realise this in my life.' I thought of Gerard—strong, sure Gerard. I missed the way he'd nuzzle my cheek or greet me with the morning paper and a poached egg on a plate with golden brown toast. He'd devoted his life to me, giving me his whole heart freely, when I let him have only a piece of mine. In my heart, I'd kept a room locked.

'Oh, Grandma, why didn't you tell me this story sooner? How lonely to keep it to yourself all these years.'

I patted my locket. 'No, dear, I have never been alone. You see, when you share love with someone, even for a time, it remains in your heart.' I unclasped the locket and let the tiny bit of wood fall into my palm. 'I have never been alone.'

Jennifer frowned. 'But didn't you ever try to find Westry?'

'No,' I said. 'The day I married your grandfather, I vowed to let it all go. I had to. It was only fair to him.'

'What about the bungalow, the painting? Remember what Tita said about finding justice?'

I felt a deep exhaustion setting in. 'I haven't forgot,' I said.

'I'm coming with you,' she said, nodding with determination. 'To Bora-Bora. We'll go together.'

I smiled. 'Oh, honey, you're very sweet, but I don't think I . . .' Retelling the story had opened up wounds that felt as painful as the day they were inflicted. 'I don't think I can.'

'Don't you understand, Grandma? Don't you see? You have to.'

**A**t the open door of the plane, a flight attendant pinned a purple orchid to my shirt, so deeply coloured I wondered if it had been spray-painted. 'Welcome to Bora-Bora. You will love this island.'

'I have always loved this island,' I said, smiling, taking in a breath of the warm, humid air. A bustling airport stood where a single runway had seventy years prior. The emerald hillside was now dotted with homes. Everything had changed, and yet the familiar floral scent lingered in the air, and the turquoise water sparkled in the distance, beckoning me to its shore. I knew it then: my heart was home.

'Take my hand, Grandma.' Jennifer reached out to steady me.

I shook my head, feeling stronger than I had in years. 'I can do this,' I said, making my way down the steps.

A shuttle deposited us at our hotel, the Outrigger Suites, just a mile from the airport. Jennifer pushed the key card into the door and set our bags down in the air-conditioned room. 'Look at that view!' she exclaimed. French doors framed a stunning picture of sand and surf.

I walked closer as something familiar caught my eye. 'I think this hotel was built on the old base! I know that beach, the way it hooks up at the shore. The reef below the sparkling water.' I shook my head, expecting to see Nurse Hildebrand or Kitty, or—I sighed—Westry walking towards me from the sea. 'To be here again, it's just . . .' I opened the doors and walked outside onto the balcony.

'Take all the time you need,' Jennifer said. 'I'll be inside.'

I sat down in a wicker chair on the balcony and let my mind, my heart, become mesmerised by the familiar waves.

**I** ventured back inside the room an hour later, and found Jennifer asleep on one of the beds. I took a spare blanket from the hall closet and spread it over her before leaving her a note. I knew where I had to go.

I reached for my straw hat and made my way outside the hotel, out to the open shore, which, aside from an occasional home nestled along the edge of the sand, was just as quiet, just as pristine as it had been the day I left. At once, I was twenty-one again, sneaking off to the beach, peeking over my shoulder to make sure I wasn't being followed, heart pounding in anticipation of seeing *him*.

I trudged along. The sand felt heavier now. I pulled my hat low, protecting my weathered face from the sun's unrelenting rays. I searched the palm-lined shore. Birds called as I scanned the thicket with every step.

Twenty minutes later, I stopped, out of breath, and sank into a shady spot on the sand, freeing a deep sigh from the depths of my heart. *Of course the bungalow is gone. How could I be so foolish to think it would still be waiting for me?*

'Excuse me, ma'am? Are you all right?'

A man, perhaps in his sixties, not much older than my eldest son, was approaching, with a woman of about the same age. She wore a blue sundress, and her dark hair was pulled back loosely in a clip.

'Why, yes,' I said, collecting myself.

'I'm Greg. This is my wife Loraine. We live right here.'

'I'm Anne. Anne Call—' I stopped myself, marvelling at the slip. I'd been Anne Godfrey the majority of my life, and yet here on the island, the name felt wrong.

'Anne Calloway,' I finished.

The woman gave her husband a look of astonishment. 'Anne *Calloway*?' she said, kneeling next to me. 'We've hoped to meet you for a very long time. You lived on this island during the war didn't you? There's an old beach bungalow near here.' She turned to her husband and then back to me. 'He always said you'd come.'

'He?'

'Mr Green,' she said.

'You know of the bungalow? And'—I gulped—'Westry?'

Greg pointed. 'It's just back this way. You must have missed it.'

I rose stiffly. 'Will you take me there?'

'Yes,' he said, smiling.

We walked in silence. Occasionally the couple glanced at me, but I did not return their gaze, preferring to let the sound of the surf absorb my thoughts. Greg stopped suddenly, pointing towards the jungle, thick with palms. 'Right through there,' he said.

I nodded. 'Thank you,' I replied. I walked on, pushing past aggressive vines reaching out to wrap their tendrils round my frail arms. I looked right, then left. Then an overgrown hibiscus caught my eye. Tiny yellow buds pushed up from its leaves. My heart pounded.

I pushed another vine out of my way, and there it was—still standing, but barely. The thatched roof had weakened and collapsed in places. The woven walls were gone on one side, and the door was missing. I took a deep breath, remembering the way Westry and I had discovered the little hut so many years ago. Now look at it.

The front step had eroded, so I had to raise my body up to the entrance. My arms ached as I hoisted myself inside. I stood and looked around with awe. The bed with its rumpled spread, the mahogany desk and chair, the curtains, though ragged—everything was still in its place. I knelt down. Under the bed lay a lonely scrap of burlap. The painting was gone.

I stood and collapsed into the chair, feeling the weight of seventy years of emotion. Of course it was gone.

When I stood up, the floor creaked below my feet, and I smiled as I thought of the makeshift mailbox. It would be silly to think there might be a letter. And yet I crouched down anyway, fighting back tears as I ceremoniously lifted the old floorboard. I pushed my hand into the little dark space below.

I pulled out a leather-bound notebook, fanning its pages to release years of dust. I opened the cover to read the first page:

Letters to Anne, from Westry . . .

My God. He returned. Just like he promised.

'Ms Calloway?' Greg's voice echoed through the air outside.

I tucked the journal into my bag. 'Yes,' I said, rising, 'I'm here.'

I stood in the doorway as he and his wife approached. 'We didn't want to leave you out here all alone too long,' he said. 'Let me help you down.'

Strong arms lowered me to the ground. Loraine looked at me. 'Did you find what you were looking for?'

'No,' I said, 'but I found something else, something better.'

She smiled. 'Would you like to come back to our terrace for some tea?'

I nodded. 'Thank you. I would like that very much.'

Loraine poured black tea from a blue and white teapot. 'Cream and sugar?'

'Yes, thank you,' I said.

The home was just a simple two-bedroom structure with an ample deck outside. 'We've lived here for thirty-five years,' Greg said. 'Loraine and I used to work in New York City, but after a trip here in the late sixties, we knew we couldn't go back to city life.'

'We opened a restaurant a few miles away,' Loraine chimed in.

I envied them, of course. This was the life that Westry and I might have had. I took a sip of tea, and then set the white china cup down on its saucer. 'You mentioned that you know Westry,' I said quietly.

Greg looked at Loraine and then back to me. 'Yes. We knew him for many years.'

'Knew him?' I asked.

'Yes,' Loraine said. 'He came here every year. His yearly pilgrimage, he called it.'

Greg smiled. 'Pilgrimage in hope of finding you. He told us how you'd fallen in love, and how war had separated you.'

I shook my head in confusion, remembering Kitty, remembering the way I'd left Westry that day in the hospital in Paris. 'But why didn't he try to find me in Seattle? Why didn't he ever write?'

'He didn't feel it was his place,' Loraine explained. 'He knew you had a life, a family in Seattle. And yet, somewhere in his heart, he believed that you might return, that one day you might be waiting for him in the bungalow, just the way you did in his memories.'

I pulled out the notebook. 'I found this. Letters he wrote to me.'

'Yes. Every year he left you a new one, hoping you'd find it,' Loraine said wistfully. 'It was the most romantic thing. Greg and I felt for him, watching him make such a strenuous journey year after year, a man in his condition.'

I sat up straight. 'What do you mean, "a man in his condition"?'

'You don't know? Mr Green was in a wheelchair. He was paralysed in the war.'

I held my hand to my heart to muffle the ache. *Paralysed.* I closed my eyes, remembering the Paris hospital. Had he refused to see me not because of Kitty, but because of his pride?

I looked down at the notebook in my hands, trying to make sense of it all. 'Where is Westry now?'

Loraine looked troubled. 'We don't know. He stopped coming about five years ago.'

'The notebook,' Greg said. 'Perhaps you'll find a clue.'

I stood up. 'Thank you ever so much,' I said, 'for everything. I should be getting back now. My granddaughter is expecting me.'

Loraine stood up beside me. 'Let us walk you to your hotel.'

I shook my head. 'Thank you,' I said. 'But I'll be fine.'

The early light shone on the balcony the next morning as I made myself comfortable in a wicker chair. Jennifer, out for a jog, would be back in an hour. I opened Westry's journal and let my eyes take in his familiar handwriting:

*August 23, 1959*

*My dearest Cleo,*

*This is the first letter I have written to you since we last saw each other on the island, that final day as the airplanes roared into the distance, taking you one place and me another. I've come back to the bungalow on this day— August 23, the very day we met so long ago—in hopes of finding you, or some memory of you, here, for nearly twenty years have passed and you have not escaped my mind or my heart. You'll be happy to know that the old place has held up well. Everything is as we left it. The curtains, still swinging in the breeze. The desk and chair. The bed. Everything but you.*

*How I wish you were here, my love. How I wish I could take you in my arms the way I used to. I know you are out there, living your life, and I do not want to disturb that life. But my heart yearns for you. It always will. And so I will return each year on this day, in hope that our paths may cross again. I will leave this journal here in our mailbox. I will eagerly anticipate your letter, and you.*

*Yours,*

*Grayson*

I marvelled at the letter that had taken some fifty years to reach my hands. I turned to the next page:

*August 23, 1960*

*My dearest Cleo,*

*I admit, my heart leapt as I opened the mailbox and retrieved this journal. I had hoped to see an entry from you, or better yet, to find you here waiting. But I've waited all these years, what's one more? I will be patient. I promise, my love.*

*I often wonder why you didn't respond to the letters I sent from the hospital in Paris. Kitty said you had married, but I didn't believe it, not at first. How could you marry after the love we shared?*

*I've come to terms with that now. I know that life must go on, but a part of me will never fully live until I am with you again.*

*Until next year, my love,*

*Grayson*

I closed the journal, too disturbed to read further. Kitty had intercepted his letters. *Why did she do it?*

I turned to the hotel room when I heard Jennifer at the door. 'It's a beautiful morning,' she said. 'You should get out for a walk.'

I stood up and nestled the journal in my suitcase, then pulled out Genevieve Thorpe's letter. 'I think we should call her now,' I said, more sure of myself than I'd been in years.

Jennifer sat beside me on the bed as I punched the numbers into the phone and then listened to the ringing.

A woman's voice answered. 'Hello, this is Genevieve speaking.'

'Genevieve, this is Anne Call—Anne Godfrey. I'm in Bora-Bora,' I said. 'Would you like to meet us for a drink this evening?'

'Just two tonight?' the hostess asked as Jennifer and I walked into the restaurant at the Outrigger Suites.

'No,' I said. 'We're expecting another guest.' Just then, a woman at the bar stood up and waved from across the room. She was striking, petite, with rosy cheeks and light brown curly hair.

'Hello,' she said, walking towards us. She couldn't have been much older than my sons. 'You must be Anne.'

'Yes,' I said, trying to place the familiar feeling I sensed when I shook her hand. 'And this is my granddaughter, Jennifer.'

'Hello to you both,' she greeted us warmly. 'I'm Genevieve.'

The hostess directed us to a table by the window. When the waiter appeared, I ordered a bottle of white wine.

Genevieve smiled. 'I can hardly believe you're here. You seemed like such a mythical figure.'

A hush fell as the waitress filled our glasses with wine.

'So I take it you know of the bungalow about a half-mile from here? A little hut you'd miss if you blinked?'

I nodded. 'I know the place.'

'It's funny,' she said, taking a sip of wine and leaning back in her chair. 'The locals won't go near the place. They say it's cursed. I avoided it as a girl. My brother and I stumbled upon it, but neither of us would dare step inside.' She shrugged. 'But at some point I suppose my curiosity got the better of me. Twenty-five years ago, I climbed through the window. A week later I found out my husband was having an affair and my mother was dying of cancer.'

'So you believe in its curse, then?' I asked.

'Part of me does, and yet part of me feels there is so much good that resides there, too. I felt it when I was there. Does that even make sense?'

'It's how I've come to feel about the bungalow myself,' I said.

She reached into her bag. 'Here,' she said, smiling. 'I found this on the floor in a corner. I believe it belongs to you.'

I took a deep breath before lifting the flap of the small white envelope. My fingers felt around inside and met something hard and cold. The sparkle of the blue jewels refracted the setting sun. My pin. The one Kitty had given me. I gasped, reading the inscription on the back, an inscription lost in time. Thick tears welled up in my eyes and the room blurred.

'How did you know this belonged to me?' I said, puzzled.

'I did my research,' Genevieve replied, smiling.

'And in your research, did you happen to come across a Westry?' I looked at Jennifer. 'Westry Green?'

Genevieve nodded. 'Yes, I found a book of his, in fact, in the bungalow. An old novel from the 1930s. His name was written on the inside cover. We spoke years ago, before I'd taken on this project. I've tried reaching him since. The number's been changed, and no one seems to know what became of him.'

I looked at my lap, folding the ivory napkin there in half, and then in half again.

'I'm sorry,' she said. 'I don't mean to imply that he—'

'What did he say?' Jennifer asked. 'When you spoke?'

Genevieve smiled. 'It was out of the pages of a novel,' she replied. 'He said that he once loved you a great deal, and that he still did.'

'Why didn't he just call or write?' I said, shaking my head.

Genevieve shrugged. 'I suppose he had his reasons. He was eccentric, Mr Green. I suppose all artists are, though.'

I frowned in confusion. '*Artists?*'

'Why, yes. Of course, I haven't seen any of his work, but he had quite an impressive collection to his name. Paintings, sculpture. He studied art in Europe after the war, and settled somewhere in the Midwest, where he taught art at the university level.'

'You said he *had* an impressive collection?' I said.

'He donated it all to various galleries. I recall him saying that art was meant to be shared, not cloistered.'

I smiled. 'That sounds like the Westry I knew.'

'Genevieve, you mentioned that Westry did sculpture,' Jennifer said, looking at me for approval. 'Do you know the medium? Clay? *Bronze?*'

I knew where her mind was going. The island had a way of drawing connections that weren't real.

'I'm not sure.' Genevieve shrugged. 'He was very brief about his work. And it was so long ago.'

Jennifer and I watched as she pulled a yellow notebook out of her bag and set it on the table. 'Do you mind if I ask you some questions?' she asked cautiously.

'Of course not,' I said, using my right hand to steady the clinking water glass in my left.

'As I said in my letter, a young woman was murdered on this island long ago. I'm trying to put the story to rest, to find justice.'

Jennifer and I exchanged a knowing look.

'I understand that you were off duty the night of the tragedy. Did you see or hear anything of significance? There's been such a shroud of secrecy around the circumstances of the murder.'

I clasped my hands in my lap, thinking of Westry's convictions about keeping the secret. Even after years of turning the story over in my brain, I'd never understood whom he'd been protecting. Perhaps bringing the secret to light would give me the answers I'd longed for.

'Atea was her name,' I said.

Genevieve's eyes widened. 'Yes.'

'She was a beautiful woman. I knew her only briefly.'

'Many of the islanders never came to terms with her death. The ones who are old enough to remember still speak of it as a great evil. It's why I've made it my mission to find justice for her.'

'I can help you,' I said. 'But I need to take you somewhere. Can you meet us in front of the hotel tomorrow morning at about nine thirty?'

'Perfect,' Genevieve said. 'I can hardly wait.'

That evening, Jennifer's cellphone rang in her bag on the balcony, where I sat watching the waves roll onto the shore. The sea sparkled in the light of the crescent moon. 'Honey,' I called in to her through the French doors, 'your phone's ringing.'

She bounded out to the terrace in a pair of green pyjamas and fumbled through her bag. 'Hello?' she said into the phone. She listened for what seemed like an eternity. 'Oh.' She paused, disturbed by something, then smiled. 'Well, I'm very grateful. Thank you so much. I'll ring you when I'm back in Seattle.'

Jennifer ended the call and sat down in the wicker chair next to mine. 'It was the woman from the archives,' she said, stunned. 'They found him. They found the artist.'

I remembered her exchange with Genevieve. 'He's not . . . is he?'

'I'm sorry, Grandma,' she said. 'No. It's not Westry.'

I nodded. 'Of course.'

She watched a sea bird fly overhead until it was out of sight. 'The artist died four years ago,' she continued.

'Sorry, honey,' I said, patting her hand.

'It's OK,' she replied, forcing a smile. 'At least the mystery's solved now—well, sort of. Now that I know who he is, I might be able to talk to his family.'

'I wish we had a bottle of champagne to toast the occasion. You finally found your guy.'

Jennifer leaned her head against my shoulder. 'You'll find yours, too,' she said. 'I have a feeling that it will all work out.'

'Maybe,' I said, hoping she couldn't hear the doubt in my voice.

Just as we had planned, Genevieve met us the next day after breakfast. "Morning,' she said with a cheerful smile. She carried a backpack, and her curly hair pushed out of her white floppy sunhat.

'Thank you so much for meeting me today,' she said once we were a good distance down the beach. 'It's exciting to be closer to the answers.'

'I hope I have the right ones,' I said quietly. 'Tell me what you know about the crime already.'

'I know only what the islanders believe they know—that the man who committed the murder was responsible for a series of pregnancies on the island, several native women and an American nurse.'

*Kitty.* I nodded. 'I didn't see him,' I said quietly, looking out at the stretch of white sand before us. 'It was too dark. But the only man it could have been was Lance.'

'Lance?' Genevieve asked.

'Yes,' I said. 'He was the man who left the nurse in a terrible predicament, pregnant and alone, while he continued his philandering with the native women.'

'Anne,' she said, 'if you knew this, why didn't you report it?'

I sighed, clasping my hands tightly together. 'I know how it must sound, but it's complicated.' The bungalow was close, so I gestured to a bit of driftwood near the shore. 'Let's sit for a moment.'

We sat down on a beam that had washed up on the shore, grey and smooth from years of battling with the surf. I pointed behind us. 'That is where I watched him put a knife to her throat.'

Genevieve covered her mouth.

'I hovered in the shadows until he was gone, then ran to her. I held her as she fought for life.' I shook my head. 'There was nothing I could do.

Westry and I remembered the stash of morphine in my bag. The nurses always kept supplies of it in their medical cases. It could end her pain; we both knew that. I was reluctant at first, but as I watched her laboured breathing and heard the way her lungs gurgled, I knew it was the only way. She died in my arms.'

'You did the right thing,' Genevieve said. 'It's what any of us would have done in the same situation.'

'It's what I told myself, but in my heart, I knew I could have done more. It was Westry's idea to keep quiet. He told me we'd be charged for the murder. But I don't think that was the real reason. Westry would never run from justice unless there was an important reason.' I looked out to the shore, remembering him on that night, so sure, so strong. He had known something I didn't. 'He spoke of protecting someone. If we went to the authorities on base, he feared that something terrible might happen. I trusted him.'

'Do you have any inkling of what he may have meant by that?'

'I don't,' I said, throwing my hands in the air. 'I'm no closer to under-standing his concerns now than I was seventy years ago.'

Genevieve sighed.

'But I do have something to show you. I tucked it away the night of the murder, hoping it may be of use one day years from then, when the truth was ready to be told. That time may be now.'

I stood up, and Genevieve and Jennifer followed my lead. Jennifer steadied me as we pushed through the brush and made our way into the jungle. *Look at me, schlepping through the jungle at my age.* But age didn't matter now. Nothing mattered but truth, and I was intent on finding it. I stared ahead, attempting to get my bearings. 'Yes.' I nodded. 'It should be over here.'

I saw the large old palm in the distance. I pushed ahead and hastened my pace until I reached its base. I knelt down and sank my hands into the moist soil, excavating as much dirt as I could. Soil caked my hands and arms, but I didn't care. My hand hit something hard about a foot below the surface, and I worked to retrieve it.

'Grandma, are you OK?' Jennifer whispered beside me.

'Yes,' I said, producing the package I'd hidden so long ago. I unwrapped the ragged fabric, now in shreds from moisture and insects, and produced the knife. 'The murder weapon,' I said.

Like a forensic expert, Genevieve pulled a ziplock bag from her back-pack and carefully placed the knife inside. 'The time is right,' she said quietly. 'Thank you.'

'Don't thank me. Just bring Atea the justice she deserves.'

'I will,' Genevieve replied, examining the knife through the bag. 'These unit and issue numbers, they have to mean something.' She tucked it into her backpack. 'I can look this up with help from the army's historical society. They keep records of everything. It's how I found you, after all.'

I smiled to myself as we walked back to the beach. It felt good to set the truth free, and I felt lighter for it. Genevieve's cellphone rang inside her backpack, and Jennifer and I excused ourselves to the shore, where I submerged my hands in the salty water, cleansing them of any residual dirt—and evil—that had clung to the knife.

'That took a lot of courage, what you did,' Jennifer said.

'Thank you, dear,' I said, patting my hands dry on my trousers. 'I should have done it years ago.'

We walked back to where Genevieve stood, talking on her cellphone. 'Yes, honey,' she said. 'I promise, I'll be home later and we can have that dinner together we talked about.' She paused. 'Love you too, Adella.'

The hair on my arms stood on end. *That name. I haven't heard it since . . .* Jennifer's face told me she'd made the connection too.

'Excuse me,' I said to Genevieve. 'I couldn't help but overhear you say the name Adella.'

'Oh,' she said, 'yes, my daughter.'

'It's such a beautiful name,' I said. 'You don't hear it often.'

'You don't,' she said. 'I've never met another Adella in my life, actually. It's my middle name. I was adopted, you know, and it was supposedly the name my birth mother had chosen for me.'

I looked away, unable to hide the emotion rising in my heart.

'My parents felt compelled to keep it,' she said, looking thoughtful for a moment. 'When my daughter was born, it was the only name that felt right.'

'Anne,' she said, concerned, 'is something wrong?'

'I was wondering if you ever tried to find your birth mother.'

'Believe me, I've tried. My parents would tell me nothing of her. And the records were destroyed long ago.'

Kitty's daughter. Right here before my eyes. The very baby I helped deliver in the bungalow.

The hotel was in sight now. 'Well,' Genevieve said, clasping her hands together. Now that I'd put the pieces together, I could see that her eyes were the eyes of Kitty in her youth. 'Here I am, going on about myself and keeping you out in the hot sun. It's been an emotional morning. I should let you rest. Why don't I come by tomorrow when I have some news about this knife? I should know something by the afternoon.'

I nodded. 'That would be lovely,' I said, my head spinning.

'We'll have a lot to talk about then.'

'We will,' I replied, tucking a stray curl behind her ear, the way I might have done if Kitty had been standing in front of me just then.

The next morning I pulled out Westry's journal and continued reading his letters. I pored over the yellowed pages, learning about the life he'd led without me, and the love he'd harboured, a love that seemed to grow stronger and clearer by the year. When I reached the final page, dated five years ago, my heart seized:

*August 23, 2006*

*My dearest Cleo,*

*Here I am again—another year, another August—too old now, to be here, to be here without you. This year hasn't been kind to me. I only hope it was kinder to you.*

*Do you remember the song we heard that night in the bungalow, 'La Vie en Rose'? One verse went, 'Give your heart and soul to me and life will always be la vie en rose.' I suppose this is true of my life. For even without your presence, without your touch, I have still had you with me, always. You gave your heart and soul to me once, and I have never let it go.*

*Whether we meet again or not, that's all that matters.*

*La vie en rose, my dearest.*

*Yours, always,*

*Grayson*

Genevieve arrived at our hotel room at three o'clock. Jennifer let her in, and she set her bag down on the desk. 'You're never going to believe what I found.'

'What?' I said eagerly.

Genevieve sat on the bed beside me. 'The inscription on the knife,' she said. 'I looked it up. It doesn't belong to Lance, Anne.'

'My God,' I said, shaking my head. 'Then who?'

She retrieved her notebook from her bag and opened it. 'The knife was issued to Colonel Matthew Donahue, the commanding officer of the entire base.' She looked at me. 'There must be some mistake.'

*I got it all wrong.* 'No mistake,' I said. Images from the past ran through my mind—of Kitty, crying on her bed; of Atea, confused and distraught the night of the Christmas service; of Westry's bloodied face in the men's barracks. It wasn't Lance, I could see that now. The colonel had been behind it all.

Genevieve looked confused. 'No one will believe that a commanding officer, a respected one, at that, could have committed such a brutal crime. The only way we can get proof is if we find the American nurse he was involved with. The knife is much too corroded for fingerprints, and the islanders who are old enough to remember won't talk.' She shrugged in defeat. 'What are the chances we could get that nurse on the phone? Not likely, huh?'

'Maybe,' I said quietly. 'I happen to know the woman. Well, I did, anyway. She was my best friend. We travelled to the island together, in fact.' I paused to survey Genevieve's face, so like Kitty's.

'What's her name?'

'Kitty Morgan.' I sighed. 'I don't know what became of her. We haven't spoken since, well, it's been a very long time.'

Genevieve's eyes lit up. 'I know that name. Yes. I believe I took down her information from the staff roster records for the infirmary. At one point I looked up her phone number, though I never called—didn't see any reason to at the time.' She thumbed through her notebook. 'Yes, here it is. Kitty Morgan Hampton. She lives in California now—well, at least she did two years ago. Anne, would you call her?'

I felt weak all over. 'Me? But this is your project.'

'She's more likely to talk to you than a stranger.'

*If you only knew.*

I thought of Kitty's coldness in our final month on the island, the way she'd acted towards Westry—the way she'd put herself between us, severing our love for ever. No, I couldn't speak to her.

I felt Jennifer's chin rest gently on my shoulder. 'Time changes people,' she whispered. 'You loved her once.'

I did love her, yes. And maybe still. Her memory still moved me, after all these years. 'All right,' I conceded. 'I'll make the call.'

Jennifer handed me the phone, and I hesitantly punched in the numbers written in Genevieve's notebook.

'Hello?' Kitty's voice was raspier now, but the tone was still the same. I froze, unable to find my voice. 'Hello?' she said again.

'Kitty?' My voice cracked, and tears began streaming down my cheeks. 'Kitty, it's Anne.'

'Anne?'

'Yes!' I cried. 'Anne Calloway, Godfrey.'

'My God, Anne,' she said. 'Is it really you?'

'Yes, it's really me.'

Jennifer handed me a tissue, and I blew my nose quietly, just as I heard Kitty do on the other end of the line.

'Anne, I—I—' Her voice faltered. 'I don't know where to begin. How are you?'

'It's funny,' I said. 'I'm not sure how to answer that question after all these years. Where do I start?'

'Well,' Kitty said softly. The edge in her voice, the one that had shaken me so in Paris, was gone. 'I can start by saying I'm sorry.'

'Kitty, I—'

'No, let me finish. I am not well, Anne. I may not be able to say this to you again, so I must say it now.' She paused, as if to collect her thoughts. 'I should have reached out to you years ago. I don't know why I didn't. I'm ashamed.'

'Oh, Kitty,' I said, wiping another tissue under my eyes.

'I regret everything about the way I behaved on the island, and in Paris. I froze after the birth. I sank into a dark place I didn't understand. I know now it was depression—what they call postpartum depression, my daughter tells me. But I . . .'

I looked at Genevieve watching quietly from the chair near the desk, so like Kitty in more ways than I could count: beautiful, vibrant, impulsive. 'Kitty, you have a daughter?'

'Well, yes, I have three—well, four . . .' Her voice trailed off. 'I married a good man, you'll be happy to know. I met him in Paris after the war, a

Marine. We moved to California. It's been a nice life.' The line went quiet for a moment. 'Has your life been nice, Anne? I've often thought of you.'

'It has,' I said quietly. 'In almost every way.'

Kitty sighed. 'Anne, there's something I need to tell you, about Westry.'

I closed my eyes tightly.

'He talked about you incessantly in Paris,' she said. 'He was always asking about you and hoping you'd come.'

'I did come,' I said. 'You remember, of course.'

'Yes.' I could hear Kitty's shame, feel it ricocheting across the Pacific. 'I was jealous of what you had,' she said.

'So you intercepted his letters to me?'

Kitty gasped. 'You know?'

'I only recently found out,' I said.

'Anne, I'm ashamed of myself,' she said tearfully. 'To think I changed the course of your life by my actions. I can hardly bear it.'

In an instant, the anger that had churned in my heart lost its steam. 'You have my forgiveness,' I said. 'What you said about time running out—I feel that too.'

'I still have my pin,' she said. 'The one I gave you at the Cabaña Club. It's in my jewellery box. I look at it and think of you.'

Her gesture of enduring friendship. If only that pin could have held our bond. Or maybe it had. I retrieved it from my pocket and turned it over, eyeing the engraving. 'I have mine, too. Right here.'

'How I'd love to see you again. Where are you? Seattle?'

'No,' I said. 'I'm in Bora-Bora.'

'*Bora-Bora?*'

'Yes, I'm here with a woman who's researching a crime that was committed on the island, a murder.'

Kitty was quiet for a moment. 'You're referring to Atea?'

'Yes,' I said. I decided not to ask her how she knew of the story. 'I wanted to ask you some questions, if you don't mind.'

'Go ahead.'

'We never spoke of the father of your baby. I'd assumed it was Lance, but now we have evidence linking the murder to—'

'To the colonel?'

'Yes,' I said. 'You know?'

'I do. And so did Westry. He was protecting me, Anne, by not telling. Before the murder, he'd got wind of my situation. He saw us together and overheard a conversation on the beach. He also knew the colonel had had encounters with island women. I was headstrong and naive. Westry warned me, but I wouldn't listen.'

I recalled the brutal beating in the barracks. 'He threatened Westry, didn't he?'

'Yes. The colonel warned him that if he tried to intervene or report any of it to his superiors, he'd do something terrible to me.'

'My God, Kitty!' I exclaimed. 'So by keeping quiet about Atea's murder, Westry was protecting *you*?'

'Yes,' she said. 'Looking back, I think I was in more danger than I ever knew. Westry spared me from all of that.'

I sighed. 'It's why you developed feelings for him, isn't it?'

'I suppose,' Kitty said honestly. 'After being treated so terribly by men all my life, here was an honest man, who wanted to protect me. And yet, he was already in love with my best friend.'

I gazed out of the window to the shore, remembering the way Kitty had looked at Westry. I couldn't blame her for loving him.

'Anyway, Atea was murdered because he got her pregnant and she refused to keep quiet like the other women. There were at least two. I should have come forward about this, but I had to move on. After I heard of his death, I decided he'd burn in hell anyway.'

'When did he die?'

'Nineteen sixty-three,' Kitty said. 'A heart attack, alone in a San Francisco hotel room.'

I sat up straighter, looking at Genevieve. 'It doesn't mean justice can't still be served,' I said. 'He's a decorated war veteran. We'll have the military revoke his status posthumously.'

Genevieve nodded in agreement. I took a deep breath, for what I was about to say would change everything.

'Kitty,' I said, gesturing for Genevieve to come over to the phone. 'There's someone I'd like you to speak to. Her name is Genevieve. I think you two have more in common than you know. Her daughter, for instance . . . Well, I think you two should talk.'

Genevieve gave me a confused look, but reached for the phone and smiled. 'Ms Hampton?'

# CHAPTER 12

THE PHONE RANG in the living room, and I groaned. Answering it meant standing up, leaving my bed, and feeling my bones ache with every step. But the persistent ringing enticed me to make the journey. I reached the phone and uttered an out-of-breath hello.

'Grandma, it's me,' chirped Jennifer. 'Today's the day.'

More than three months had passed since we'd returned from Bora-Bora. While I'd made peace for Genevieve, Atea, Kitty, and perhaps even for the island, I had left with a tsunami in my own heart, with only whispers of Westry and a book of old letters to cling to.

'Grandma?'

'I'm here, dear. I'm just not feeling like myself today.'

'But you're still coming, right?'

'Oh, honey,' I said into the phone, sinking to the sofa before pulling a blanket over my icy feet. 'I don't think I can.'

Jennifer's silence pierced my heart. She had turned in her article a week prior, and the newspaper had got wind of the project, as did the university's public relations team.

'Oh, Grandma,' she said. 'I know you haven't been feeling well, but so many people will be there, and I can hardly stand to face them alone. We'll park close so you won't have to walk far.'

I forced my legs out in front of me and stood up. *I can do this. For Jennifer.* 'Well,' I said, taking a deep breath, 'then I will come. For you, dear.'

'Oh, Grandma, thank you!' she exclaimed. 'I'll be over soon.'

I set the phone down and reached for the letter on the coffee table. It had arrived yesterday, and I'd already read it a dozen times.

*Dear Anne,*

*I wanted to thank you for coming to Bora-Bora. Your visit was transformative, and I write with good news: The army has agreed to put a case*

*together against Colonel Donahue. It all feels very strange, knowing my*
*relation to this man, but it doesn't stop me from seeking justice for Atea, for*
*my unborn sister or brother. While the army can't prosecute him in death, he*
*will most likely be stripped of his honours, at least in all military records.*
*Island officials are talking about erecting a memorial for Atea somewhere in*
*town. None of this would have happened without your courage.*

*I'm meeting Kitty next month. She's invited me to stay with her. I'm*
*bringing Adella. I have to pinch myself, as I can hardly believe this is real.*
*But it is, wonderfully real.*

*I will always think of you with fondness and appreciation.*
*With love,*
*Genevieve*

**Q**uiet lingered on campus, and my heels clicked loudly on the brick path, shiny from a recent rain shower. A clock chimed in the distance: noon. 'Just a little farther,' Jennifer said, gauging my face for signs of strain.

'I'm all right, dear.' The crisp fall air felt good on my skin. It energised me in a way I hadn't anticipated. 'You lead the way.'

We walked past a row of maples, their leaves tinged orange and red. A stately brick building stood nearby. I recognised it instantly, of course. Gerard taught finance here after he retired from the bank. How I'd loved taking walks with him through campus.

'Right through here,' Jennifer said, taking my arm in hers as we approached a narrow path that curved round the ivy-covered building. Of all the times I'd been on campus with Gerard, I'd never thought to walk behind the building. Not even once.

'There it is,' she said, pointing ahead proudly.

I could see why the sculpture captivated her. It told a story. I walked closer, intrigued, and eyed the bronze couple huddled in a crude doorway. *Why is my heart racing?* The man looked at the woman with longing, while her gaze drifted out to the distance.

'It's beautiful,' I said. The man held in his hands a large box with a lock, and at his feet lay a painter's canvas and a book. My hands trembled as I knelt down. In that moment, my heart *knew.*

Jennifer stood quietly behind me. *Where are all the people, the fanfare she spoke of?* I ran my hand along the bronze book at the base of the sculpture, cold, wet from the rain, until I secured the corner of its cover.

*Could it be?* I lifted the heavy edge and stared at the tarnished steel key inside, my heart beating faster by the second.

I gestured for Jennifer to come closer. 'I can't do this alone,' I said, wiping a tear from my cheek.

She steadied me as I slid the key into the lock on the tightly sealed box. *A perfect match.* I turned it to the right but it jammed.

'The weather must have corroded it,' I said. 'I'll try it again.'

I pulled the key out and inserted it a second time, giving it a light shake. A faint click sounded as the lock released its stubborn grip.

Jennifer hovered as I peered inside to find a blue velvet case. I removed it from its bronze crypt and walked to a nearby bench.

'Are you going to open it?' Jennifer whispered.

I turned to her with heavy, moist eyes. 'You knew, didn't you?'

She smiled, nodding. 'When the woman from the archives called in Bora-Bora, she told me the artist's name, Grayson Hodge, but I didn't recognise it. The name didn't click until a few weeks after we were home.' She paused. 'He used the pseudonym in his work. I didn't want to keep it from you, but I wanted you to see this for yourself.'

I carefully opened the case and peeled back the brown wrapping.

Jennifer gasped. 'The painting? The one from the bungalow?'

I nodded in awe. The old Gauguin warmed my hands as I held it, as if the Bora-Bora sun had lingered in the canvas all these years. The colours, just as vibrant; the composition, just as moving. And for a moment, I was there again, on the island, feeling the warm air on my cheeks, the sand on my feet, the love of Westry all around me.

'He found it!' I cried. 'Just as he promised.' *Of course he kept his promise.* 'And to think it was here, waiting for me, all these years.' I turned to Jennifer with eyes of gratitude. 'Thank you, dear.' I looked at the statue and then back at the painting. 'This is a gift.'

She eyed the nearby building anxiously before turning back to me. 'Grandma,' she whispered, 'are you ready?'

'Ready for what?'

'To see *him*.'

My heart swelled. 'But you said, you said he was . . .'

'Dead?' She shook her head. 'Yes, Grayson Hodge, a ninety-year-old man from Barkley, Utah, died. But not Westry Green.'

Westry. Here? Can it be true?

'I don't know,' I said, choking back tears. 'But your project?'

Jennifer smiled. 'It's concluded beautifully.'

I felt weak, unsure. 'I've been dreaming about this day for as long as I can remember, and now that it's here I'm . . .'

'Scared?'

'Yes,' I muttered, smoothing my wispy hair—what was left of it, anyway. *Why didn't I put on a dress? And some lipstick?*

Jennifer shook her head, sensing my insecurity. 'Westry will only see what I see: your true *beauty*.'

She handed me a handkerchief to dry my eyes. 'Now, you wait here. I'll go round front and tell them we're ready.'

'You mean,' I said, fumbling, 'he's here already?'

'Yes,' she said, smiling proudly. 'His son brought him over this morning. They travelled all the way from New York.'

She turned towards the path, disappearing round the old building. Alone, I looked up at the sculpture, gazing at the man's eyes. Even cast in bronze, they did look like Westry's, very much so. All those times I'd walked this stretch of campus—I exhaled deeply—if I had only stopped once to notice, to see the clue he'd placed in my path, I might have found him.

I heard the crunch of gravel in the distance, and I turned my eyes back to the pathway. When a man appeared, a flock of sparrows startled, fluttering away to a nearby tree. Even in a wheelchair, he had a familiar presence—the way he held himself, the outline of his chin. When our eyes met, he waved away the middle-aged man behind him and took the wheels in his hands, pushing the chair with a strength that didn't match the white of his hair, the wrinkles on his face. His eyes remained fixed on my face, holding me in his gaze.

He stopped in front of the bench where I sat, reaching his hands out to me, cradling my icy fingers in his strong, warm palms. 'Hello, Cleo,' he said, extending a hand to my face. He stroked my cheek lightly, before his fingers found my locket.

'Hello, Grayson,' I said, wiping the tears from my cheek.

'You're a little late, my dear,' he said, with the same mischievous grin I'd been so charmed by on the day we met.

I searched his face. 'How can you ever forgive me? For not knowing, for not looking . . . I was—'

Westry brushed his finger against my lips and smiled in a way that calmed me. *He could always calm me.* 'Just a little late,' he said softly, 'but not too late.' In an instant, he was twenty-five, and I, twenty-one. Age disappeared. Time faded into the distance.

He buttoned his brown corduroy jacket and set the brakes of the wheelchair, then inched closer to the edge of the seat before pushing his body to a standing position.

I gasped. 'But I thought . . .'

He grinned. 'That you'd like to take an autumn stroll?' He retrieved a grey cane from the side of the chair, securing it in his left hand and holding his right out to me. 'Ready?'

'Yes,' I said, beaming, marvelling at him standing next to me, so tall, so sure. I tucked the painting under my arm before taking his hand in mine, blinking hard to make sure I wasn't dreaming.

We started down the path through campus, unsure of our destination. But none of that mattered, not now. For our story had an ending that suited me. I loved him, and he loved me, up until the very end. This is the story that would whistle in the winds of Bora-Bora, haunt the weathered remains of the bungalow, and live on in my heart for ever.

Westry came. The curse ended. Together, we walked slowly, but surely. I nestled closer to him, wrapping my arm round his just as two wine-coloured leaves fell from a nearby tree branch, dancing in the autumn breeze on separate paths before falling softly to the ground, where they settled on the damp earth, side by side.

*Sarah Jio*

**Can you tell us a little about your background?**

I grew up in the Kitsap Peninsula in Poulsbo, Washington, a small town a ferry's ride away from Seattle. I always knew I wanted to be a writer. In the first grade I penned the book *A Tug Boat's Dream*, which stemmed from my fascination with tug boats (I also loved cabooses on trains back then!).

**You started professionally as a journalist?**

I've written for women's magazines and newspapers for more than twelve years, and have had the privilege of breaking news, reporting on important health stories and major studies, and even interviewing celebrities like Gwyneth Paltrow. Because of my interest in healthy living, I have specialised in health, fitness, nutrition and happiness in my reporting. I love staying up to date on health news, so I'm always sifting through the medical journals in search of the latest thinking on living your best and healthiest life. I'm in my fourth year as the health and fitness blogger for *Glamour* magazine, so this is an area where my interests and career collide.

But I always hoped to realise my dream of writing a novel. After finishing one 'practice novel' that was never published, I sat down to write my first real novel, *The Violets of March*. It was sold to Penguin/Plume in 2010.

**How does the magazine work differ from fiction?**

I've found that writing for magazines has helped keep me disciplined as a novelist. Because I have daily magazine deadlines, I'm always writing, which exercises my creative muscles and keeps my brain agile. I do find that writing fiction is very freeing. After a long day working on articles, it's nice to be able to write whatever I want without having to stick to facts.

**How do you raise three young sons and write at the same time?**

It isn't always easy, but I love both of my jobs: being a mother and being a writer. And I find that they work together quite nicely. My little boys are as rambunctious as can be, but they all go to bed early enough to allow their mama to be productive in the evenings. I love writing at night after they're in bed, when the house is quiet. I also have an incredibly supportive husband, Jason, who is very hands-on with the children and takes them out on adventures to the park and the zoo while I'm trying to meet my deadlines. And I watch very little TV—aside from *Downton Abbey*, which has recently captured my attention.

**Where do you write and do you have any writing rituals?**

I have to have a clean office to write well. Before I attempt to have a productive writing session, I always tidy my desk and empty my recycle bin. Oddly, this helps me clear my mind and get myself in the place I need to write. I also have two funny quirks when it comes to novel writing: I always write the last chapter first. Oddly, I find it satisfying to type 'The End' before I've even really begun the story. This helps me write towards a goal. And I usually come up with the titles of my novels first. There is just something very motivating about a great title.

**What was your inspiration for *The Bungalow*?**

I first became fascinated with the South Pacific when my late grandfather shared stories of his military service during World War II. He was always very quiet about his time there, as many war veterans are, but he shared just enough to pique my curiosity, which simmered over the course of my lifetime. Also, while beginning to research this novel, I discovered the wartime journal of my great uncle, who fought in the South Pacific and wrote in great detail about his adventures and challenges there. His journal entries fascinated me and provided valuable information for the setting and landscape of my story.

**Any other snippets of information about yourself that you'd like to share with us?**

I've a golden retriever named Paisley, who likes to steal socks. I always sneeze without fail after taking my first bite of chocolate. I am a Christmas freak and begin listening to Christmas music in October (shamelessly) every year. I love running, and it fuels my creativity. (I always think of the most interesting ideas and character quirks while jogging, so I take my phone to email myself my thoughts mid-jog.)